Part V.
The Book of Elements
Volume 2

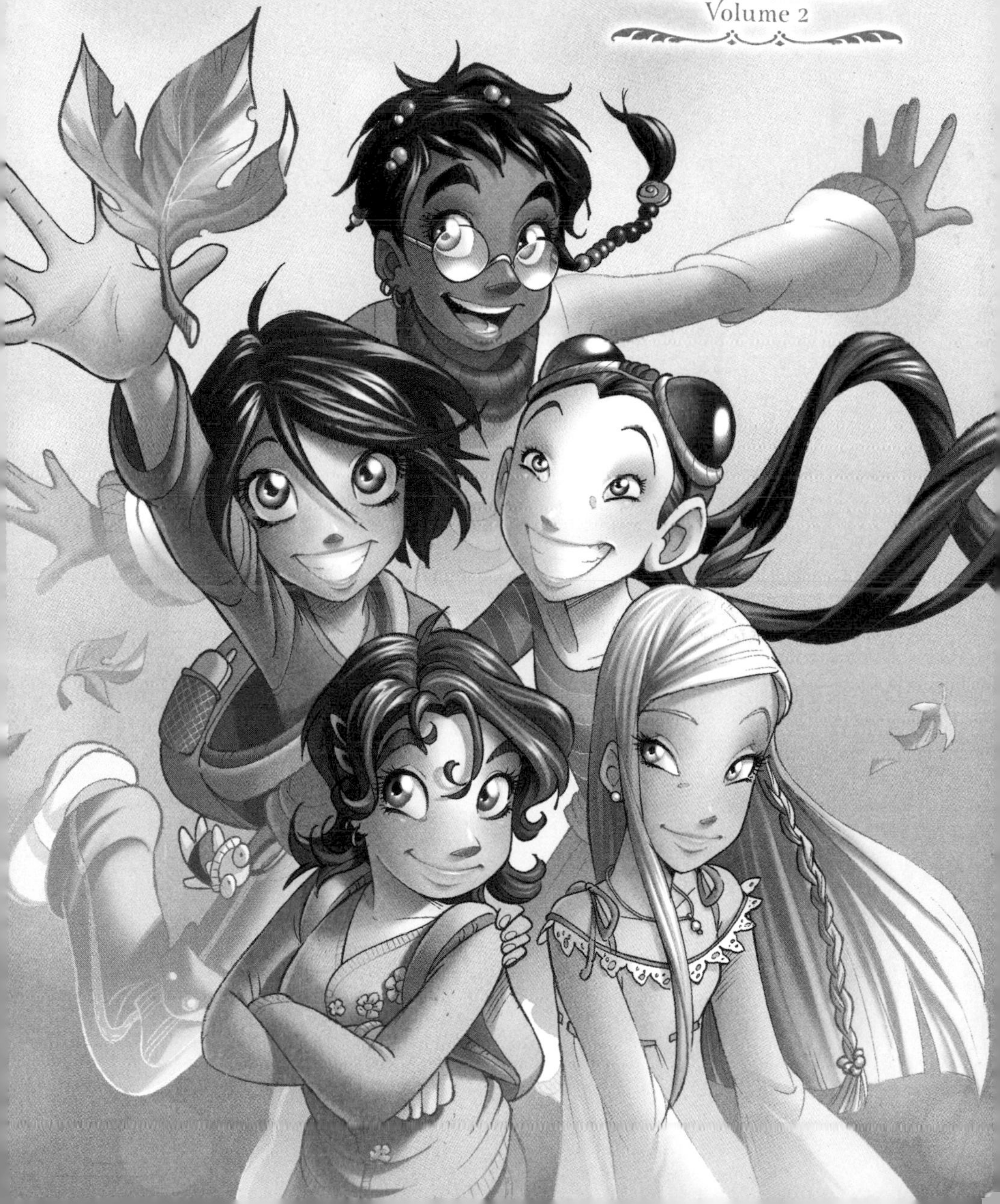

W.i.t.c.h.

Will   Irma   Taranee   Cornelia   Hay Lin

Part V.
The Book of Elements
Volume 2

CONTENTS

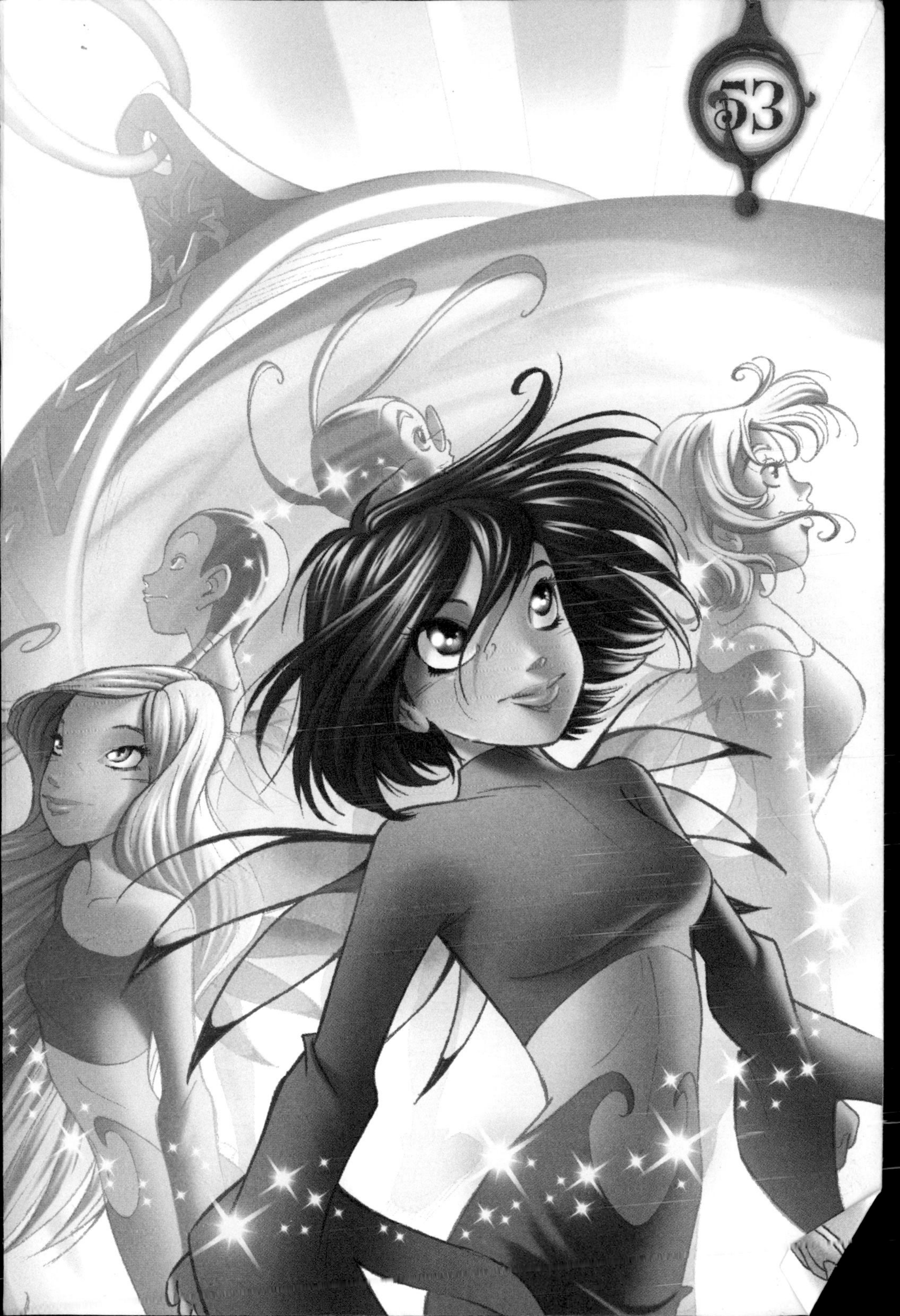
53

Dancing to a Different Tune

"There's nothing better than everyone being happy together..."

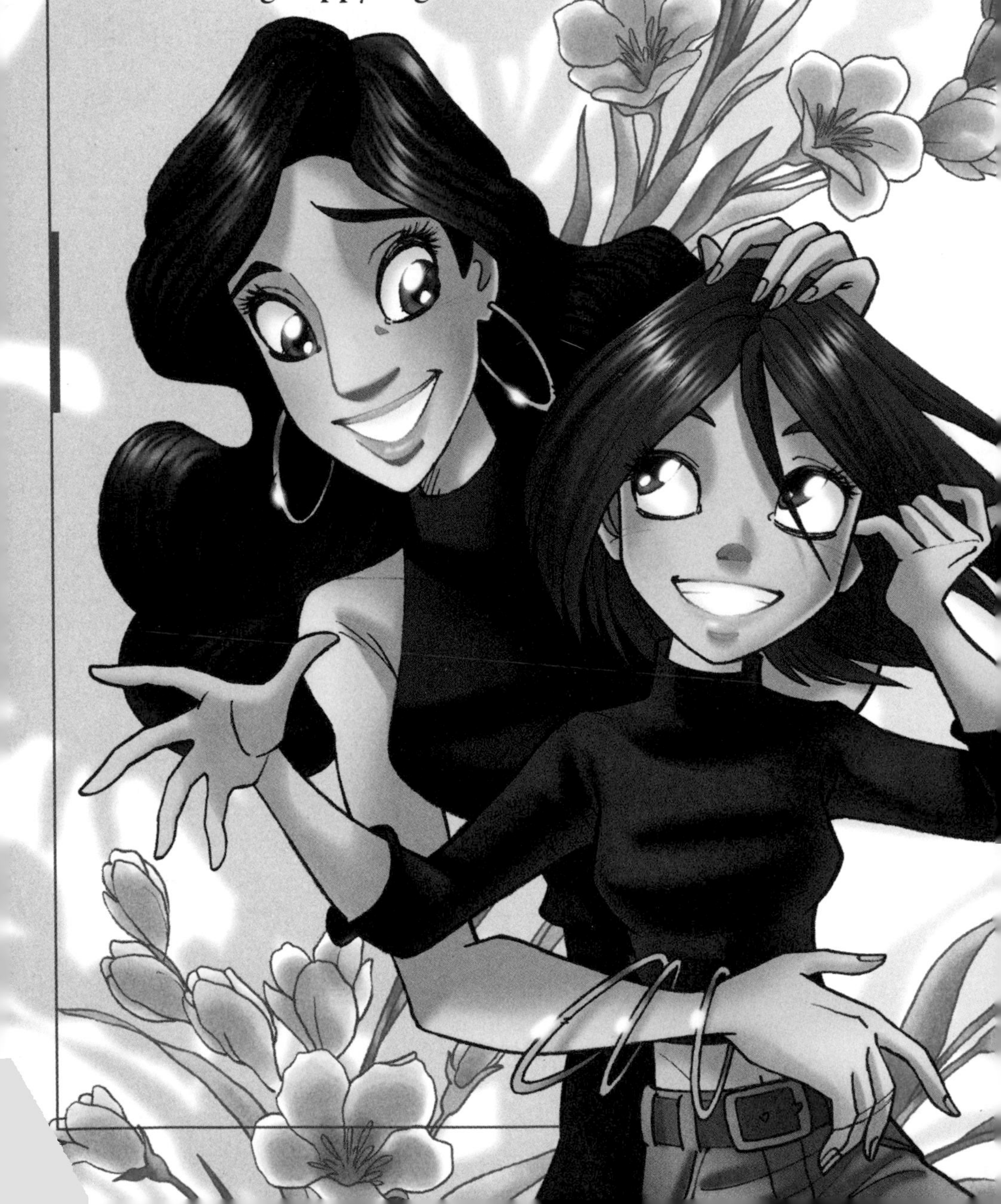

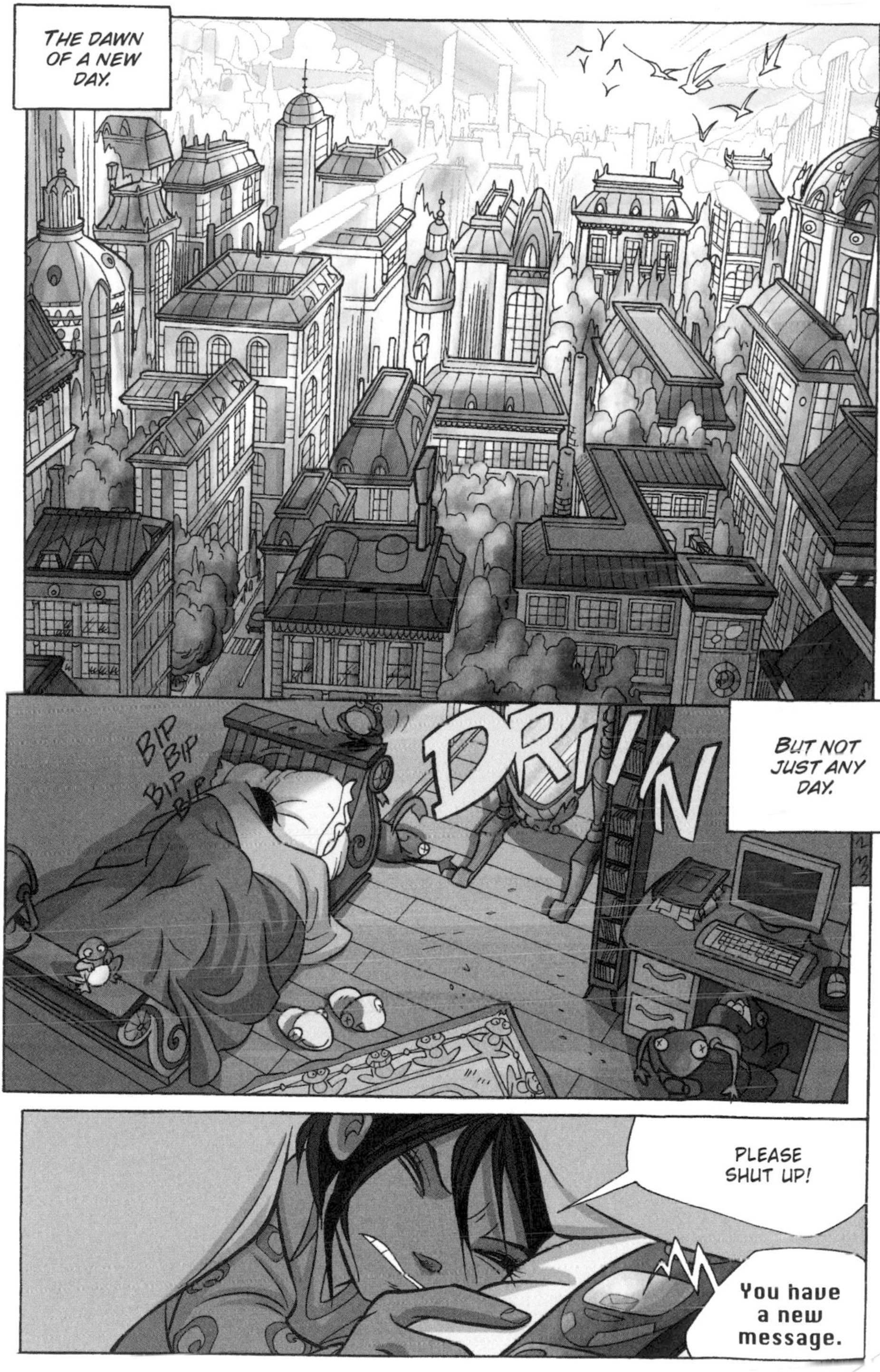
THE DAWN OF A NEW DAY.
BIP BIP BIP BIP
DRIIIN
BUT NOT JUST ANY DAY.
PLEASE SHUT UP!
You have a new message.

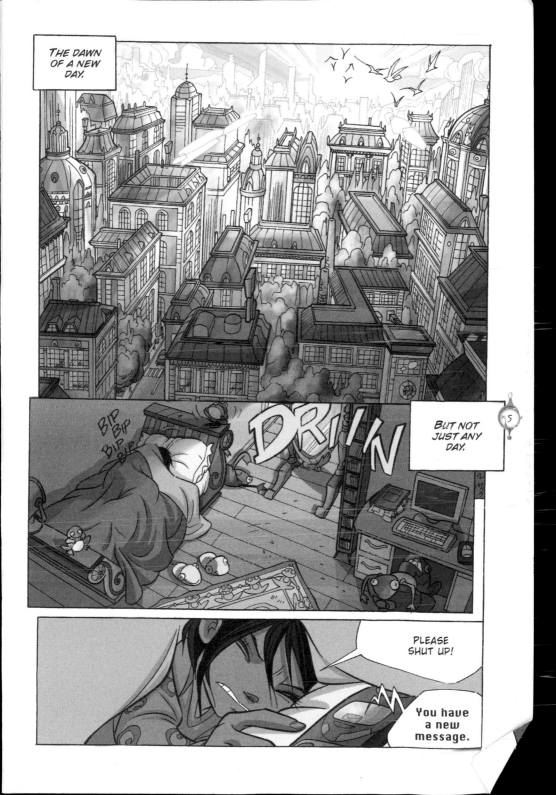

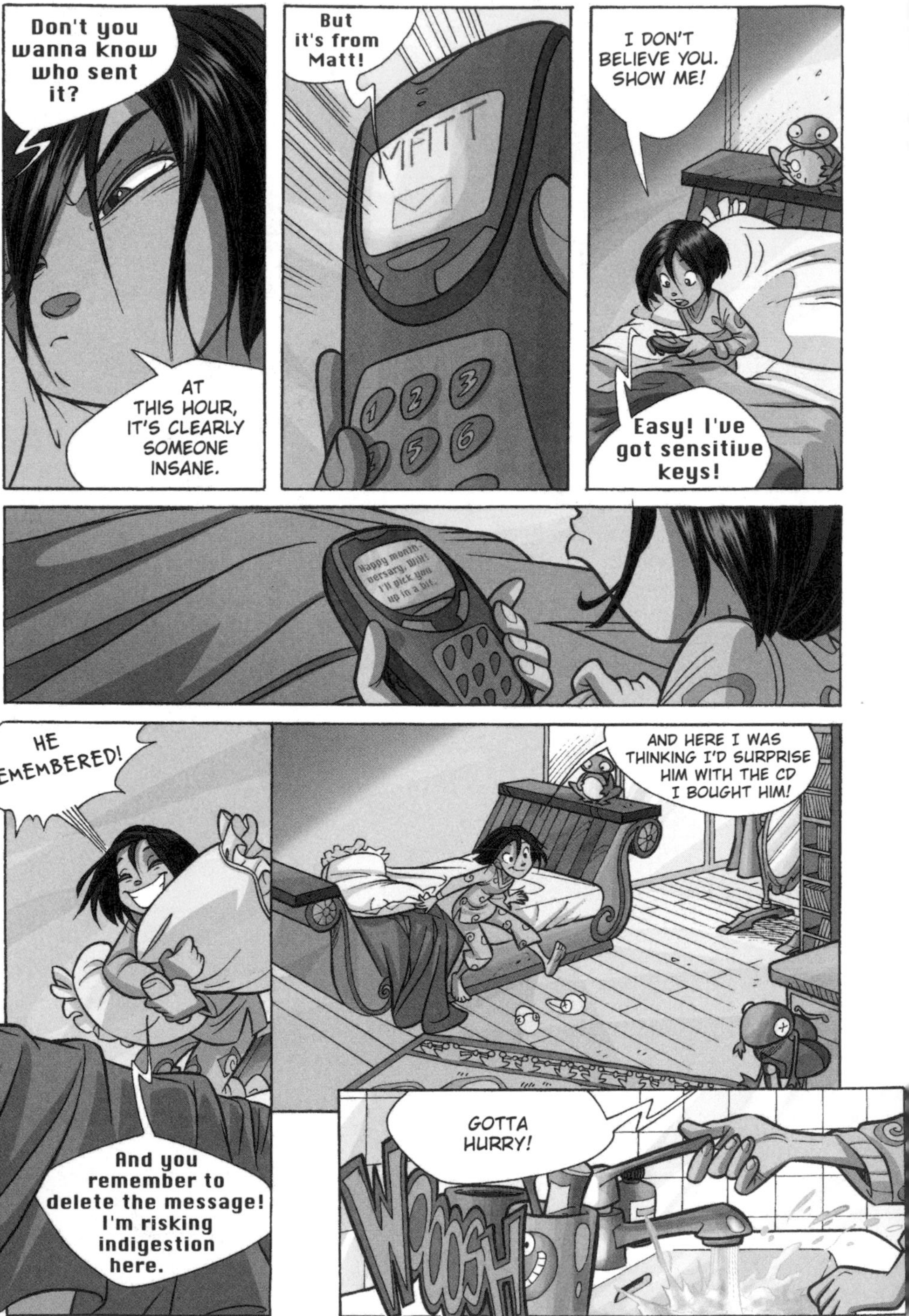
Don't you wanna know who sent it?
AT THIS HOUR, IT'S CLEARLY SOMEONE INSANE.
But it's from Matt!
I DON'T BELIEVE YOU. SHOW ME!
Easy! I've got sensitive keys!
Happy month-versary, Will! I'll pick you up in a bit.
HE REMEMBERED!
And you remember to delete the message! I'm risking indigestion here.
AND HERE I WAS THINKING I'D SURPRISE HIM WITH THE CD I BOUGHT HIM!
GOTTA HURRY!
WOOSH

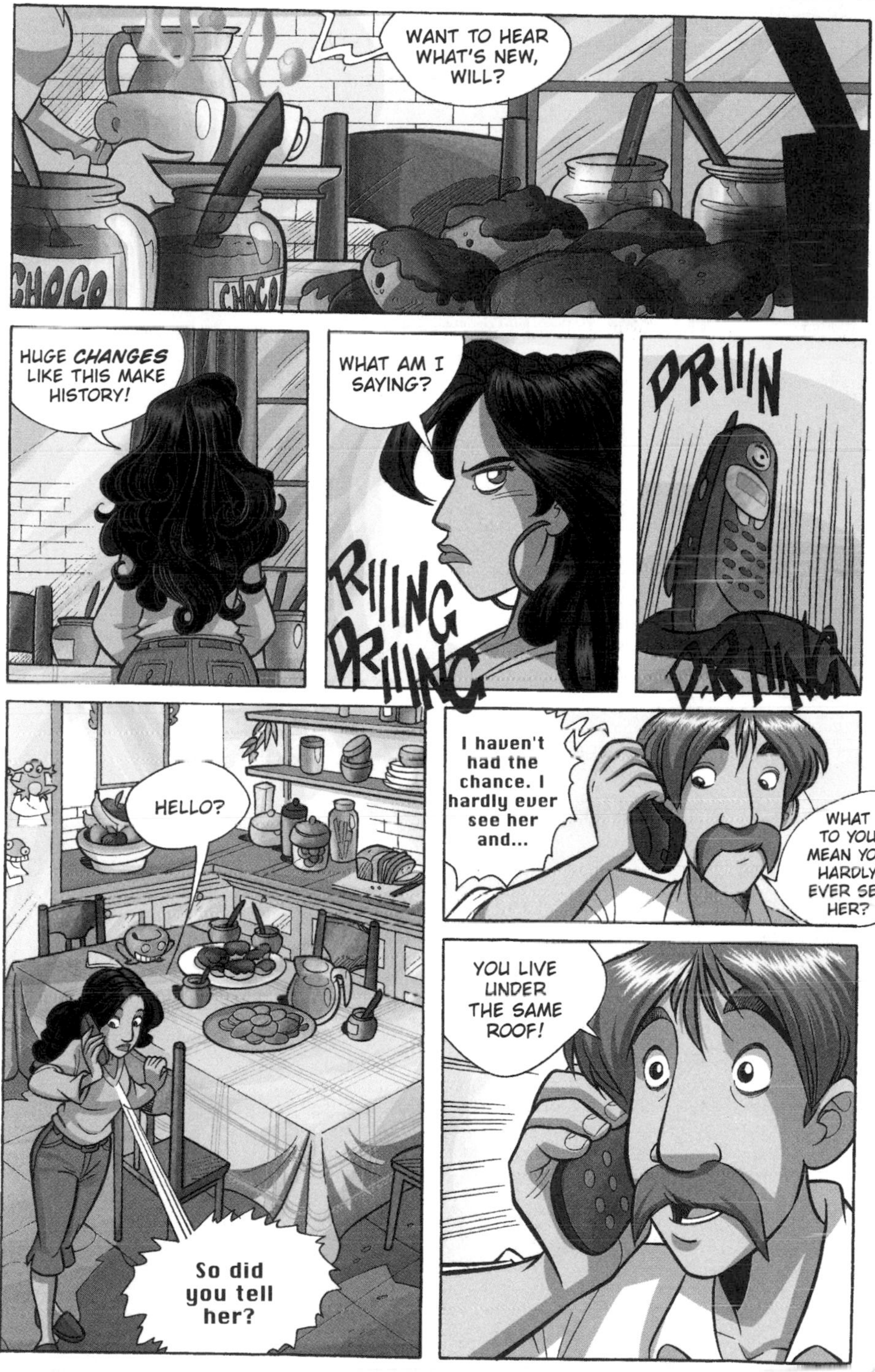

WANT TO HEAR WHAT'S NEW, WILL?
HUGE **CHANGES** LIKE THIS MAKE HISTORY!
WHAT AM I SAYING?
RIIING
DRIIING
DRIIIN
HELLO?
So did you tell her?
I haven't had the chance. I hardly ever see her and...
WHAT TO YOU MEAN YOU HARDLY EVER SEE HER?
YOU LIVE UNDER THE SAME ROOF!

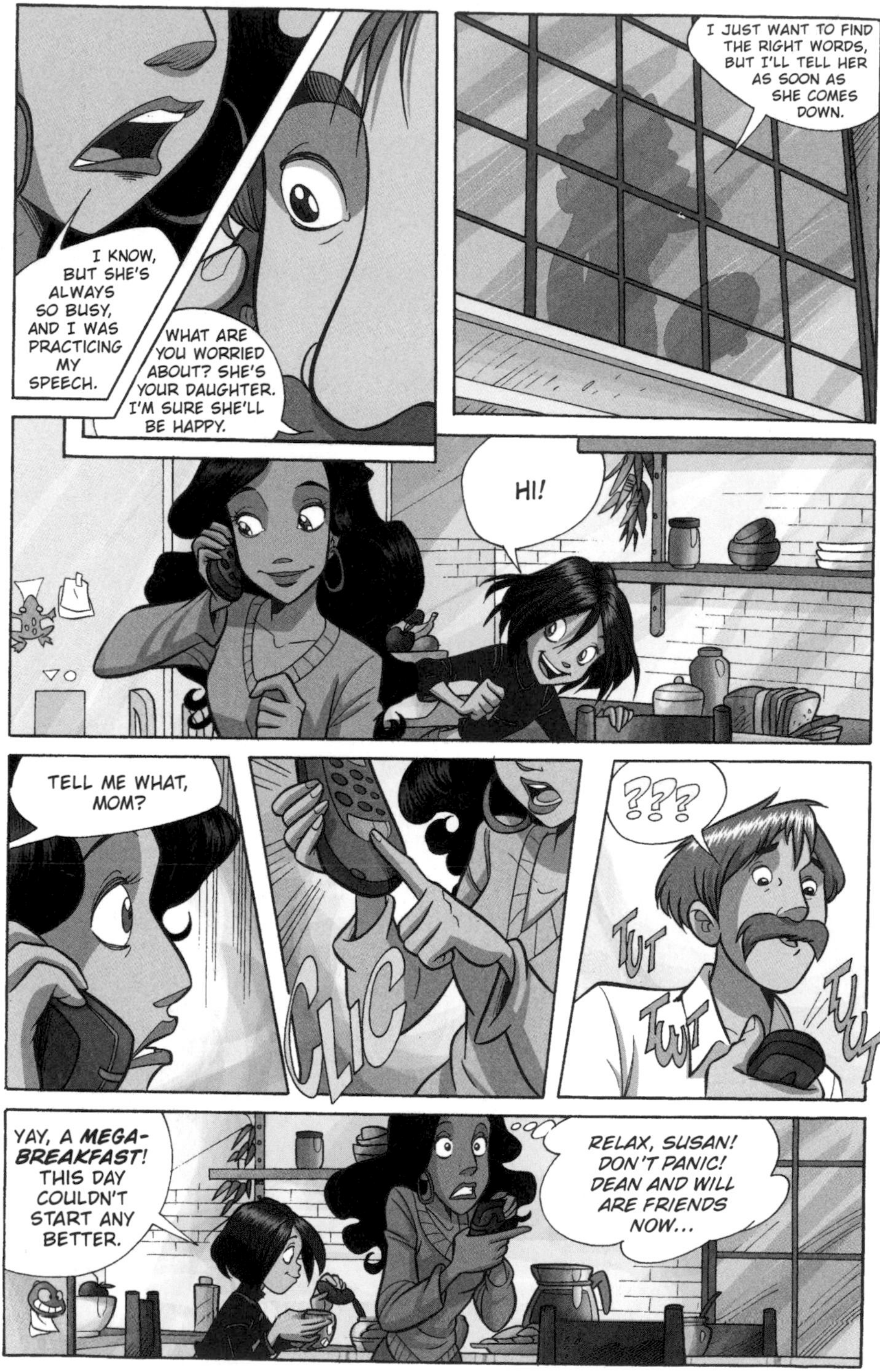
I KNOW, BUT SHE'S ALWAYS SO BUSY, AND I WAS PRACTICING MY SPEECH.
WHAT ARE YOU WORRIED ABOUT? SHE'S YOUR DAUGHTER. I'M SURE SHE'LL BE HAPPY.
I JUST WANT TO FIND THE RIGHT WORDS, BUT I'LL TELL HER AS SOON AS SHE COMES DOWN.
HI!
TELL ME WHAT, MOM?
CLIC
???
TUT
TUT
TUT
YAY, A MEGA-BREAKFAST! THIS DAY COULDN'T START ANY BETTER.
RELAX, SUSAN! DON'T PANIC! DEAN AND WILL ARE FRIENDS NOW...

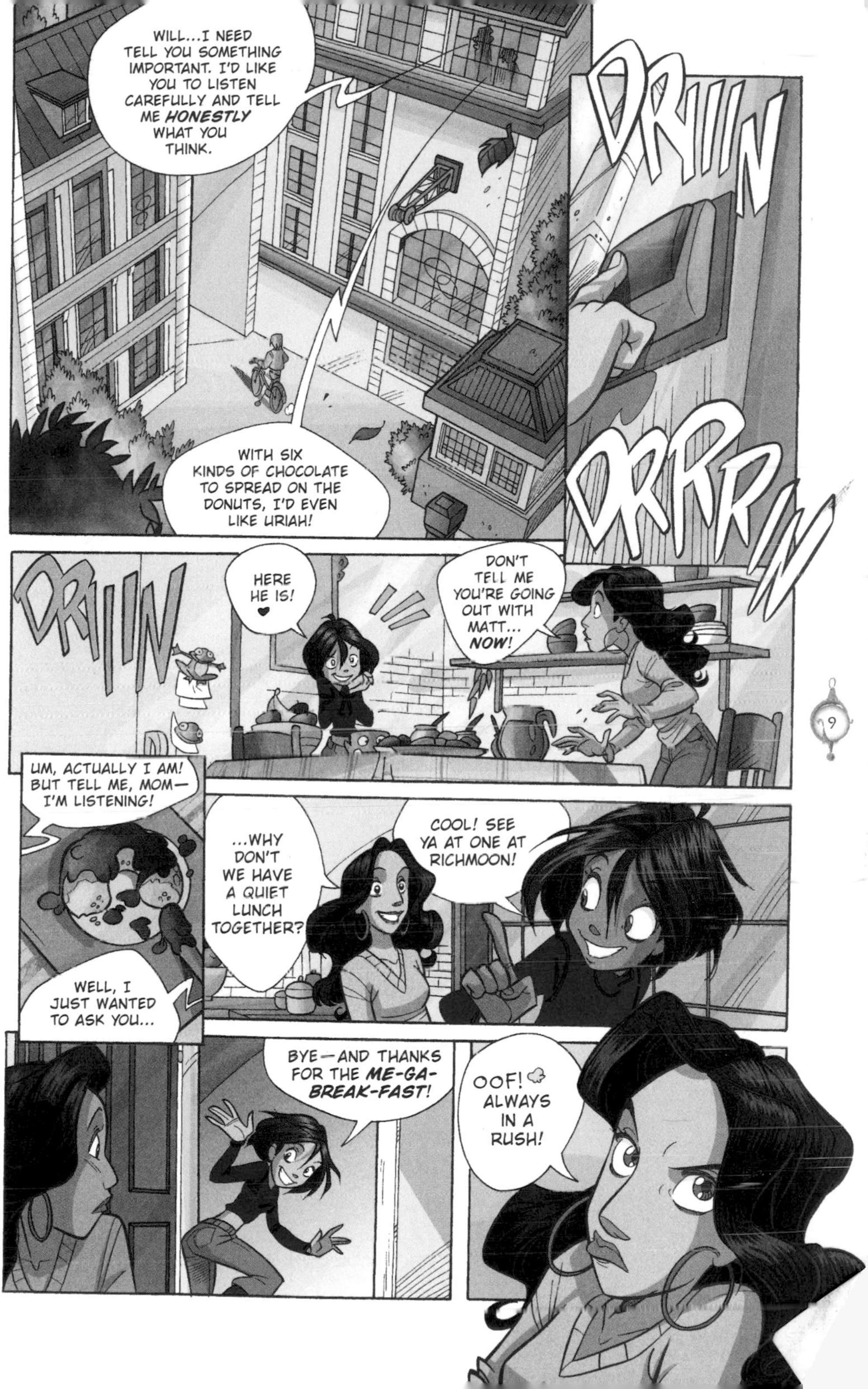

WILL...I NEED TELL YOU SOMETHING IMPORTANT. I'D LIKE YOU TO LISTEN CAREFULLY AND TELL ME **HONESTLY** WHAT YOU THINK.
WITH SIX KINDS OF CHOCOLATE TO SPREAD ON THE DONUTS, I'D EVEN LIKE URIAH!
DRIIIN
DRRRRIN
DRIIIN
HERE HE IS! ❤
DON'T TELL ME YOU'RE GOING OUT WITH MATT... **NOW**!
UM, ACTUALLY I AM! BUT TELL ME, MOM—I'M LISTENING!
WELL, I JUST WANTED TO ASK YOU...
...WHY DON'T WE HAVE A QUIET LUNCH TOGETHER?
COOL! SEE YA AT ONE AT RICHMOON!
BYE—AND THANKS FOR THE **ME-GA-BREAK-FAST**!
OOF! ALWAYS IN A RUSH!

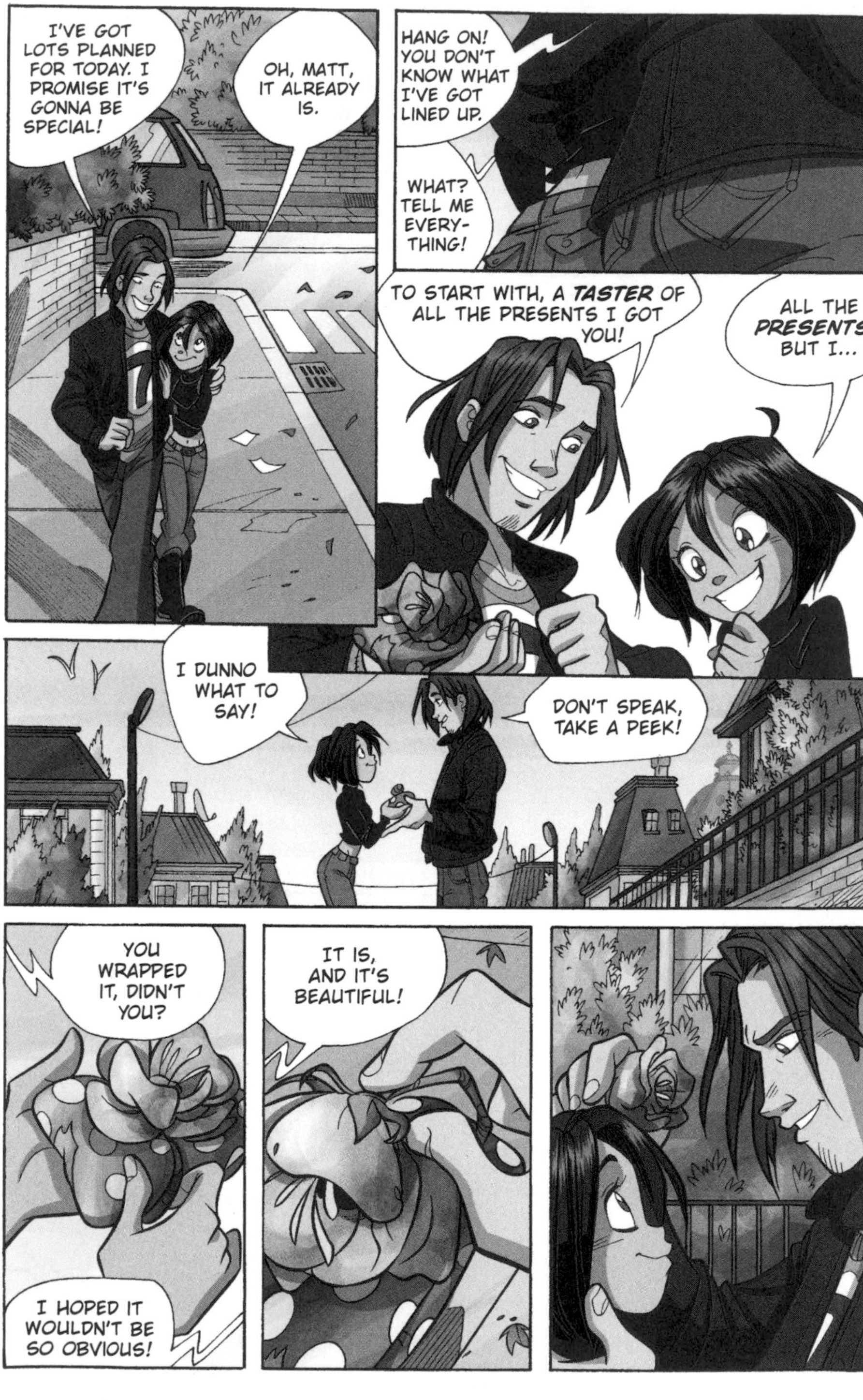
I'VE GOT LOTS PLANNED FOR TODAY. I PROMISE IT'S GONNA BE SPECIAL!
OH, MATT, IT ALREADY IS.
HANG ON! YOU DON'T KNOW WHAT I'VE GOT LINED UP.
WHAT? TELL ME EVERY-THING!
TO START WITH, A TASTER OF ALL THE PRESENTS I GOT YOU!
ALL THE PRESENTS? BUT I...
I DUNNO WHAT TO SAY!
DON'T SPEAK, TAKE A PEEK!
YOU WRAPPED IT, DIDN'T YOU?
I HOPED IT WOULDN'T BE SO OBVIOUS!
IT IS, AND IT'S BEAUTIFUL!

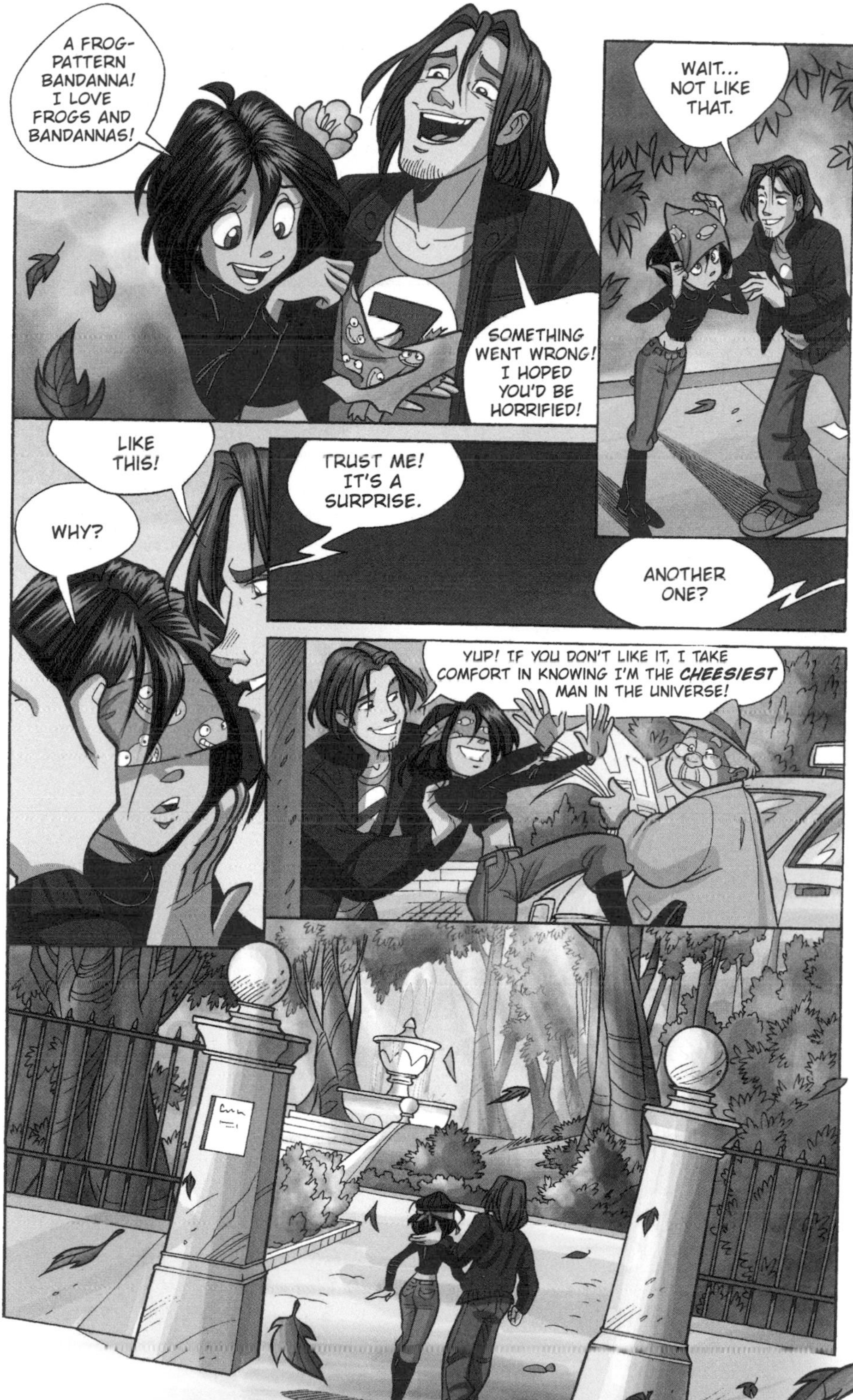
A FROG-PATTERN BANDANNA! I LOVE FROGS AND BANDANNAS!
SOMETHING WENT WRONG! I HOPED YOU'D BE HORRIFIED!
WAIT... NOT LIKE THAT.
LIKE THIS!
WHY?
TRUST ME! IT'S A SURPRISE.
ANOTHER ONE?
YUP! IF YOU DON'T LIKE IT, I TAKE COMFORT IN KNOWING I'M THE CHEESIEST MAN IN THE UNIVERSE!

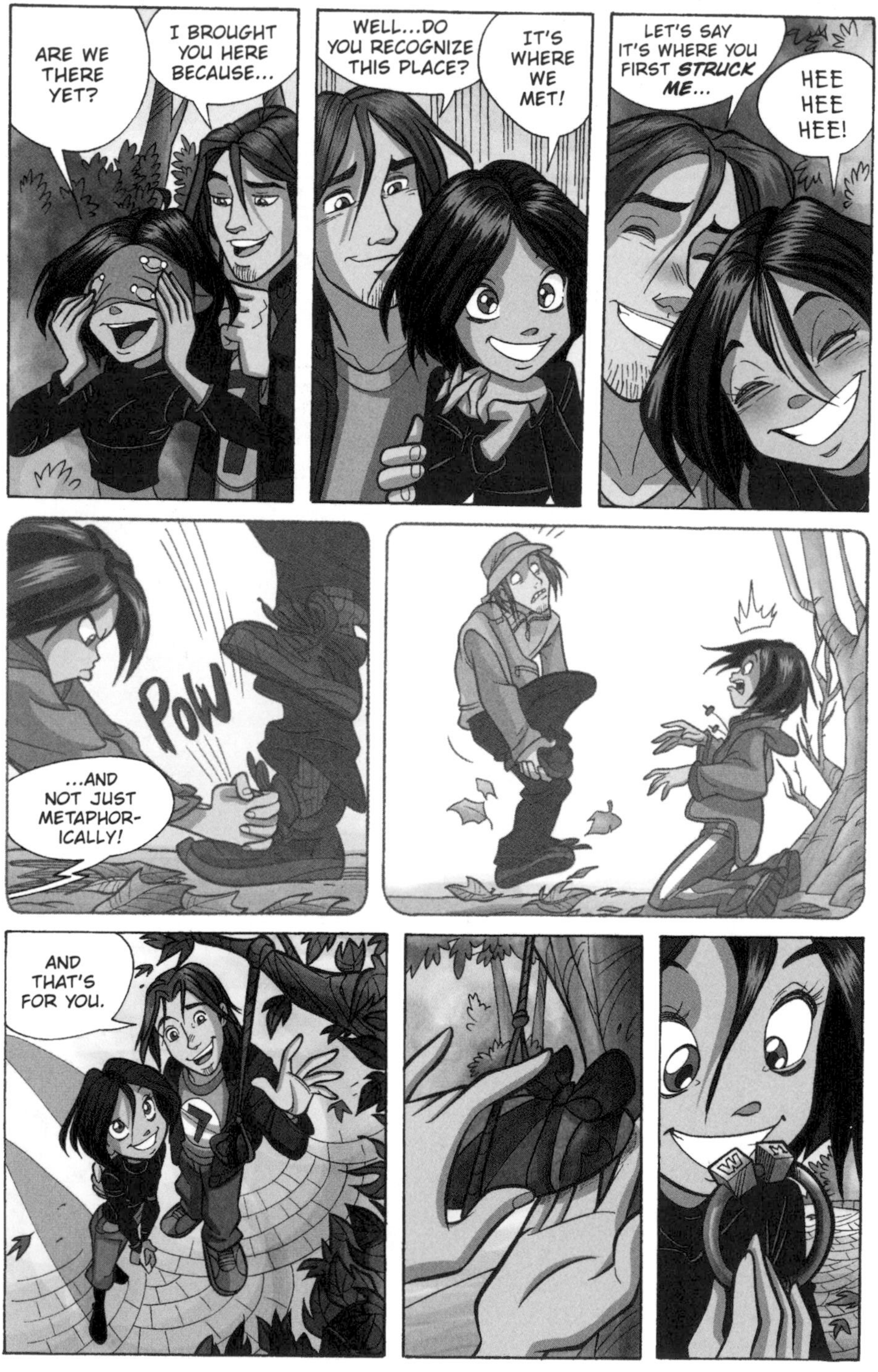
ARE WE THERE YET?
I BROUGHT YOU HERE BECAUSE...
WELL...DO YOU RECOGNIZE THIS PLACE?
IT'S WHERE WE MET!
LET'S SAY IT'S WHERE YOU FIRST STRUCK ME...
HEE HEE HEE!
POW
...AND NOT JUST METAPHOR-ICALLY!
AND THAT'S FOR YOU.

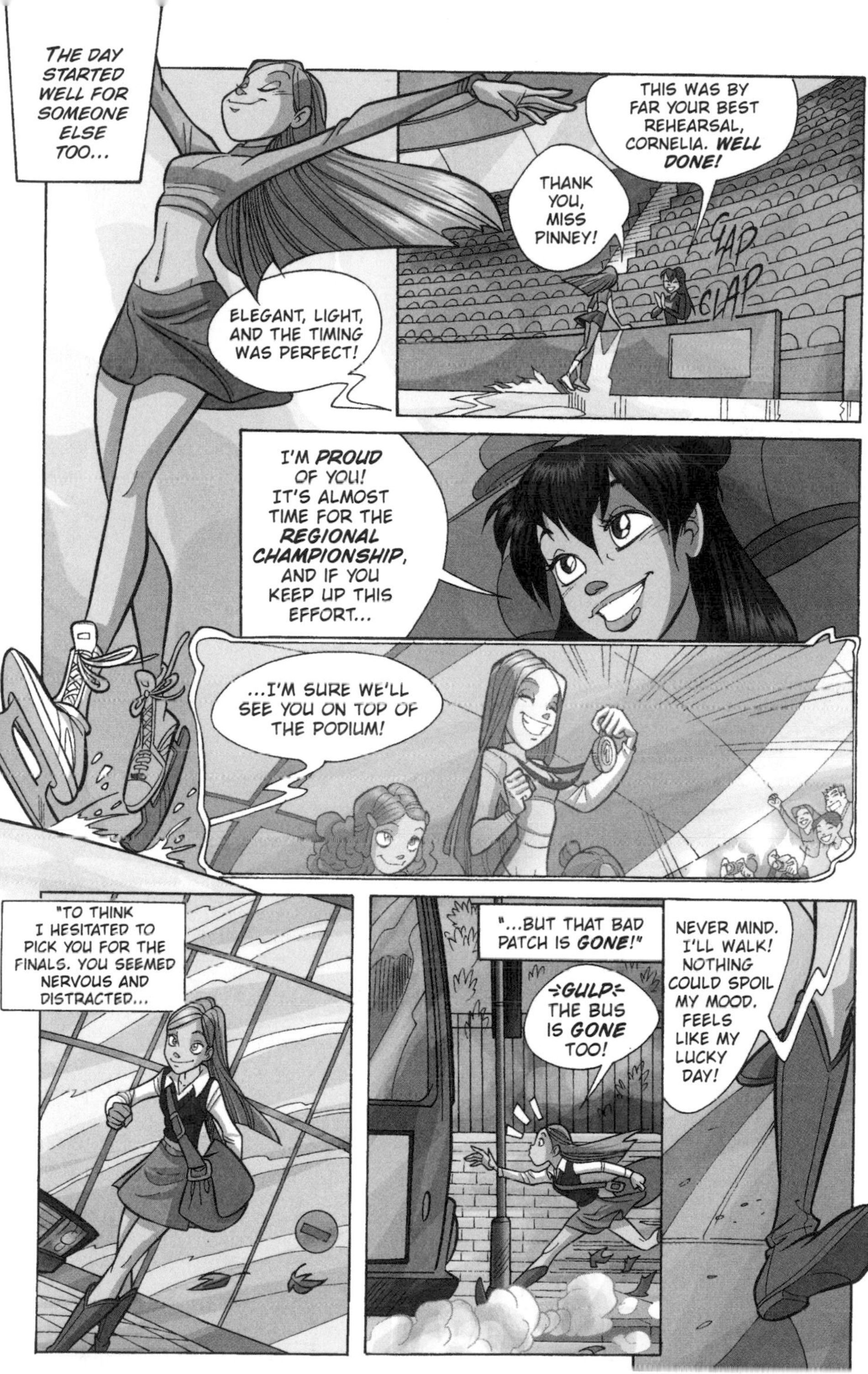
THE DAY STARTED WELL FOR SOMEONE ELSE TOO...
THIS WAS BY FAR YOUR BEST REHEARSAL, CORNELIA. **WELL DONE!**
THANK YOU, MISS PINNEY!
CLAP
CLAP
ELEGANT, LIGHT, AND THE TIMING WAS PERFECT!
I'M **PROUD** OF YOU! IT'S ALMOST TIME FOR THE **REGIONAL CHAMPIONSHIP**, AND IF YOU KEEP UP THIS EFFORT...
...I'M SURE WE'LL SEE YOU ON TOP OF THE PODIUM!
"TO THINK I HESITATED TO PICK YOU FOR THE FINALS. YOU SEEMED NERVOUS AND DISTRACTED...
"...BUT THAT BAD PATCH IS **GONE!**"
GULP THE BUS IS **GONE** TOO!
NEVER MIND. I'LL WALK! NOTHING COULD SPOIL MY MOOD. FEELS LIKE MY LUCKY DAY!

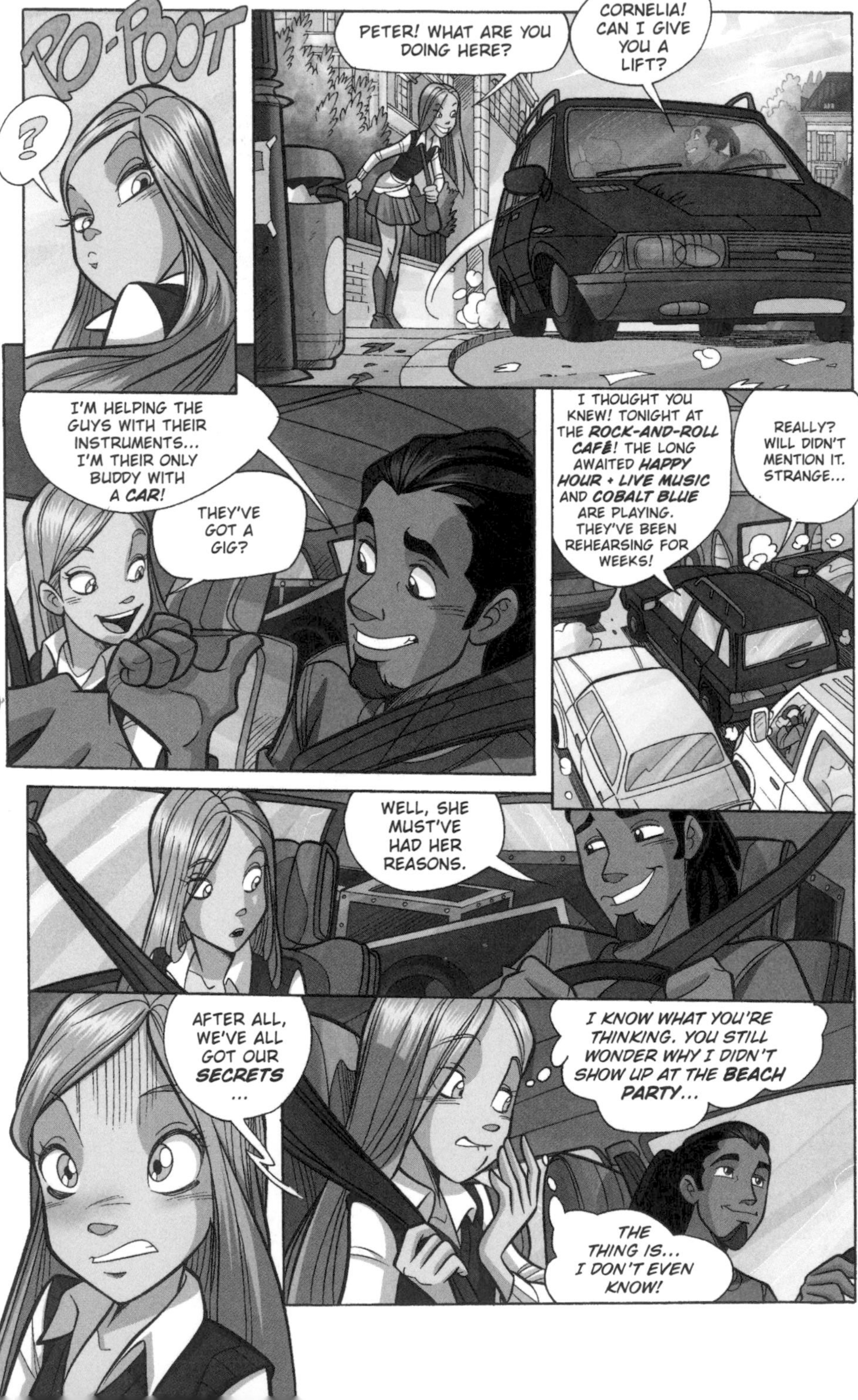
PO-POOT
?
PETER! WHAT ARE YOU DOING HERE?
HI, CORNELIA! CAN I GIVE YOU A LIFT?
I'M HELPING THE GUYS WITH THEIR INSTRUMENTS... I'M THEIR ONLY BUDDY WITH A **CAR**!
THEY'VE GOT A GIG?
I THOUGHT YOU KNEW! TONIGHT AT THE **ROCK-AND-ROLL CAFÉ**! THE LONG AWAITED **HAPPY HOUR + LIVE MUSIC** AND **COBALT BLUE** ARE PLAYING. THEY'VE BEEN REHEARSING FOR WEEKS!
REALLY? WILL DIDN'T MENTION IT. STRANGE...
WELL, SHE MUST'VE HAD HER REASONS.
AFTER ALL, WE'VE ALL GOT OUR **SECRETS** ...
*I KNOW WHAT YOU'RE THINKING. YOU STILL WONDER WHY I DIDN'T SHOW UP AT THE **BEACH PARTY**...*
THE THING IS... I DON'T EVEN KNOW!

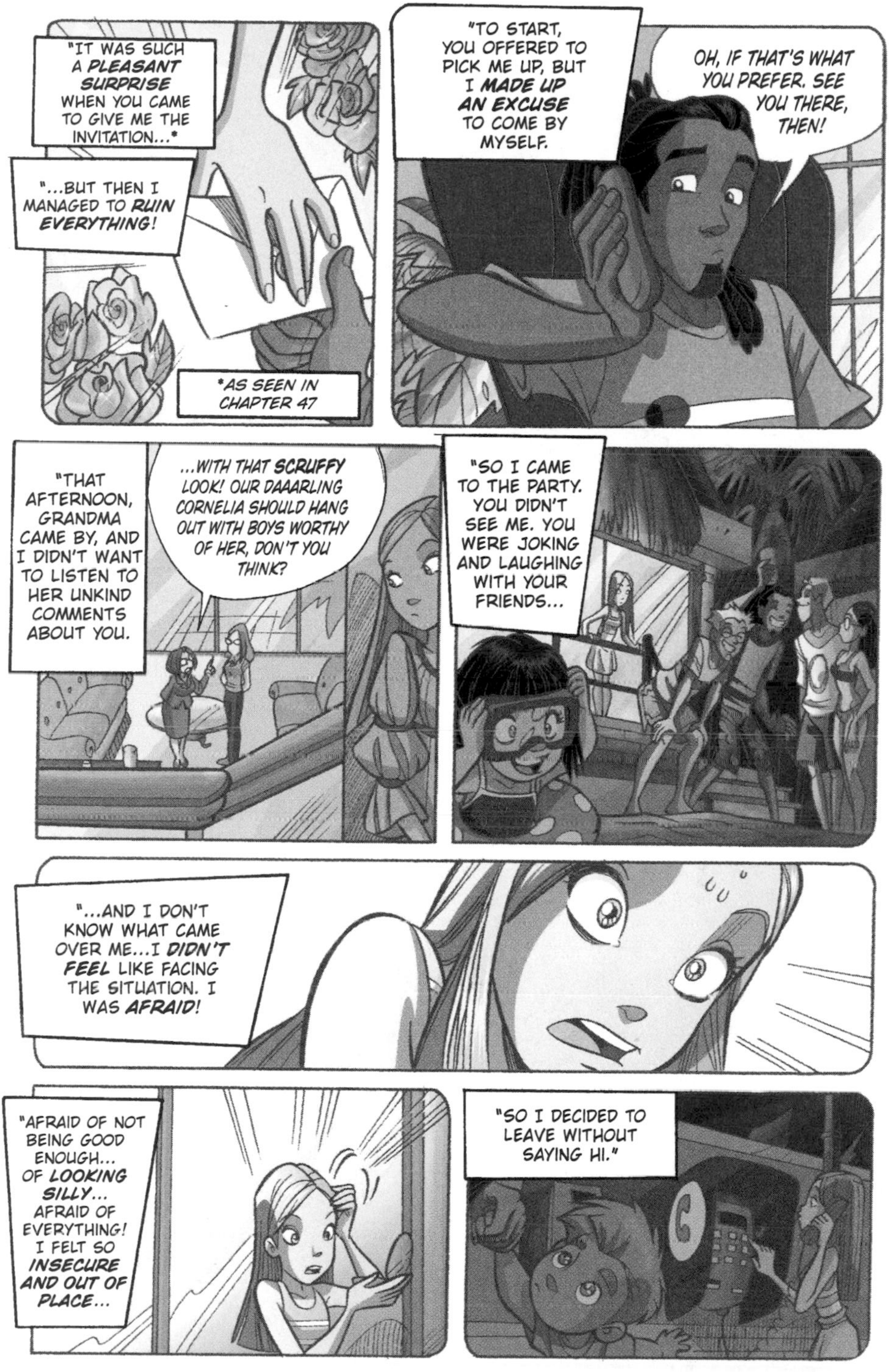
"IT WAS SUCH A PLEASANT SURPRISE WHEN YOU CAME TO GIVE ME THE INVITATION...*
"...BUT THEN I MANAGED TO RUIN EVERYTHING!
*AS SEEN IN CHAPTER 47
"TO START, YOU OFFERED TO PICK ME UP, BUT I MADE UP AN EXCUSE TO COME BY MYSELF.
OH, IF THAT'S WHAT YOU PREFER. SEE YOU THERE, THEN!
"THAT AFTERNOON, GRANDMA CAME BY, AND I DIDN'T WANT TO LISTEN TO HER UNKIND COMMENTS ABOUT YOU.
...WITH THAT SCRUFFY LOOK! OUR DAAARLING CORNELIA SHOULD HANG OUT WITH BOYS WORTHY OF HER, DON'T YOU THINK?
"SO I CAME TO THE PARTY. YOU DIDN'T SEE ME. YOU WERE JOKING AND LAUGHING WITH YOUR FRIENDS...
"...AND I DON'T KNOW WHAT CAME OVER ME...I DIDN'T FEEL LIKE FACING THE SITUATION. I WAS AFRAID!
"AFRAID OF NOT BEING GOOD ENOUGH... OF LOOKING SILLY... AFRAID OF EVERYTHING! I FELT SO INSECURE AND OUT OF PLACE...
"SO I DECIDED TO LEAVE WITHOUT SAYING HI."

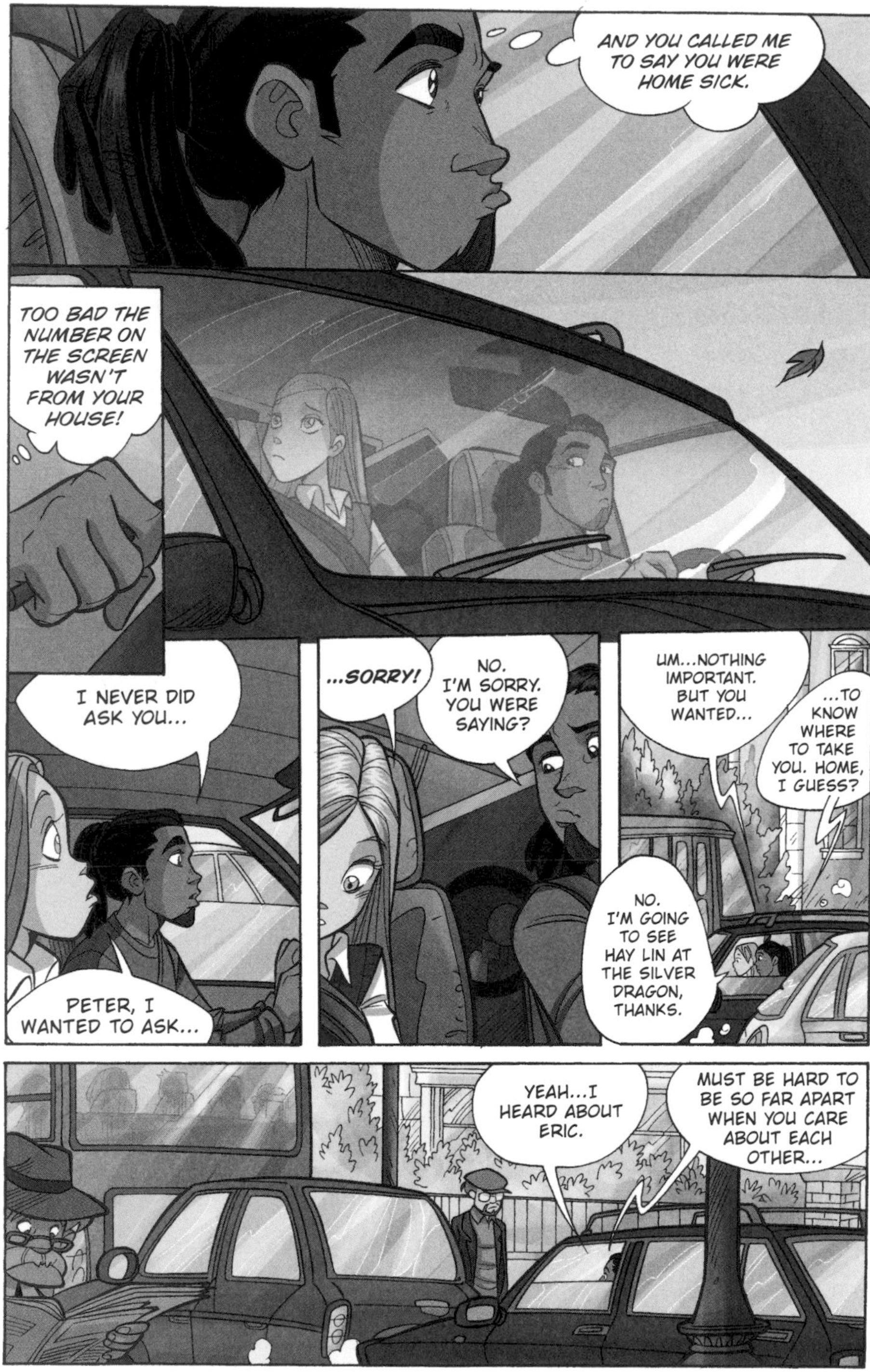
AND YOU CALLED ME TO SAY YOU WERE HOME SICK.
TOO BAD THE NUMBER ON THE SCREEN WASN'T FROM YOUR HOUSE!
I NEVER DID ASK YOU...
PETER, I WANTED TO ASK...
...SORRY!
NO. I'M SORRY. YOU WERE SAYING?
UM...NOTHING IMPORTANT. BUT YOU WANTED...
...TO KNOW WHERE TO TAKE YOU. HOME, I GUESS?
NO. I'M GOING TO SEE HAY LIN AT THE SILVER DRAGON, THANKS.
YEAH...I HEARD ABOUT ERIC.
MUST BE HARD TO BE SO FAR APART WHEN YOU CARE ABOUT EACH OTHER...

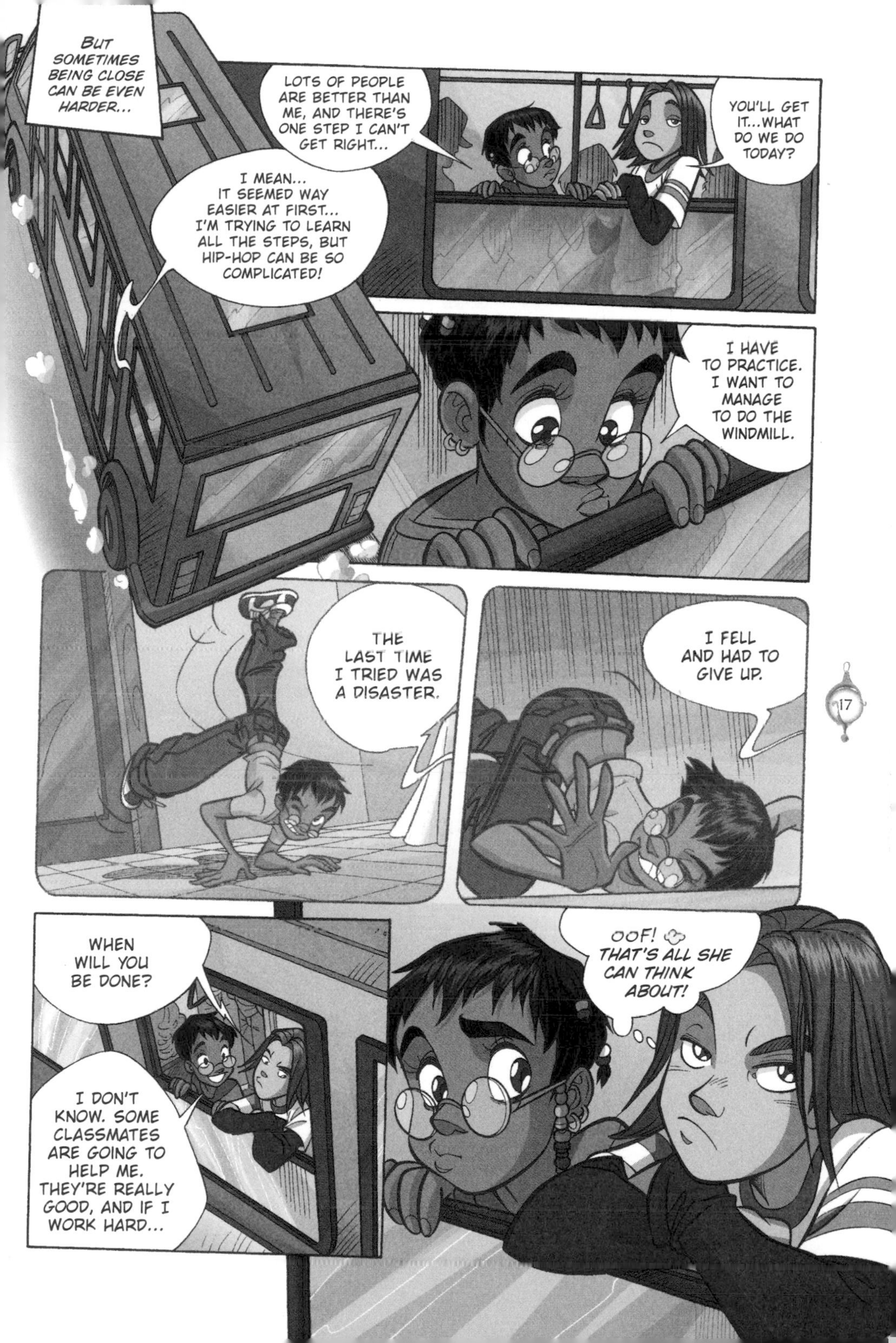

BUT SOMETIMES BEING CLOSE CAN BE EVEN HARDER...
LOTS OF PEOPLE ARE BETTER THAN ME, AND THERE'S ONE STEP I CAN'T GET RIGHT...
YOU'LL GET IT...WHAT DO WE DO TODAY?
I MEAN... IT SEEMED WAY EASIER AT FIRST... I'M TRYING TO LEARN ALL THE STEPS, BUT HIP-HOP CAN BE SO COMPLICATED!
I HAVE TO PRACTICE. I WANT TO MANAGE TO DO THE WINDMILL.
THE LAST TIME I TRIED WAS A DISASTER.
I FELL AND HAD TO GIVE UP.
WHEN WILL YOU BE DONE?
I DON'T KNOW. SOME CLASSMATES ARE GOING TO HELP ME. THEY'RE REALLY GOOD, AND IF I WORK HARD...
OOF! THAT'S ALL SHE CAN THINK ABOUT!

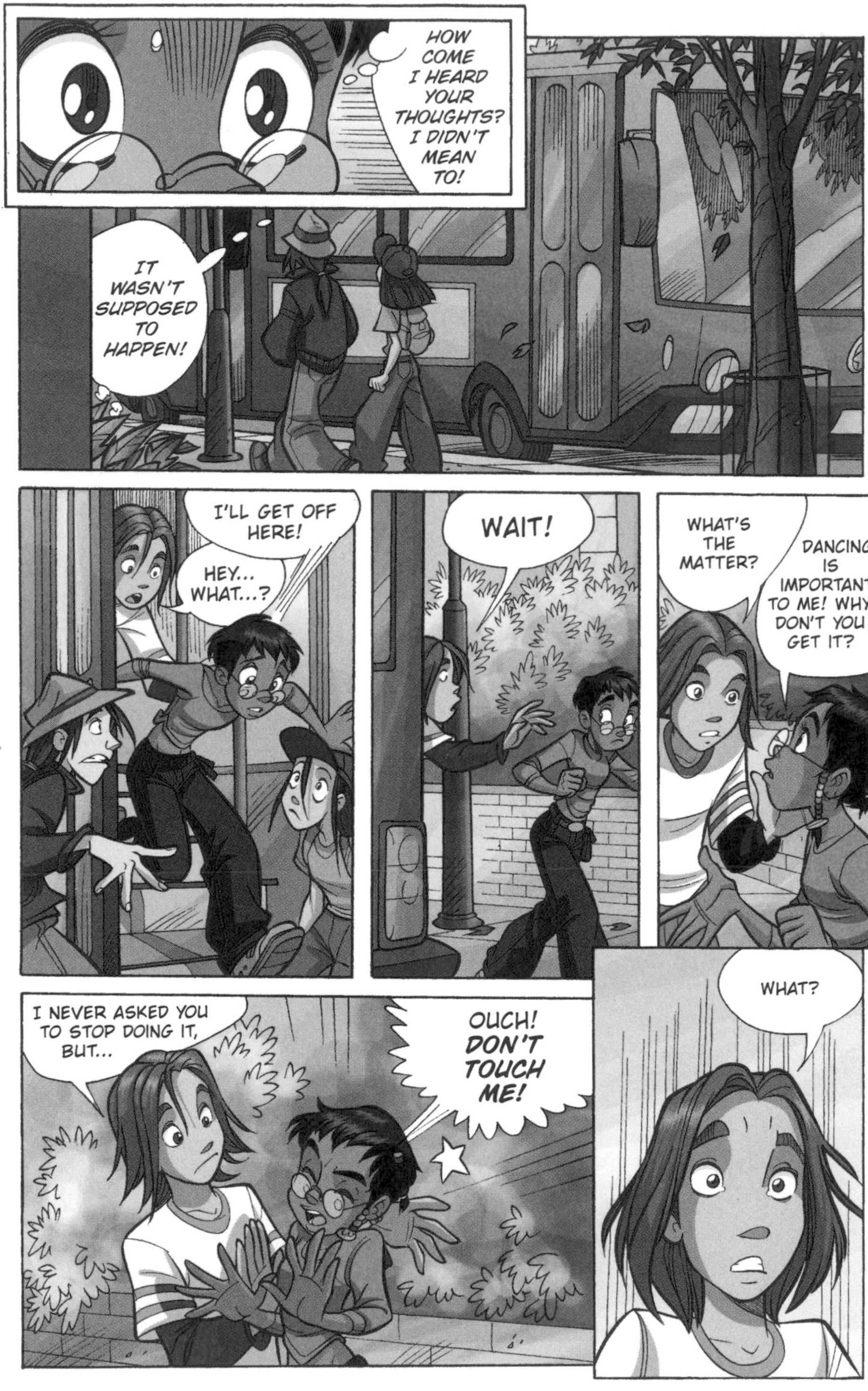
HOW COME I HEARD YOUR THOUGHTS? I DIDN'T MEAN TO!
IT WASN'T SUPPOSED TO HAPPEN!
I'LL GET OFF HERE!
HEY... WHAT...?
WAIT!
WHAT'S THE MATTER?
DANCING IS IMPORTANT TO ME! WHY DON'T YOU GET IT?
I NEVER ASKED YOU TO STOP DOING IT, BUT...
OUCH! DON'T TOUCH ME!
WHAT?

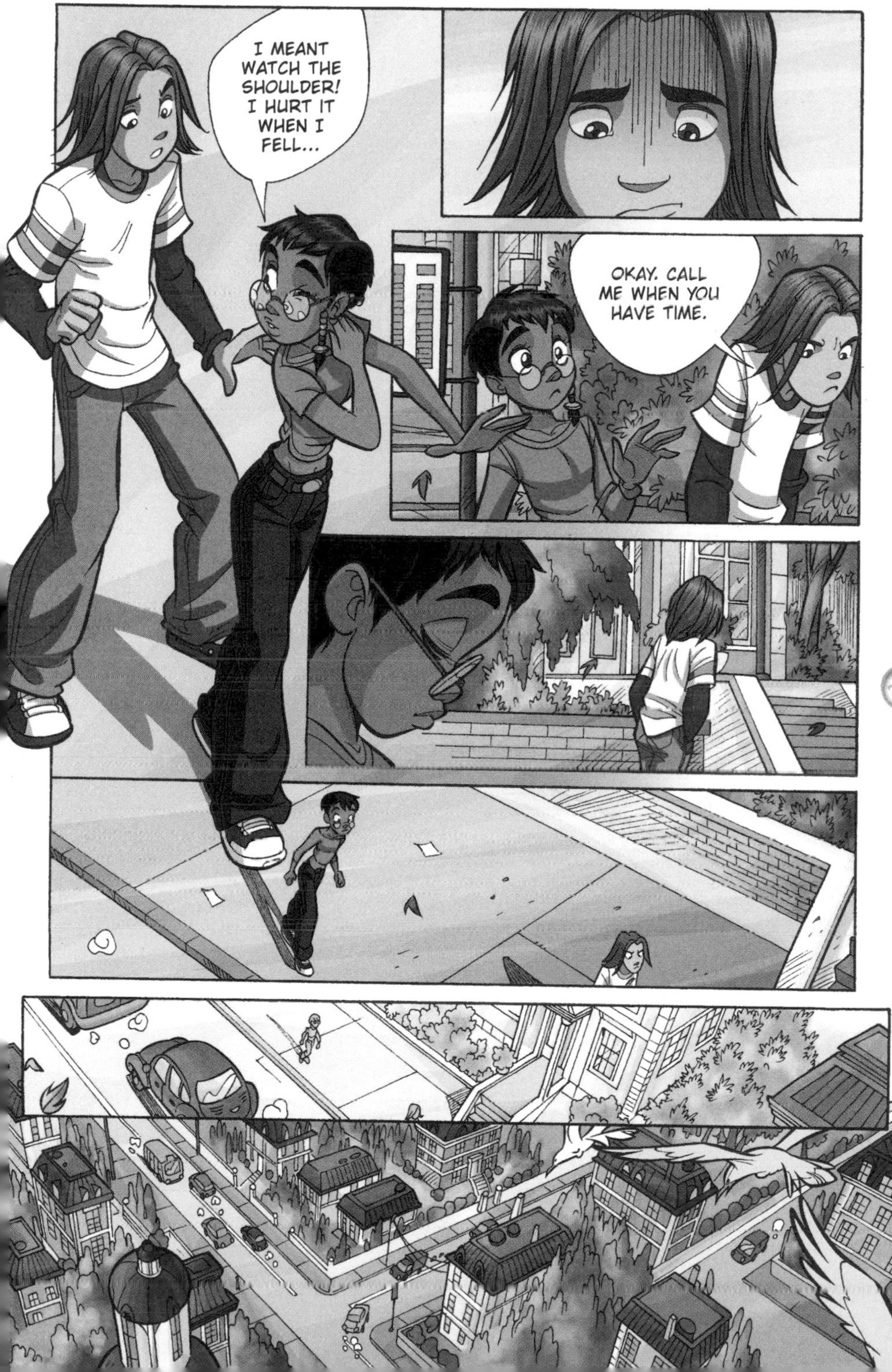
I MEANT WATCH THE SHOULDER! I HURT IT WHEN I FELL...
OKAY. CALL ME WHEN YOU HAVE TIME.

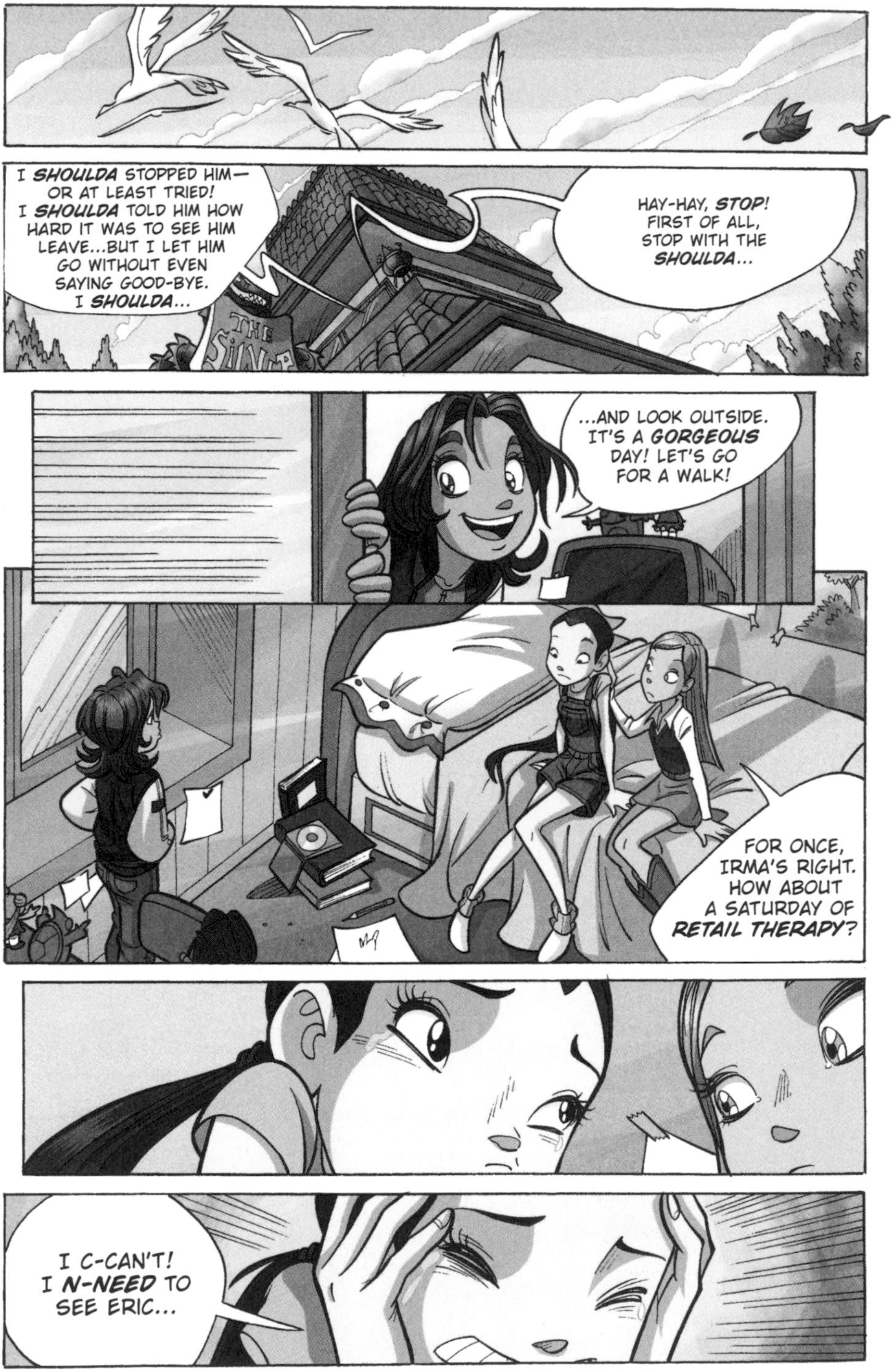
I SHOULDA STOPPED HIM— OR AT LEAST TRIED! I SHOULDA TOLD HIM HOW HARD IT WAS TO SEE HIM LEAVE...BUT I LET HIM GO WITHOUT EVEN SAYING GOOD-BYE. I SHOULDA...
HAY-HAY, STOP! FIRST OF ALL, STOP WITH THE SHOULDA...
...AND LOOK OUTSIDE. IT'S A GORGEOUS DAY! LET'S GO FOR A WALK!
FOR ONCE, IRMA'S RIGHT. HOW ABOUT A SATURDAY OF RETAIL THERAPY?
I C-CAN'T! I N-NEED TO SEE ERIC...

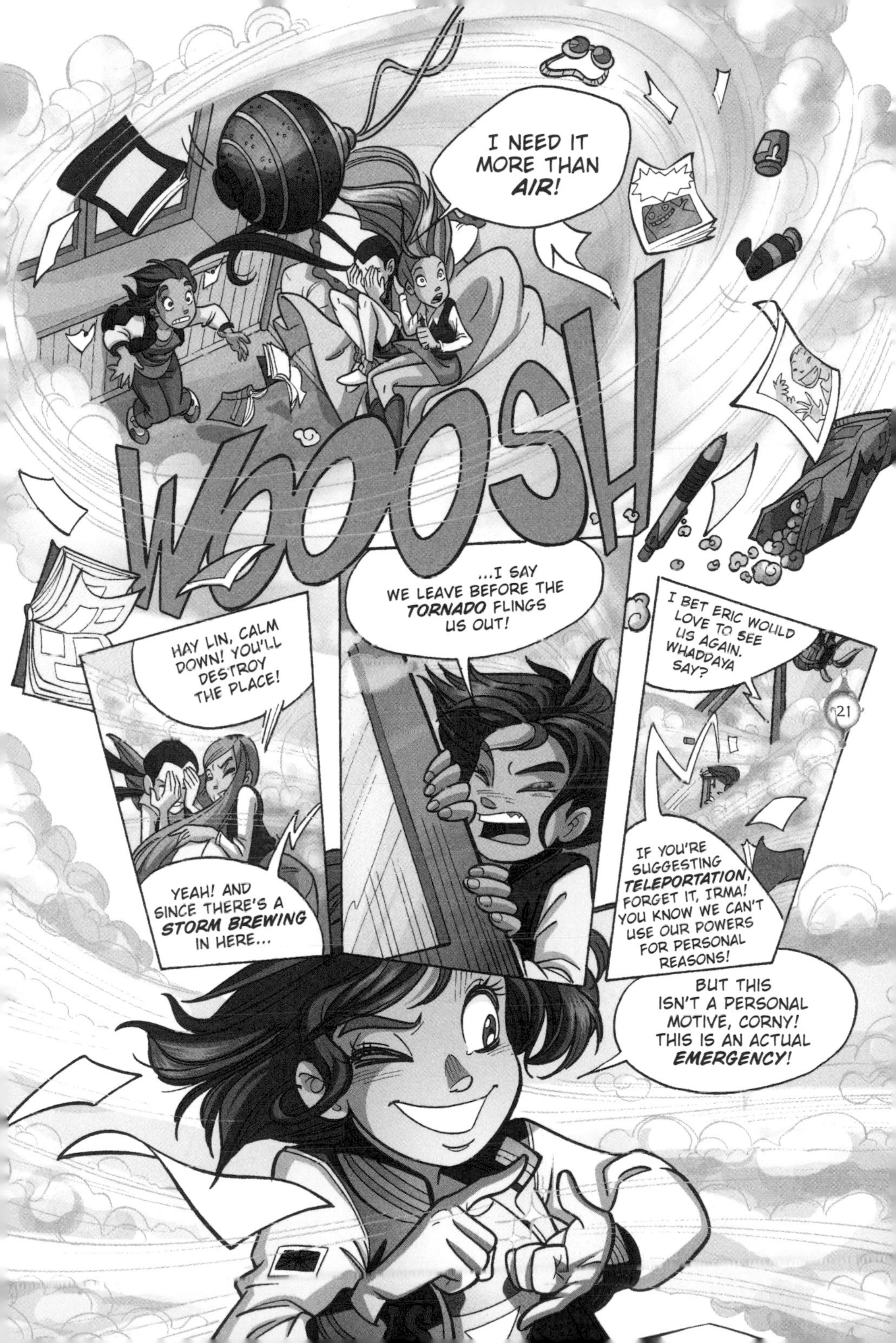
I NEED IT MORE THAN AIR!
WOOOSH
HAY LIN, CALM DOWN! YOU'LL DESTROY THE PLACE!
YEAH! AND SINCE THERE'S A STORM BREWING IN HERE...
...I SAY WE LEAVE BEFORE THE TORNADO FLINGS US OUT!
I BET ERIC WOULD LOVE TO SEE US AGAIN. WHADDAYA SAY?
IF YOU'RE SUGGESTING TELEPORTATION, FORGET IT, IRMA! YOU KNOW WE CAN'T USE OUR POWERS FOR PERSONAL REASONS!
BUT THIS ISN'T A PERSONAL MOTIVE, CORNY! THIS IS AN ACTUAL EMERGENCY!

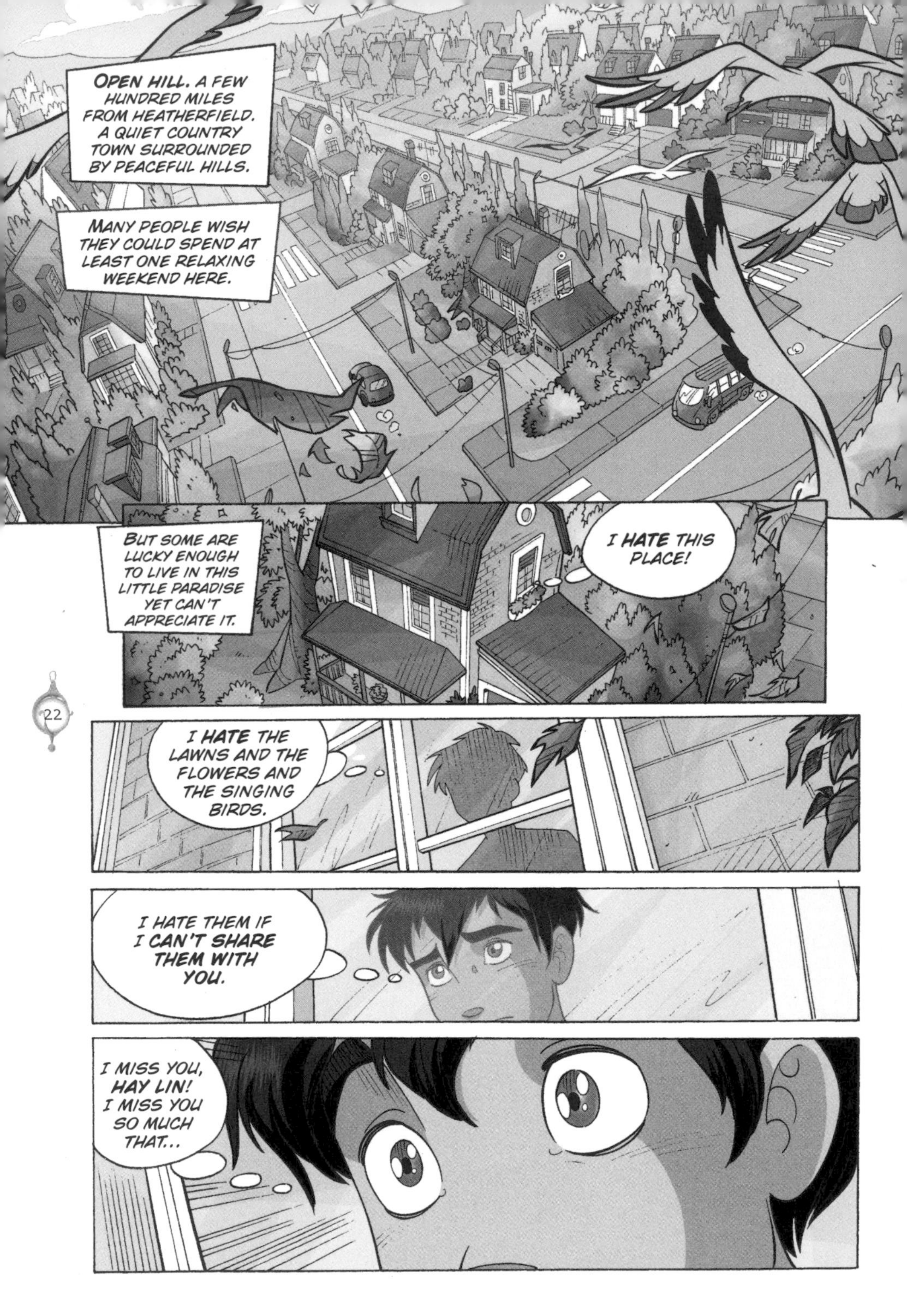

OPEN HILL. A FEW HUNDRED MILES FROM HEATHERFIELD. A QUIET COUNTRY TOWN SURROUNDED BY PEACEFUL HILLS.
MANY PEOPLE WISH THEY COULD SPEND AT LEAST ONE RELAXING WEEKEND HERE.
BUT SOME ARE LUCKY ENOUGH TO LIVE IN THIS LITTLE PARADISE YET CAN'T APPRECIATE IT.
I HATE THIS PLACE!
I HATE THE LAWNS AND THE FLOWERS AND THE SINGING BIRDS.
I HATE THEM IF I CAN'T SHARE THEM WITH YOU.
I MISS YOU, HAY LIN! I MISS YOU SO MUCH THAT...

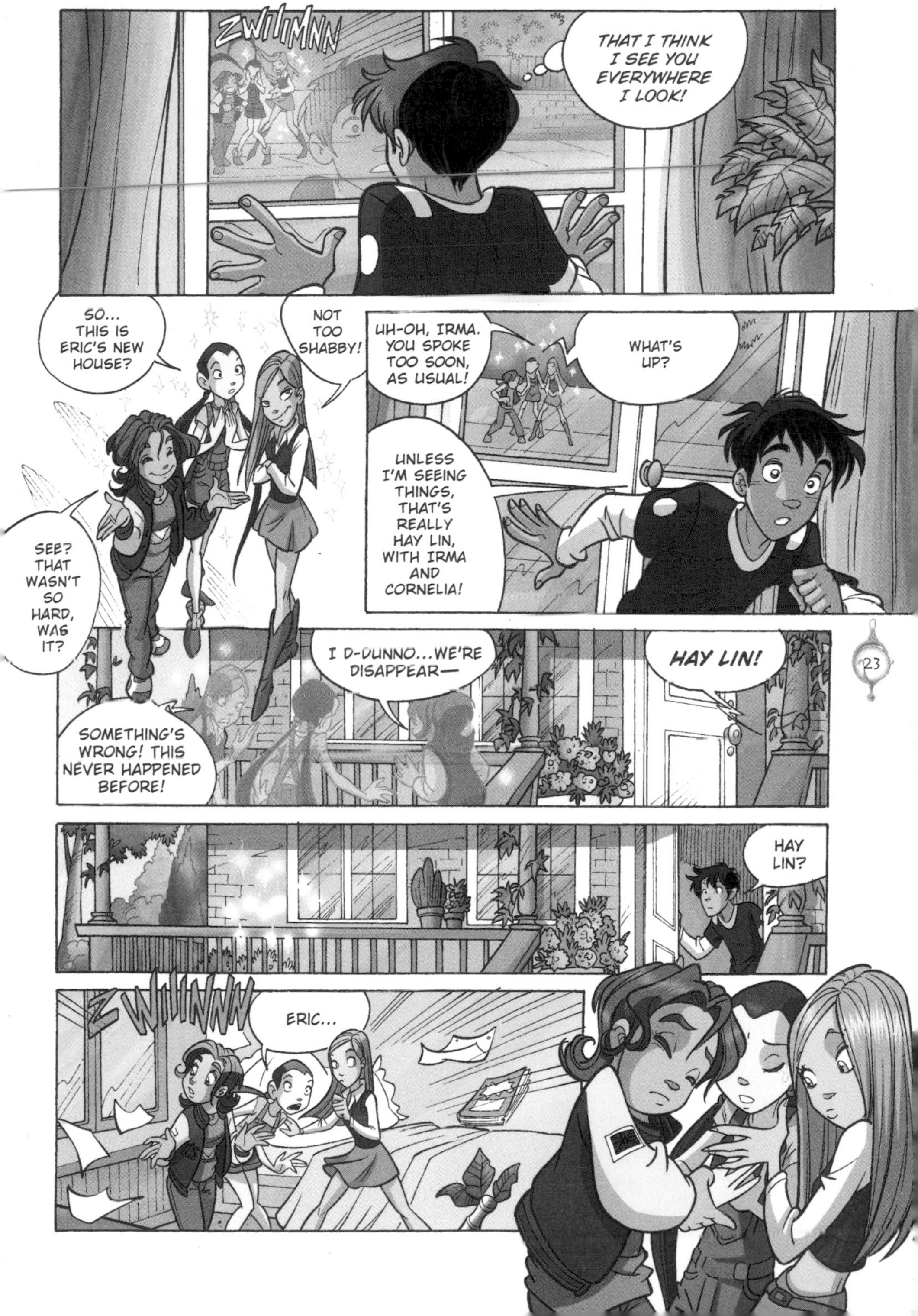
ZWIIIMNN
THAT I THINK I SEE YOU EVERYWHERE I LOOK!
SO... THIS IS ERIC'S NEW HOUSE?
NOT TOO SHABBY!
SEE? THAT WASN'T SO HARD, WAS IT?
UH-OH, IRMA. YOU SPOKE TOO SOON, AS USUAL!
WHAT'S UP?
UNLESS I'M SEEING THINGS, THAT'S REALLY HAY LIN, WITH IRMA AND CORNELIA!
SOMETHING'S WRONG! THIS NEVER HAPPENED BEFORE!
I D-DUNNO...WE'RE DISAPPEAR—
HAY LIN!
HAY LIN?
ZWIIINNN
ERIC...

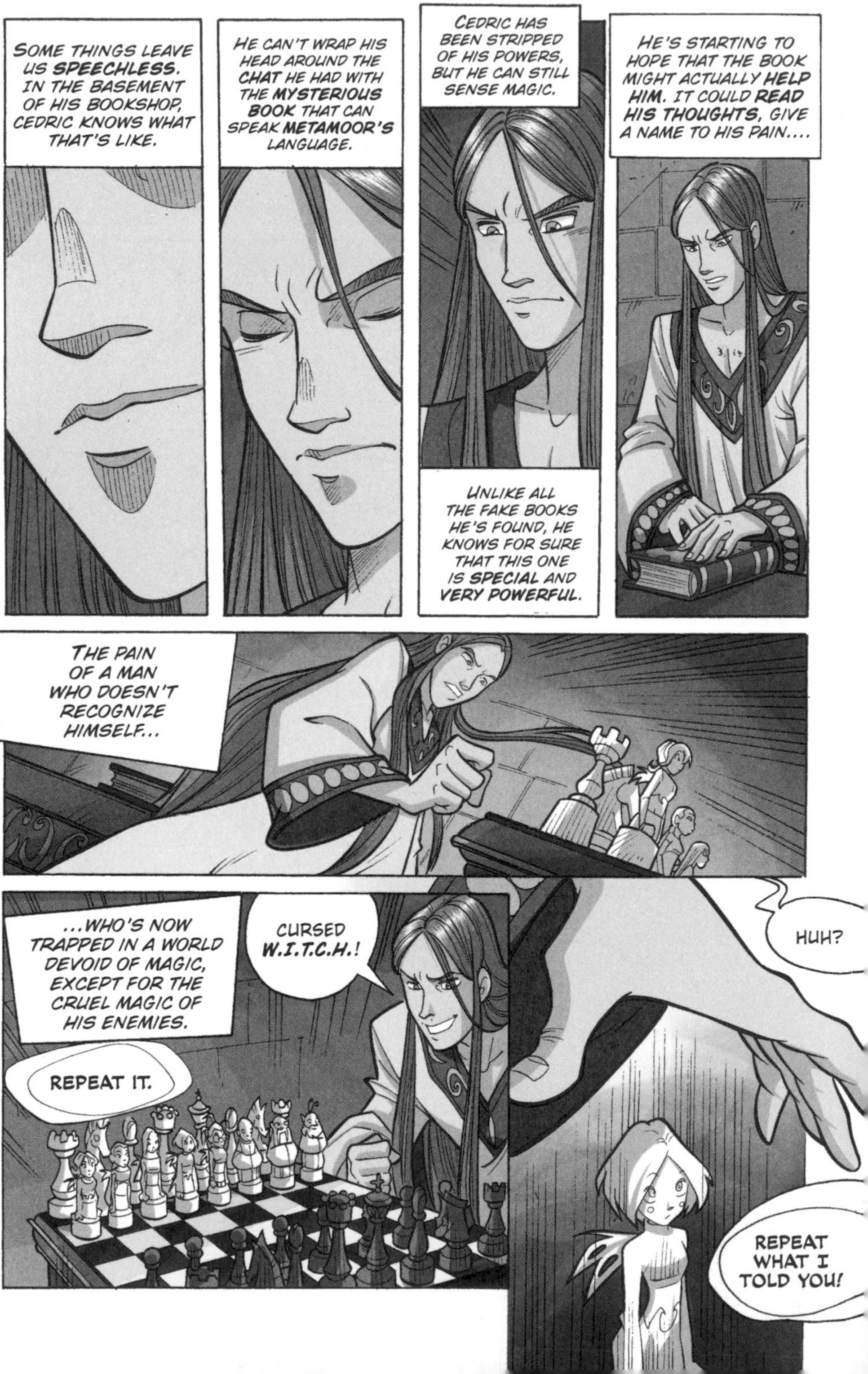
SOME THINGS LEAVE US SPEECHLESS. IN THE BASEMENT OF HIS BOOKSHOP, CEDRIC KNOWS WHAT THAT'S LIKE.
HE CAN'T WRAP HIS HEAD AROUND THE CHAT HE HAD WITH THE MYSTERIOUS BOOK THAT CAN SPEAK METAMOOR'S LANGUAGE.
CEDRIC HAS BEEN STRIPPED OF HIS POWERS, BUT HE CAN STILL SENSE MAGIC.
UNLIKE ALL THE FAKE BOOKS HE'S FOUND, HE KNOWS FOR SURE THAT THIS ONE IS SPECIAL AND VERY POWERFUL.
HE'S STARTING TO HOPE THAT THE BOOK MIGHT ACTUALLY HELP HIM. IT COULD READ HIS THOUGHTS, GIVE A NAME TO HIS PAIN....
THE PAIN OF A MAN WHO DOESN'T RECOGNIZE HIMSELF...
...WHO'S NOW TRAPPED IN A WORLD DEVOID OF MAGIC, EXCEPT FOR THE CRUEL MAGIC OF HIS ENEMIES.
CURSED W.I.T.C.H.!
REPEAT IT.
HUH?
REPEAT WHAT I TOLD YOU!

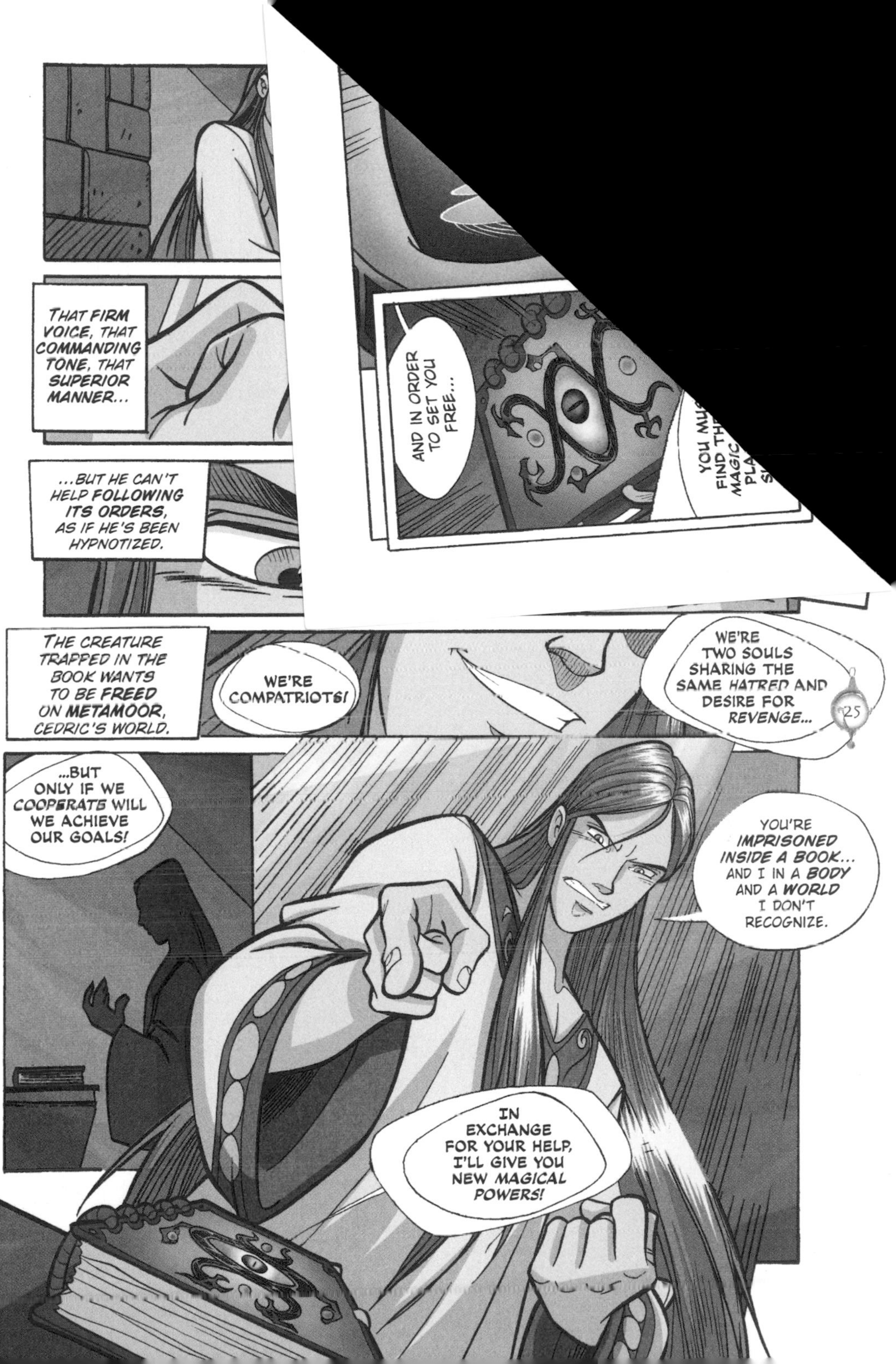
THAT FIRM VOICE, THAT COMMANDING TONE, THAT SUPERIOR MANNER...
...BUT HE CAN'T HELP FOLLOWING ITS ORDERS, AS IF HE'S BEEN HYPNOTIZED.
AND IN ORDER TO SET YOU FREE...
THE CREATURE TRAPPED IN THE BOOK WANTS TO BE FREED ON METAMOOR, CEDRIC'S WORLD.
WE'RE COMPATRIOTS!
WE'RE TWO SOULS SHARING THE SAME HATRED AND DESIRE FOR REVENGE...
...BUT ONLY IF WE COOPERATE WILL WE ACHIEVE OUR GOALS!
YOU'RE IMPRISONED INSIDE A BOOK... AND I IN A BODY AND A WORLD I DON'T RECOGNIZE.
IN EXCHANGE FOR YOUR HELP, I'LL GIVE YOU NEW MAGICAL POWERS!

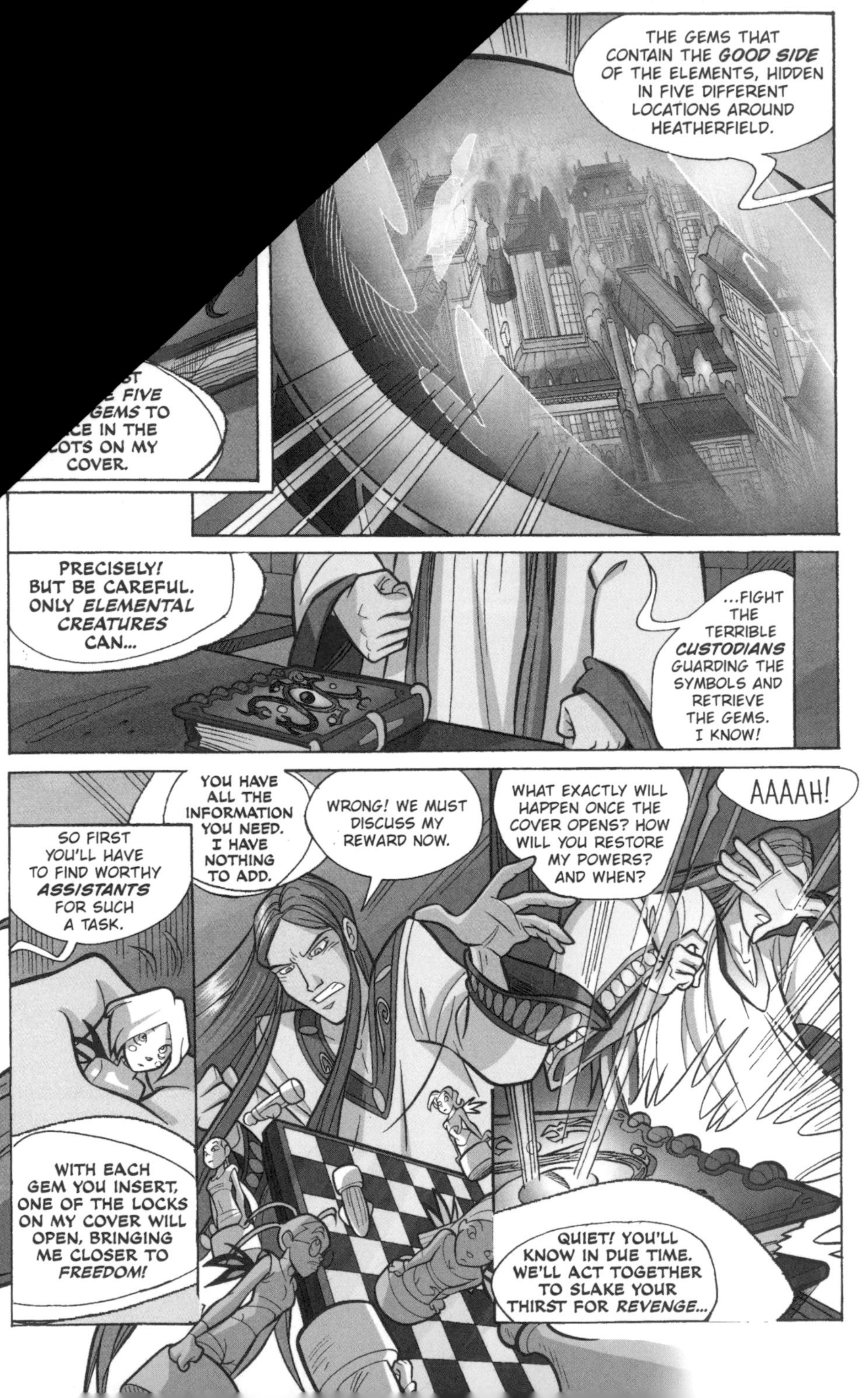

FIVE GEMS TO IN THE ON MY COVER.
THE GEMS THAT CONTAIN THE *GOOD SIDE* OF THE ELEMENTS, HIDDEN IN FIVE DIFFERENT LOCATIONS AROUND HEATHERFIELD.
PRECISELY! BUT BE CAREFUL. ONLY *ELEMENTAL CREATURES* CAN...
...FIGHT THE TERRIBLE *CUSTODIANS* GUARDING THE SYMBOLS AND RETRIEVE THE GEMS. I KNOW!
SO FIRST YOU'LL HAVE TO FIND WORTHY *ASSISTANTS* FOR SUCH A TASK.
YOU HAVE ALL THE INFORMATION YOU NEED. I HAVE NOTHING TO ADD.
WRONG! WE MUST DISCUSS MY REWARD NOW.
WHAT EXACTLY WILL HAPPEN ONCE THE COVER OPENS? HOW WILL YOU RESTORE MY POWERS? AND WHEN?
AAAAH!
WITH EACH GEM YOU INSERT, ONE OF THE LOCKS ON MY COVER WILL OPEN, BRINGING ME CLOSER TO *FREEDOM!*
QUIET! YOU'LL KNOW IN DUE TIME. WE'LL ACT TOGETHER TO SLAKE YOUR THIRST FOR *REVENGE...*

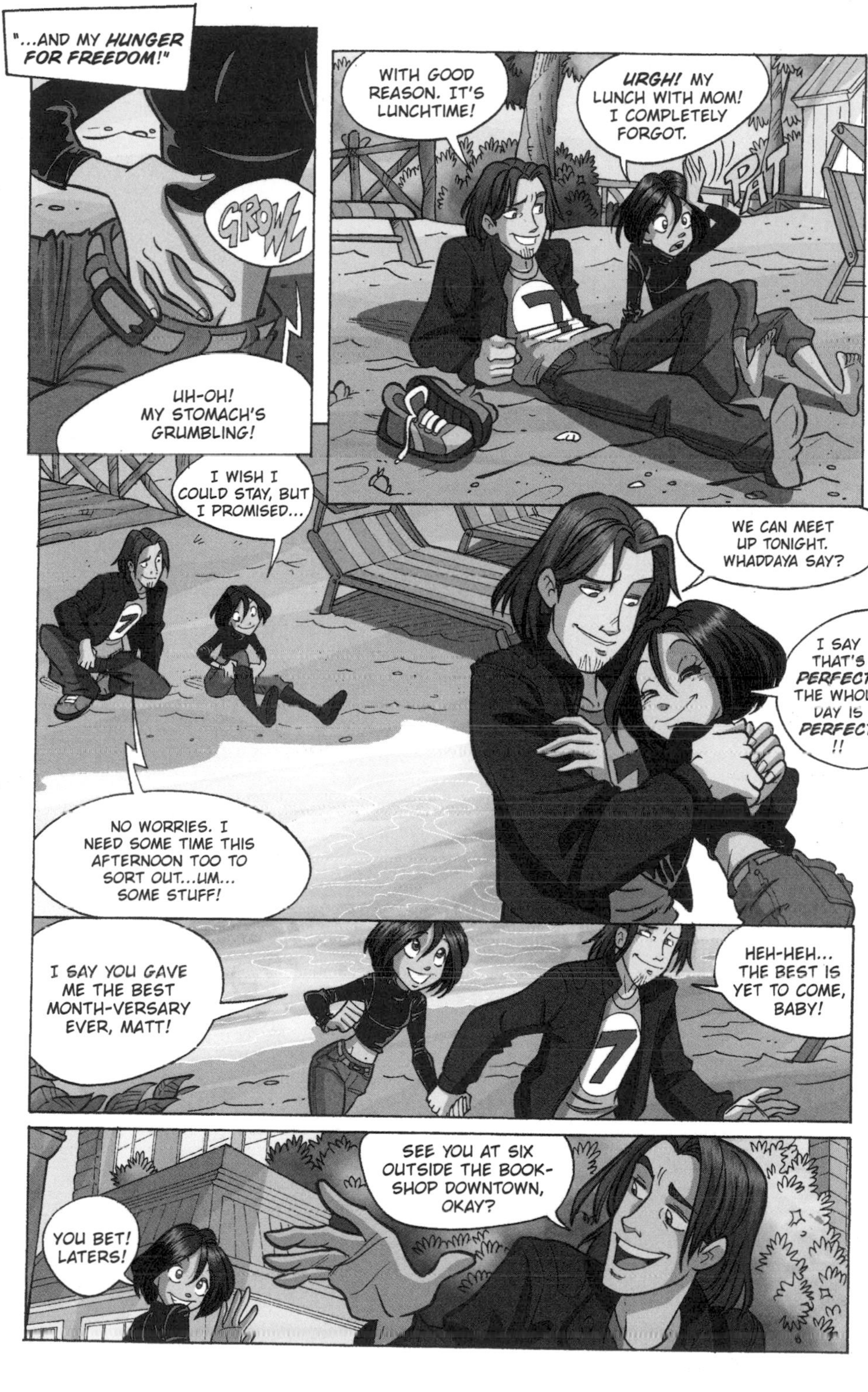

"...AND MY *HUNGER FOR FREEDOM!*"
GROWL
UH-OH! MY STOMACH'S GRUMBLING!
WITH GOOD REASON. IT'S LUNCHTIME!
URGH! MY LUNCH WITH MOM! I COMPLETELY FORGOT.
PAT
I WISH I COULD STAY, BUT I PROMISED...
NO WORRIES. I NEED SOME TIME THIS AFTERNOON TOO TO SORT OUT...UM... SOME STUFF!
WE CAN MEET UP TONIGHT. WHADDAYA SAY?
I SAY THAT'S *PERFECT*. THE WHOLE DAY IS *PERFECT*!!
I SAY YOU GAVE ME THE BEST MONTH-VERSARY EVER, MATT!
HEH-HEH... THE BEST IS YET TO COME, BABY!
SEE YOU AT SIX OUTSIDE THE BOOK-SHOP DOWNTOWN, OKAY?
YOU BET! LATERS!

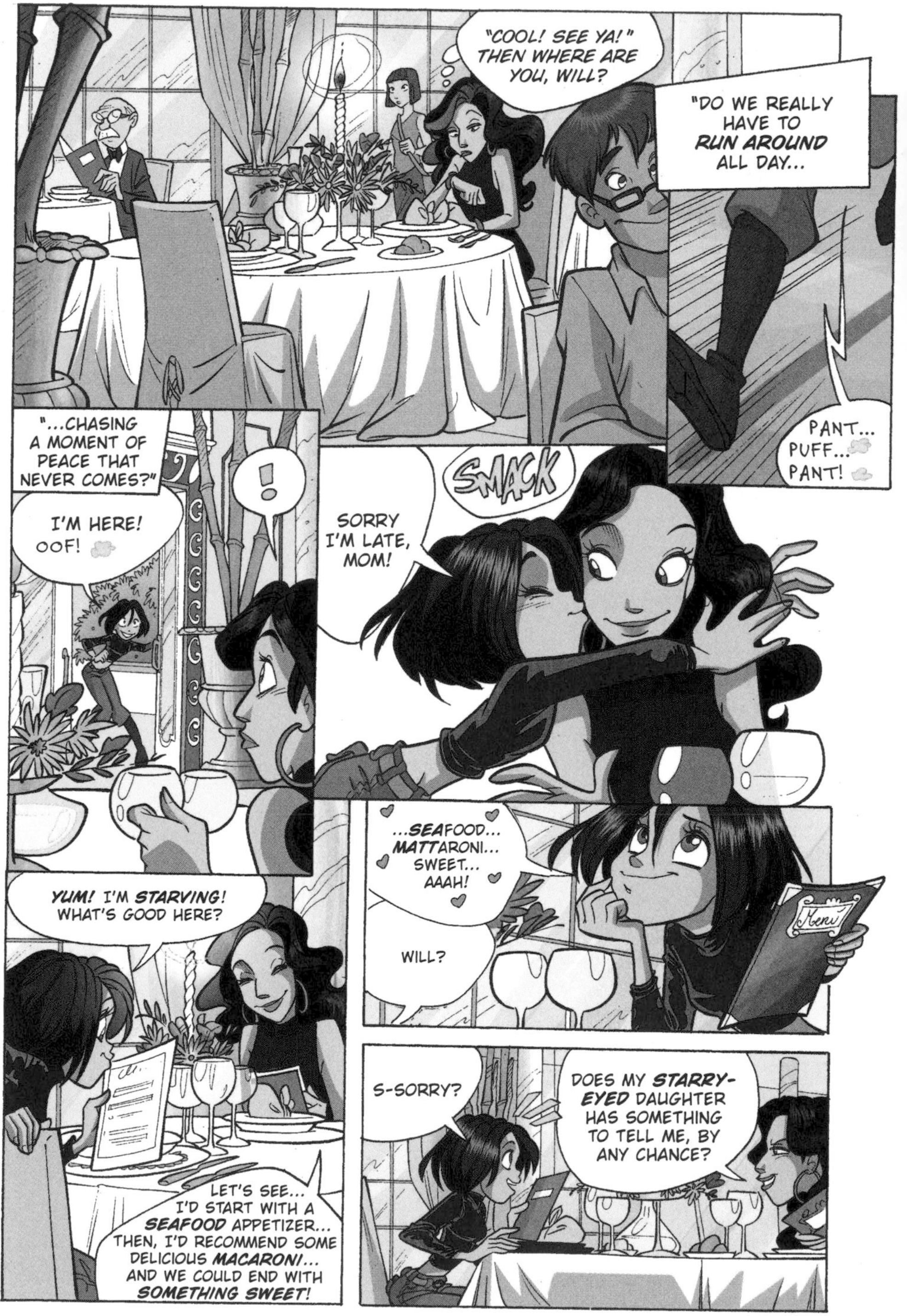
"COOL! SEE YA!" THEN WHERE ARE YOU, WILL?
"DO WE REALLY HAVE TO RUN AROUND ALL DAY...
PANT... PUFF... PANT!
"...CHASING A MOMENT OF PEACE THAT NEVER COMES?"
I'M HERE! OOF!
!
SMACK
SORRY I'M LATE, MOM!
YUM! I'M STARVING! WHAT'S GOOD HERE?
LET'S SEE... I'D START WITH A SEAFOOD APPETIZER... THEN, I'D RECOMMEND SOME DELICIOUS MACARONI... AND WE COULD END WITH SOMETHING SWEET!
...SEAFOOD... MATTARONI... SWEET... AAAH!
WILL?
S-SORRY?
DOES MY STARRY-EYED DAUGHTER HAS SOMETHING TO TELL ME, BY ANY CHANCE?

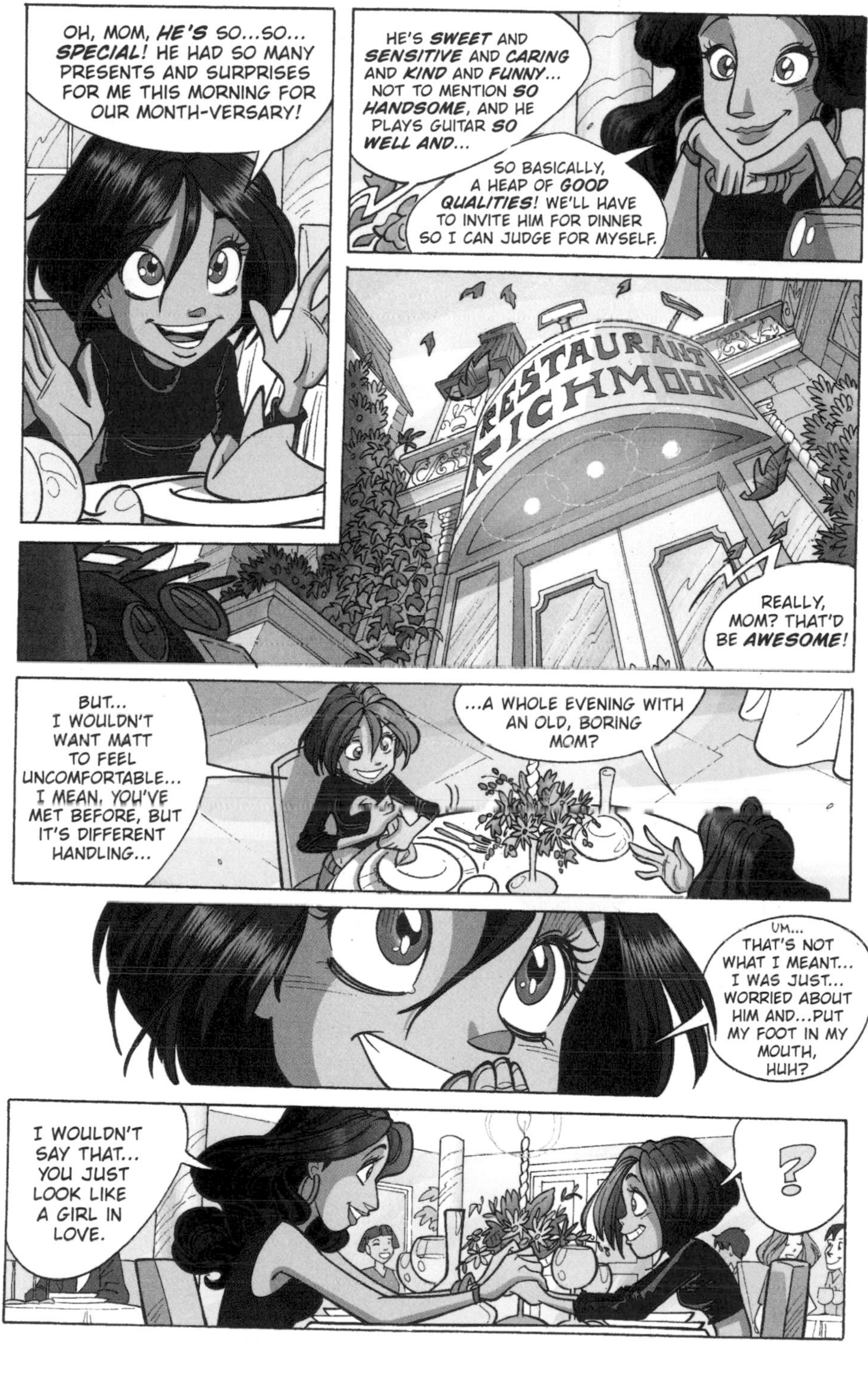
OH, MOM, HE'S SO...SO... SPECIAL! HE HAD SO MANY PRESENTS AND SURPRISES FOR ME THIS MORNING FOR OUR MONTH-VERSARY!
HE'S SWEET AND SENSITIVE AND CARING AND KIND AND FUNNY... NOT TO MENTION SO HANDSOME, AND HE PLAYS GUITAR SO WELL AND...
SO BASICALLY, A HEAP OF GOOD QUALITIES! WE'LL HAVE TO INVITE HIM FOR DINNER SO I CAN JUDGE FOR MYSELF.
RESTAURANT RICHMOOD
REALLY, MOM? THAT'D BE AWESOME!
BUT... I WOULDN'T WANT MATT TO FEEL UNCOMFORTABLE... I MEAN, YOU'VE MET BEFORE, BUT IT'S DIFFERENT HANDLING...
...A WHOLE EVENING WITH AN OLD, BORING MOM?
UM... THAT'S NOT WHAT I MEANT... I WAS JUST... WORRIED ABOUT HIM AND...PUT MY FOOT IN MY MOUTH, HUH?
I WOULDN'T SAY THAT... YOU JUST LOOK LIKE A GIRL IN LOVE.
?

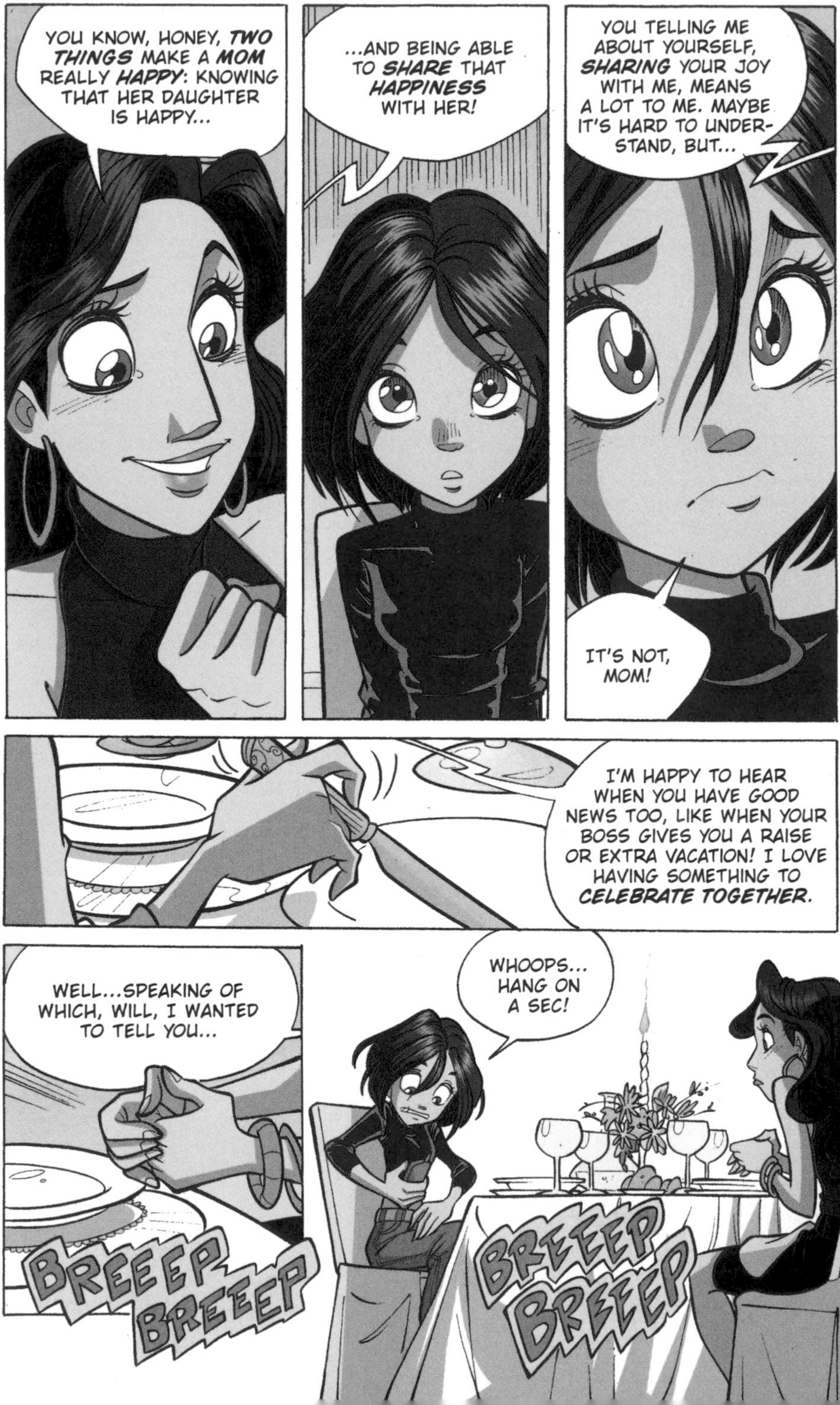
YOU KNOW, HONEY, TWO THINGS MAKE A MOM REALLY HAPPY: KNOWING THAT HER DAUGHTER IS HAPPY...
...AND BEING ABLE TO SHARE THAT HAPPINESS WITH HER!
YOU TELLING ME ABOUT YOURSELF, SHARING YOUR JOY WITH ME, MEANS A LOT TO ME. MAYBE IT'S HARD TO UNDER-STAND, BUT...
IT'S NOT, MOM!
I'M HAPPY TO HEAR WHEN YOU HAVE GOOD NEWS TOO, LIKE WHEN YOUR BOSS GIVES YOU A RAISE OR EXTRA VACATION! I LOVE HAVING SOMETHING TO CELEBRATE TOGETHER.
WELL...SPEAKING OF WHICH, WILL, I WANTED TO TELL YOU...
BREEEP BREEEP
WHOOPS... HANG ON A SEC!
BREEEP BREEEP

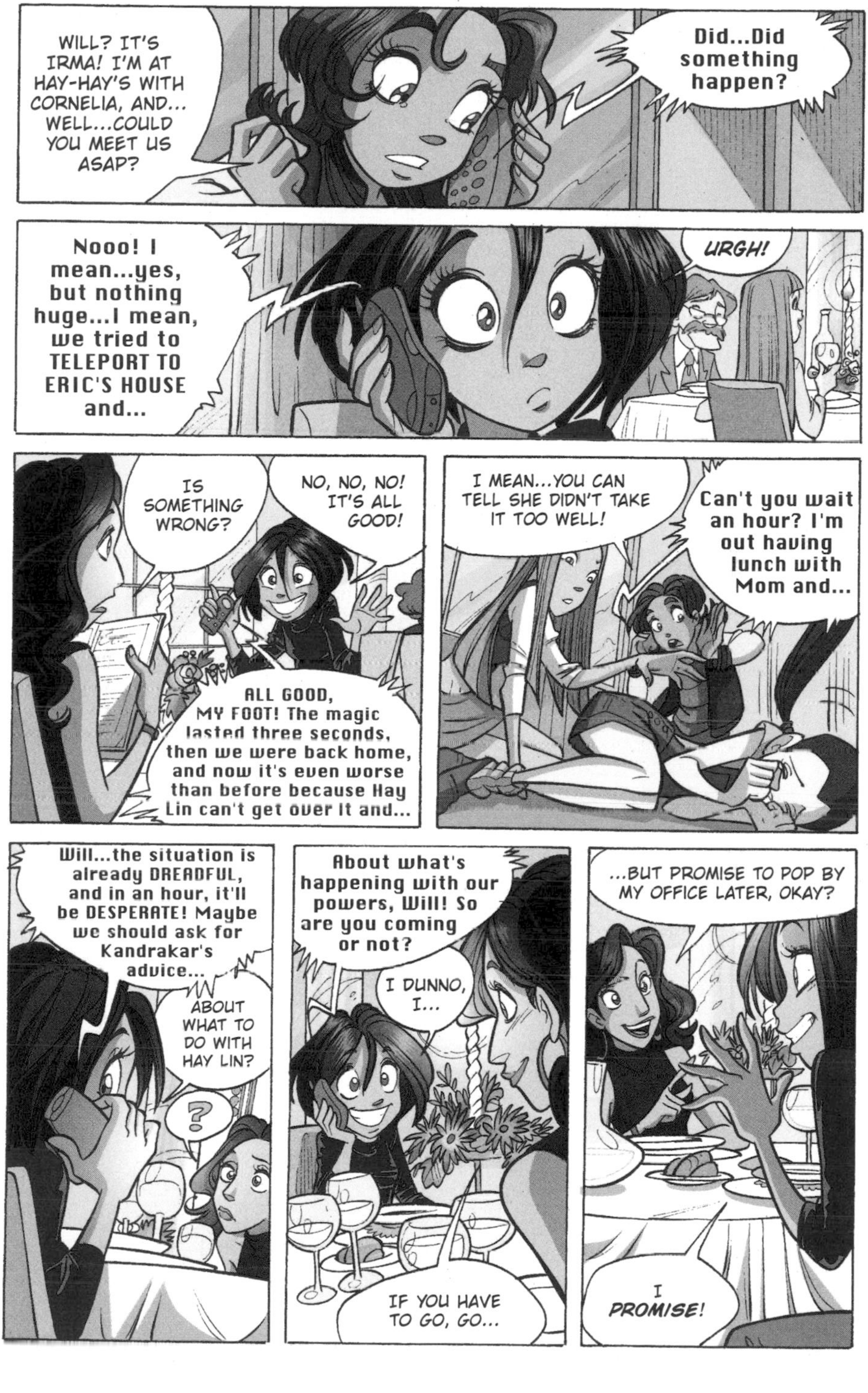
WILL? IT'S IRMA! I'M AT HAY-HAY'S WITH CORNELIA, AND... WELL...COULD YOU MEET US ASAP?
Did...Did something happen?
Nooo! I mean...yes, but nothing huge...I mean, we tried to TELEPORT TO ERIC'S HOUSE and...
URGH!
IS SOMETHING WRONG?
NO, NO, NO! IT'S ALL GOOD!
ALL GOOD, MY FOOT! The magic lasted three seconds, then we were back home, and now it's even worse than before because Hay Lin can't get over it and...
I MEAN...YOU CAN TELL SHE DIDN'T TAKE IT TOO WELL!
Can't you wait an hour? I'm out having lunch with Mom and...
Will...the situation is already DREADFUL, and in an hour, it'll be DESPERATE! Maybe we should ask for Kandrakar's advice...
ABOUT WHAT TO DO WITH HAY LIN?
?
About what's happening with our powers, Will! So are you coming or not?
I DUNNO, I...
IF YOU HAVE TO GO, GO...
...BUT PROMISE TO POP BY MY OFFICE LATER, OKAY?
I PROMISE!

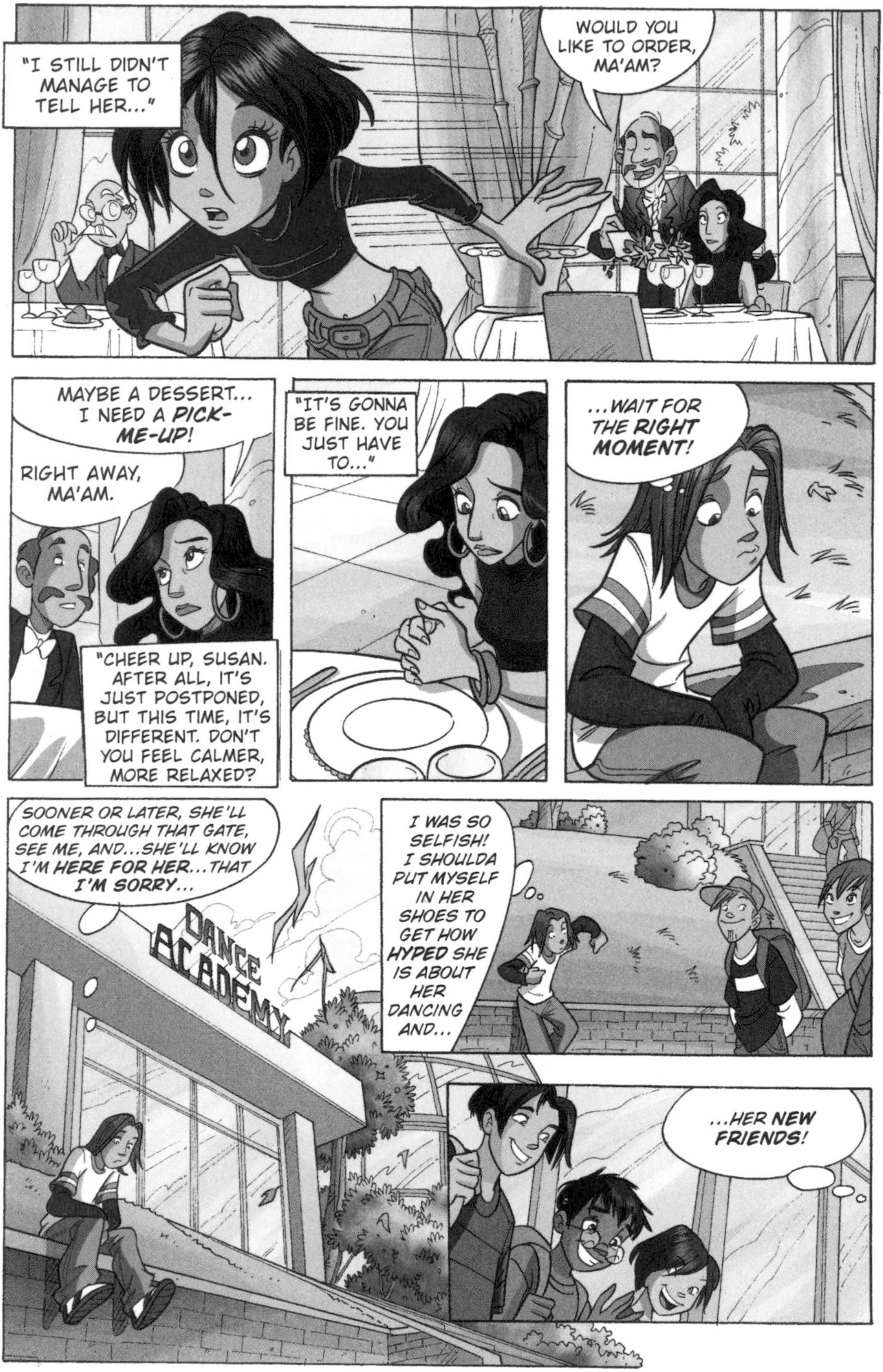

"I STILL DIDN'T MANAGE TO TELL HER..."
WOULD YOU LIKE TO ORDER, MA'AM?
MAYBE A DESSERT... I NEED A PICK-ME-UP!
RIGHT AWAY, MA'AM.
"CHEER UP, SUSAN. AFTER ALL, IT'S JUST POSTPONED, BUT THIS TIME, IT'S DIFFERENT. DON'T YOU FEEL CALMER, MORE RELAXED?
"IT'S GONNA BE FINE. YOU JUST HAVE TO..."
...WAIT FOR THE RIGHT MOMENT!
SOONER OR LATER, SHE'LL COME THROUGH THAT GATE, SEE ME, AND...SHE'LL KNOW I'M HERE FOR HER...THAT I'M SORRY...
DANCE ACADEMY
I WAS SO SELFISH! I SHOULDA PUT MYSELF IN HER SHOES TO GET HOW HYPED SHE IS ABOUT HER DANCING AND...
...HER NEW FRIENDS!

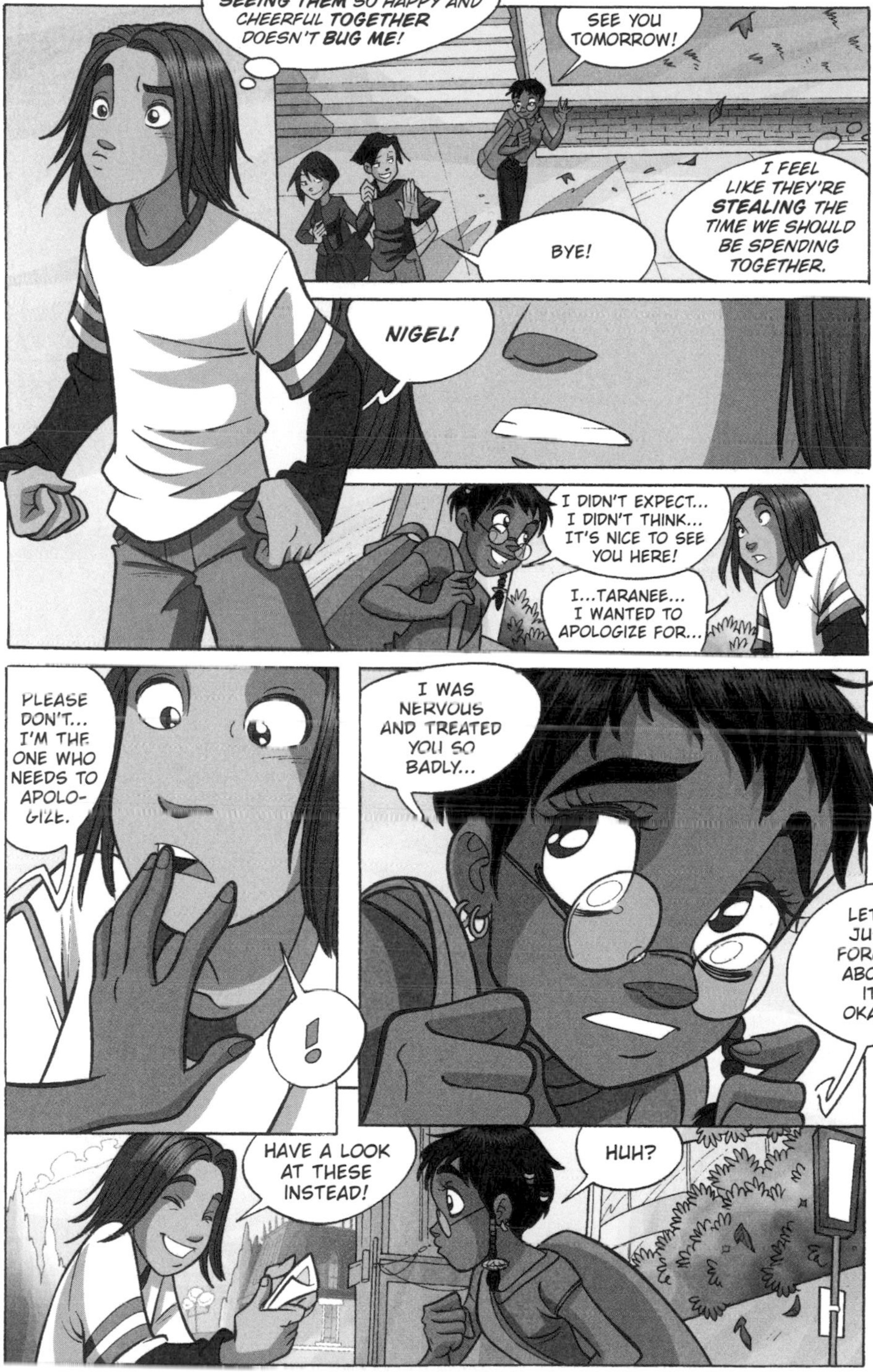
BUT I'D BE LYING IF I SAID SEEING THEM SO HAPPY AND CHEERFUL TOGETHER DOESN'T BUG ME!
SEE YOU TOMORROW!
I FEEL LIKE THEY'RE STEALING THE TIME WE SHOULD BE SPENDING TOGETHER.
BYE!
NIGEL!
I DIDN'T EXPECT... I DIDN'T THINK... IT'S NICE TO SEE YOU HERE!
I...TARANEE... I WANTED TO APOLOGIZE FOR...
PLEASE DON'T... I'M THE ONE WHO NEEDS TO APOLOGIZE.
I WAS NERVOUS AND TREATED YOU SO BADLY...
!
LET'S JUST FORGET ABOUT IT, OKAY?
HAVE A LOOK AT THESE INSTEAD!
HUH?

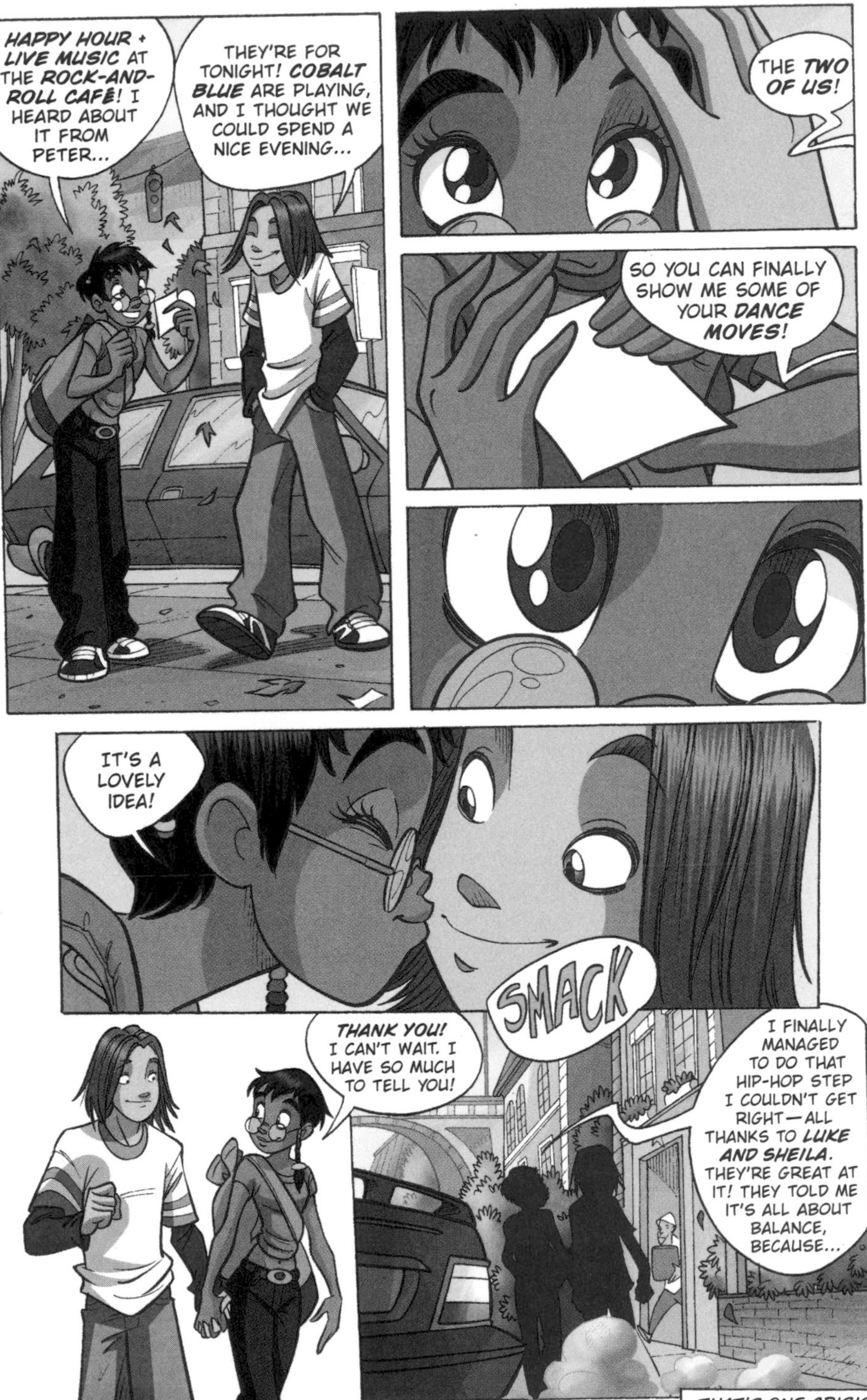

HAPPY HOUR + LIVE MUSIC AT THE ROCK-AND-ROLL CAFÉ! I HEARD ABOUT IT FROM PETER...
THEY'RE FOR TONIGHT! COBALT BLUE ARE PLAYING, AND I THOUGHT WE COULD SPEND A NICE EVENING...
THE TWO OF US!
SO YOU CAN FINALLY SHOW ME SOME OF YOUR DANCE MOVES!
IT'S A LOVELY IDEA!
SMACK
THANK YOU! I CAN'T WAIT. I HAVE SO MUCH TO TELL YOU!
I FINALLY MANAGED TO DO THAT HIP-HOP STEP I COULDN'T GET RIGHT—ALL THANKS TO LUKE AND SHEILA. THEY'RE GREAT AT IT! THEY TOLD ME IT'S ALL ABOUT BALANCE, BECAUSE...
THAT'S ONE CRISIS AVERTED...

W.i.t.c.h.

Will Irma Taranee Cornelia Hay Lin

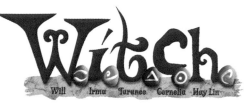

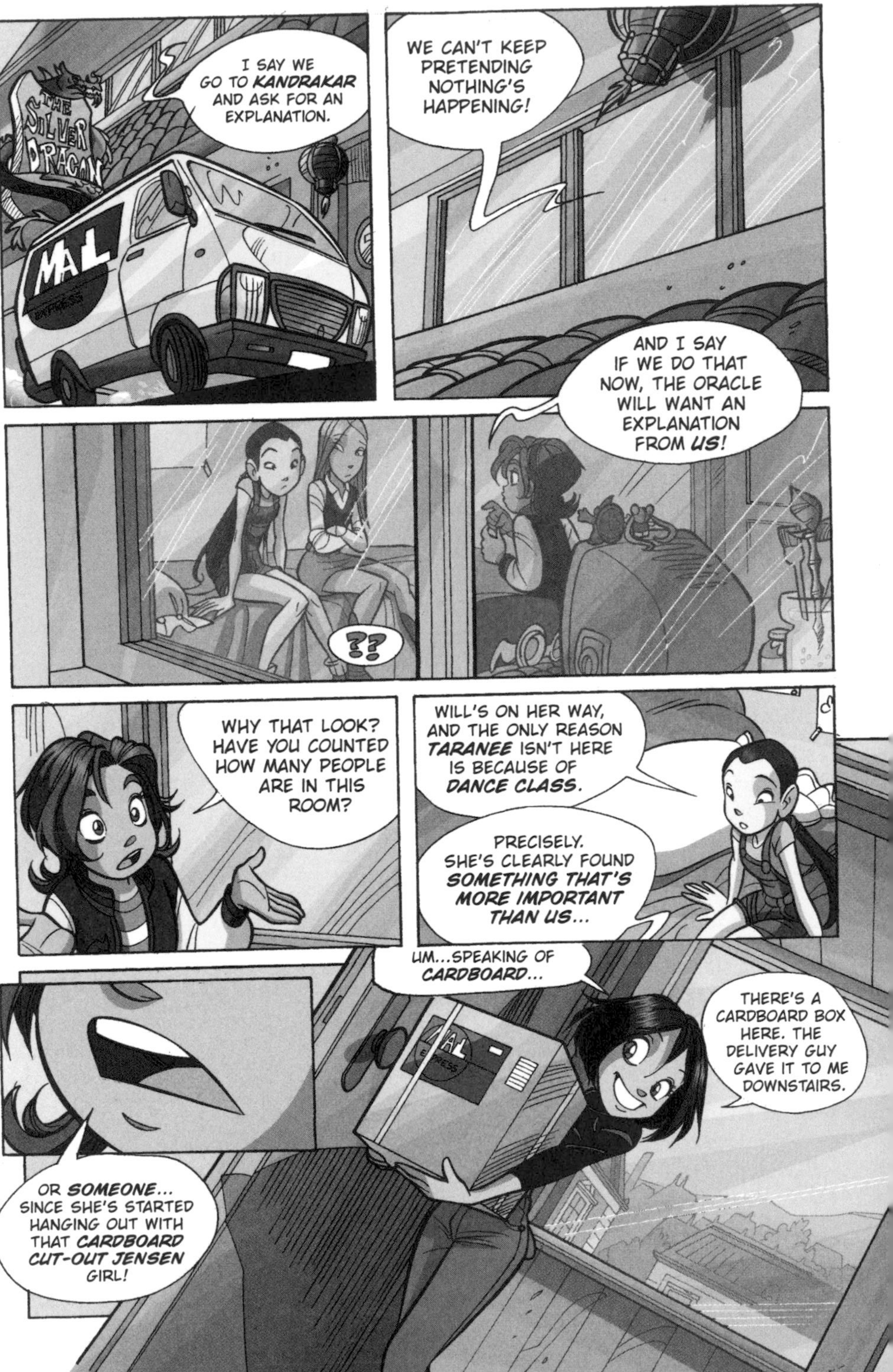

THE SILVER DRAGON
MAIL EXPRESS
I SAY WE GO TO KANDRAKAR AND ASK FOR AN EXPLANATION.
WE CAN'T KEEP PRETENDING NOTHING'S HAPPENING!
AND I SAY IF WE DO THAT NOW, THE ORACLE WILL WANT AN EXPLANATION FROM US!
??
WHY THAT LOOK? HAVE YOU COUNTED HOW MANY PEOPLE ARE IN THIS ROOM?
WILL'S ON HER WAY, AND THE ONLY REASON TARANEE ISN'T HERE IS BECAUSE OF DANCE CLASS.
PRECISELY. SHE'S CLEARLY FOUND SOMETHING THAT'S MORE IMPORTANT THAN US...
OR SOMEONE... SINCE SHE'S STARTED HANGING OUT WITH THAT CARDBOARD CUT-OUT JENSEN GIRL!
UM...SPEAKING OF CARDBOARD...
THERE'S A CARDBOARD BOX HERE. THE DELIVERY GUY GAVE IT TO ME DOWNSTAIRS.

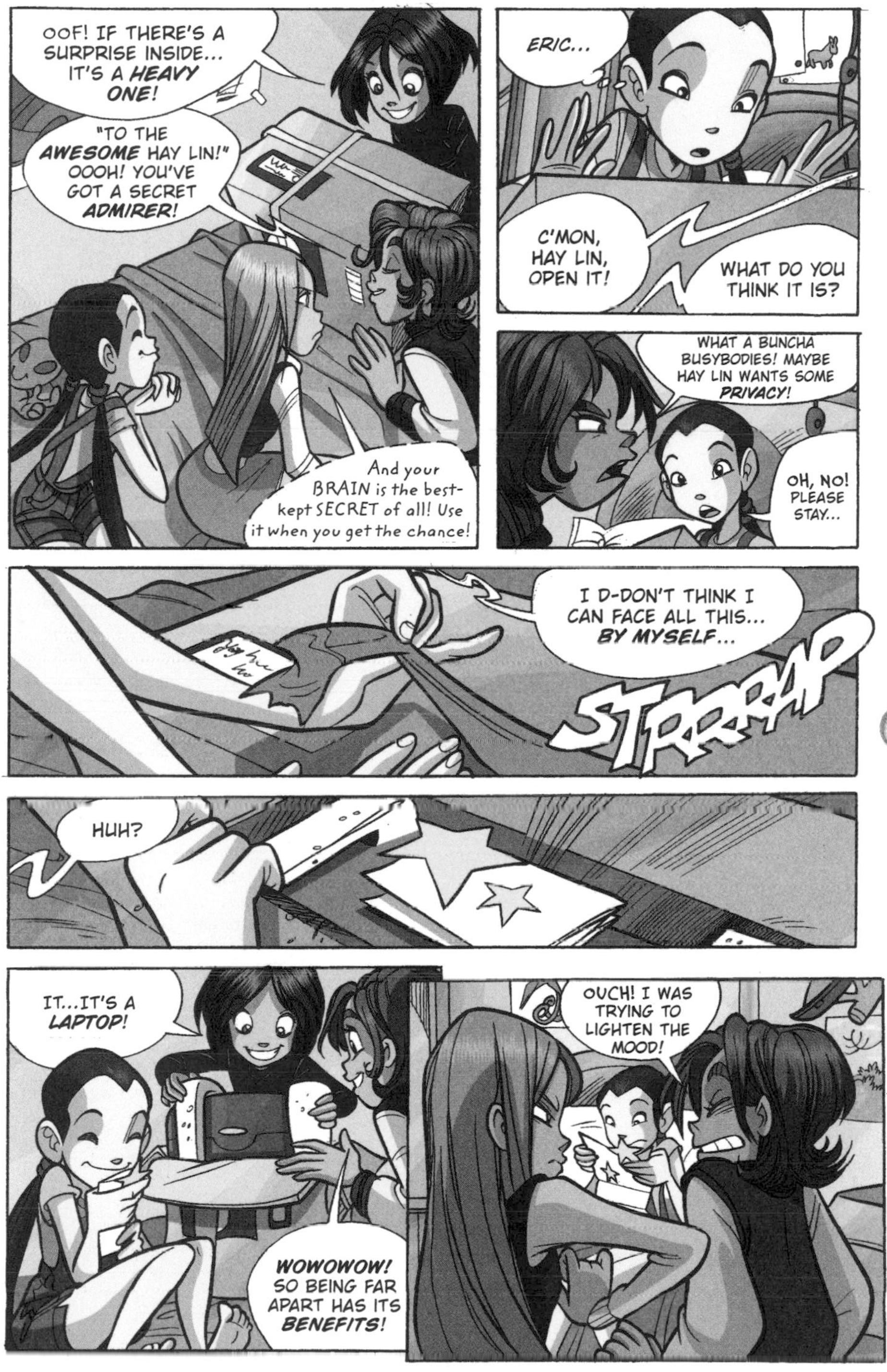
OOF! IF THERE'S A SURPRISE INSIDE... IT'S A HEAVY ONE!
"TO THE AWESOME HAY LIN!" OOOH! YOU'VE GOT A SECRET ADMIRER!
And your BRAIN is the best-kept SECRET of all! Use it when you get the chance!
ERIC...
C'MON, HAY LIN, OPEN IT!
WHAT DO YOU THINK IT IS?
WHAT A BUNCHA BUSYBODIES! MAYBE HAY LIN WANTS SOME PRIVACY!
OH, NO! PLEASE STAY...
I D-DON'T THINK I CAN FACE ALL THIS... BY MYSELF...
STRRRAP
HUH?
IT...IT'S A LAPTOP!
WOWOWOW! SO BEING FAR APART HAS ITS BENEFITS!
OUCH! I WAS TRYING TO LIGHTEN THE MOOD!

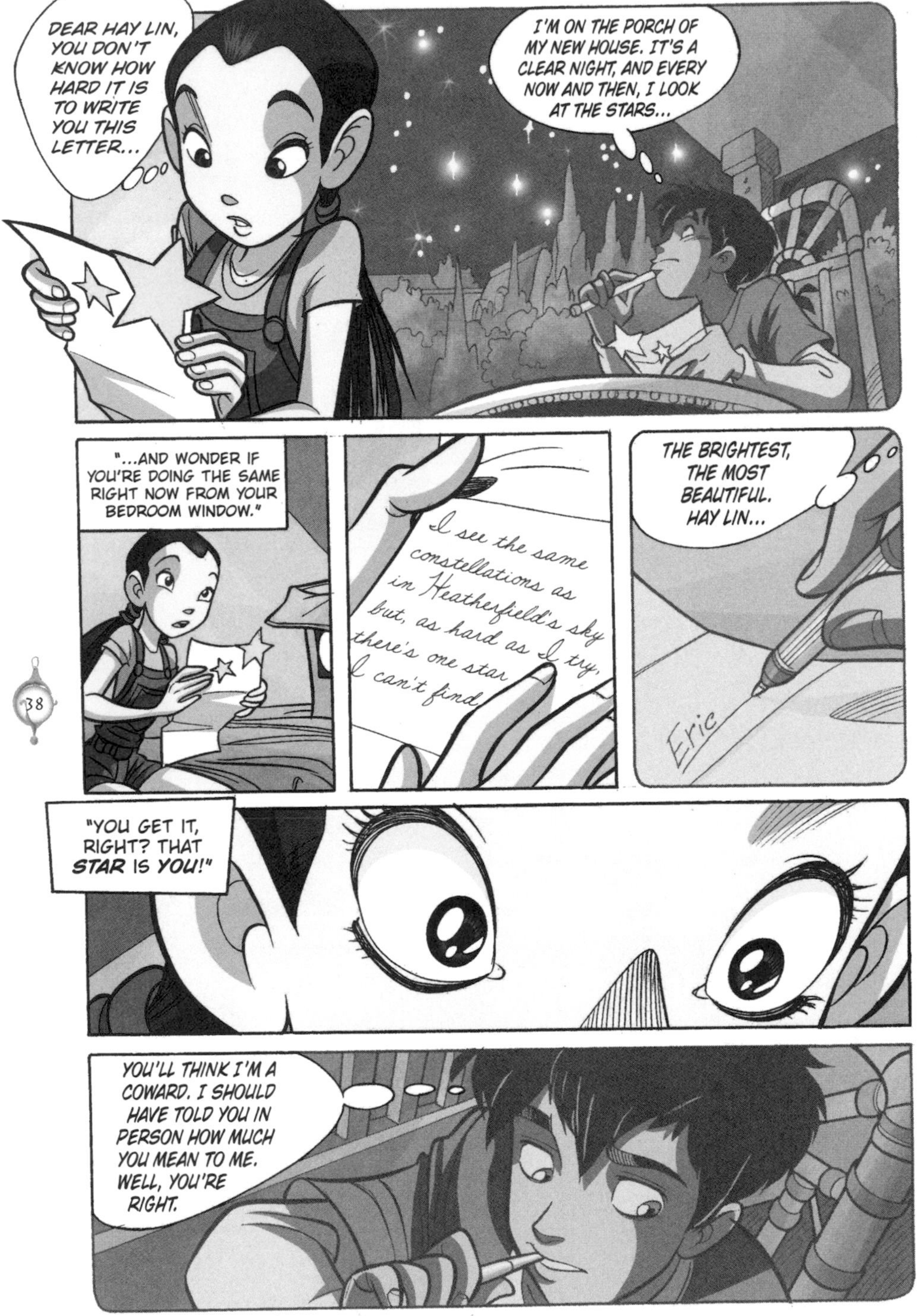
DEAR HAY LIN, YOU DON'T KNOW HOW HARD IT IS TO WRITE YOU THIS LETTER...
I'M ON THE PORCH OF MY NEW HOUSE. IT'S A CLEAR NIGHT, AND EVERY NOW AND THEN, I LOOK AT THE STARS...
"...AND WONDER IF YOU'RE DOING THE SAME RIGHT NOW FROM YOUR BEDROOM WINDOW."
I see the same constellations as in Heatherfield's sky but, as hard as I try, there's one star I can't find
THE BRIGHTEST, THE MOST BEAUTIFUL. HAY LIN...
Eric
"YOU GET IT, RIGHT? THAT STAR IS YOU!"
YOU'LL THINK I'M A COWARD. I SHOULD HAVE TOLD YOU IN PERSON HOW MUCH YOU MEAN TO ME. WELL, YOU'RE RIGHT.

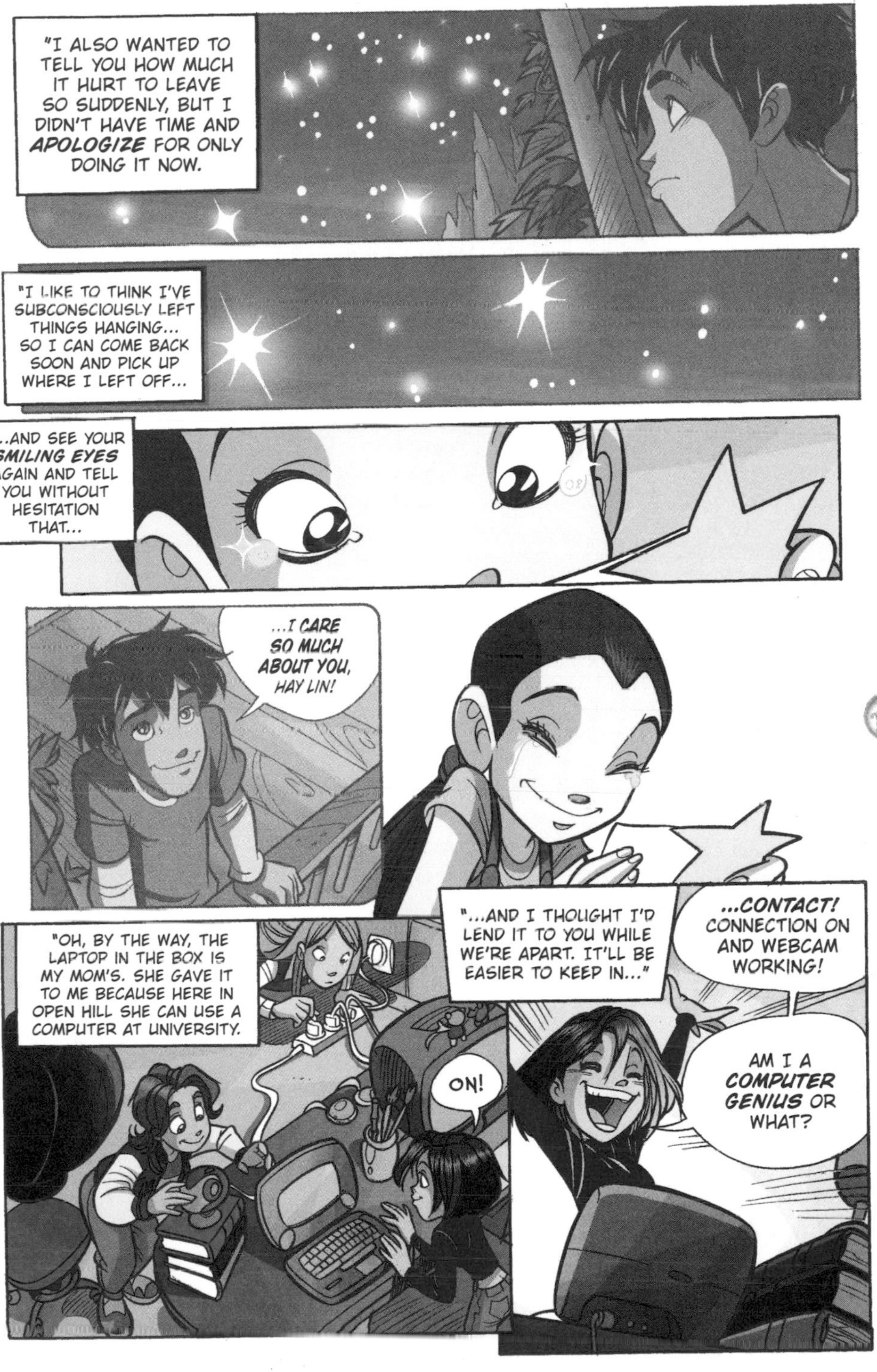
"I ALSO WANTED TO TELL YOU HOW MUCH IT HURT TO LEAVE SO SUDDENLY, BUT I DIDN'T HAVE TIME AND APOLOGIZE FOR ONLY DOING IT NOW.
"I LIKE TO THINK I'VE SUBCONSCIOUSLY LEFT THINGS HANGING... SO I CAN COME BACK SOON AND PICK UP WHERE I LEFT OFF...
"...AND SEE YOUR SMILING EYES AGAIN AND TELL YOU WITHOUT HESITATION THAT...
...I CARE SO MUCH ABOUT YOU, HAY LIN!
"OH, BY THE WAY, THE LAPTOP IN THE BOX IS MY MOM'S. SHE GAVE IT TO ME BECAUSE HERE IN OPEN HILL SHE CAN USE A COMPUTER AT UNIVERSITY.
ON!
"...AND I THOUGHT I'D LEND IT TO YOU WHILE WE'RE APART. IT'LL BE EASIER TO KEEP IN..."
...CONTACT! CONNECTION ON AND WEBCAM WORKING!
AM I A COMPUTER GENIUS OR WHAT?

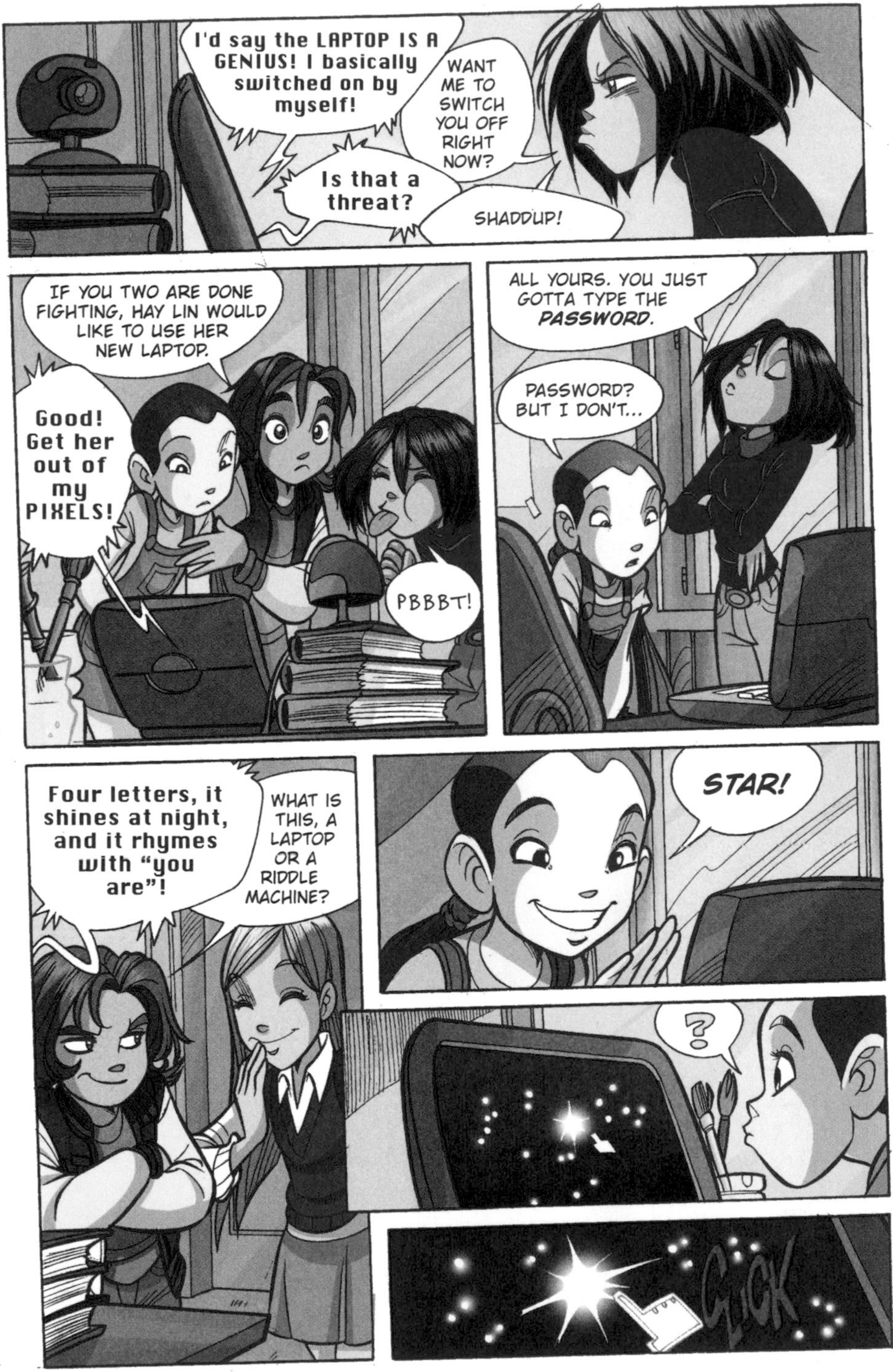
I'd say the LAPTOP IS A GENIUS! I basically switched on by myself!
WANT ME TO SWITCH YOU OFF RIGHT NOW?
Is that a threat?
SHADDUP!
IF YOU TWO ARE DONE FIGHTING, HAY LIN WOULD LIKE TO USE HER NEW LAPTOP.
Good! Get her out of my PIXELS!
PBBBT!
ALL YOURS. YOU JUST GOTTA TYPE THE PASSWORD.
PASSWORD? BUT I DON'T...
Four letters, it shines at night, and it rhymes with "you are"!
WHAT IS THIS, A LAPTOP OR A RIDDLE MACHINE?
STAR!
?
CLICK

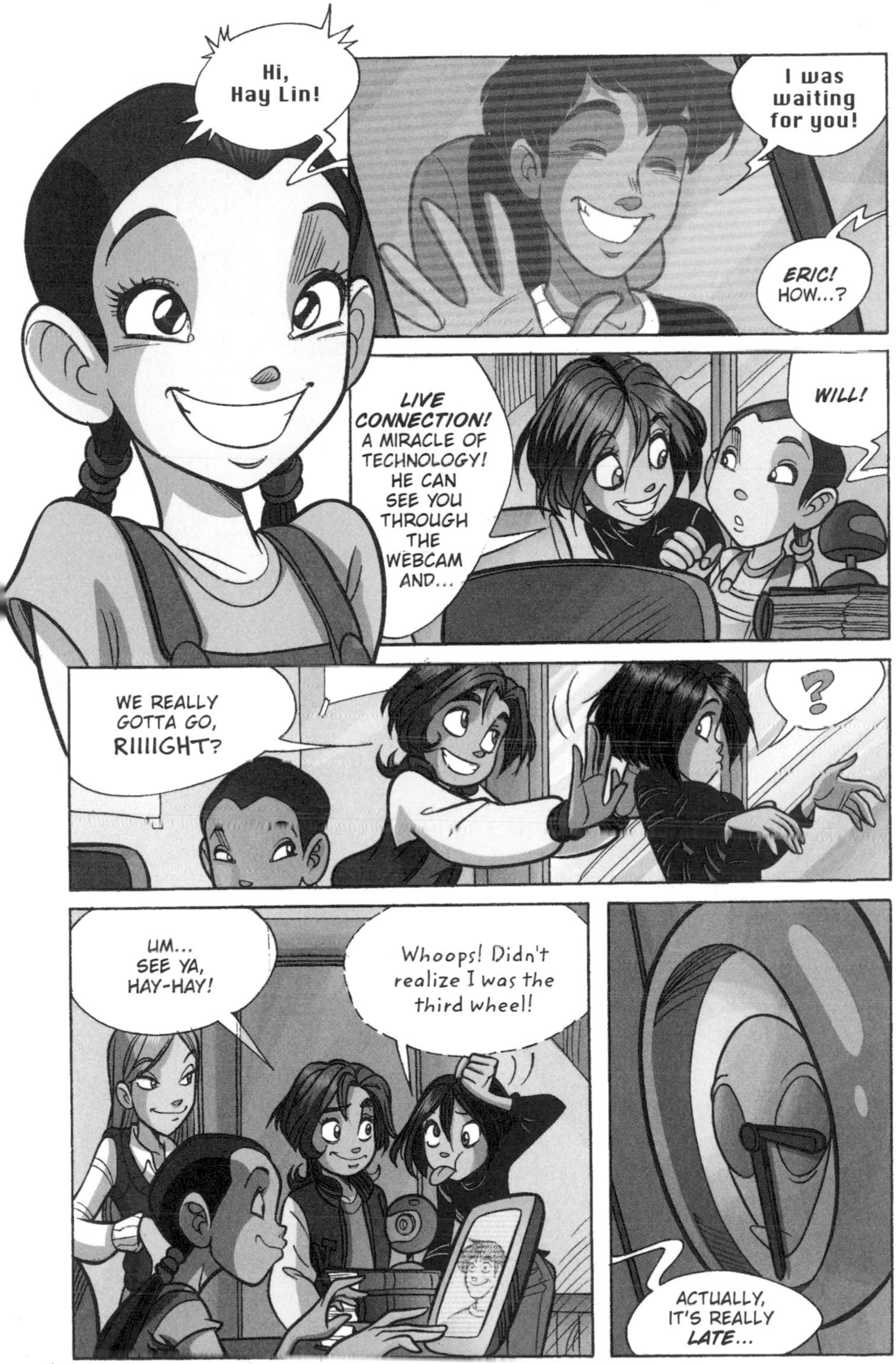
Hi, Hay Lin!
I was waiting for you!
ERIC! HOW...?
LIVE CONNECTION! A MIRACLE OF TECHNOLOGY! HE CAN SEE YOU THROUGH THE WEBCAM AND...
WILL!
WE REALLY GOTTA GO, RIIIIGHT?
?
UM... SEE YA, HAY-HAY!
Whoops! Didn't realize I was the third wheel!
ACTUALLY, IT'S REALLY LATE...

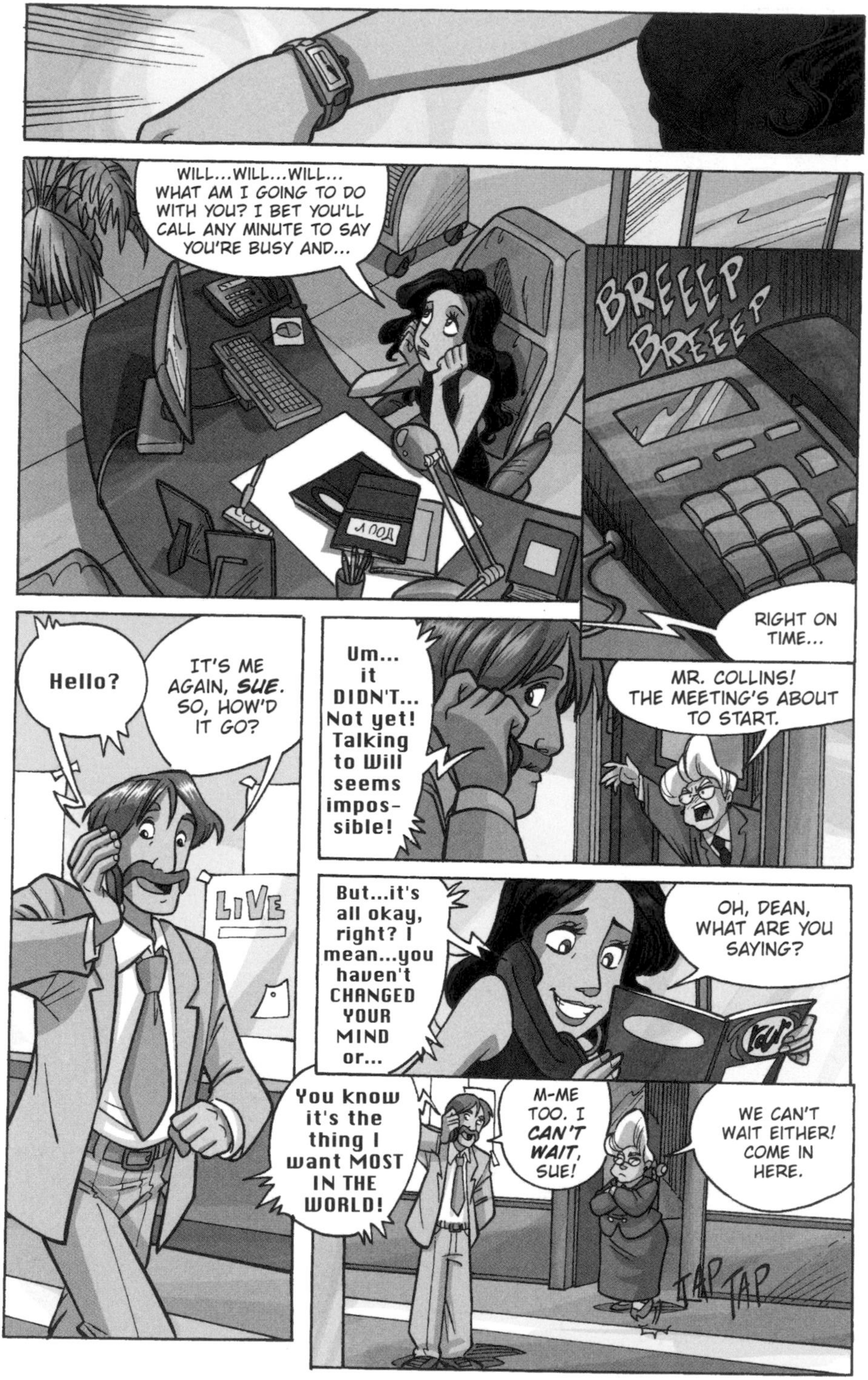
WILL...WILL...WILL... WHAT AM I GOING TO DO WITH YOU? I BET YOU'LL CALL ANY MINUTE TO SAY YOU'RE BUSY AND...
BREEEP
BREEEP
RIGHT ON TIME...
Hello?
IT'S ME AGAIN, SUE. SO, HOW'D IT GO?
Um... it DIDN'T... Not yet! Talking to Will seems impos-sible!
MR. COLLINS! THE MEETING'S ABOUT TO START.
LIVE
But...it's all okay, right? I mean...you haven't CHANGED YOUR MIND or...
OH, DEAN, WHAT ARE YOU SAYING?
You know it's the thing I want MOST IN THE WORLD!
M-ME TOO. I CAN'T WAIT, SUE!
WE CAN'T WAIT EITHER! COME IN HERE.
TAP TAP

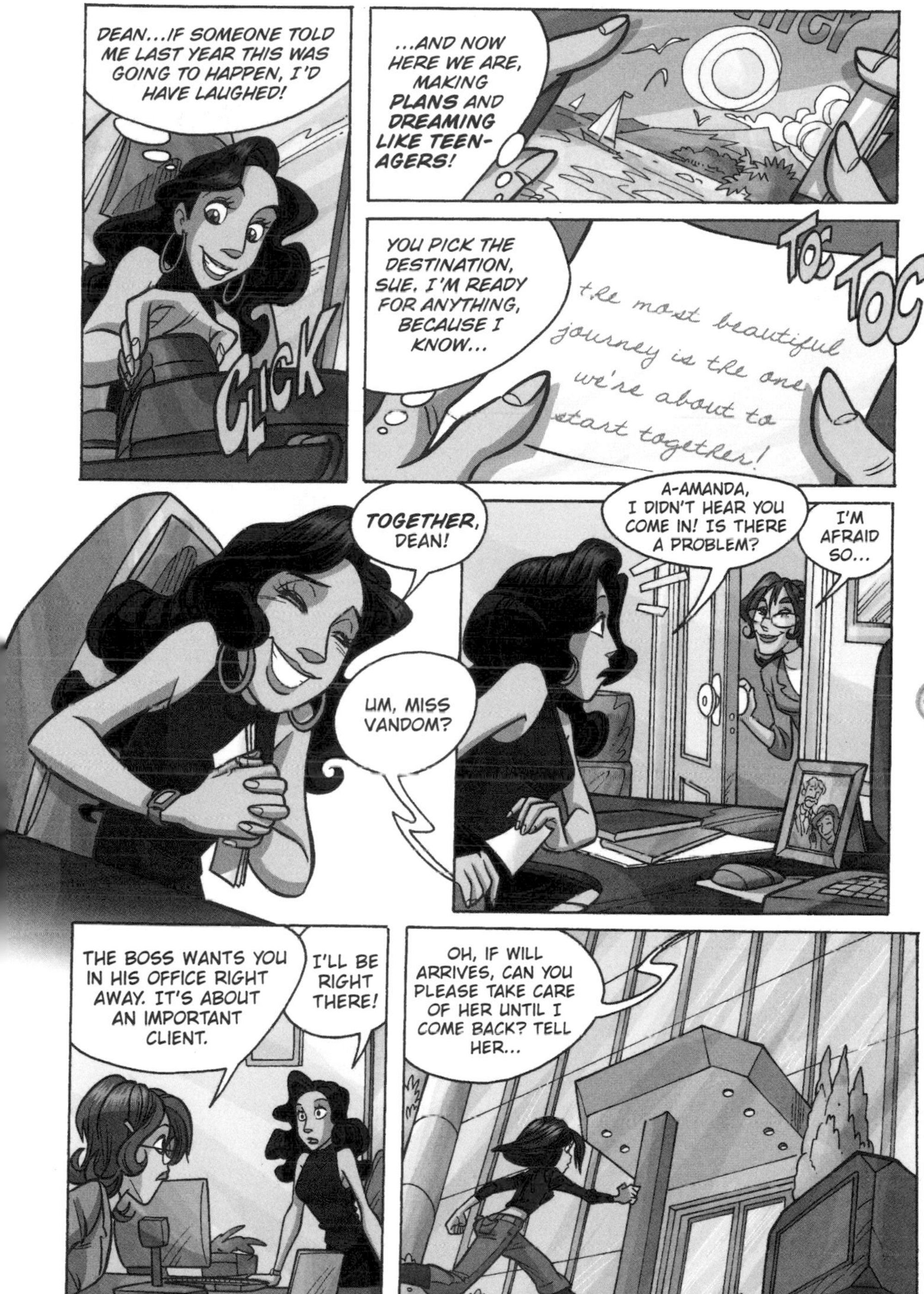
DEAN...IF SOMEONE TOLD ME LAST YEAR THIS WAS GOING TO HAPPEN, I'D HAVE LAUGHED!
CLICK
...AND NOW HERE WE ARE, MAKING PLANS AND DREAMING LIKE TEEN-AGERS!
YOU PICK THE DESTINATION, SUE. I'M READY FOR ANYTHING, BECAUSE I KNOW...
the most beautiful journey is the one we're about to start together!
TOC TOC
TOGETHER, DEAN!
UM, MISS VANDOM?
A-AMANDA, I DIDN'T HEAR YOU COME IN! IS THERE A PROBLEM?
I'M AFRAID SO...
THE BOSS WANTS YOU IN HIS OFFICE RIGHT AWAY. IT'S ABOUT AN IMPORTANT CLIENT.
I'LL BE RIGHT THERE!
OH, IF WILL ARRIVES, CAN YOU PLEASE TAKE CARE OF HER UNTIL I COME BACK? TELL HER...

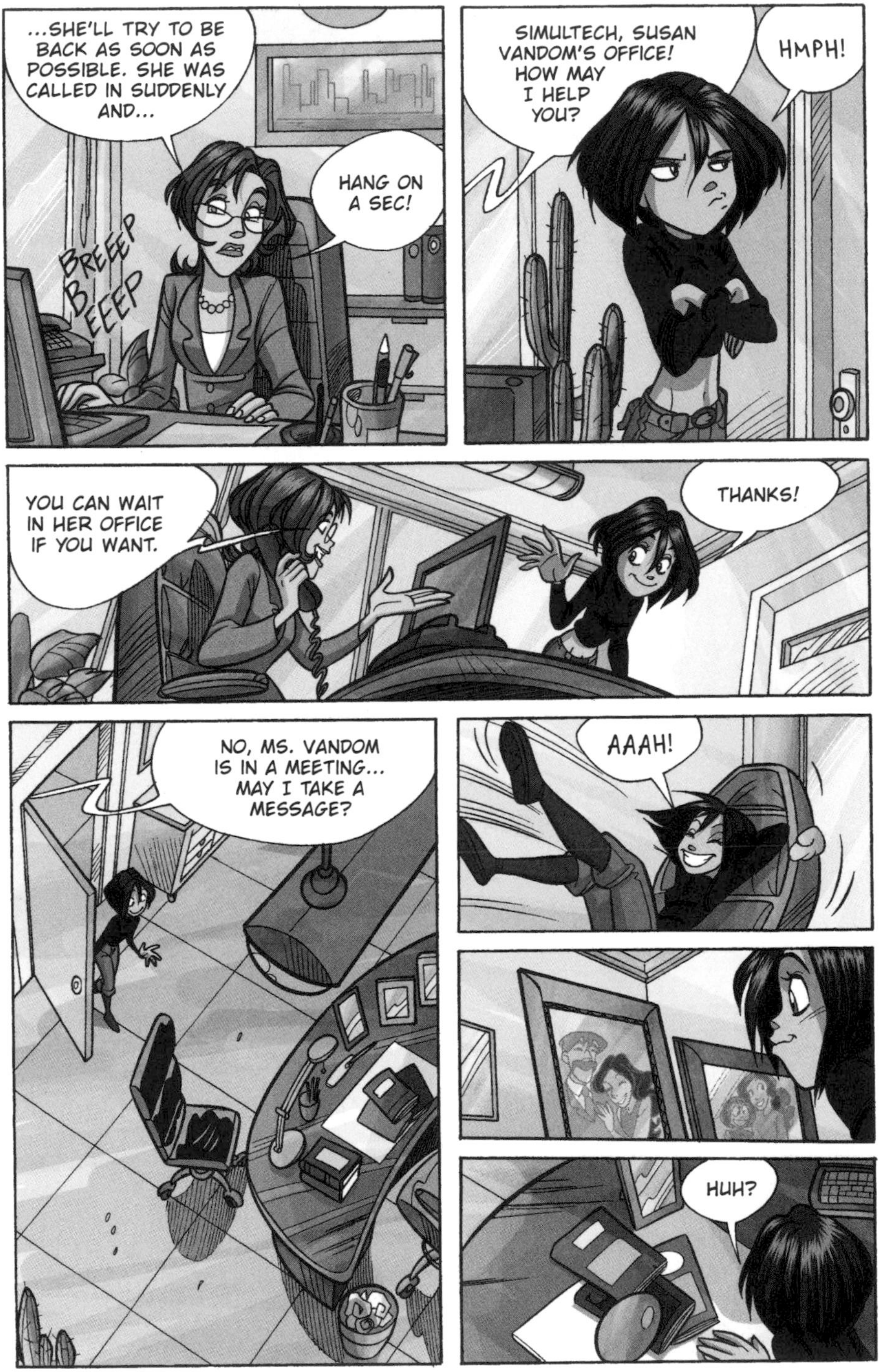
...SHE'LL TRY TO BE BACK AS SOON AS POSSIBLE. SHE WAS CALLED IN SUDDENLY AND...
BREEEP BEEEP
HANG ON A SEC!
SIMULTECH, SUSAN VANDOM'S OFFICE! HOW MAY I HELP YOU?
HMPH!
YOU CAN WAIT IN HER OFFICE IF YOU WANT.
THANKS!
NO, MS. VANDOM IS IN A MEETING... MAY I TAKE A MESSAGE?
AAAH!
HUH?

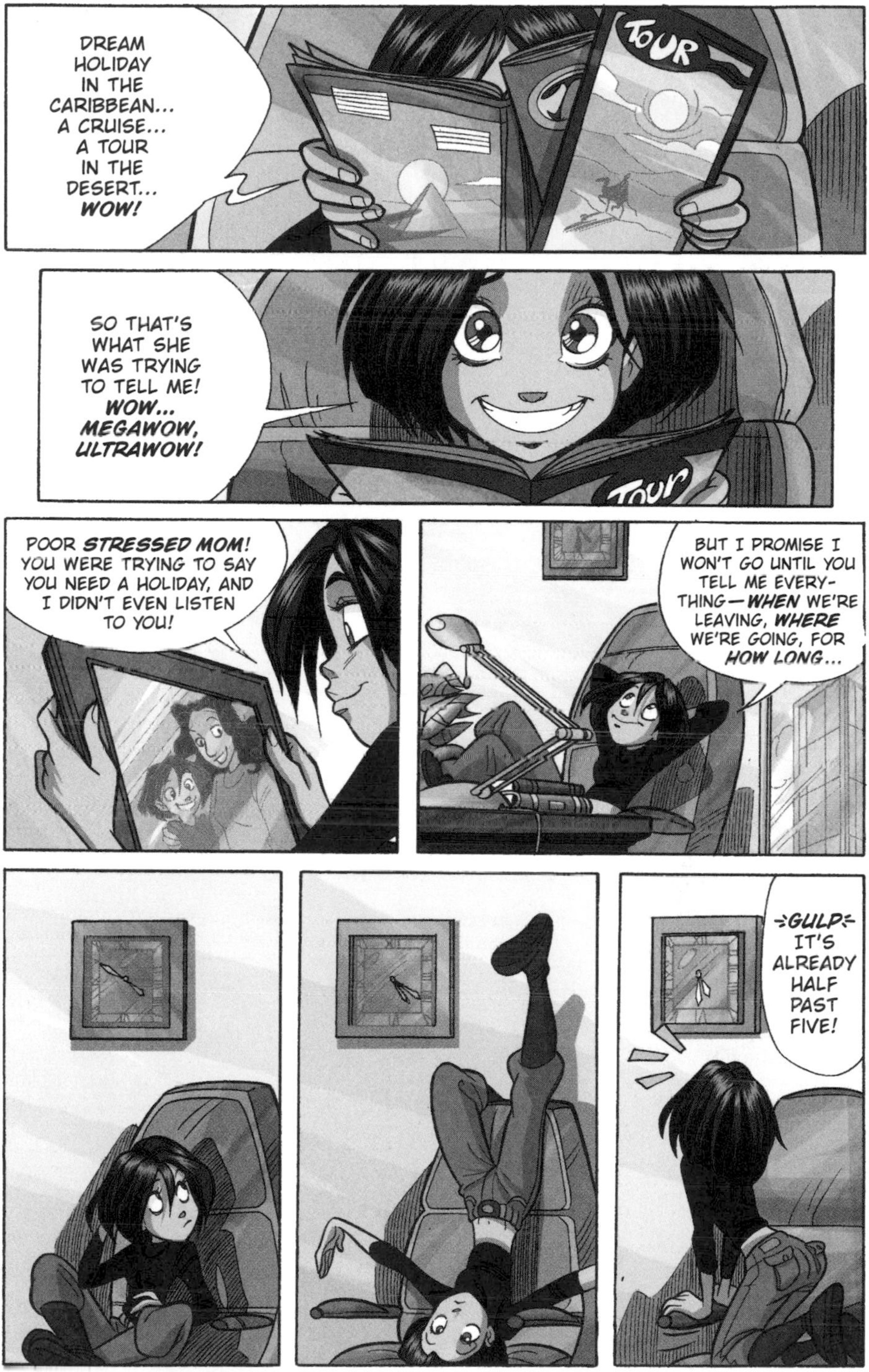
DREAM HOLIDAY IN THE CARIBBEAN... A CRUISE... A TOUR IN THE DESERT... WOW!
TOUR
SO THAT'S WHAT SHE WAS TRYING TO TELL ME! WOW... MEGAWOW, ULTRAWOW!
TOUR
POOR STRESSED MOM! YOU WERE TRYING TO SAY YOU NEED A HOLIDAY, AND I DIDN'T EVEN LISTEN TO YOU!
BUT I PROMISE I WON'T GO UNTIL YOU TELL ME EVERY-THING—WHEN WE'RE LEAVING, WHERE WE'RE GOING, FOR HOW LONG...
GULP IT'S ALREADY HALF PAST FIVE!

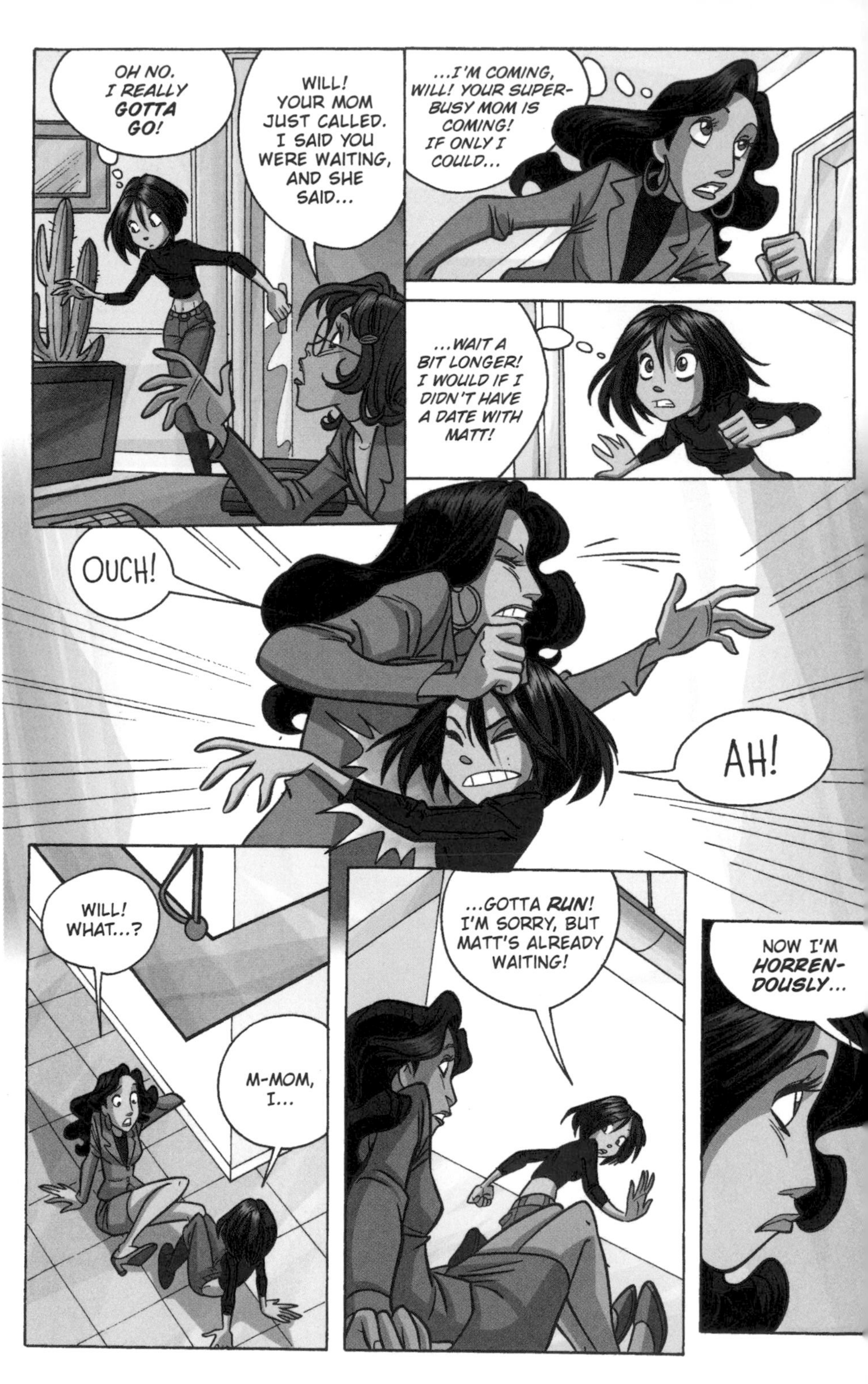
OH NO. I REALLY GOTTA GO!
WILL! YOUR MOM JUST CALLED. I SAID YOU WERE WAITING, AND SHE SAID...
...I'M COMING, WILL! YOUR SUPER-BUSY MOM IS COMING! IF ONLY I COULD...
...WAIT A BIT LONGER! I WOULD IF I DIDN'T HAVE A DATE WITH MATT!
OUCH!
AH!
WILL! WHAT...?
M-MOM, I...
...GOTTA RUN! I'M SORRY, BUT MATT'S ALREADY WAITING!
NOW I'M HORREN-DOUSLY...

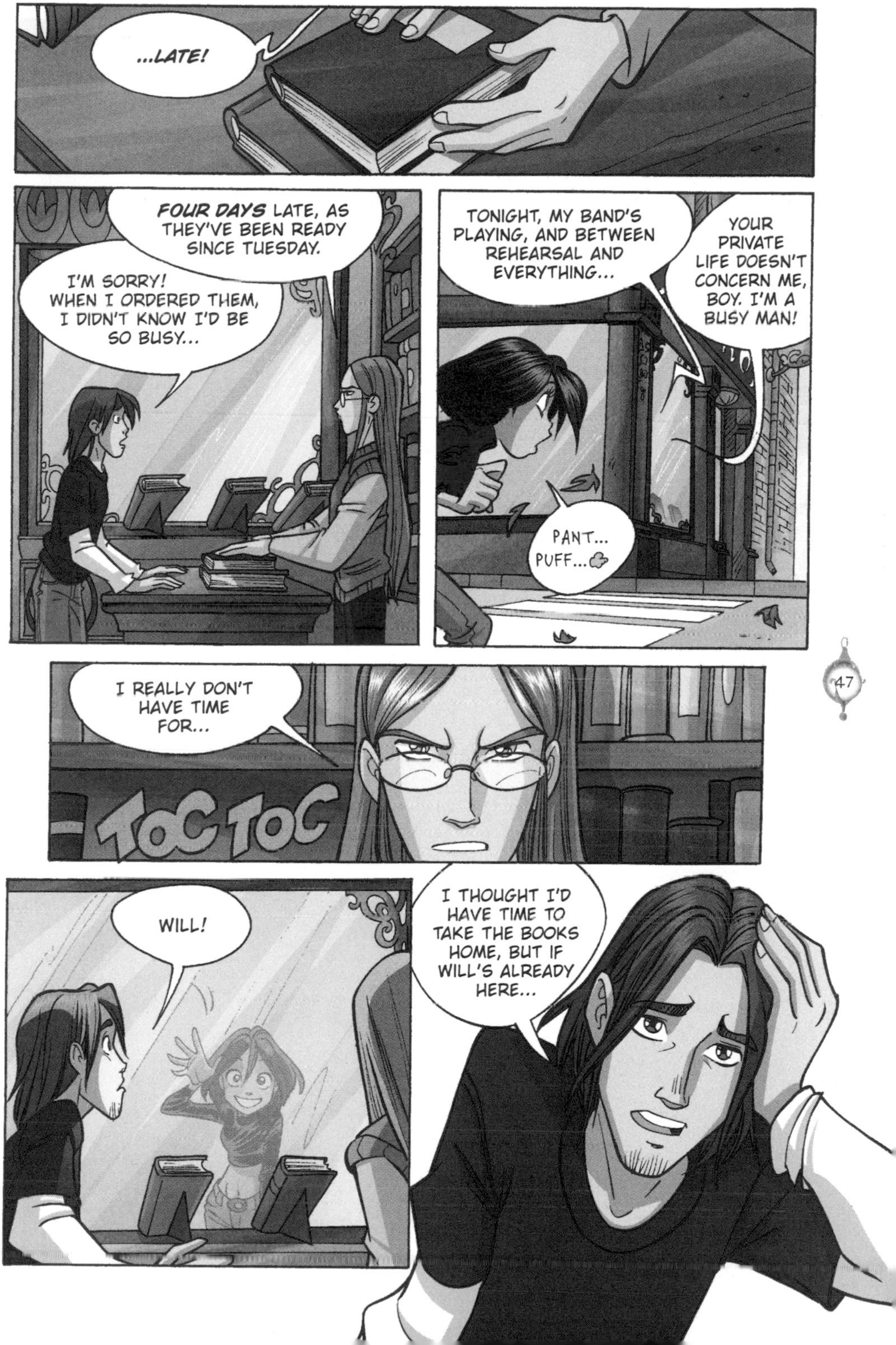
...LATE!
FOUR DAYS LATE, AS THEY'VE BEEN READY SINCE TUESDAY.
I'M SORRY! WHEN I ORDERED THEM, I DIDN'T KNOW I'D BE SO BUSY...
TONIGHT, MY BAND'S PLAYING, AND BETWEEN REHEARSAL AND EVERYTHING...
YOUR PRIVATE LIFE DOESN'T CONCERN ME, BOY. I'M A BUSY MAN!
PANT... PUFF...
I REALLY DON'T HAVE TIME FOR...
TOC TOC
WILL!
I THOUGHT I'D HAVE TIME TO TAKE THE BOOKS HOME, BUT IF WILL'S ALREADY HERE...

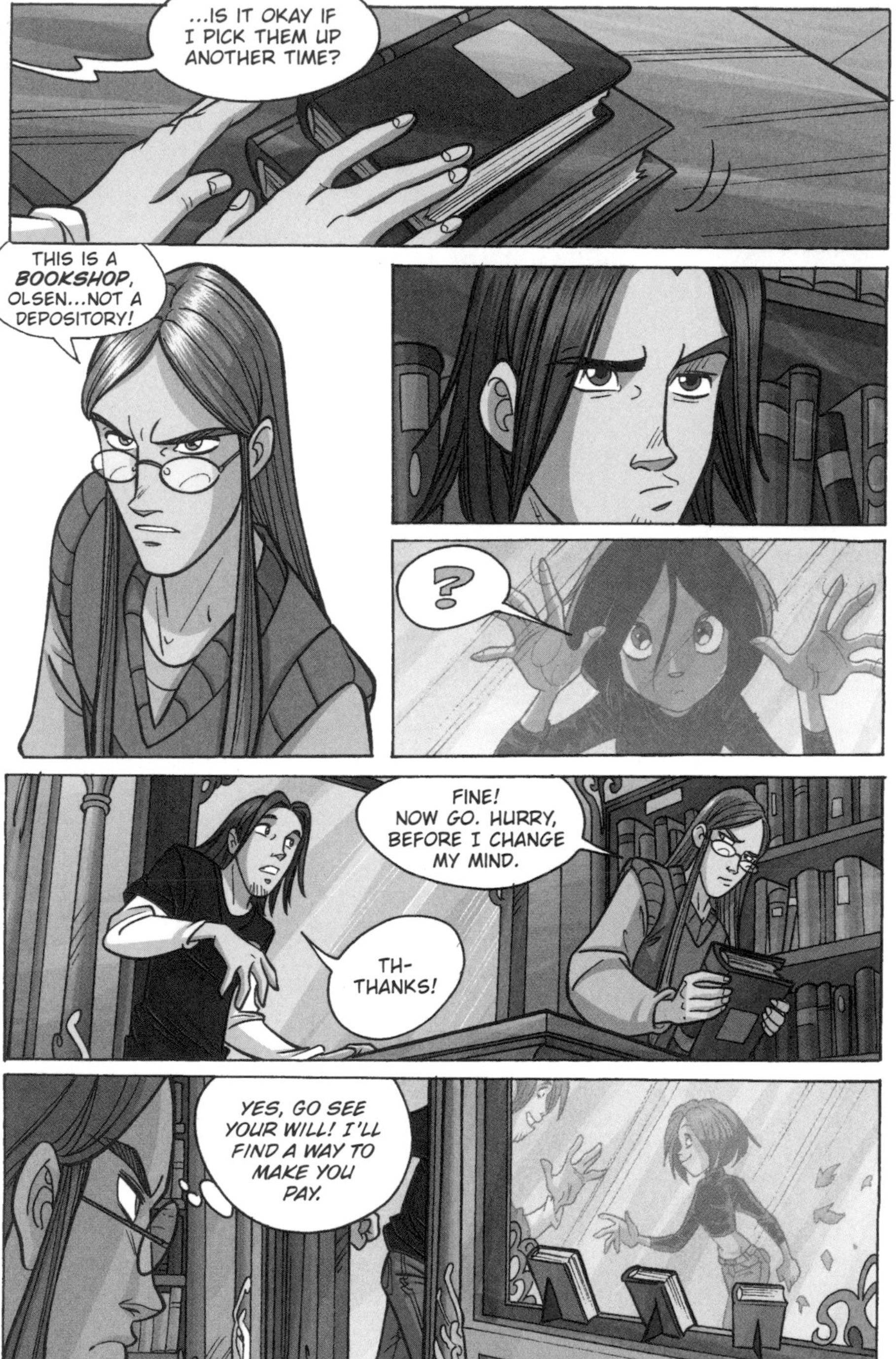

...IS IT OKAY IF I PICK THEM UP ANOTHER TIME?
THIS IS A ***BOOKSHOP***, OLSEN...NOT A DEPOSITORY!
?
FINE! NOW GO. HURRY, BEFORE I CHANGE MY MIND.
TH- THANKS!
YES, GO SEE YOUR WILL! I'LL FIND A WAY TO MAKE YOU PAY.

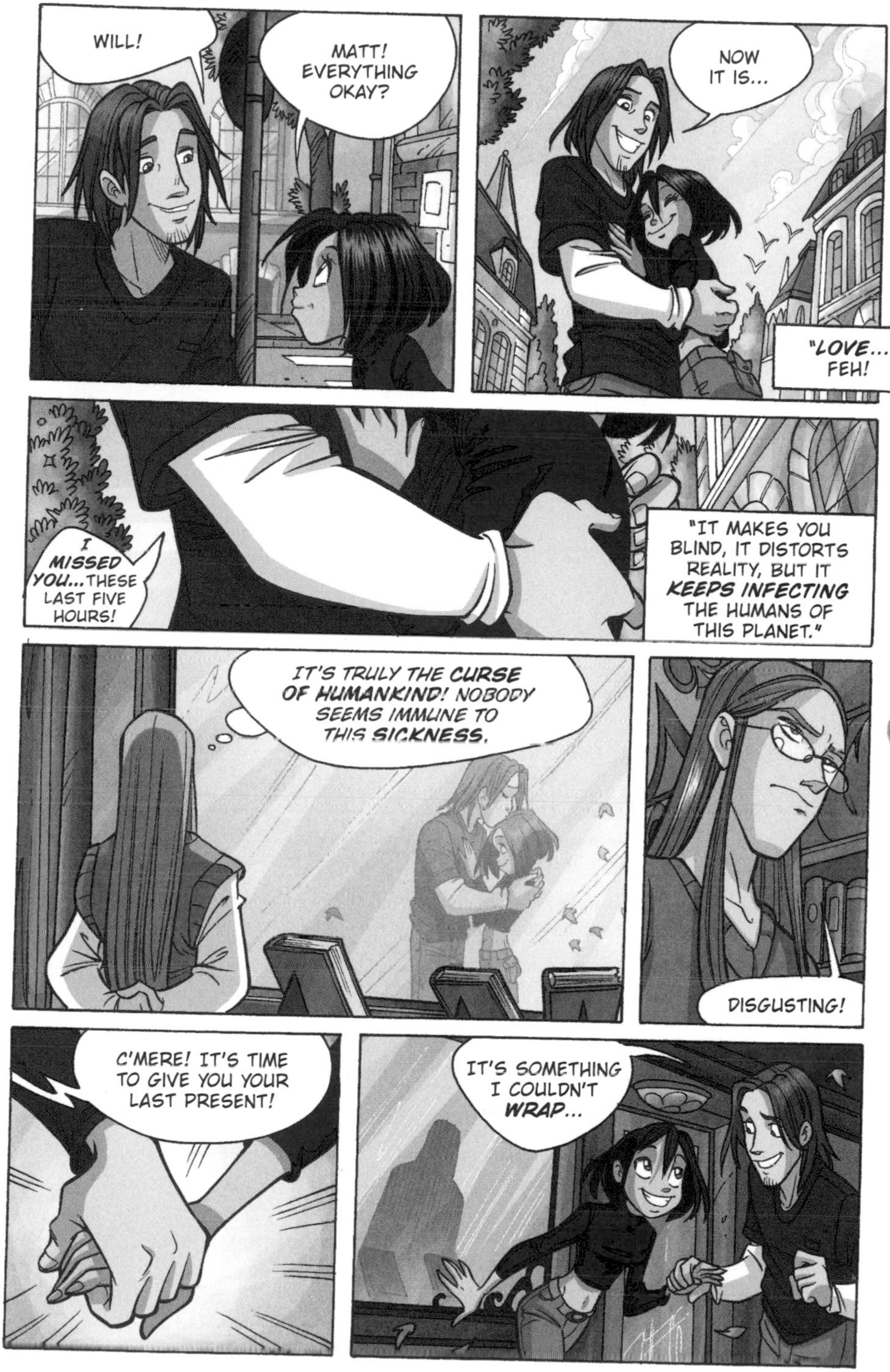
WILL!
MATT! EVERYTHING OKAY?
NOW IT IS...
"LOVE... FEH!
I MISSED YOU... THESE LAST FIVE HOURS!
"IT MAKES YOU BLIND, IT DISTORTS REALITY, BUT IT KEEPS INFECTING THE HUMANS OF THIS PLANET."
IT'S TRULY THE CURSE OF HUMANKIND! NOBODY SEEMS IMMUNE TO THIS SICKNESS.
DISGUSTING!
C'MERE! IT'S TIME TO GIVE YOU YOUR LAST PRESENT!
IT'S SOMETHING I COULDN'T WRAP...

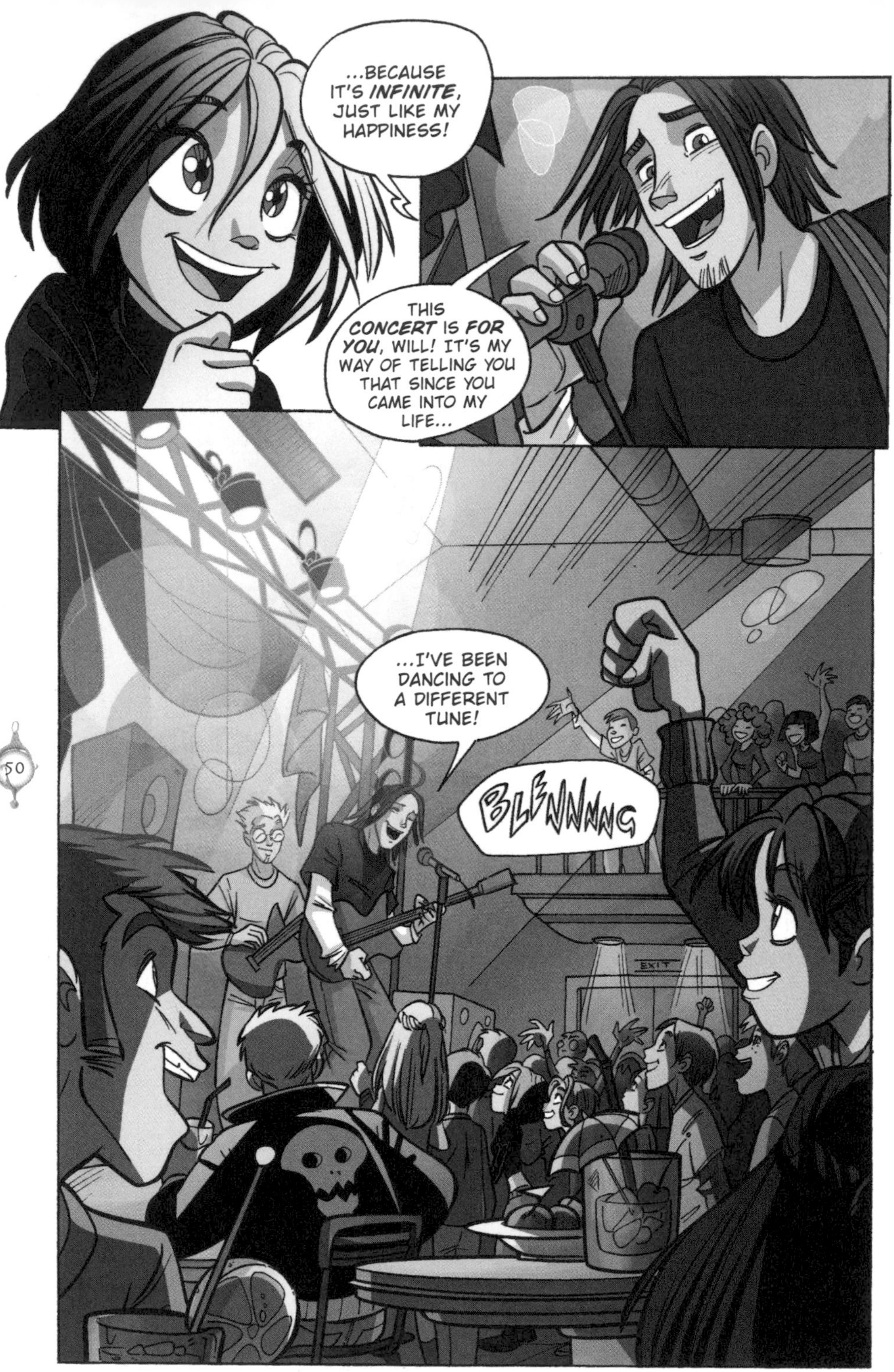
...BECAUSE IT'S INFINITE, JUST LIKE MY HAPPINESS!
THIS CONCERT IS FOR YOU, WILL! IT'S MY WAY OF TELLING YOU THAT SINCE YOU CAME INTO MY LIFE...
...I'VE BEEN DANCING TO A DIFFERENT TUNE!
BLENNNNG
EXIT

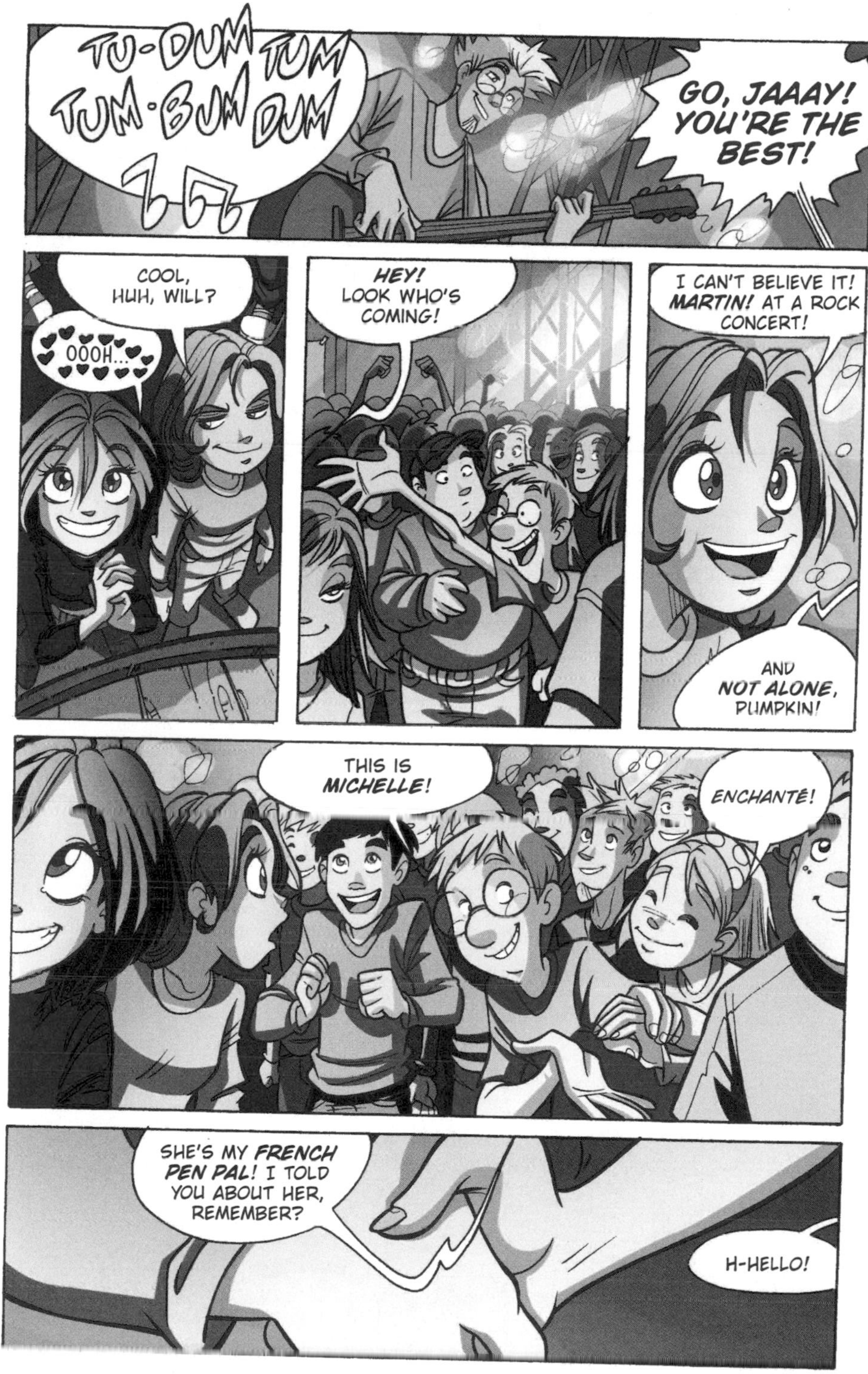
TU-DUM TUM
TUM-BUM DUM
GO, JAAAY! YOU'RE THE BEST!
COOL, HUH, WILL?
OOOH...
HEY! LOOK WHO'S COMING!
I CAN'T BELIEVE IT! MARTIN! AT A ROCK CONCERT!
AND NOT ALONE, PUMPKIN!
THIS IS MICHELLE!
ENCHANTÉ!
SHE'S MY FRENCH PEN PAL! I TOLD YOU ABOUT HER, REMEMBER?
H-HELLO!

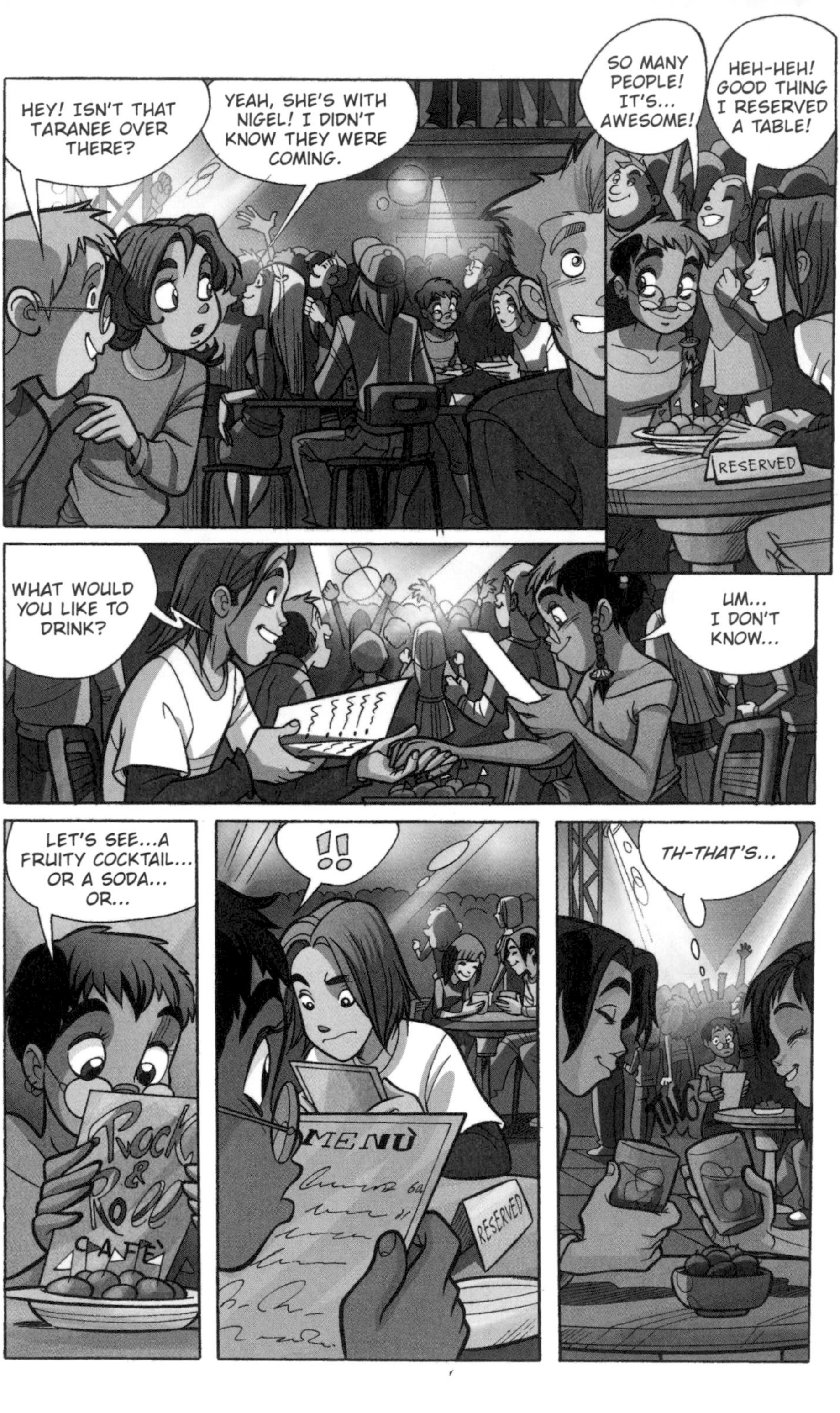
HEY! ISN'T THAT TARANEE OVER THERE?
YEAH, SHE'S WITH NIGEL! I DIDN'T KNOW THEY WERE COMING.
SO MANY PEOPLE! IT'S... AWESOME!
HEH-HEH! GOOD THING I RESERVED A TABLE!
RESERVED
WHAT WOULD YOU LIKE TO DRINK?
UM... I DON'T KNOW...
LET'S SEE...A FRUITY COCKTAIL... OR A SODA... OR...
Rock & Roll CAFÈ
!!
MENÙ
RESERVED
TH-THAT'S...
TING

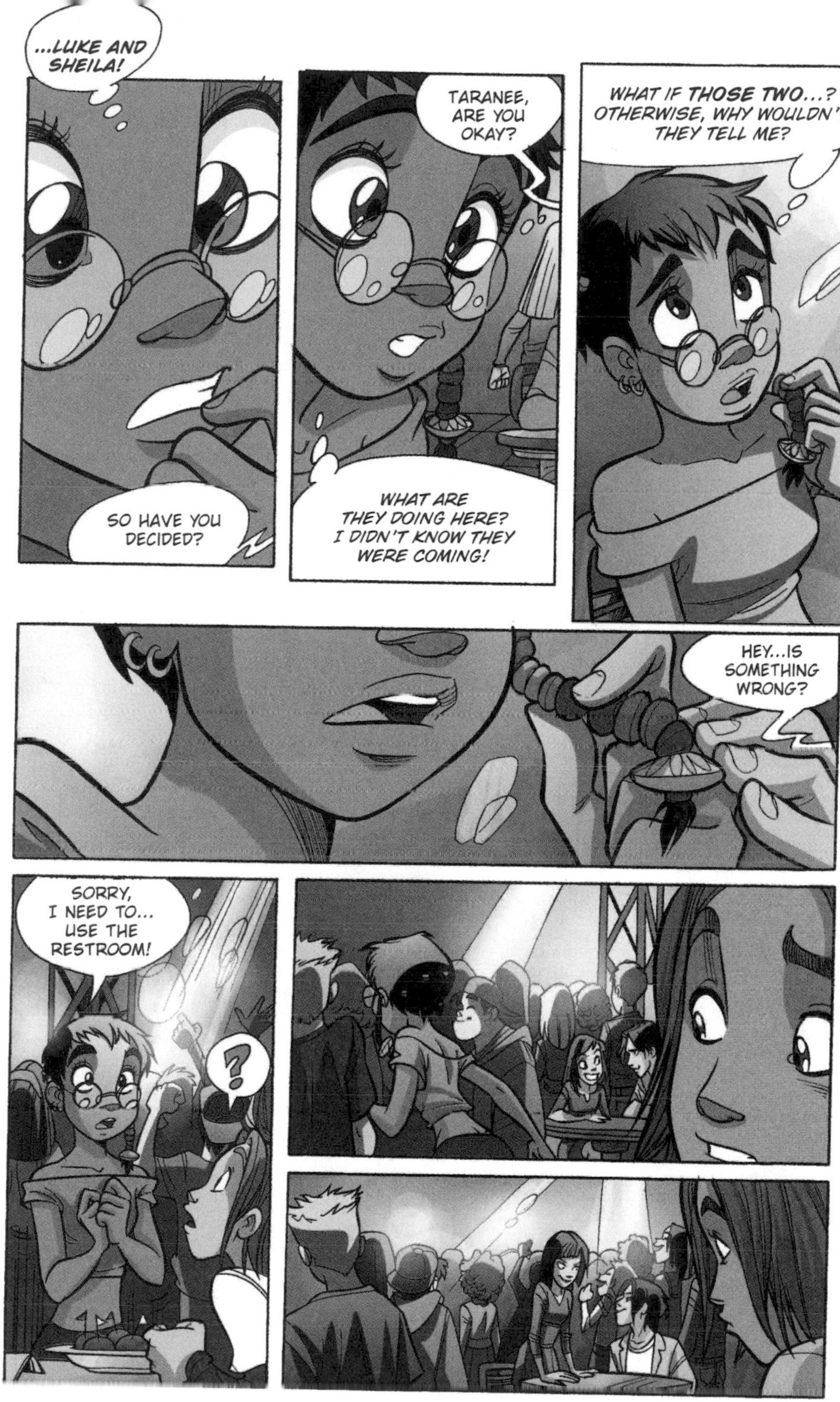

...LUKE AND SHEILA!
SO HAVE YOU DECIDED?
TARANEE, ARE YOU OKAY?
WHAT ARE THEY DOING HERE? I DIDN'T KNOW THEY WERE COMING!
WHAT IF THOSE TWO...? OTHERWISE, WHY WOULDN'T THEY TELL ME?
HEY...IS SOMETHING WRONG?
SORRY, I NEED TO... USE THE RESTROOM!
?

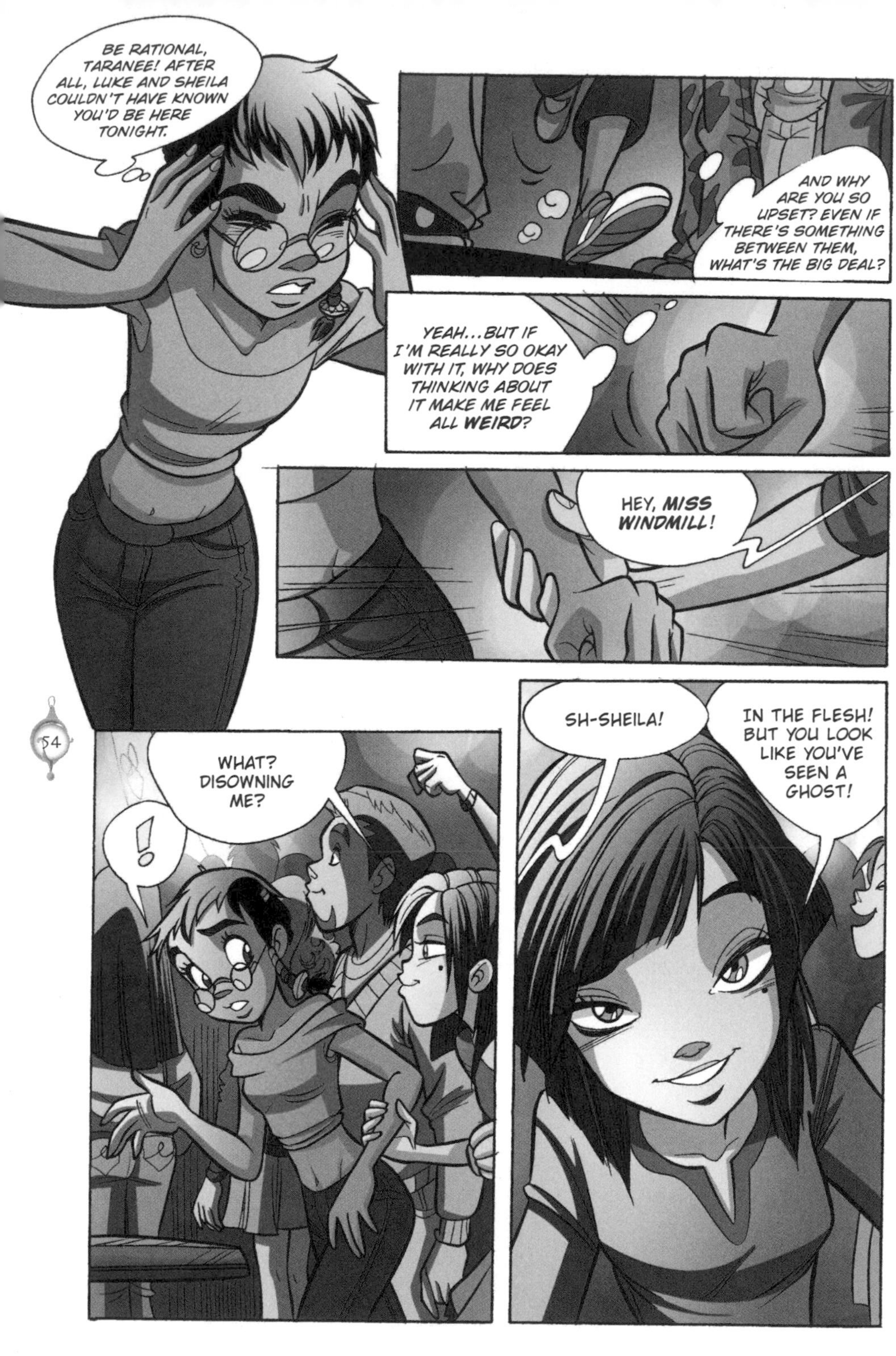

BE RATIONAL, TARANEE! AFTER ALL, LUKE AND SHEILA COULDN'T HAVE KNOWN YOU'D BE HERE TONIGHT.
AND WHY ARE YOU SO UPSET? EVEN IF THERE'S SOMETHING BETWEEN THEM, WHAT'S THE BIG DEAL?
YEAH...BUT IF I'M REALLY SO OKAY WITH IT, WHY DOES THINKING ABOUT IT MAKE ME FEEL ALL WEIRD?
HEY, MISS WINDMILL!
WHAT? DISOWNING ME?
!
SH-SHEILA!
IN THE FLESH! BUT YOU LOOK LIKE YOU'VE SEEN A GHOST!

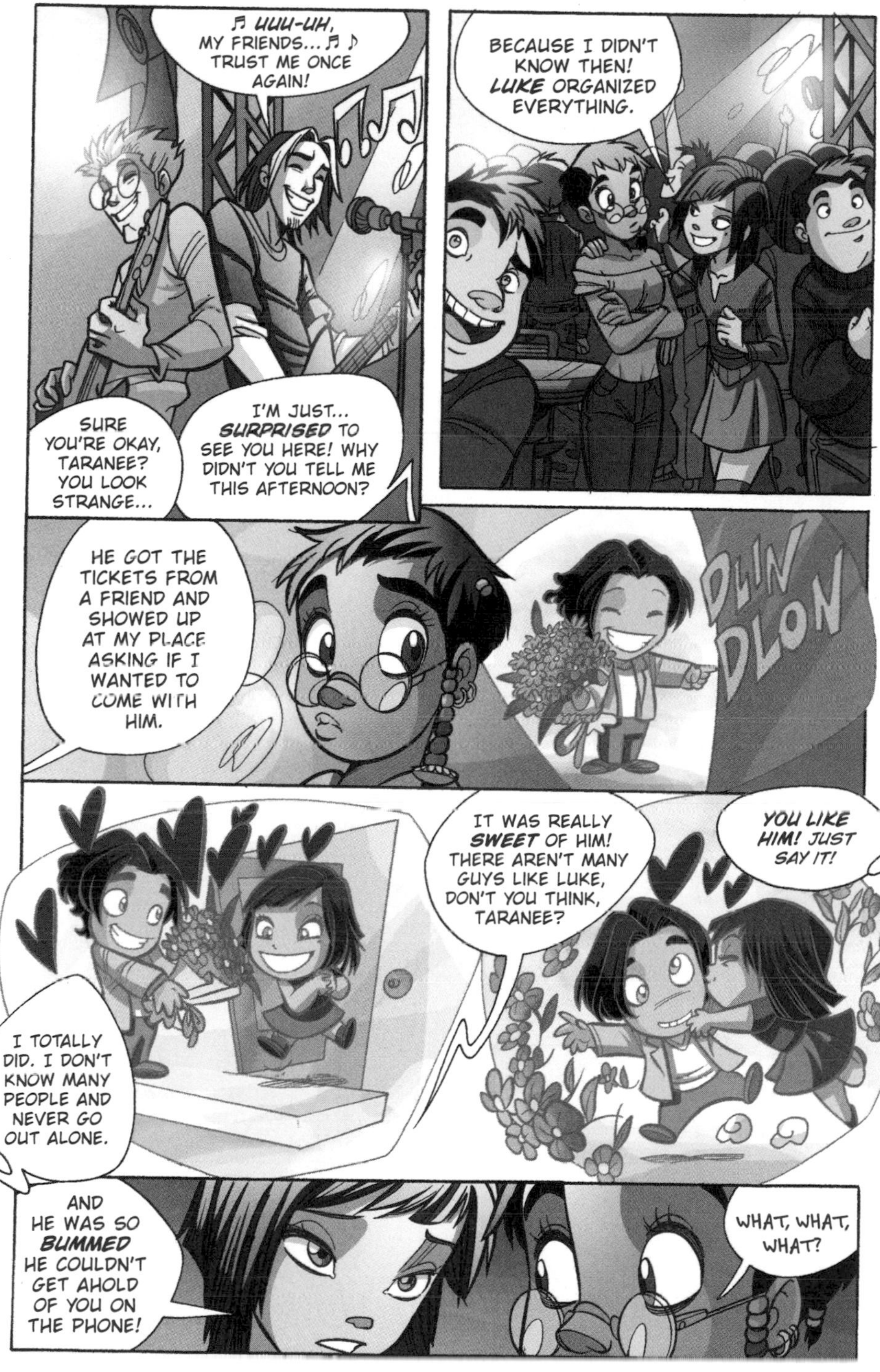
♬ UUU-UH, MY FRIENDS... ♬ ♪ TRUST ME ONCE AGAIN!
SURE YOU'RE OKAY, TARANEE? YOU LOOK STRANGE...
I'M JUST... SURPRISED TO SEE YOU HERE! WHY DIDN'T YOU TELL ME THIS AFTERNOON?
BECAUSE I DIDN'T KNOW THEN! LUKE ORGANIZED EVERYTHING.
HE GOT THE TICKETS FROM A FRIEND AND SHOWED UP AT MY PLACE ASKING IF I WANTED TO COME WITH HIM.
DLIN DLON
I TOTALLY DID. I DON'T KNOW MANY PEOPLE AND NEVER GO OUT ALONE.
IT WAS REALLY SWEET OF HIM! THERE AREN'T MANY GUYS LIKE LUKE, DON'T YOU THINK, TARANEE?
YOU LIKE HIM! JUST SAY IT!
AND HE WAS SO BUMMED HE COULDN'T GET AHOLD OF YOU ON THE PHONE!
WHAT, WHAT, WHAT?

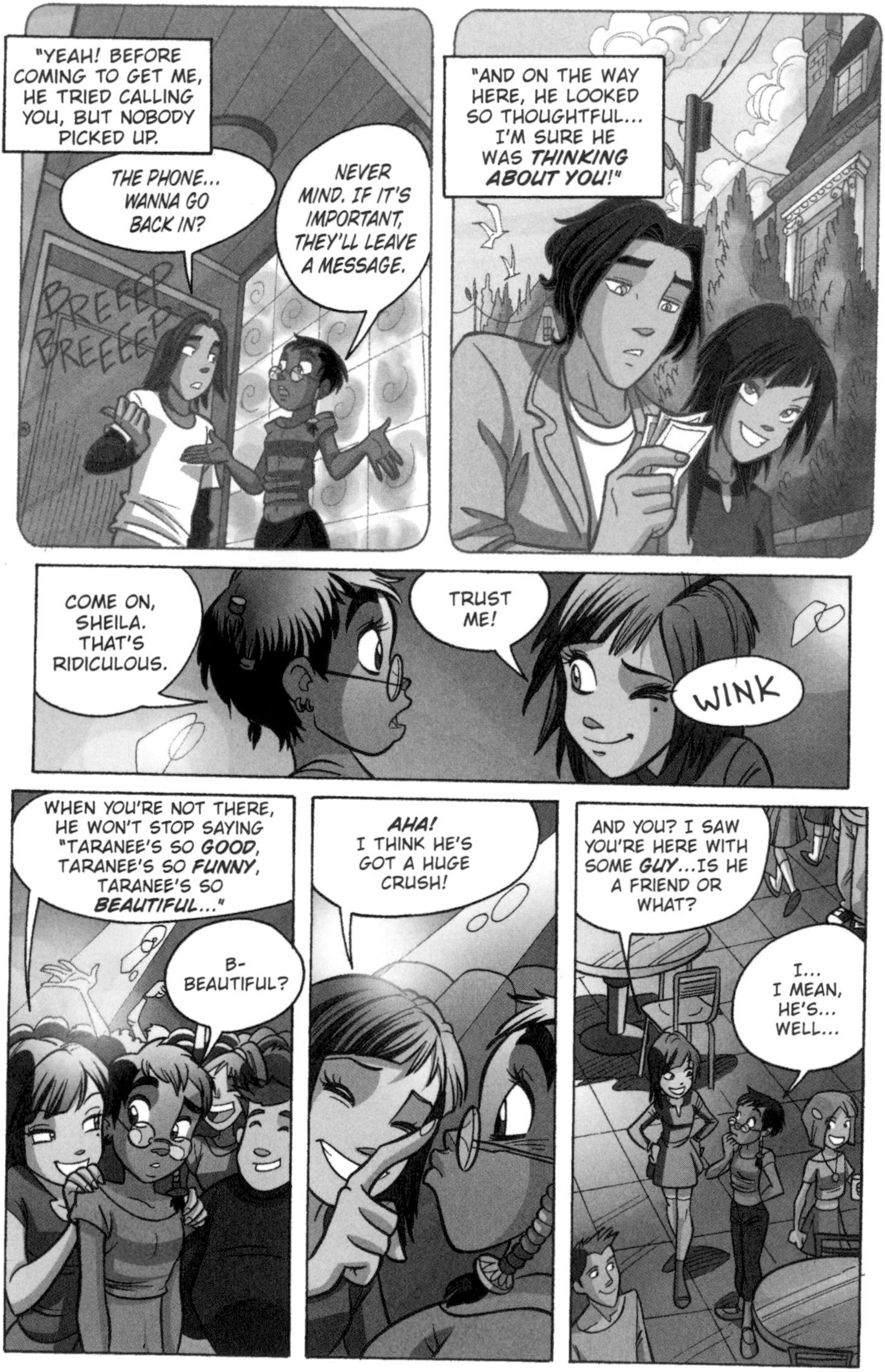
"YEAH! BEFORE COMING TO GET ME, HE TRIED CALLING YOU, BUT NOBODY PICKED UP.
BREEEP BREEEEP
THE PHONE... WANNA GO BACK IN?
NEVER MIND. IF IT'S IMPORTANT, THEY'LL LEAVE A MESSAGE.
"AND ON THE WAY HERE, HE LOOKED SO THOUGHTFUL... I'M SURE HE WAS THINKING ABOUT YOU!"
COME ON, SHEILA. THAT'S RIDICULOUS.
TRUST ME!
WINK
WHEN YOU'RE NOT THERE, HE WON'T STOP SAYING "TARANEE'S SO GOOD, TARANEE'S SO FUNNY, TARANEE'S SO BEAUTIFUL..."
B- BEAUTIFUL?
AHA! I THINK HE'S GOT A HUGE CRUSH!
AND YOU? I SAW YOU'RE HERE WITH SOME GUY...IS HE A FRIEND OR WHAT?
I... I MEAN, HE'S... WELL...

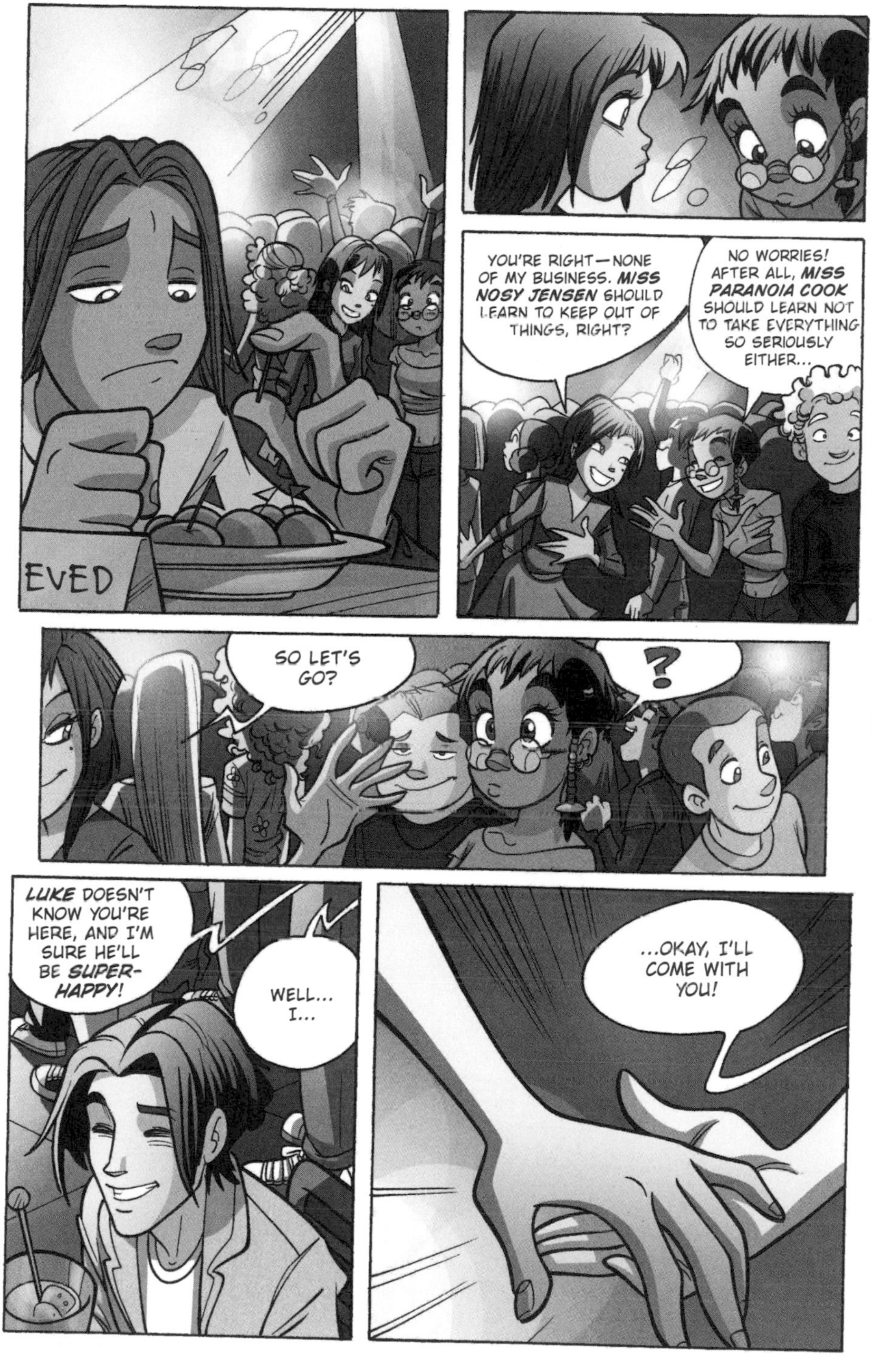
EVED
YOU'RE RIGHT—NONE OF MY BUSINESS. MISS NOSY JENSEN SHOULD LEARN TO KEEP OUT OF THINGS, RIGHT?
NO WORRIES! AFTER ALL, MISS PARANOIA COOK SHOULD LEARN NOT TO TAKE EVERYTHING SO SERIOUSLY EITHER...
SO LET'S GO?
?
LUKE DOESN'T KNOW YOU'RE HERE, AND I'M SURE HE'LL BE SUPER-HAPPY!
WELL... I...
...OKAY, I'LL COME WITH YOU!

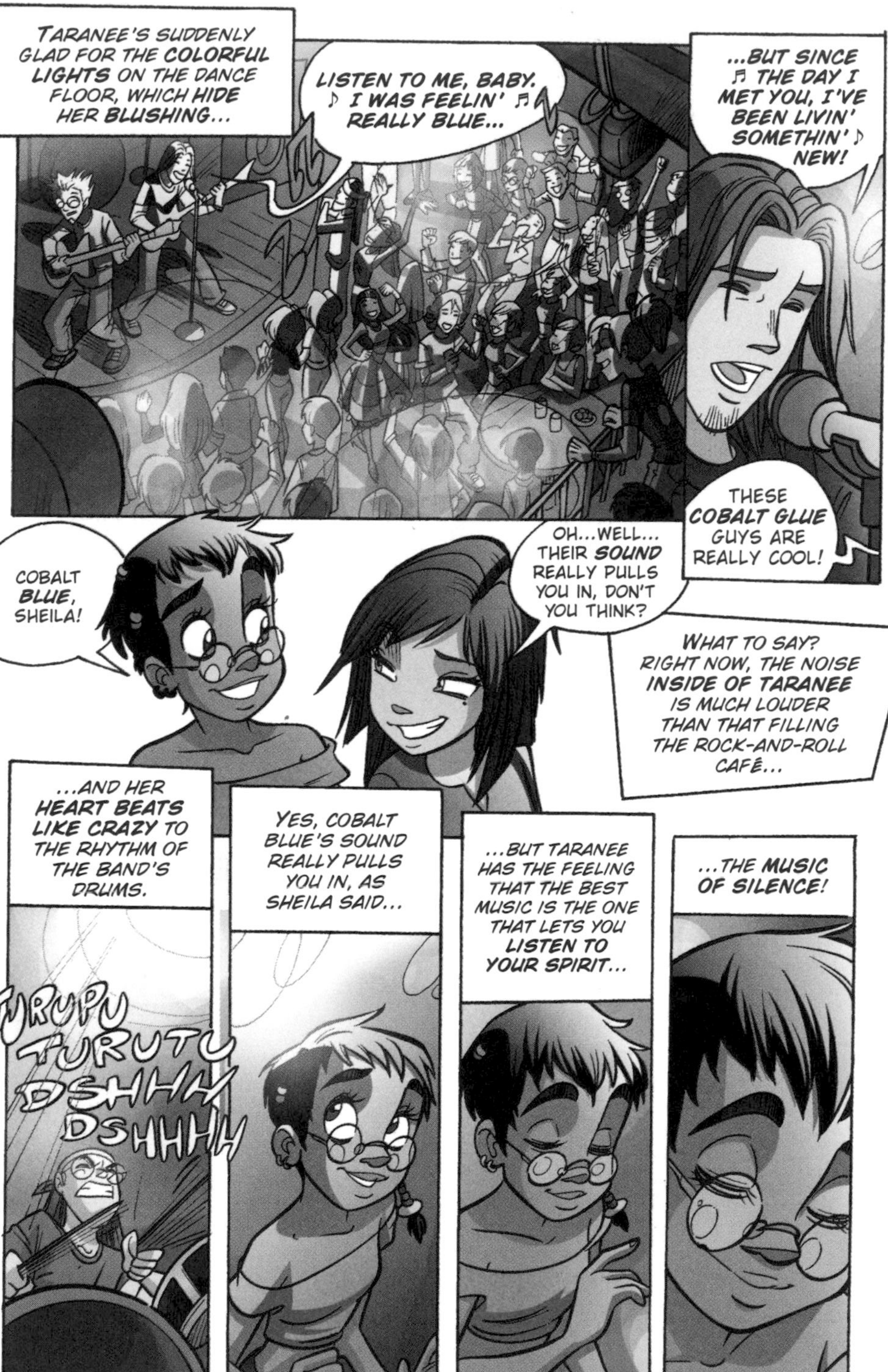
TARANEE'S SUDDENLY GLAD FOR THE COLORFUL LIGHTS ON THE DANCE FLOOR, WHICH HIDE HER BLUSHING...
LISTEN TO ME, BABY. ♪ I WAS FEELIN' ♬ REALLY BLUE...
...BUT SINCE ♬ THE DAY I MET YOU, I'VE BEEN LIVIN' SOMETHIN' ♪ NEW!
THESE COBALT GLUE GUYS ARE REALLY COOL!
OH...WELL... THEIR SOUND REALLY PULLS YOU IN, DON'T YOU THINK?
COBALT BLUE, SHEILA!
WHAT TO SAY? RIGHT NOW, THE NOISE INSIDE OF TARANEE IS MUCH LOUDER THAN THAT FILLING THE ROCK-AND-ROLL CAFÉ...
...AND HER HEART BEATS LIKE CRAZY TO THE RHYTHM OF THE BAND'S DRUMS.
TURUPU TURUTU DSHHH DSHHHH
YES, COBALT BLUE'S SOUND REALLY PULLS YOU IN, AS SHEILA SAID...
...BUT TARANEE HAS THE FEELING THAT THE BEST MUSIC IS THE ONE THAT LETS YOU LISTEN TO YOUR SPIRIT...
...THE MUSIC OF SILENCE!

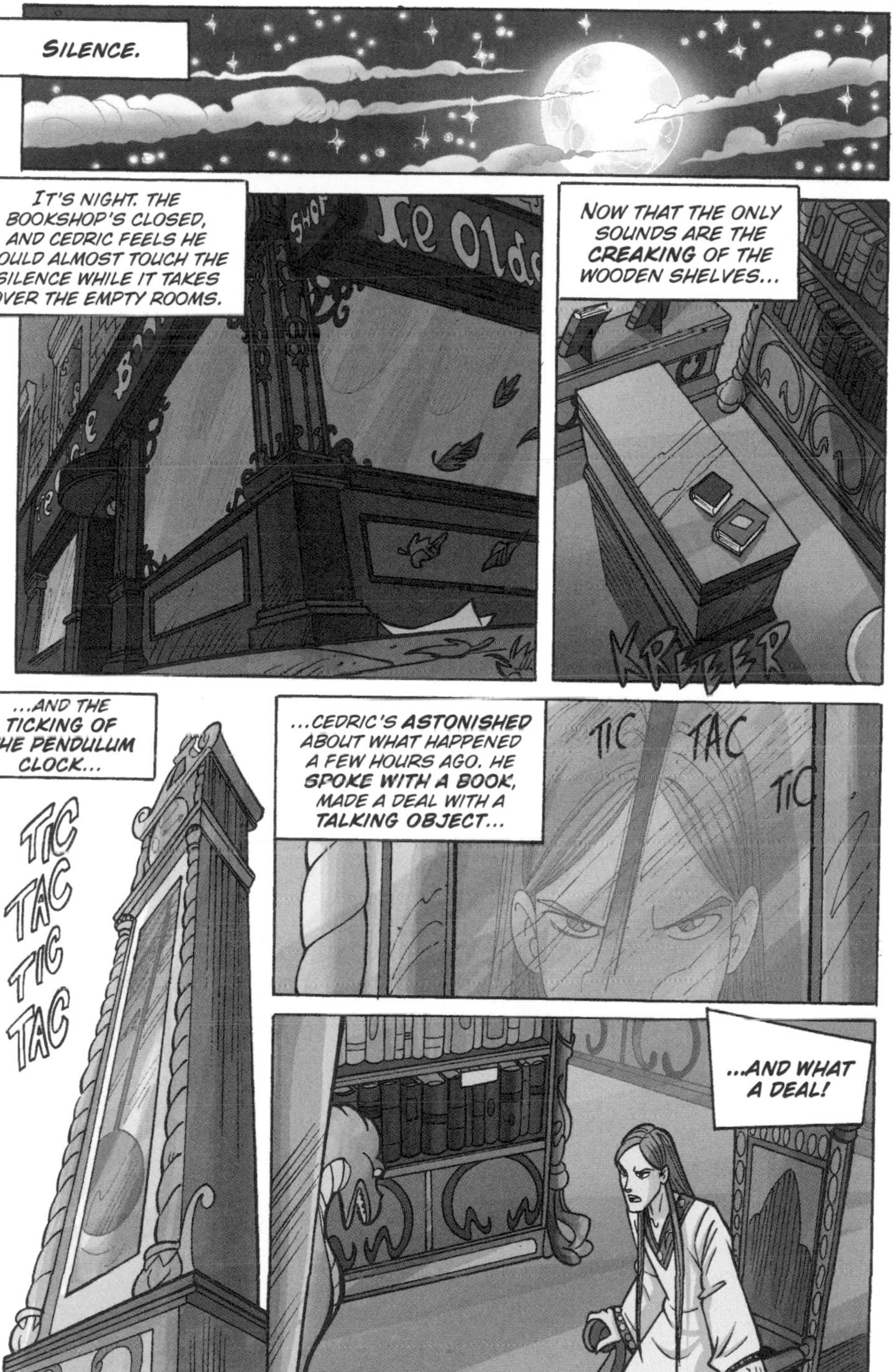
SILENCE.
IT'S NIGHT. THE BOOKSHOP'S CLOSED, AND CEDRIC FEELS HE COULD ALMOST TOUCH THE SILENCE WHILE IT TAKES OVER THE EMPTY ROOMS.
NOW THAT THE ONLY SOUNDS ARE THE CREAKING OF THE WOODEN SHELVES...
KREEER
...AND THE TICKING OF THE PENDULUM CLOCK...
TIC TAC TIC TAC
...CEDRIC'S ASTONISHED ABOUT WHAT HAPPENED A FEW HOURS AGO. HE SPOKE WITH A BOOK, MADE A DEAL WITH A TALKING OBJECT...
TIC TAC TIC
...AND WHAT A DEAL!

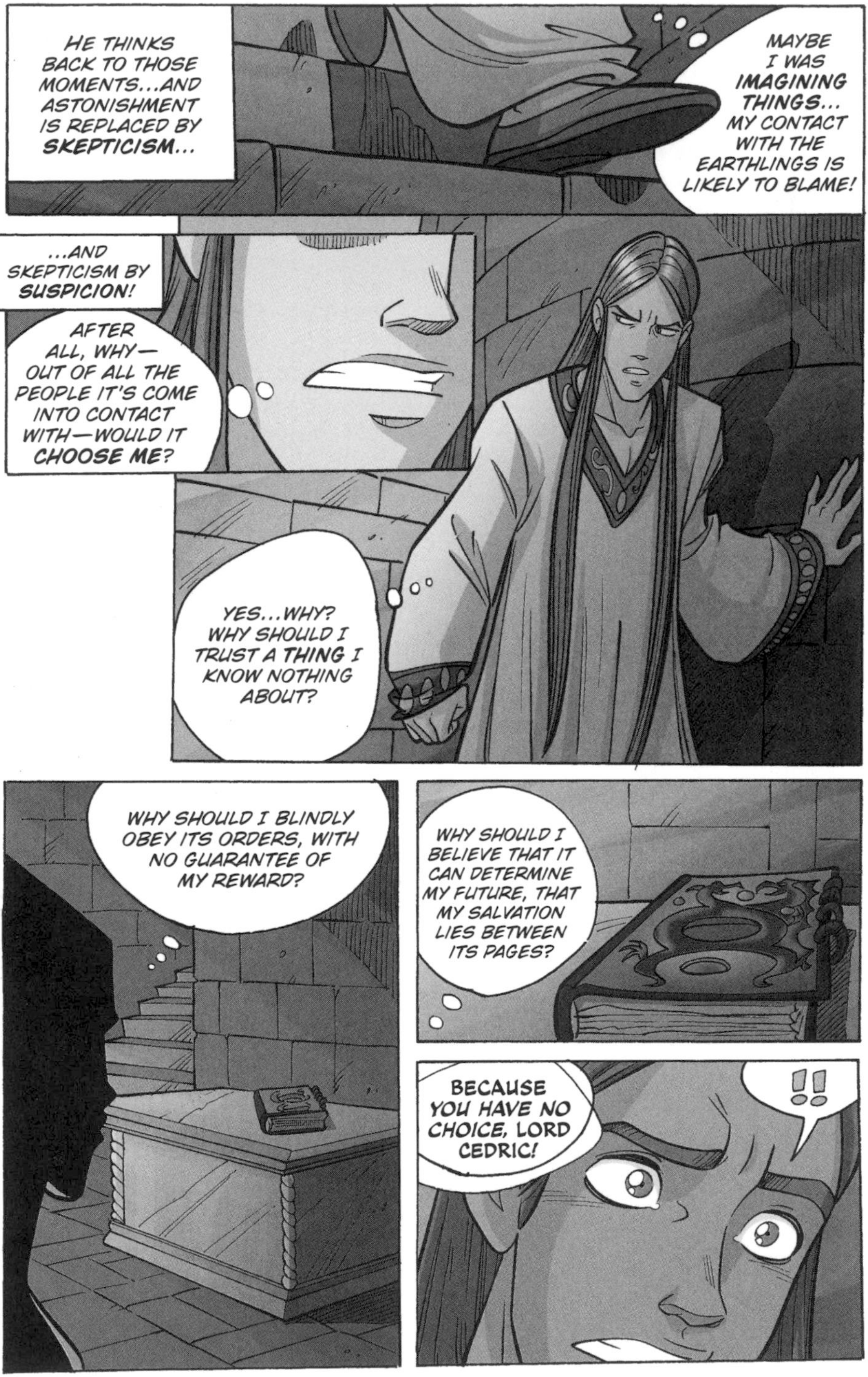
HE THINKS BACK TO THOSE MOMENTS...AND ASTONISHMENT IS REPLACED BY SKEPTICISM...
MAYBE I WAS IMAGINING THINGS... MY CONTACT WITH THE EARTHLINGS IS LIKELY TO BLAME!
...AND SKEPTICISM BY SUSPICION!
AFTER ALL, WHY—OUT OF ALL THE PEOPLE IT'S COME INTO CONTACT WITH—WOULD IT CHOOSE ME?
YES...WHY? WHY SHOULD I TRUST A THING I KNOW NOTHING ABOUT?
WHY SHOULD I BLINDLY OBEY ITS ORDERS, WITH NO GUARANTEE OF MY REWARD?
WHY SHOULD I BELIEVE THAT IT CAN DETERMINE MY FUTURE, THAT MY SALVATION LIES BETWEEN ITS PAGES?
BECAUSE YOU HAVE NO CHOICE, LORD CEDRIC!
!!

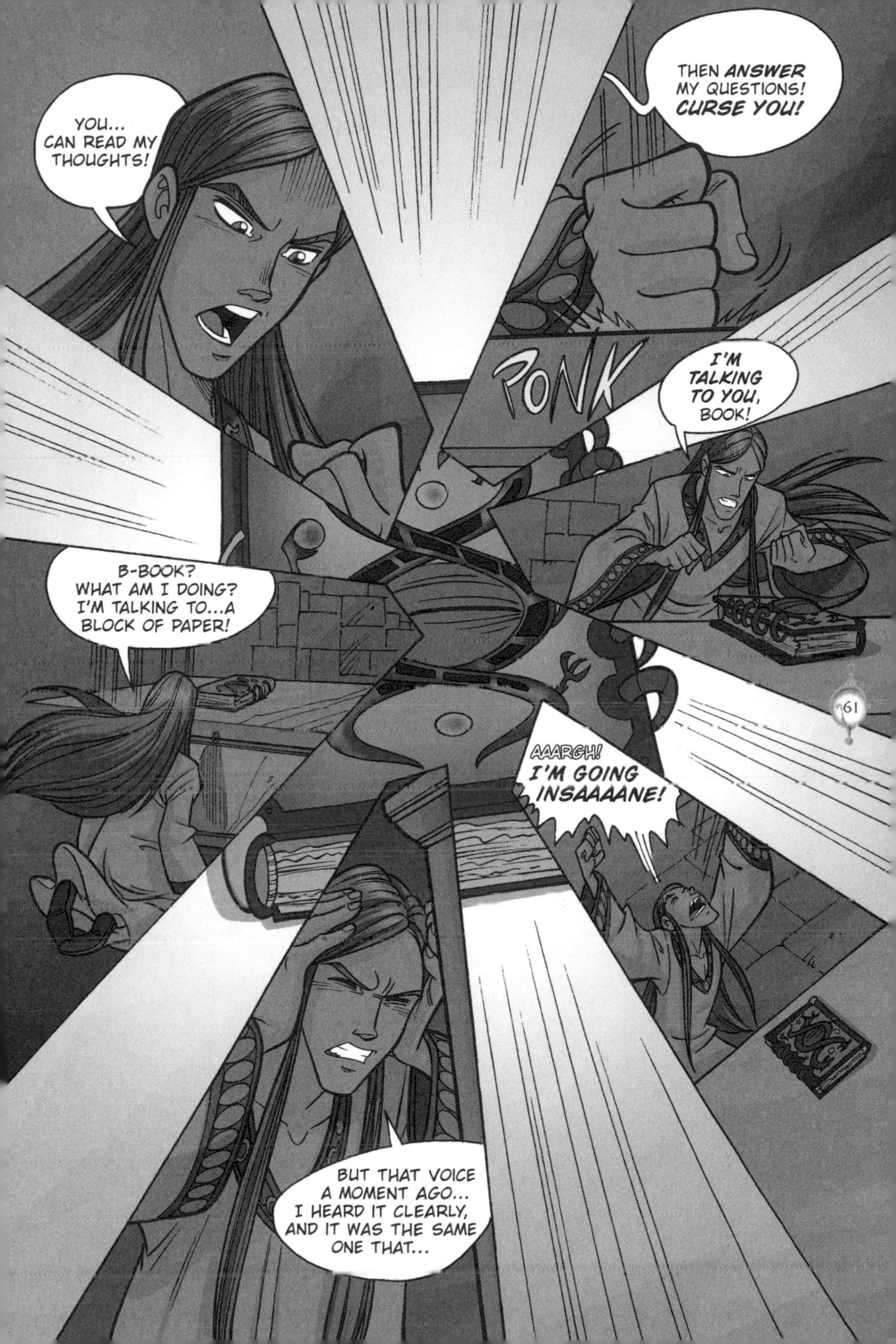

YOU... CAN READ MY THOUGHTS!
THEN ANSWER MY QUESTIONS! CURSE YOU!
PONK
I'M TALKING TO YOU, BOOK!
B-BOOK? WHAT AM I DOING? I'M TALKING TO...A BLOCK OF PAPER!
AAARGH! I'M GOING INSAAAANE!
BUT THAT VOICE A MOMENT AGO... I HEARD IT CLEARLY, AND IT WAS THE SAME ONE THAT...

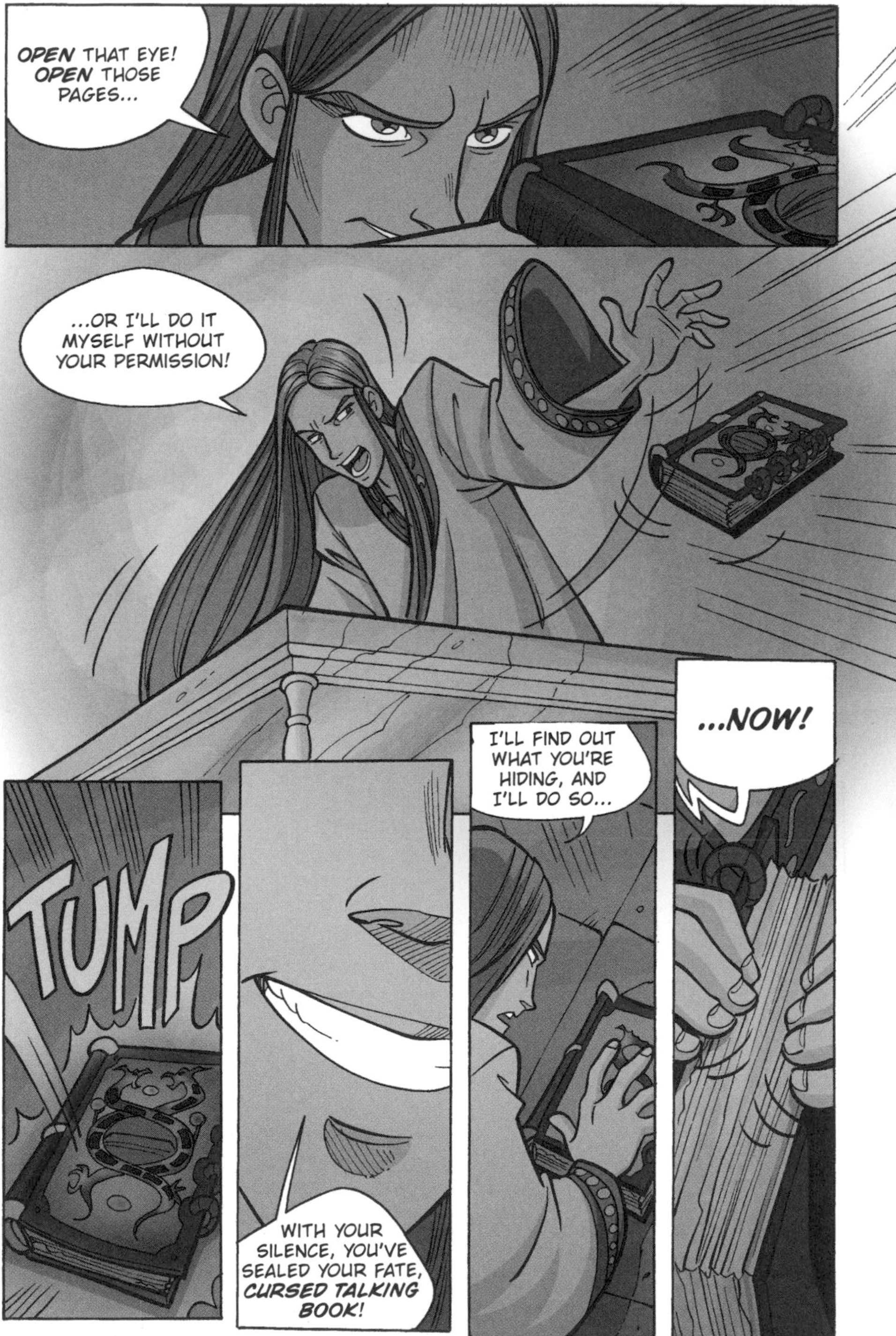
OPEN THAT EYE! OPEN THOSE PAGES...
...OR I'LL DO IT MYSELF WITHOUT YOUR PERMISSION!
TUMP
WITH YOUR SILENCE, YOU'VE SEALED YOUR FATE, CURSED TALKING BOOK!
I'LL FIND OUT WHAT YOU'RE HIDING, AND I'LL DO SO...
...NOW!

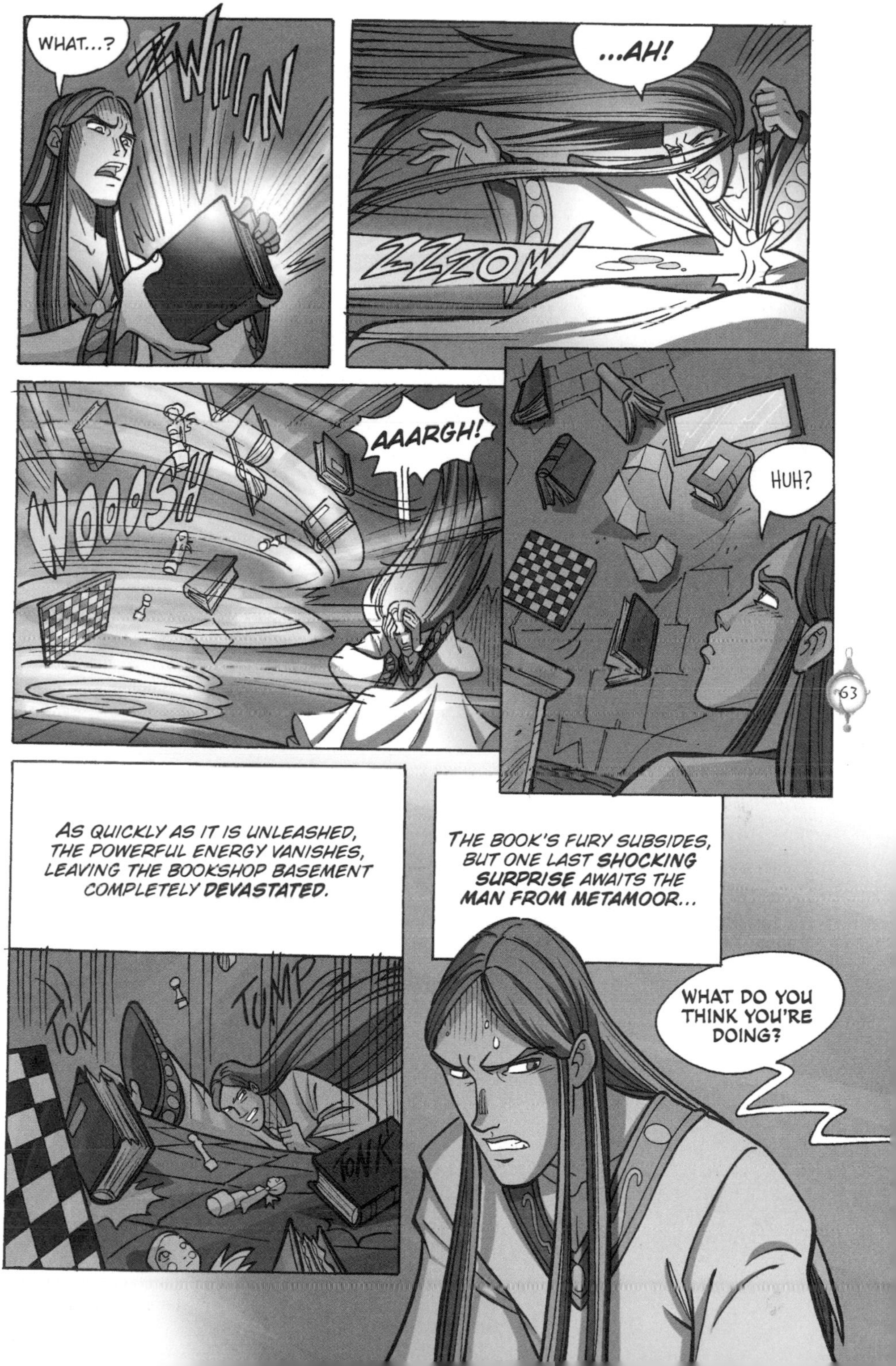
WHAT...?
ZWIIIIN
...AH!
ZZZOW
WOOOSH
AAARGH!
HUH?
AS QUICKLY AS IT IS UNLEASHED, THE POWERFUL ENERGY VANISHES, LEAVING THE BOOKSHOP BASEMENT COMPLETELY DEVASTATED.
TOK
TUMP
TONK
THE BOOK'S FURY SUBSIDES, BUT ONE LAST SHOCKING SURPRISE AWAITS THE MAN FROM METAMOOR...
WHAT DO YOU THINK YOU'RE DOING?

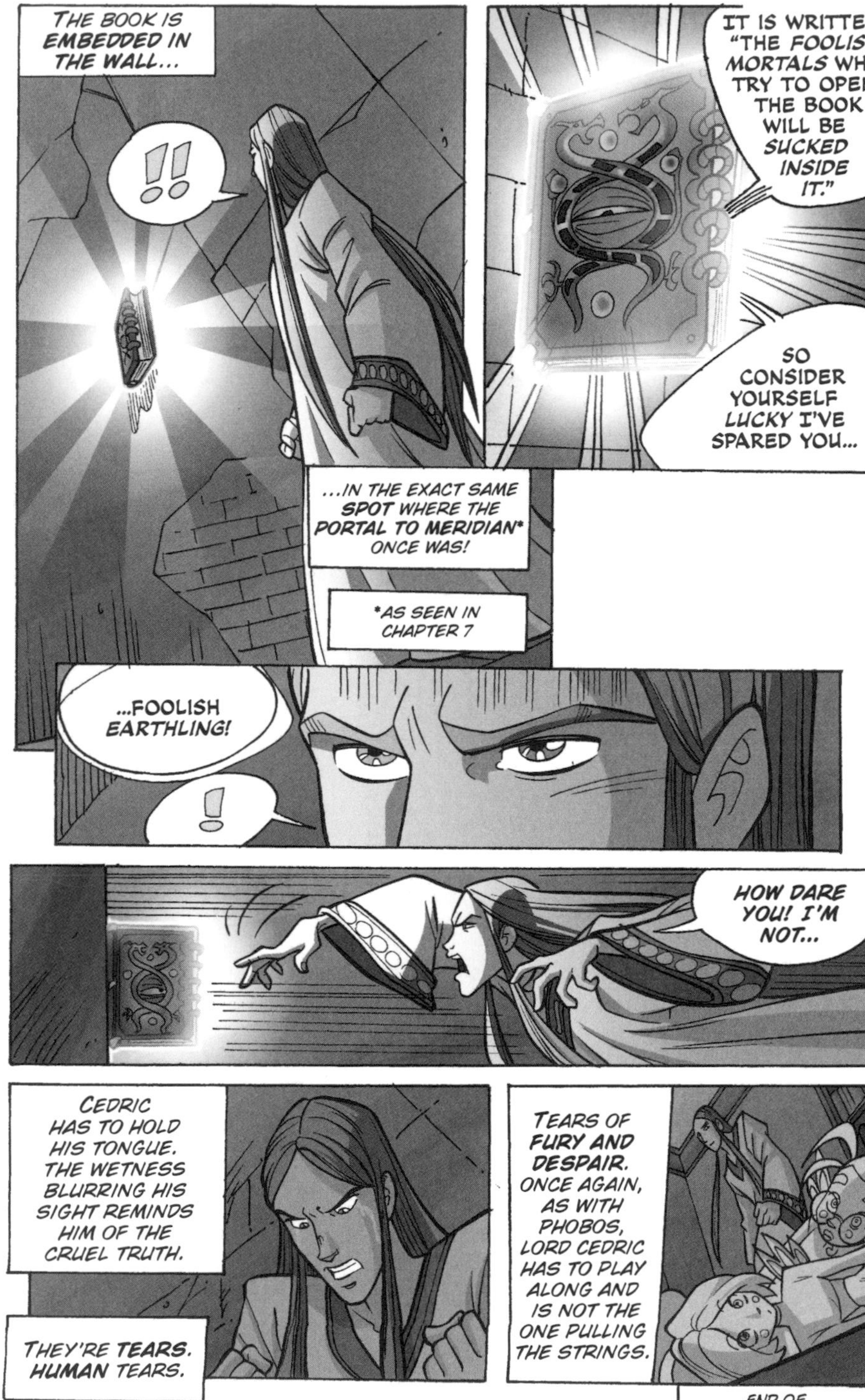
THE BOOK IS EMBEDDED IN THE WALL...
!!
IT IS WRITTEN: "THE FOOLISH MORTALS WHO TRY TO OPEN THE BOOK WILL BE SUCKED INSIDE IT."
SO CONSIDER YOURSELF LUCKY I'VE SPARED YOU...
...IN THE EXACT SAME SPOT WHERE THE PORTAL TO MERIDIAN* ONCE WAS!
*AS SEEN IN CHAPTER 7
...FOOLISH EARTHLING!
!
HOW DARE YOU! I'M NOT...
CEDRIC HAS TO HOLD HIS TONGUE. THE WETNESS BLURRING HIS SIGHT REMINDS HIM OF THE CRUEL TRUTH.
THEY'RE TEARS. HUMAN TEARS.
TEARS OF FURY AND DESPAIR. ONCE AGAIN, AS WITH PHOBOS, LORD CEDRIC HAS TO PLAY ALONG AND IS NOT THE ONE PULLING THE STRINGS.
END OF CHAPTER 53

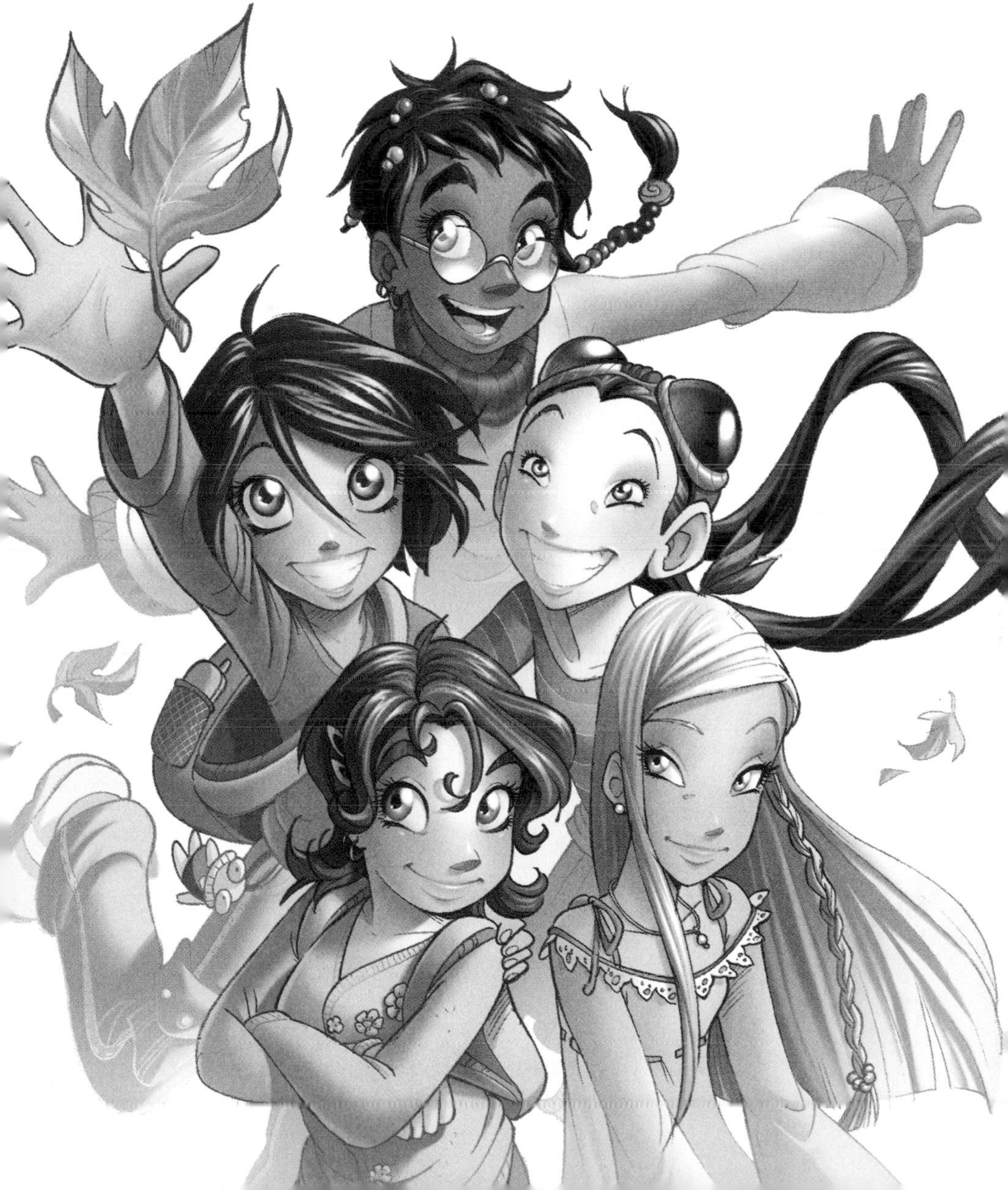

One More Hug

"I gotta find out what's going on around here..."

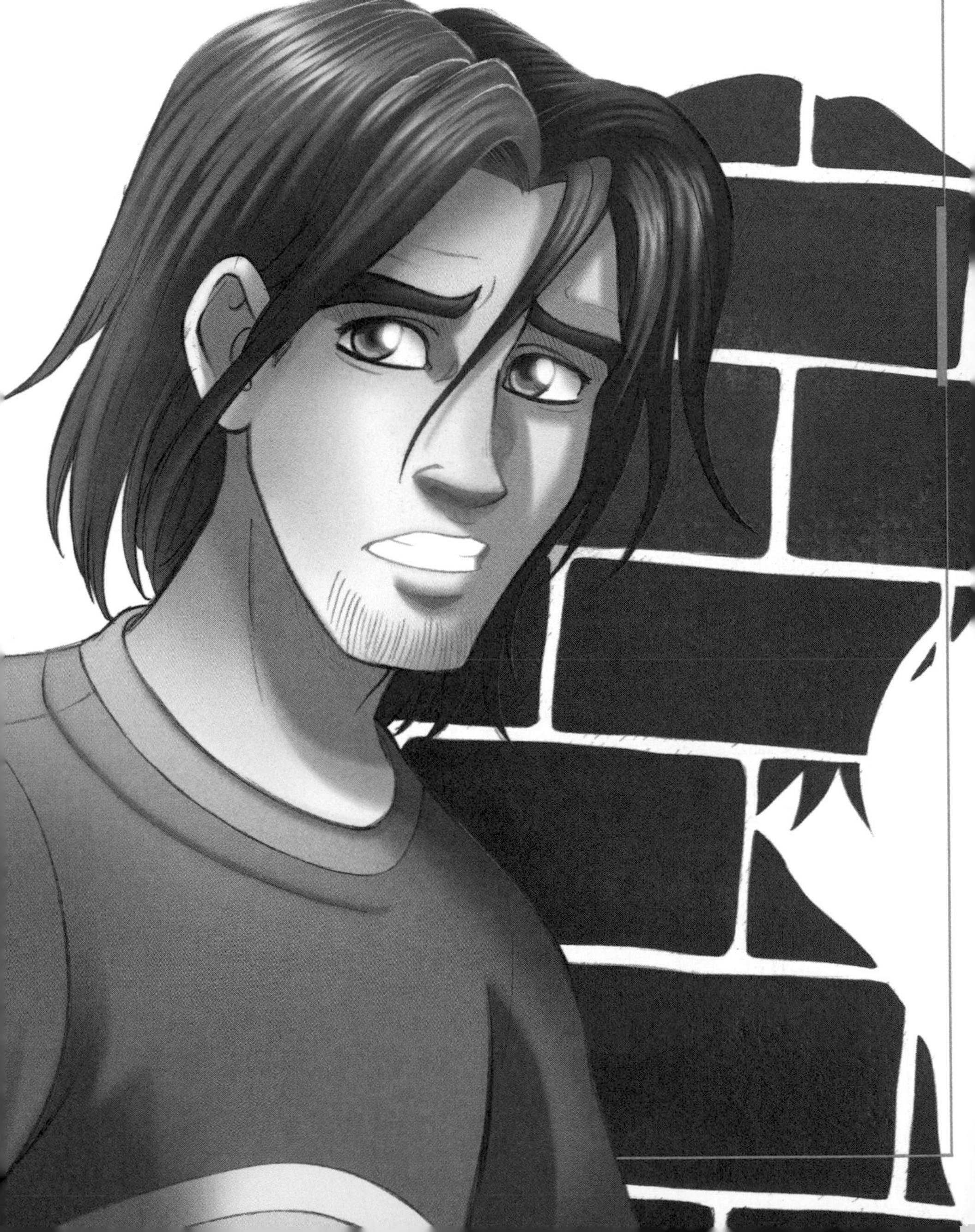

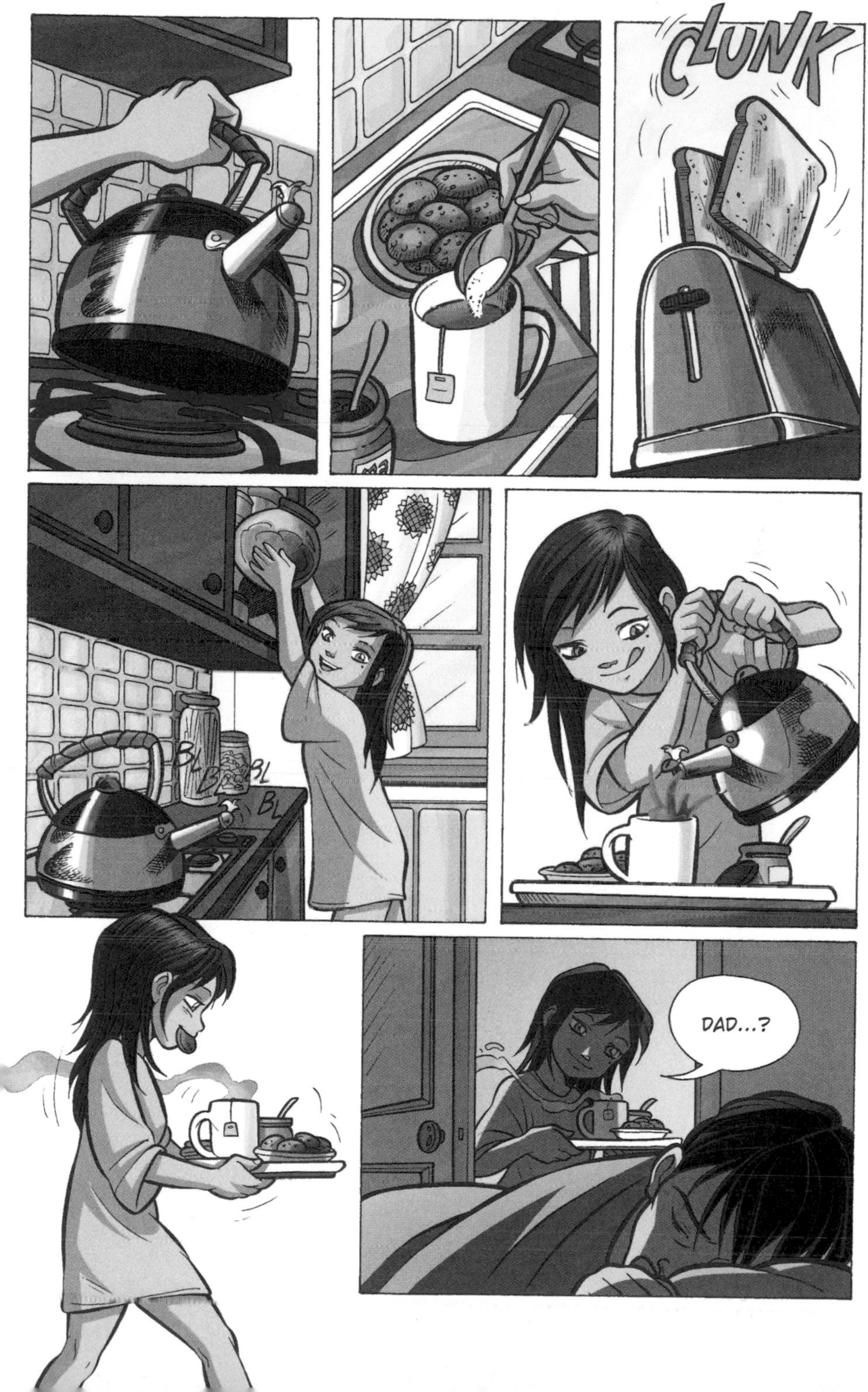
CLUNK
BL
BL
BL
DAD...?

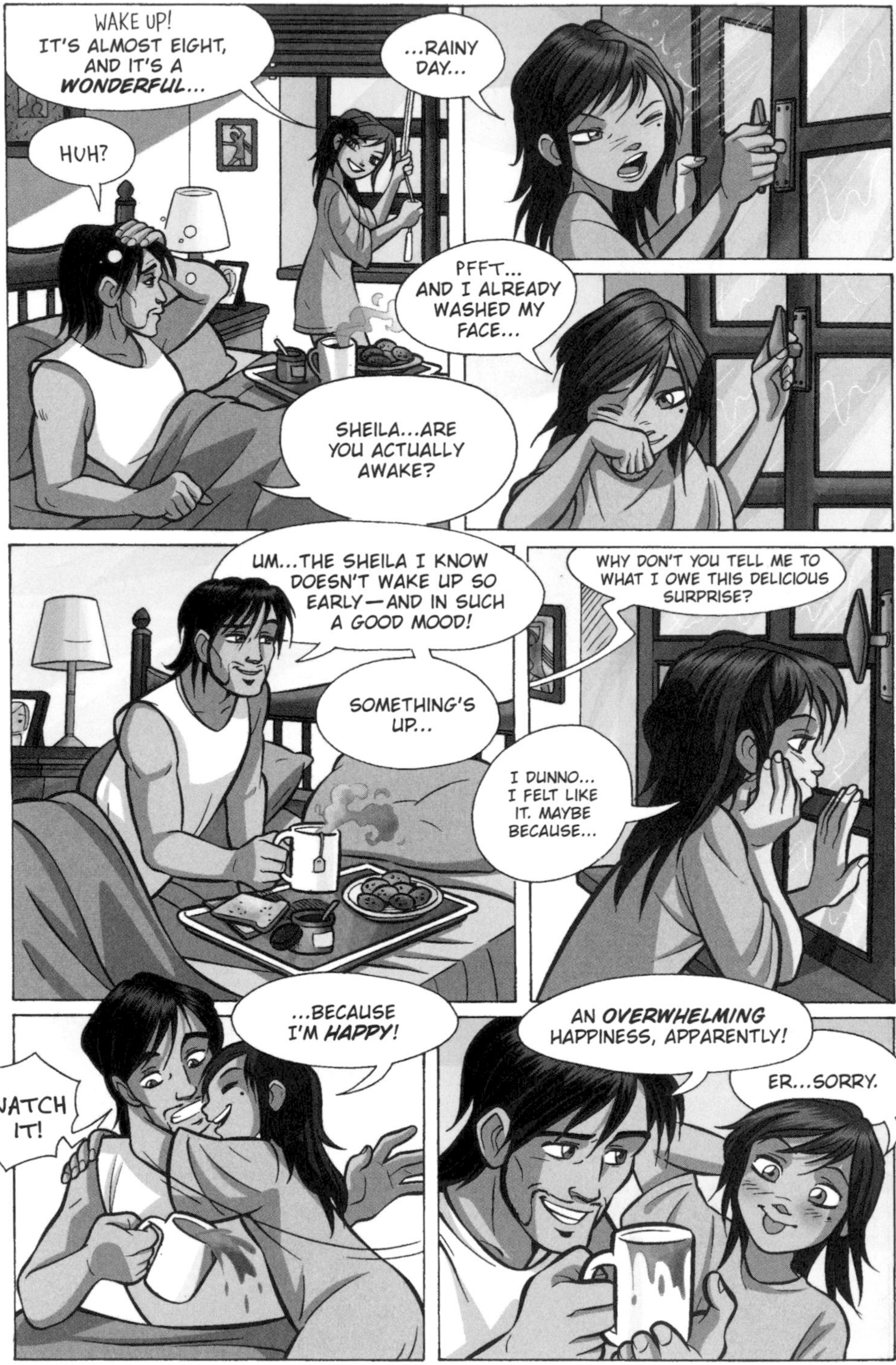
WAKE UP! IT'S ALMOST EIGHT, AND IT'S A WONDERFUL...
HUH?
...RAINY DAY...
PFFT... AND I ALREADY WASHED MY FACE...
SHEILA...ARE YOU ACTUALLY AWAKE?
UM...THE SHEILA I KNOW DOESN'T WAKE UP SO EARLY—AND IN SUCH A GOOD MOOD!
SOMETHING'S UP...
WHY DON'T YOU TELL ME TO WHAT I OWE THIS DELICIOUS SURPRISE?
I DUNNO... I FELT LIKE IT. MAYBE BECAUSE...
...BECAUSE I'M HAPPY!
WATCH IT!
AN OVERWHELMING HAPPINESS, APPARENTLY!
ER...SORRY.

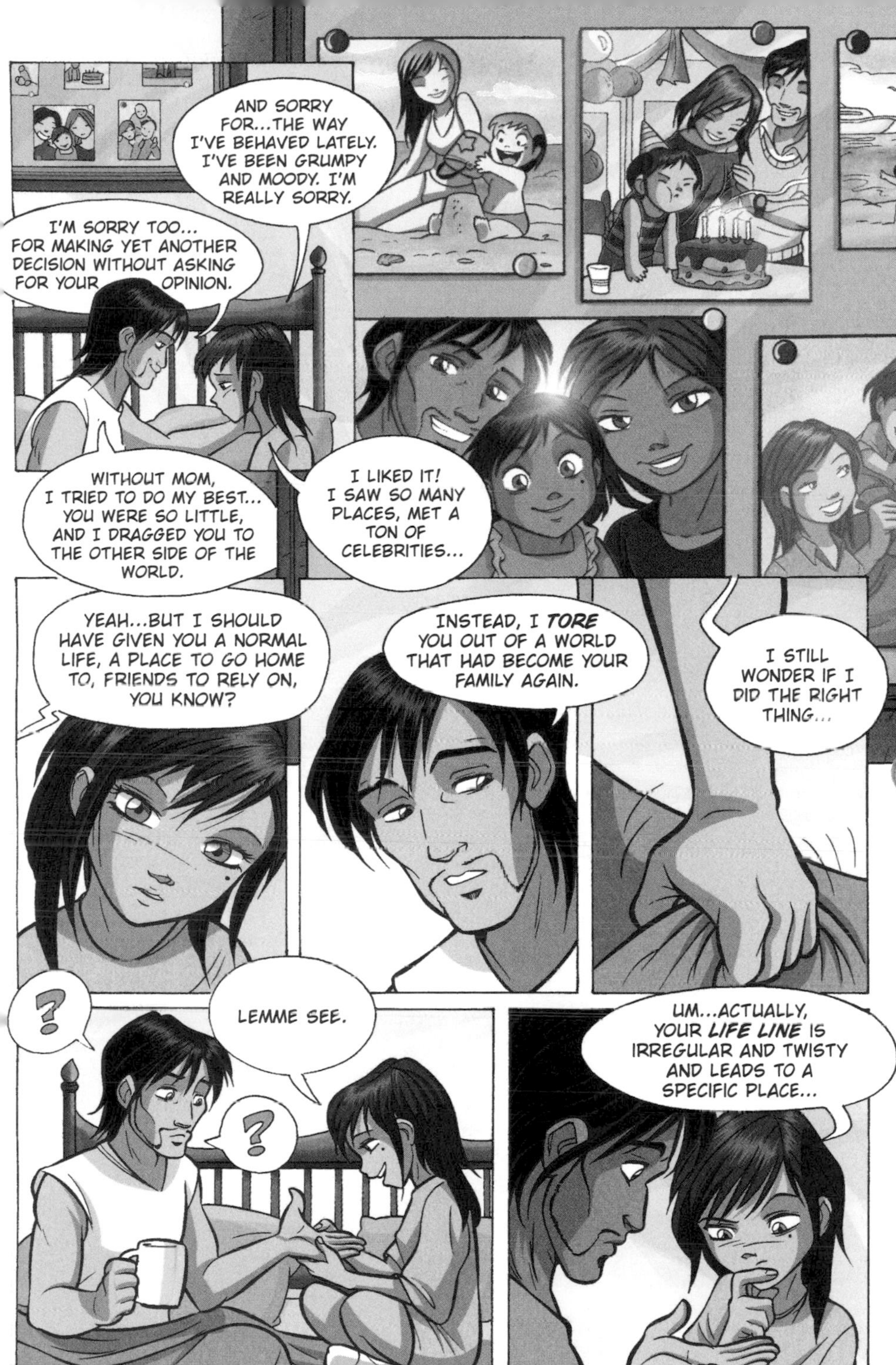
AND SORRY FOR...THE WAY I'VE BEHAVED LATELY. I'VE BEEN GRUMPY AND MOODY. I'M REALLY SORRY.
I'M SORRY TOO... FOR MAKING YET ANOTHER DECISION WITHOUT ASKING FOR YOUR OPINION.
WITHOUT MOM, I TRIED TO DO MY BEST... YOU WERE SO LITTLE, AND I DRAGGED YOU TO THE OTHER SIDE OF THE WORLD.
I LIKED IT! I SAW SO MANY PLACES, MET A TON OF CELEBRITIES...
YEAH...BUT I SHOULD HAVE GIVEN YOU A NORMAL LIFE, A PLACE TO GO HOME TO, FRIENDS TO RELY ON, YOU KNOW?
INSTEAD, I *TORE* YOU OUT OF A WORLD THAT HAD BECOME YOUR FAMILY AGAIN.
I STILL WONDER IF I DID THE RIGHT THING...
?
LEMME SEE.
?
UM...ACTUALLY, YOUR ***LIFE LINE*** IS IRREGULAR AND TWISTY AND LEADS TO A SPECIFIC PLACE...

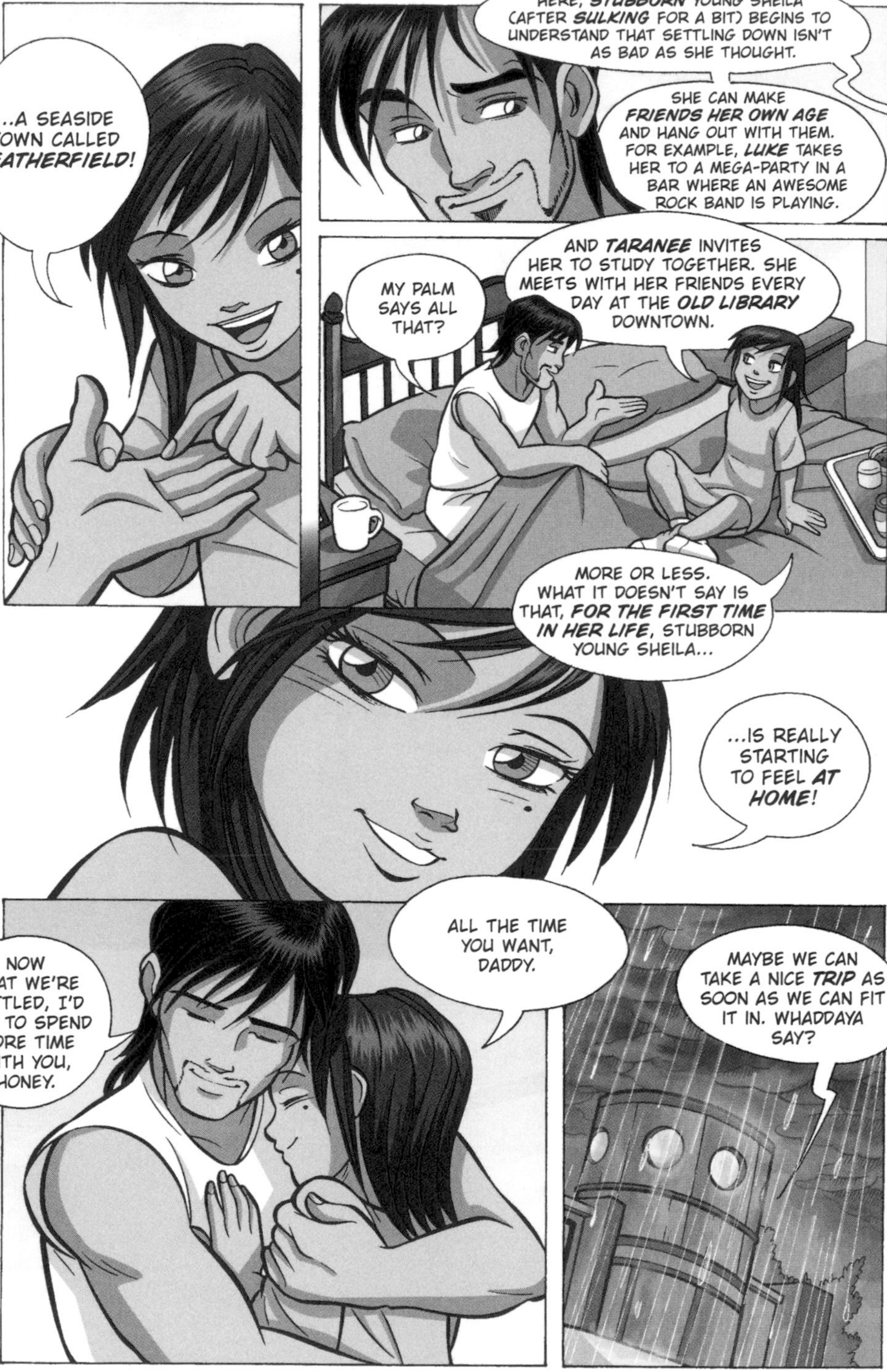
...A SEASIDE TOWN CALLED HEATHERFIELD!
HERE, STUBBORN YOUNG SHEILA (AFTER SULKING FOR A BIT) BEGINS TO UNDERSTAND THAT SETTLING DOWN ISN'T AS BAD AS SHE THOUGHT.
SHE CAN MAKE FRIENDS HER OWN AGE AND HANG OUT WITH THEM. FOR EXAMPLE, LUKE TAKES HER TO A MEGA-PARTY IN A BAR WHERE AN AWESOME ROCK BAND IS PLAYING.
MY PALM SAYS ALL THAT?
AND TARANEE INVITES HER TO STUDY TOGETHER. SHE MEETS WITH HER FRIENDS EVERY DAY AT THE OLD LIBRARY DOWNTOWN.
MORE OR LESS. WHAT IT DOESN'T SAY IS THAT, FOR THE FIRST TIME IN HER LIFE, STUBBORN YOUNG SHEILA...
...IS REALLY STARTING TO FEEL AT HOME!
NOW THAT WE'RE SETTLED, I'D LIKE TO SPEND MORE TIME WITH YOU, HONEY.
ALL THE TIME YOU WANT, DADDY.
MAYBE WE CAN TAKE A NICE TRIP AS SOON AS WE CAN FIT IT IN. WHADDAYA SAY?

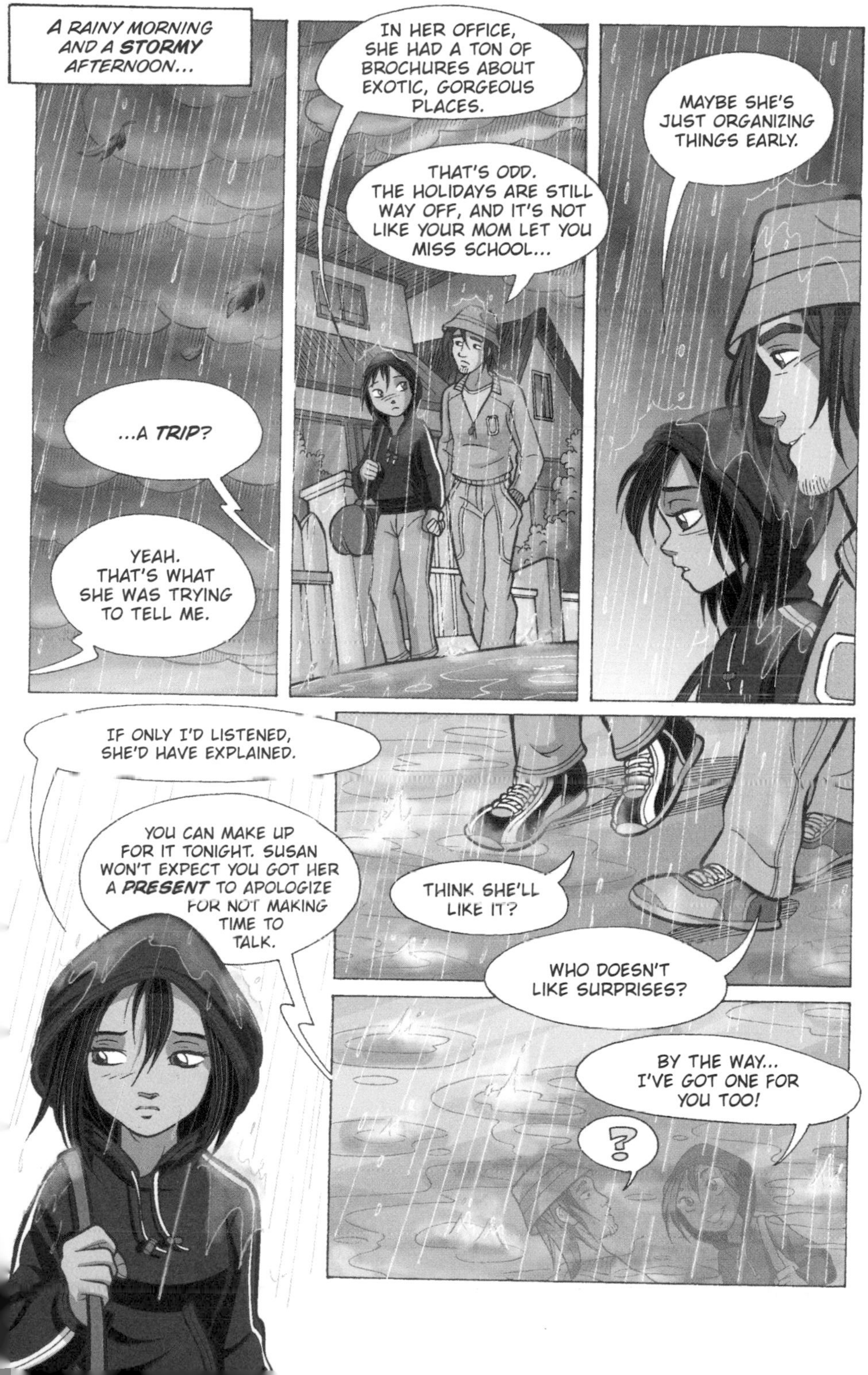
A RAINY MORNING AND A STORMY AFTERNOON...
...A TRIP?
YEAH. THAT'S WHAT SHE WAS TRYING TO TELL ME.
IN HER OFFICE, SHE HAD A TON OF BROCHURES ABOUT EXOTIC, GORGEOUS PLACES.
THAT'S ODD. THE HOLIDAYS ARE STILL WAY OFF, AND IT'S NOT LIKE YOUR MOM LET YOU MISS SCHOOL...
MAYBE SHE'S JUST ORGANIZING THINGS EARLY.
IF ONLY I'D LISTENED, SHE'D HAVE EXPLAINED.
YOU CAN MAKE UP FOR IT TONIGHT. SUSAN WON'T EXPECT YOU GOT HER A PRESENT TO APOLOGIZE FOR NOT MAKING TIME TO TALK.
THINK SHE'LL LIKE IT?
WHO DOESN'T LIKE SURPRISES?
BY THE WAY... I'VE GOT ONE FOR YOU TOO!
?

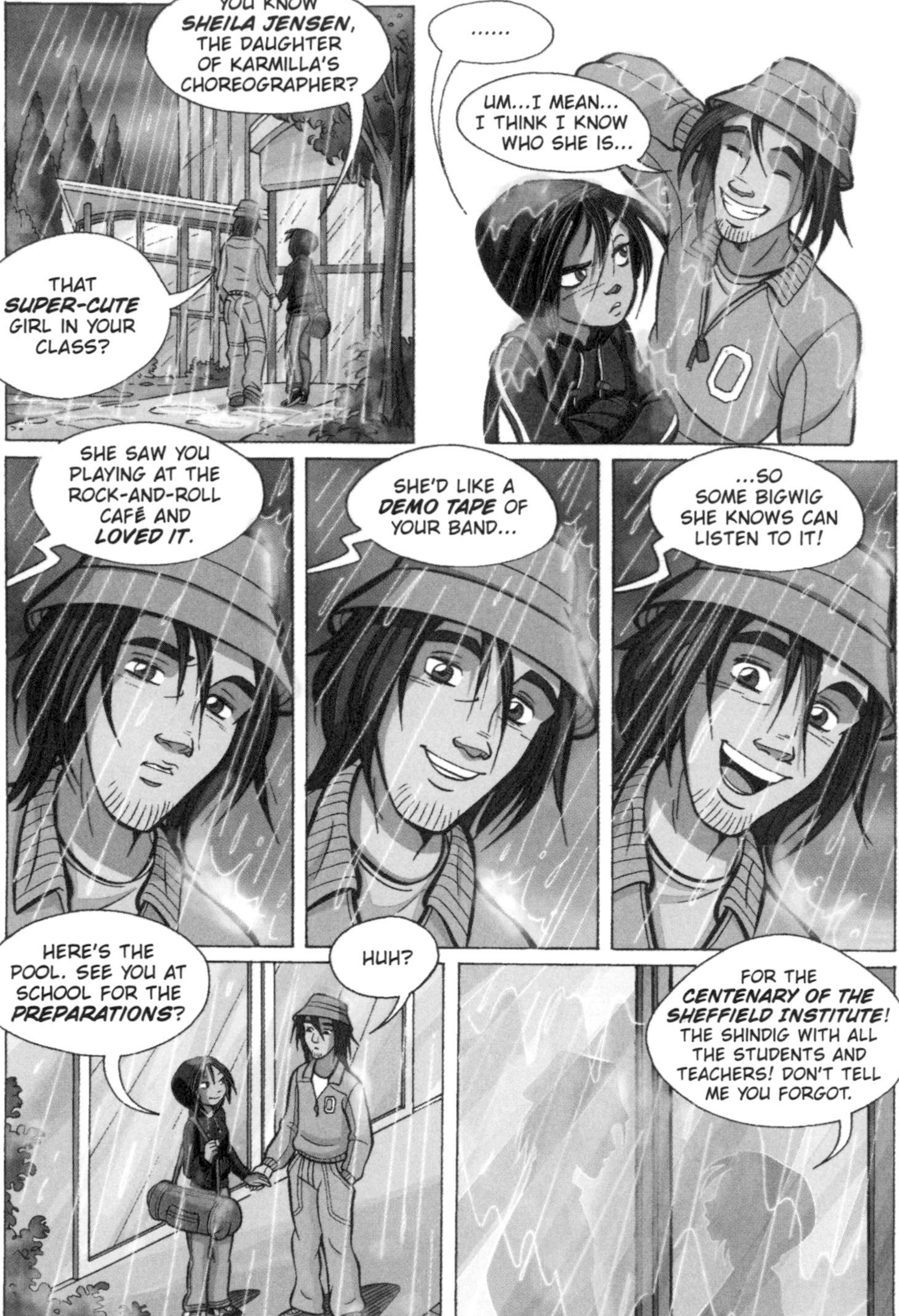
YOU KNOW SHEILA JENSEN, THE DAUGHTER OF KARMILLA'S CHOREOGRAPHER?
THAT SUPER-CUTE GIRL IN YOUR CLASS?
......
UM...I MEAN... I THINK I KNOW WHO SHE IS...
SHE SAW YOU PLAYING AT THE ROCK-AND-ROLL CAFÉ AND LOVED IT.
SHE'D LIKE A DEMO TAPE OF YOUR BAND...
...SO SOME BIGWIG SHE KNOWS CAN LISTEN TO IT!
HERE'S THE POOL. SEE YOU AT SCHOOL FOR THE PREPARATIONS?
HUH?
FOR THE CENTENARY OF THE SHEFFIELD INSTITUTE! THE SHINDIG WITH ALL THE STUDENTS AND TEACHERS! DON'T TELL ME YOU FORGOT.

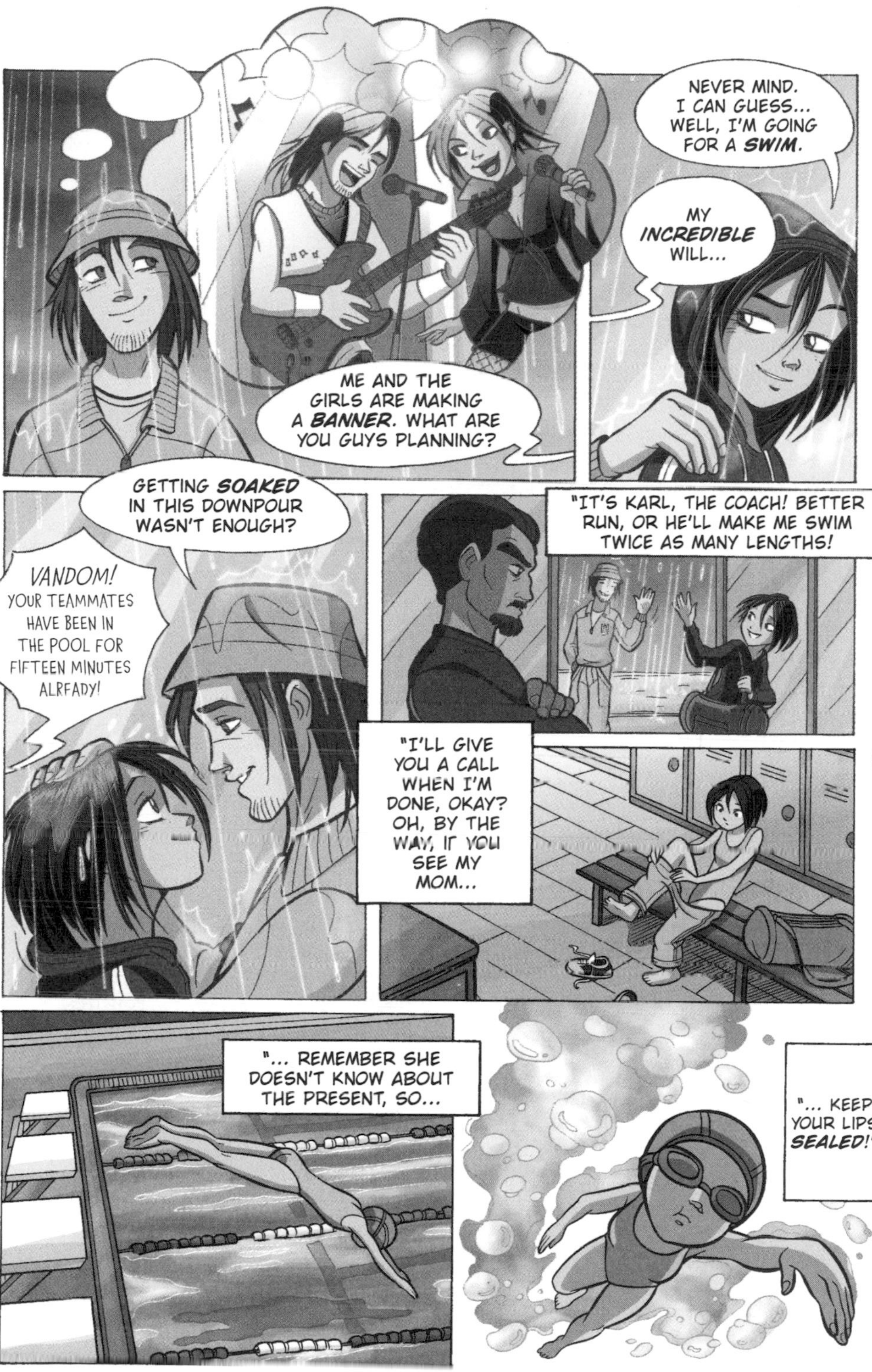
ME AND THE GIRLS ARE MAKING A BANNER. WHAT ARE YOU GUYS PLANNING?
NEVER MIND. I CAN GUESS... WELL, I'M GOING FOR A SWIM.
MY INCREDIBLE WILL...
GETTING SOAKED IN THIS DOWNPOUR WASN'T ENOUGH?
VANDOM! YOUR TEAMMATES HAVE BEEN IN THE POOL FOR FIFTEEN MINUTES ALREADY!
"IT'S KARL, THE COACH! BETTER RUN, OR HE'LL MAKE ME SWIM TWICE AS MANY LENGTHS!
"I'LL GIVE YOU A CALL WHEN I'M DONE, OKAY? OH, BY THE WAY, IF YOU SEE MY MOM...
"... REMEMBER SHE DOESN'T KNOW ABOUT THE PRESENT, SO...
"... KEEP YOUR LIPS SEALED!"

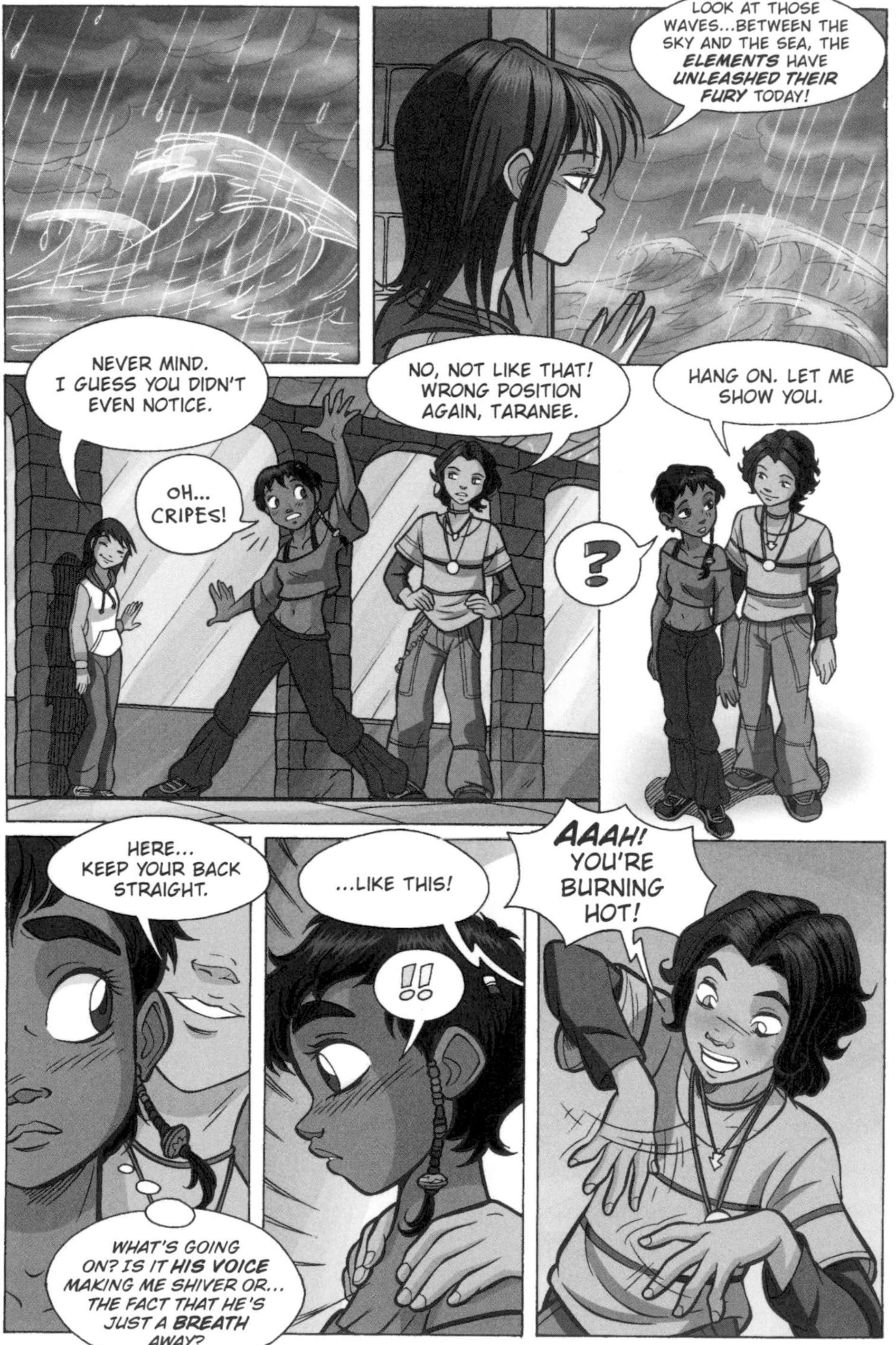
LOOK AT THOSE WAVES...BETWEEN THE SKY AND THE SEA, THE ELEMENTS HAVE UNLEASHED THEIR FURY TODAY!
NEVER MIND. I GUESS YOU DIDN'T EVEN NOTICE.
OH... CRIPES!
NO, NOT LIKE THAT! WRONG POSITION AGAIN, TARANEE.
HANG ON. LET ME SHOW YOU.
?
HERE... KEEP YOUR BACK STRAIGHT.
WHAT'S GOING ON? IS IT HIS VOICE MAKING ME SHIVER OR... THE FACT THAT HE'S JUST A BREATH AWAY?
...LIKE THIS!
!!
AAAH! YOU'RE BURNING HOT!

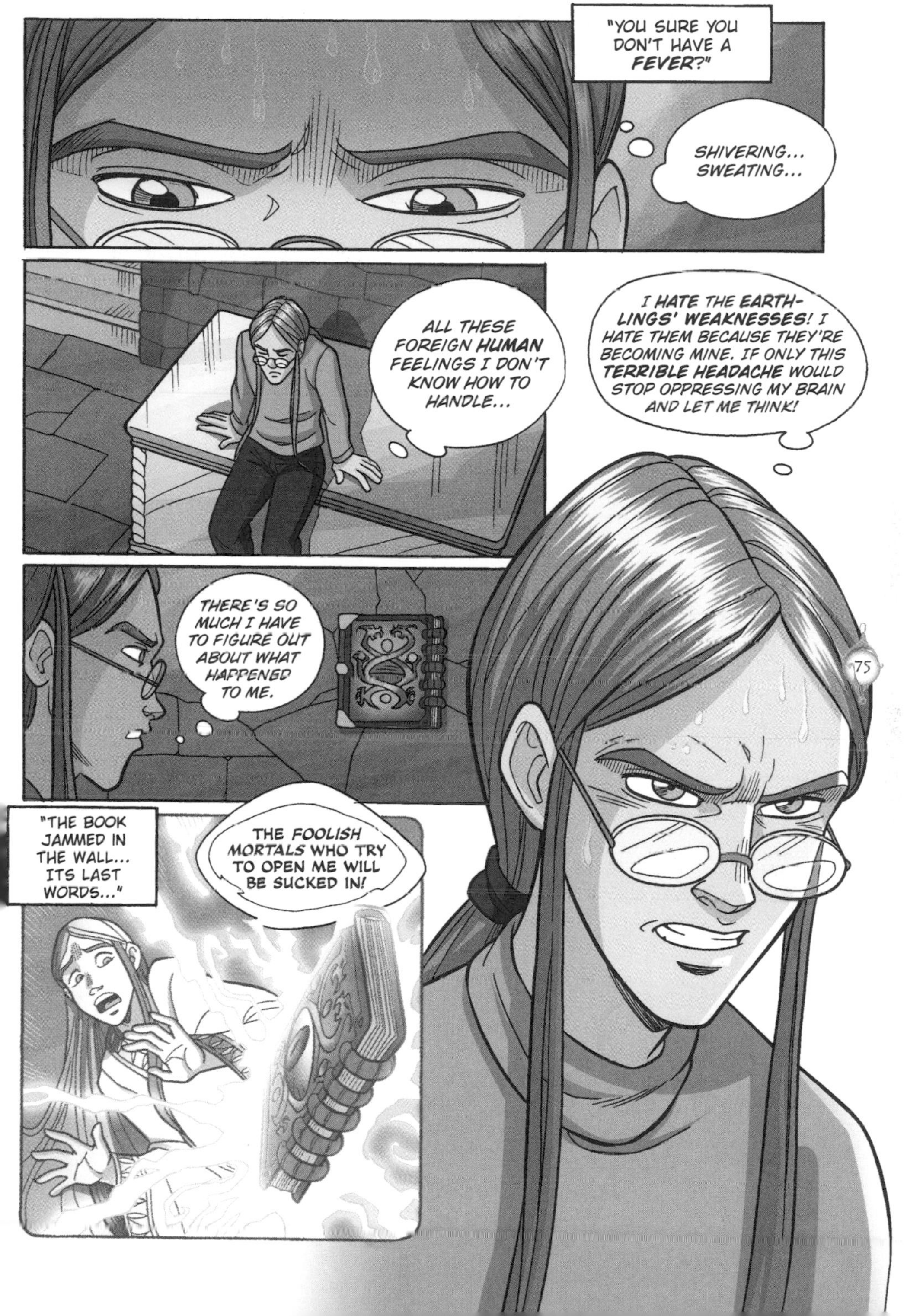
"YOU SURE YOU DON'T HAVE A FEVER?"
SHIVERING... SWEATING...
ALL THESE FOREIGN HUMAN FEELINGS I DON'T KNOW HOW TO HANDLE...
I HATE THE EARTHLINGS' WEAKNESSES! I HATE THEM BECAUSE THEY'RE BECOMING MINE. IF ONLY THIS TERRIBLE HEADACHE WOULD STOP OPPRESSING MY BRAIN AND LET ME THINK!
THERE'S SO MUCH I HAVE TO FIGURE OUT ABOUT WHAT HAPPENED TO ME.
"THE BOOK JAMMED IN THE WALL... ITS LAST WORDS..."
THE FOOLISH MORTALS WHO TRY TO OPEN ME WILL BE SUCKED IN!

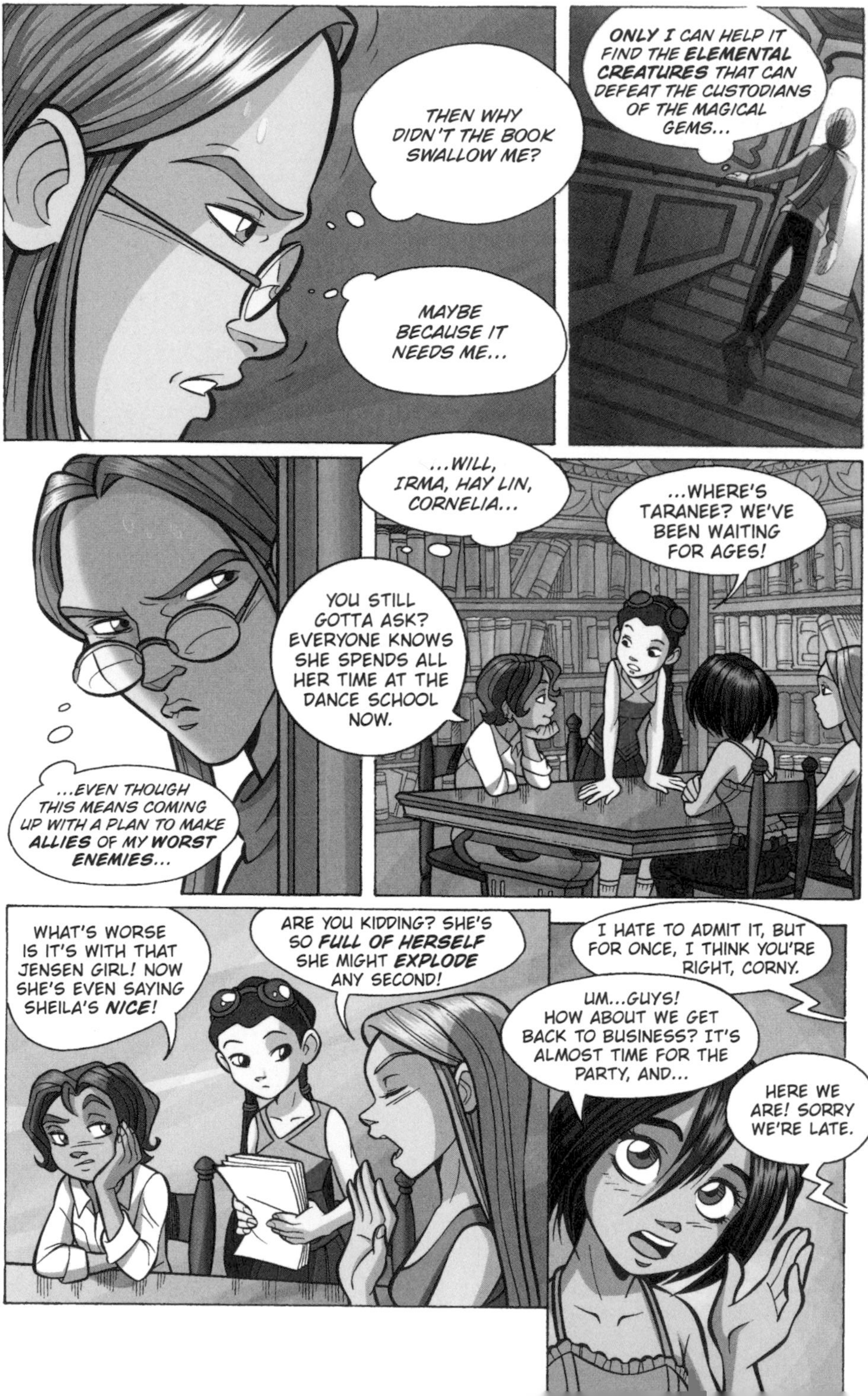
THEN WHY DIDN'T THE BOOK SWALLOW ME?
MAYBE BECAUSE IT NEEDS ME...
ONLY I CAN HELP IT FIND THE ELEMENTAL CREATURES THAT CAN DEFEAT THE CUSTODIANS OF THE MAGICAL GEMS...
...EVEN THOUGH THIS MEANS COMING UP WITH A PLAN TO MAKE ALLIES OF MY WORST ENEMIES...
...WILL, IRMA, HAY LIN, CORNELIA...
...WHERE'S TARANEE? WE'VE BEEN WAITING FOR AGES!
YOU STILL GOTTA ASK? EVERYONE KNOWS SHE SPENDS ALL HER TIME AT THE DANCE SCHOOL NOW.
WHAT'S WORSE IS IT'S WITH THAT JENSEN GIRL! NOW SHE'S EVEN SAYING SHEILA'S NICE!
ARE YOU KIDDING? SHE'S SO FULL OF HERSELF SHE MIGHT EXPLODE ANY SECOND!
I HATE TO ADMIT IT, BUT FOR ONCE, I THINK YOU'RE RIGHT, CORNY.
UM...GUYS! HOW ABOUT WE GET BACK TO BUSINESS? IT'S ALMOST TIME FOR THE PARTY, AND...
HERE WE ARE! SORRY WE'RE LATE.

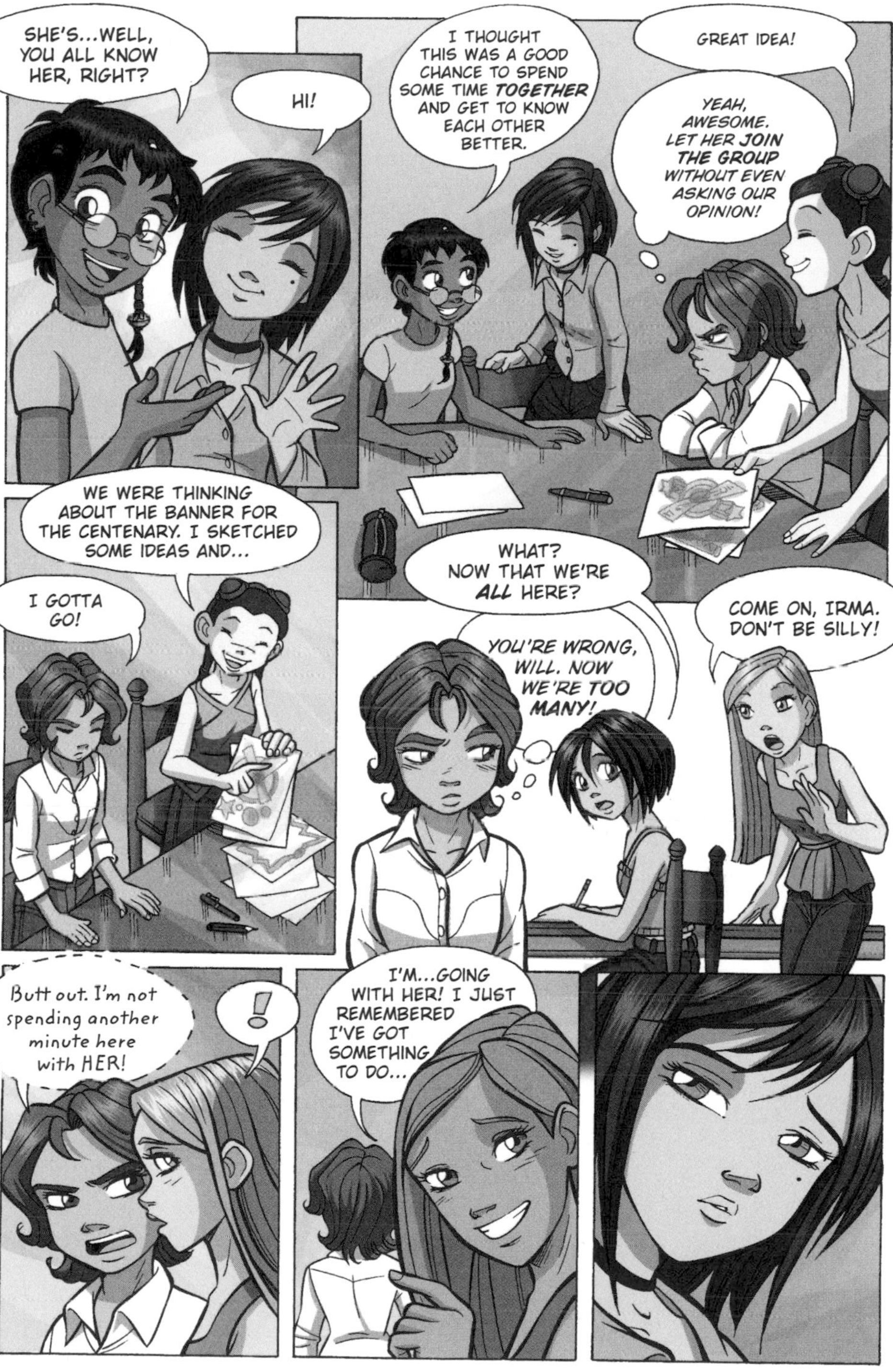

SHE'S...WELL, YOU ALL KNOW HER, RIGHT?
HI!
I THOUGHT THIS WAS A GOOD CHANCE TO SPEND SOME TIME TOGETHER AND GET TO KNOW EACH OTHER BETTER.
GREAT IDEA!
YEAH, AWESOME. LET HER JOIN THE GROUP WITHOUT EVEN ASKING OUR OPINION!
WE WERE THINKING ABOUT THE BANNER FOR THE CENTENARY. I SKETCHED SOME IDEAS AND...
I GOTTA GO!
WHAT? NOW THAT WE'RE ALL HERE?
YOU'RE WRONG, WILL. NOW WE'RE TOO MANY!
COME ON, IRMA. DON'T BE SILLY!
Butt out. I'm not spending another minute here with HER!
!
I'M...GOING WITH HER! I JUST REMEMBERED I'VE GOT SOMETHING TO DO...

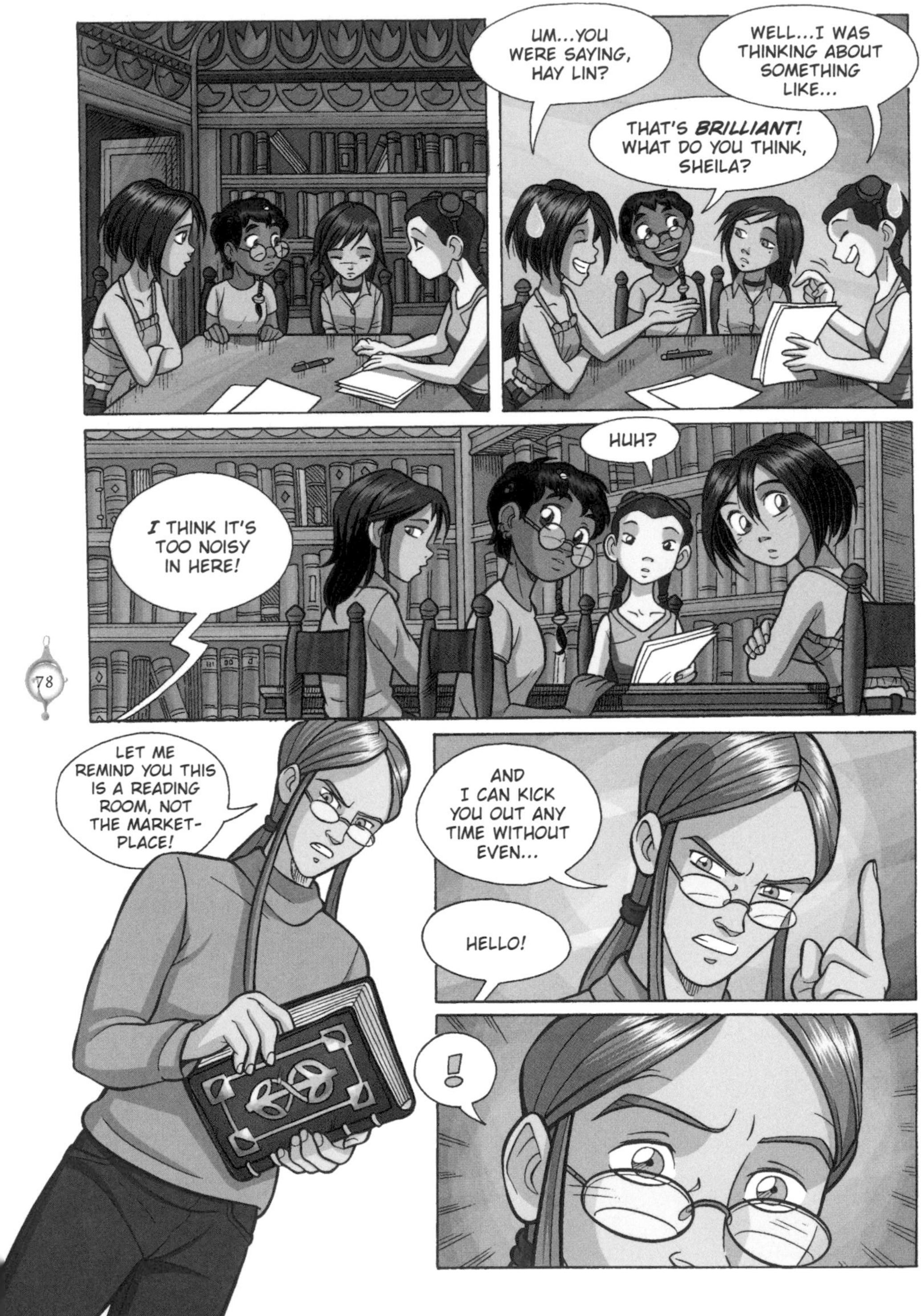
UM...YOU WERE SAYING, HAY LIN?
WELL...I WAS THINKING ABOUT SOMETHING LIKE...
THAT'S BRILLIANT! WHAT DO YOU THINK, SHEILA?
I THINK IT'S TOO NOISY IN HERE!
HUH?
LET ME REMIND YOU THIS IS A READING ROOM, NOT THE MARKET-PLACE!
AND I CAN KICK YOU OUT ANY TIME WITHOUT EVEN...
HELLO!
!

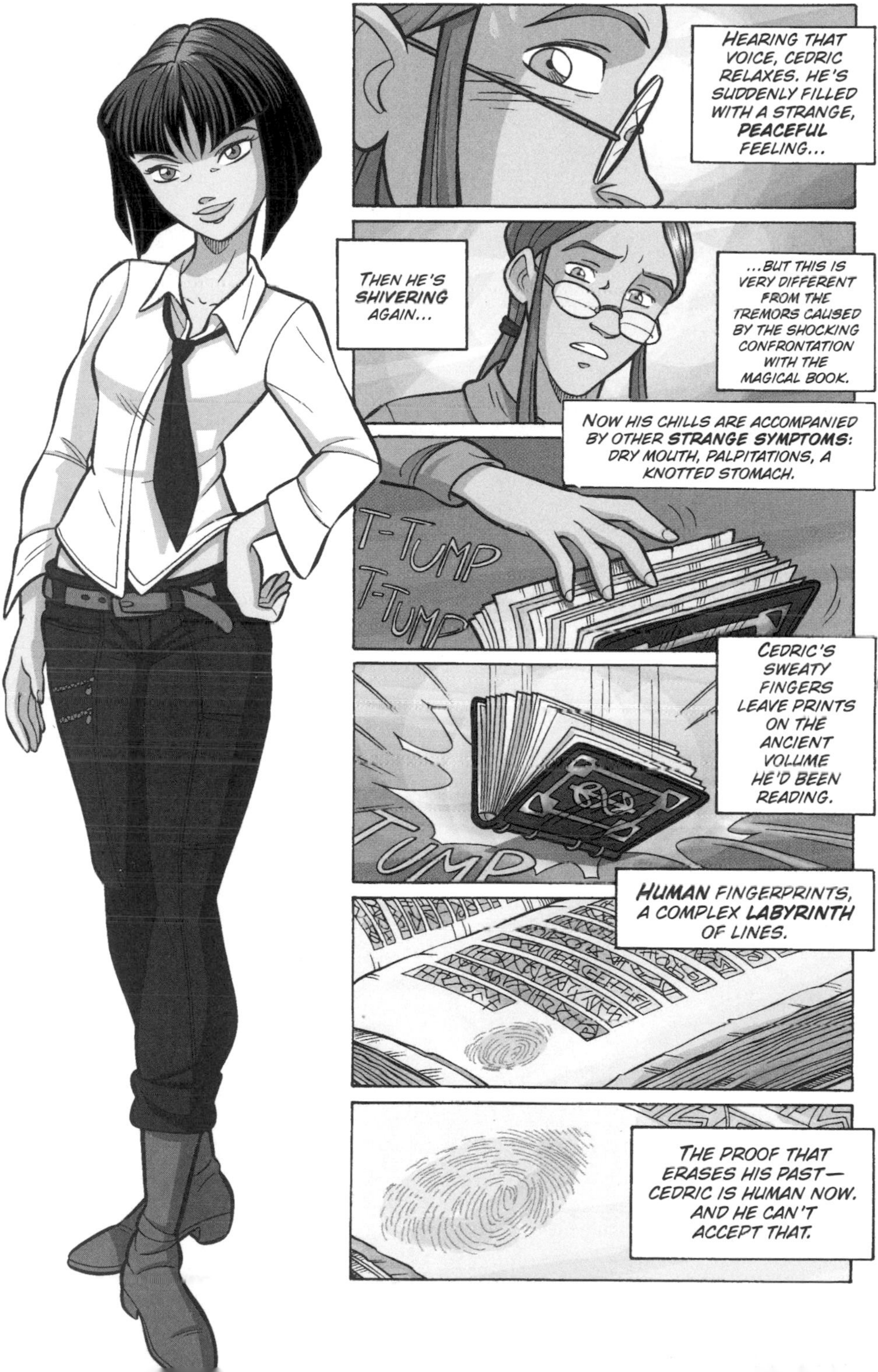
HEARING THAT VOICE, CEDRIC RELAXES. HE'S SUDDENLY FILLED WITH A STRANGE, PEACEFUL FEELING...
THEN HE'S SHIVERING AGAIN...
...BUT THIS IS VERY DIFFERENT FROM THE TREMORS CAUSED BY THE SHOCKING CONFRONTATION WITH THE MAGICAL BOOK.
NOW HIS CHILLS ARE ACCOMPANIED BY OTHER STRANGE SYMPTOMS: DRY MOUTH, PALPITATIONS, A KNOTTED STOMACH.
T-TUMP
T-TUMP
CEDRIC'S SWEATY FINGERS LEAVE PRINTS ON THE ANCIENT VOLUME HE'D BEEN READING.
TUMP
HUMAN FINGERPRINTS, A COMPLEX LABYRINTH OF LINES.
THE PROOF THAT ERASES HIS PAST—CEDRIC IS HUMAN NOW. AND HE CAN'T ACCEPT THAT.

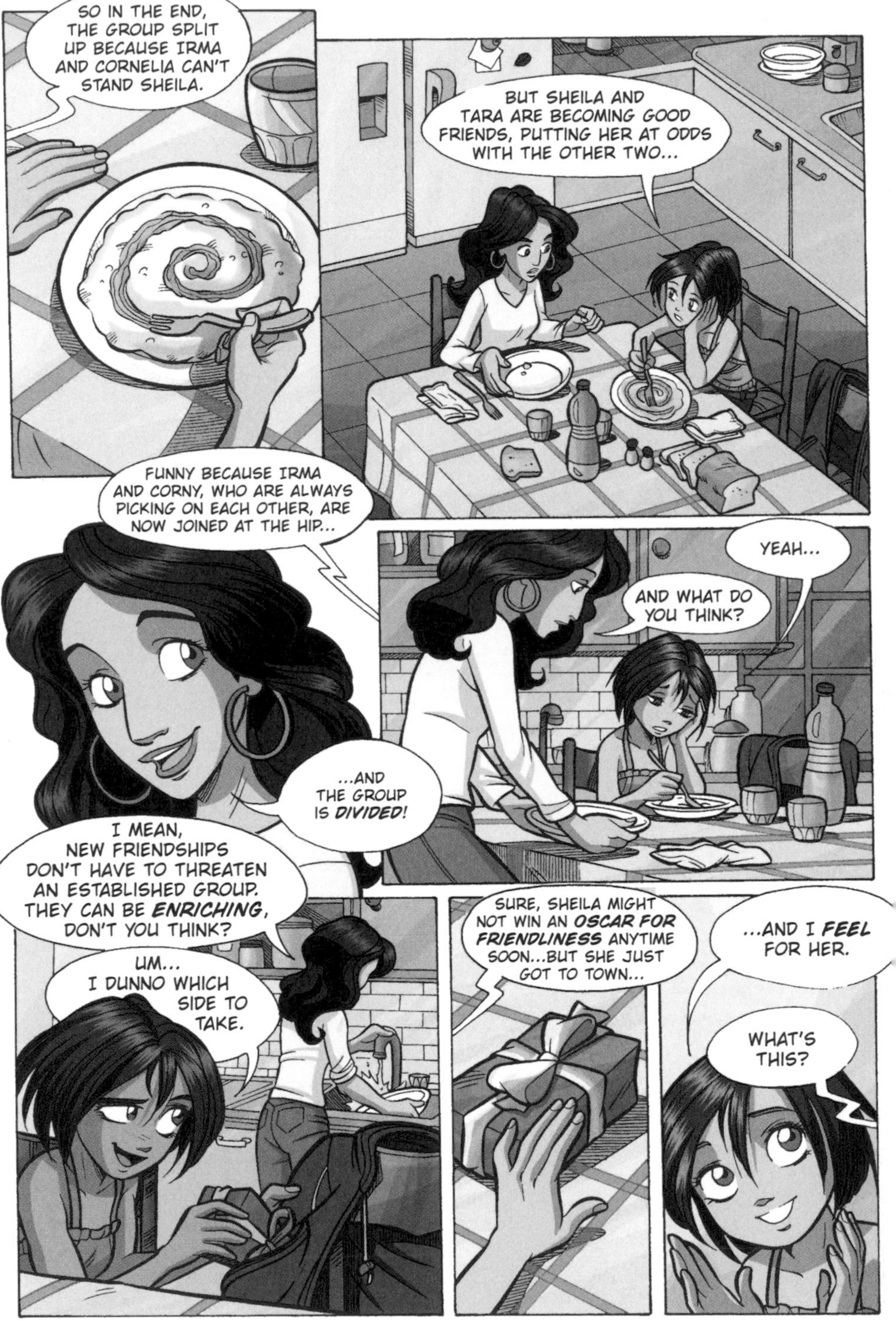
SO IN THE END, THE GROUP SPLIT UP BECAUSE IRMA AND CORNELIA CAN'T STAND SHEILA.
BUT SHEILA AND TARA ARE BECOMING GOOD FRIENDS, PUTTING HER AT ODDS WITH THE OTHER TWO...
FUNNY BECAUSE IRMA AND CORNY, WHO ARE ALWAYS PICKING ON EACH OTHER, ARE NOW JOINED AT THE HIP...
...AND THE GROUP IS *DIVIDED*!
YEAH...
AND WHAT DO YOU THINK?
I MEAN, NEW FRIENDSHIPS DON'T HAVE TO THREATEN AN ESTABLISHED GROUP. THEY CAN BE ***ENRICHING***, DON'T YOU THINK?
UM... I DUNNO WHICH SIDE TO TAKE.
SURE, SHEILA MIGHT NOT WIN AN ***OSCAR FOR FRIENDLINESS*** ANYTIME SOON...BUT SHE JUST GOT TO TOWN...
...AND I ***FEEL*** FOR HER.
WHAT'S THIS?

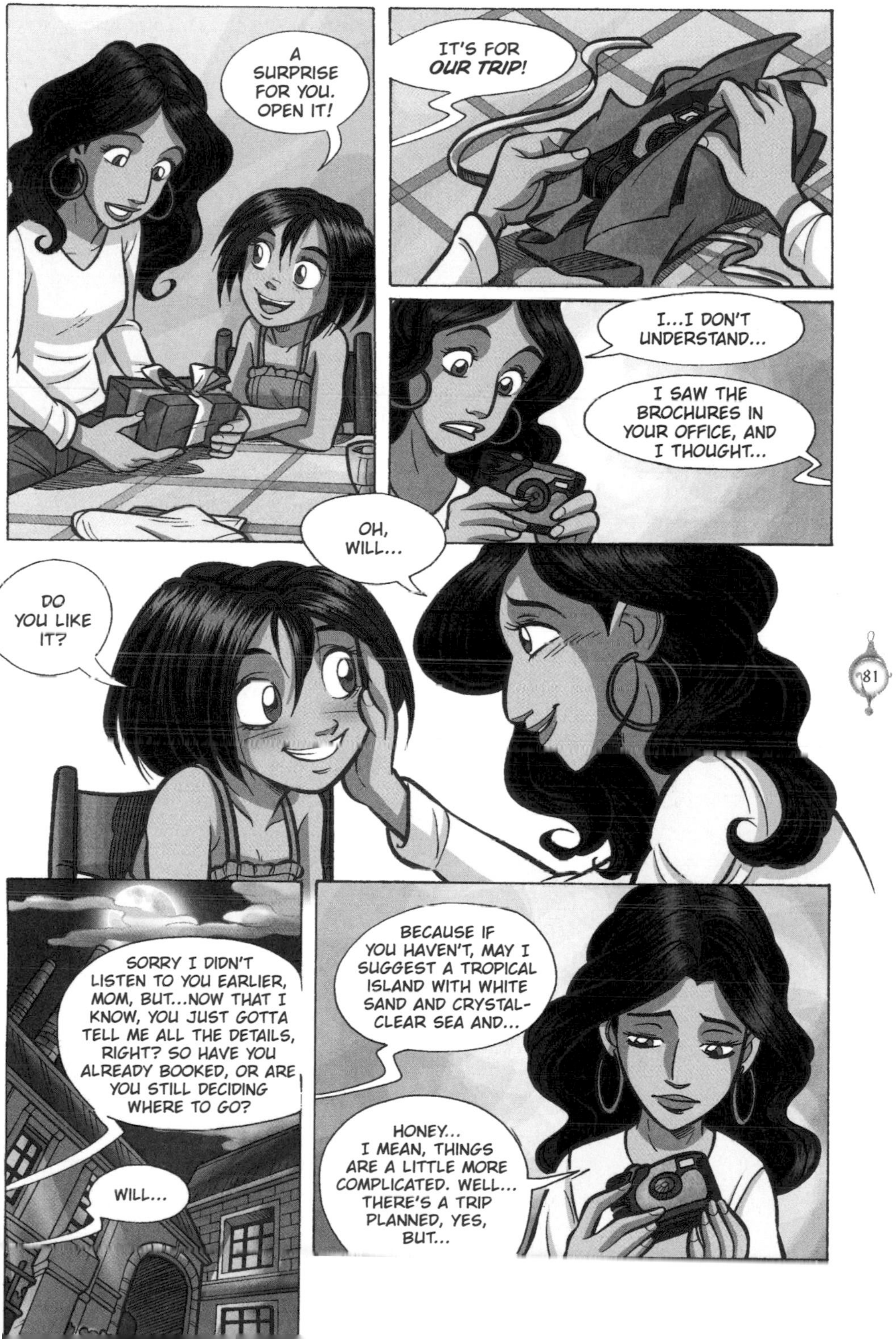
A SURPRISE FOR YOU. OPEN IT!
IT'S FOR *OUR TRIP!*
I...I DON'T UNDERSTAND...
I SAW THE BROCHURES IN YOUR OFFICE, AND I THOUGHT...
OH, WILL...
DO YOU LIKE IT?
SORRY I DIDN'T LISTEN TO YOU EARLIER, MOM, BUT...NOW THAT I KNOW, YOU JUST GOTTA TELL ME ALL THE DETAILS, RIGHT? SO HAVE YOU ALREADY BOOKED, OR ARE YOU STILL DECIDING WHERE TO GO?
WILL...
BECAUSE IF YOU HAVEN'T, MAY I SUGGEST A TROPICAL ISLAND WITH WHITE SAND AND CRYSTAL-CLEAR SEA AND...
HONEY... I MEAN, THINGS ARE A LITTLE MORE COMPLICATED. WELL... THERE'S A TRIP PLANNED, YES, BUT...

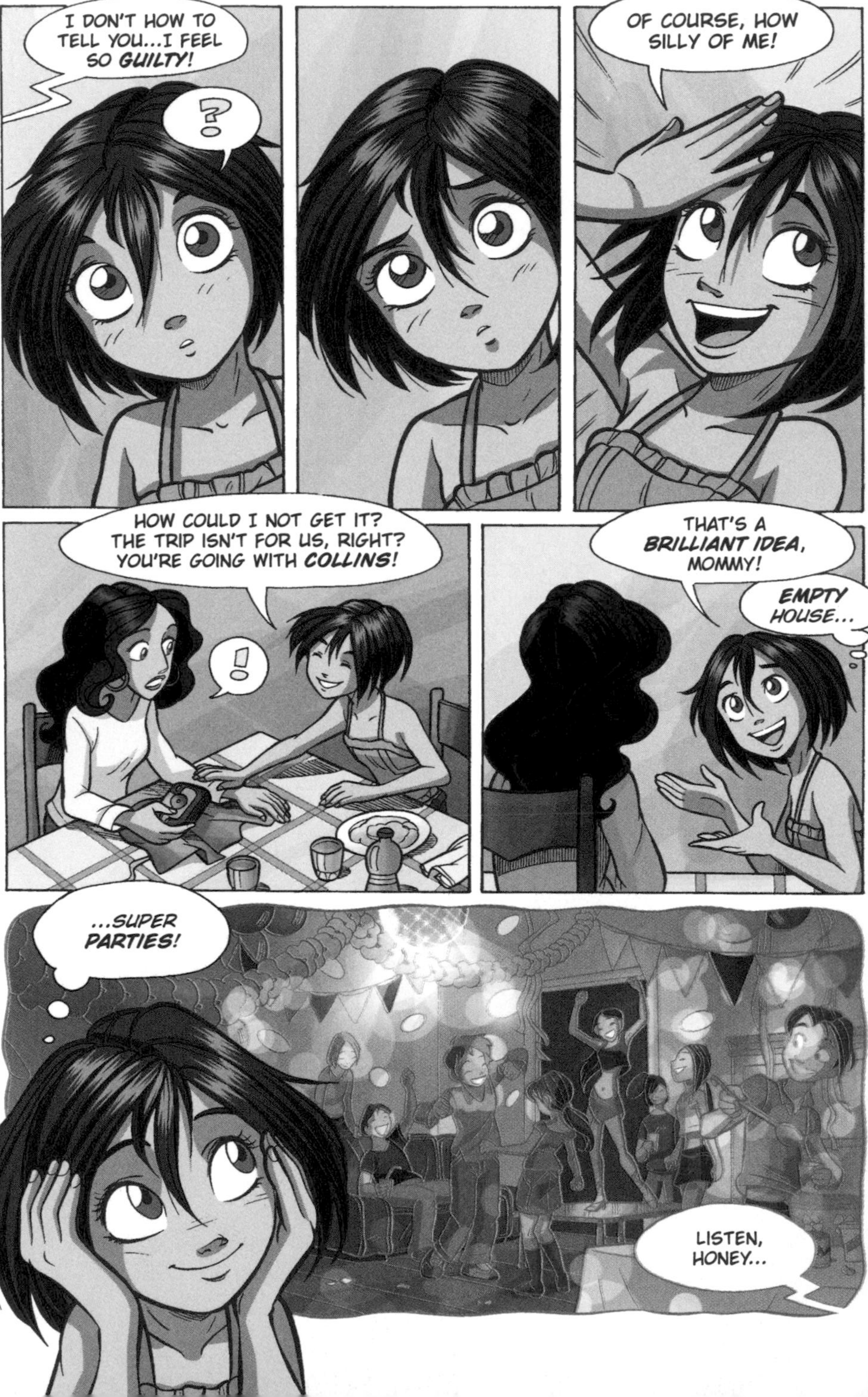
I DON'T HOW TO TELL YOU...I FEEL SO GUILTY!
?
OF COURSE, HOW SILLY OF ME!
HOW COULD I NOT GET IT? THE TRIP ISN'T FOR US, RIGHT? YOU'RE GOING WITH COLLINS!
!
THAT'S A BRILLIANT IDEA, MOMMY!
EMPTY HOUSE...
...SUPER PARTIES!
LISTEN, HONEY...

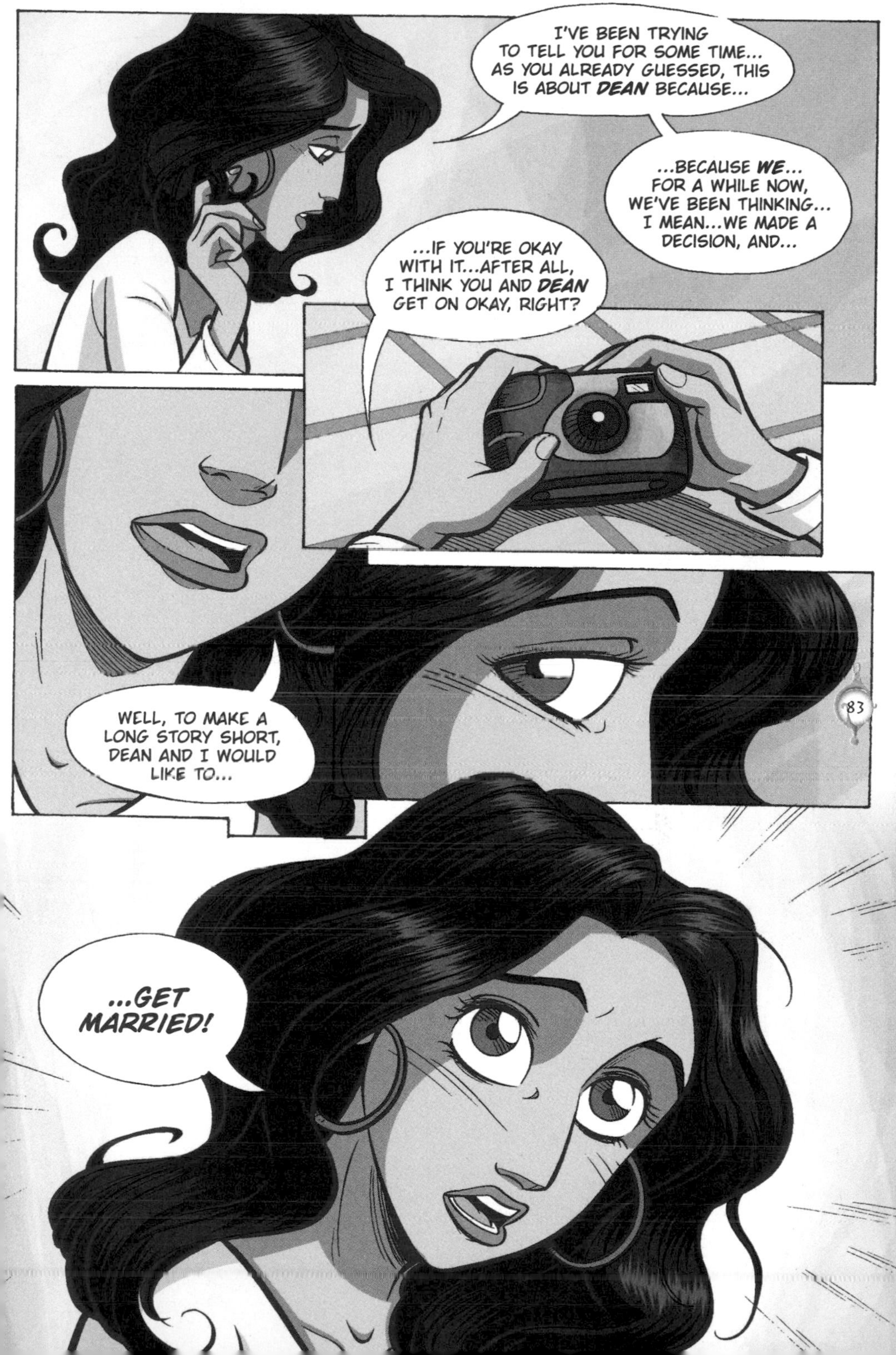
I'VE BEEN TRYING TO TELL YOU FOR SOME TIME... AS YOU ALREADY GUESSED, THIS IS ABOUT ***DEAN*** BECAUSE...
...BECAUSE ***WE***... FOR A WHILE NOW, WE'VE BEEN THINKING... I MEAN...WE MADE A DECISION, AND...
...IF YOU'RE OKAY WITH IT...AFTER ALL, I THINK YOU AND ***DEAN*** GET ON OKAY, RIGHT?
WELL, TO MAKE A LONG STORY SHORT, DEAN AND I WOULD LIKE TO...
...GET MARRIED!

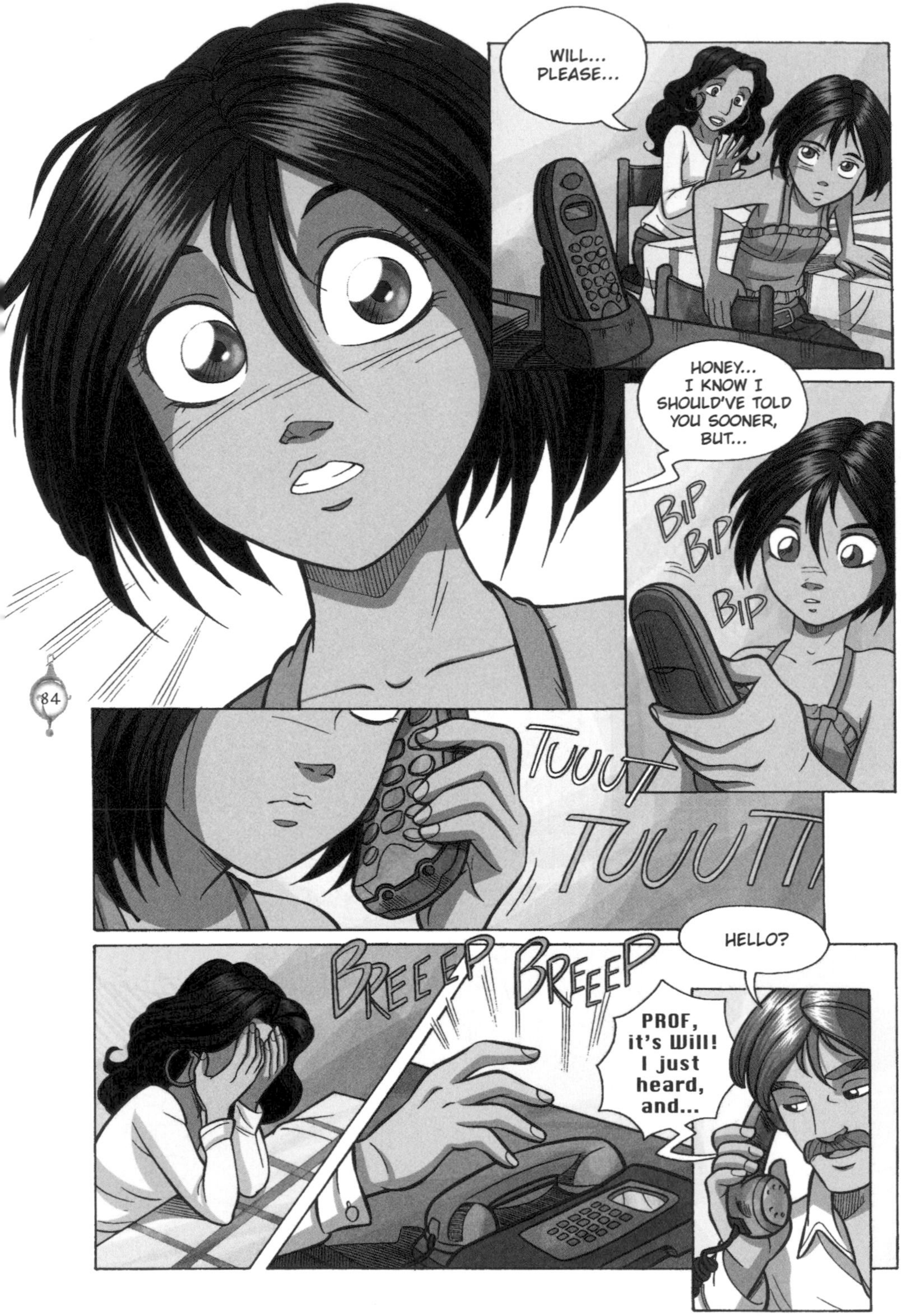
WILL... PLEASE...
HONEY... I KNOW I SHOULD'VE TOLD YOU SOONER, BUT...
BIP
BIP
BIP
TUUUT
TUUUTT
BREEEP
BREEEP
HELLO?
PROF, it's Will! I just heard, and...

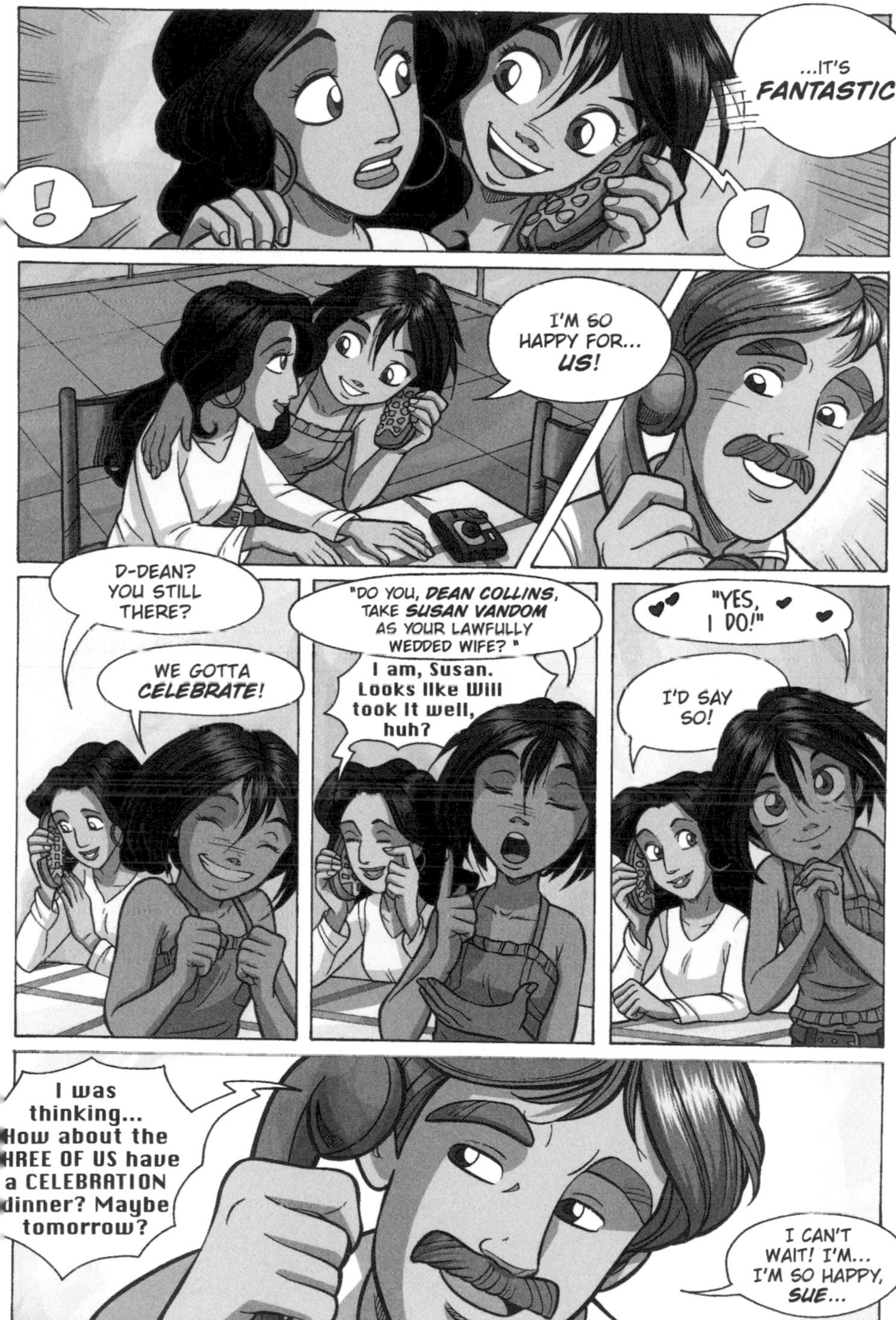
!
...IT'S FANTASTIC!
!
I'M SO HAPPY FOR... US!
D-DEAN? YOU STILL THERE?
WE GOTTA CELEBRATE!
"DO YOU, DEAN COLLINS, TAKE SUSAN VANDOM AS YOUR LAWFULLY WEDDED WIFE?"
I am, Susan. Looks like Will took it well, huh?
"YES, I DO!"
I'D SAY SO!
I was thinking... How about the HREE OF US have a CELEBRATION dinner? Maybe tomorrow?
I CAN'T WAIT! I'M... I'M SO HAPPY, SUE...

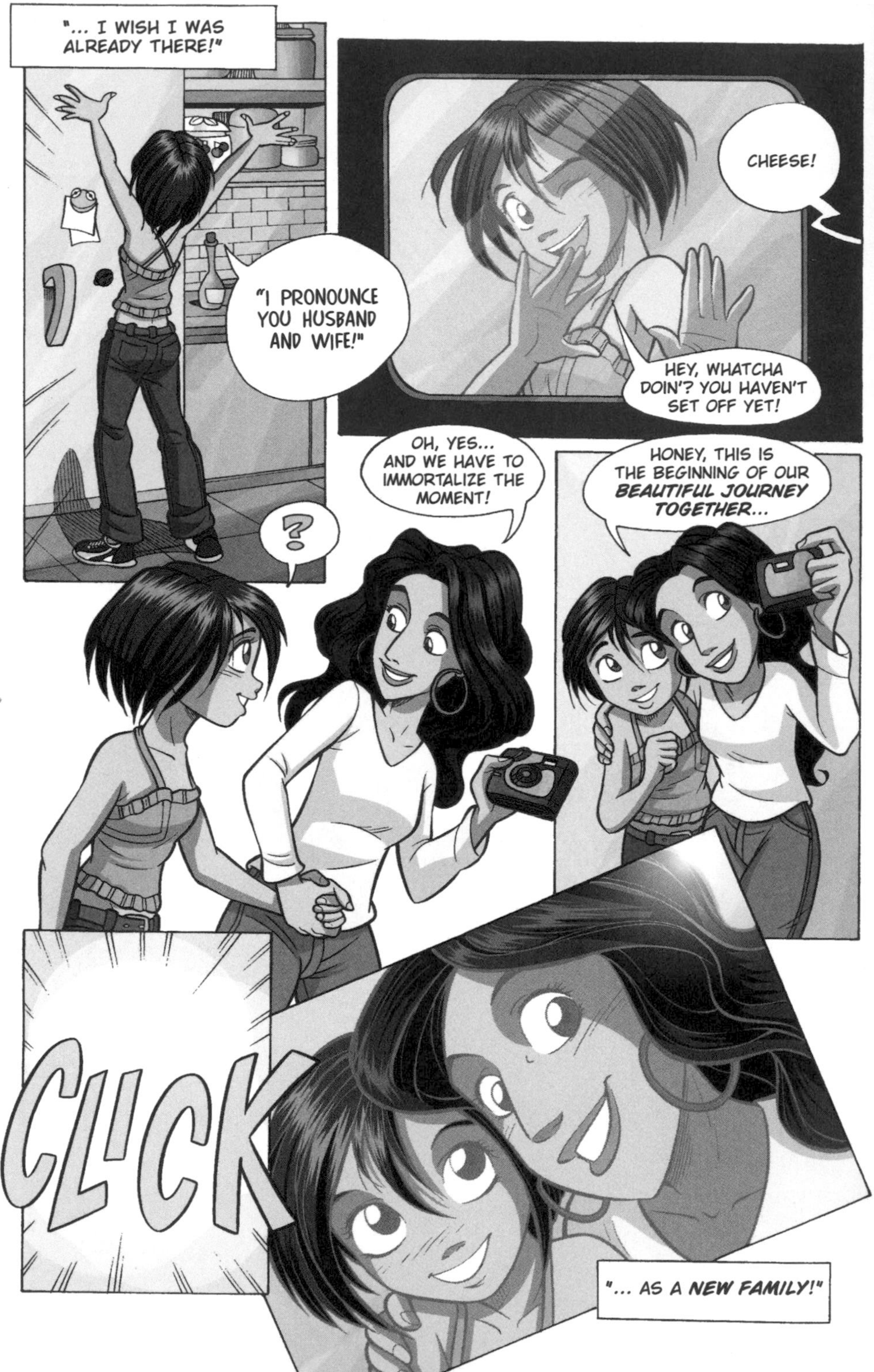

"... I WISH I WAS ALREADY THERE!"
"I PRONOUNCE YOU HUSBAND AND WIFE!"
CHEESE!
HEY, WHATCHA DOIN'? YOU HAVEN'T SET OFF YET!
?
OH, YES... AND WE HAVE TO IMMORTALIZE THE MOMENT!
HONEY, THIS IS THE BEGINNING OF OUR BEAUTIFUL JOURNEY TOGETHER...
CLICK
"... AS A NEW FAMILY!"

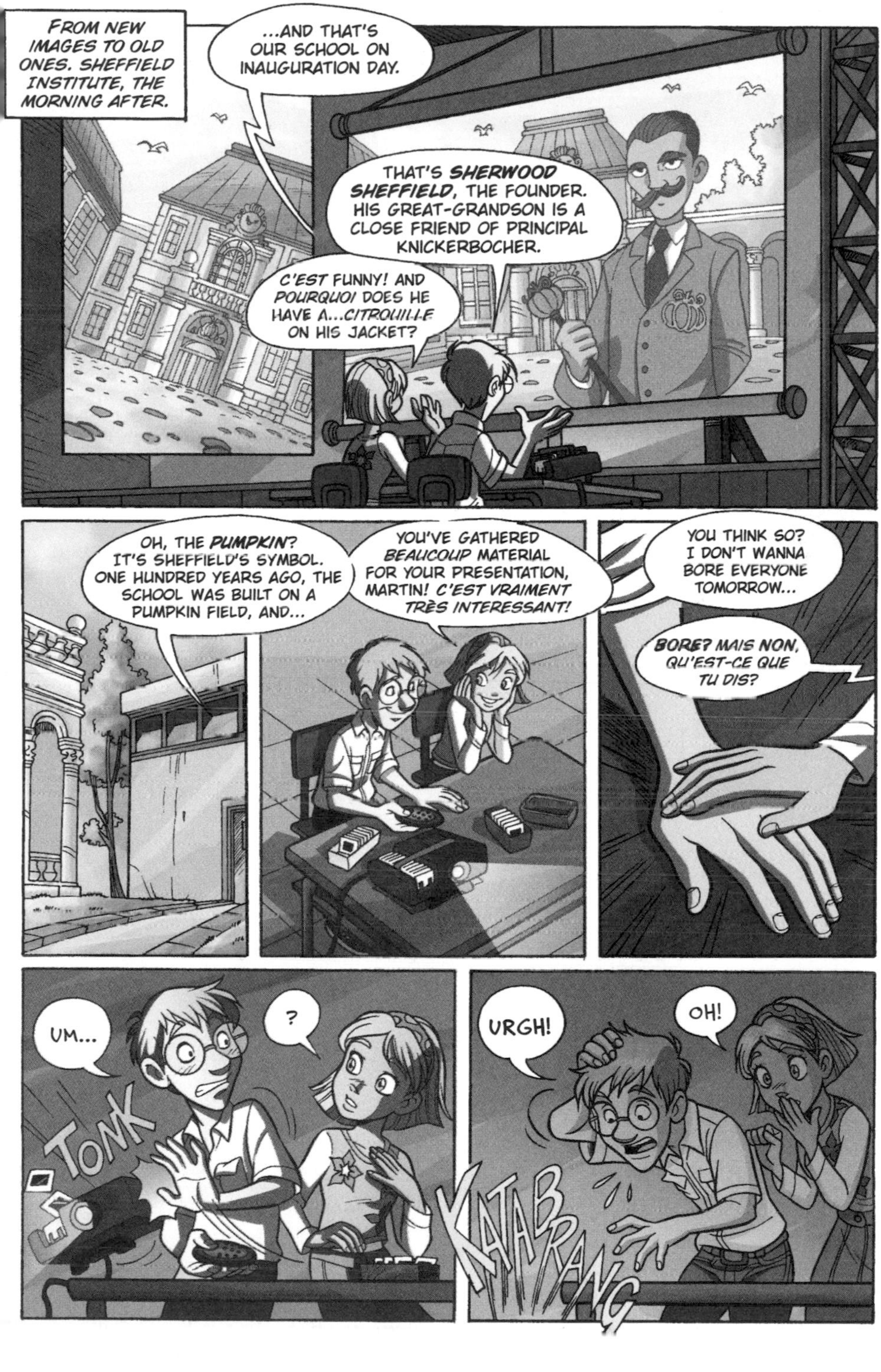
FROM NEW IMAGES TO OLD ONES. SHEFFIELD INSTITUTE, THE MORNING AFTER.
...AND THAT'S OUR SCHOOL ON INAUGURATION DAY.
THAT'S SHERWOOD SHEFFIELD, THE FOUNDER. HIS GREAT-GRANDSON IS A CLOSE FRIEND OF PRINCIPAL KNICKERBOCHER.
C'EST FUNNY! AND POURQUOI DOES HE HAVE A...CITROUILLE ON HIS JACKET?
OH, THE PUMPKIN? IT'S SHEFFIELD'S SYMBOL. ONE HUNDRED YEARS AGO, THE SCHOOL WAS BUILT ON A PUMPKIN FIELD, AND...
YOU'VE GATHERED BEAUCOUP MATERIAL FOR YOUR PRESENTATION, MARTIN! C'EST VRAIMENT TRÈS INTERESSANT!
YOU THINK SO? I DON'T WANNA BORE EVERYONE TOMORROW...
BORE? MAIS NON, QU'EST-CE QUE TU DIS?
UM...
?
TONK
URGH!
OH!
KATABRANG

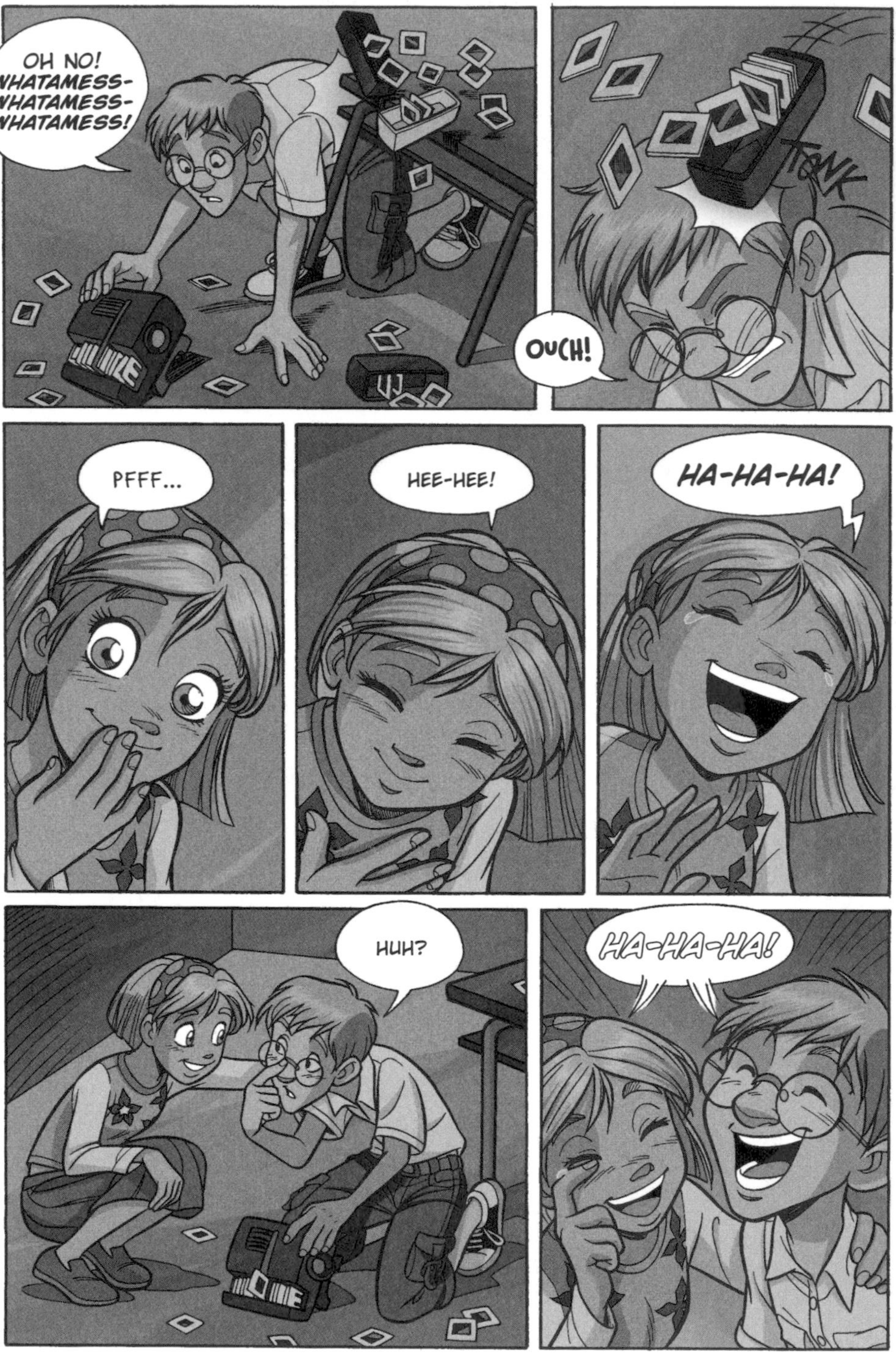
OH NO! WHATAMESS-WHATAMESS-WHATAMESS!
TONK
OUCH!
PFFF...
HEE-HEE!
HA-HA-HA!
HUH?
HA-HA-HA!

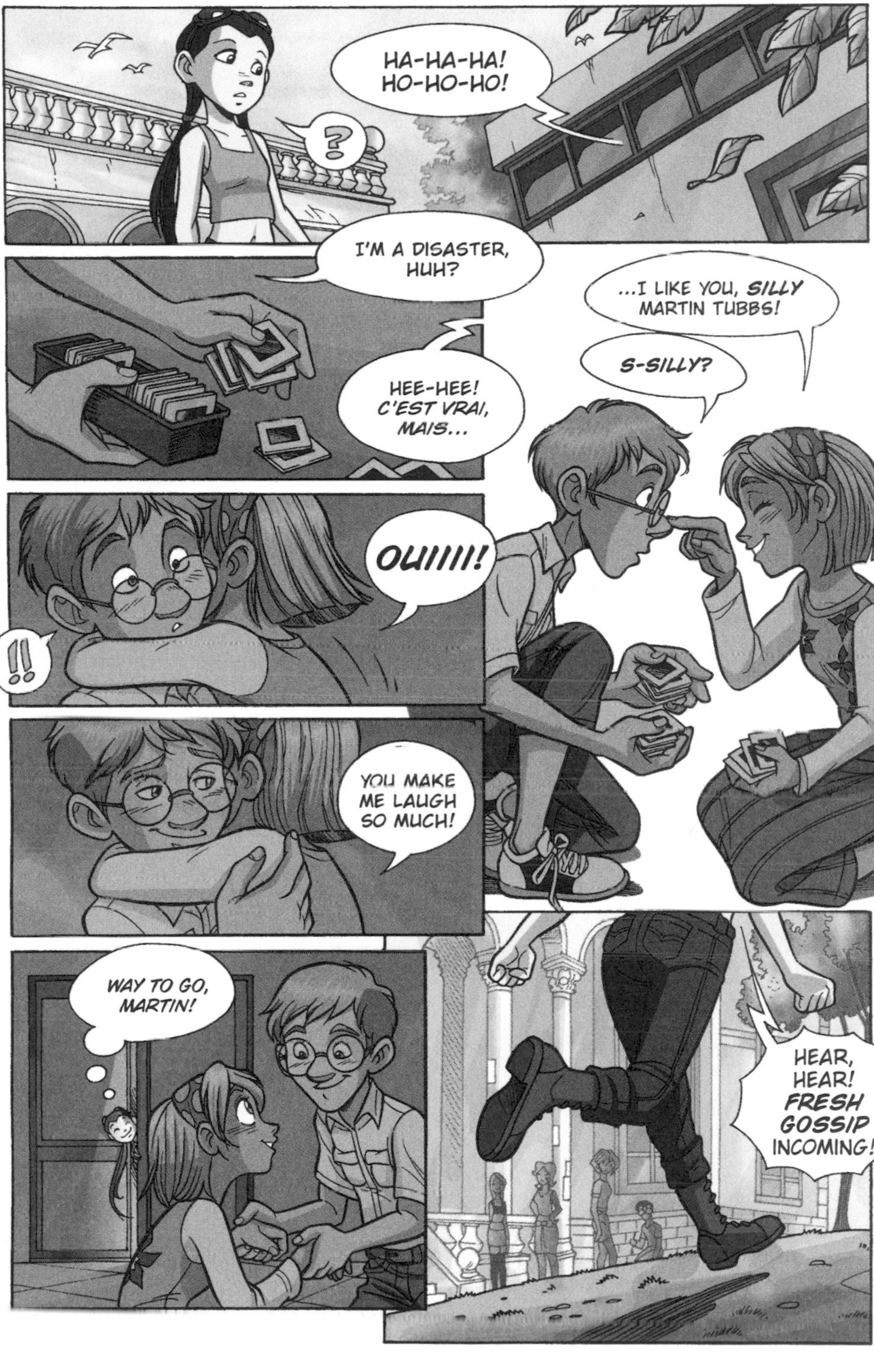
HA-HA-HA!
HO-HO-HO!
?
I'M A DISASTER, HUH?
HEE-HEE! C'EST VRAI, MAIS...
OUIIIII!
!!
YOU MAKE ME LAUGH SO MUCH!
...I LIKE YOU, SILLY MARTIN TUBBS!
S-SILLY?
WAY TO GO, MARTIN!
HEAR, HEAR! FRESH GOSSIP INCOMING!

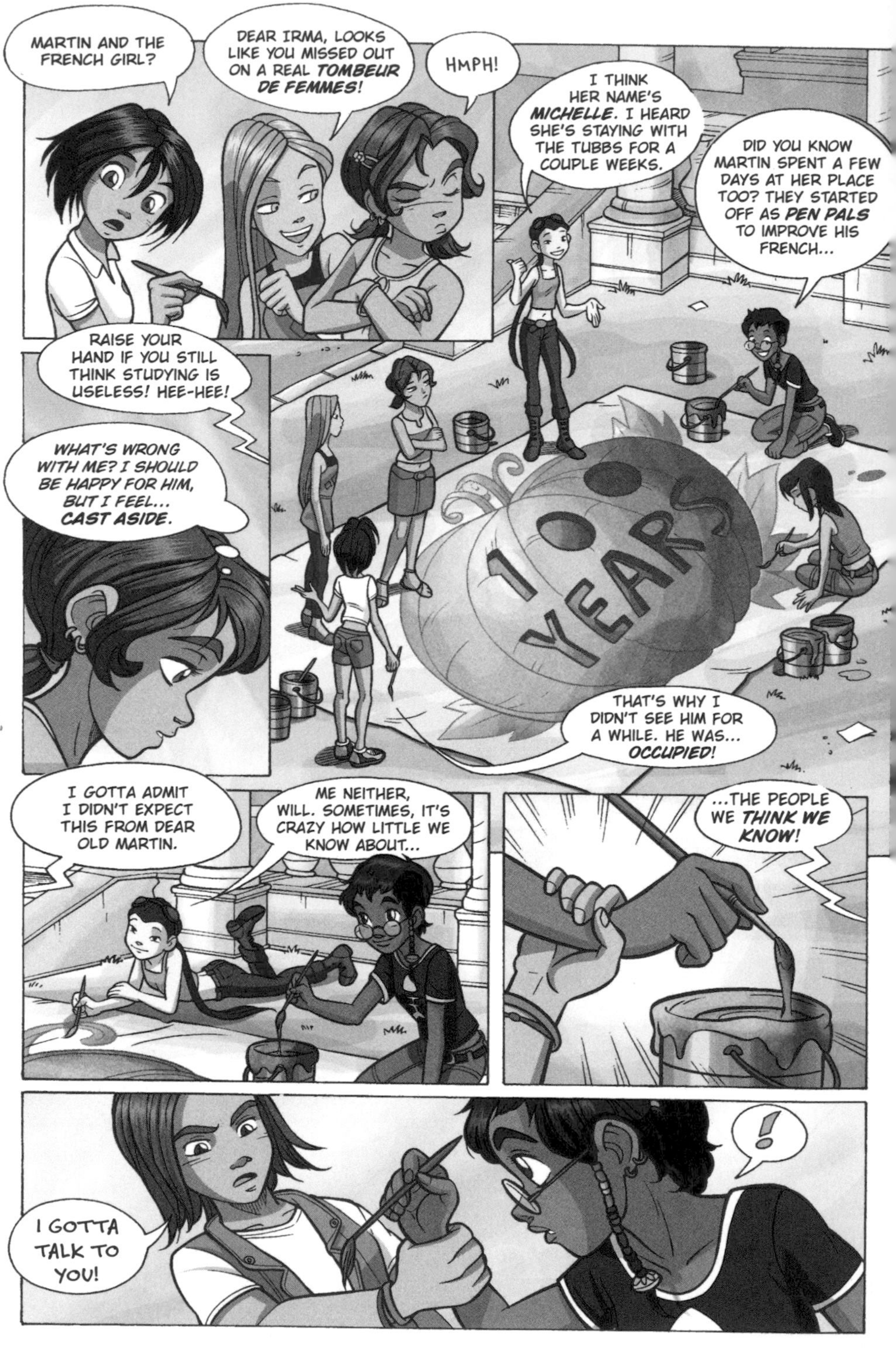
MARTIN AND THE FRENCH GIRL?
DEAR IRMA, LOOKS LIKE YOU MISSED OUT ON A REAL TOMBEUR DE FEMMES!
HMPH!
I THINK HER NAME'S MICHELLE. I HEARD SHE'S STAYING WITH THE TUBBS FOR A COUPLE WEEKS.
DID YOU KNOW MARTIN SPENT A FEW DAYS AT HER PLACE TOO? THEY STARTED OFF AS PEN PALS TO IMPROVE HIS FRENCH...
RAISE YOUR HAND IF YOU STILL THINK STUDYING IS USELESS! HEE-HEE!
WHAT'S WRONG WITH ME? I SHOULD BE HAPPY FOR HIM, BUT I FEEL... CAST ASIDE.
10 YEARS
THAT'S WHY I DIDN'T SEE HIM FOR A WHILE. HE WAS... OCCUPIED!
I GOTTA ADMIT I DIDN'T EXPECT THIS FROM DEAR OLD MARTIN.
ME NEITHER, WILL. SOMETIMES, IT'S CRAZY HOW LITTLE WE KNOW ABOUT...
...THE PEOPLE WE THINK WE KNOW!
I GOTTA TALK TO YOU!
!

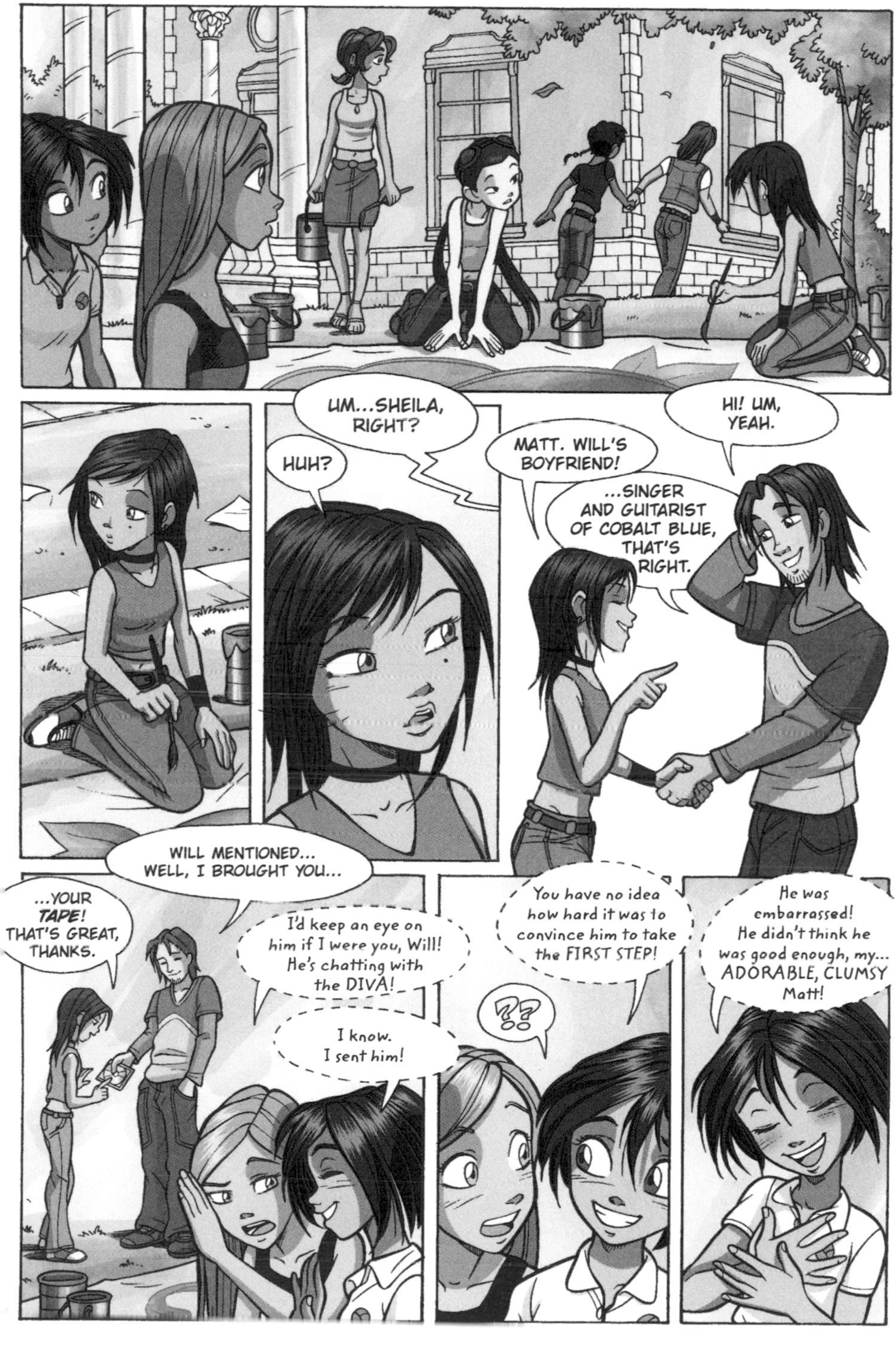
UM...SHEILA, RIGHT?
HUH?
HI! UM, YEAH.
MATT. WILL'S BOYFRIEND!
...SINGER AND GUITARIST OF COBALT BLUE, THAT'S RIGHT.
WILL MENTIONED... WELL, I BROUGHT YOU...
...YOUR TAPE! THAT'S GREAT, THANKS.
I'd keep an eye on him if I were you, Will! He's chatting with the DIVA!
I know. I sent him!
You have no idea how hard it was to convince him to take the FIRST STEP!
??
He was embarrassed! He didn't think he was good enough, my... ADORABLE, CLUMSY Matt!

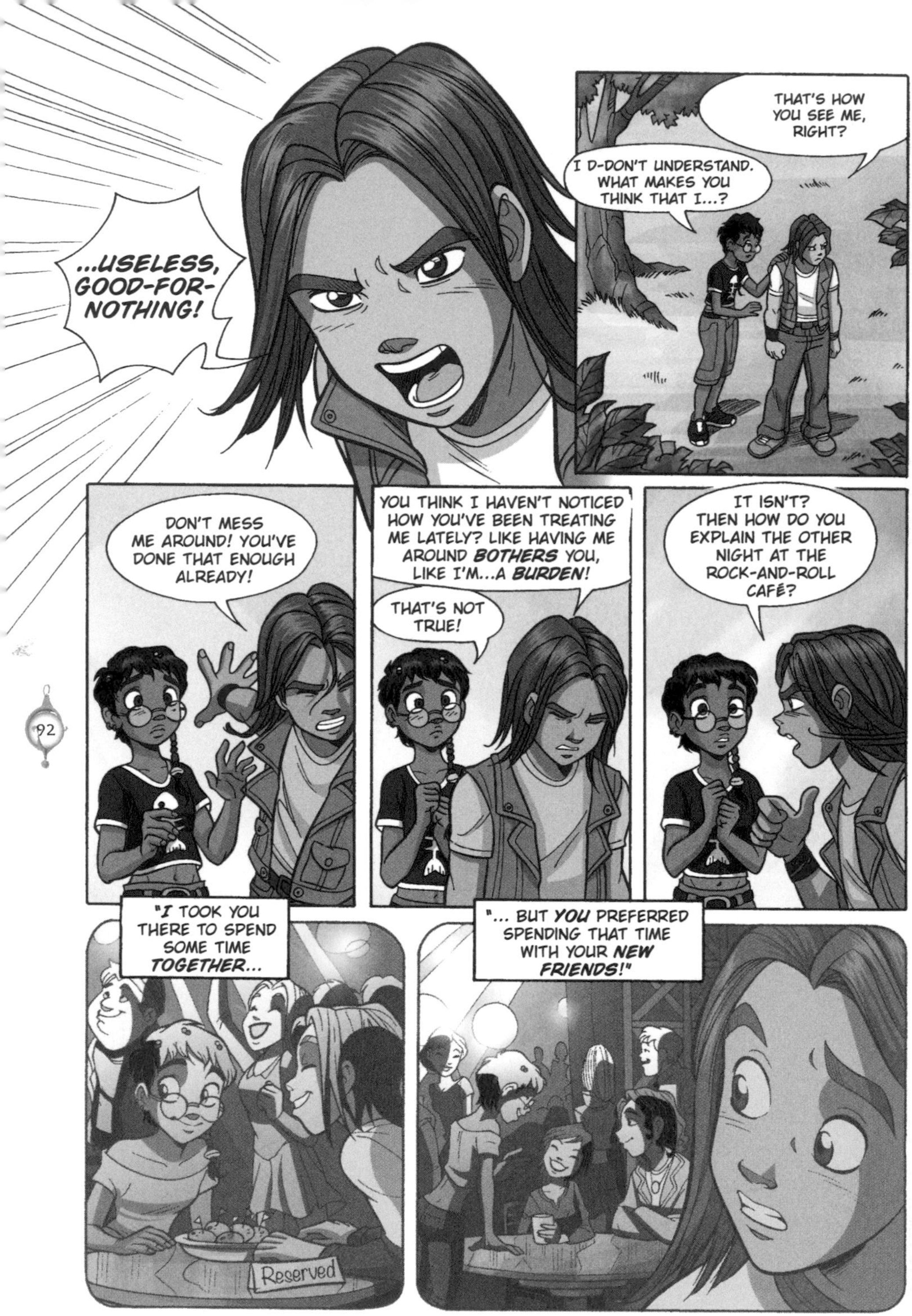
...USELESS, GOOD-FOR-NOTHING!
THAT'S HOW YOU SEE ME, RIGHT?
I D-DON'T UNDERSTAND. WHAT MAKES YOU THINK THAT I...?
DON'T MESS ME AROUND! YOU'VE DONE THAT ENOUGH ALREADY!
YOU THINK I HAVEN'T NOTICED HOW YOU'VE BEEN TREATING ME LATELY? LIKE HAVING ME AROUND BOTHERS YOU, LIKE I'M...A BURDEN!
THAT'S NOT TRUE!
IT ISN'T? THEN HOW DO YOU EXPLAIN THE OTHER NIGHT AT THE ROCK-AND-ROLL CAFÉ?
"I TOOK YOU THERE TO SPEND SOME TIME TOGETHER...
Reserved
"... BUT YOU PREFERRED SPENDING THAT TIME WITH YOUR NEW FRIENDS!"

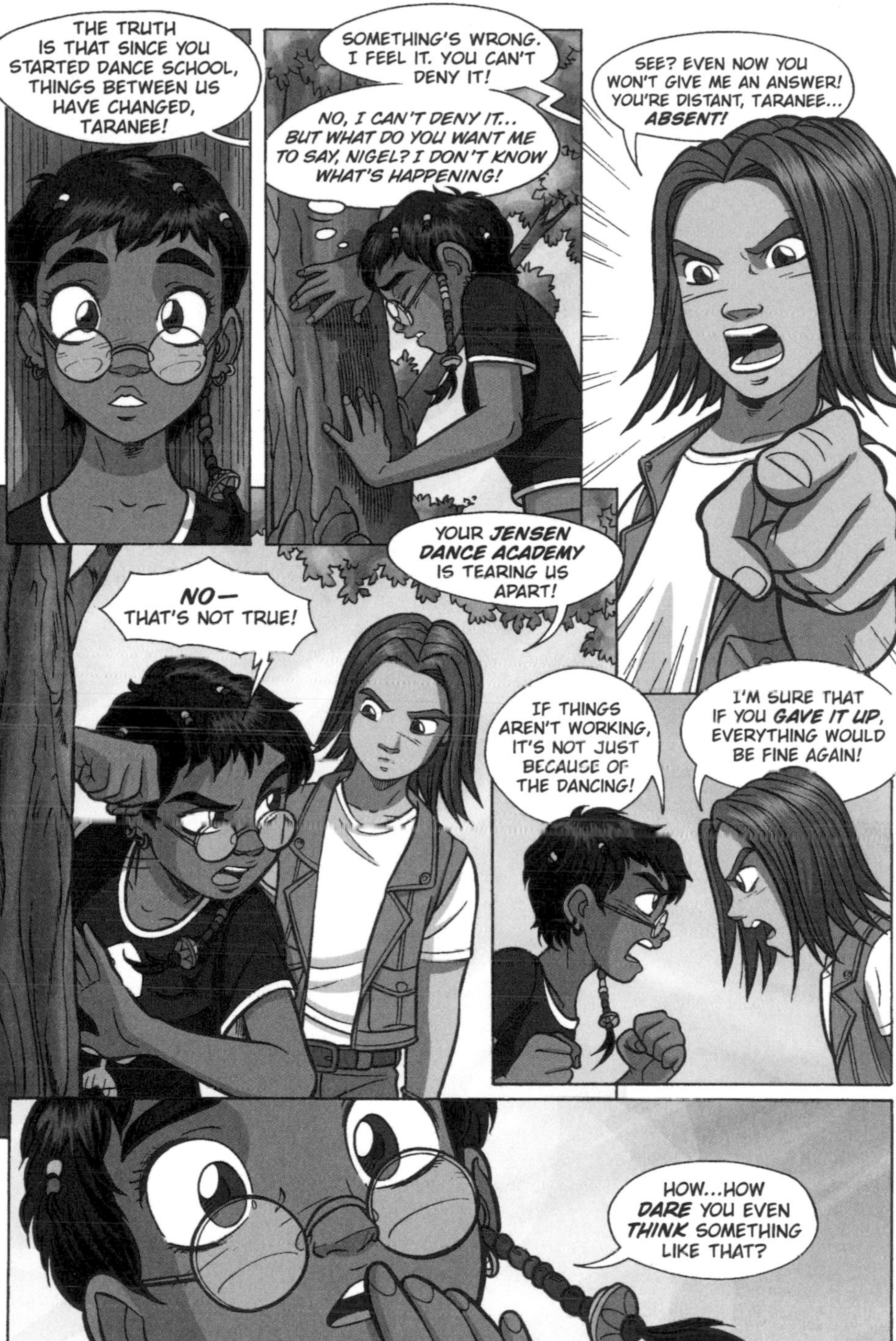
THE TRUTH IS THAT SINCE YOU STARTED DANCE SCHOOL, THINGS BETWEEN US HAVE CHANGED, TARANEE!
SOMETHING'S WRONG. I FEEL IT. YOU CAN'T DENY IT!
NO, I CAN'T DENY IT... BUT WHAT DO YOU WANT ME TO SAY, NIGEL? I DON'T KNOW WHAT'S HAPPENING!
SEE? EVEN NOW YOU WON'T GIVE ME AN ANSWER! YOU'RE DISTANT, TARANEE... ABSENT!
YOUR JENSEN DANCE ACADEMY IS TEARING US APART!
NO— THAT'S NOT TRUE!
IF THINGS AREN'T WORKING, IT'S NOT JUST BECAUSE OF THE DANCING!
I'M SURE THAT IF YOU GAVE IT UP, EVERYTHING WOULD BE FINE AGAIN!
HOW...HOW DARE YOU EVEN THINK SOMETHING LIKE THAT?

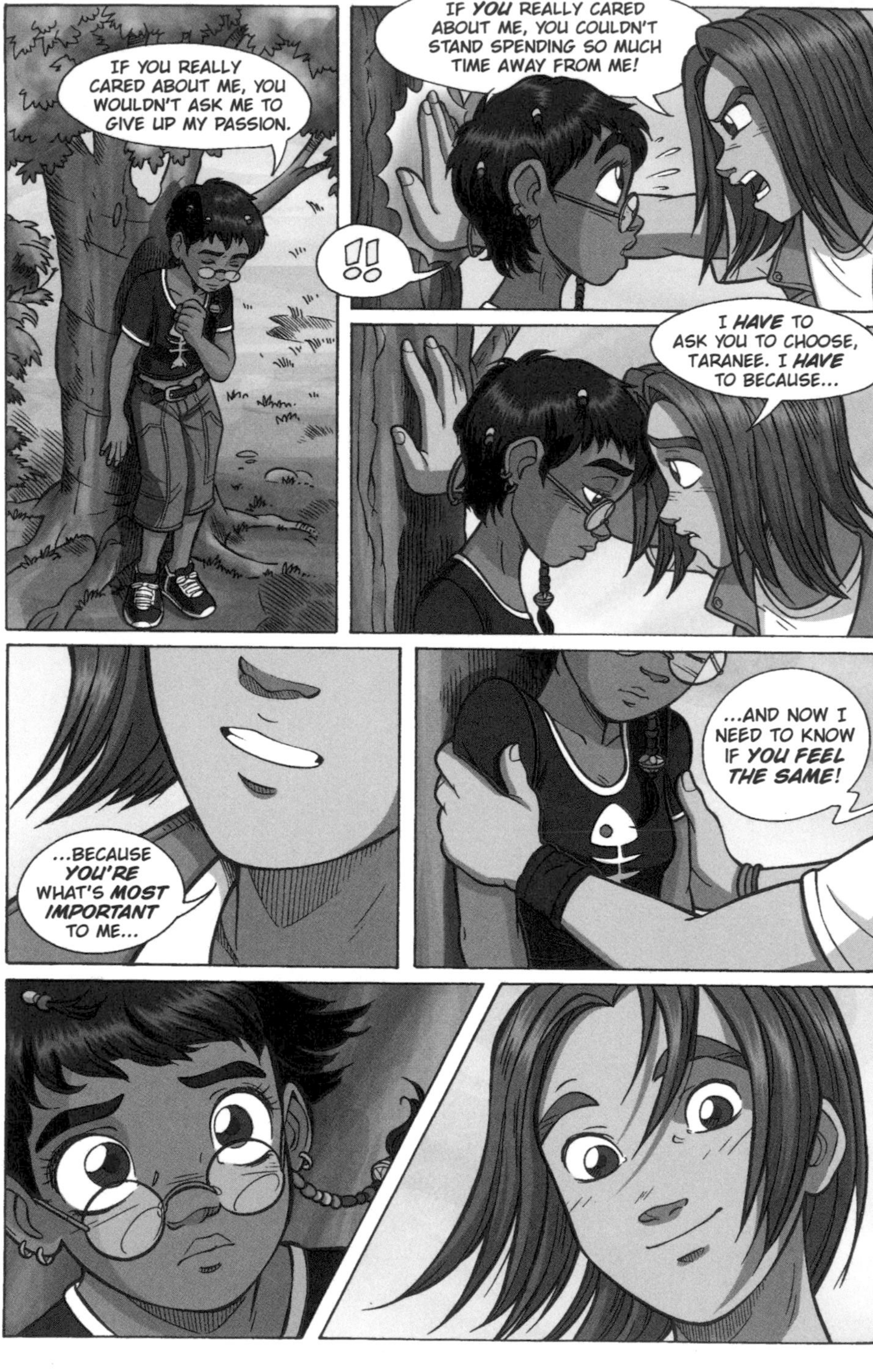
IF YOU REALLY CARED ABOUT ME, YOU WOULDN'T ASK ME TO GIVE UP MY PASSION.
IF YOU REALLY CARED ABOUT ME, YOU COULDN'T STAND SPENDING SO MUCH TIME AWAY FROM ME!
!!
I HAVE TO ASK YOU TO CHOOSE, TARANEE. I HAVE TO BECAUSE...
...BECAUSE YOU'RE WHAT'S MOST IMPORTANT TO ME...
...AND NOW I NEED TO KNOW IF YOU FEEL THE SAME!

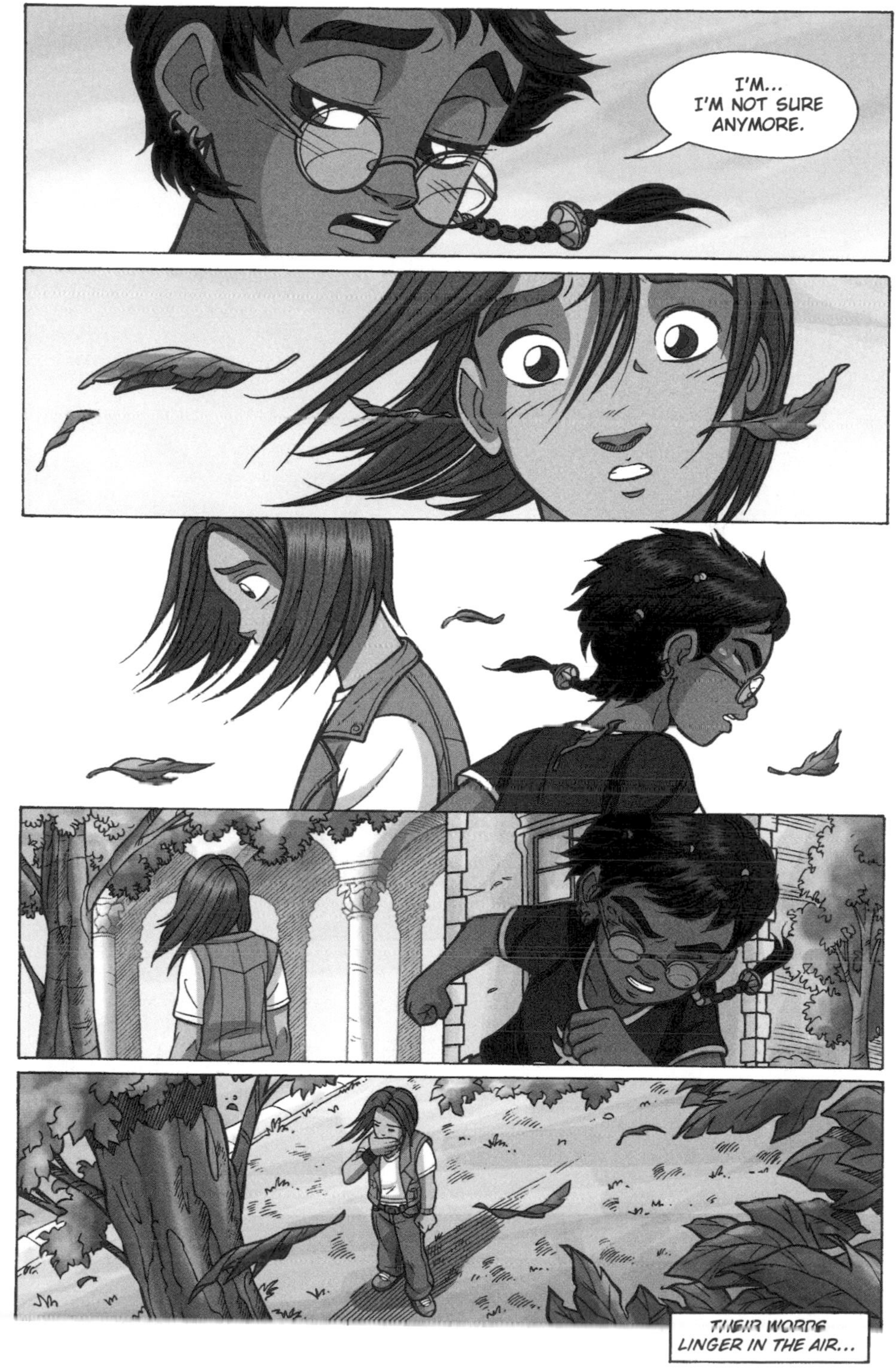
I'M... I'M NOT SURE ANYMORE.
THEIR WORDS LINGER IN THE AIR...

W.i.t.c.h.

Will Irma Taranee Cornelia Hay Lin

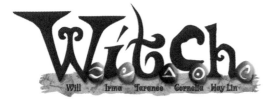

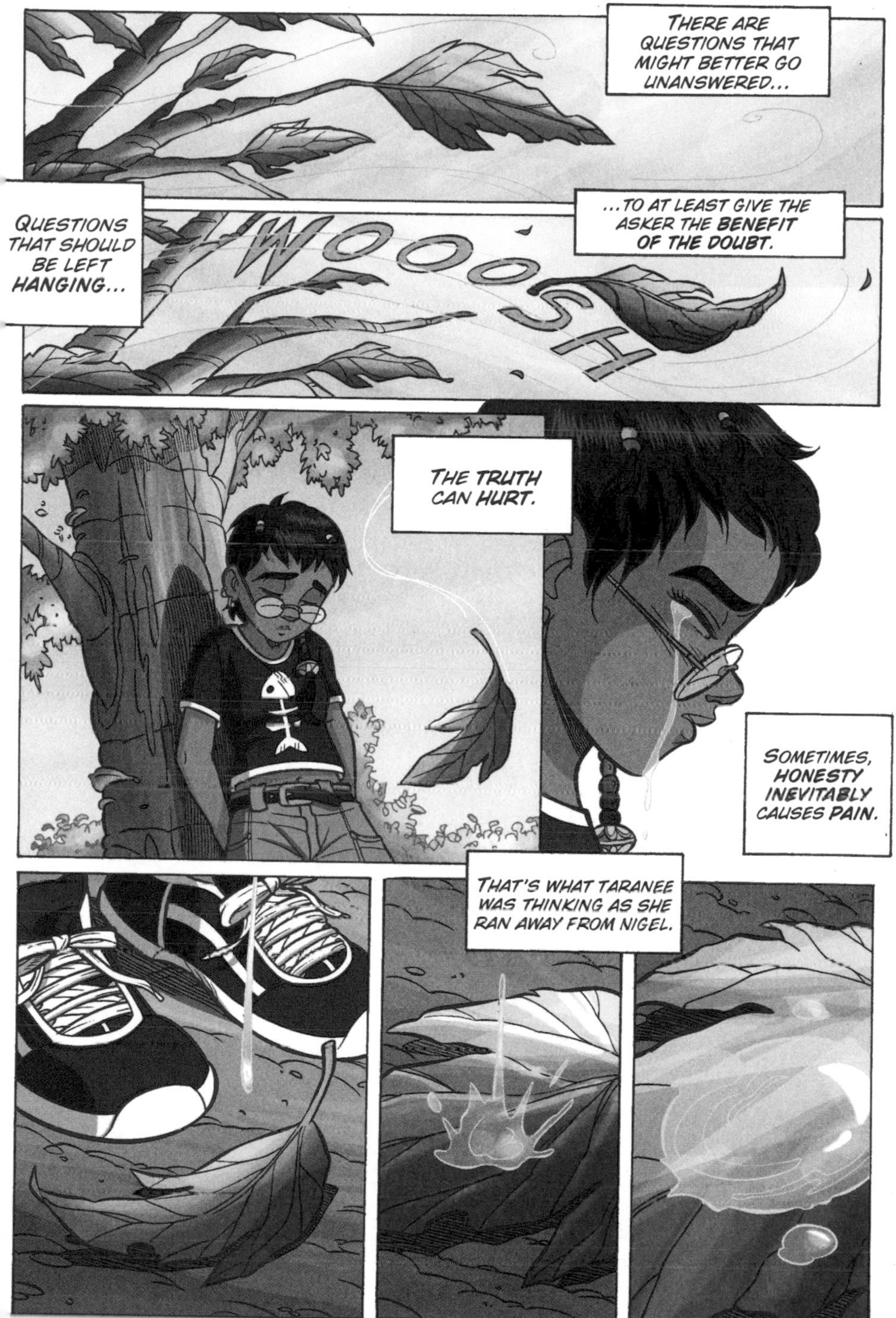

THERE ARE QUESTIONS THAT MIGHT BETTER GO UNANSWERED...
QUESTIONS THAT SHOULD BE LEFT HANGING...
...TO AT LEAST GIVE THE ASKER THE BENEFIT OF THE DOUBT.
WOOOSH
THE TRUTH CAN HURT.
SOMETIMES, HONESTY INEVITABLY CAUSES PAIN.
THAT'S WHAT TARANEE WAS THINKING AS SHE RAN AWAY FROM NIGEL.

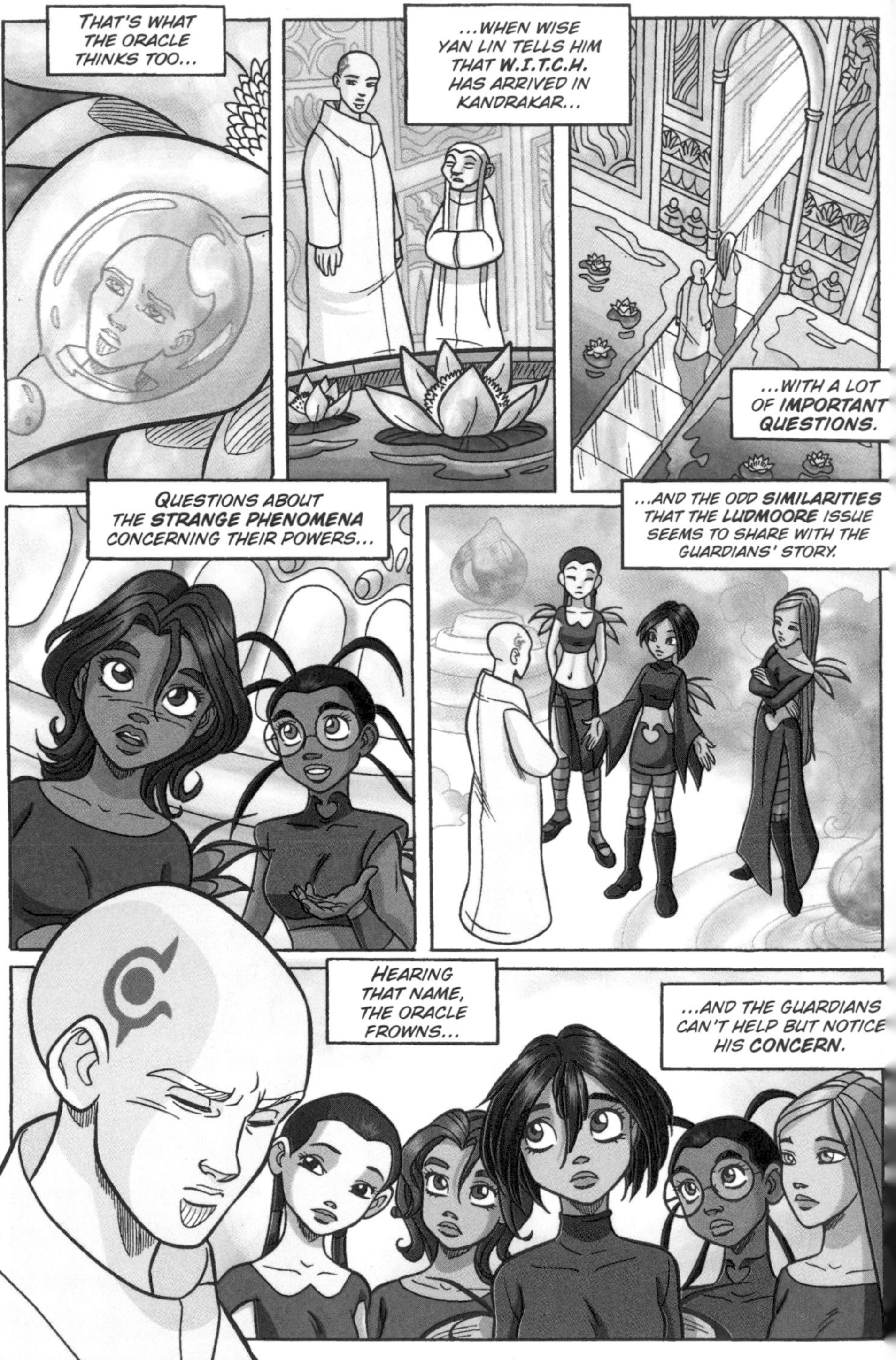
THAT'S WHAT THE ORACLE THINKS TOO...
...WHEN WISE YAN LIN TELLS HIM THAT W.I.T.C.H. HAS ARRIVED IN KANDRAKAR...
...WITH A LOT OF IMPORTANT QUESTIONS.
QUESTIONS ABOUT THE STRANGE PHENOMENA CONCERNING THEIR POWERS...
...AND THE ODD SIMILARITIES THAT THE LUDMOORE ISSUE SEEMS TO SHARE WITH THE GUARDIANS' STORY.
HEARING THAT NAME, THE ORACLE FROWNS...
...AND THE GUARDIANS CAN'T HELP BUT NOTICE HIS CONCERN.

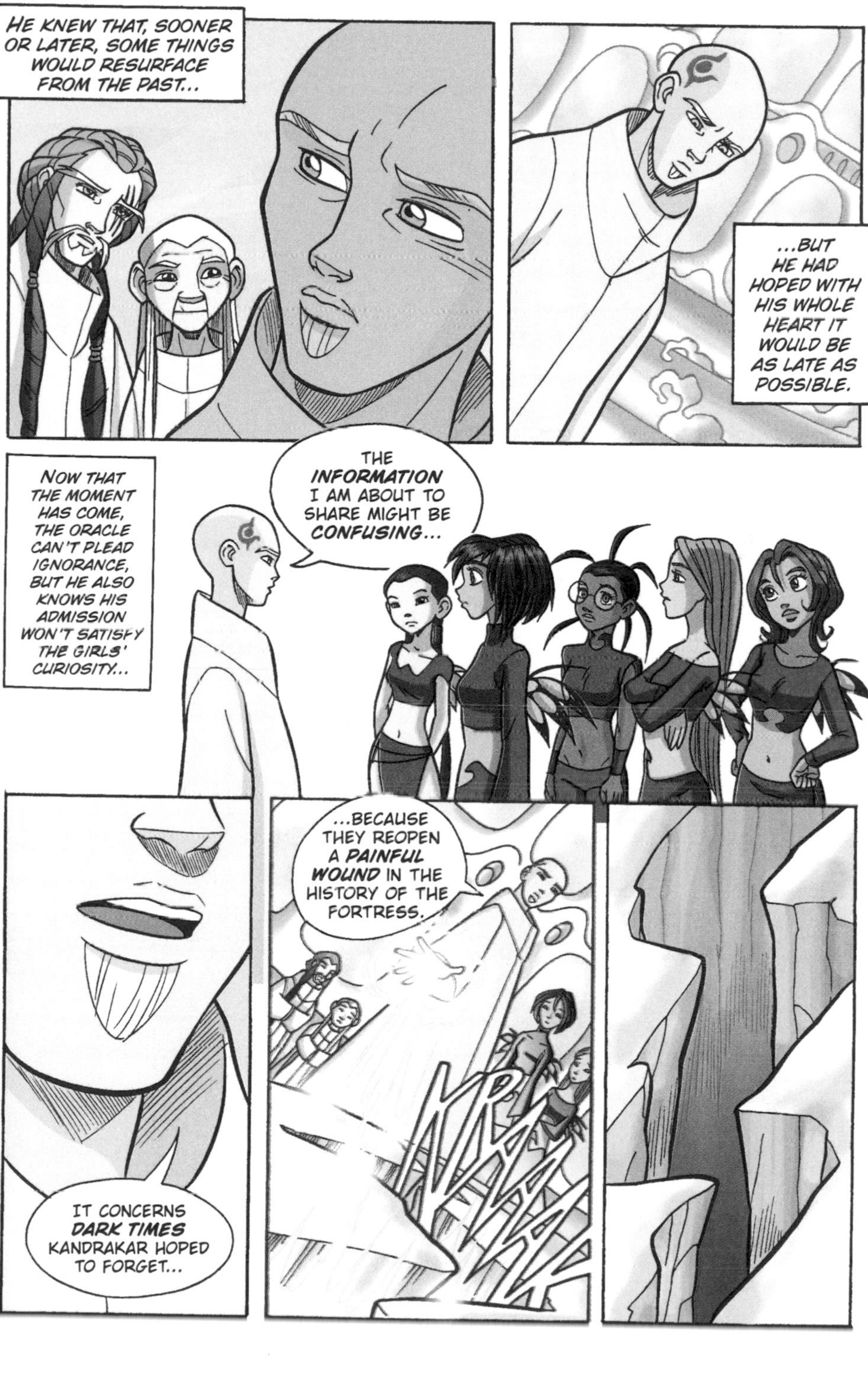
HE KNEW THAT, SOONER OR LATER, SOME THINGS WOULD RESURFACE FROM THE PAST...
...BUT HE HAD HOPED WITH HIS WHOLE HEART IT WOULD BE AS LATE AS POSSIBLE.
NOW THAT THE MOMENT HAS COME, THE ORACLE CAN'T PLEAD IGNORANCE, BUT HE ALSO KNOWS HIS ADMISSION WON'T SATISFY THE GIRLS' CURIOSITY...
THE INFORMATION I AM ABOUT TO SHARE MIGHT BE CONFUSING...
IT CONCERNS DARK TIMES KANDRAKAR HOPED TO FORGET...
...BECAUSE THEY REOPEN A PAINFUL WOUND IN THE HISTORY OF THE FORTRESS.

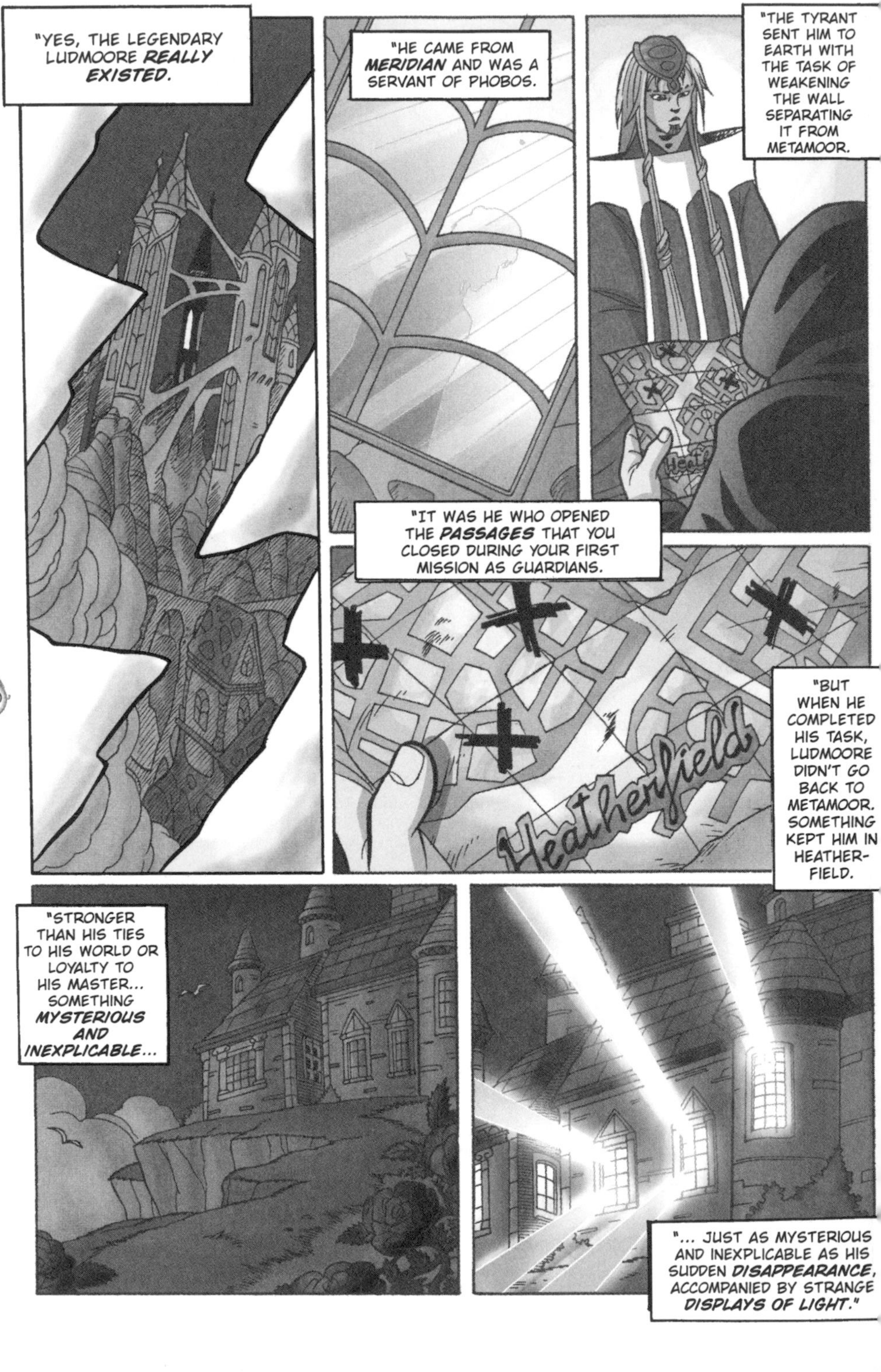
"YES, THE LEGENDARY LUDMOORE REALLY EXISTED.
"HE CAME FROM MERIDIAN AND WAS A SERVANT OF PHOBOS.
"THE TYRANT SENT HIM TO EARTH WITH THE TASK OF WEAKENING THE WALL SEPARATING IT FROM METAMOOR.
"IT WAS HE WHO OPENED THE PASSAGES THAT YOU CLOSED DURING YOUR FIRST MISSION AS GUARDIANS.
Heatherfield
"BUT WHEN HE COMPLETED HIS TASK, LUDMOORE DIDN'T GO BACK TO METAMOOR. SOMETHING KEPT HIM IN HEATHER-FIELD.
"STRONGER THAN HIS TIES TO HIS WORLD OR LOYALTY TO HIS MASTER... SOMETHING MYSTERIOUS AND INEXPLICABLE...
"... JUST AS MYSTERIOUS AND INEXPLICABLE AS HIS SUDDEN DISAPPEARANCE, ACCOMPANIED BY STRANGE DISPLAYS OF LIGHT."

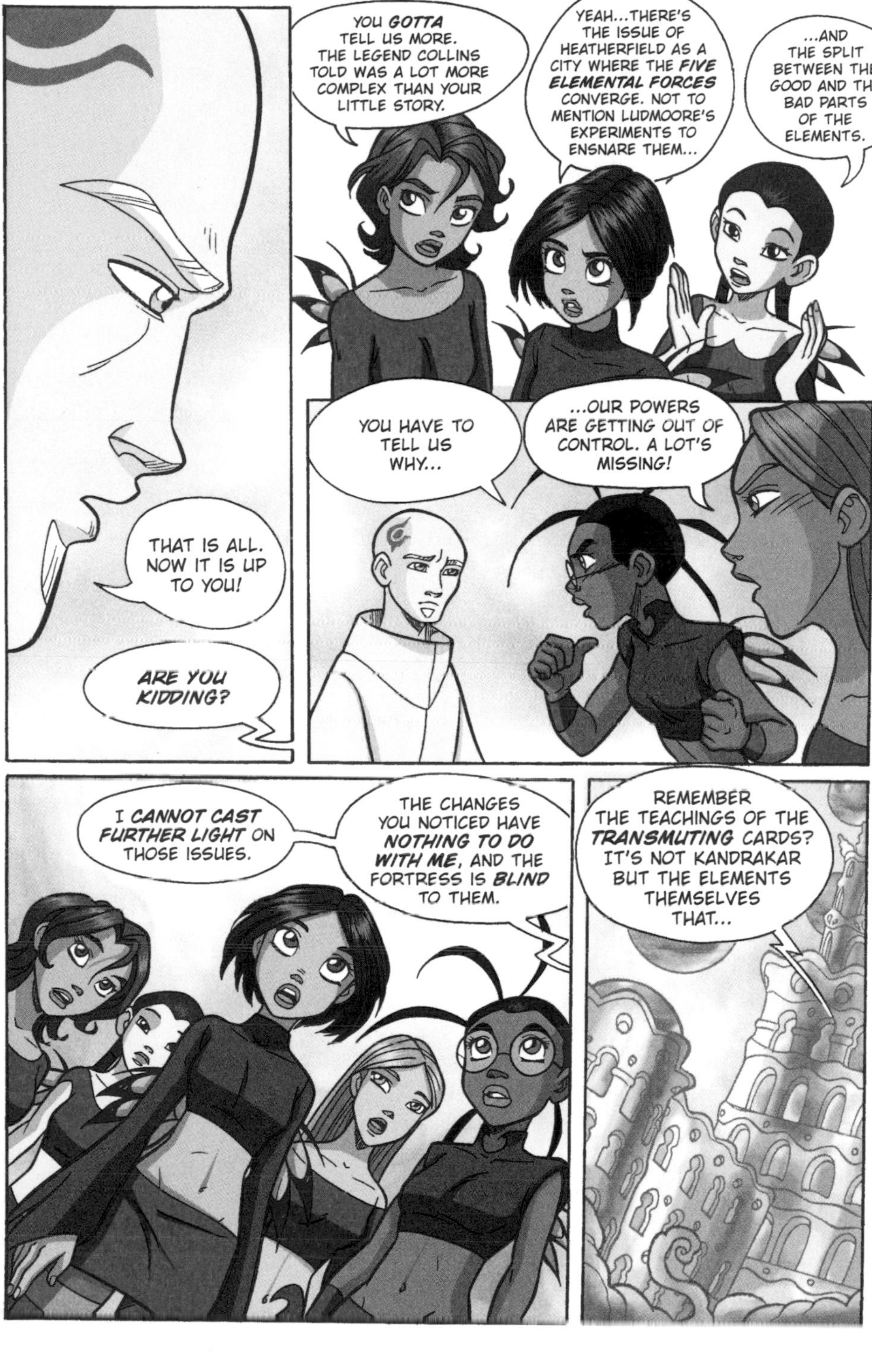
YOU *GOTTA* TELL US MORE. THE LEGEND COLLINS TOLD WAS A LOT MORE COMPLEX THAN YOUR LITTLE STORY.
YEAH...THERE'S THE ISSUE OF HEATHERFIELD AS A CITY WHERE THE *FIVE ELEMENTAL FORCES* CONVERGE. NOT TO MENTION LUDMOORE'S EXPERIMENTS TO ENSNARE THEM...
...AND THE SPLIT BETWEEN THE GOOD AND THE BAD PARTS OF THE ELEMENTS.
THAT IS ALL. NOW IT IS UP TO YOU!
ARE YOU KIDDING?
YOU HAVE TO TELL US WHY...
...OUR POWERS ARE GETTING OUT OF CONTROL. A LOT'S MISSING!
I *CANNOT CAST FURTHER LIGHT* ON THOSE ISSUES.
THE CHANGES YOU NOTICED HAVE *NOTHING TO DO WITH ME*, AND THE FORTRESS IS *BLIND* TO THEM.
REMEMBER THE TEACHINGS OF THE *TRANSMUTING* CARDS? IT'S NOT KANDRAKAR BUT THE ELEMENTS THEMSELVES THAT...

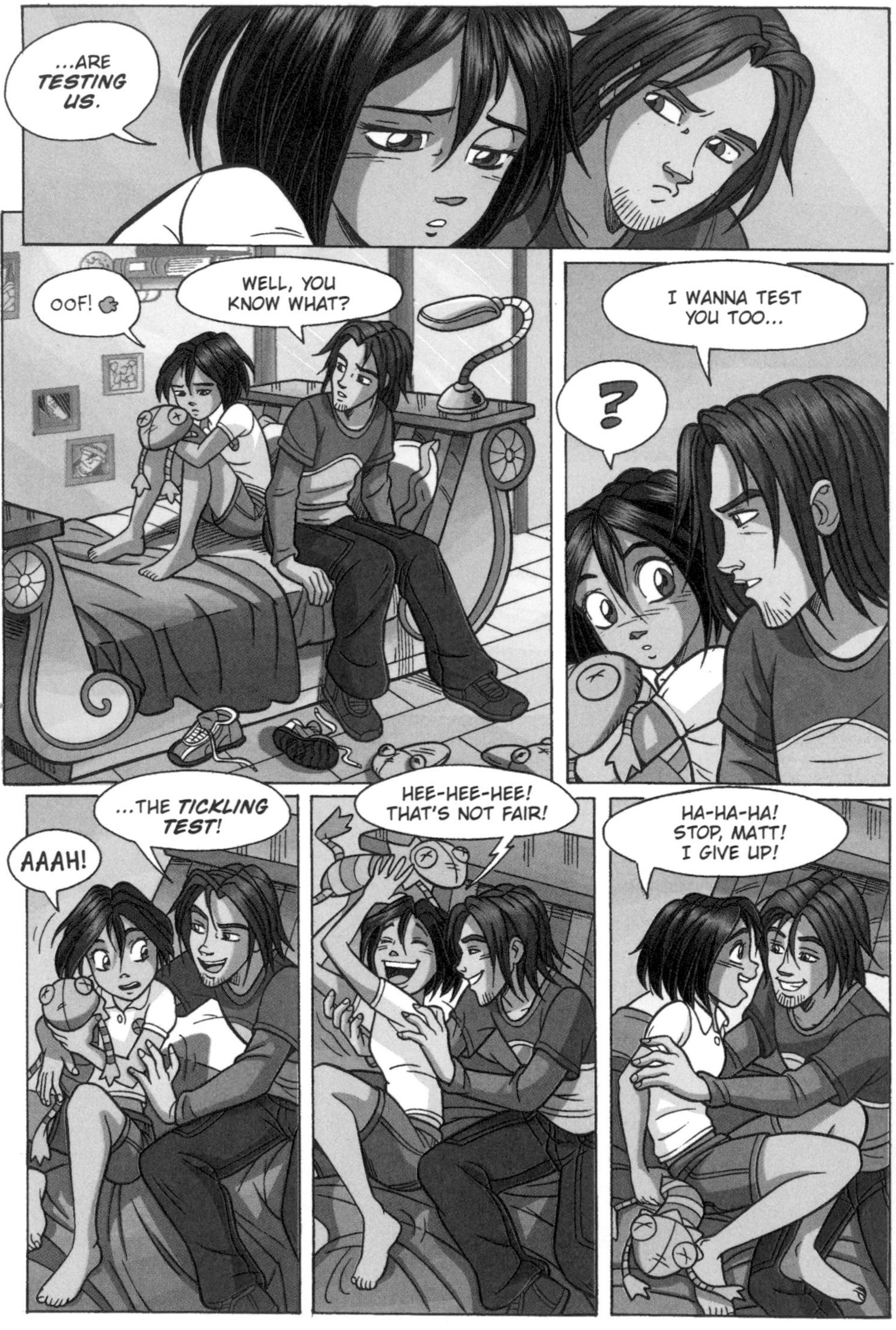
...ARE TESTING US.
OOF!
WELL, YOU KNOW WHAT?
I WANNA TEST YOU TOO...
?
...THE TICKLING TEST!
AAAH!
HEE-HEE-HEE! THAT'S NOT FAIR!
HA-HA-HA! STOP, MATT! I GIVE UP!

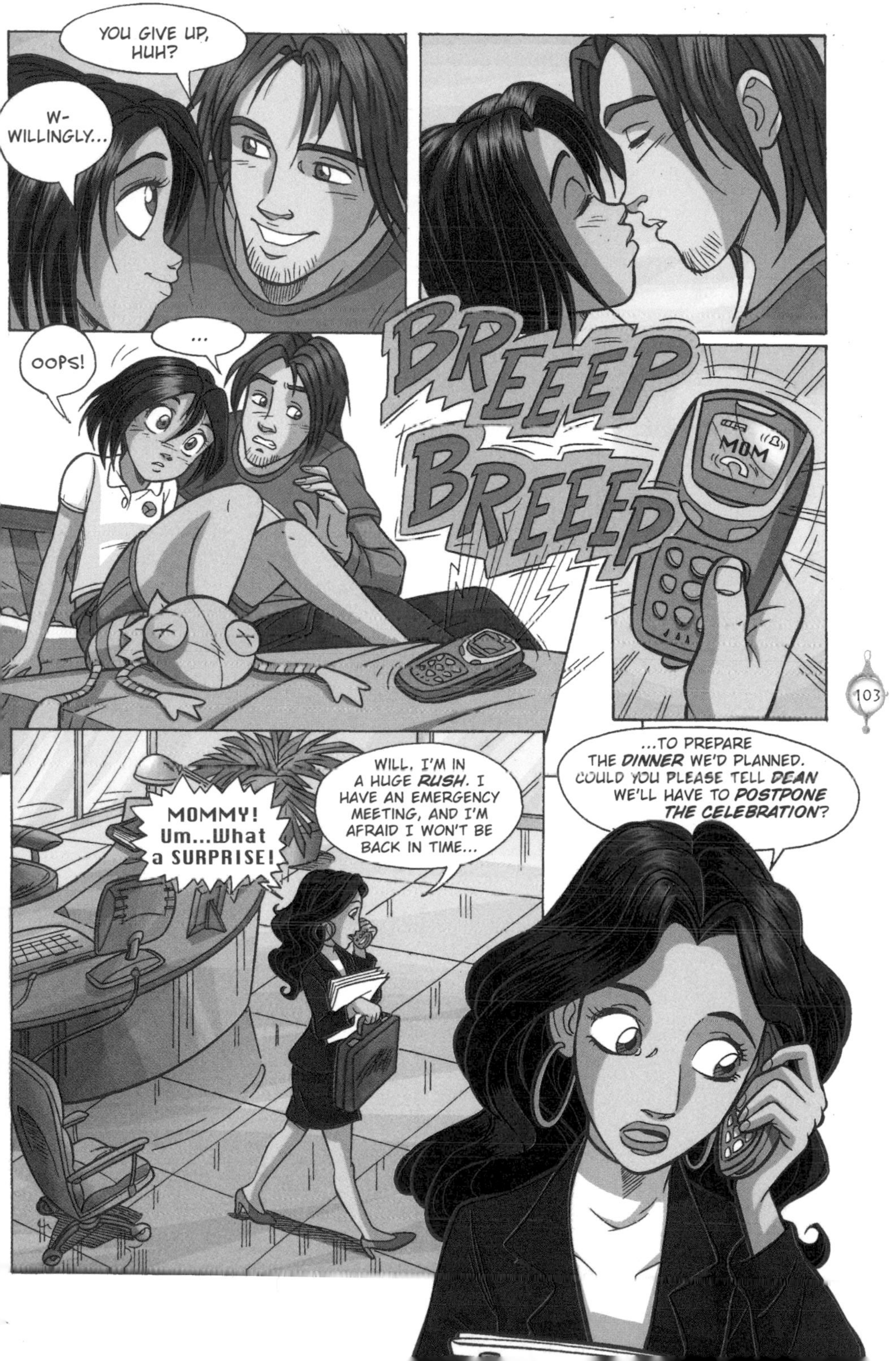

YOU GIVE UP, HUH?
W- WILLINGLY...
OOPS!
...
BREEEP BREEEP
MOM
MOMMY! Um...What a SURPRISE!
WILL, I'M IN A HUGE *RUSH*. I HAVE AN EMERGENCY MEETING, AND I'M AFRAID I WON'T BE BACK IN TIME...
...TO PREPARE THE *DINNER* WE'D PLANNED. COULD YOU PLEASE TELL *DEAN* WE'LL HAVE TO *POSTPONE THE CELEBRATION*?

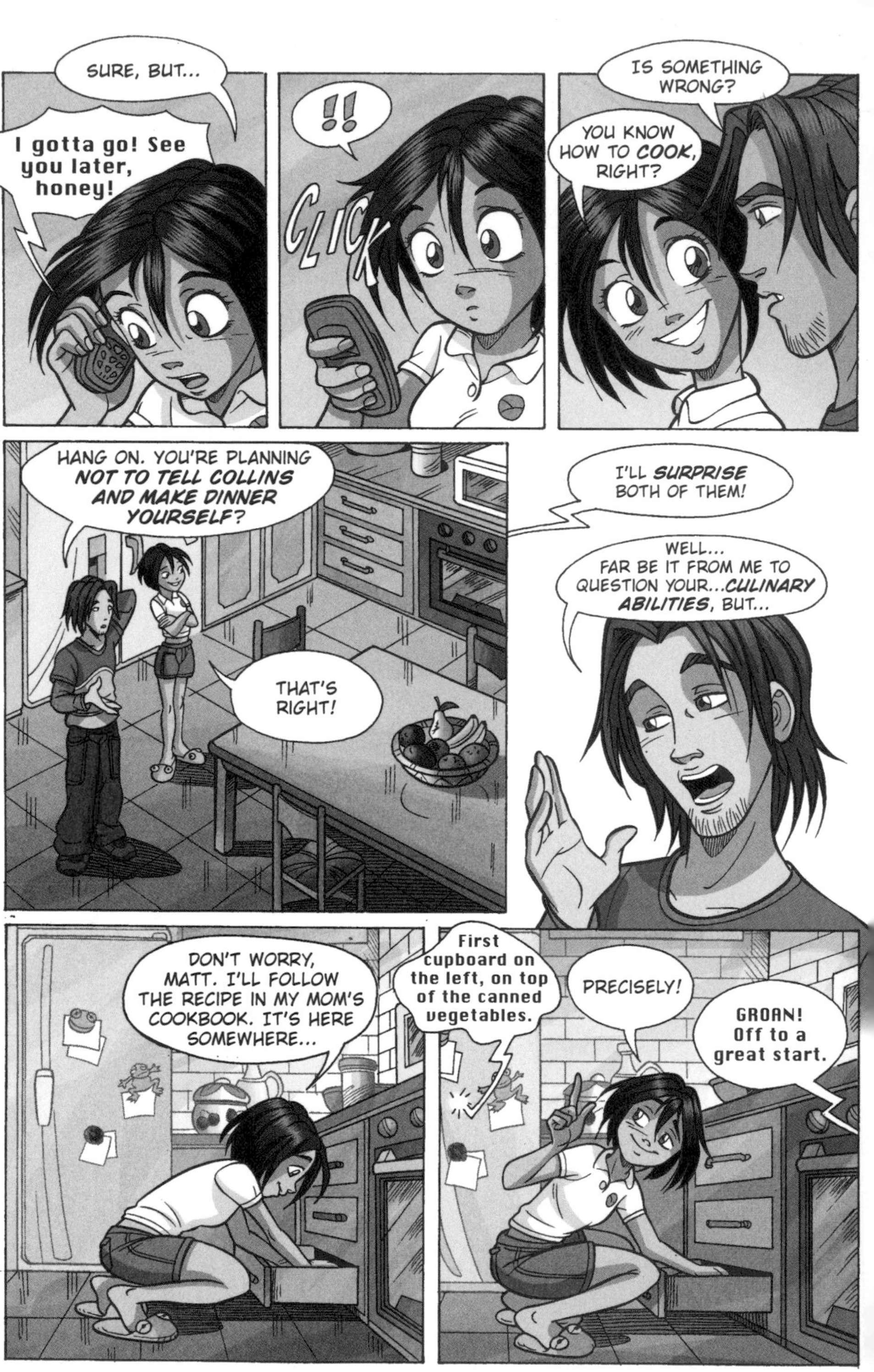
SURE, BUT...
I gotta go! See you later, honey!
!!
CLICK
IS SOMETHING WRONG?
YOU KNOW HOW TO COOK, RIGHT?
HANG ON. YOU'RE PLANNING NOT TO TELL COLLINS AND MAKE DINNER YOURSELF?
THAT'S RIGHT!
I'LL SURPRISE BOTH OF THEM!
WELL... FAR BE IT FROM ME TO QUESTION YOUR...CULINARY ABILITIES, BUT...
DON'T WORRY, MATT. I'LL FOLLOW THE RECIPE IN MY MOM'S COOKBOOK. IT'S HERE SOMEWHERE...
First cupboard on the left, on top of the canned vegetables.
PRECISELY!
GROAN! Off to a great start.

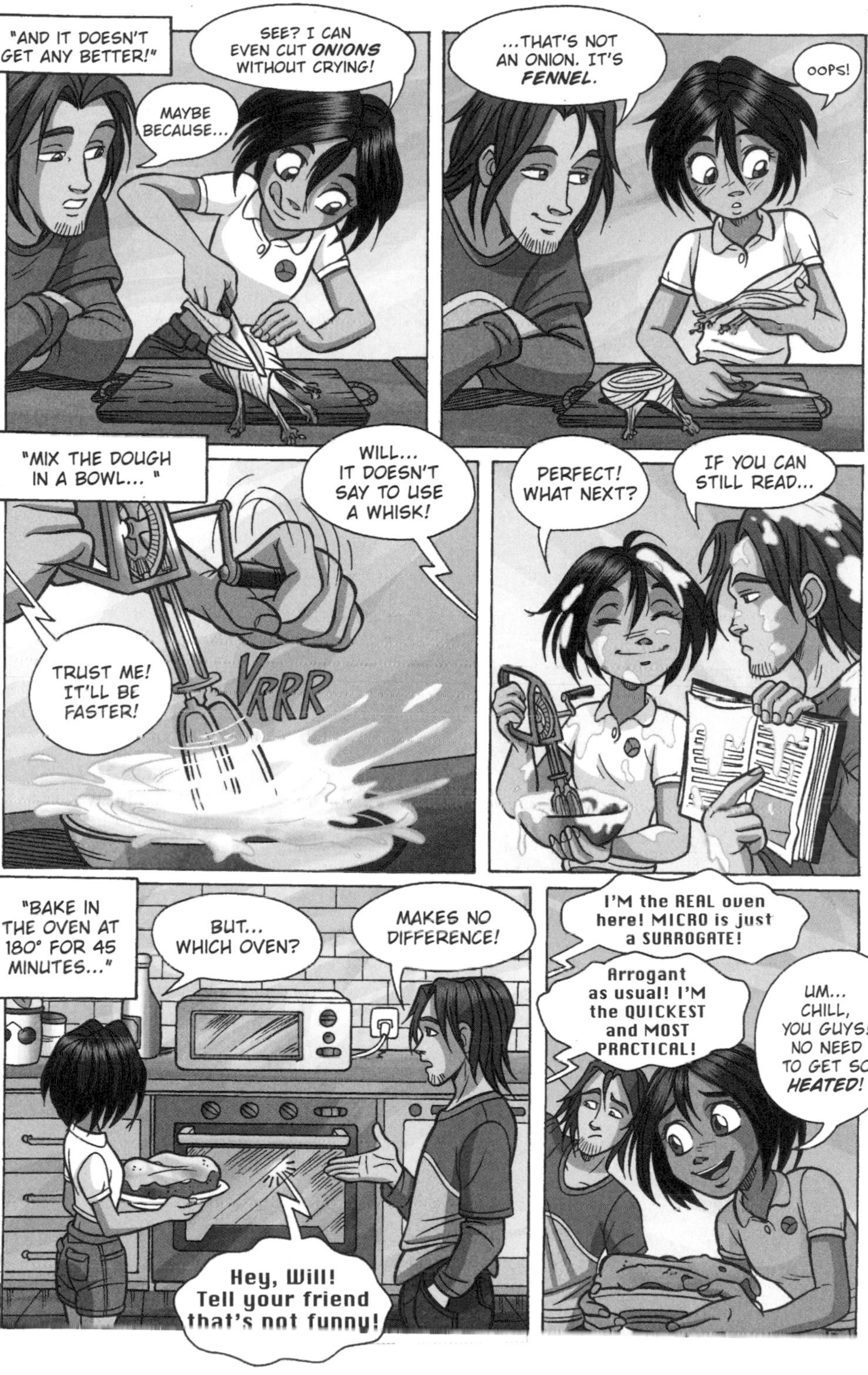
"AND IT DOESN'T GET ANY BETTER!"
SEE? I CAN EVEN CUT ONIONS WITHOUT CRYING!
MAYBE BECAUSE...
...THAT'S NOT AN ONION. IT'S FENNEL.
OOPS!
"MIX THE DOUGH IN A BOWL..."
WILL... IT DOESN'T SAY TO USE A WHISK!
TRUST ME! IT'LL BE FASTER!
VRRR
PERFECT! WHAT NEXT?
IF YOU CAN STILL READ...
"BAKE IN THE OVEN AT 180° FOR 45 MINUTES..."
BUT... WHICH OVEN?
MAKES NO DIFFERENCE!
Hey, Will! Tell your friend that's not funny!
I'M the REAL oven here! MICRO is just a SURROGATE!
Arrogant as usual! I'M the QUICKEST and MOST PRACTICAL!
UM... CHILL, YOU GUYS! NO NEED TO GET SO HEATED!

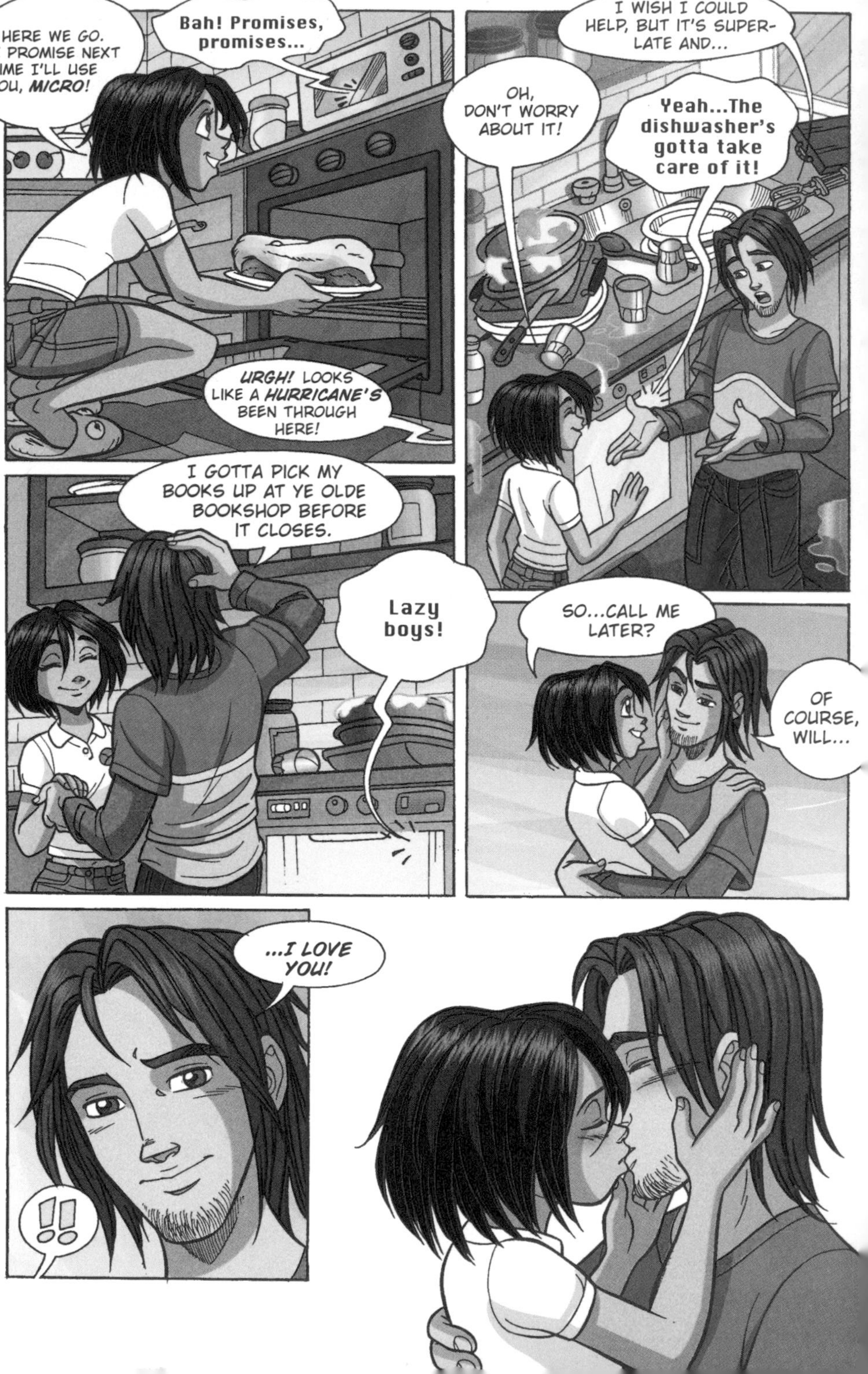

HERE WE GO. I PROMISE NEXT TIME I'LL USE YOU, MICRO!
Bah! Promises, promises...
URGH! LOOKS LIKE A HURRICANE'S BEEN THROUGH HERE!
I WISH I COULD HELP, BUT IT'S SUPER-LATE AND...
OH, DON'T WORRY ABOUT IT!
Yeah...The dishwasher's gotta take care of it!
I GOTTA PICK MY BOOKS UP AT YE OLDE BOOKSHOP BEFORE IT CLOSES.
Lazy boys!
SO...CALL ME LATER?
OF COURSE, WILL...
...I LOVE YOU!
!!

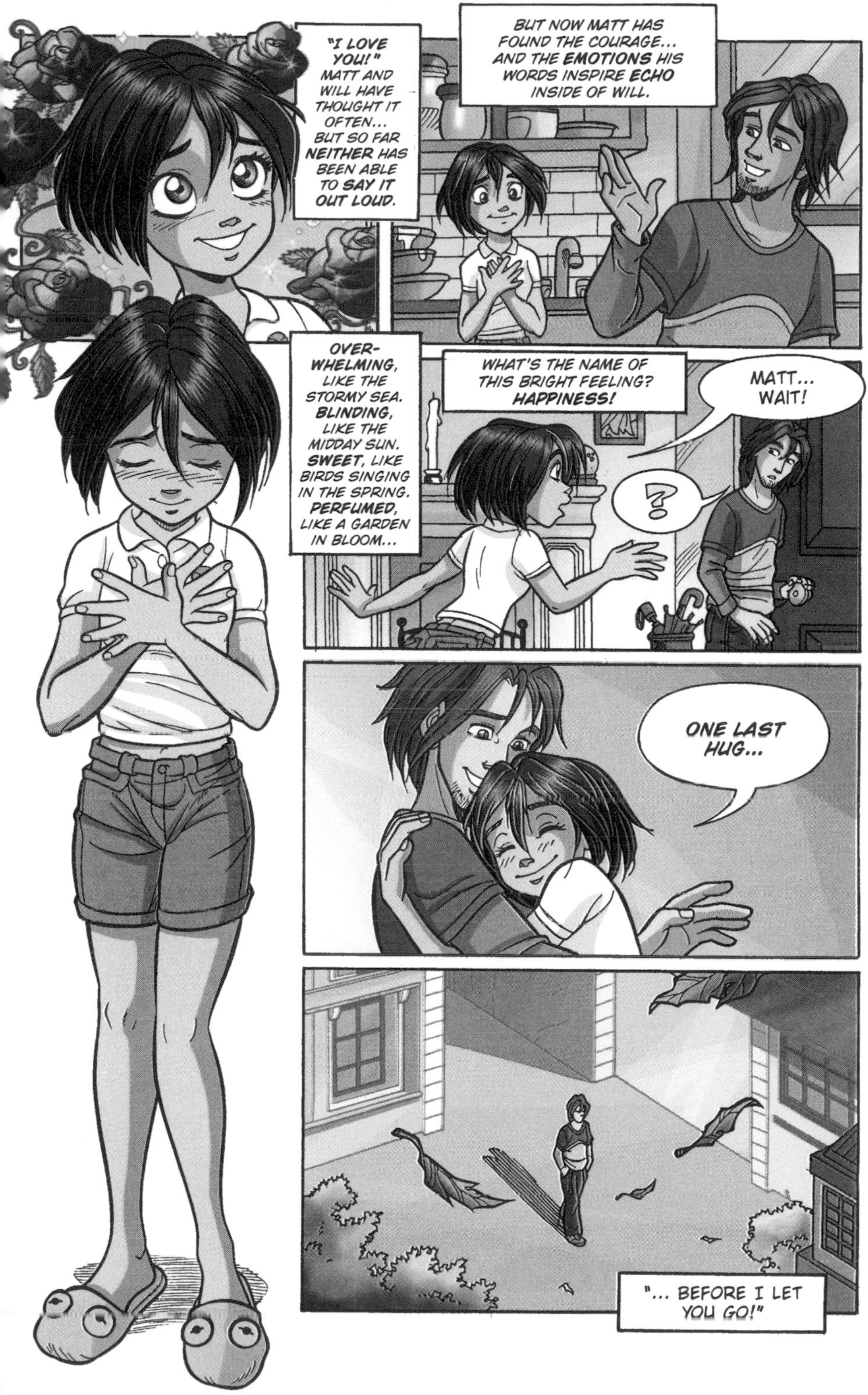
"I LOVE YOU!" MATT AND WILL HAVE THOUGHT IT OFTEN... BUT SO FAR NEITHER HAS BEEN ABLE TO SAY IT OUT LOUD.
BUT NOW MATT HAS FOUND THE COURAGE... AND THE EMOTIONS HIS WORDS INSPIRE ECHO INSIDE OF WILL.
OVER-WHELMING, LIKE THE STORMY SEA. BLINDING, LIKE THE MIDDAY SUN. SWEET, LIKE BIRDS SINGING IN THE SPRING. PERFUMED, LIKE A GARDEN IN BLOOM...
WHAT'S THE NAME OF THIS BRIGHT FEELING? HAPPINESS!
MATT... WAIT!
?
ONE LAST HUG...
"... BEFORE I LET YOU GO!"

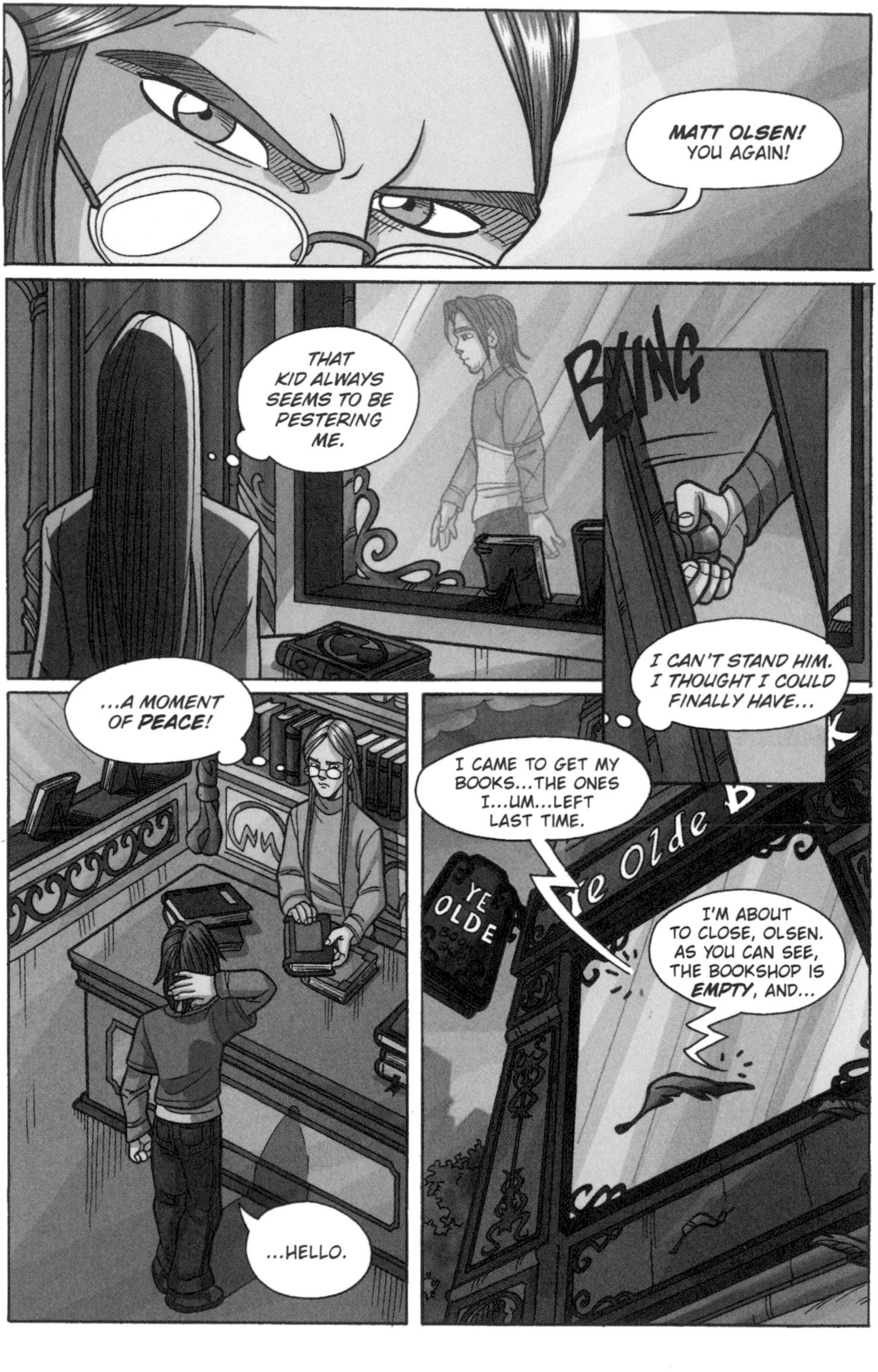
MATT OLSEN! YOU AGAIN!
THAT KID ALWAYS SEEMS TO BE PESTERING ME.
BLING
I CAN'T STAND HIM. I THOUGHT I COULD FINALLY HAVE...
...A MOMENT OF PEACE!
I CAME TO GET MY BOOKS...THE ONES I...UM...LEFT LAST TIME.
Ye Olde
YE OLDE
I'M ABOUT TO CLOSE, OLSEN. AS YOU CAN SEE, THE BOOKSHOP IS EMPTY, AND...
...HELLO.

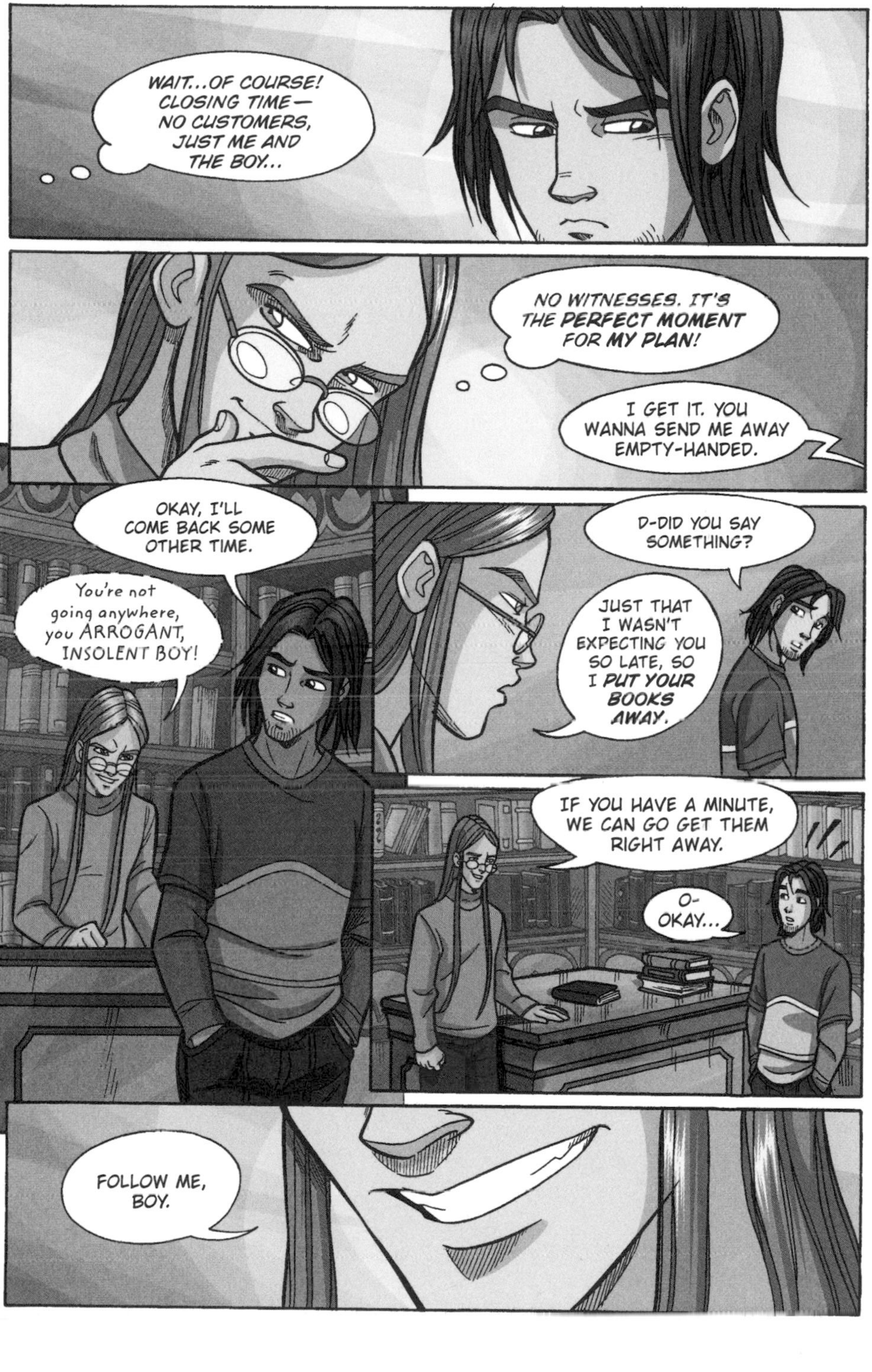
WAIT...OF COURSE! CLOSING TIME— NO CUSTOMERS, JUST ME AND THE BOY...
NO WITNESSES. IT'S THE PERFECT MOMENT FOR MY PLAN!
I GET IT. YOU WANNA SEND ME AWAY EMPTY-HANDED.
OKAY, I'LL COME BACK SOME OTHER TIME.
You're not going anywhere, you ARROGANT, INSOLENT BOY!
D-DID YOU SAY SOMETHING?
JUST THAT I WASN'T EXPECTING YOU SO LATE, SO I PUT YOUR BOOKS AWAY.
IF YOU HAVE A MINUTE, WE CAN GO GET THEM RIGHT AWAY.
O-OKAY...
FOLLOW ME, BOY.

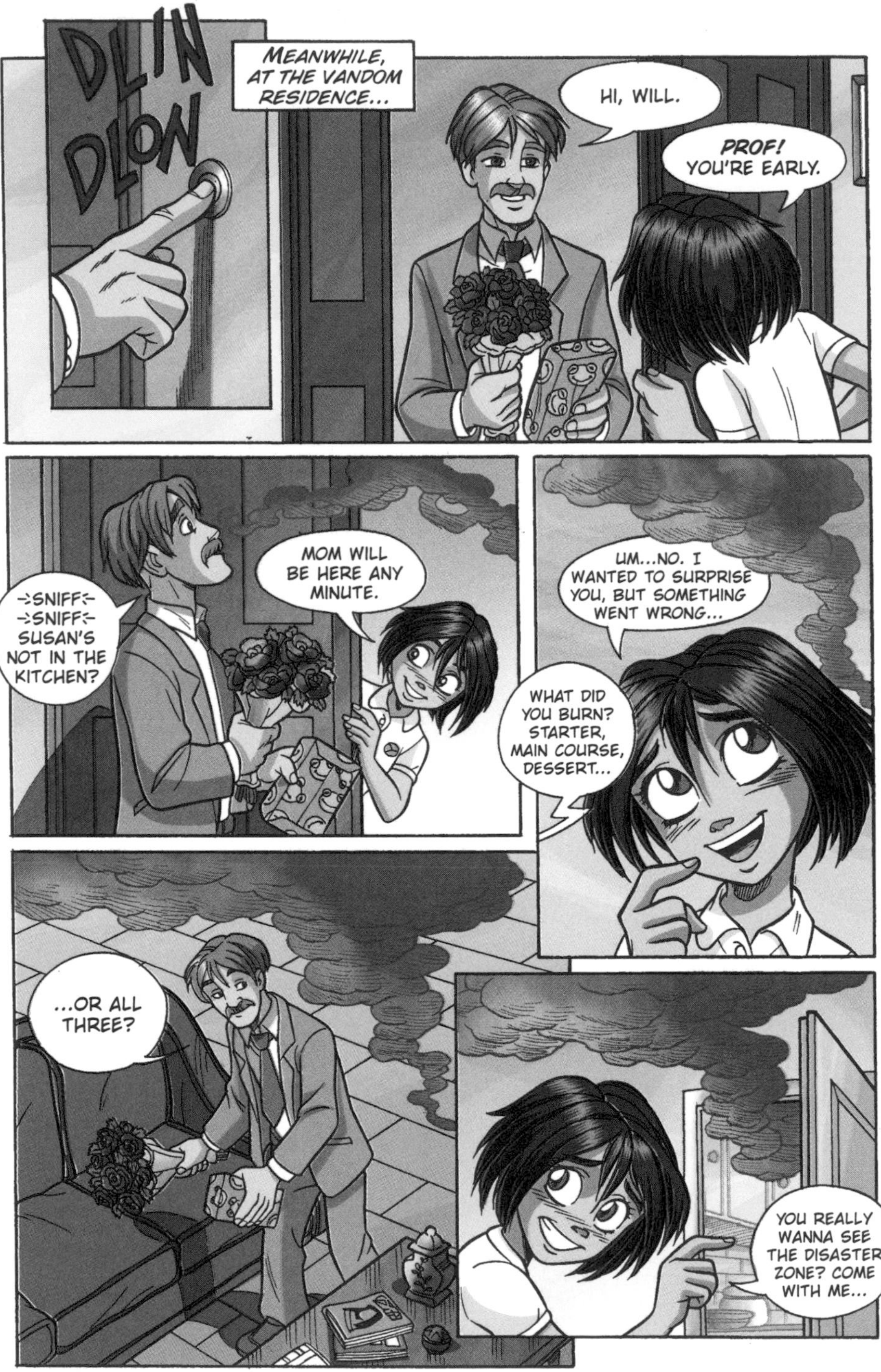
DLIN DLON
MEANWHILE, AT THE VANDOM RESIDENCE...
HI, WILL.
PROF! YOU'RE EARLY.
-SNIFF- -SNIFF- SUSAN'S NOT IN THE KITCHEN?
MOM WILL BE HERE ANY MINUTE.
UM...NO. I WANTED TO SURPRISE YOU, BUT SOMETHING WENT WRONG...
WHAT DID YOU BURN? STARTER, MAIN COURSE, DESSERT...
...OR ALL THREE?
YOU REALLY WANNA SEE THE DISASTER ZONE? COME WITH ME...

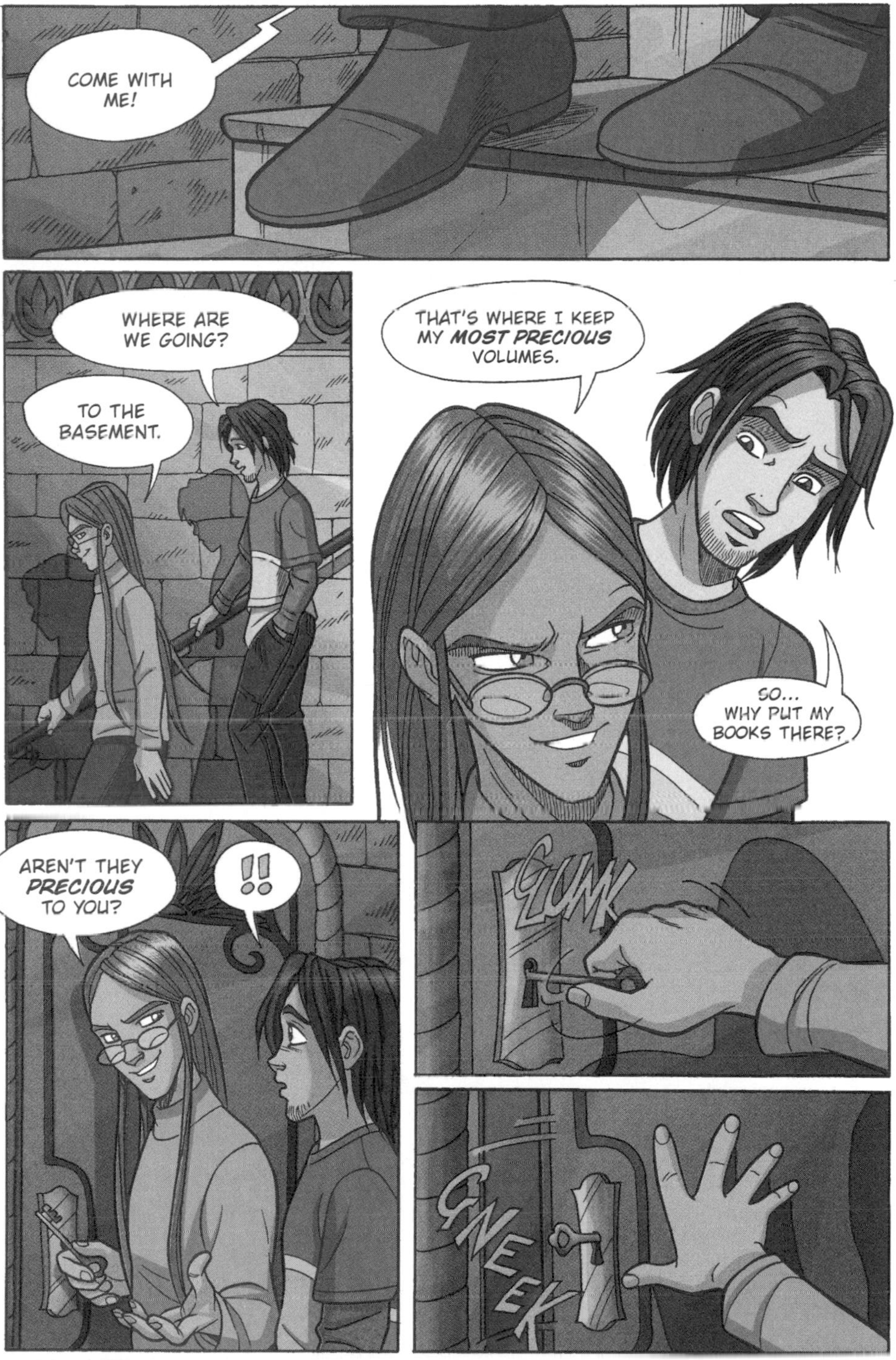
COME WITH ME!
WHERE ARE WE GOING?
TO THE BASEMENT.
THAT'S WHERE I KEEP MY ***MOST PRECIOUS*** VOLUMES.
SO... WHY PUT MY BOOKS THERE?
AREN'T THEY ***PRECIOUS*** TO YOU?
!!
CLUNK
GNEEK

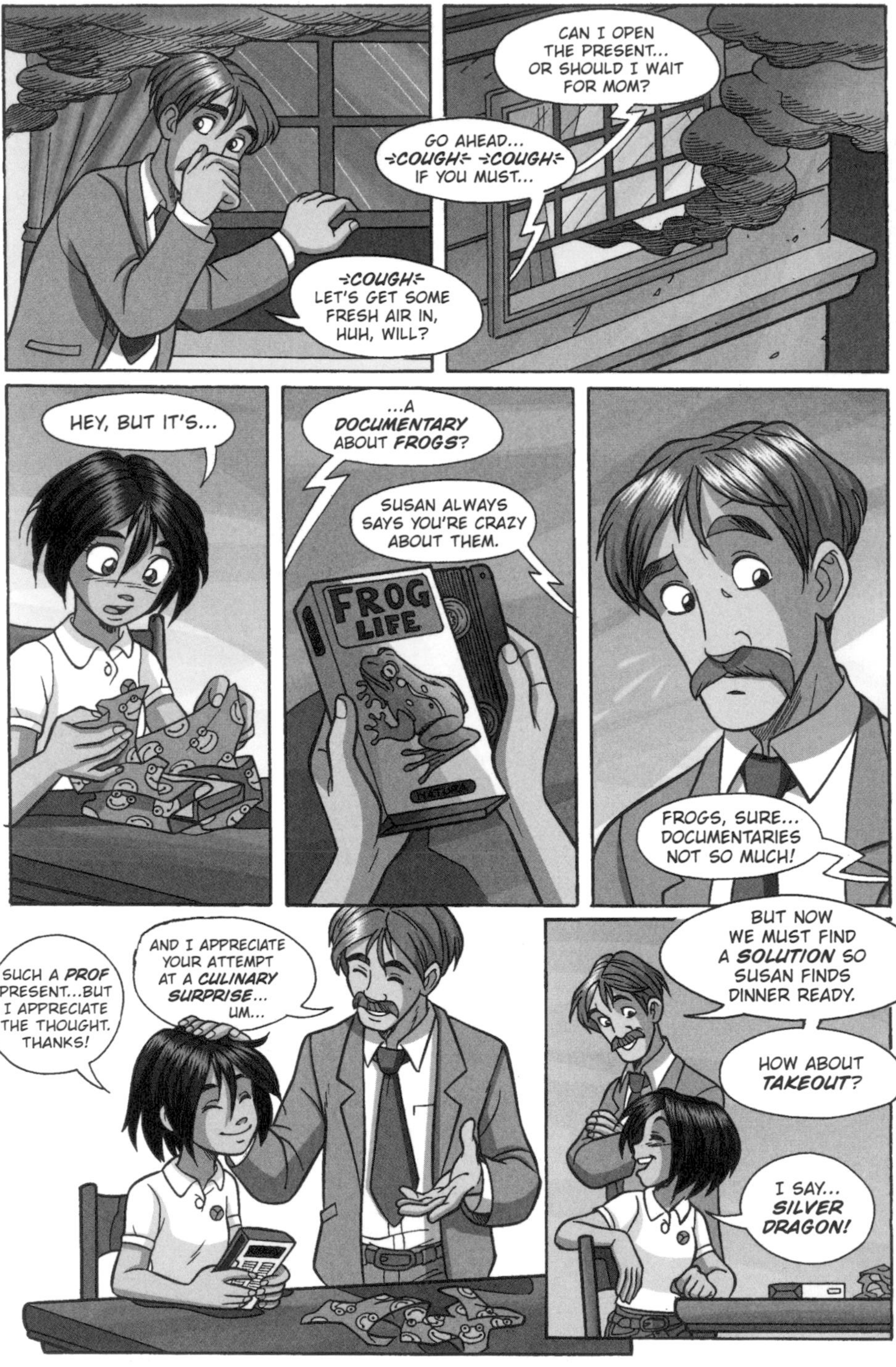

=COUGH=
LET'S GET SOME FRESH AIR IN, HUH, WILL?
CAN I OPEN THE PRESENT... OR SHOULD I WAIT FOR MOM?
GO AHEAD... =COUGH= =COUGH= IF YOU MUST...
HEY, BUT IT'S...
...A DOCUMENTARY ABOUT FROGS?
SUSAN ALWAYS SAYS YOU'RE CRAZY ABOUT THEM.
FROG LIFE
FROGS, SURE... DOCUMENTARIES NOT SO MUCH!
SUCH A PROF PRESENT...BUT I APPRECIATE THE THOUGHT. THANKS!
AND I APPRECIATE YOUR ATTEMPT AT A CULINARY SURPRISE... UM...
BUT NOW WE MUST FIND A SOLUTION SO SUSAN FINDS DINNER READY.
HOW ABOUT TAKEOUT?
I SAY... SILVER DRAGON!

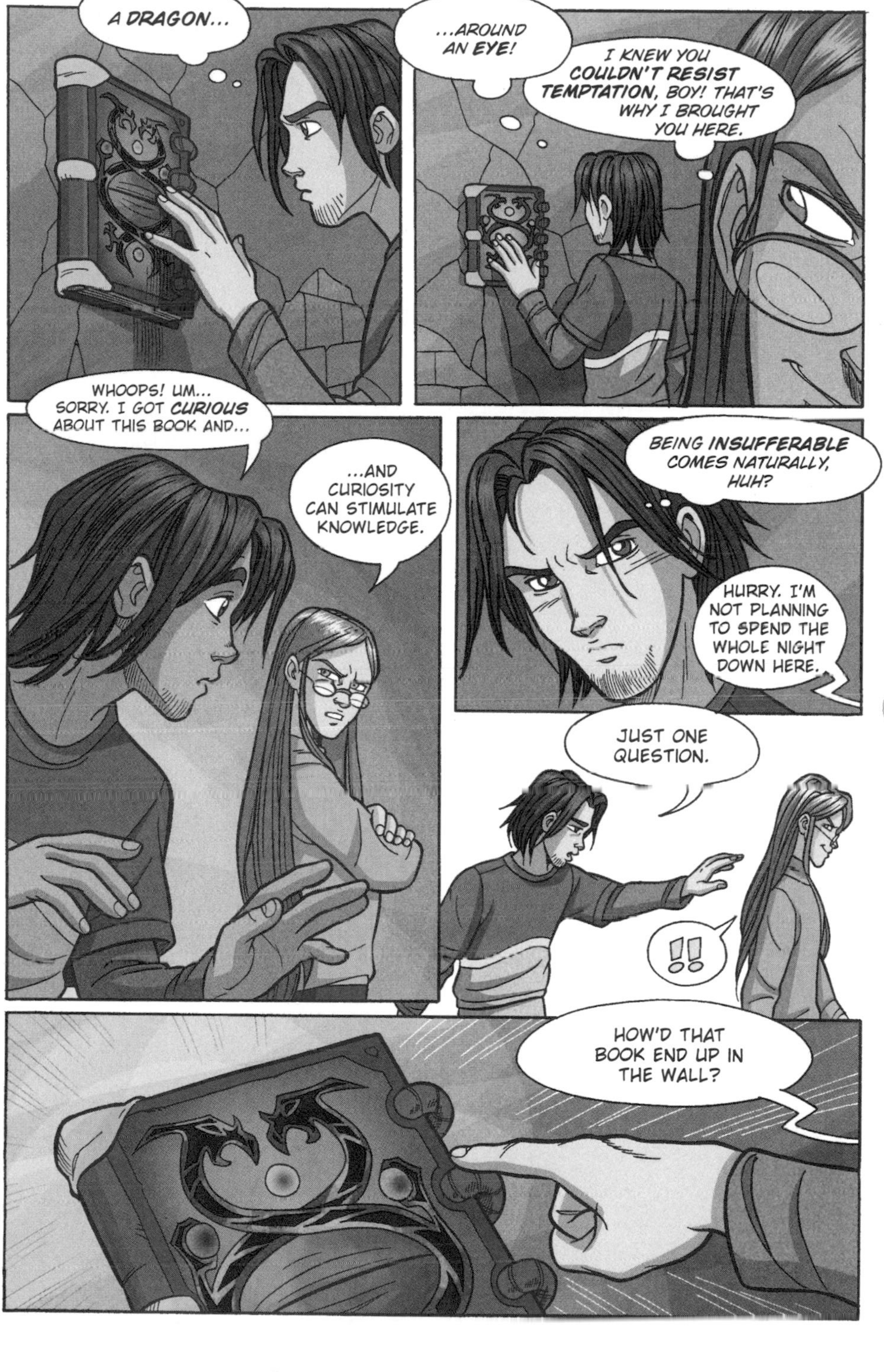

A DRAGON...
...AROUND AN EYE!
I KNEW YOU COULDN'T RESIST TEMPTATION, BOY! THAT'S WHY I BROUGHT YOU HERE.
WHOOPS! UM... SORRY. I GOT CURIOUS ABOUT THIS BOOK AND...
...AND CURIOSITY CAN STIMULATE KNOWLEDGE.
BEING INSUFFERABLE COMES NATURALLY, HUH?
HURRY. I'M NOT PLANNING TO SPEND THE WHOLE NIGHT DOWN HERE.
JUST ONE QUESTION.
!!
HOW'D THAT BOOK END UP IN THE WALL?

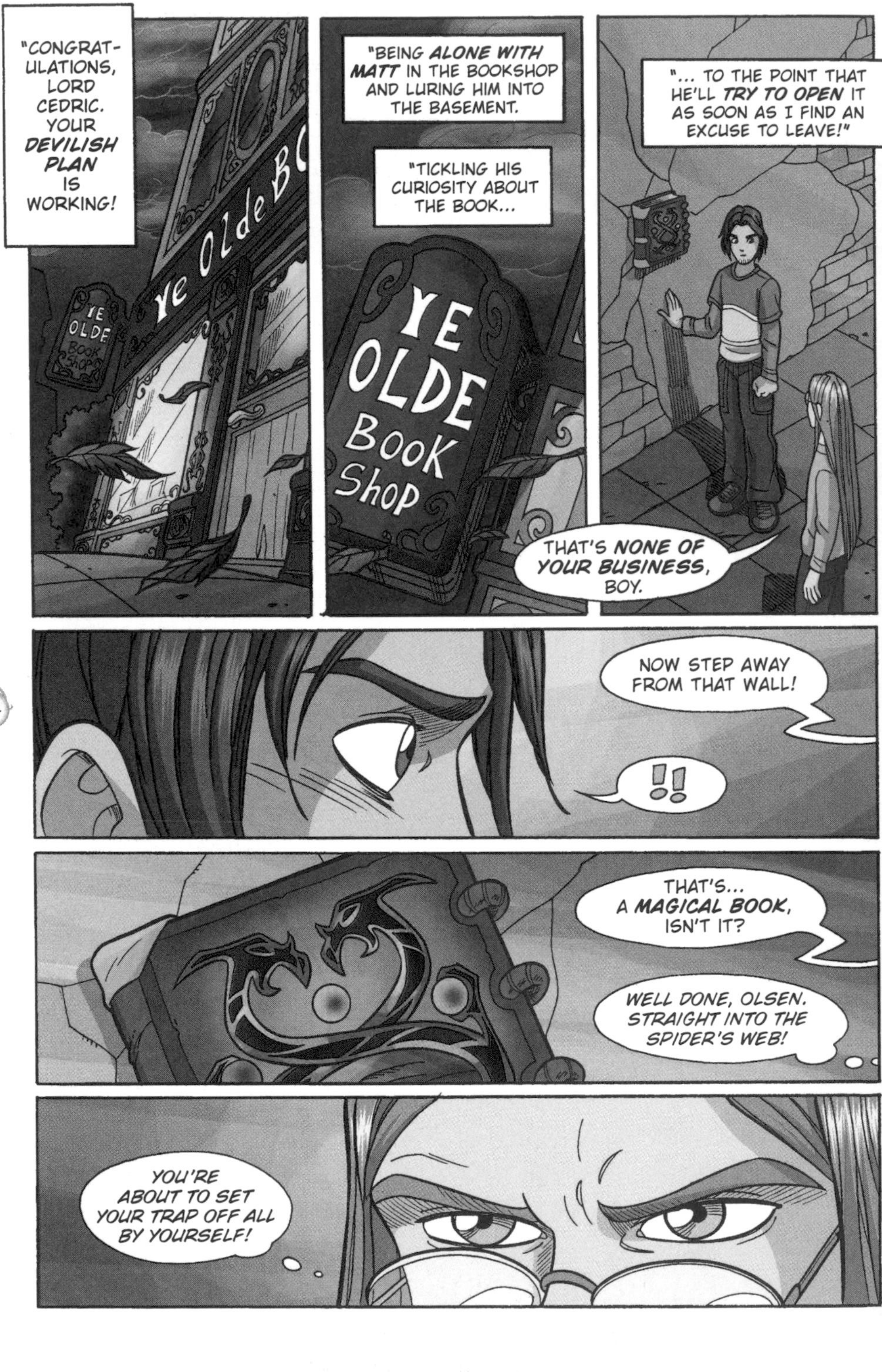
"CONGRATULATIONS, LORD CEDRIC. YOUR DEVILISH PLAN IS WORKING!
YE OLDE BO
YE OLDE BOOK SHOP
"BEING ALONE WITH MATT IN THE BOOKSHOP AND LURING HIM INTO THE BASEMENT.
"TICKLING HIS CURIOSITY ABOUT THE BOOK...
YE OLDE BOOK SHOP
"... TO THE POINT THAT HE'LL TRY TO OPEN IT AS SOON AS I FIND AN EXCUSE TO LEAVE!"
THAT'S NONE OF YOUR BUSINESS, BOY.
NOW STEP AWAY FROM THAT WALL!
!!
THAT'S... A MAGICAL BOOK, ISN'T IT?
WELL DONE, OLSEN. STRAIGHT INTO THE SPIDER'S WEB!
YOU'RE ABOUT TO SET YOUR TRAP OFF ALL BY YOURSELF!

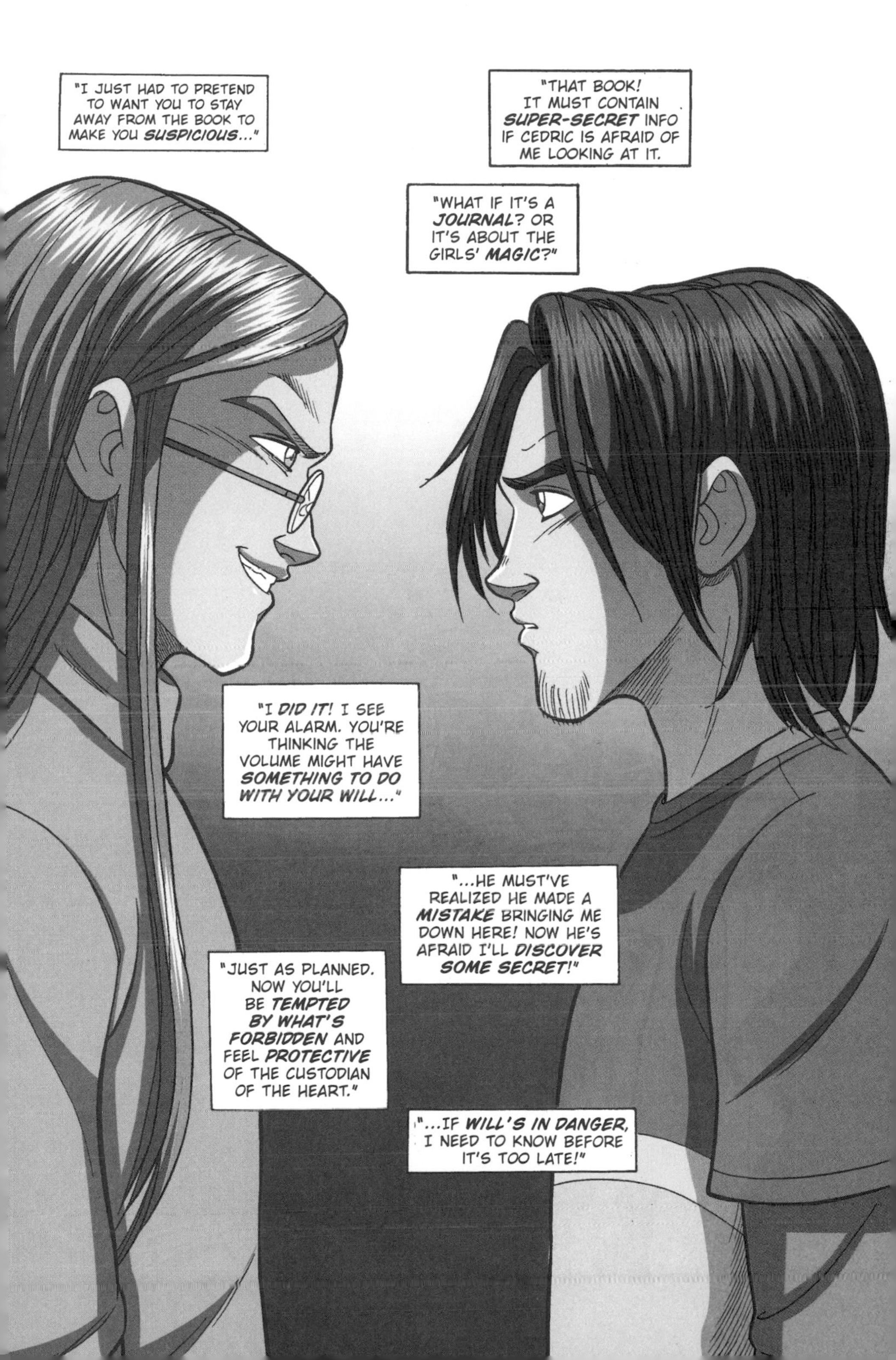
"I JUST HAD TO PRETEND TO WANT YOU TO STAY AWAY FROM THE BOOK TO MAKE YOU *SUSPICIOUS*..."
"THAT BOOK! IT MUST CONTAIN *SUPER-SECRET* INFO IF CEDRIC IS AFRAID OF ME LOOKING AT IT.
"WHAT IF IT'S A *JOURNAL*? OR IT'S ABOUT THE GIRLS' *MAGIC*?"
"I *DID IT*! I SEE YOUR ALARM. YOU'RE THINKING THE VOLUME MIGHT HAVE *SOMETHING TO DO WITH YOUR WILL*..."
"...HE MUST'VE REALIZED HE MADE A *MISTAKE* BRINGING ME DOWN HERE! NOW HE'S AFRAID I'LL *DISCOVER SOME SECRET*!"
"JUST AS PLANNED. NOW YOU'LL BE *TEMPTED BY WHAT'S FORBIDDEN* AND FEEL *PROTECTIVE* OF THE CUSTODIAN OF THE HEART."
"...IF *WILL'S IN DANGER*, I NEED TO KNOW BEFORE IT'S TOO LATE!"

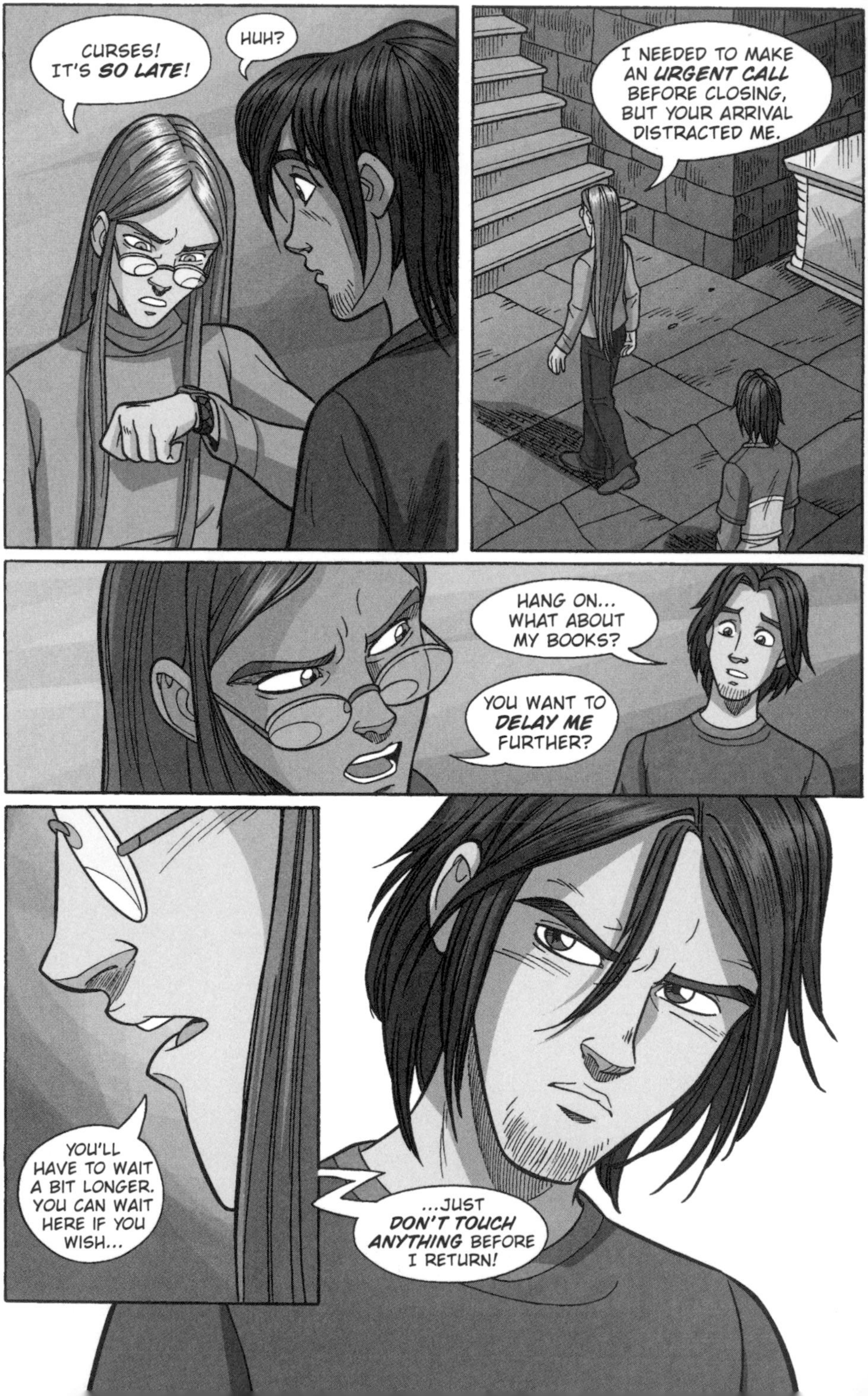
CURSES! IT'S SO LATE!
HUH?
I NEEDED TO MAKE AN URGENT CALL BEFORE CLOSING, BUT YOUR ARRIVAL DISTRACTED ME.
HANG ON... WHAT ABOUT MY BOOKS?
YOU WANT TO DELAY ME FURTHER?
YOU'LL HAVE TO WAIT A BIT LONGER. YOU CAN WAIT HERE IF YOU WISH...
...JUST DON'T TOUCH ANYTHING BEFORE I RETURN!

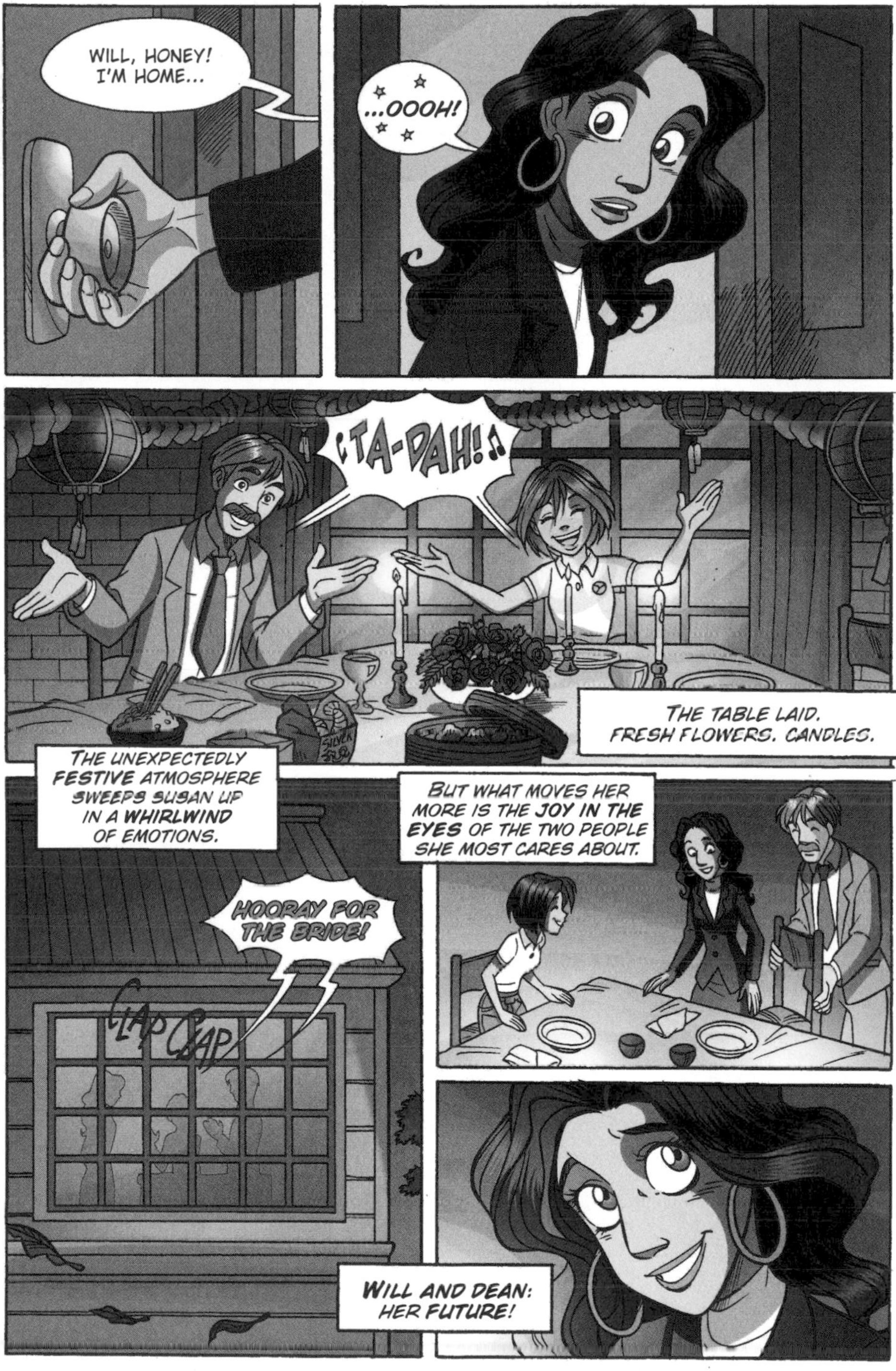
WILL, HONEY! I'M HOME...
...OOOH!
TA-DAH!
THE TABLE LAID. FRESH FLOWERS. CANDLES.
THE UNEXPECTEDLY FESTIVE ATMOSPHERE SWEEPS SUSAN UP IN A WHIRLWIND OF EMOTIONS.
BUT WHAT MOVES HER MORE IS THE JOY IN THE EYES OF THE TWO PEOPLE SHE MOST CARES ABOUT.
HOORAY FOR THE BRIDE!
CLAP CLAP
WILL AND DEAN: HER FUTURE!

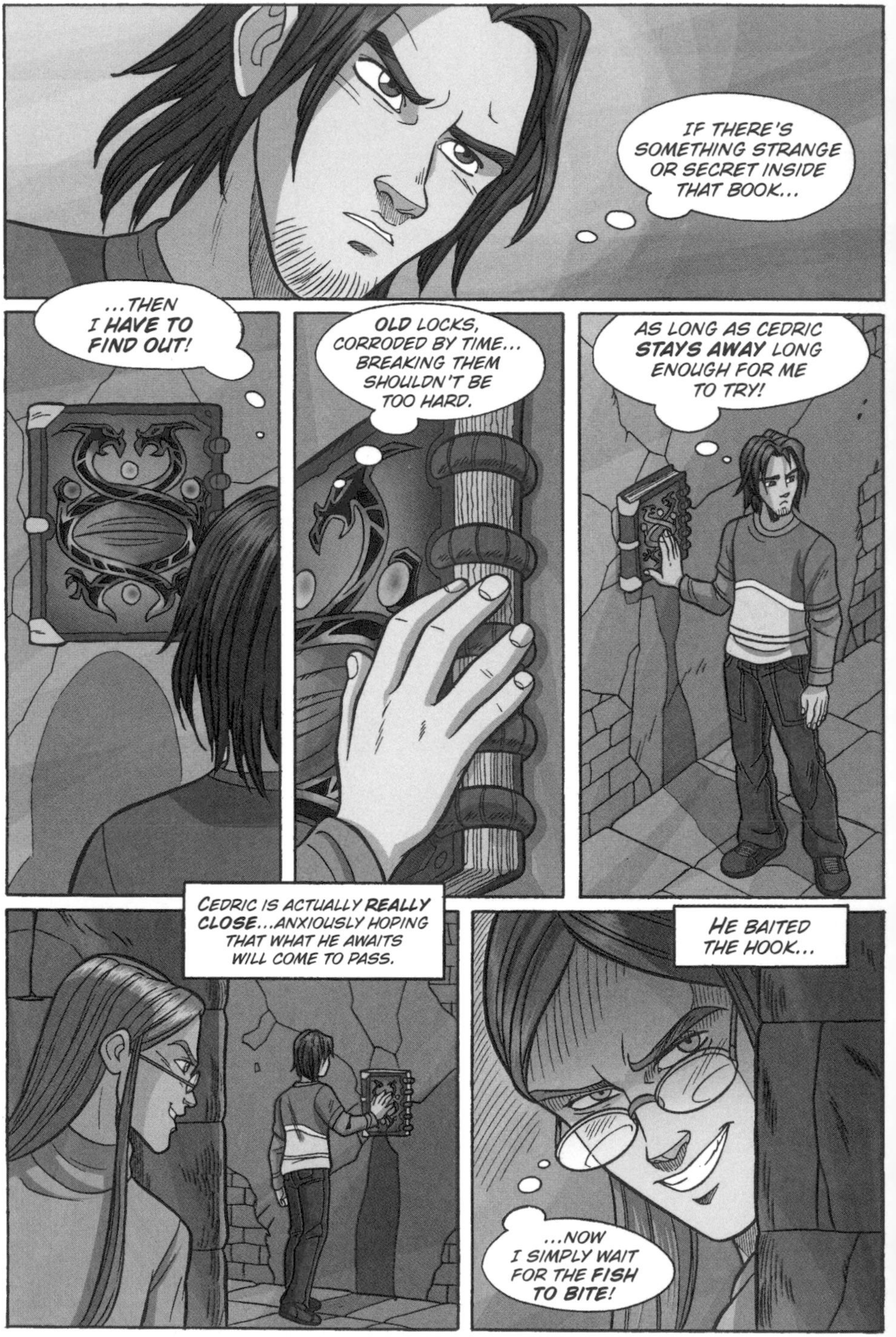
IF THERE'S SOMETHING STRANGE OR SECRET INSIDE THAT BOOK...
...THEN I **HAVE TO FIND OUT**!
OLD LOCKS, CORRODED BY TIME... BREAKING THEM SHOULDN'T BE TOO HARD.
AS LONG AS CEDRIC **STAYS AWAY** LONG ENOUGH FOR ME TO TRY!
CEDRIC IS ACTUALLY **REALLY CLOSE**...ANXIOUSLY HOPING THAT WHAT HE AWAITS WILL COME TO PASS.
HE BAITED THE HOOK...
...NOW I SIMPLY WAIT FOR THE **FISH TO BITE**!

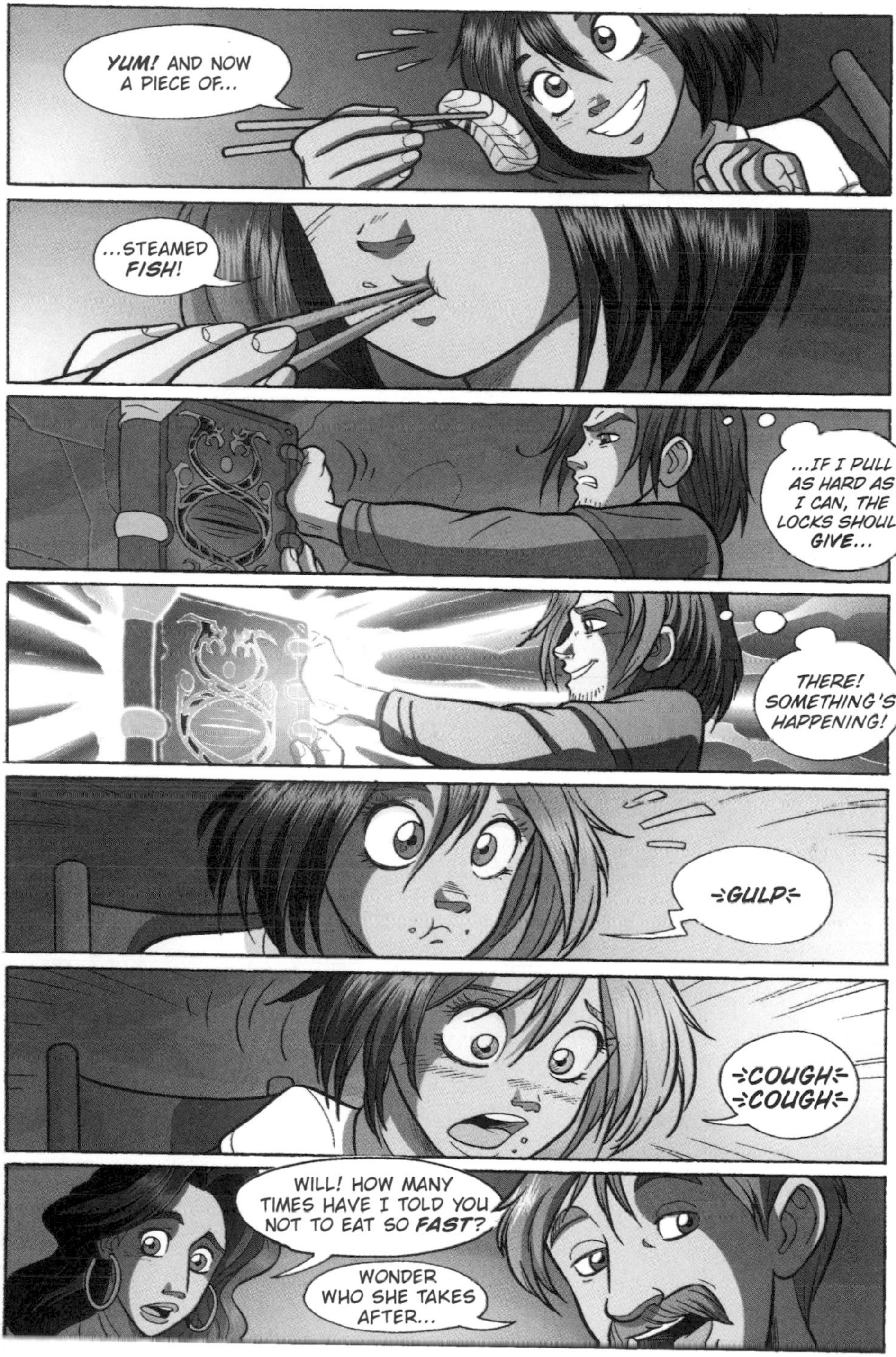
YUM! AND NOW A PIECE OF...
...STEAMED FISH!
...IF I PULL AS HARD AS I CAN, THE LOCKS SHOULD GIVE...
THERE! SOMETHING'S HAPPENING!
GULP
COUGH COUGH
WILL! HOW MANY TIMES HAVE I TOLD YOU NOT TO EAT SO FAST?
WONDER WHO SHE TAKES AFTER...

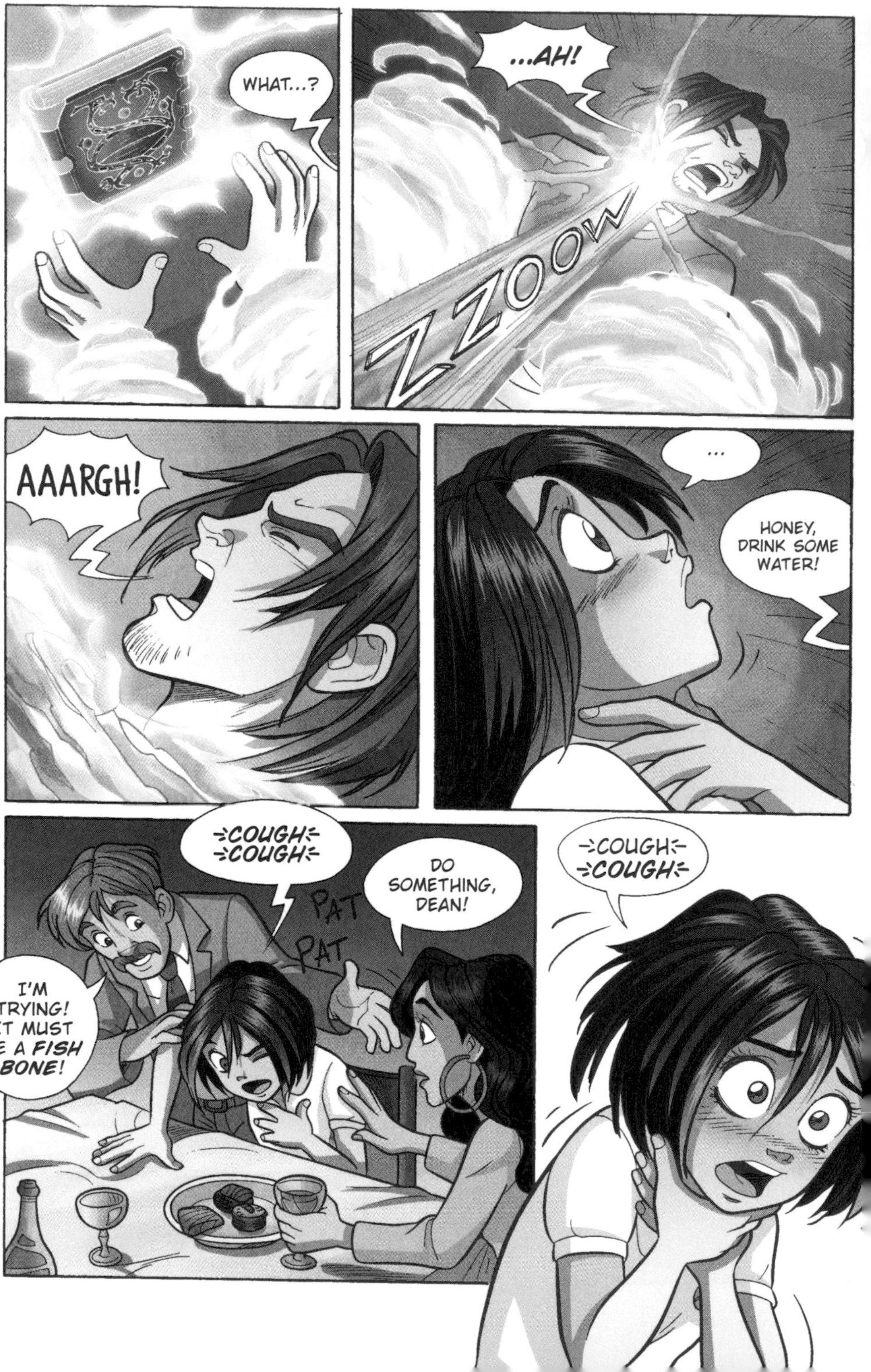
WHAT...?
...AH!
ZZOOOW
AAARGH!
...
HONEY, DRINK SOME WATER!
COUGH COUGH
PAT PAT
DO SOMETHING, DEAN!
I'M TRYING! IT MUST BE A FISH BONE!
COUGH COUGH

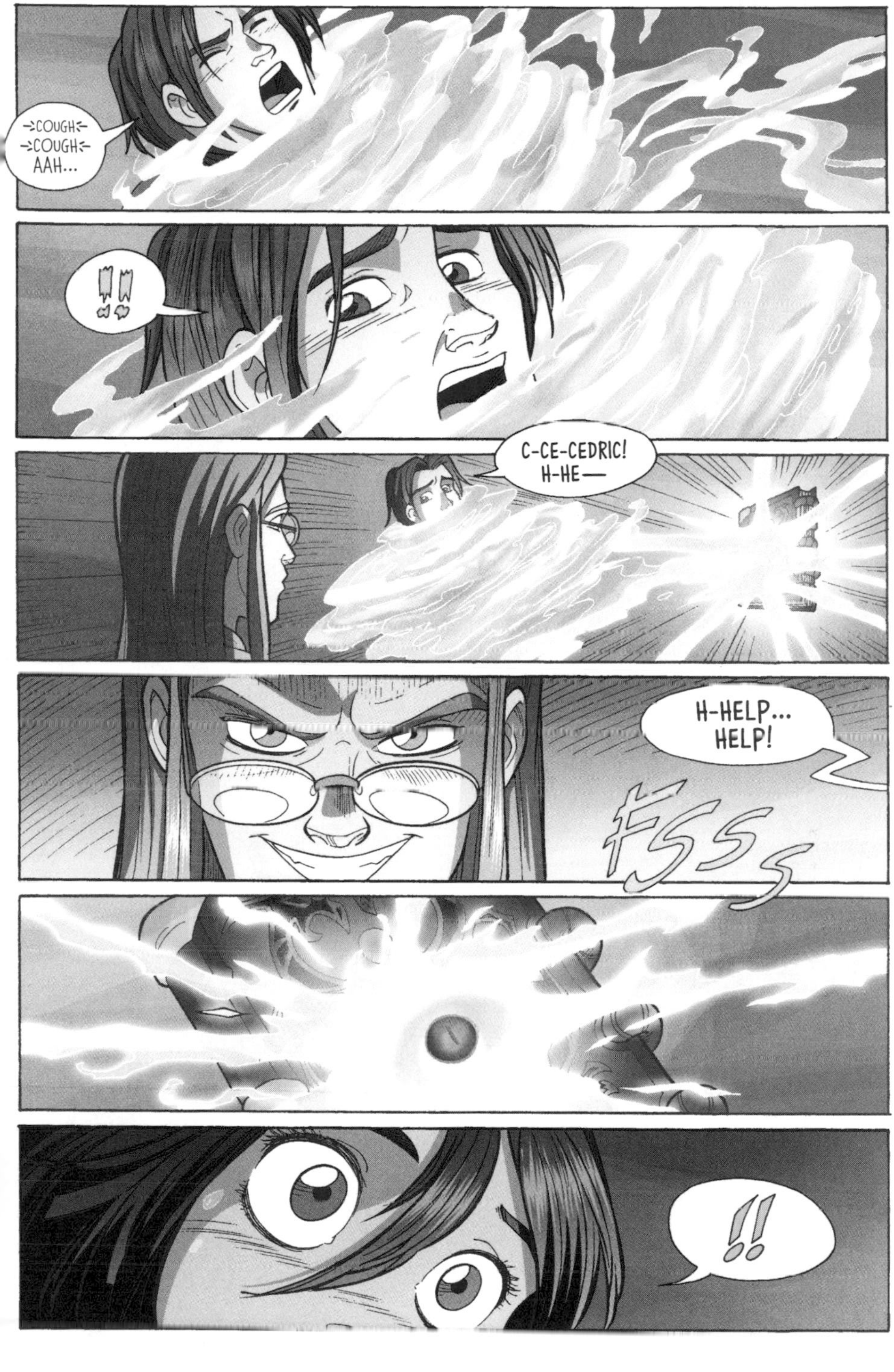

COUGH
COUGH
AAH...
!!
C-CE-CEDRIC! H-HE—
H-HELP... HELP!
FSSS
!!

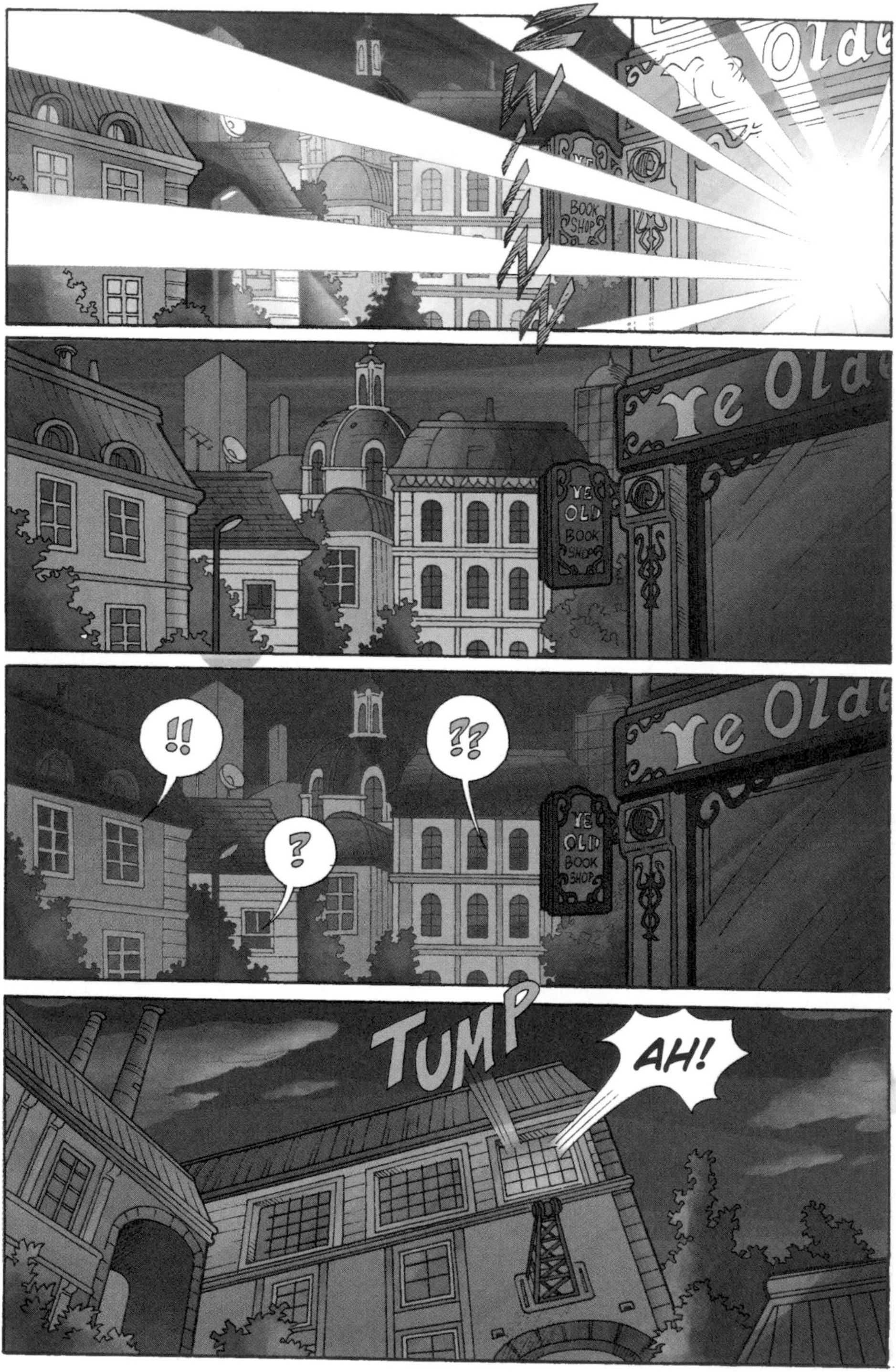
ZWIINN
BOOK SHOP
Ye Old
YE OLD BOOK SHOP
!!
??
?
TUMP
AH!

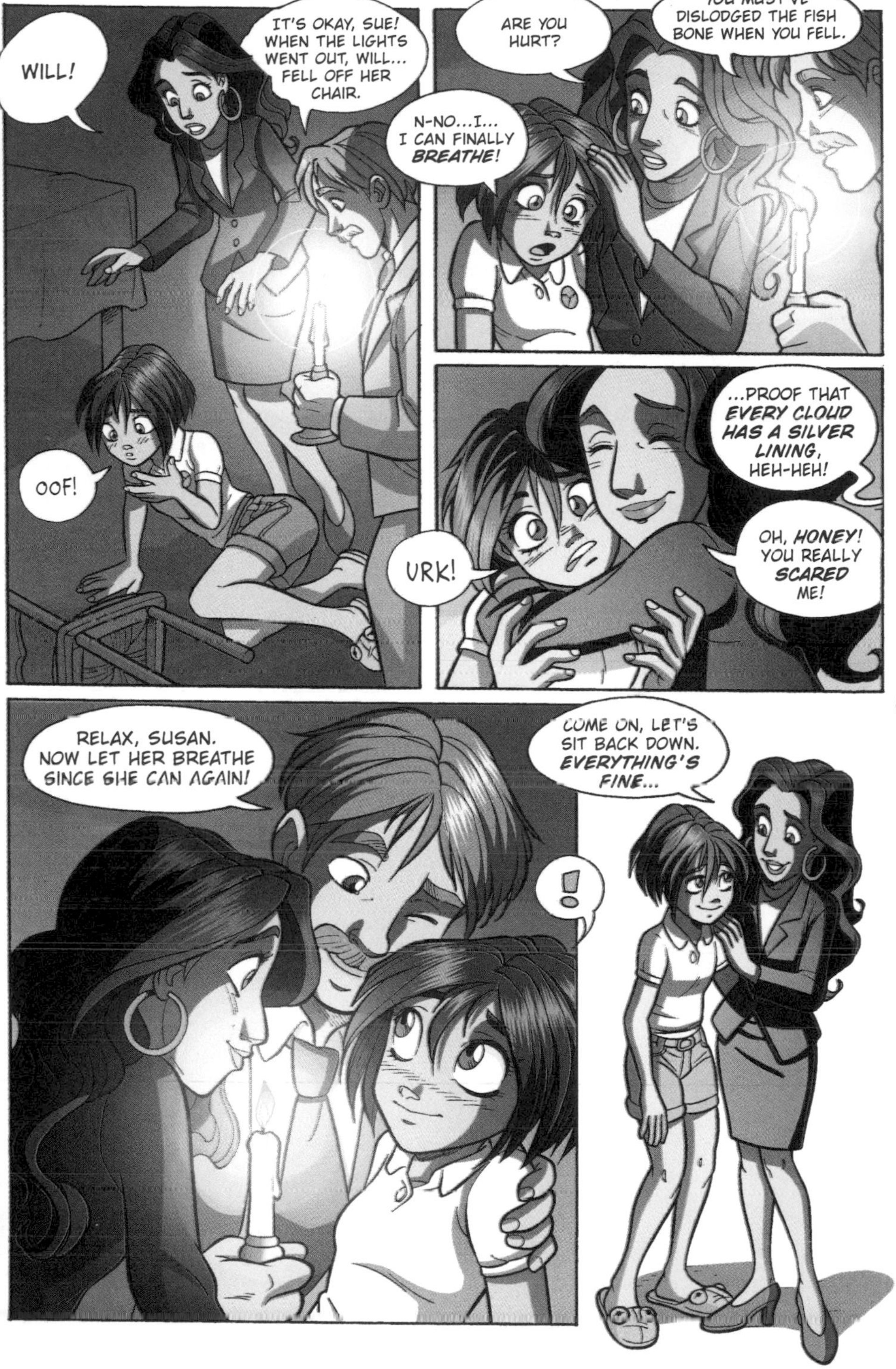
WILL!
IT'S OKAY, SUE! WHEN THE LIGHTS WENT OUT, WILL... FELL OFF HER CHAIR.
OOF!
ARE YOU HURT?
YOU MUST'VE DISLODGED THE FISH BONE WHEN YOU FELL.
N-NO...I... I CAN FINALLY BREATHE!
...PROOF THAT EVERY CLOUD HAS A SILVER LINING, HEH-HEH!
OH, HONEY! YOU REALLY SCARED ME!
URK!
RELAX, SUSAN. NOW LET HER BREATHE SINCE SHE CAN AGAIN!
COME ON, LET'S SIT BACK DOWN. EVERYTHING'S FINE...
!

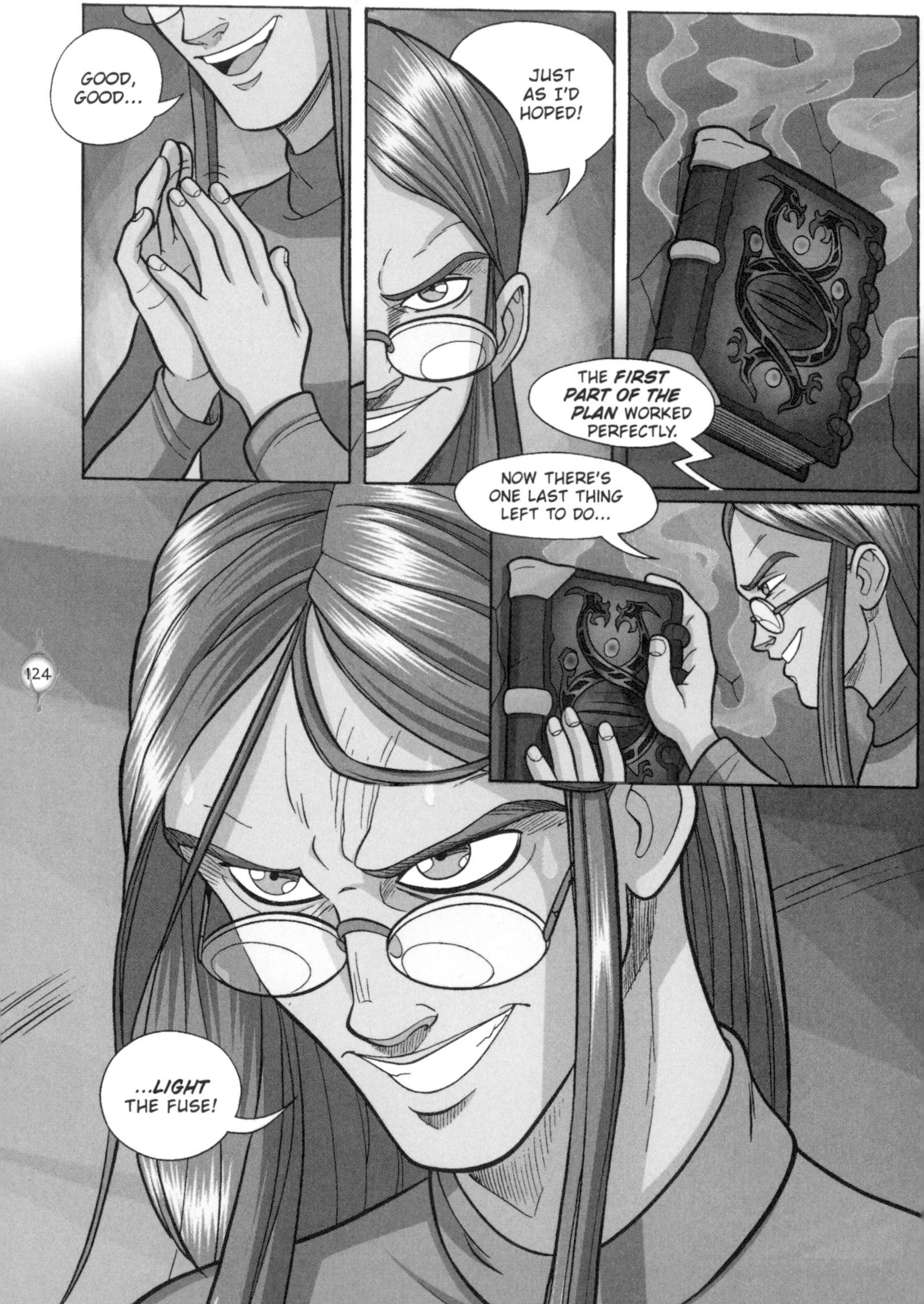
GOOD, GOOD...
JUST AS I'D HOPED!
THE **FIRST PART OF THE PLAN** WORKED PERFECTLY.
NOW THERE'S ONE LAST THING LEFT TO DO...
...**LIGHT** THE FUSE!

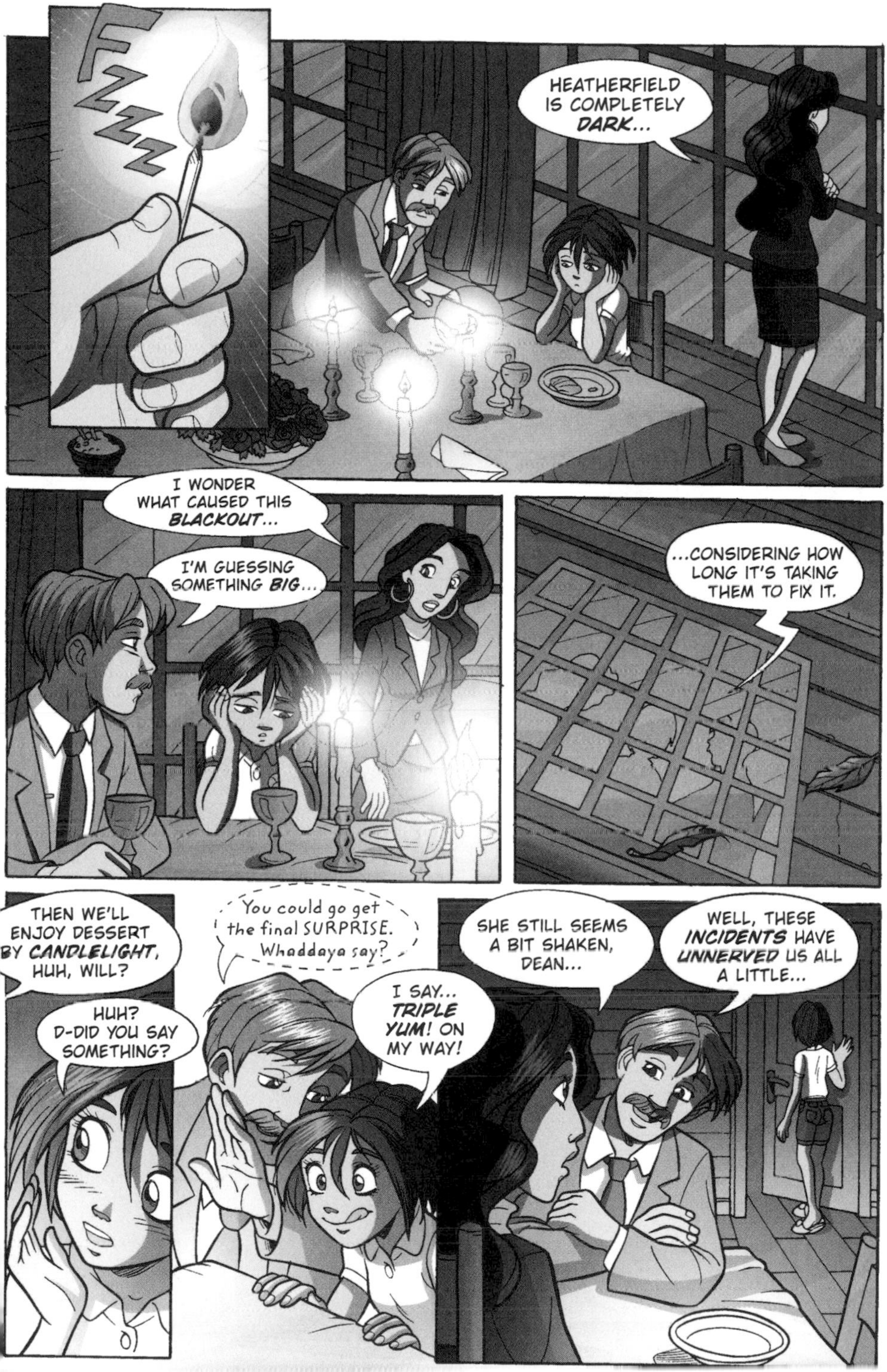
FZZZ
HEATHERFIELD IS COMPLETELY DARK...
I WONDER WHAT CAUSED THIS BLACKOUT...
I'M GUESSING SOMETHING BIG...
...CONSIDERING HOW LONG IT'S TAKING THEM TO FIX IT.
THEN WE'LL ENJOY DESSERT BY CANDLELIGHT, HUH, WILL?
HUH? D-DID YOU SAY SOMETHING?
You could go get the final SURPRISE. Whaddaya say?
I SAY... TRIPLE YUM! ON MY WAY!
SHE STILL SEEMS A BIT SHAKEN, DEAN...
WELL, THESE INCIDENTS HAVE UNNERVED US ALL A LITTLE...

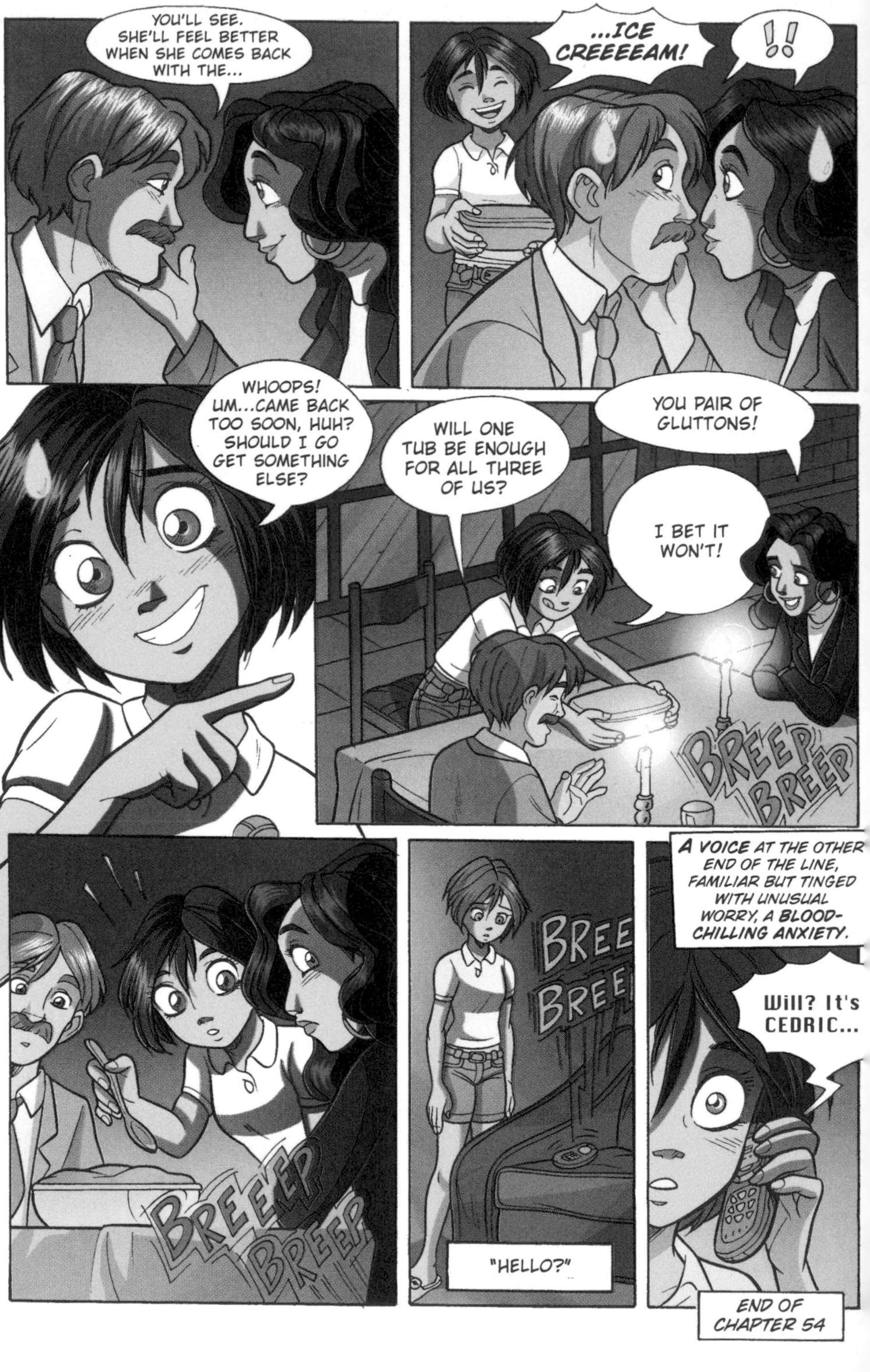
YOU'LL SEE. SHE'LL FEEL BETTER WHEN SHE COMES BACK WITH THE...
...ICE CREEEEAM!
!!
WHOOPS! UM...CAME BACK TOO SOON, HUH? SHOULD I GO GET SOMETHING ELSE?
WILL ONE TUB BE ENOUGH FOR ALL THREE OF US?
YOU PAIR OF GLUTTONS!
I BET IT WON'T!
BREEP BREEP
BREEEP BREEP
BREE BREE
"HELLO?"
A VOICE AT THE OTHER END OF THE LINE, FAMILIAR BUT TINGED WITH UNUSUAL WORRY, A BLOOD-CHILLING ANXIETY.
Will? It's CEDRIC...
END OF CHAPTER 54

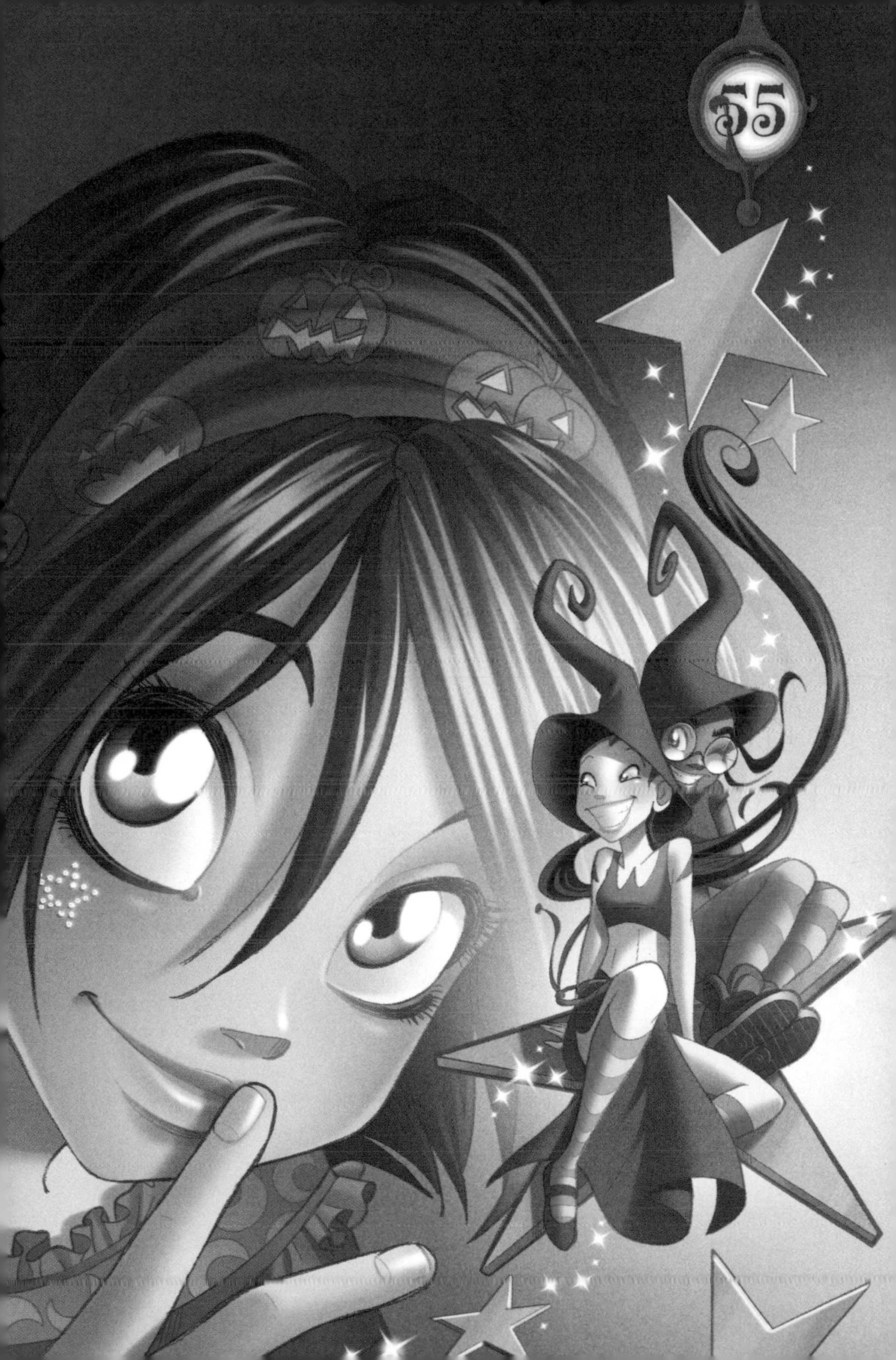
55

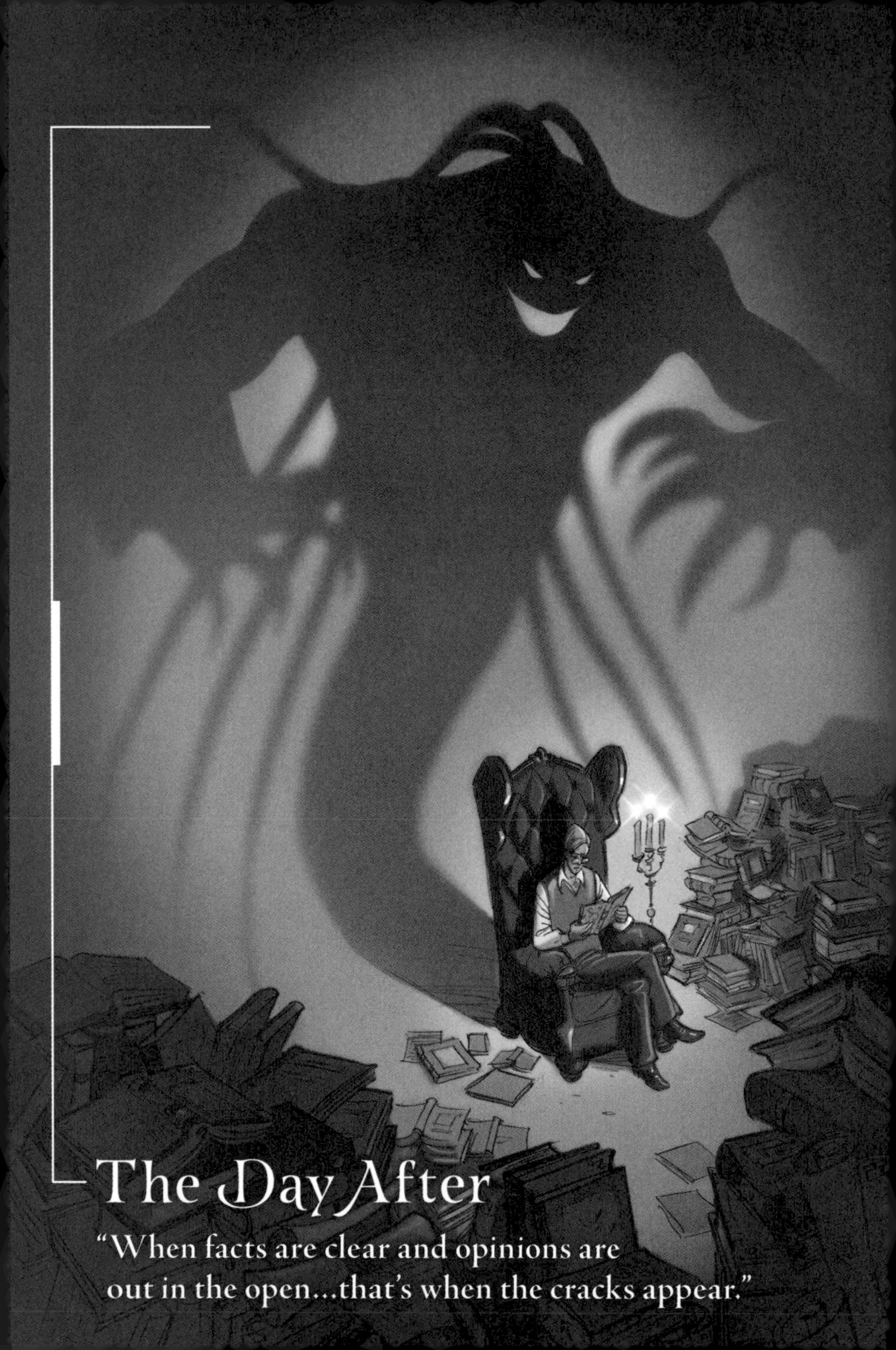

The Day After

"When facts are clear and opinions are out in the open…that's when the cracks appear."

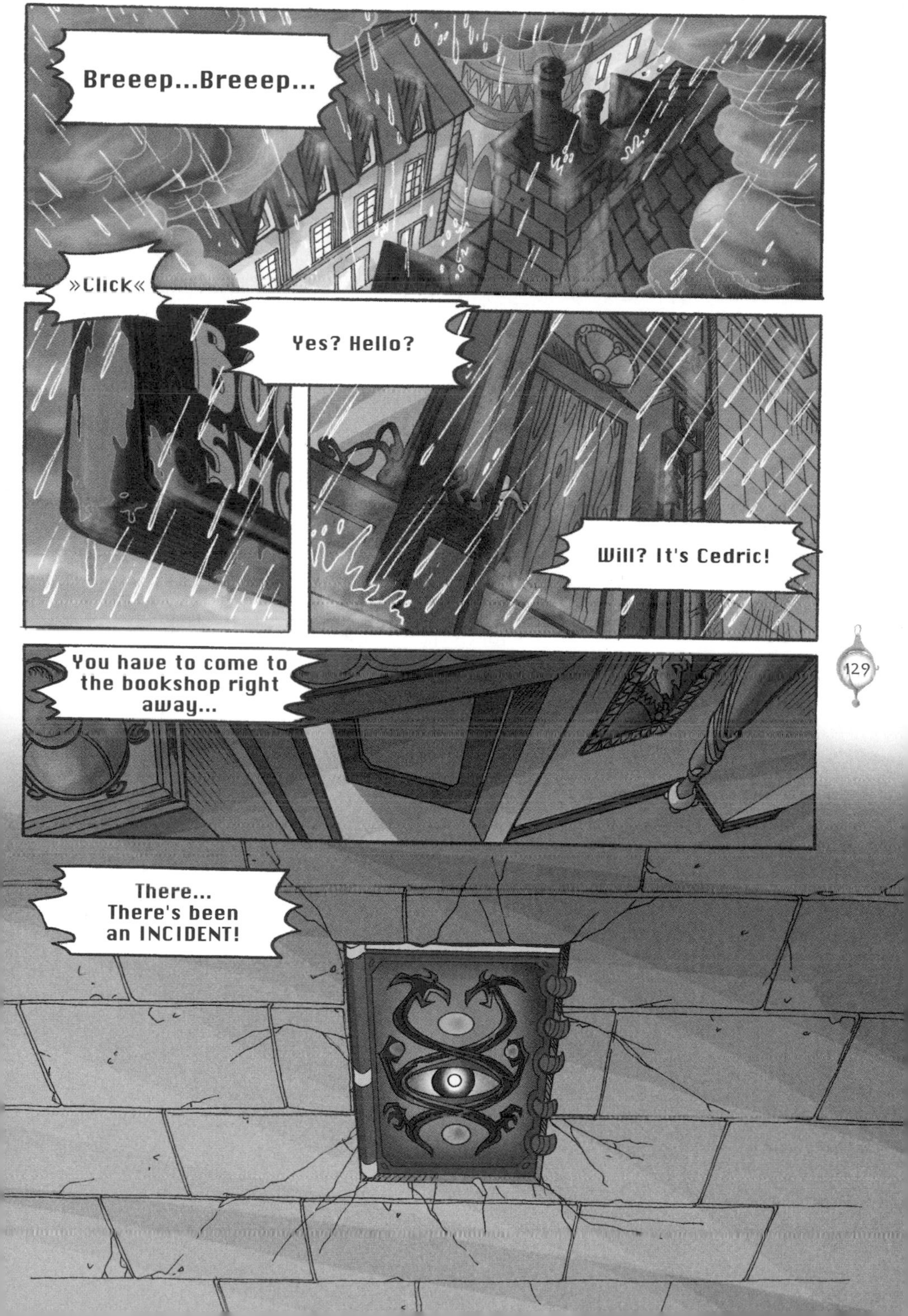
Breeep...Breeep...
»Click«
Yes? Hello?
Will? It's Cedric!
You have to come to the bookshop right away...
There... There's been an INCIDENT!

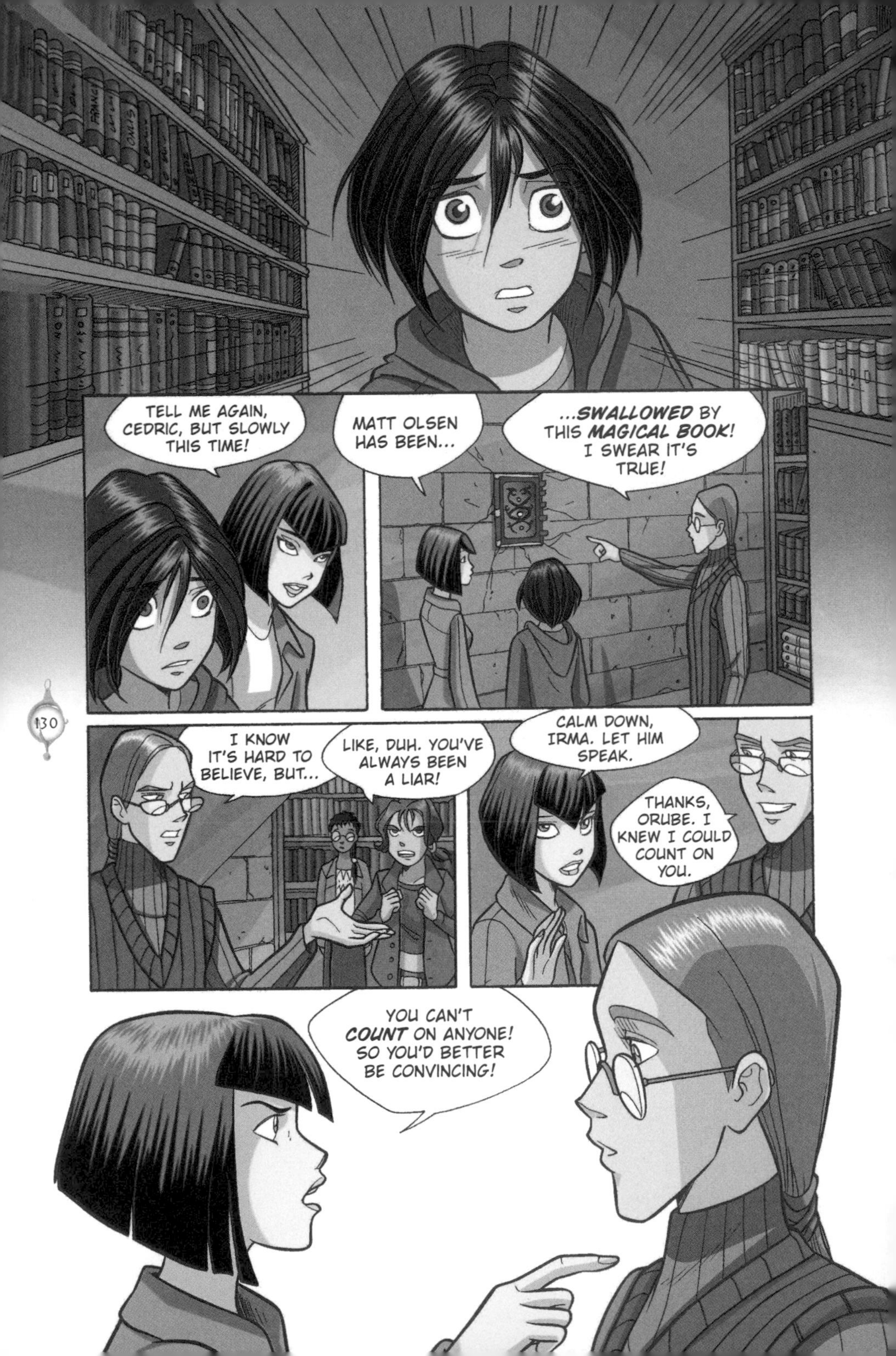
TELL ME AGAIN, CEDRIC, BUT SLOWLY THIS TIME!
MATT OLSEN HAS BEEN...
...SWALLOWED BY THIS MAGICAL BOOK! I SWEAR IT'S TRUE!
I KNOW IT'S HARD TO BELIEVE, BUT...
LIKE, DUH. YOU'VE ALWAYS BEEN A LIAR!
CALM DOWN, IRMA. LET HIM SPEAK.
THANKS, ORUBE. I KNEW I COULD COUNT ON YOU.
YOU CAN'T COUNT ON ANYONE! SO YOU'D BETTER BE CONVINCING!

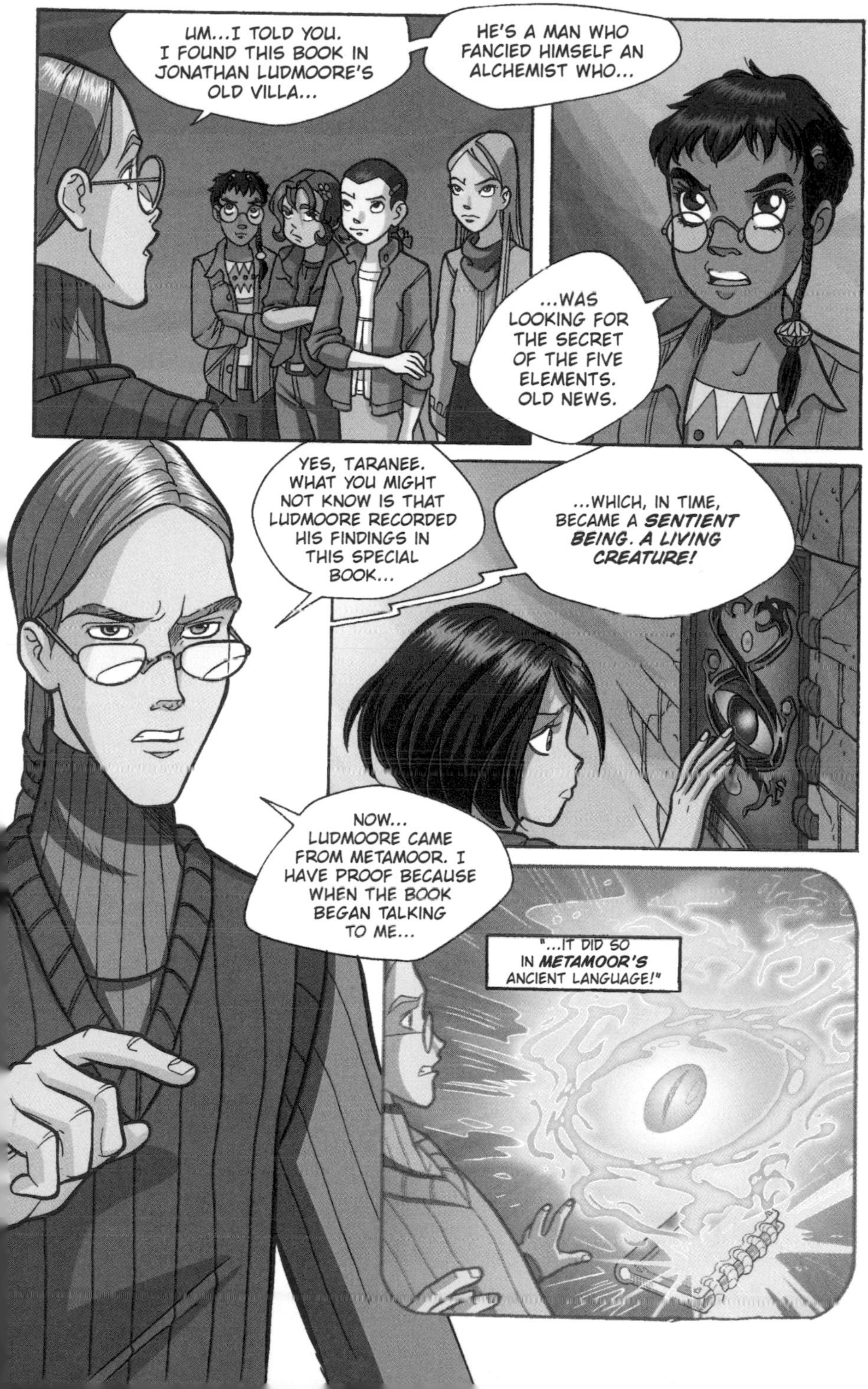
UM...I TOLD YOU. I FOUND THIS BOOK IN JONATHAN LUDMOORE'S OLD VILLA...
HE'S A MAN WHO FANCIED HIMSELF AN ALCHEMIST WHO...
...WAS LOOKING FOR THE SECRET OF THE FIVE ELEMENTS. OLD NEWS.
YES, TARANEE. WHAT YOU MIGHT NOT KNOW IS THAT LUDMOORE RECORDED HIS FINDINGS IN THIS SPECIAL BOOK...
...WHICH, IN TIME, BECAME A ***SENTIENT BEING. A LIVING CREATURE!***
NOW... LUDMOORE CAME FROM METAMOOR. I HAVE PROOF BECAUSE WHEN THE BOOK BEGAN TALKING TO ME...
"...IT DID SO IN ***METAMOOR'S*** ANCIENT LANGUAGE!"

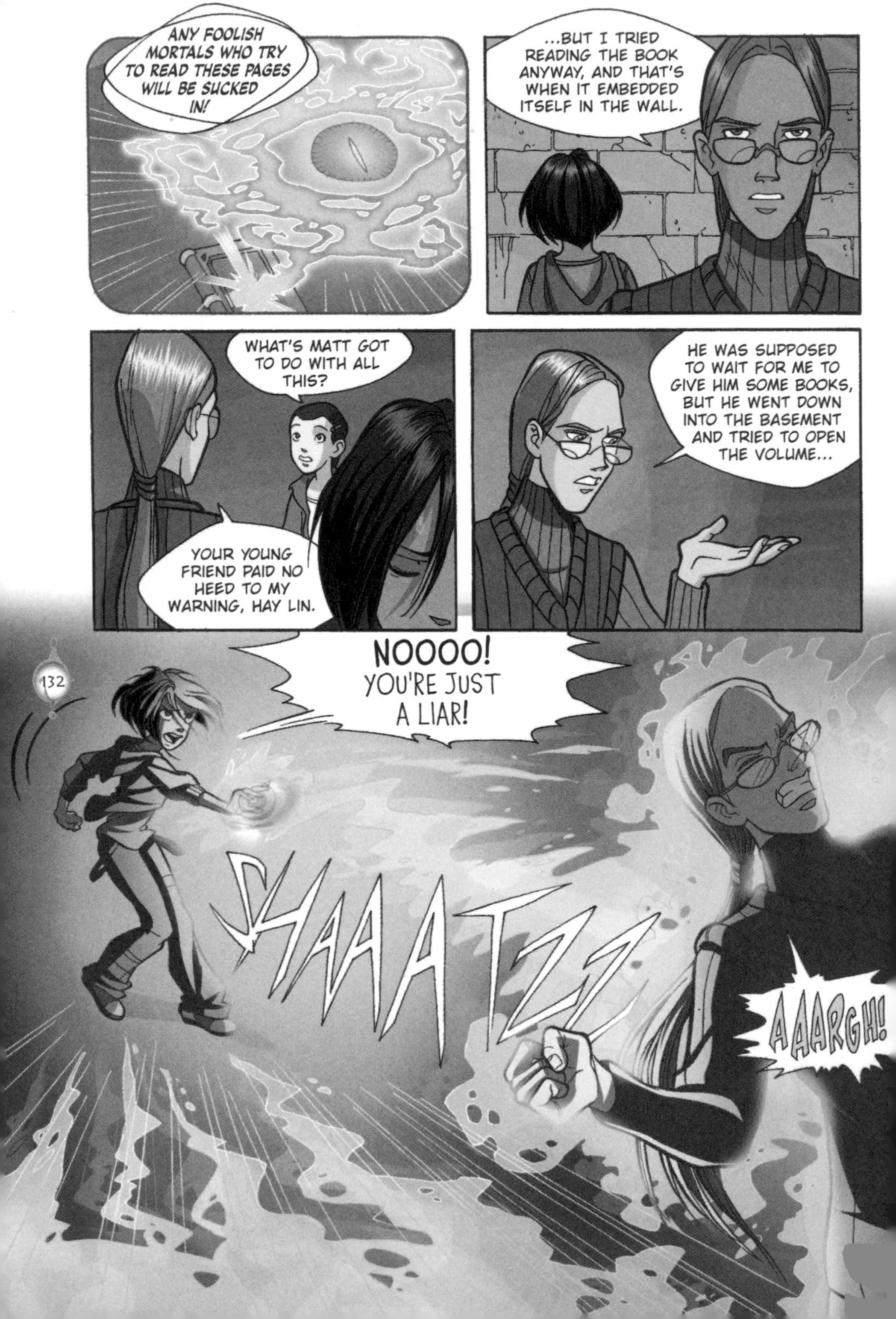
ANY FOOLISH MORTALS WHO TRY TO READ THESE PAGES WILL BE SUCKED IN!
...BUT I TRIED READING THE BOOK ANYWAY, AND THAT'S WHEN IT EMBEDDED ITSELF IN THE WALL.
WHAT'S MATT GOT TO DO WITH ALL THIS?
YOUR YOUNG FRIEND PAID NO HEED TO MY WARNING, HAY LIN.
HE WAS SUPPOSED TO WAIT FOR ME TO GIVE HIM SOME BOOKS, BUT HE WENT DOWN INTO THE BASEMENT AND TRIED TO OPEN THE VOLUME...
NOOOO! YOU'RE JUST A LIAR!
SHAAATZZ
AAARGH!

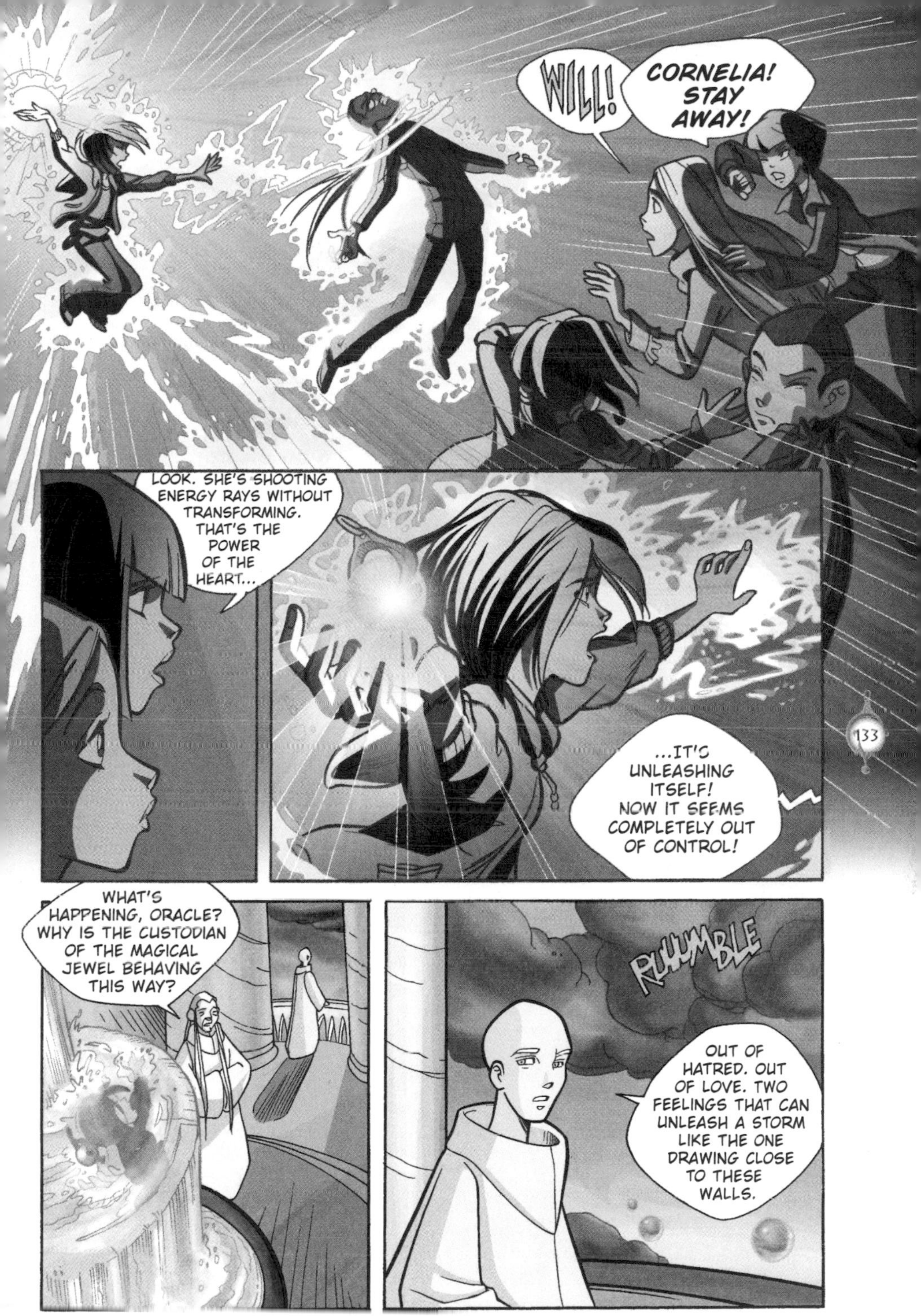
WILL!
CORNELIA! STAY AWAY!
LOOK. SHE'S SHOOTING ENERGY RAYS WITHOUT TRANSFORMING. THAT'S THE POWER OF THE HEART...
...IT'S UNLEASHING ITSELF! NOW IT SEEMS COMPLETELY OUT OF CONTROL!
WHAT'S HAPPENING, ORACLE? WHY IS THE CUSTODIAN OF THE MAGICAL JEWEL BEHAVING THIS WAY?
RUHUMBLE
OUT OF HATRED. OUT OF LOVE. TWO FEELINGS THAT CAN UNLEASH A STORM LIKE THE ONE DRAWING CLOSE TO THESE WALLS.

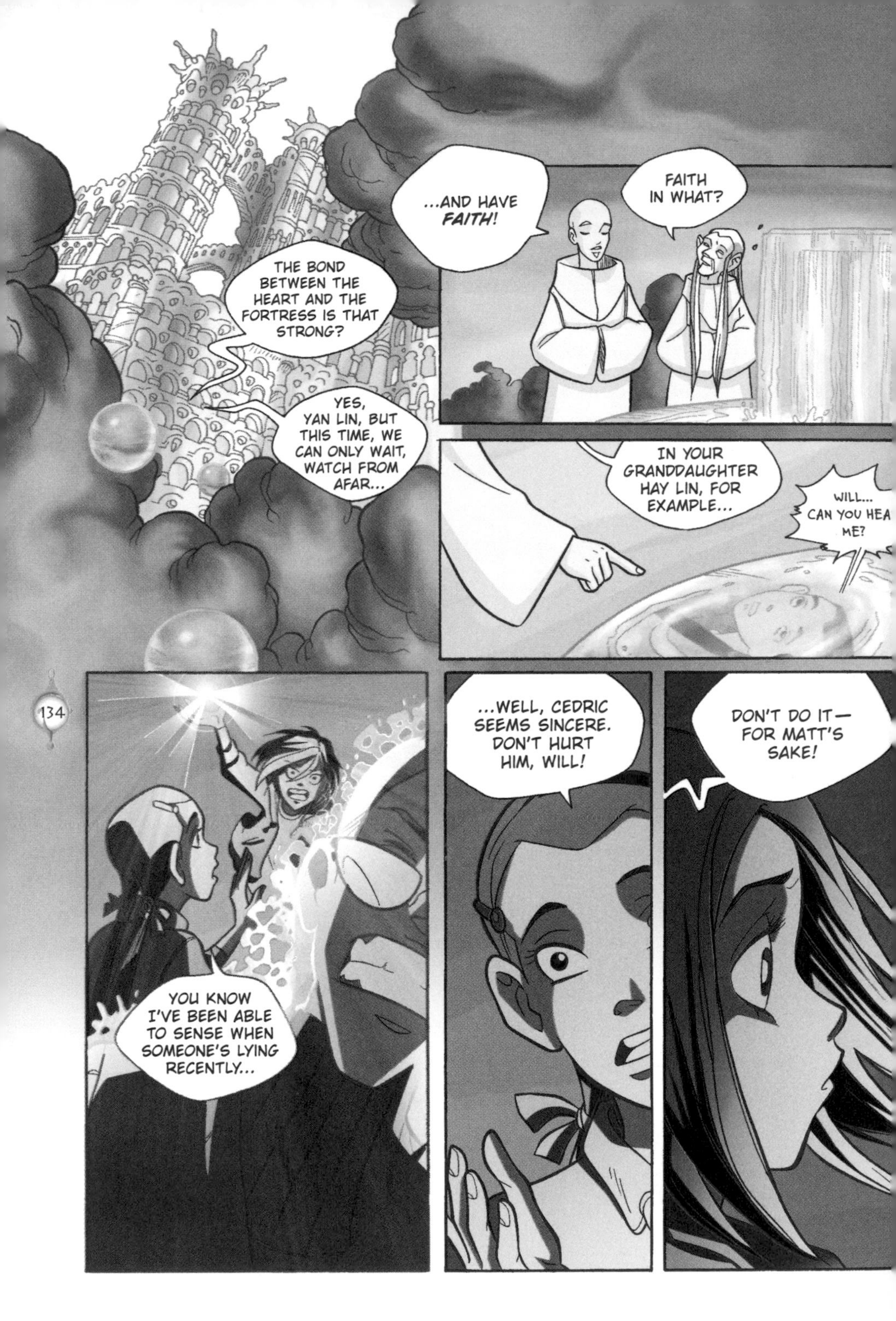
THE BOND BETWEEN THE HEART AND THE FORTRESS IS THAT STRONG?
YES, YAN LIN, BUT THIS TIME, WE CAN ONLY WAIT, WATCH FROM AFAR...
...AND HAVE *FAITH*!
FAITH IN WHAT?
IN YOUR GRANDDAUGHTER HAY LIN, FOR EXAMPLE...
WILL... CAN YOU HEA ME?
YOU KNOW I'VE BEEN ABLE TO SENSE WHEN SOMEONE'S LYING RECENTLY...
...WELL, CEDRIC SEEMS SINCERE. DON'T HURT HIM, WILL!
DON'T DO IT— FOR MATT'S SAKE!

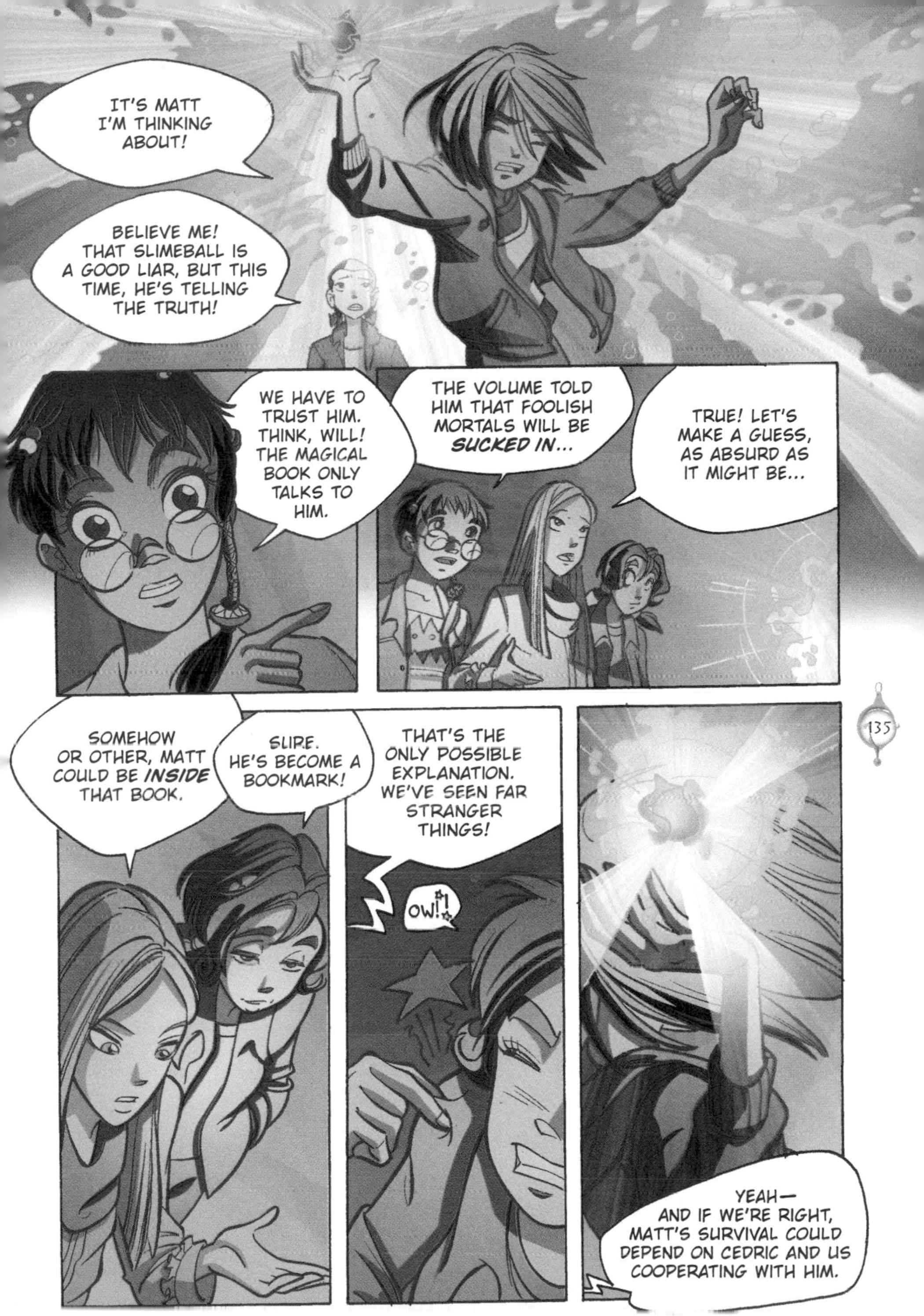
IT'S MATT I'M THINKING ABOUT!
BELIEVE ME! THAT SLIMEBALL IS A GOOD LIAR, BUT THIS TIME, HE'S TELLING THE TRUTH!
WE HAVE TO TRUST HIM. THINK, WILL! THE MAGICAL BOOK ONLY TALKS TO HIM.
THE VOLUME TOLD HIM THAT FOOLISH MORTALS WILL BE SUCKED IN...
TRUE! LET'S MAKE A GUESS, AS ABSURD AS IT MIGHT BE...
SOMEHOW OR OTHER, MATT COULD BE INSIDE THAT BOOK.
SURE. HE'S BECOME A BOOKMARK!
THAT'S THE ONLY POSSIBLE EXPLANATION. WE'VE SEEN FAR STRANGER THINGS!
OW!
YEAH— AND IF WE'RE RIGHT, MATT'S SURVIVAL COULD DEPEND ON CEDRIC AND US COOPERATING WITH HIM.

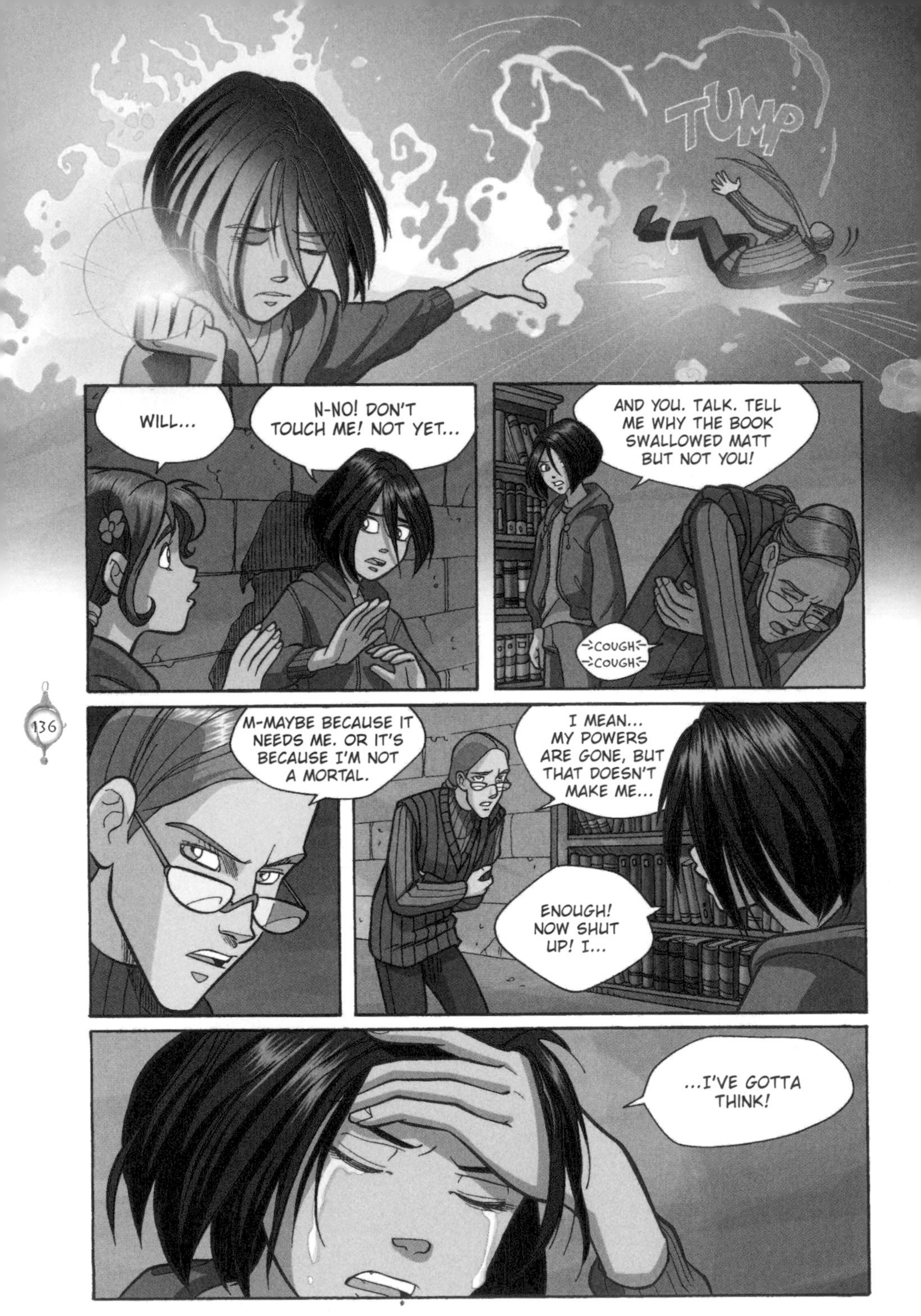
TUMP
WILL...
N-NO! DON'T TOUCH ME! NOT YET...
AND YOU. TALK. TELL ME WHY THE BOOK SWALLOWED MATT BUT NOT YOU!
COUGH COUGH
M-MAYBE BECAUSE IT NEEDS ME. OR IT'S BECAUSE I'M NOT A MORTAL.
I MEAN... MY POWERS ARE GONE, BUT THAT DOESN'T MAKE ME...
ENOUGH! NOW SHUT UP! I...
...I'VE GOTTA THINK!

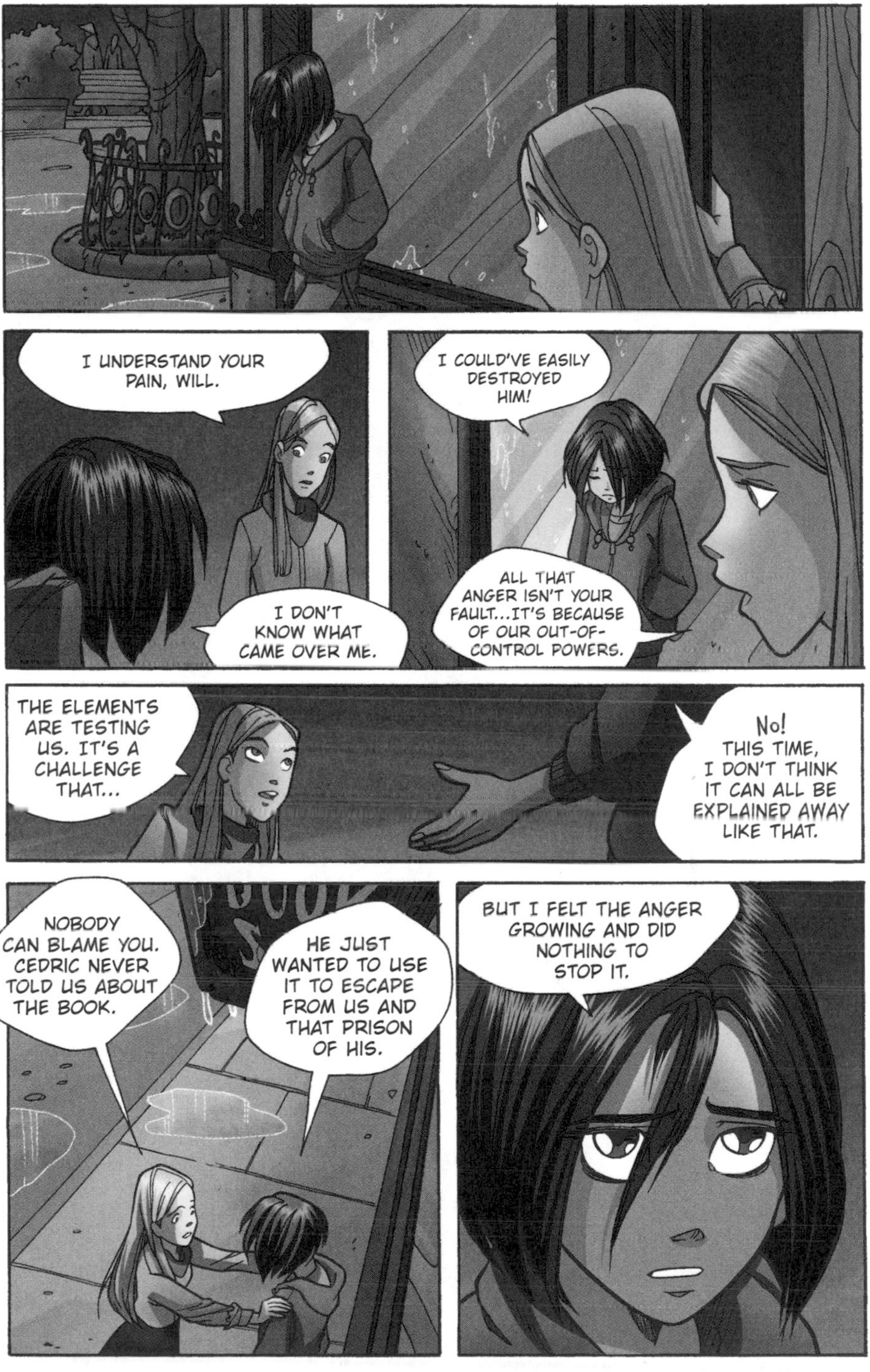

I UNDERSTAND YOUR PAIN, WILL.
I DON'T KNOW WHAT CAME OVER ME.
I COULD'VE EASILY DESTROYED HIM!
ALL THAT ANGER ISN'T YOUR FAULT...IT'S BECAUSE OF OUR OUT-OF-CONTROL POWERS.
THE ELEMENTS ARE TESTING US. IT'S A CHALLENGE THAT...
No! THIS TIME, I DON'T THINK IT CAN ALL BE EXPLAINED AWAY LIKE THAT.
NOBODY CAN BLAME YOU. CEDRIC NEVER TOLD US ABOUT THE BOOK.
HE JUST WANTED TO USE IT TO ESCAPE FROM US AND THAT PRISON OF HIS.
BUT I FELT THE ANGER GROWING AND DID NOTHING TO STOP IT.

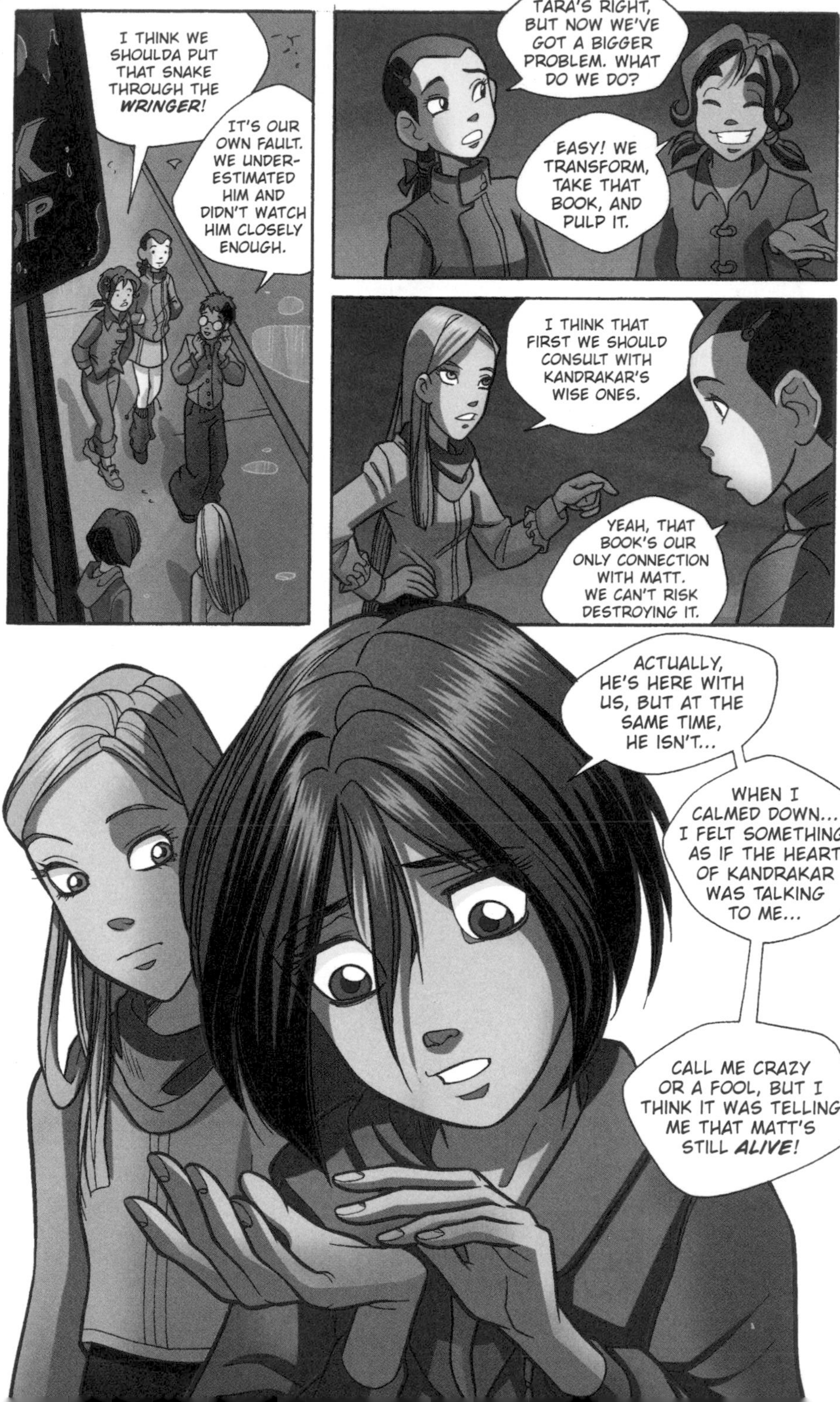
I THINK WE SHOULDA PUT THAT SNAKE THROUGH THE *WRINGER*!
IT'S OUR OWN FAULT. WE UNDER-ESTIMATED HIM AND DIDN'T WATCH HIM CLOSELY ENOUGH.
TARA'S RIGHT, BUT NOW WE'VE GOT A BIGGER PROBLEM. WHAT DO WE DO?
EASY! WE TRANSFORM, TAKE THAT BOOK, AND PULP IT.
I THINK THAT FIRST WE SHOULD CONSULT WITH KANDRAKAR'S WISE ONES.
YEAH, THAT BOOK'S OUR ONLY CONNECTION WITH MATT. WE CAN'T RISK DESTROYING IT.
ACTUALLY, HE'S HERE WITH US, BUT AT THE SAME TIME, HE ISN'T...
WHEN I CALMED DOWN... I FELT SOMETHING. AS IF THE HEART OF KANDRAKAR WAS TALKING TO ME...
CALL ME CRAZY OR A FOOL, BUT I THINK IT WAS TELLING ME THAT MATT'S STILL *ALIVE*!

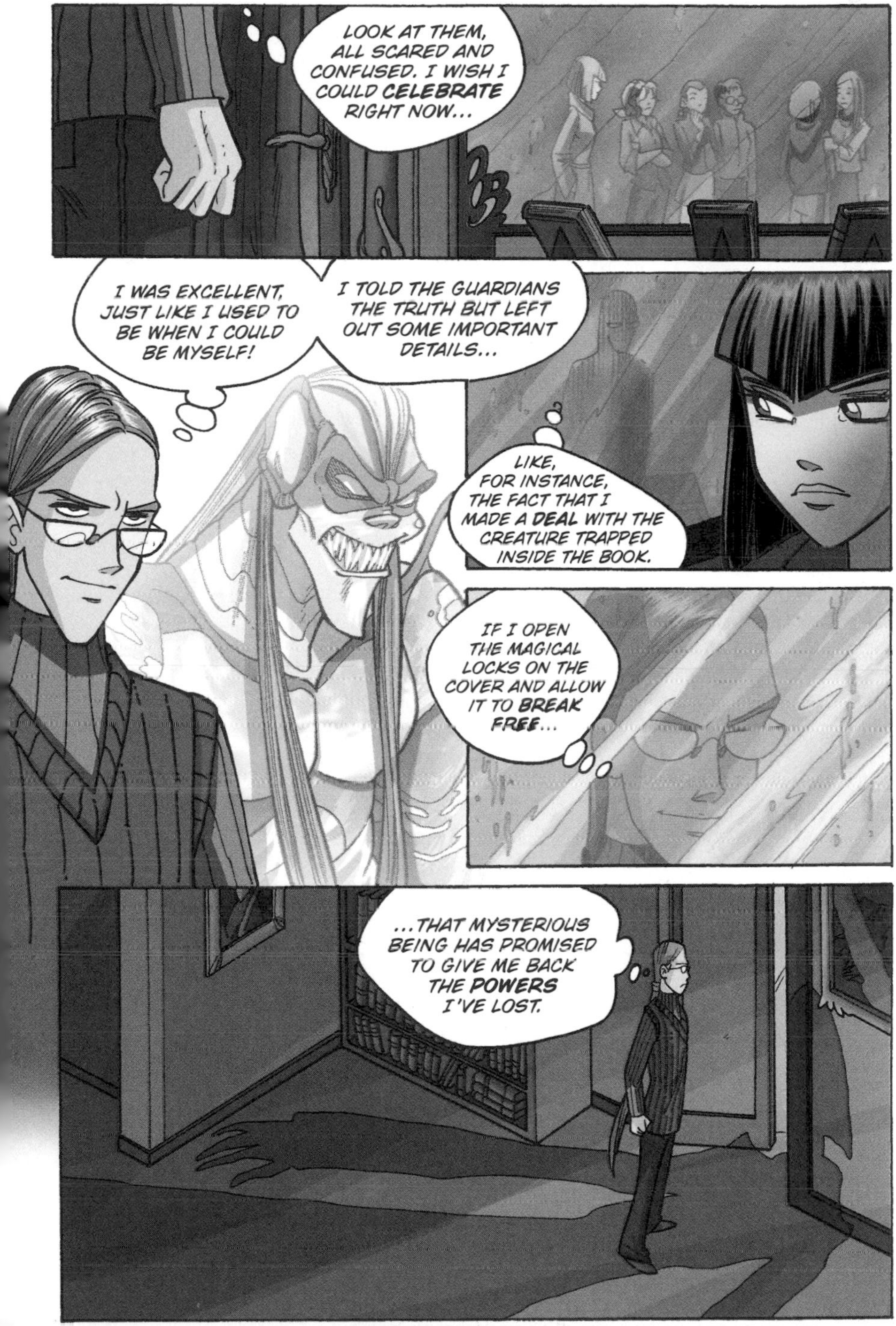
LOOK AT THEM, ALL SCARED AND CONFUSED. I WISH I COULD CELEBRATE RIGHT NOW...
I WAS EXCELLENT, JUST LIKE I USED TO BE WHEN I COULD BE MYSELF!
I TOLD THE GUARDIANS THE TRUTH BUT LEFT OUT SOME IMPORTANT DETAILS...
LIKE, FOR INSTANCE, THE FACT THAT I MADE A DEAL WITH THE CREATURE TRAPPED INSIDE THE BOOK.
IF I OPEN THE MAGICAL LOCKS ON THE COVER AND ALLOW IT TO BREAK FREE...
...THAT MYSTERIOUS BEING HAS PROMISED TO GIVE ME BACK THE POWERS I'VE LOST.

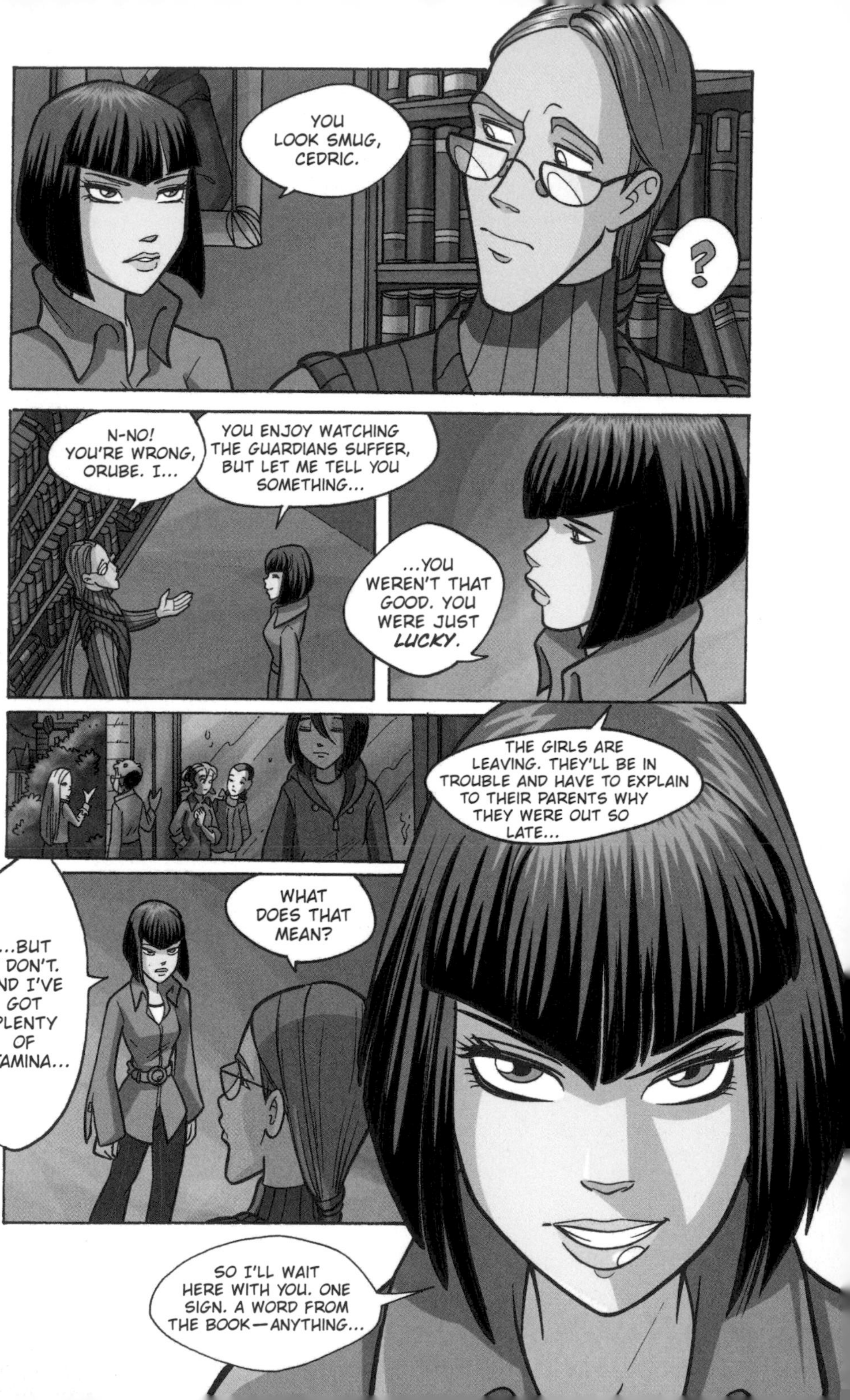
YOU LOOK SMUG, CEDRIC.
?
N-NO! YOU'RE WRONG, ORUBE. I...
YOU ENJOY WATCHING THE GUARDIANS SUFFER, BUT LET ME TELL YOU SOMETHING...
...YOU WEREN'T THAT GOOD. YOU WERE JUST *LUCKY*.
THE GIRLS ARE LEAVING. THEY'LL BE IN TROUBLE AND HAVE TO EXPLAIN TO THEIR PARENTS WHY THEY WERE OUT SO LATE...
...BUT I DON'T. AND I'VE GOT PLENTY OF STAMINA...
WHAT DOES THAT MEAN?
SO I'LL WAIT HERE WITH YOU. ONE SIGN. A WORD FROM THE BOOK—ANYTHING...

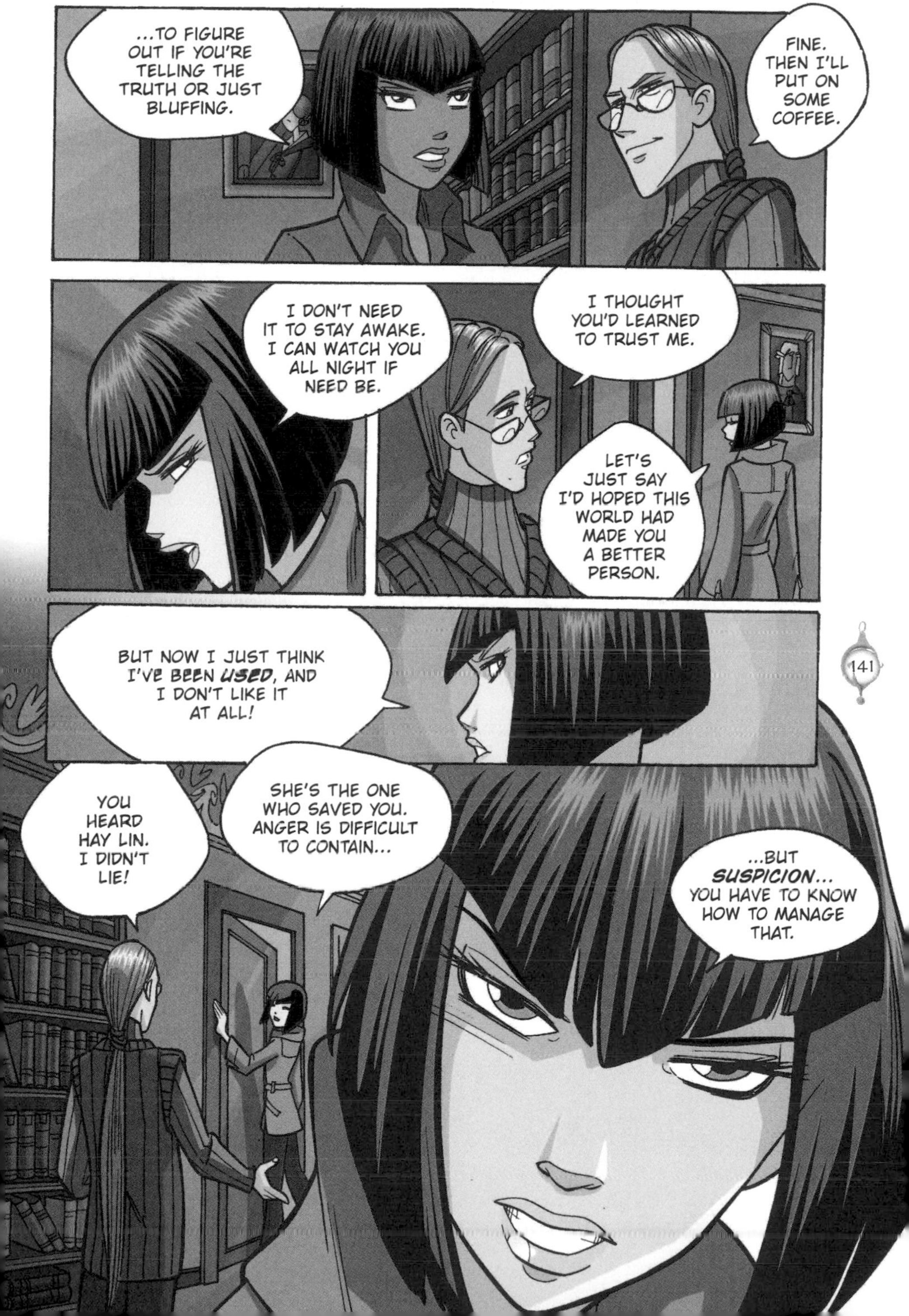
...TO FIGURE OUT IF YOU'RE TELLING THE TRUTH OR JUST BLUFFING.
FINE. THEN I'LL PUT ON SOME COFFEE.
I DON'T NEED IT TO STAY AWAKE. I CAN WATCH YOU ALL NIGHT IF NEED BE.
I THOUGHT YOU'D LEARNED TO TRUST ME.
LET'S JUST SAY I'D HOPED THIS WORLD HAD MADE YOU A BETTER PERSON.
BUT NOW I JUST THINK I'VE BEEN *USED*, AND I DON'T LIKE IT AT ALL!
YOU HEARD HAY LIN. I DIDN'T LIE!
SHE'S THE ONE WHO SAVED YOU. ANGER IS DIFFICULT TO CONTAIN...
...BUT *SUSPICION*... YOU HAVE TO KNOW HOW TO MANAGE THAT.

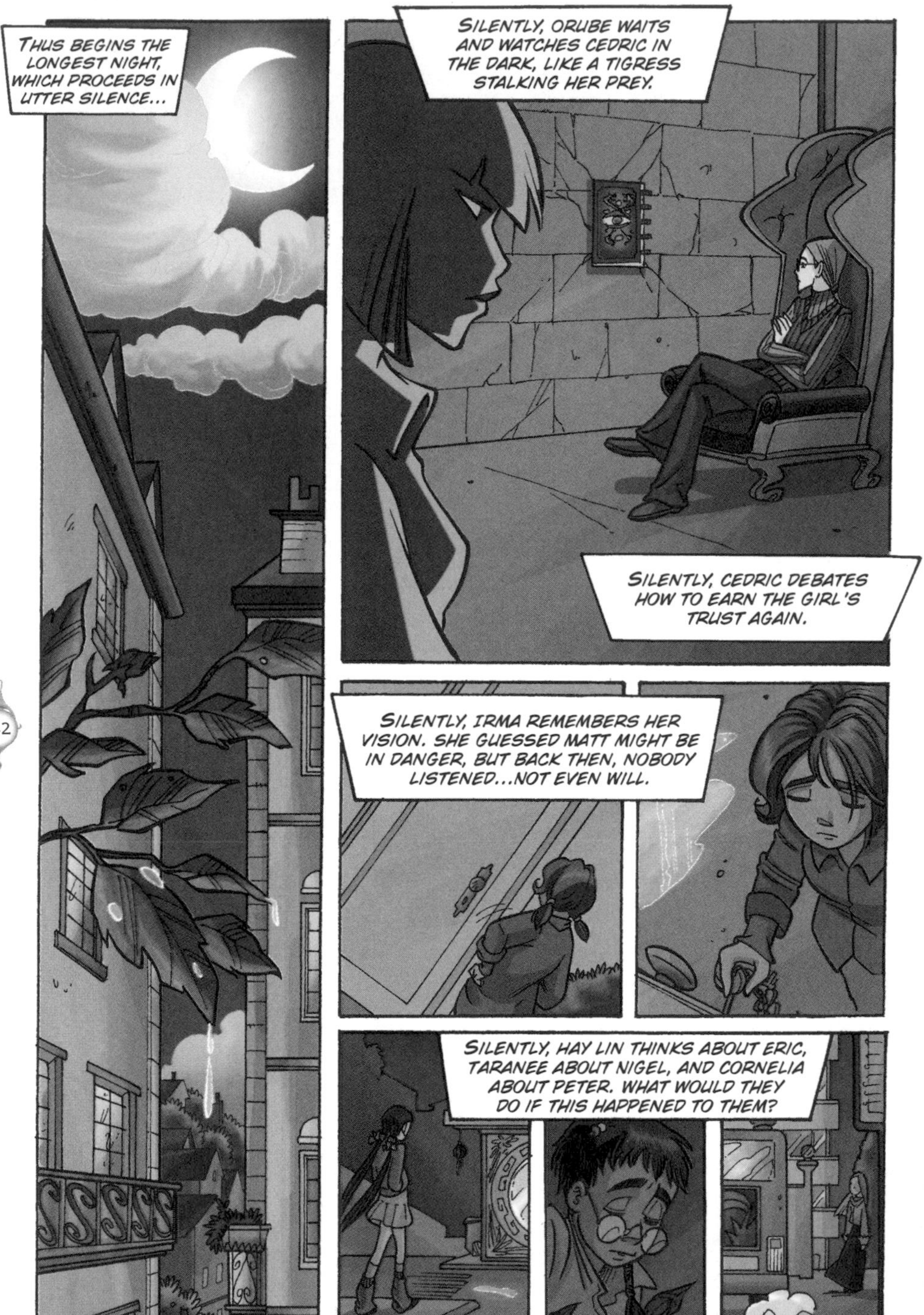
THUS BEGINS THE LONGEST NIGHT, WHICH PROCEEDS IN UTTER SILENCE...
SILENTLY, ORUBE WAITS AND WATCHES CEDRIC IN THE DARK, LIKE A TIGRESS STALKING HER PREY.
SILENTLY, CEDRIC DEBATES HOW TO EARN THE GIRL'S TRUST AGAIN.
SILENTLY, IRMA REMEMBERS HER VISION. SHE GUESSED MATT MIGHT BE IN DANGER, BUT BACK THEN, NOBODY LISTENED...NOT EVEN WILL.
SILENTLY, HAY LIN THINKS ABOUT ERIC, TARANEE ABOUT NIGEL, AND CORNELIA ABOUT PETER. WHAT WOULD THEY DO IF THIS HAPPENED TO THEM?

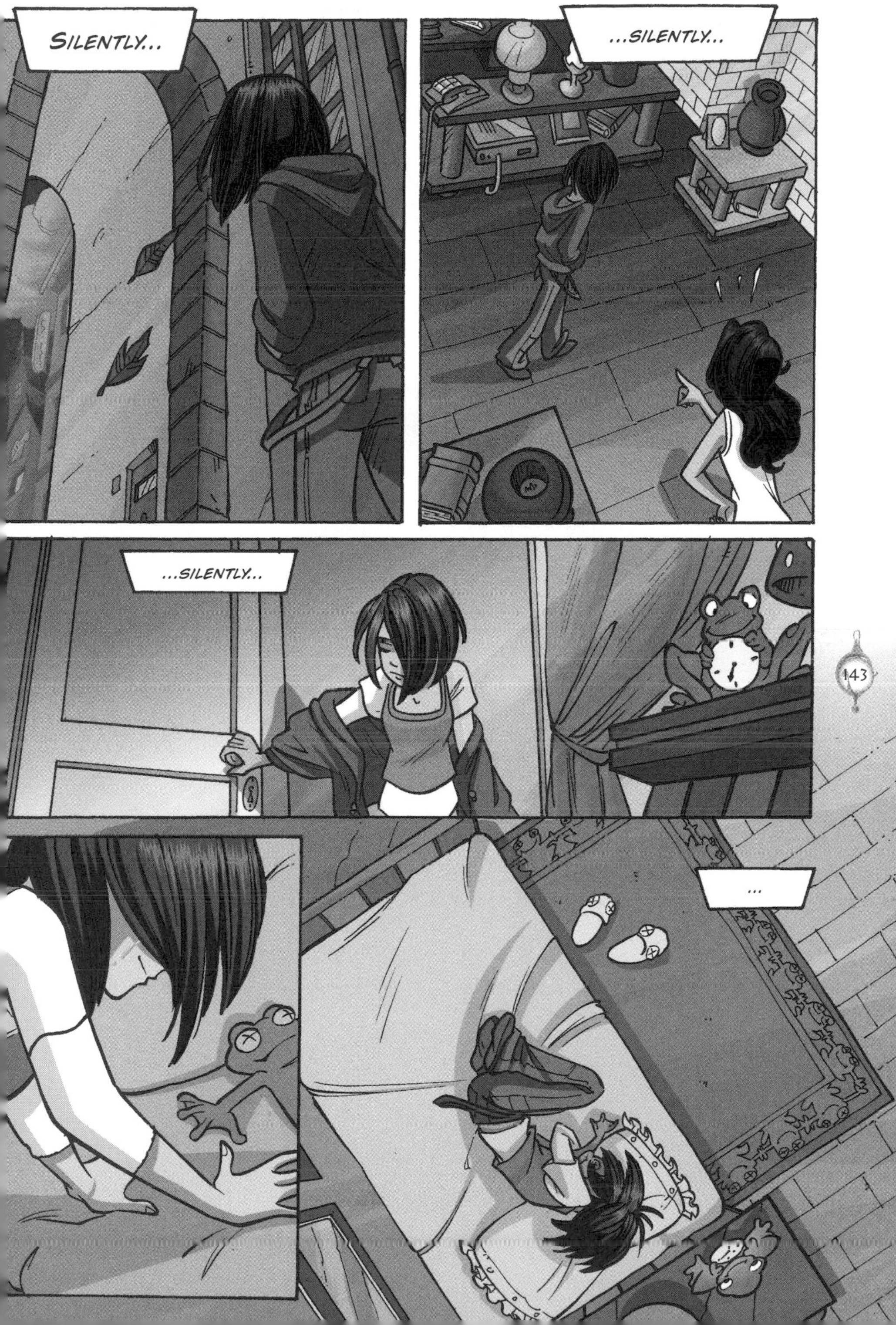
SILENTLY...
...SILENTLY...
...SILENTLY...
...

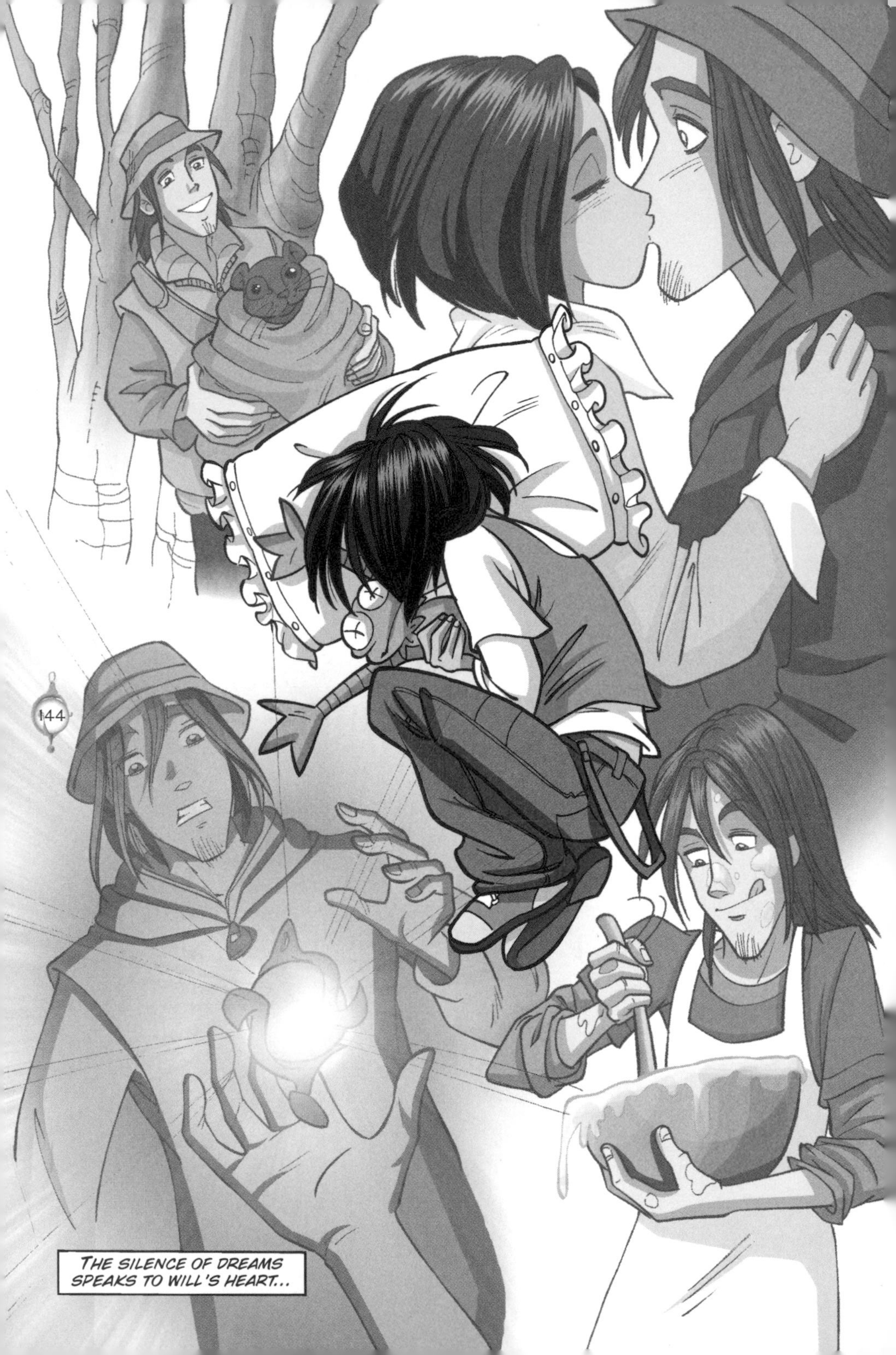
THE SILENCE OF DREAMS SPEAKS TO WILL'S HEART...

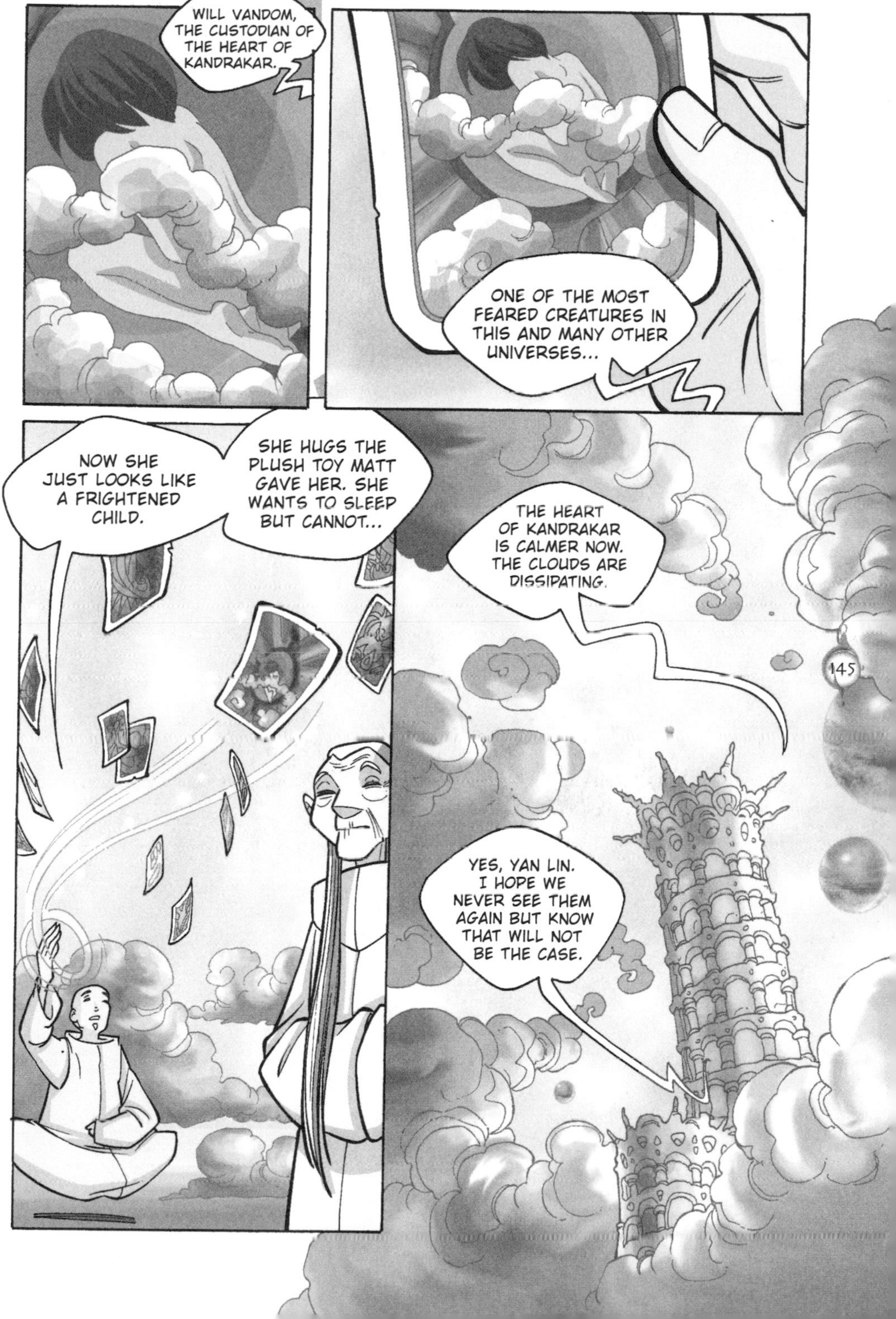

WILL VANDOM, THE CUSTODIAN OF THE HEART OF KANDRAKAR.
ONE OF THE MOST FEARED CREATURES IN THIS AND MANY OTHER UNIVERSES...
NOW SHE JUST LOOKS LIKE A FRIGHTENED CHILD.
SHE HUGS THE PLUSH TOY MATT GAVE HER. SHE WANTS TO SLEEP BUT CANNOT...
THE HEART OF KANDRAKAR IS CALMER NOW. THE CLOUDS ARE DISSIPATING.
YES, YAN LIN. I HOPE WE NEVER SEE THEM AGAIN BUT KNOW THAT WILL NOT BE THE CASE.

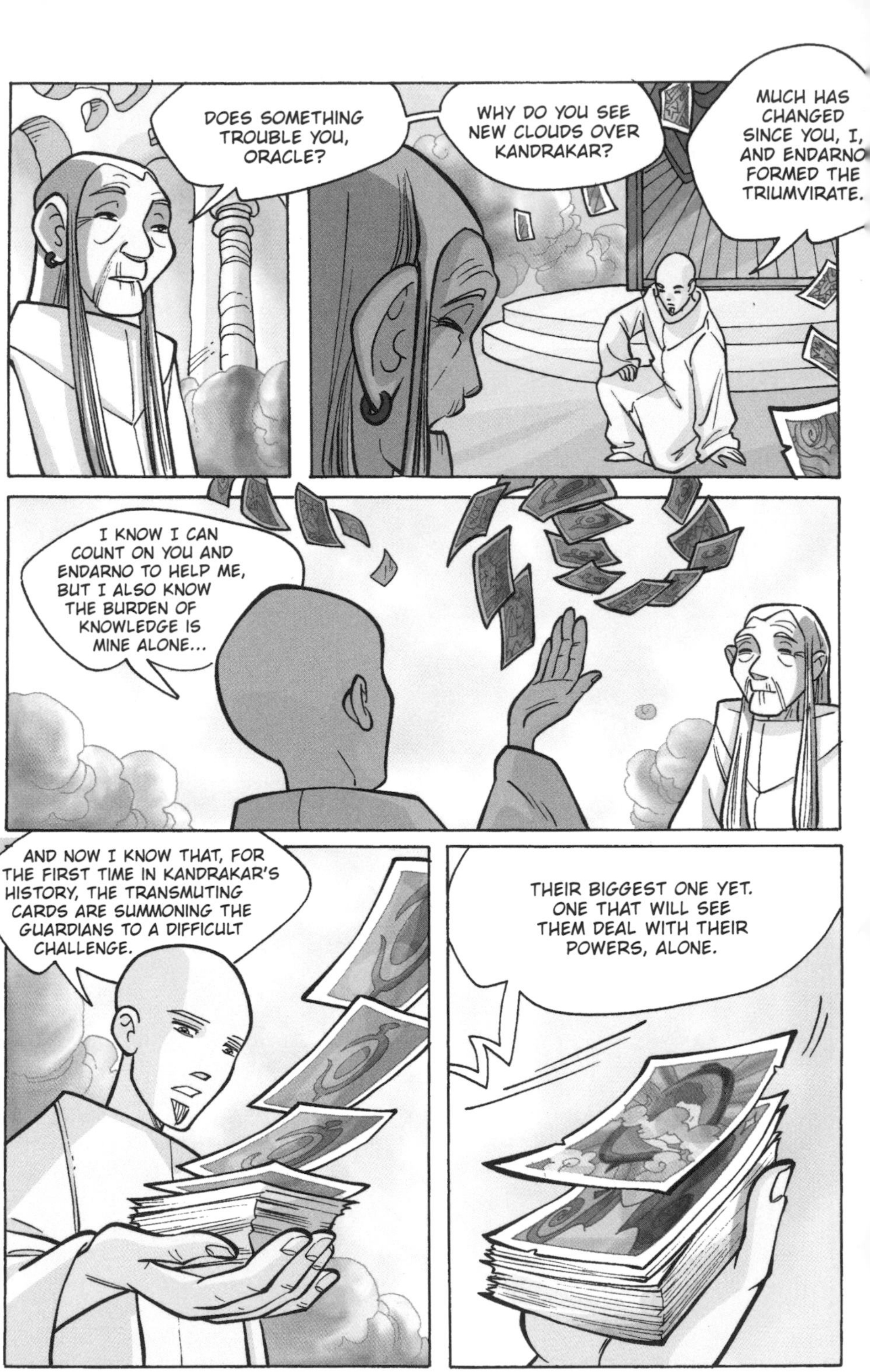
DOES SOMETHING TROUBLE YOU, ORACLE?
WHY DO YOU SEE NEW CLOUDS OVER KANDRAKAR?
MUCH HAS CHANGED SINCE YOU, I, AND ENDARNO FORMED THE TRIUMVIRATE.
I KNOW I CAN COUNT ON YOU AND ENDARNO TO HELP ME, BUT I ALSO KNOW THE BURDEN OF KNOWLEDGE IS MINE ALONE...
AND NOW I KNOW THAT, FOR THE FIRST TIME IN KANDRAKAR'S HISTORY, THE TRANSMUTING CARDS ARE SUMMONING THE GUARDIANS TO A DIFFICULT CHALLENGE.
THEIR BIGGEST ONE YET. ONE THAT WILL SEE THEM DEAL WITH THEIR POWERS, ALONE.

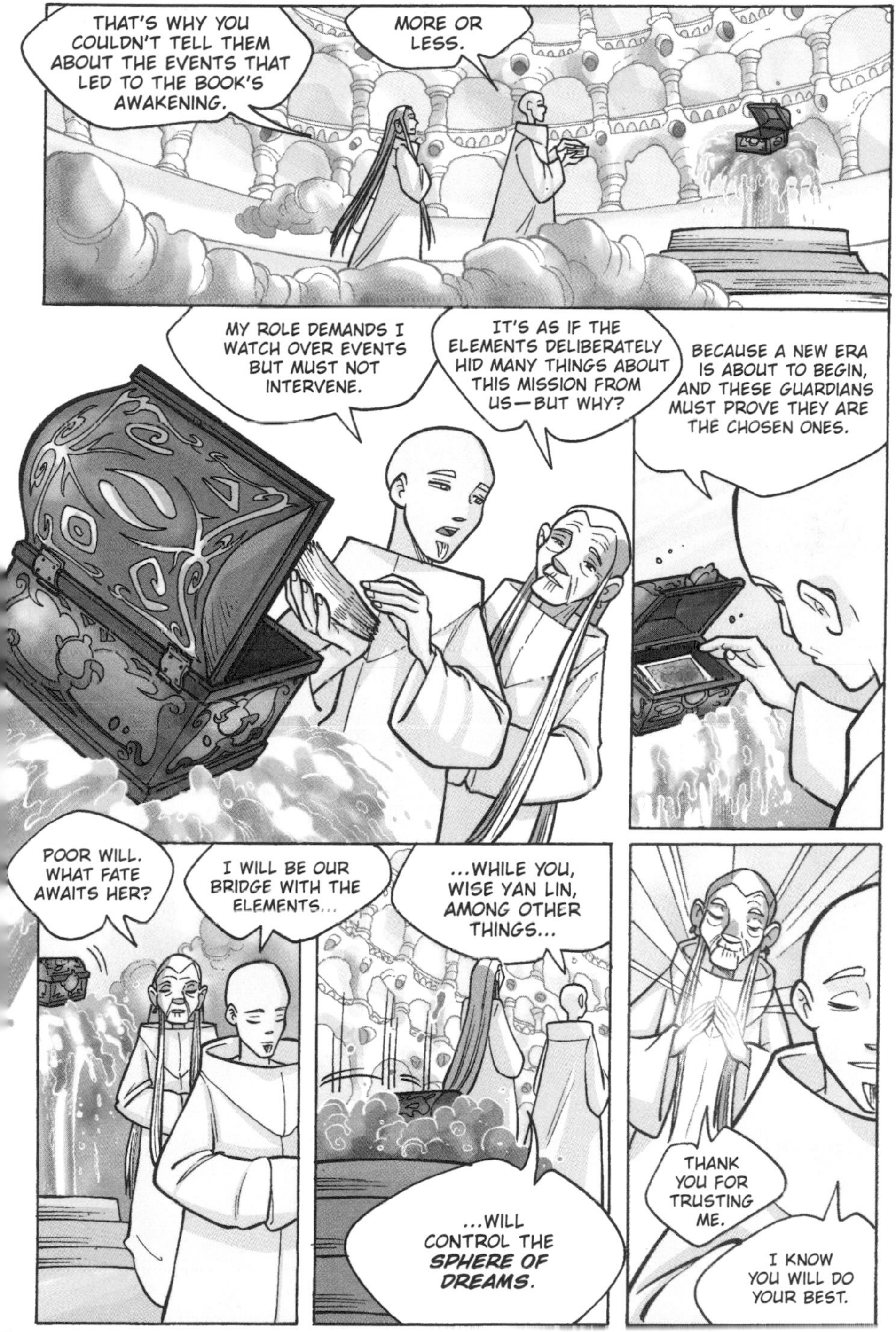
THAT'S WHY YOU COULDN'T TELL THEM ABOUT THE EVENTS THAT LED TO THE BOOK'S AWAKENING.
MORE OR LESS.
MY ROLE DEMANDS I WATCH OVER EVENTS BUT MUST NOT INTERVENE.
IT'S AS IF THE ELEMENTS DELIBERATELY HID MANY THINGS ABOUT THIS MISSION FROM US—BUT WHY?
BECAUSE A NEW ERA IS ABOUT TO BEGIN, AND THESE GUARDIANS MUST PROVE THEY ARE THE CHOSEN ONES.
POOR WILL. WHAT FATE AWAITS HER?
I WILL BE OUR BRIDGE WITH THE ELEMENTS...
...WHILE YOU, WISE YAN LIN, AMONG OTHER THINGS...
...WILL CONTROL THE ***SPHERE OF DREAMS***.
THANK YOU FOR TRUSTING ME.
I KNOW YOU WILL DO YOUR BEST.

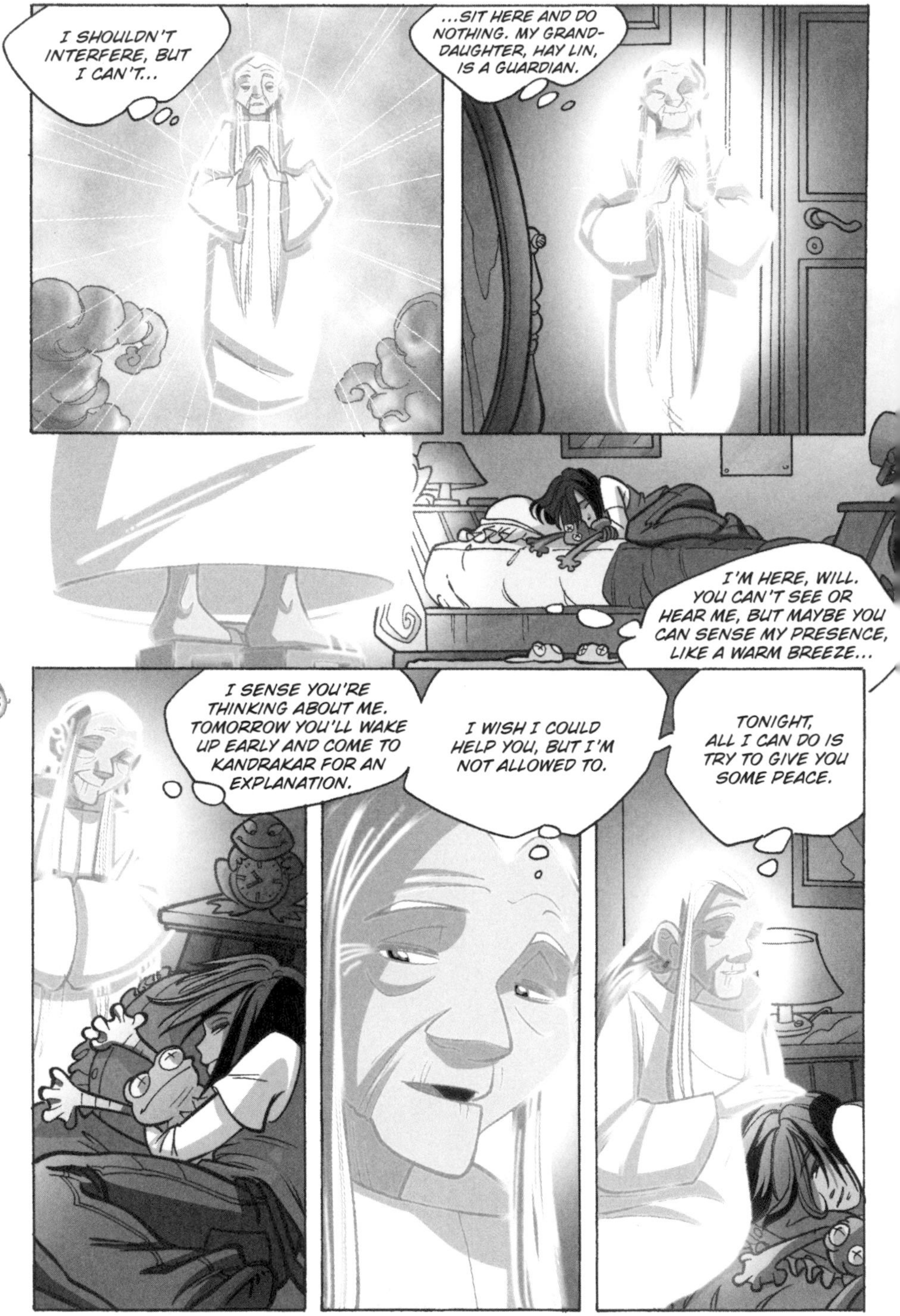

I SHOULDN'T INTERFERE, BUT I CAN'T...
...SIT HERE AND DO NOTHING. MY GRAND-DAUGHTER, HAY LIN, IS A GUARDIAN.
I'M HERE, WILL. YOU CAN'T SEE OR HEAR ME, BUT MAYBE YOU CAN SENSE MY PRESENCE, LIKE A WARM BREEZE...
I SENSE YOU'RE THINKING ABOUT ME. TOMORROW YOU'LL WAKE UP EARLY AND COME TO KANDRAKAR FOR AN EXPLANATION.
I WISH I COULD HELP YOU, BUT I'M NOT ALLOWED TO.
TONIGHT, ALL I CAN DO IS TRY TO GIVE YOU SOME PEACE.

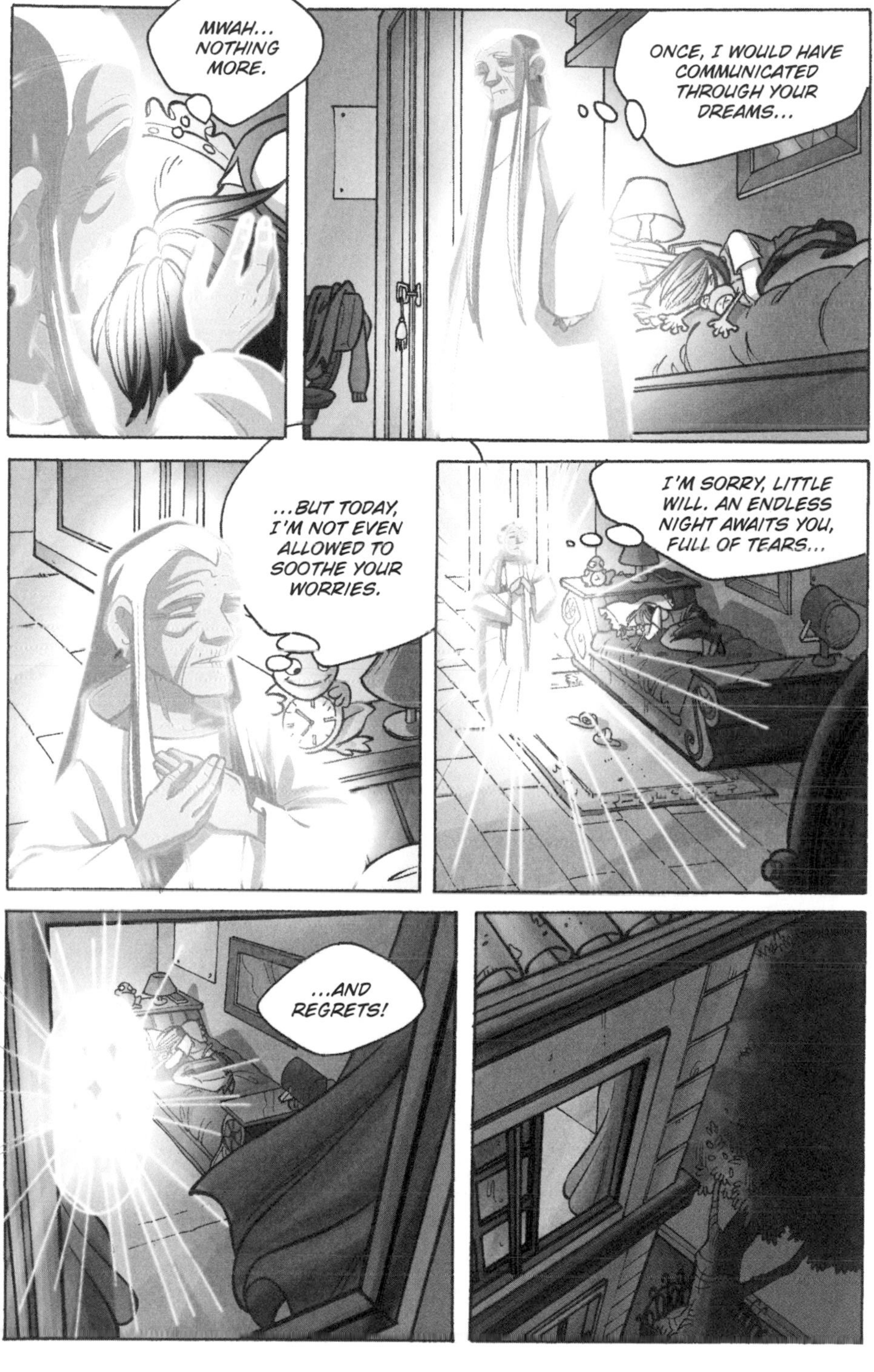
MWAH... NOTHING MORE.
ONCE, I WOULD HAVE COMMUNICATED THROUGH YOUR DREAMS...
...BUT TODAY, I'M NOT EVEN ALLOWED TO SOOTHE YOUR WORRIES.
I'M SORRY, LITTLE WILL. AN ENDLESS NIGHT AWAITS YOU, FULL OF TEARS...
...AND REGRETS!

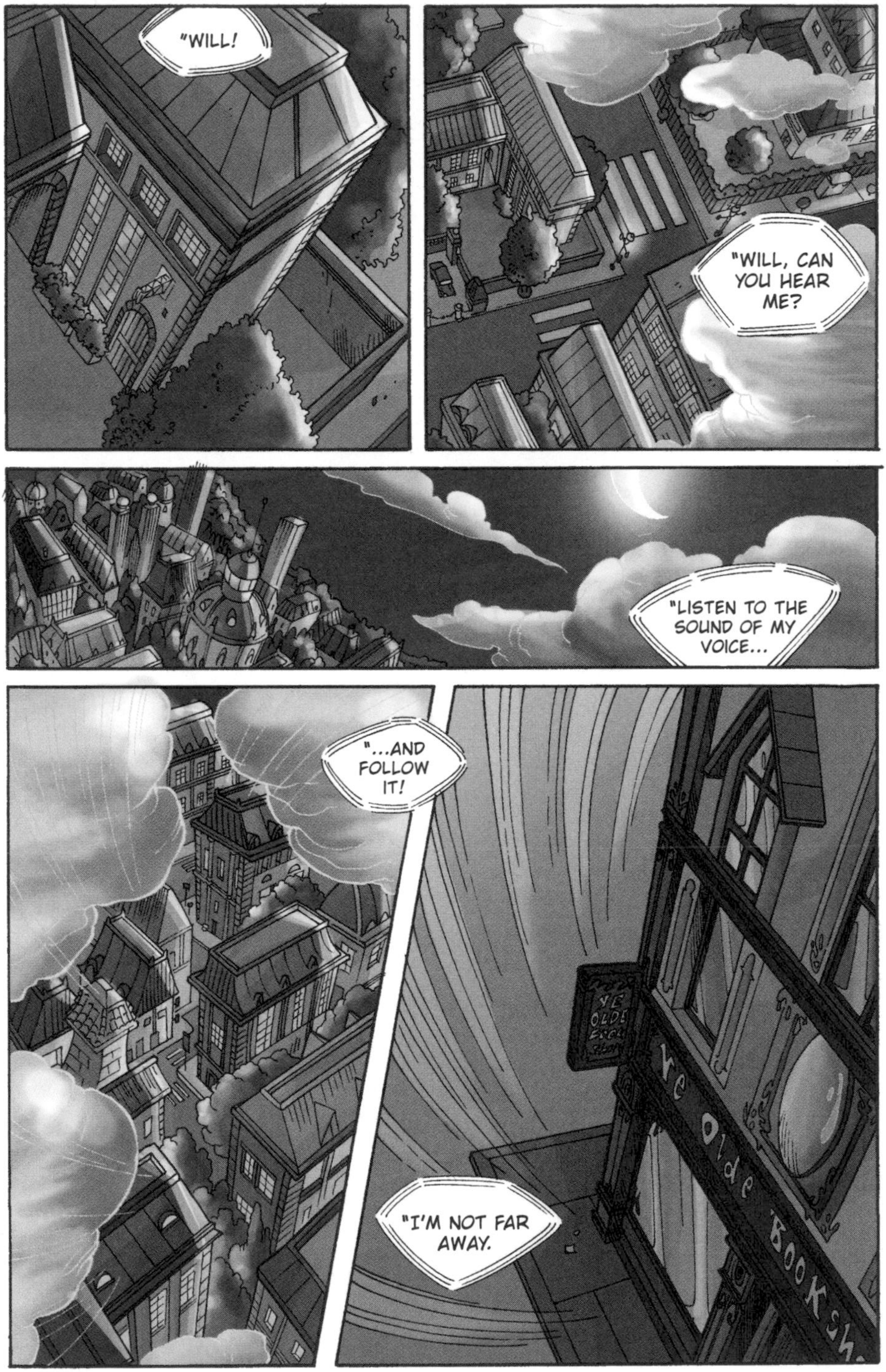
"WILL!
"WILL, CAN YOU HEAR ME?
"LISTEN TO THE SOUND OF MY VOICE...
"...AND FOLLOW IT!
"I'M NOT FAR AWAY.

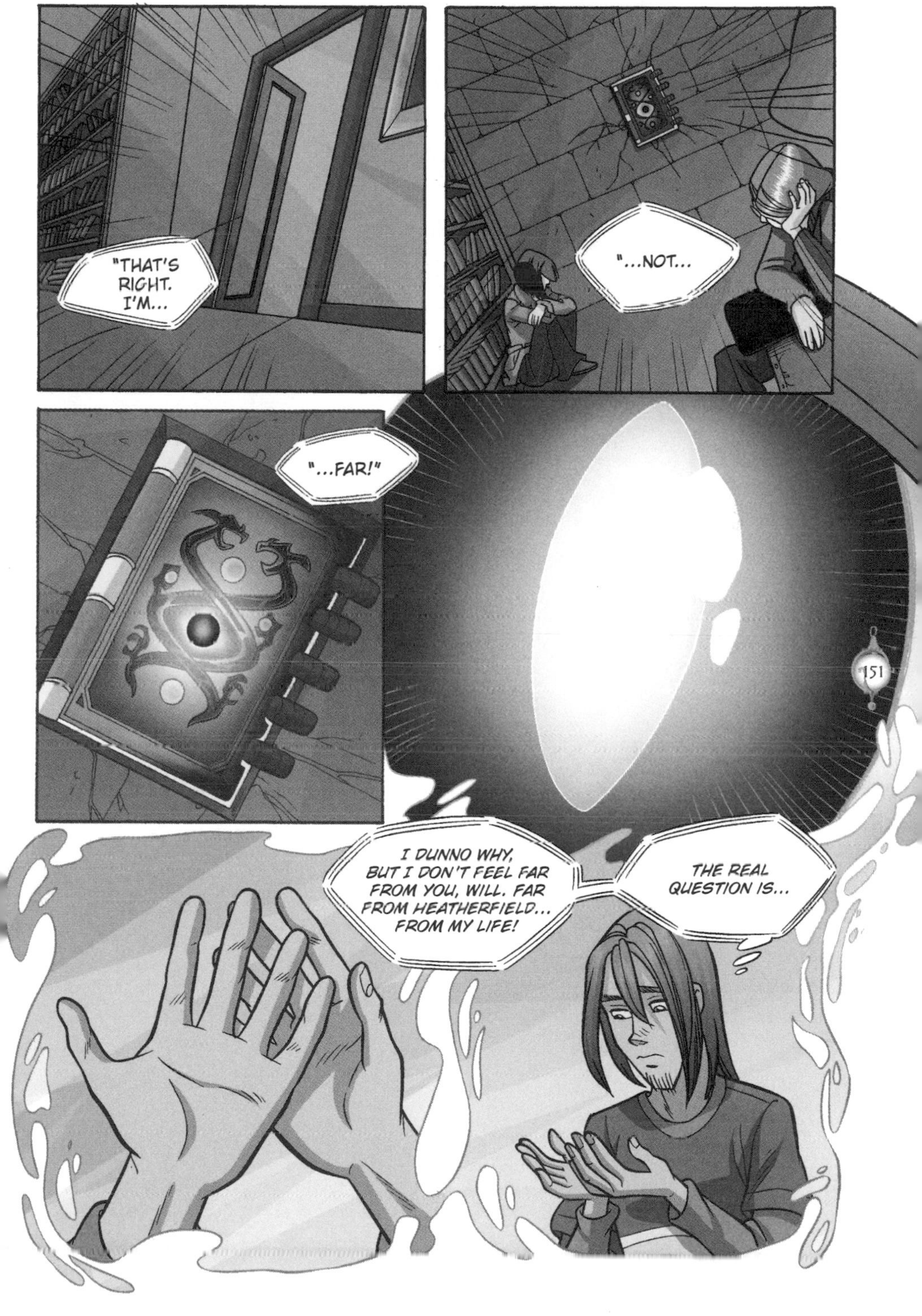
"THAT'S RIGHT. I'M...
"...NOT...
"...FAR!"
I DUNNO WHY, BUT I DON'T FEEL FAR FROM YOU, WILL. FAR FROM HEATHERFIELD... FROM MY LIFE!
THE REAL QUESTION IS...

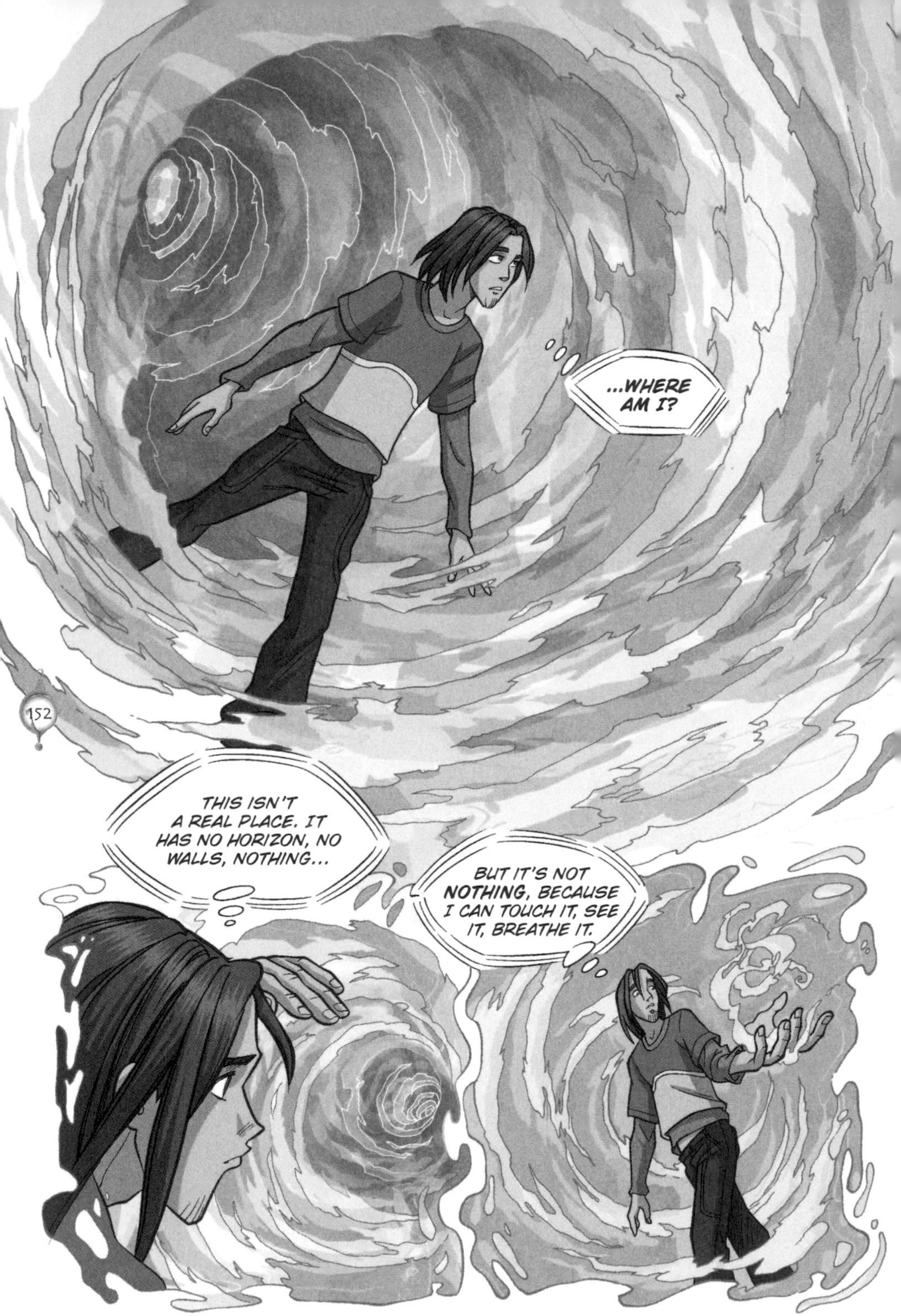
...WHERE AM I?
THIS ISN'T A REAL PLACE. IT HAS NO HORIZON, NO WALLS, NOTHING...
BUT IT'S NOT NOTHING, BECAUSE I CAN TOUCH IT, SEE IT, BREATHE IT.

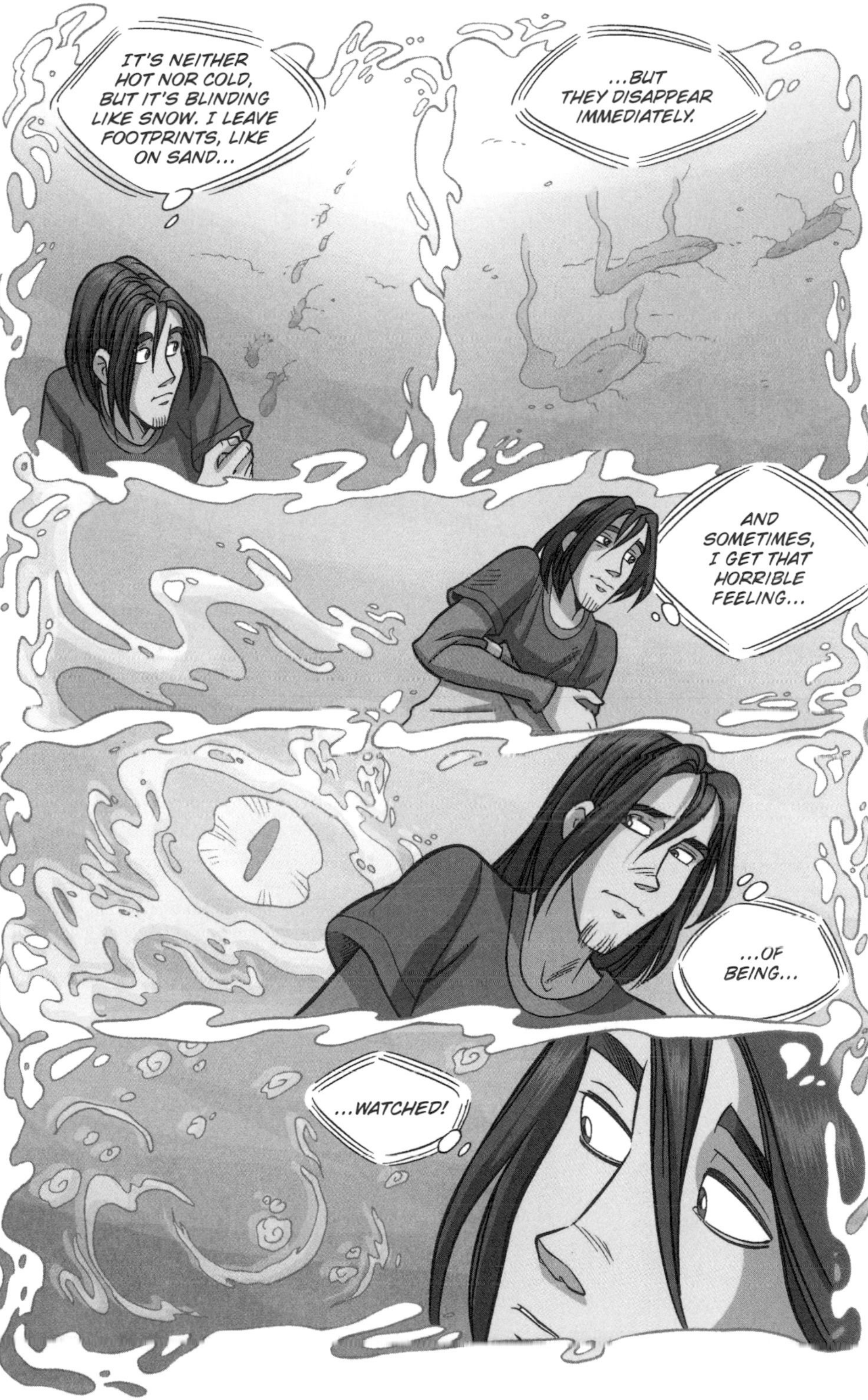
IT'S NEITHER HOT NOR COLD, BUT IT'S BLINDING LIKE SNOW. I LEAVE FOOTPRINTS, LIKE ON SAND...
...BUT THEY DISAPPEAR IMMEDIATELY.
AND SOMETIMES, I GET THAT HORRIBLE FEELING...
...OF BEING...
...WATCHED!

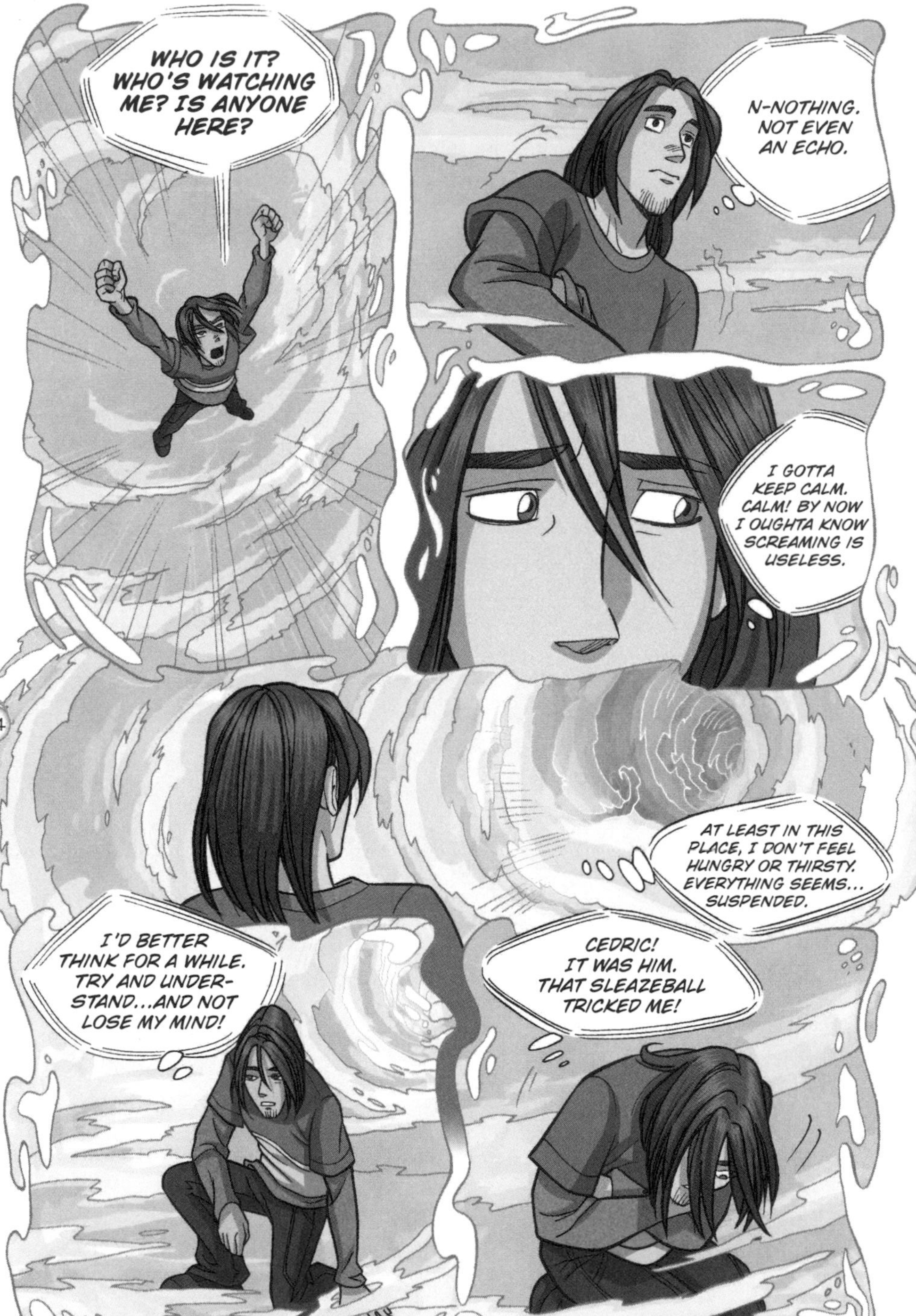
WHO IS IT? WHO'S WATCHING ME? IS ANYONE HERE?
N-NOTHING. NOT EVEN AN ECHO.
I GOTTA KEEP CALM. CALM! BY NOW I OUGHTA KNOW SCREAMING IS USELESS.
AT LEAST IN THIS PLACE, I DON'T FEEL HUNGRY OR THIRSTY. EVERYTHING SEEMS... SUSPENDED.
I'D BETTER THINK FOR A WHILE. TRY AND UNDER-STAND...AND NOT LOSE MY MIND!
CEDRIC! IT WAS HIM. THAT SLEAZEBALL TRICKED ME!

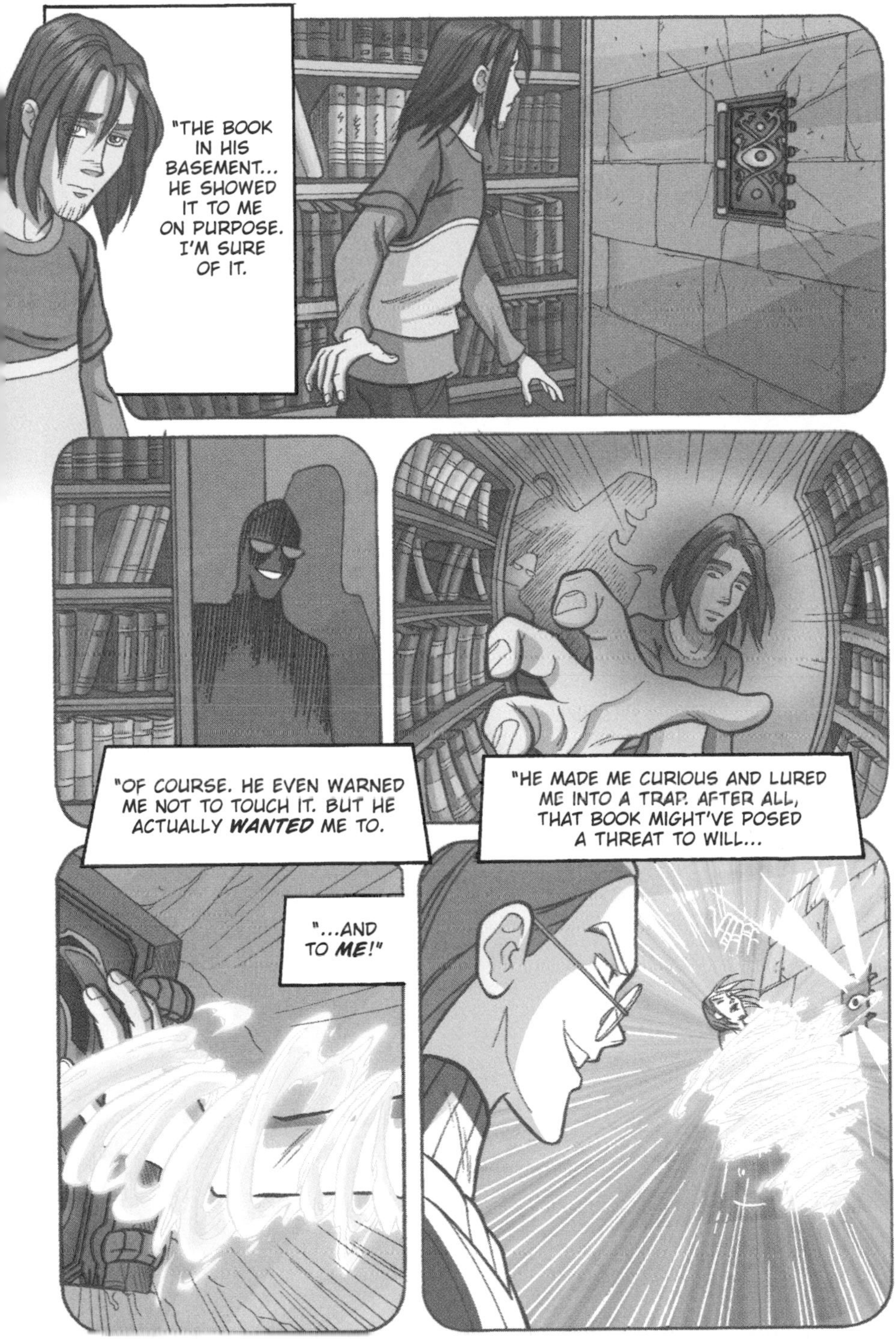
"THE BOOK IN HIS BASEMENT... HE SHOWED IT TO ME ON PURPOSE. I'M SURE OF IT.
"OF COURSE. HE EVEN WARNED ME NOT TO TOUCH IT. BUT HE ACTUALLY ***WANTED*** ME TO.
"HE MADE ME CURIOUS AND LURED ME INTO A TRAP. AFTER ALL, THAT BOOK MIGHT'VE POSED A THREAT TO WILL...
"...AND TO ***ME!***"

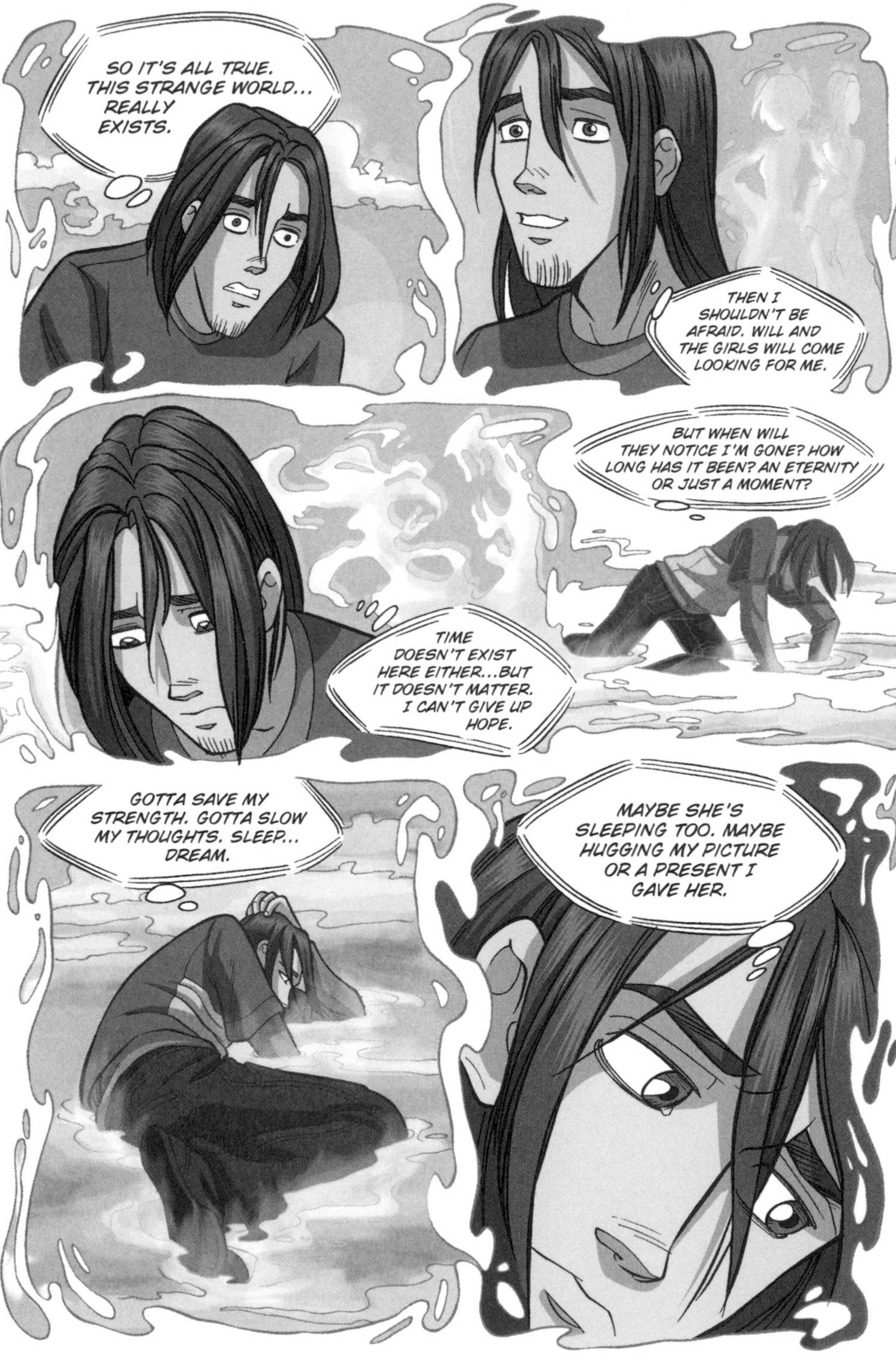
SO IT'S ALL TRUE. THIS STRANGE WORLD... REALLY EXISTS.
THEN I SHOULDN'T BE AFRAID. WILL AND THE GIRLS WILL COME LOOKING FOR ME.
BUT WHEN WILL THEY NOTICE I'M GONE? HOW LONG HAS IT BEEN? AN ETERNITY OR JUST A MOMENT?
TIME DOESN'T EXIST HERE EITHER...BUT IT DOESN'T MATTER. I CAN'T GIVE UP HOPE.
GOTTA SAVE MY STRENGTH. GOTTA SLOW MY THOUGHTS. SLEEP... DREAM.
MAYBE SHE'S SLEEPING TOO. MAYBE HUGGING MY PICTURE OR A PRESENT I GAVE HER.

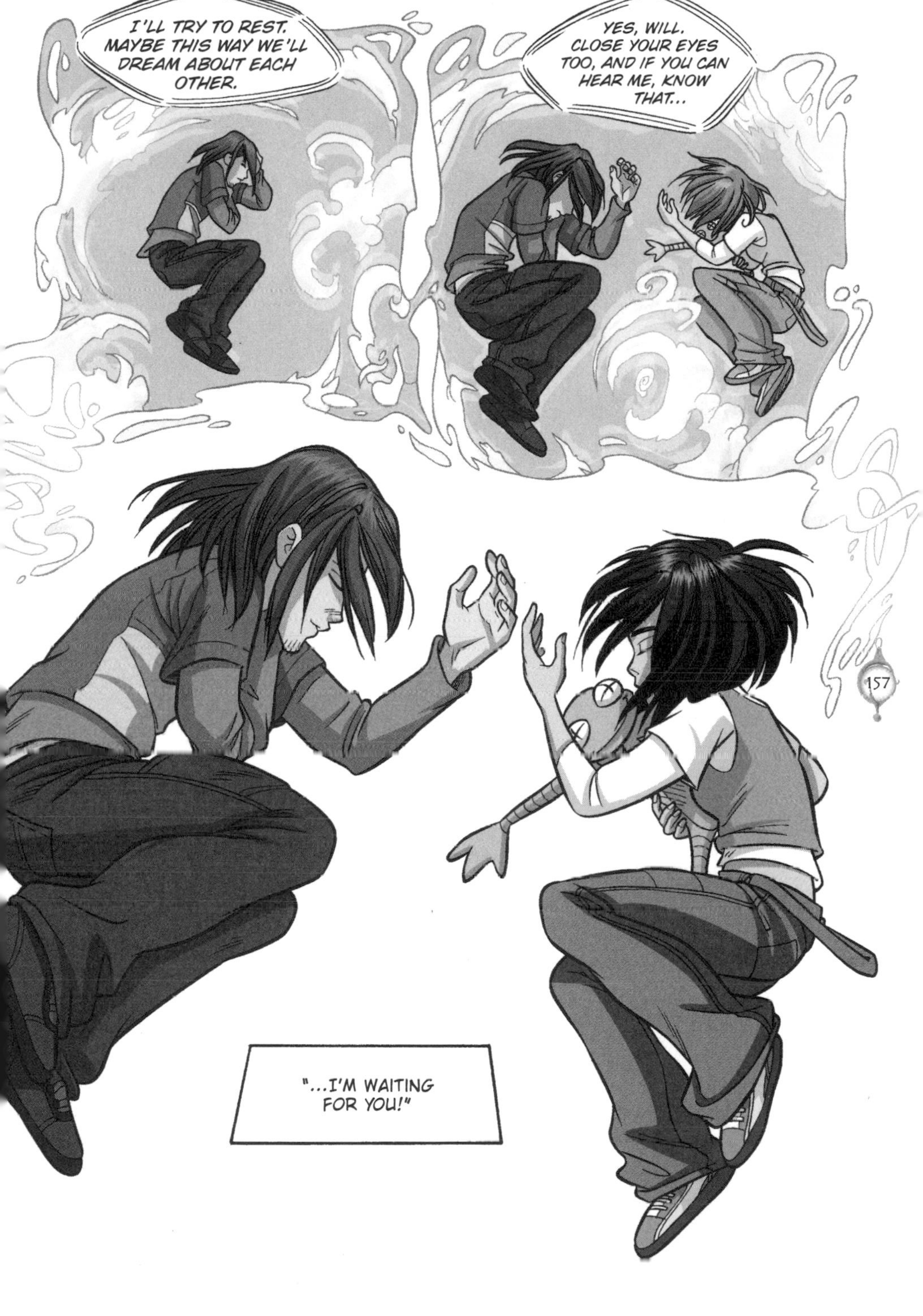
I'LL TRY TO REST. MAYBE THIS WAY WE'LL DREAM ABOUT EACH OTHER.
YES, WILL. CLOSE YOUR EYES TOO, AND IF YOU CAN HEAR ME, KNOW THAT...
"...I'M WAITING FOR YOU!"

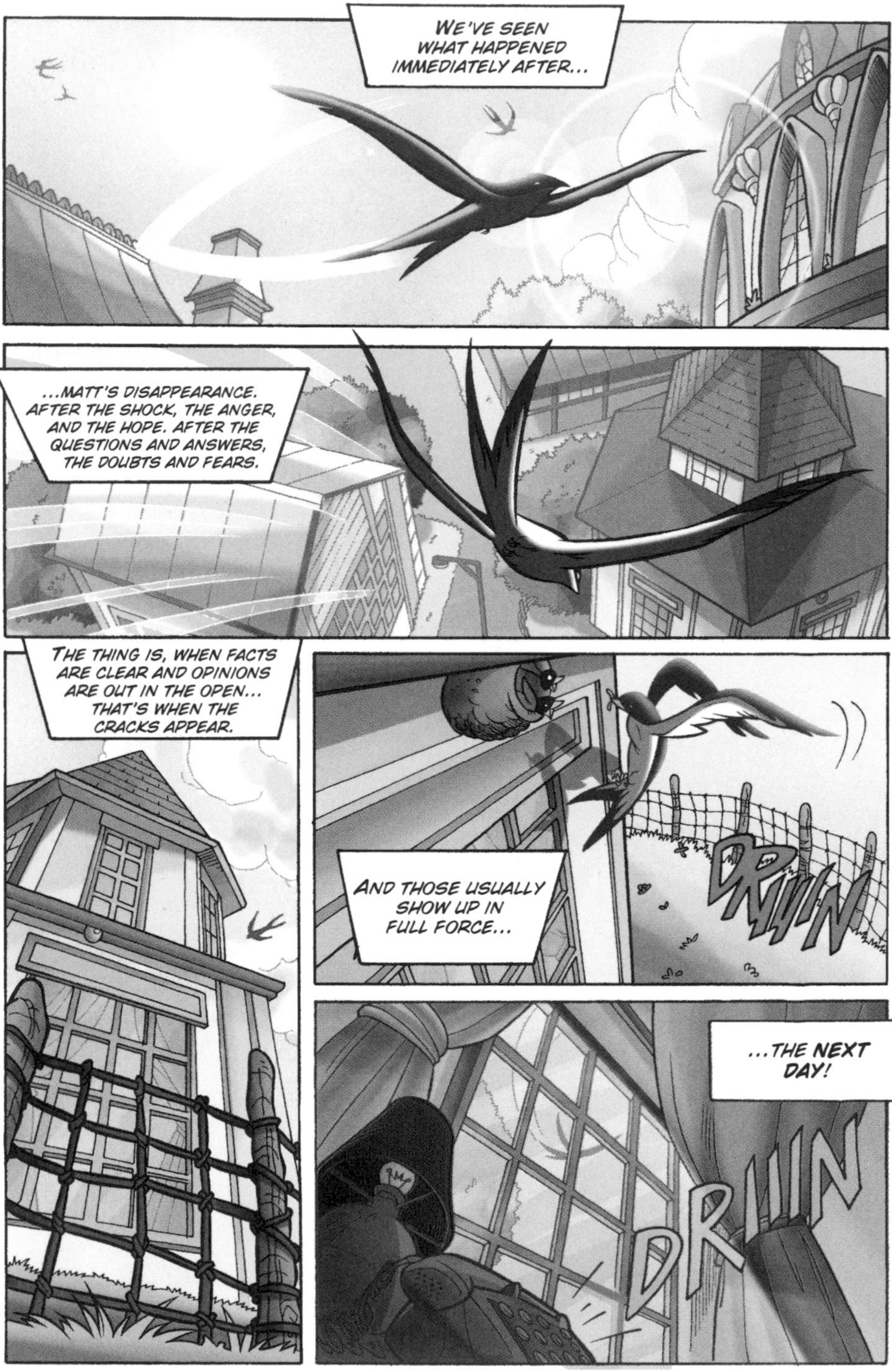

WE'VE SEEN WHAT HAPPENED IMMEDIATELY AFTER...
...MATT'S DISAPPEARANCE. AFTER THE SHOCK, THE ANGER, AND THE HOPE. AFTER THE QUESTIONS AND ANSWERS, THE DOUBTS AND FEARS.
THE THING IS, WHEN FACTS ARE CLEAR AND OPINIONS ARE OUT IN THE OPEN... THAT'S WHEN THE CRACKS APPEAR.
AND THOSE USUALLY SHOW UP IN FULL FORCE...
DRIIIN
...THE NEXT DAY!
DRIIIN

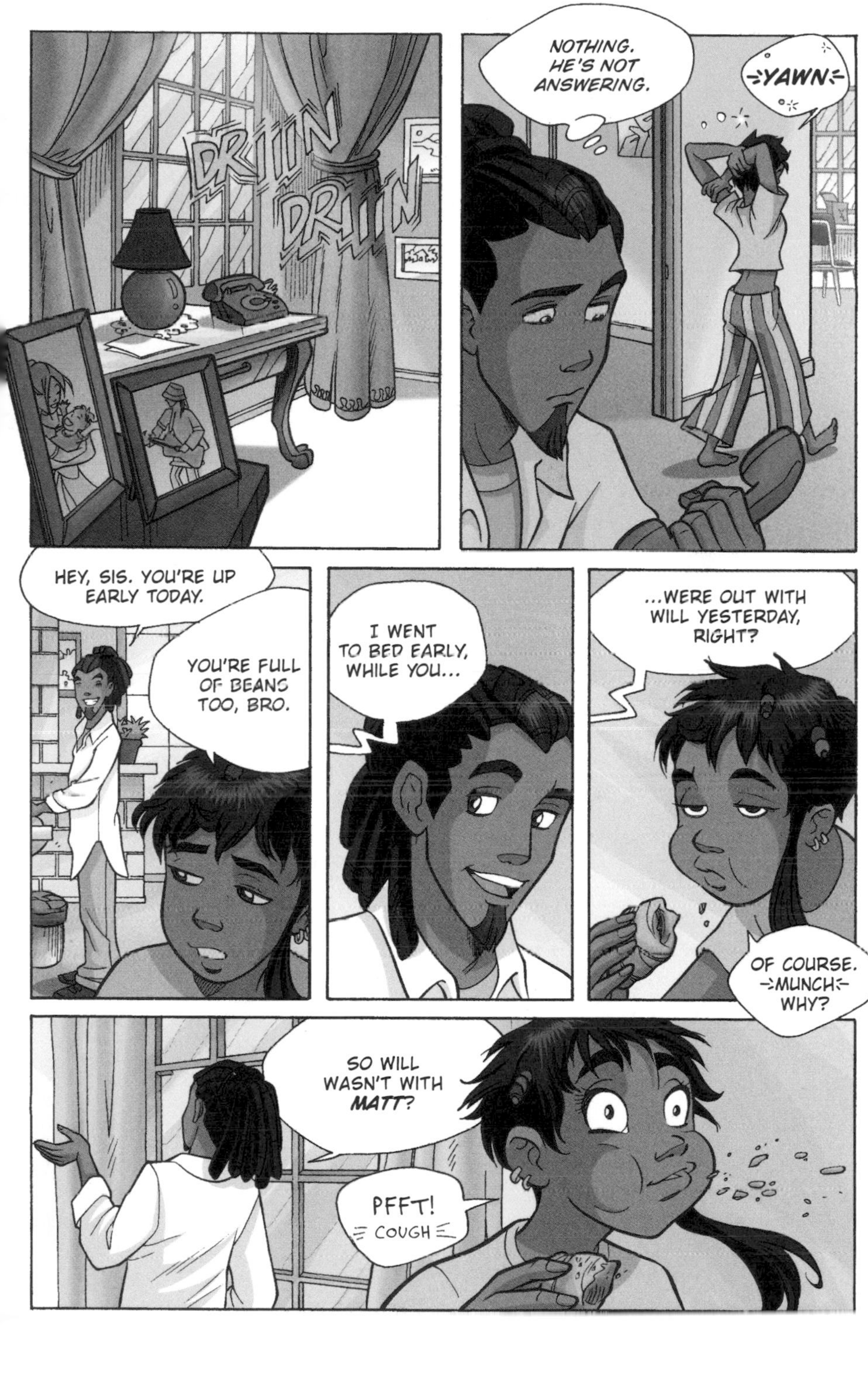
DRIIIN
DRIIIN
NOTHING. HE'S NOT ANSWERING.
YAWN
HEY, SIS. YOU'RE UP EARLY TODAY.
YOU'RE FULL OF BEANS TOO, BRO.
I WENT TO BED EARLY, WHILE YOU...
...WERE OUT WITH WILL YESTERDAY, RIGHT?
OF COURSE. MUNCH WHY?
SO WILL WASN'T WITH MATT?
PFFT! COUGH

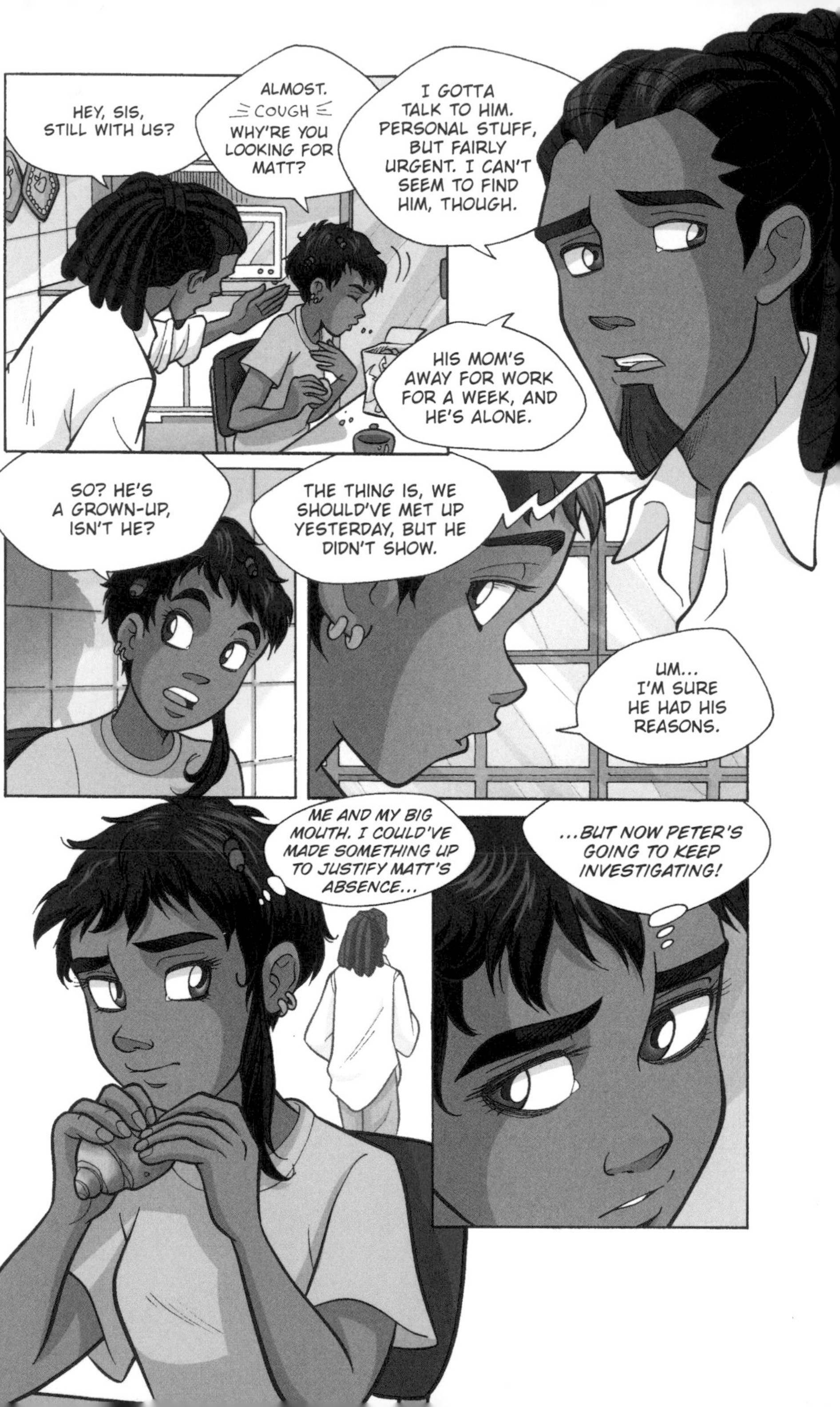
HEY, SIS, STILL WITH US?
ALMOST. COUGH WHY'RE YOU LOOKING FOR MATT?
I GOTTA TALK TO HIM. PERSONAL STUFF, BUT FAIRLY URGENT. I CAN'T SEEM TO FIND HIM, THOUGH.
HIS MOM'S AWAY FOR WORK FOR A WEEK, AND HE'S ALONE.
SO? HE'S A GROWN-UP, ISN'T HE?
THE THING IS, WE SHOULD'VE MET UP YESTERDAY, BUT HE DIDN'T SHOW.
UM... I'M SURE HE HAD HIS REASONS.
ME AND MY BIG MOUTH. I COULD'VE MADE SOMETHING UP TO JUSTIFY MATT'S ABSENCE...
...BUT NOW PETER'S GOING TO KEEP INVESTIGATING!

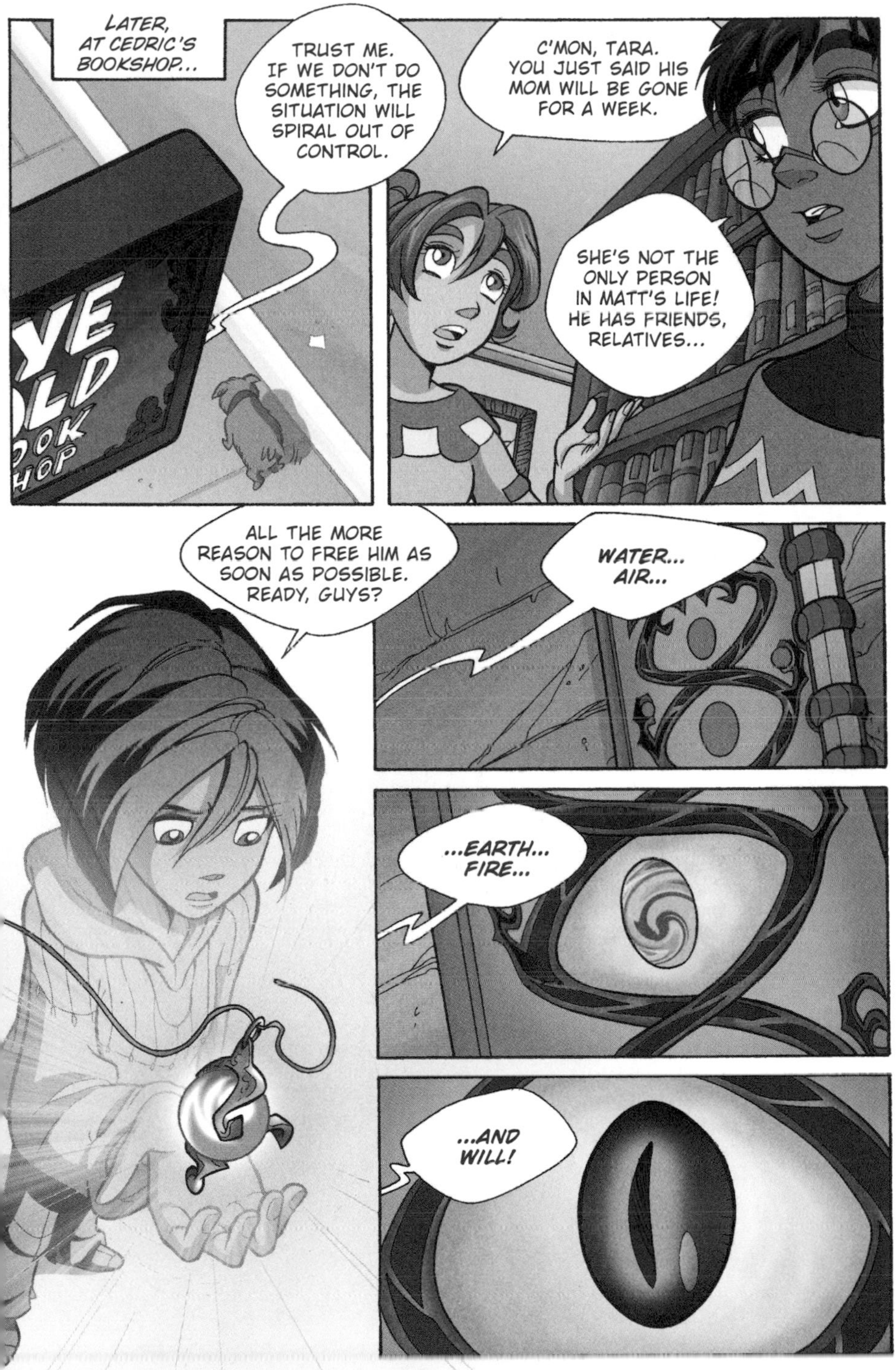
LATER, AT CEDRIC'S BOOKSHOP...
YE OLD BOOK SHOP
TRUST ME. IF WE DON'T DO SOMETHING, THE SITUATION WILL SPIRAL OUT OF CONTROL.
C'MON, TARA. YOU JUST SAID HIS MOM WILL BE GONE FOR A WEEK.
SHE'S NOT THE ONLY PERSON IN MATT'S LIFE! HE HAS FRIENDS, RELATIVES...
ALL THE MORE REASON TO FREE HIM AS SOON AS POSSIBLE. READY, GUYS?
WATER... AIR...
...EARTH... FIRE...
...AND WILL!

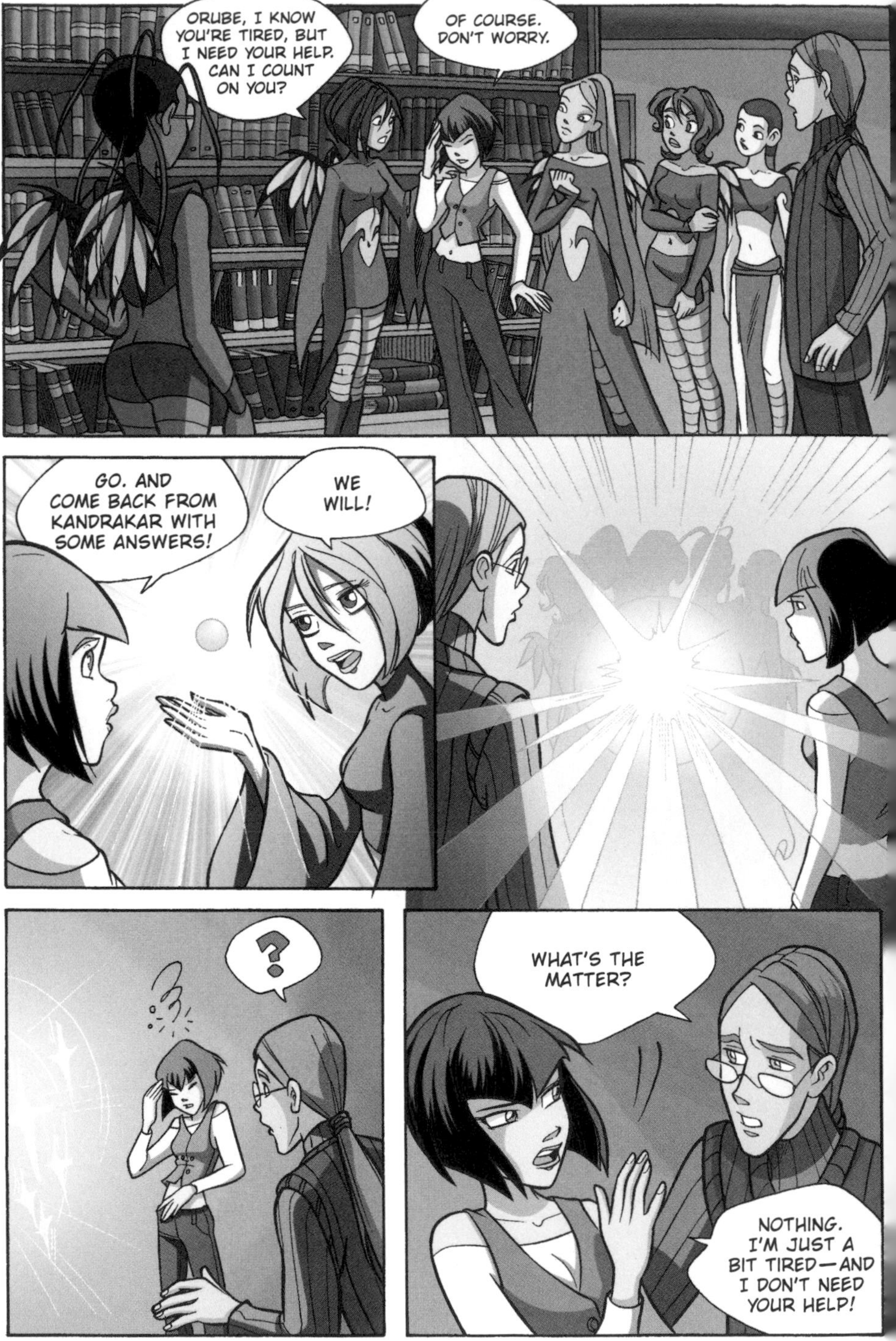
ORUBE, I KNOW YOU'RE TIRED, BUT I NEED YOUR HELP. CAN I COUNT ON YOU?
OF COURSE. DON'T WORRY.
GO. AND COME BACK FROM KANDRAKAR WITH SOME ANSWERS!
WE WILL!
?
WHAT'S THE MATTER?
NOTHING. I'M JUST A BIT TIRED—AND I DON'T NEED YOUR HELP!

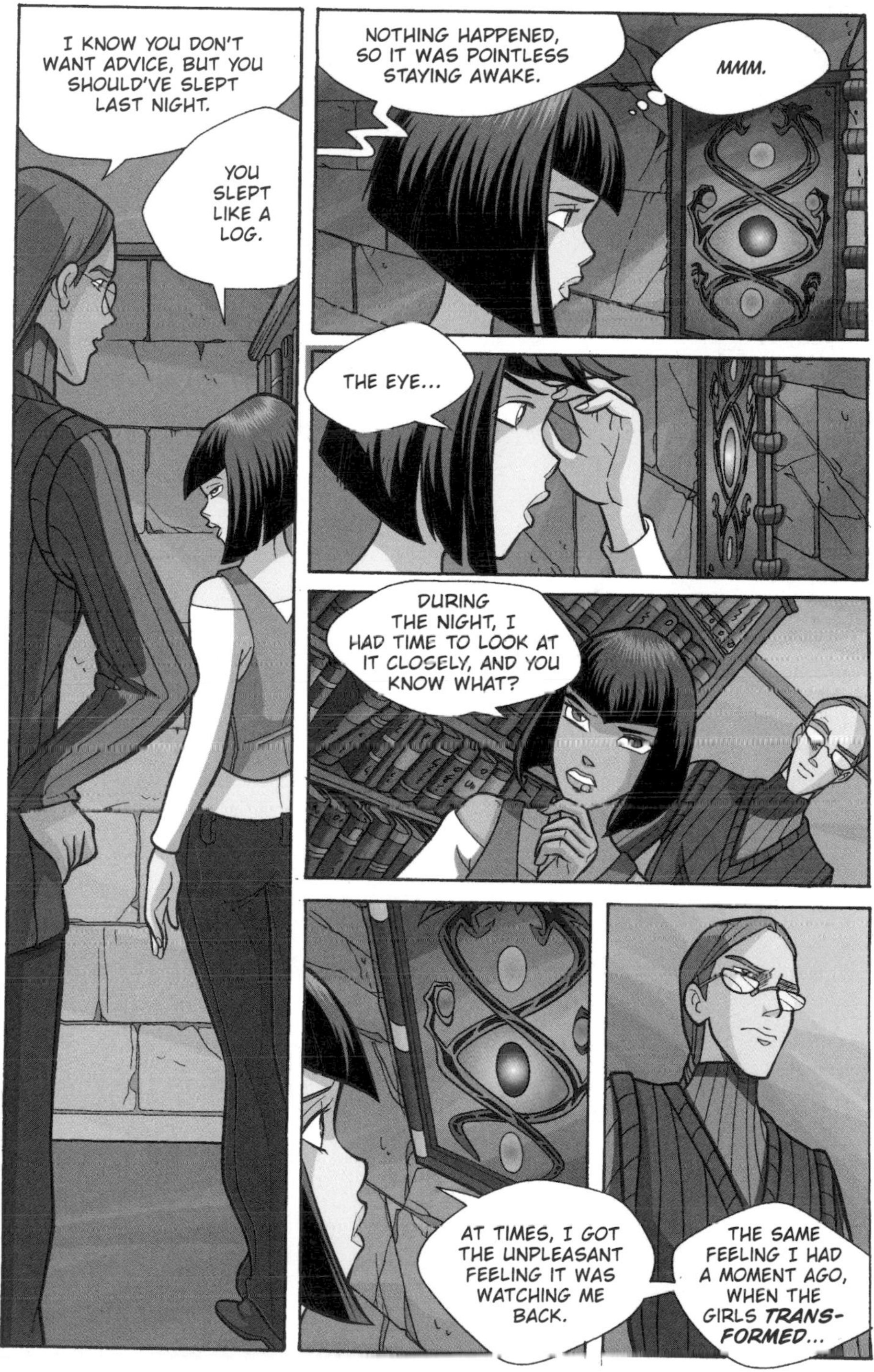
I KNOW YOU DON'T WANT ADVICE, BUT YOU SHOULD'VE SLEPT LAST NIGHT.
YOU SLEPT LIKE A LOG.
NOTHING HAPPENED, SO IT WAS POINTLESS STAYING AWAKE.
MMM.
THE EYE...
DURING THE NIGHT, I HAD TIME TO LOOK AT IT CLOSELY, AND YOU KNOW WHAT?
AT TIMES, I GOT THE UNPLEASANT FEELING IT WAS WATCHING ME BACK.
THE SAME FEELING I HAD A MOMENT AGO, WHEN THE GIRLS ***TRANS-FORMED***...

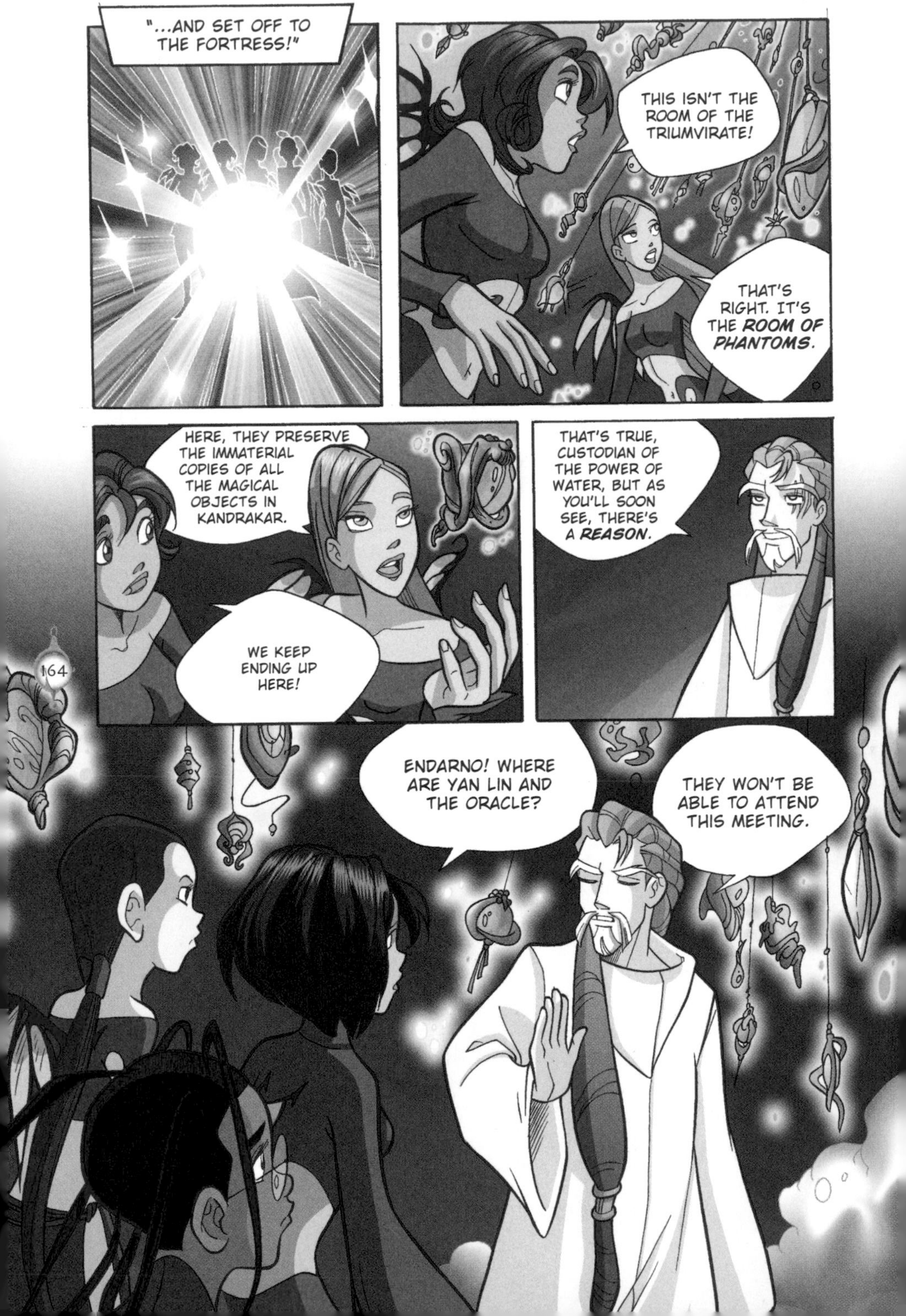
"...AND SET OFF TO THE FORTRESS!"
THIS ISN'T THE ROOM OF THE TRIUMVIRATE!
THAT'S RIGHT. IT'S THE **ROOM OF PHANTOMS**.
HERE, THEY PRESERVE THE IMMATERIAL COPIES OF ALL THE MAGICAL OBJECTS IN KANDRAKAR.
WE KEEP ENDING UP HERE!
THAT'S TRUE, CUSTODIAN OF THE POWER OF WATER, BUT AS YOU'LL SOON SEE, THERE'S A **REASON**.
ENDARNO! WHERE ARE YAN LIN AND THE ORACLE?
THEY WON'T BE ABLE TO ATTEND THIS MEETING.

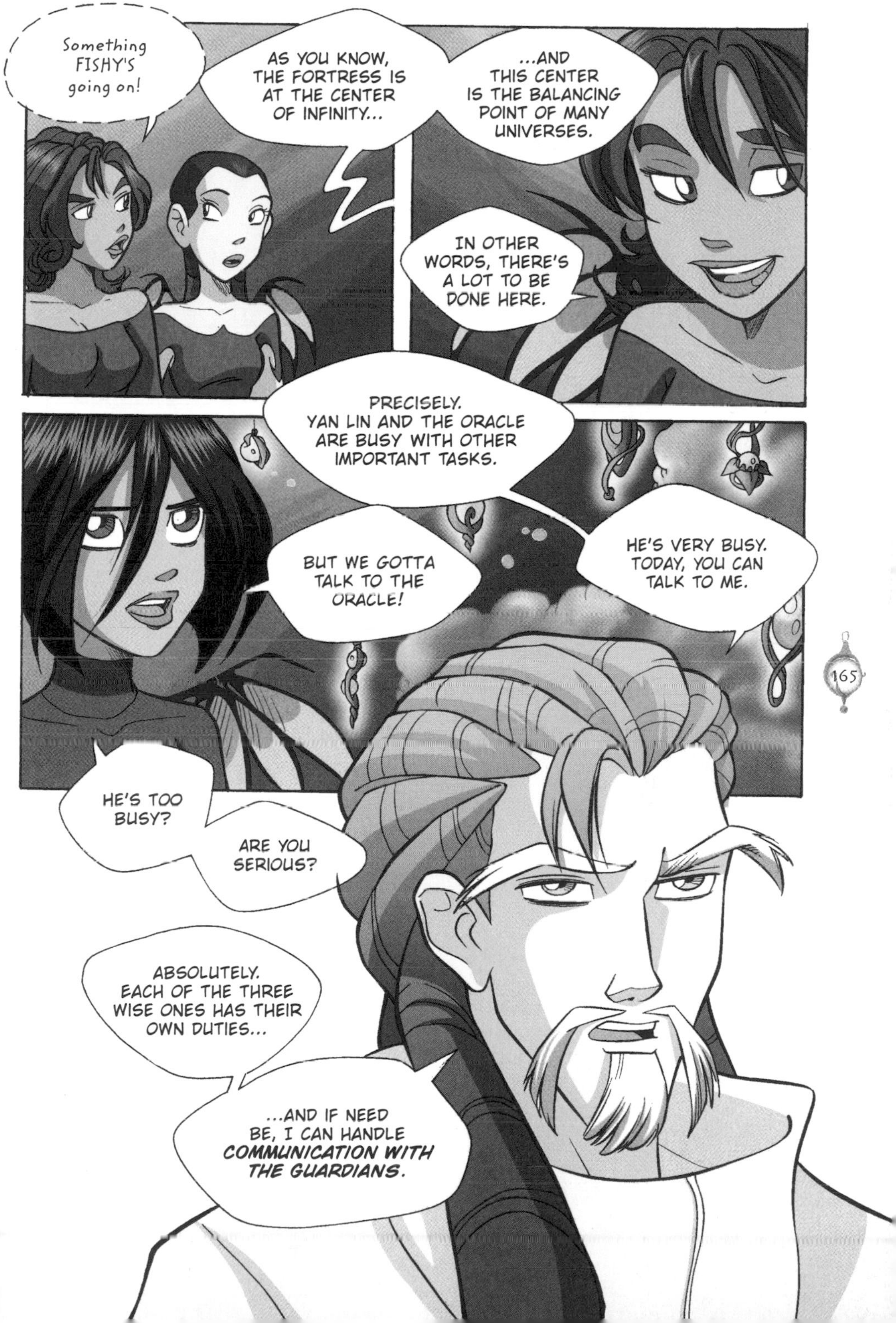
Something FISHY'S going on!
AS YOU KNOW, THE FORTRESS IS AT THE CENTER OF INFINITY...
...AND THIS CENTER IS THE BALANCING POINT OF MANY UNIVERSES.
IN OTHER WORDS, THERE'S A LOT TO BE DONE HERE.
PRECISELY. YAN LIN AND THE ORACLE ARE BUSY WITH OTHER IMPORTANT TASKS.
BUT WE GOTTA TALK TO THE ORACLE!
HE'S VERY BUSY. TODAY, YOU CAN TALK TO ME.
HE'S TOO BUSY?
ARE YOU SERIOUS?
ABSOLUTELY. EACH OF THE THREE WISE ONES HAS THEIR OWN DUTIES...
...AND IF NEED BE, I CAN HANDLE ***COMMUNICATION WITH THE GUARDIANS.***

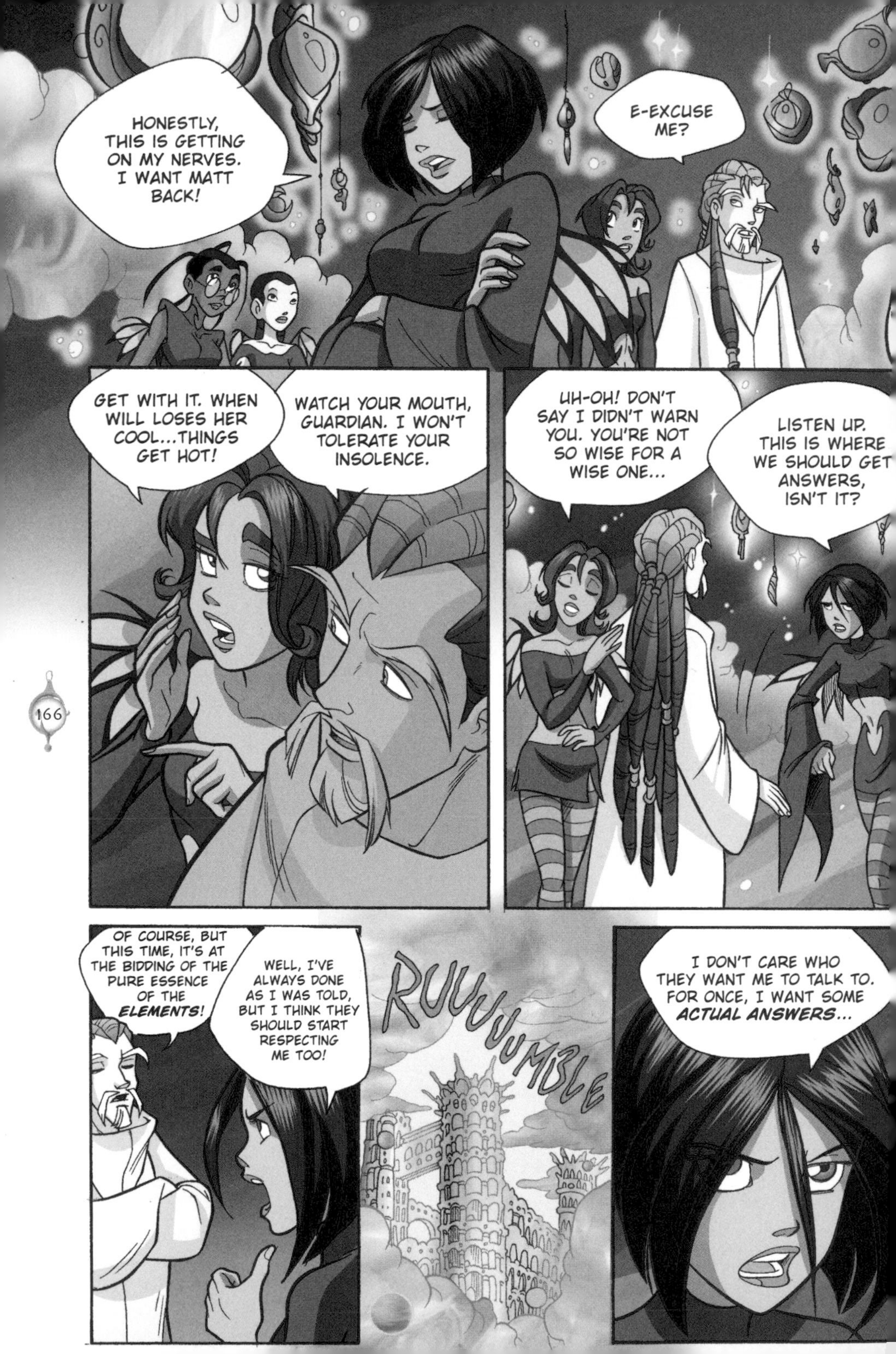
HONESTLY, THIS IS GETTING ON MY NERVES. I WANT MATT BACK!
E-EXCUSE ME?
GET WITH IT. WHEN WILL LOSES HER COOL...THINGS GET HOT!
WATCH YOUR MOUTH, GUARDIAN. I WON'T TOLERATE YOUR INSOLENCE.
UH-OH! DON'T SAY I DIDN'T WARN YOU. YOU'RE NOT SO WISE FOR A WISE ONE...
LISTEN UP. THIS IS WHERE WE SHOULD GET ANSWERS, ISN'T IT?
OF COURSE, BUT THIS TIME, IT'S AT THE BIDDING OF THE PURE ESSENCE OF THE ELEMENTS!
WELL, I'VE ALWAYS DONE AS I WAS TOLD, BUT I THINK THEY SHOULD START RESPECTING ME TOO!
RUUUUUMBLE
I DON'T CARE WHO THEY WANT ME TO TALK TO. FOR ONCE, I WANT SOME ACTUAL ANSWERS...

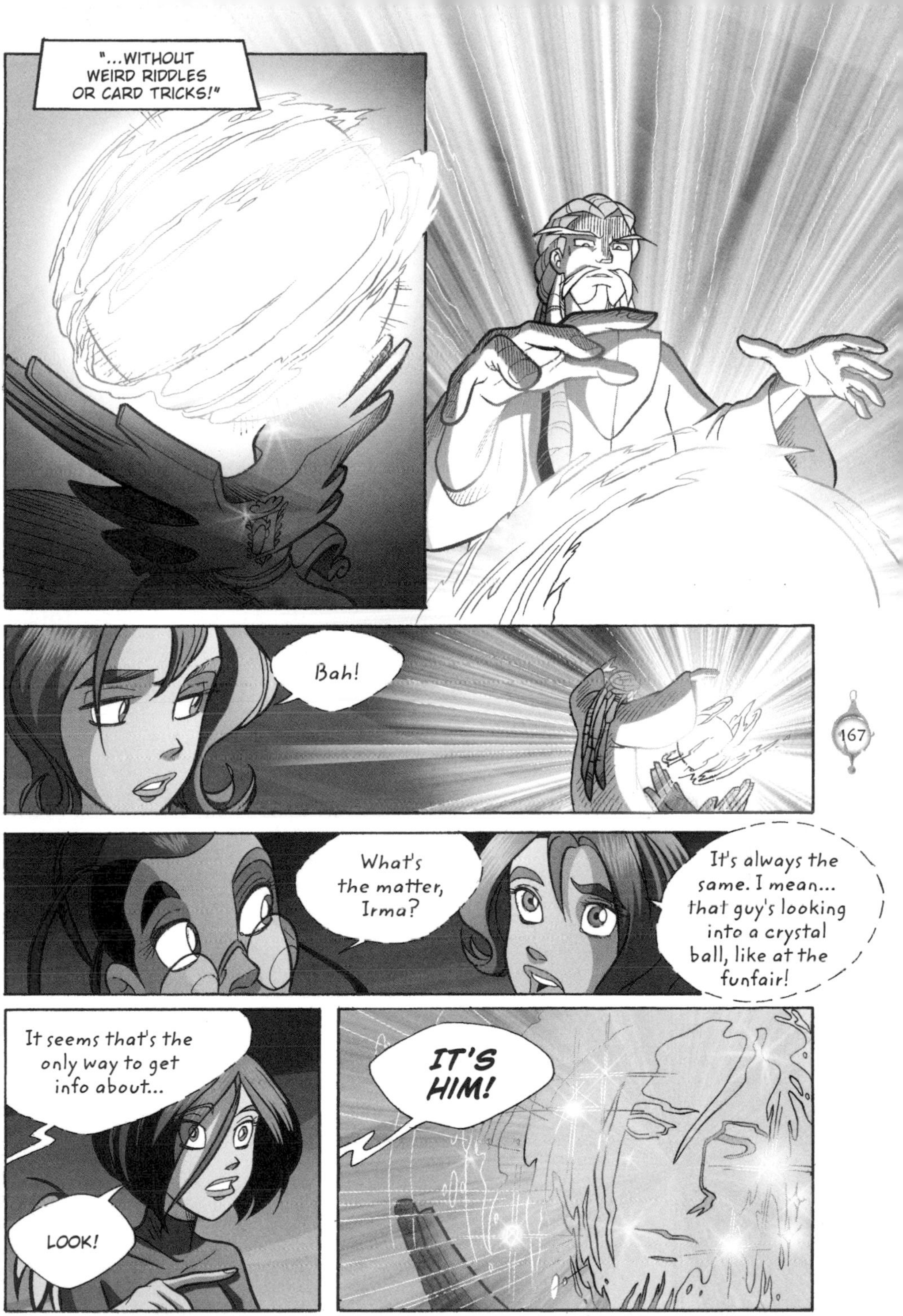
"...WITHOUT WEIRD RIDDLES OR CARD TRICKS!"
Bah!
What's the matter, Irma?
It's always the same. I mean... that guy's looking into a crystal ball, like at the funfair!
It seems that's the only way to get info about...
LOOK!
IT'S HIM!

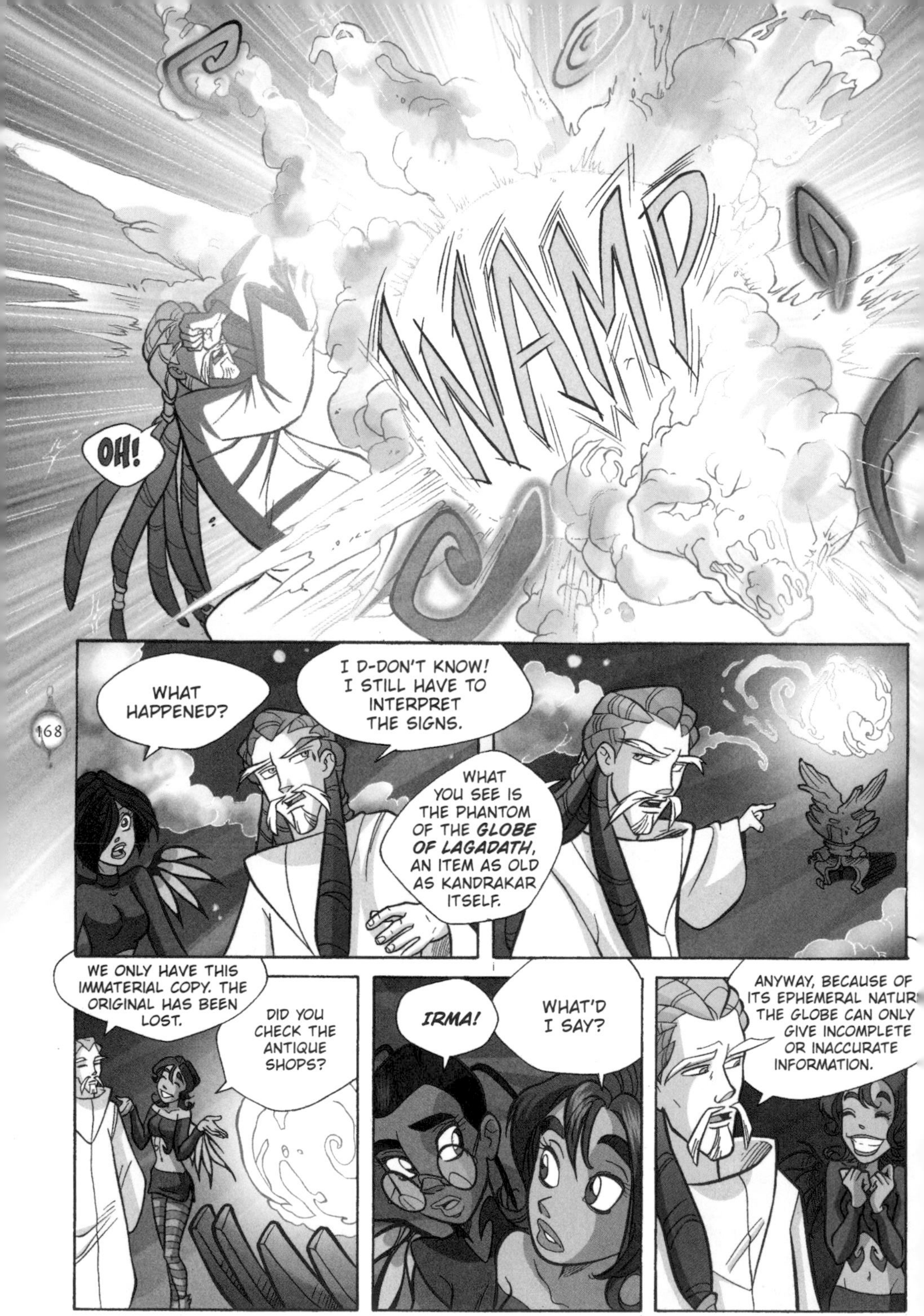
WAMP
OH!
WHAT HAPPENED?
I D-DON'T KNOW! I STILL HAVE TO INTERPRET THE SIGNS.
WHAT YOU SEE IS THE PHANTOM OF THE **GLOBE OF LAGADATH**, AN ITEM AS OLD AS KANDRAKAR ITSELF.
WE ONLY HAVE THIS IMMATERIAL COPY. THE ORIGINAL HAS BEEN LOST.
DID YOU CHECK THE ANTIQUE SHOPS?
IRMA!
WHAT'D I SAY?
ANYWAY, BECAUSE OF ITS EPHEMERAL NATUR
THE GLOBE CAN ONLY GIVE INCOMPLETE OR INACCURATE INFORMATION.

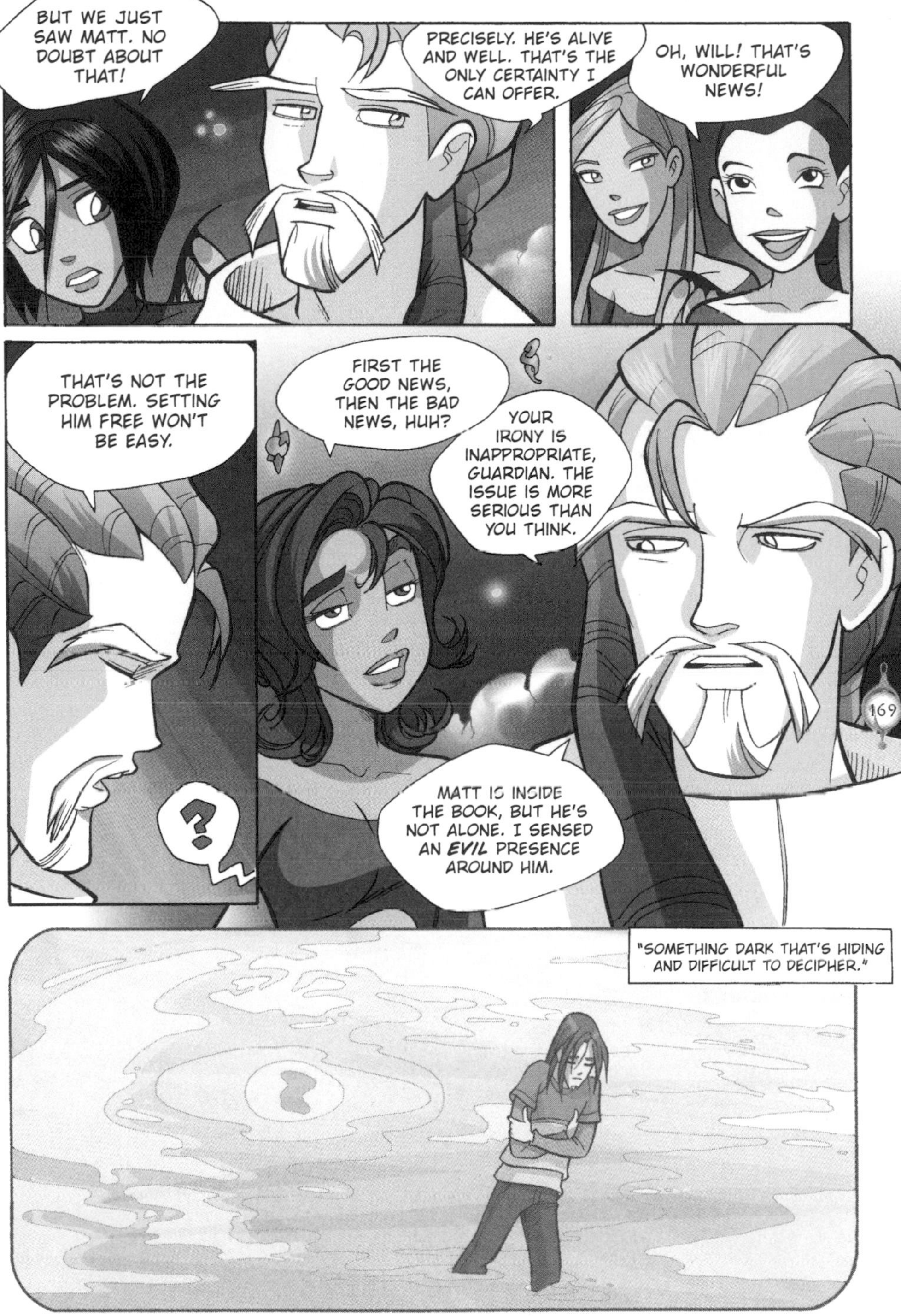
BUT WE JUST SAW MATT. NO DOUBT ABOUT THAT!
PRECISELY. HE'S ALIVE AND WELL. THAT'S THE ONLY CERTAINTY I CAN OFFER.
OH, WILL! THAT'S WONDERFUL NEWS!
THAT'S NOT THE PROBLEM. SETTING HIM FREE WON'T BE EASY.
FIRST THE GOOD NEWS, THEN THE BAD NEWS, HUH?
YOUR IRONY IS INAPPROPRIATE, GUARDIAN. THE ISSUE IS MORE SERIOUS THAN YOU THINK.
?
MATT IS INSIDE THE BOOK, BUT HE'S NOT ALONE. I SENSED AN *EVIL* PRESENCE AROUND HIM.
"SOMETHING DARK THAT'S HIDING AND DIFFICULT TO DECIPHER."

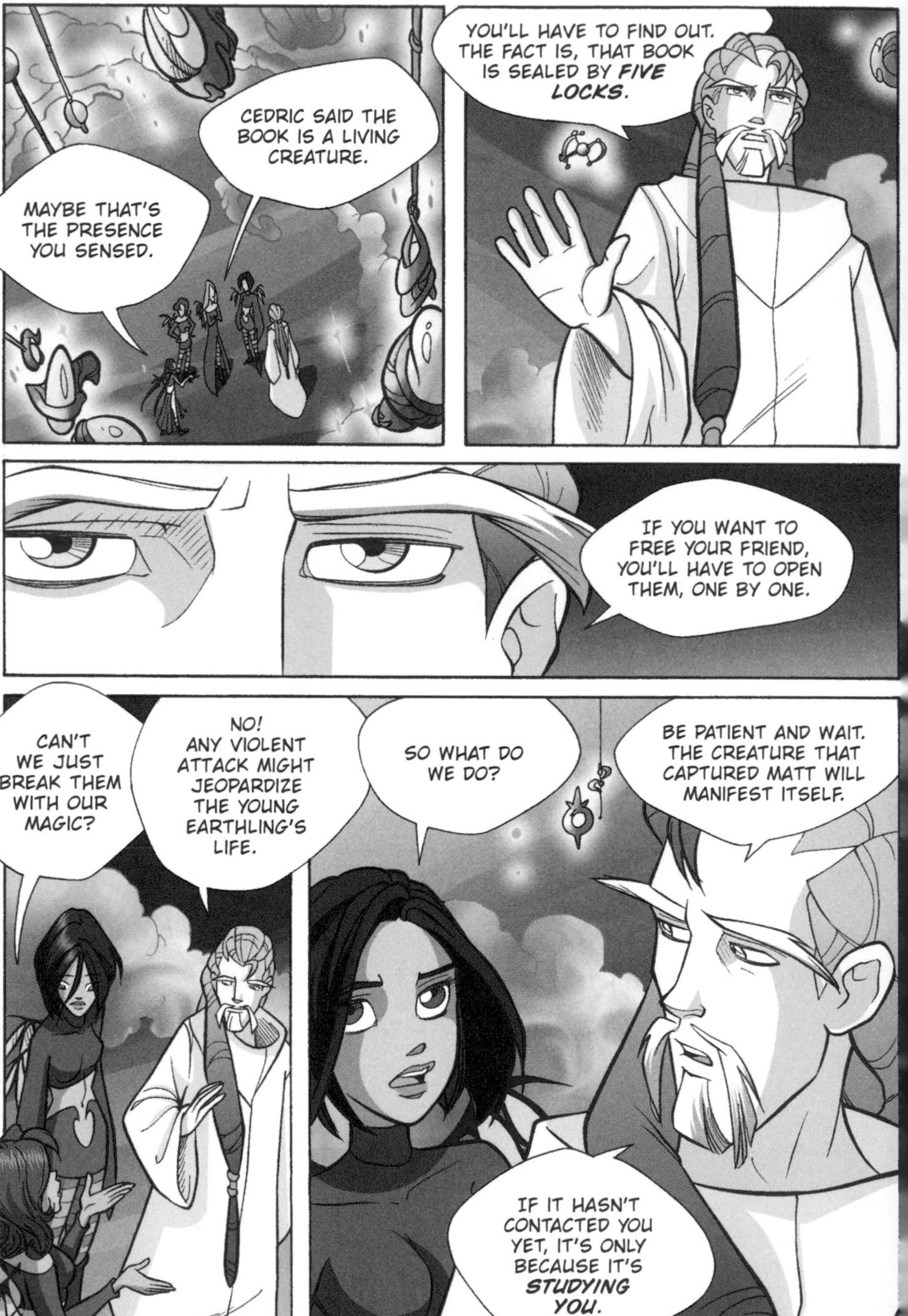
MAYBE THAT'S THE PRESENCE YOU SENSED.
CEDRIC SAID THE BOOK IS A LIVING CREATURE.
YOU'LL HAVE TO FIND OUT. THE FACT IS, THAT BOOK IS SEALED BY ***FIVE LOCKS***.
IF YOU WANT TO FREE YOUR FRIEND, YOU'LL HAVE TO OPEN THEM, ONE BY ONE.
CAN'T WE JUST BREAK THEM WITH OUR MAGIC?
NO! ANY VIOLENT ATTACK MIGHT JEOPARDIZE THE YOUNG EARTHLING'S LIFE.
SO WHAT DO WE DO?
BE PATIENT AND WAIT. THE CREATURE THAT CAPTURED MATT WILL MANIFEST ITSELF.
IF IT HASN'T CONTACTED YOU YET, IT'S ONLY BECAUSE IT'S ***STUDYING YOU***.

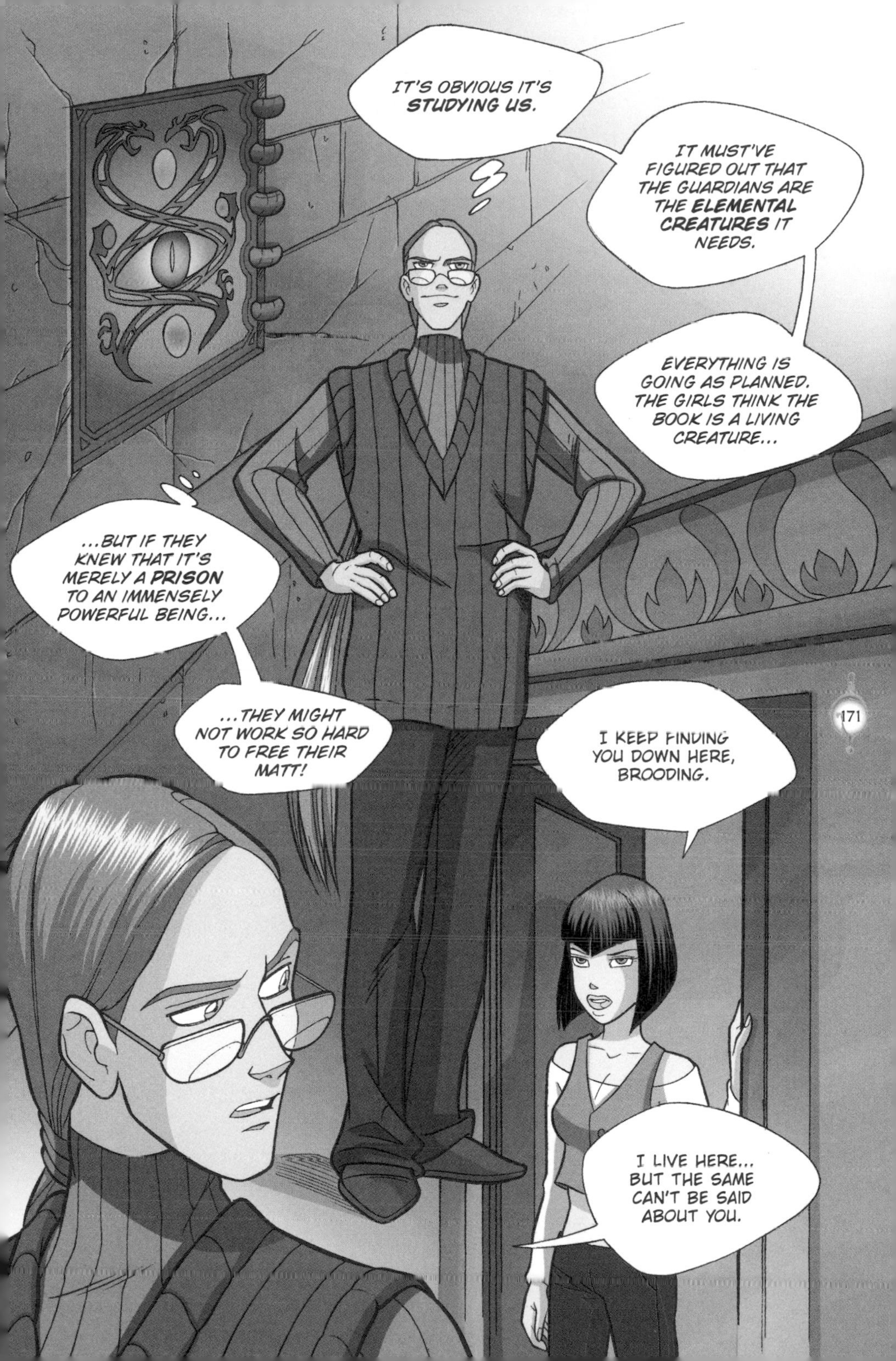
IT'S OBVIOUS IT'S STUDYING US.
IT MUST'VE FIGURED OUT THAT THE GUARDIANS ARE THE ELEMENTAL CREATURES IT NEEDS.
EVERYTHING IS GOING AS PLANNED. THE GIRLS THINK THE BOOK IS A LIVING CREATURE...
...BUT IF THEY KNEW THAT IT'S MERELY A PRISON TO AN IMMENSELY POWERFUL BEING...
...THEY MIGHT NOT WORK SO HARD TO FREE THEIR MATT!
I KEEP FINDING YOU DOWN HERE, BROODING.
I LIVE HERE... BUT THE SAME CAN'T BE SAID ABOUT YOU.

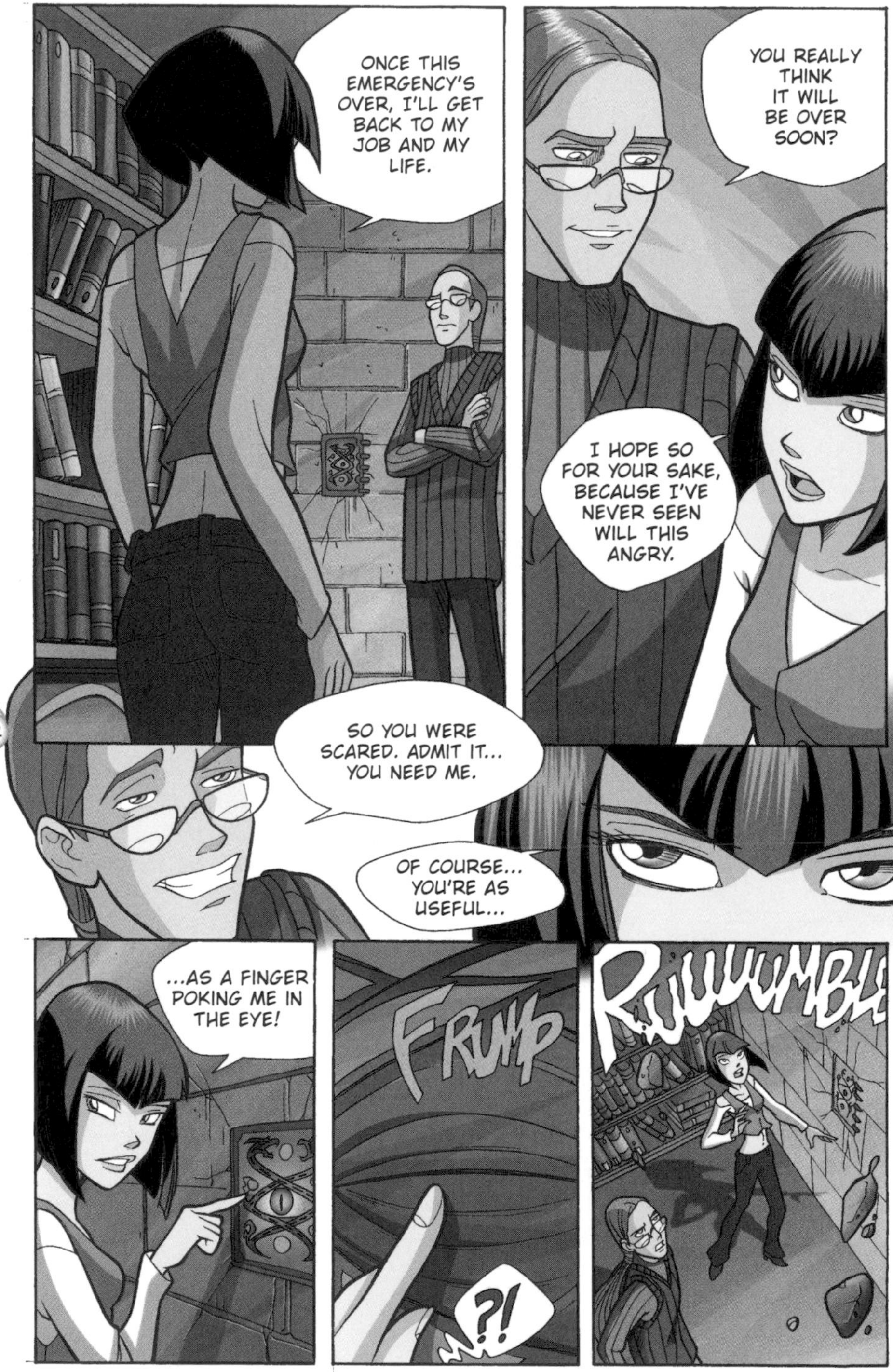
ONCE THIS EMERGENCY'S OVER, I'LL GET BACK TO MY JOB AND MY LIFE.
YOU REALLY THINK IT WILL BE OVER SOON?
I HOPE SO FOR YOUR SAKE, BECAUSE I'VE NEVER SEEN WILL THIS ANGRY.
SO YOU WERE SCARED. ADMIT IT... YOU NEED ME.
OF COURSE... YOU'RE AS USEFUL...
...AS A FINGER POKING ME IN THE EYE!
FRUMP
?!
RUUUUMBLE

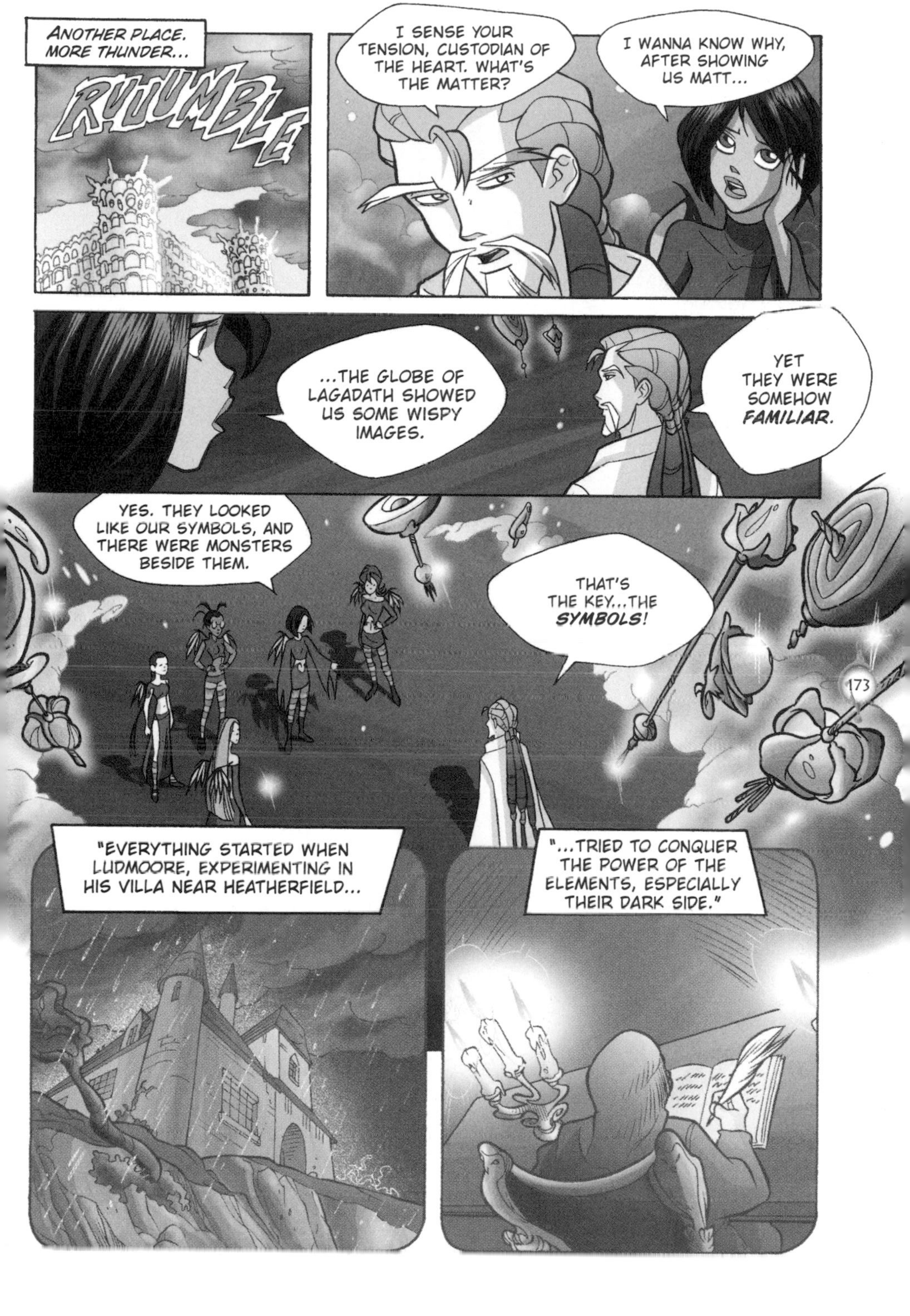
ANOTHER PLACE. MORE THUNDER...
RUUUMBLE
I SENSE YOUR TENSION, CUSTODIAN OF THE HEART. WHAT'S THE MATTER?
I WANNA KNOW WHY, AFTER SHOWING US MATT...
...THE GLOBE OF LAGADATH SHOWED US SOME WISPY IMAGES.
YET THEY WERE SOMEHOW *FAMILIAR*.
YES. THEY LOOKED LIKE OUR SYMBOLS, AND THERE WERE MONSTERS BESIDE THEM.
THAT'S THE KEY...THE *SYMBOLS*!
"EVERYTHING STARTED WHEN LUDMOORE, EXPERIMENTING IN HIS VILLA NEAR HEATHERFIELD...
"...TRIED TO CONQUER THE POWER OF THE ELEMENTS, ESPECIALLY THEIR DARK SIDE."

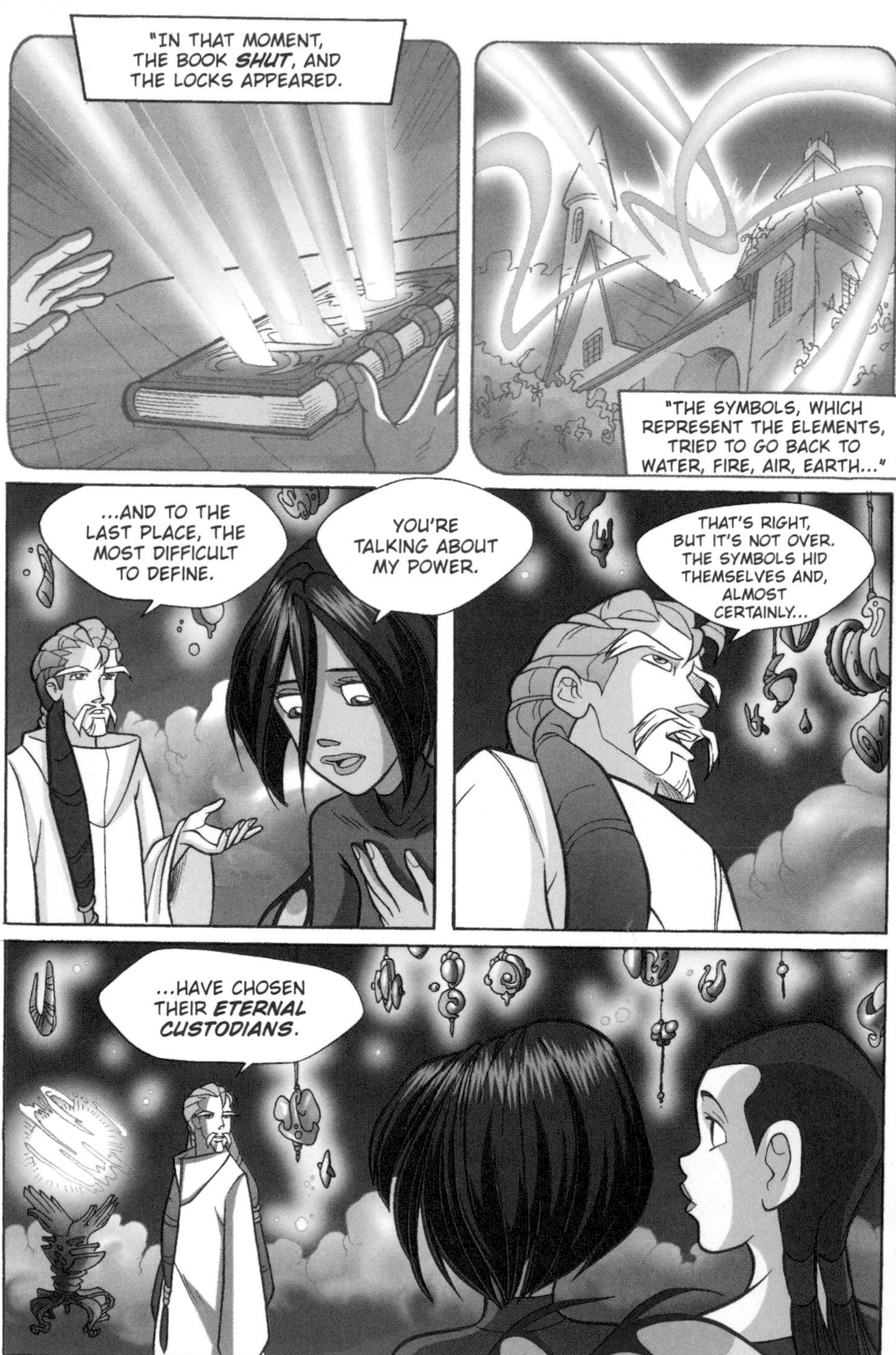
"IN THAT MOMENT, THE BOOK *SHUT*, AND THE LOCKS APPEARED.
"THE SYMBOLS, WHICH REPRESENT THE ELEMENTS, TRIED TO GO BACK TO WATER, FIRE, AIR, EARTH..."
...AND TO THE LAST PLACE, THE MOST DIFFICULT TO DEFINE.
YOU'RE TALKING ABOUT MY POWER.
THAT'S RIGHT, BUT IT'S NOT OVER. THE SYMBOLS HID THEMSELVES AND, ALMOST CERTAINLY...
...HAVE CHOSEN THEIR *ETERNAL CUSTODIANS*.

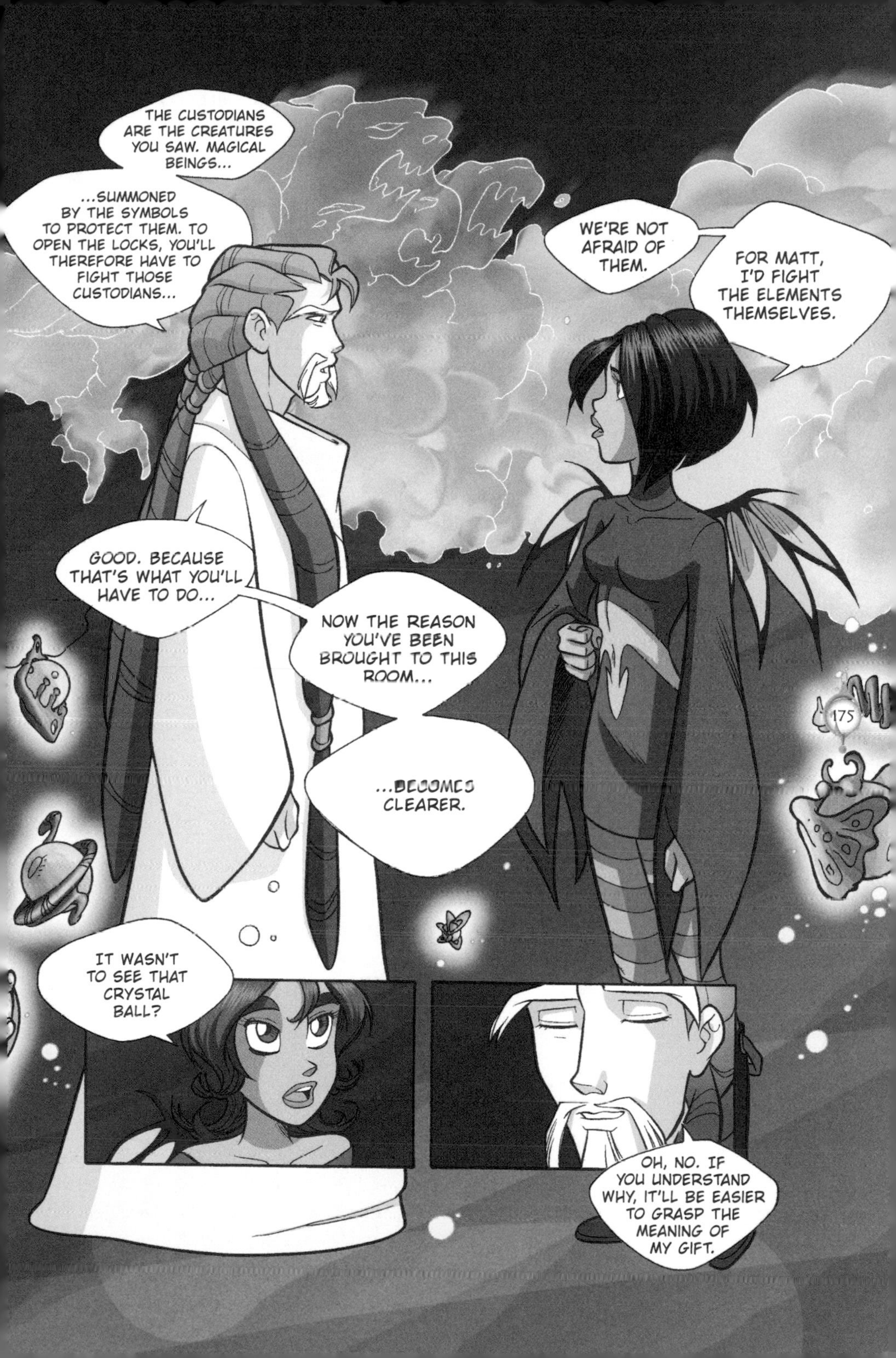
THE CUSTODIANS ARE THE CREATURES YOU SAW. MAGICAL BEINGS...
...SUMMONED BY THE SYMBOLS TO PROTECT THEM. TO OPEN THE LOCKS, YOU'LL THEREFORE HAVE TO FIGHT THOSE CUSTODIANS...
WE'RE NOT AFRAID OF THEM.
FOR MATT, I'D FIGHT THE ELEMENTS THEMSELVES.
GOOD. BECAUSE THAT'S WHAT YOU'LL HAVE TO DO...
NOW THE REASON YOU'VE BEEN BROUGHT TO THIS ROOM...
...BECOMES CLEARER.
IT WASN'T TO SEE THAT CRYSTAL BALL?
OH, NO. IF YOU UNDERSTAND WHY, IT'LL BE EASIER TO GRASP THE MEANING OF MY GIFT.

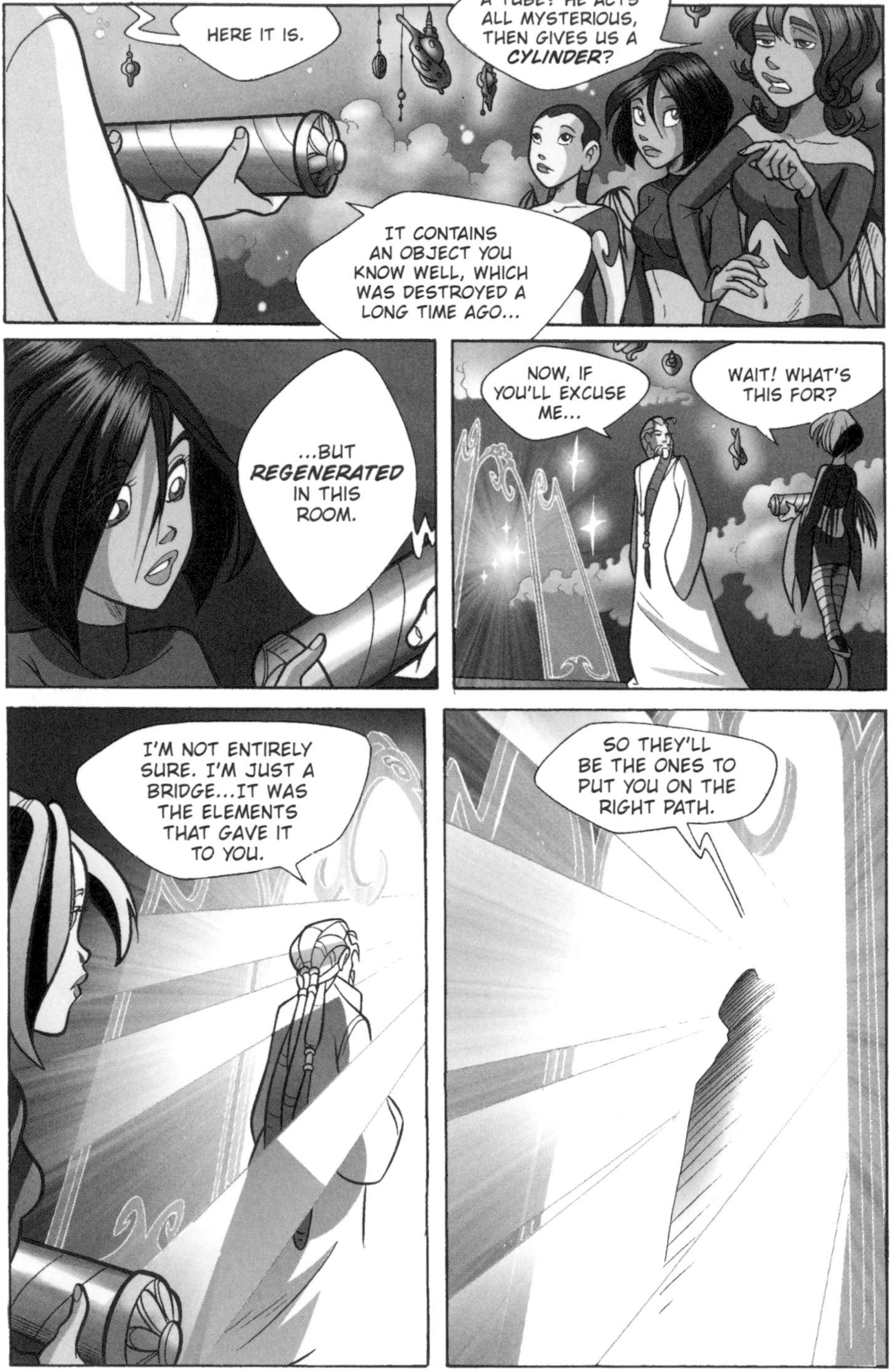
HERE IT IS.
A TUBE? HE ACTS ALL MYSTERIOUS, THEN GIVES US A *CYLINDER*?
IT CONTAINS AN OBJECT YOU KNOW WELL, WHICH WAS DESTROYED A LONG TIME AGO...
...BUT *REGENERATED* IN THIS ROOM.
NOW, IF YOU'LL EXCUSE ME...
WAIT! WHAT'S THIS FOR?
I'M NOT ENTIRELY SURE. I'M JUST A BRIDGE...IT WAS THE ELEMENTS THAT GAVE IT TO YOU.
SO THEY'LL BE THE ONES TO PUT YOU ON THE RIGHT PATH.

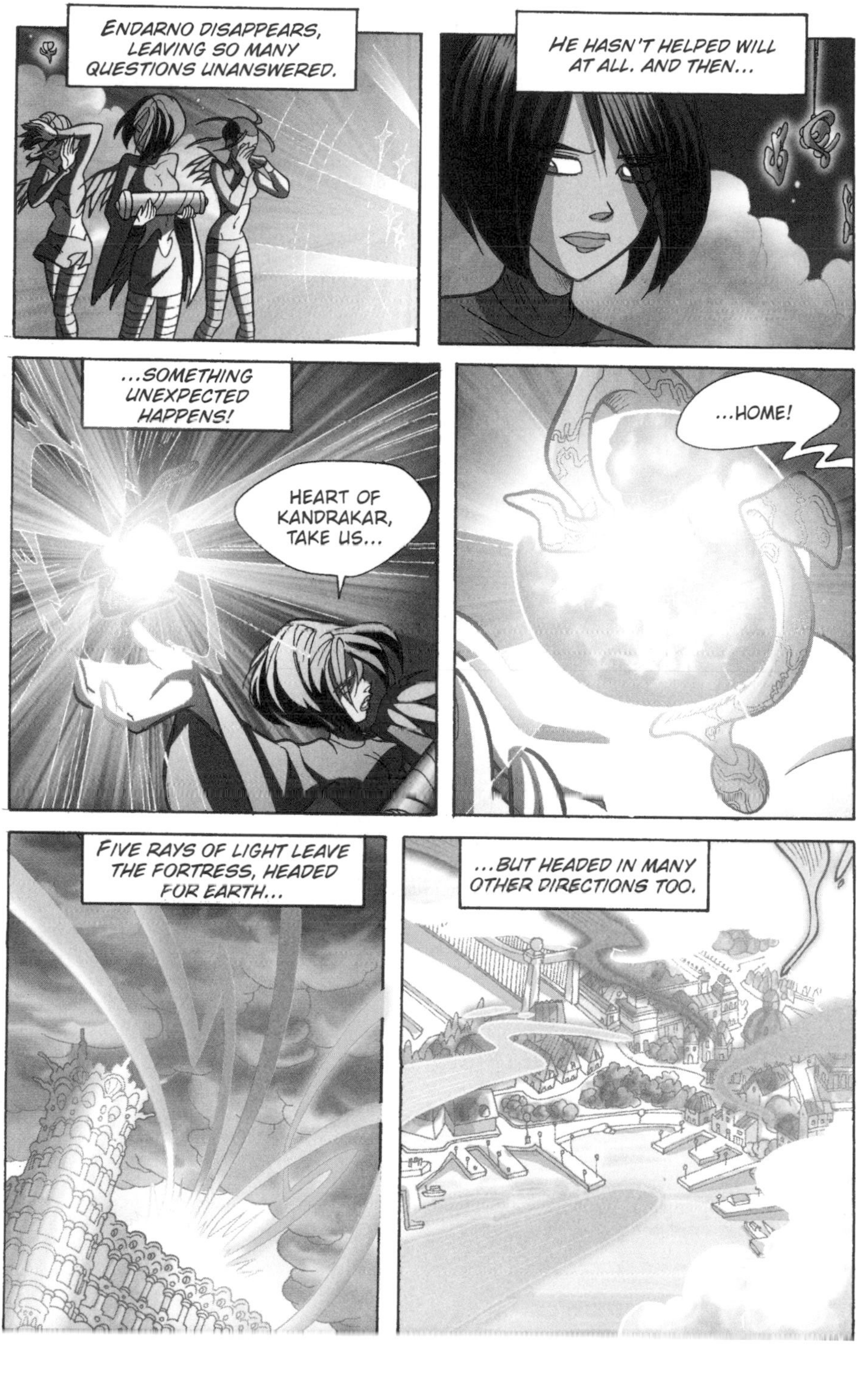
ENDARNO DISAPPEARS, LEAVING SO MANY QUESTIONS UNANSWERED.
HE HASN'T HELPED WILL AT ALL. AND THEN...
...SOMETHING UNEXPECTED HAPPENS!
HEART OF KANDRAKAR, TAKE US...
...HOME!
FIVE RAYS OF LIGHT LEAVE THE FORTRESS, HEADED FOR EARTH...
...BUT HEADED IN MANY OTHER DIRECTIONS TOO.

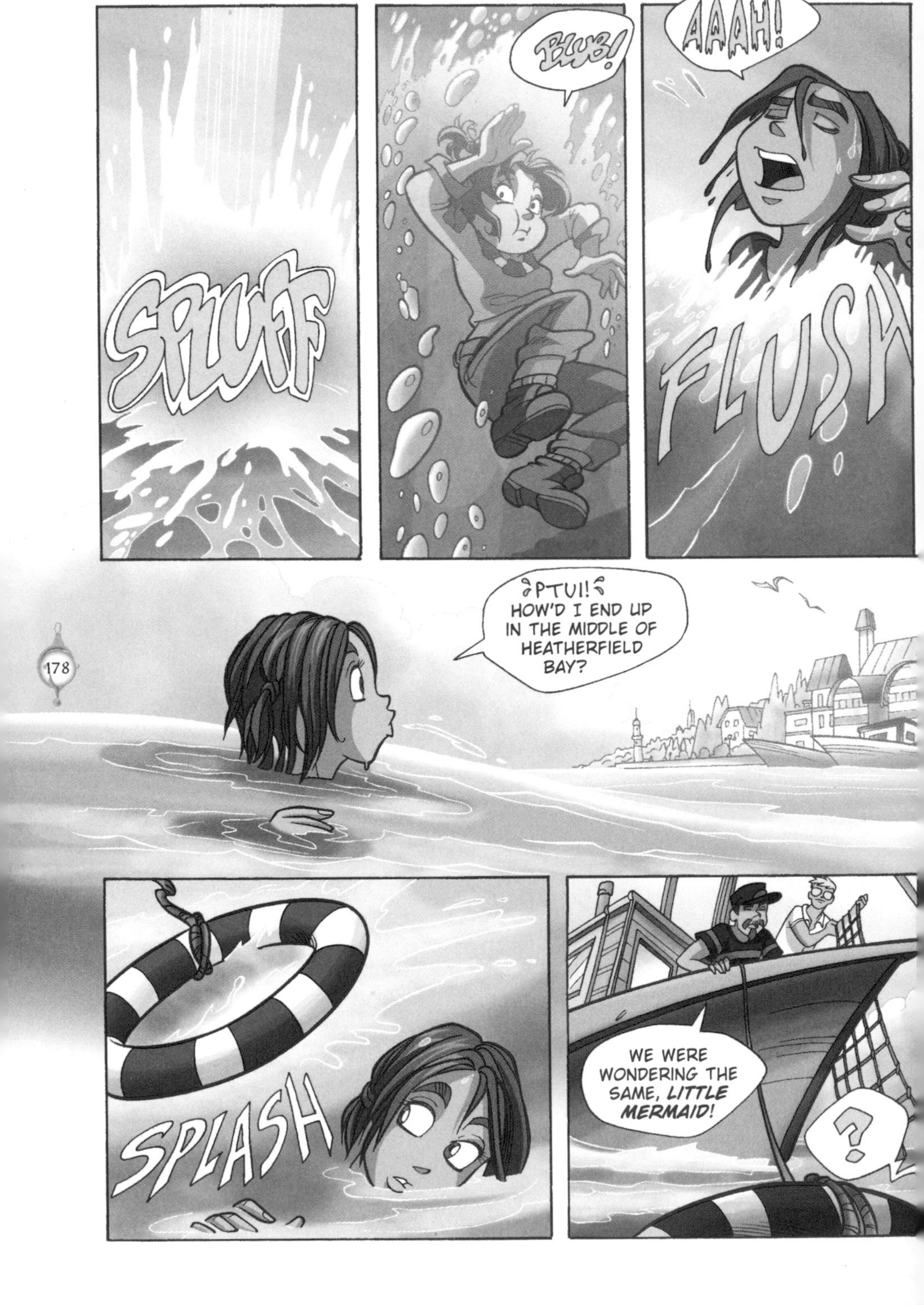
SPLUFF
BLUB!
AAAH!
FLUSH
PTUI!
HOW'D I END UP IN THE MIDDLE OF HEATHERFIELD BAY?
SPLASH
WE WERE WONDERING THE SAME, *LITTLE MERMAID*!
?

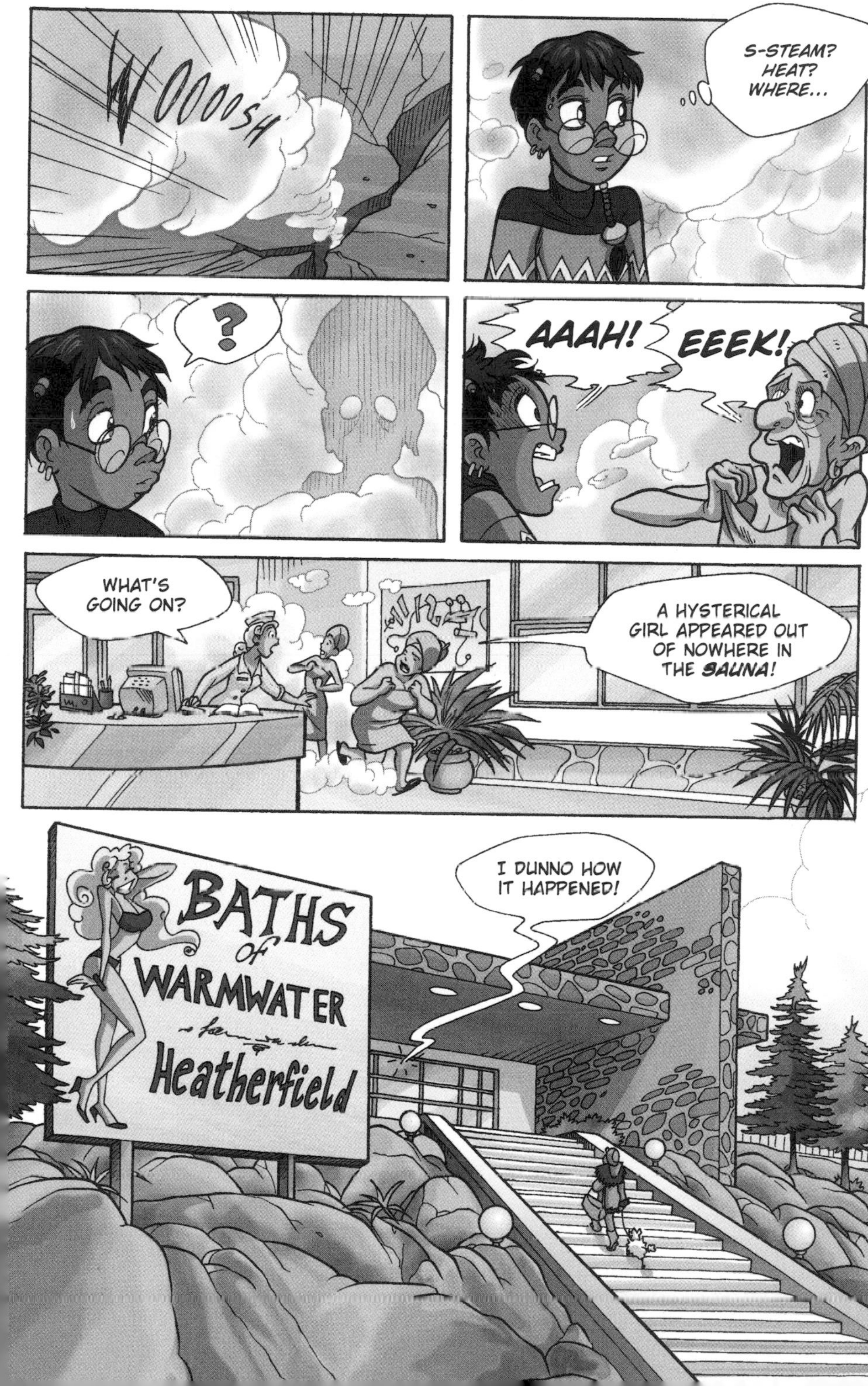
WOOOOSH
S-STEAM? HEAT? WHERE...
?
AAAH!
EEEK!
WHAT'S GOING ON?
A HYSTERICAL GIRL APPEARED OUT OF NOWHERE IN THE SAUNA!
BATHS of WARMWATER
Heatherfield
I DUNNO HOW IT HAPPENED!

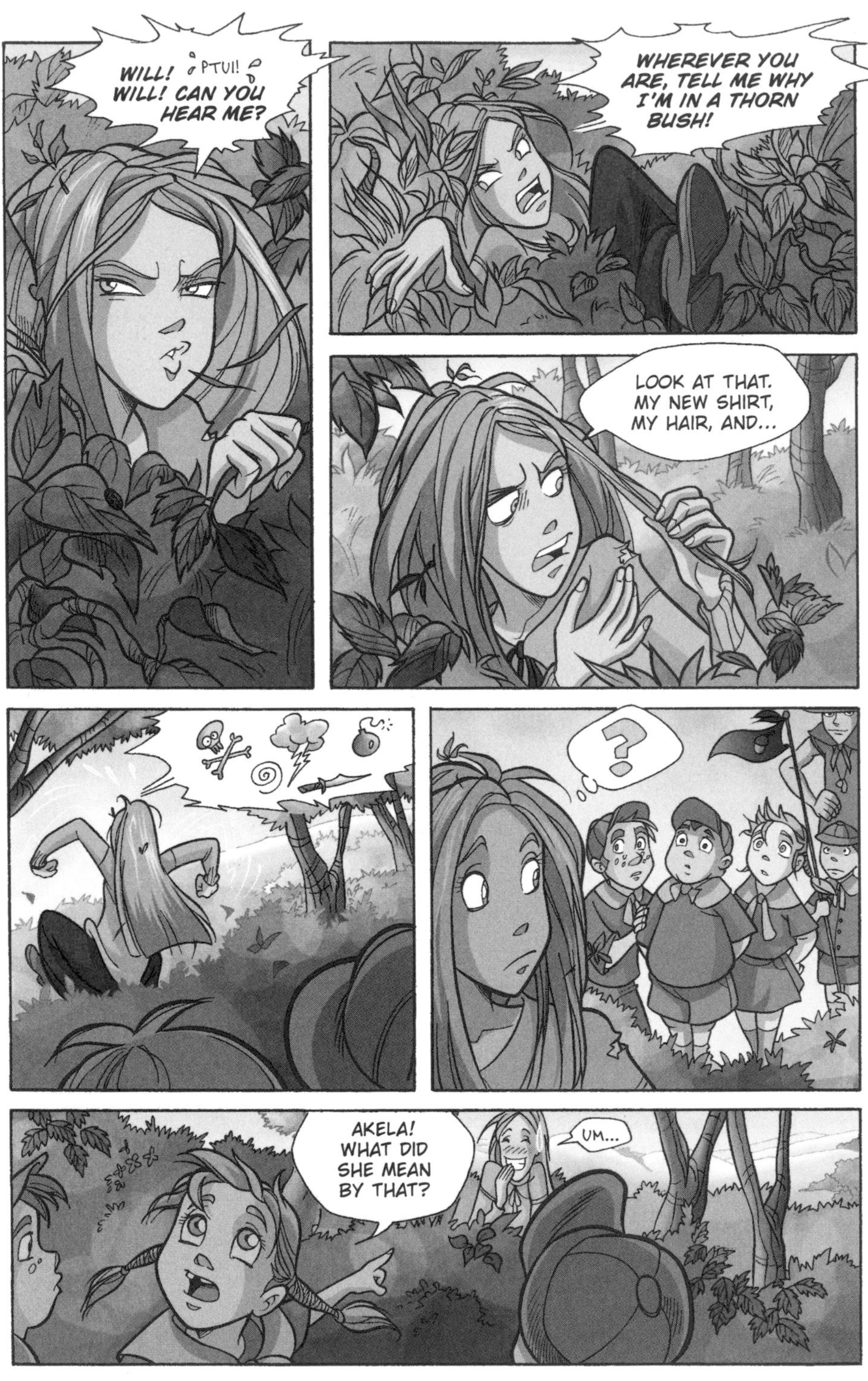
WILL! PTUI! WILL! CAN YOU HEAR ME?
WHEREVER YOU ARE, TELL ME WHY I'M IN A THORN BUSH!
LOOK AT THAT. MY NEW SHIRT, MY HAIR, AND...
?
AKELA! WHAT DID SHE MEAN BY THAT?
UM...

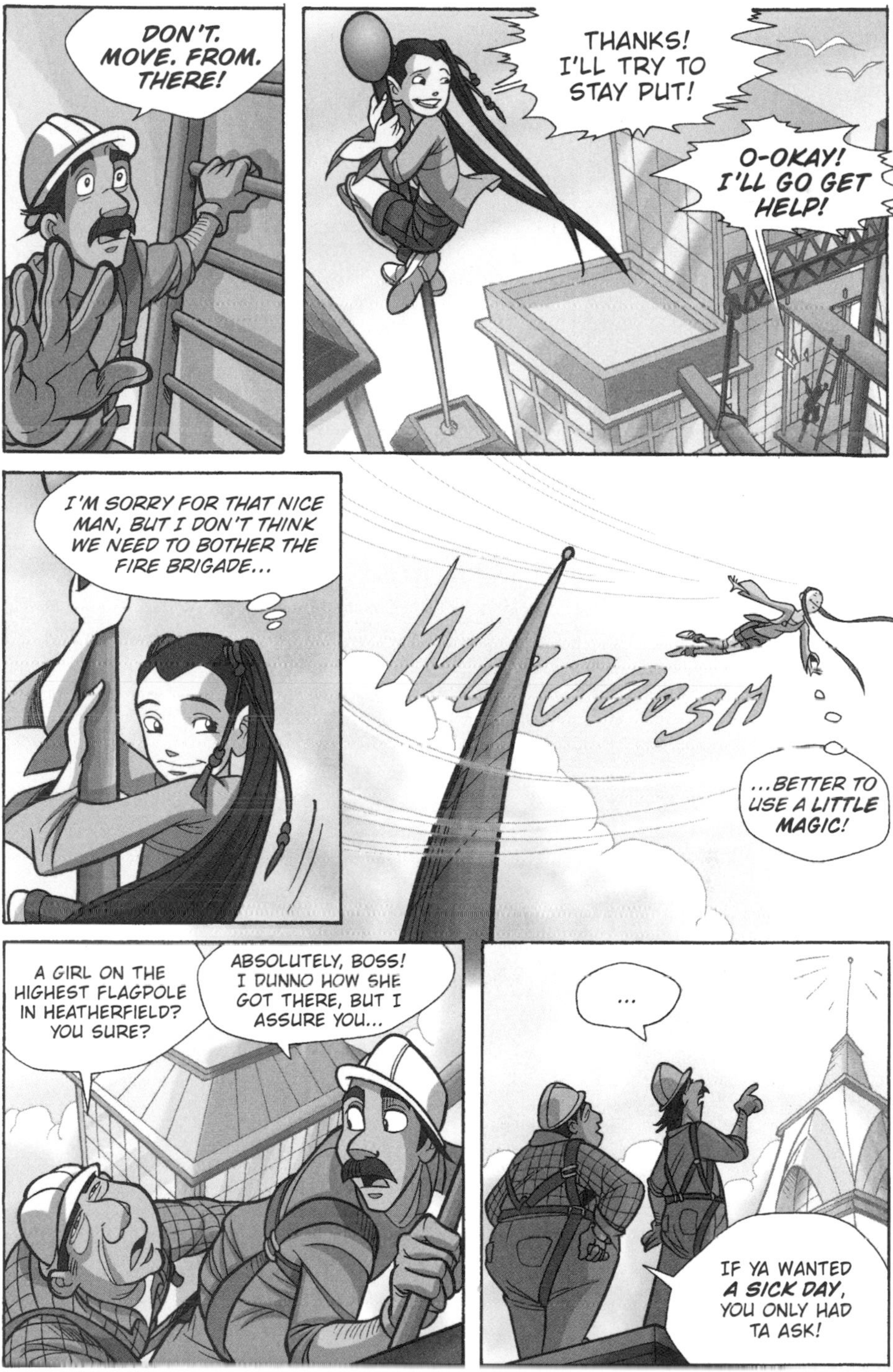

DON'T. MOVE. FROM. THERE!
THANKS! I'LL TRY TO STAY PUT!
O-OKAY! I'LL GO GET HELP!
I'M SORRY FOR THAT NICE MAN, BUT I DON'T THINK WE NEED TO BOTHER THE FIRE BRIGADE...
WHOOOOSH
...BETTER TO USE A LITTLE MAGIC!
A GIRL ON THE HIGHEST FLAGPOLE IN HEATHERFIELD? YOU SURE?
ABSOLUTELY, BOSS! I DUNNO HOW SHE GOT THERE, BUT I ASSURE YOU...
...
IF YA WANTED A SICK DAY, YOU ONLY HAD TA ASK!

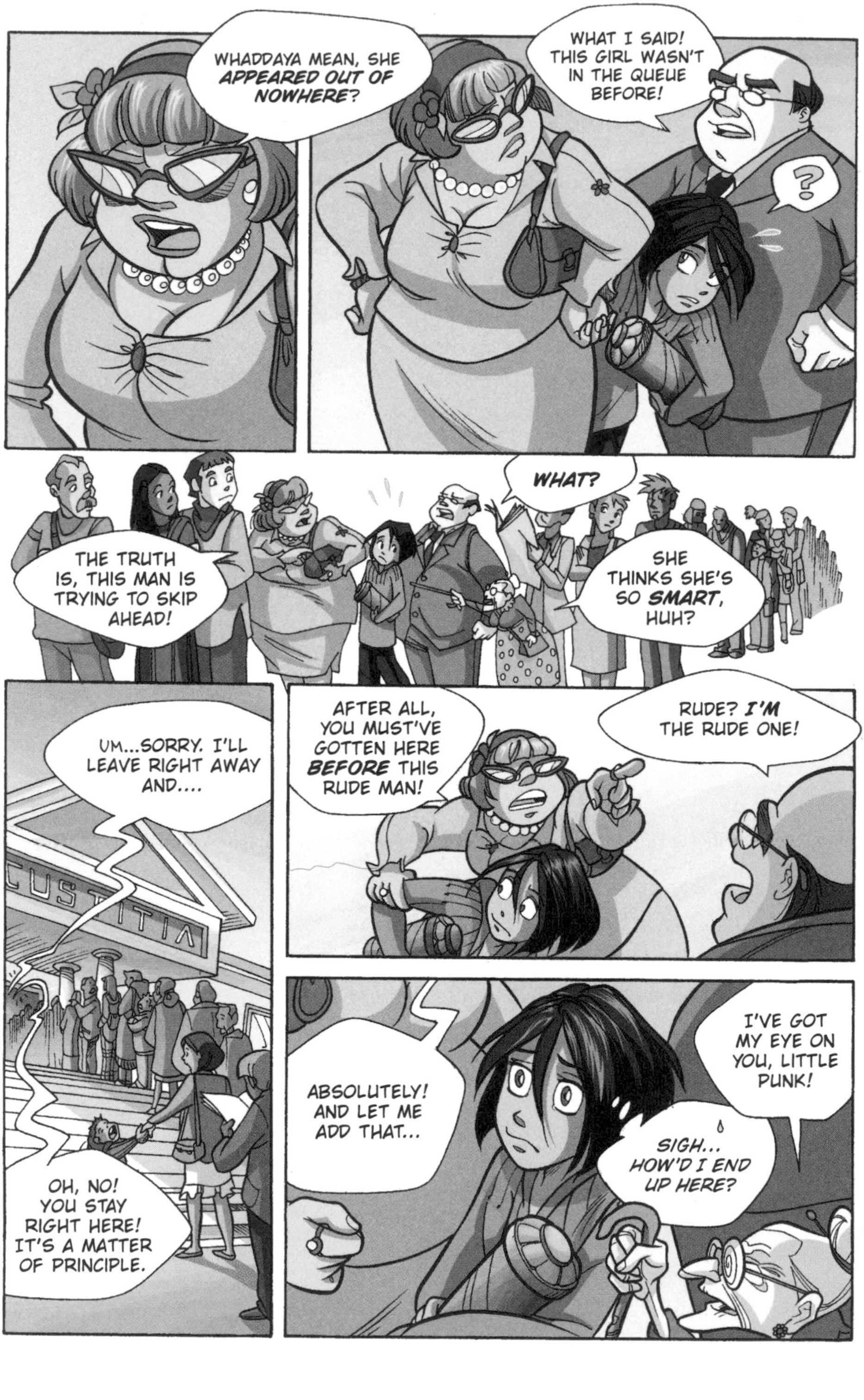

WHADDAYA MEAN, SHE *APPEARED OUT OF NOWHERE*?
WHAT I SAID! THIS GIRL WASN'T IN THE QUEUE BEFORE!
?
WHAT?
THE TRUTH IS, THIS MAN IS TRYING TO SKIP AHEAD!
SHE THINKS SHE'S SO ***SMART***, HUH?
CUSTITIA
UM...SORRY. I'LL LEAVE RIGHT AWAY AND....
OH, NO! YOU STAY RIGHT HERE! IT'S A MATTER OF PRINCIPLE.
AFTER ALL, YOU MUST'VE GOTTEN HERE ***BEFORE*** THIS RUDE MAN!
RUDE? ***I'M*** THE RUDE ONE!
ABSOLUTELY! AND LET ME ADD THAT...
I'VE GOT MY EYE ON YOU, LITTLE PUNK!
SIGH... HOW'D I END UP HERE?

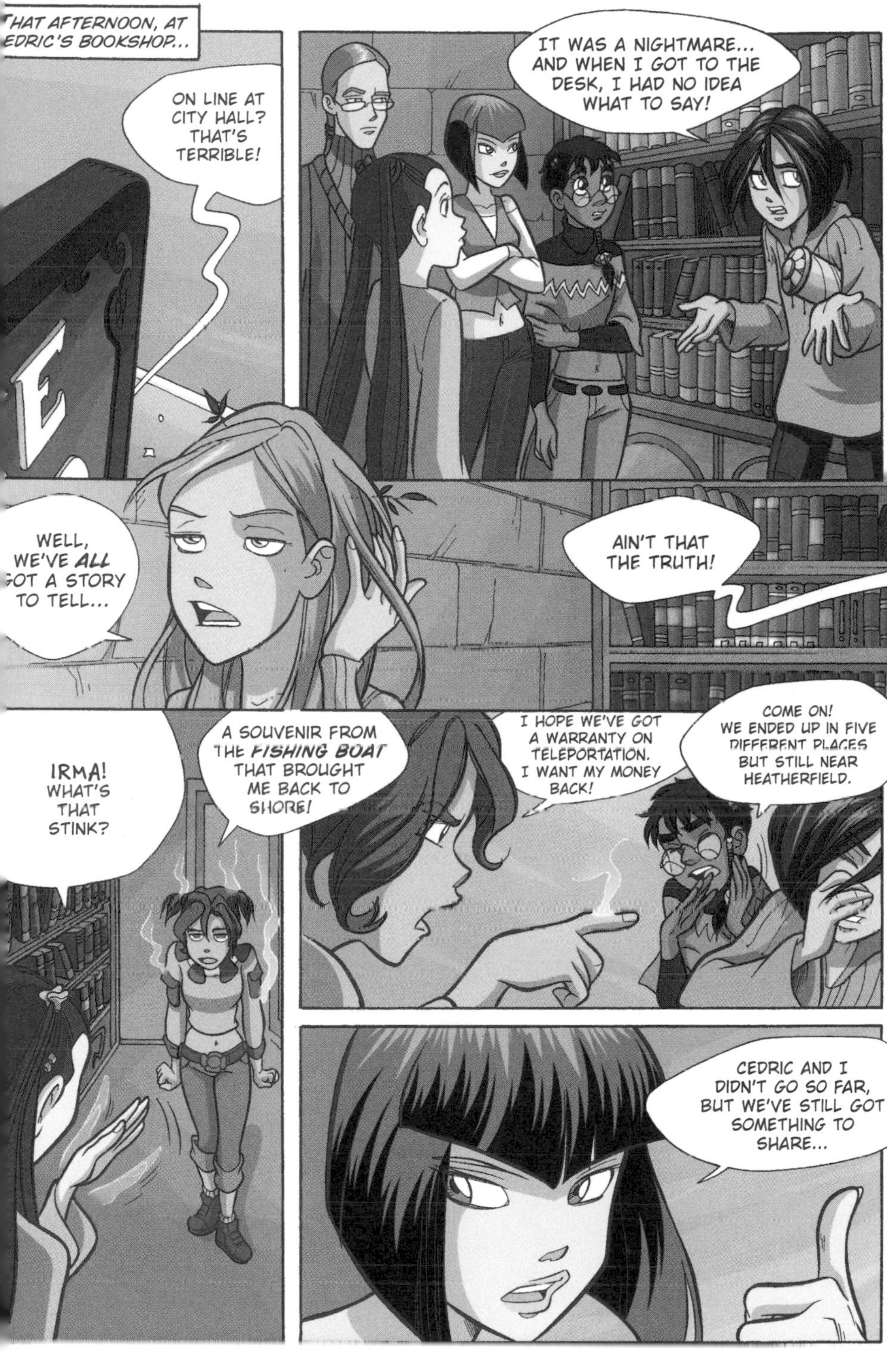
THAT AFTERNOON, AT EDRIC'S BOOKSHOP...
ON LINE AT CITY HALL? THAT'S TERRIBLE!
IT WAS A NIGHTMARE... AND WHEN I GOT TO THE DESK, I HAD NO IDEA WHAT TO SAY!
WELL, WE'VE ALL GOT A STORY TO TELL...
AIN'T THAT THE TRUTH!
IRMA! WHAT'S THAT STINK?
A SOUVENIR FROM THE FISHING BOAT THAT BROUGHT ME BACK TO SHORE!
I HOPE WE'VE GOT A WARRANTY ON TELEPORTATION. I WANT MY MONEY BACK!
COME ON! WE ENDED UP IN FIVE DIFFERENT PLACES BUT STILL NEAR HEATHERFIELD.
CEDRIC AND I DIDN'T GO SO FAR, BUT WE'VE STILL GOT SOMETHING TO SHARE...

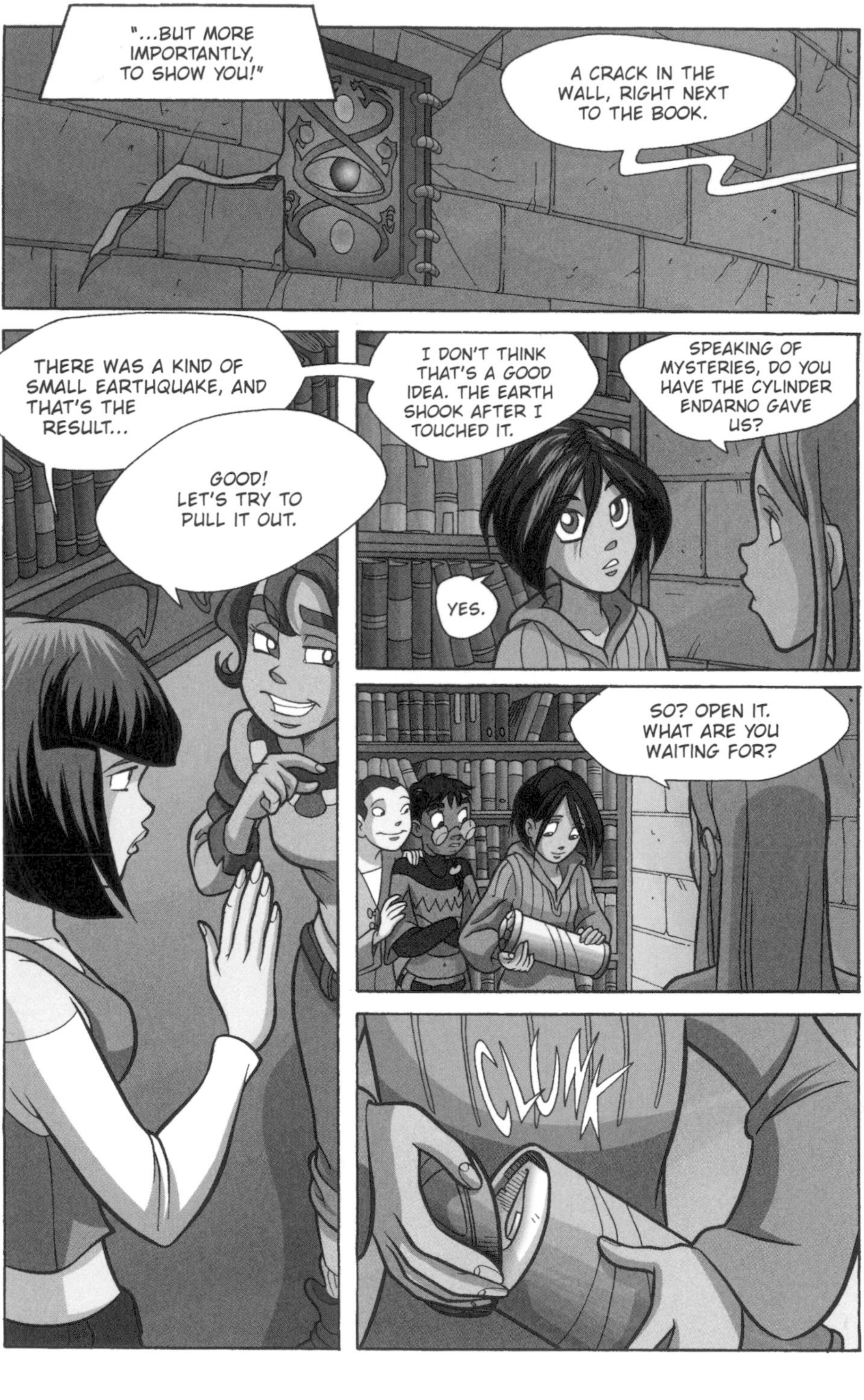

"...BUT MORE IMPORTANTLY, TO SHOW YOU!"
A CRACK IN THE WALL, RIGHT NEXT TO THE BOOK.
THERE WAS A KIND OF SMALL EARTHQUAKE, AND THAT'S THE RESULT...
GOOD! LET'S TRY TO PULL IT OUT.
I DON'T THINK THAT'S A GOOD IDEA. THE EARTH SHOOK AFTER I TOUCHED IT.
SPEAKING OF MYSTERIES, DO YOU HAVE THE CYLINDER ENDARNO GAVE US?
YES.
SO? OPEN IT. WHAT ARE YOU WAITING FOR?
CLUNK

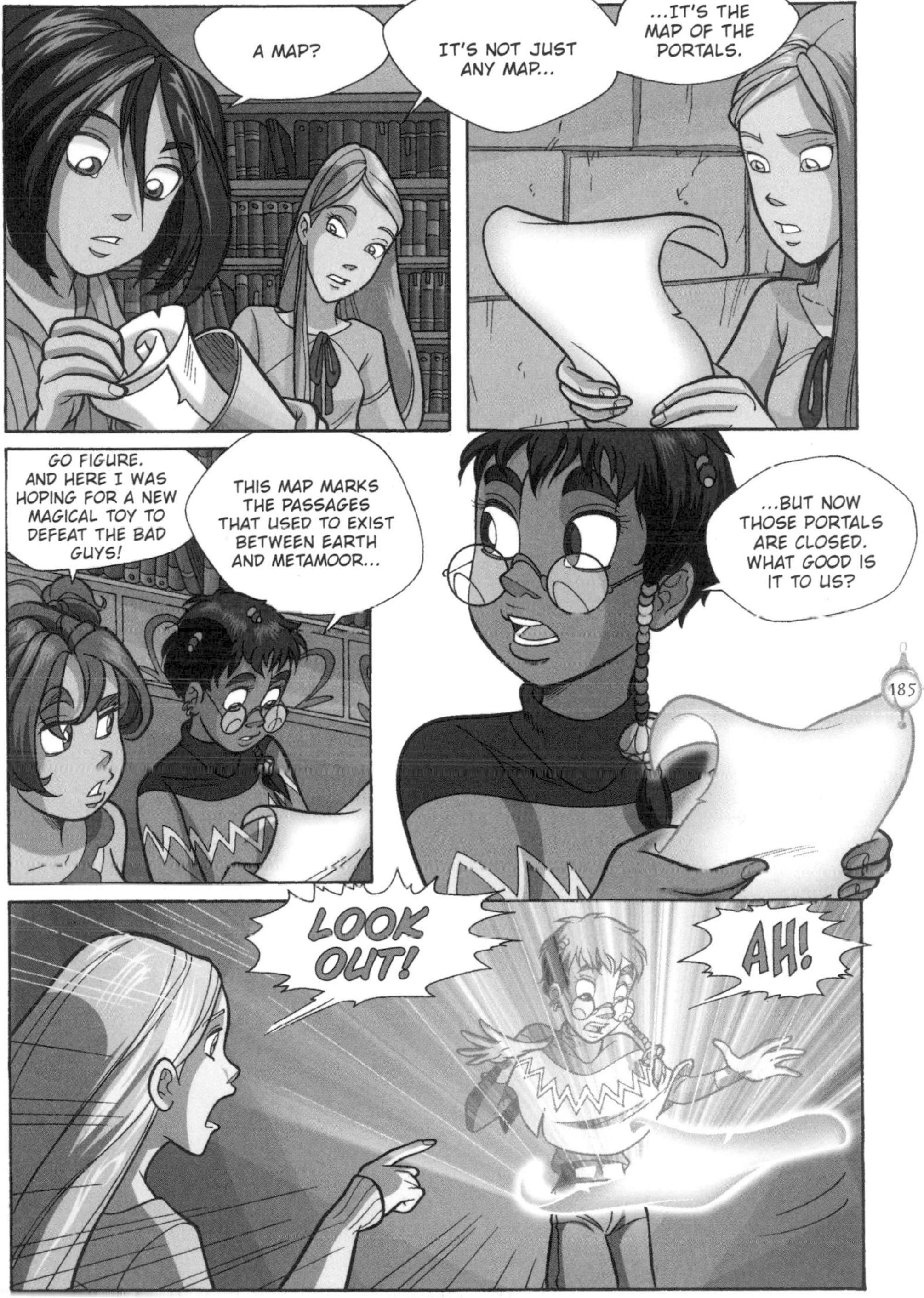

A MAP?
IT'S NOT JUST ANY MAP...
...IT'S THE MAP OF THE PORTALS.
GO FIGURE. AND HERE I WAS HOPING FOR A NEW MAGICAL TOY TO DEFEAT THE BAD GUYS!
THIS MAP MARKS THE PASSAGES THAT USED TO EXIST BETWEEN EARTH AND METAMOOR...
...BUT NOW THOSE PORTALS ARE CLOSED. WHAT GOOD IS IT TO US?
LOOK OUT!
AH!

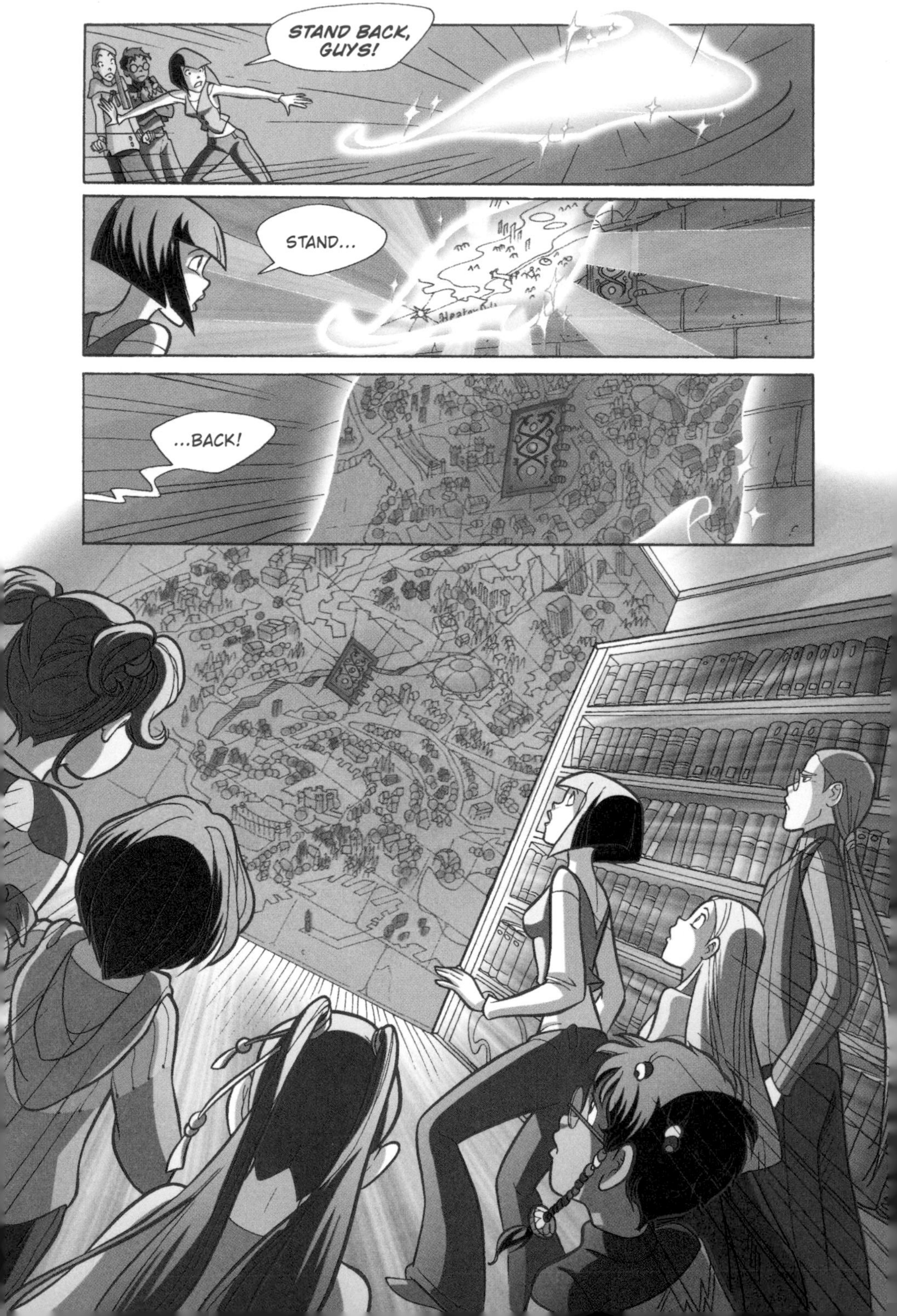
STAND BACK, GUYS!
STAND...
...BACK!

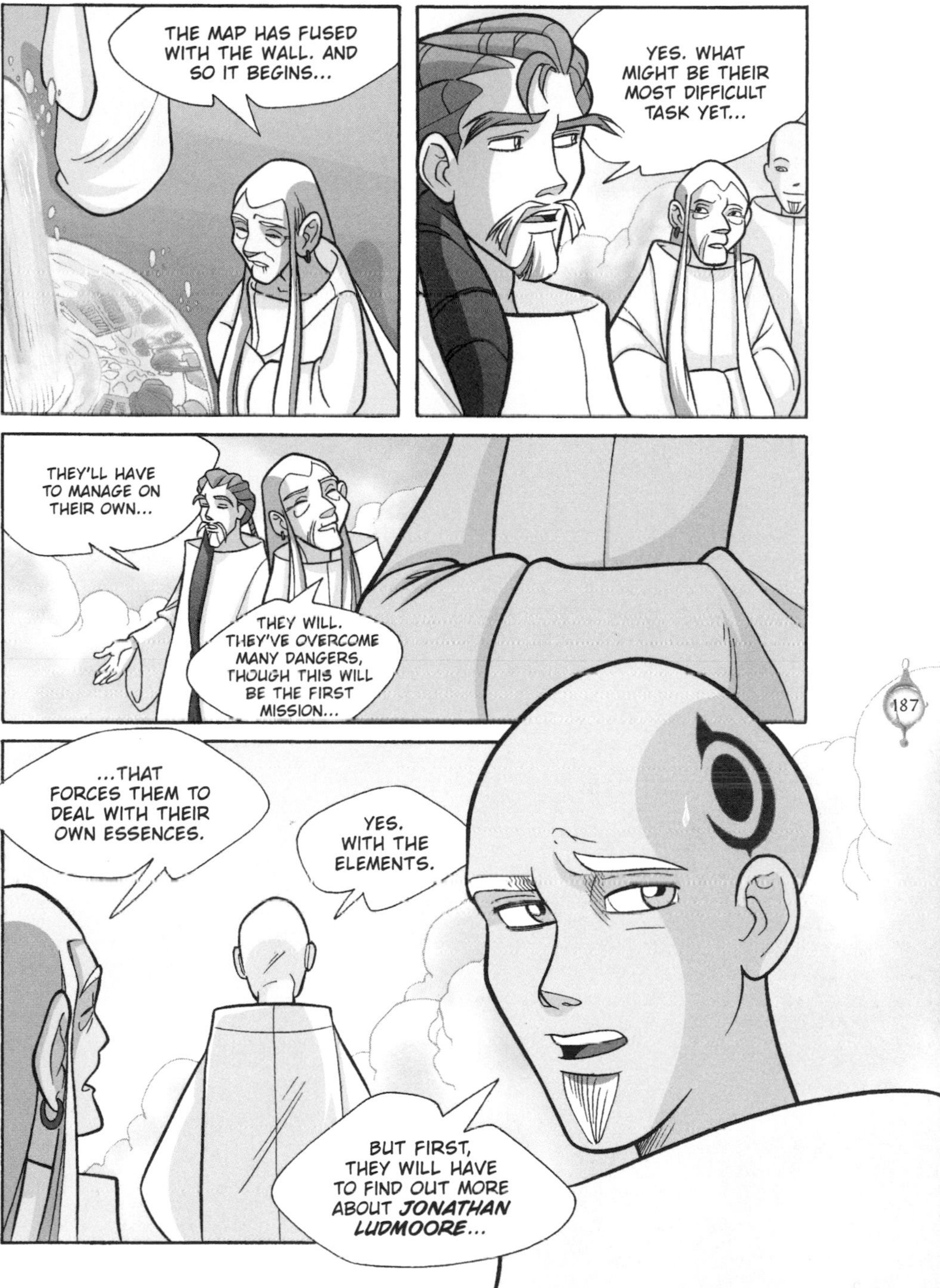
THE MAP HAS FUSED WITH THE WALL. AND SO IT BEGINS...
YES. WHAT MIGHT BE THEIR MOST DIFFICULT TASK YET...
THEY'LL HAVE TO MANAGE ON THEIR OWN...
THEY WILL. THEY'VE OVERCOME MANY DANGERS, THOUGH THIS WILL BE THE FIRST MISSION...
...THAT FORCES THEM TO DEAL WITH THEIR OWN ESSENCES.
YES. WITH THE ELEMENTS.
BUT FIRST, THEY WILL HAVE TO FIND OUT MORE ABOUT JONATHAN LUDMOORE...
END OF CHAPTER 55

W.i.t.c.h.

Will Irma Taranee Cornelia Hay Lin

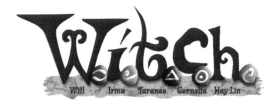

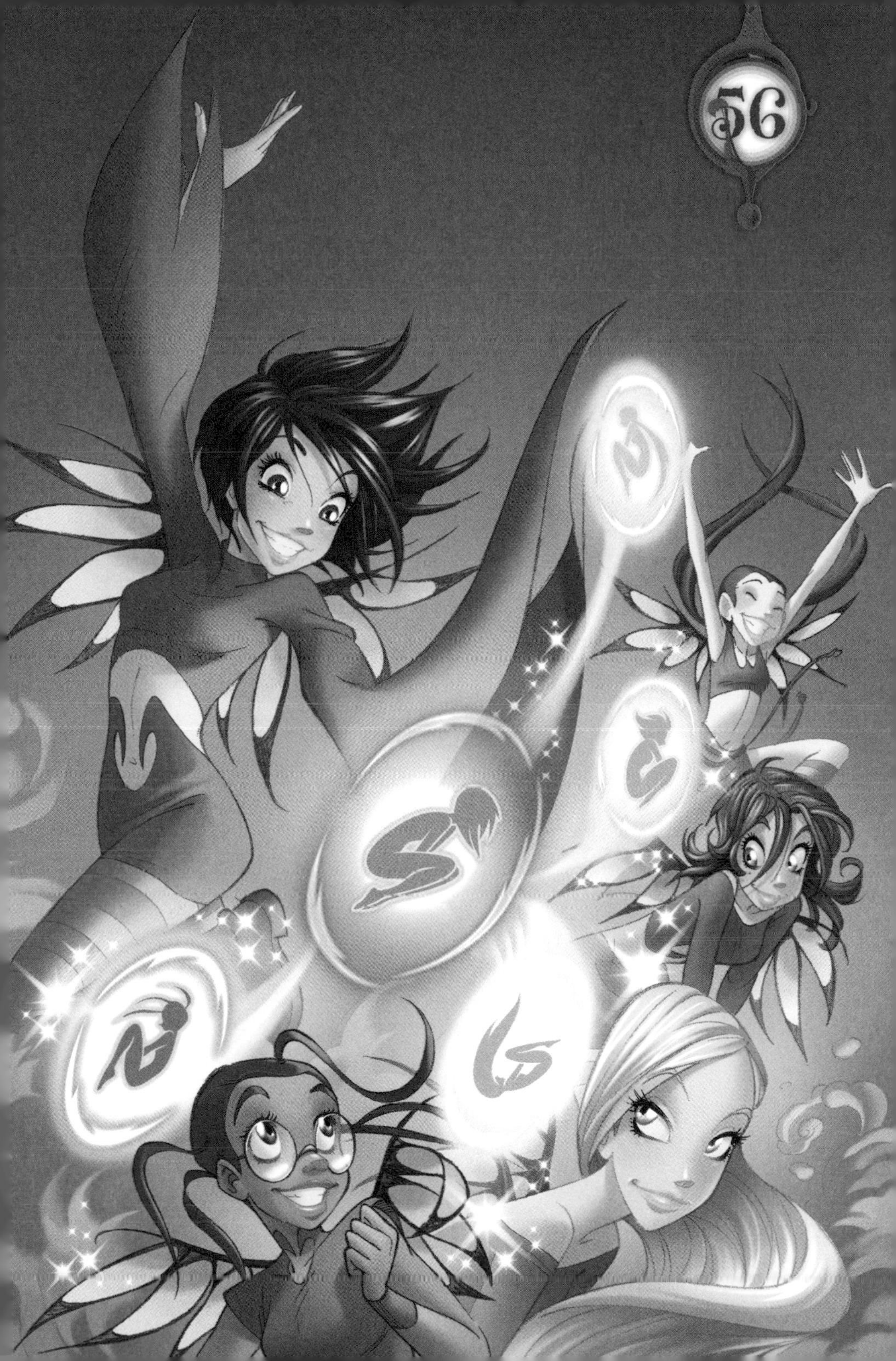
56

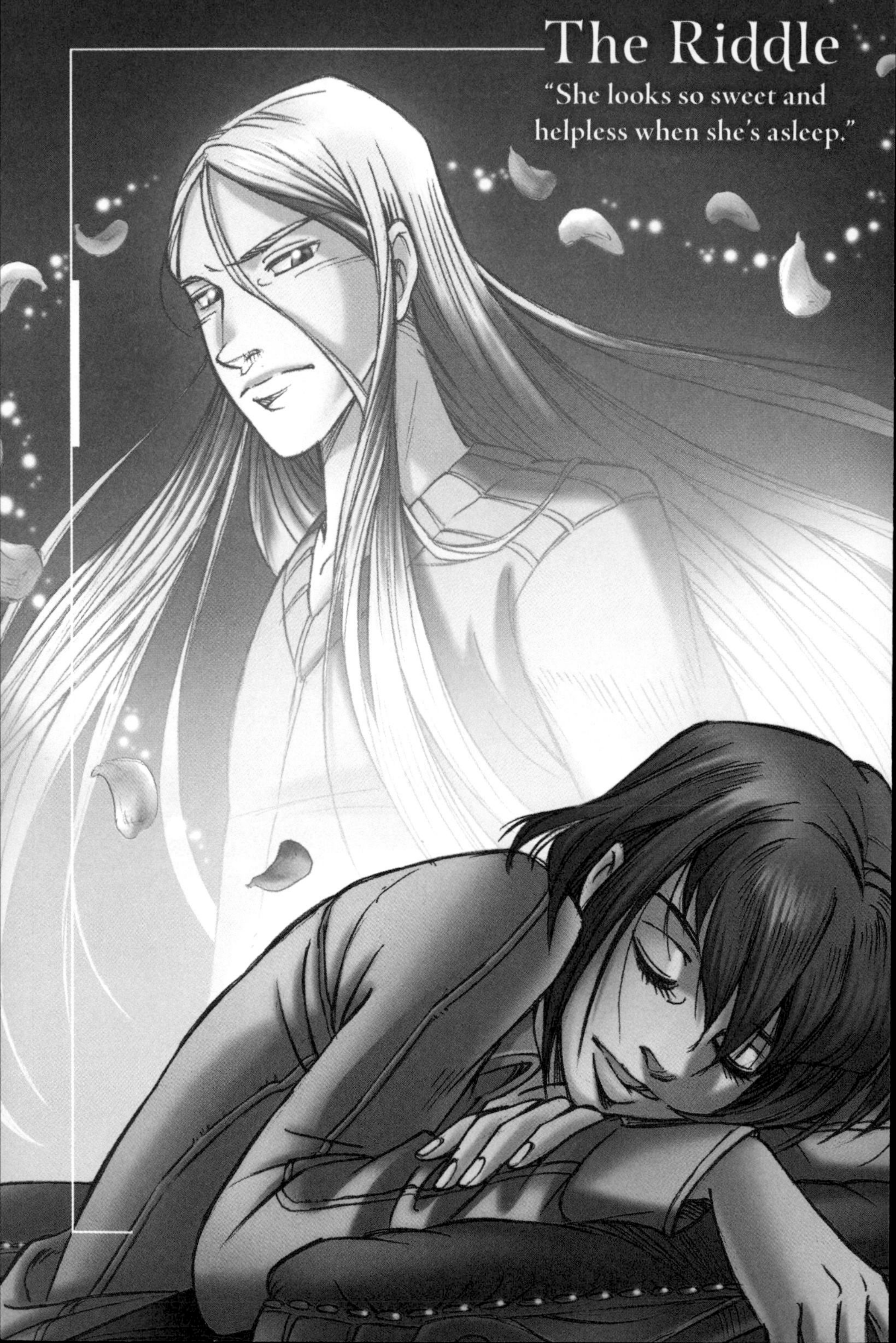
The Riddle
"She looks so sweet and
helpless when she's asleep."

W.i.t.c.h.

Will Irma Taranee Cornelia Hay Lin

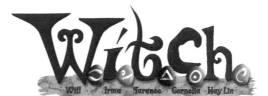

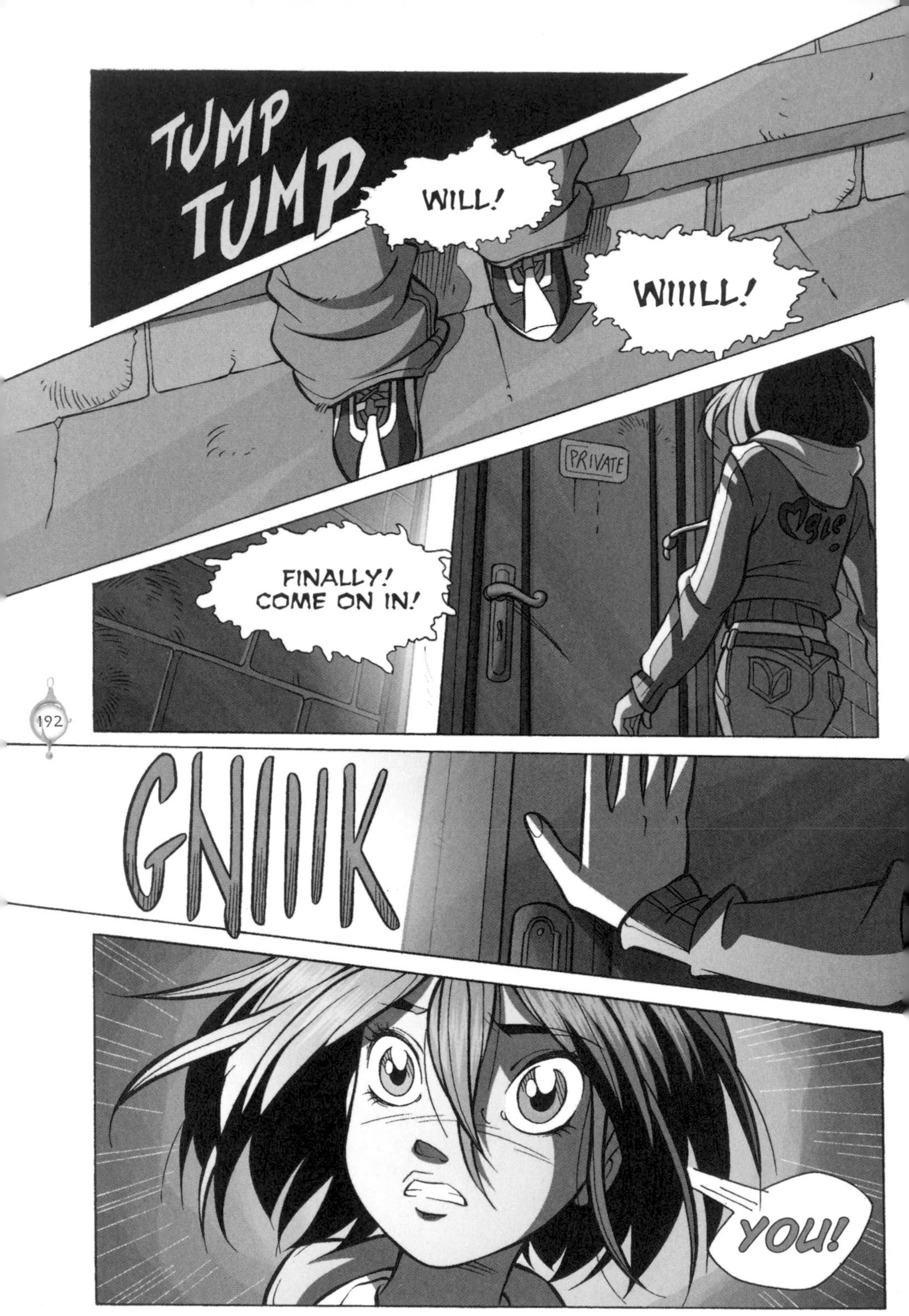
TUMP TUMP
WILL!
WIIILL!
PRIVATE
FINALLY! COME ON IN!
GNIIIK
YOU!

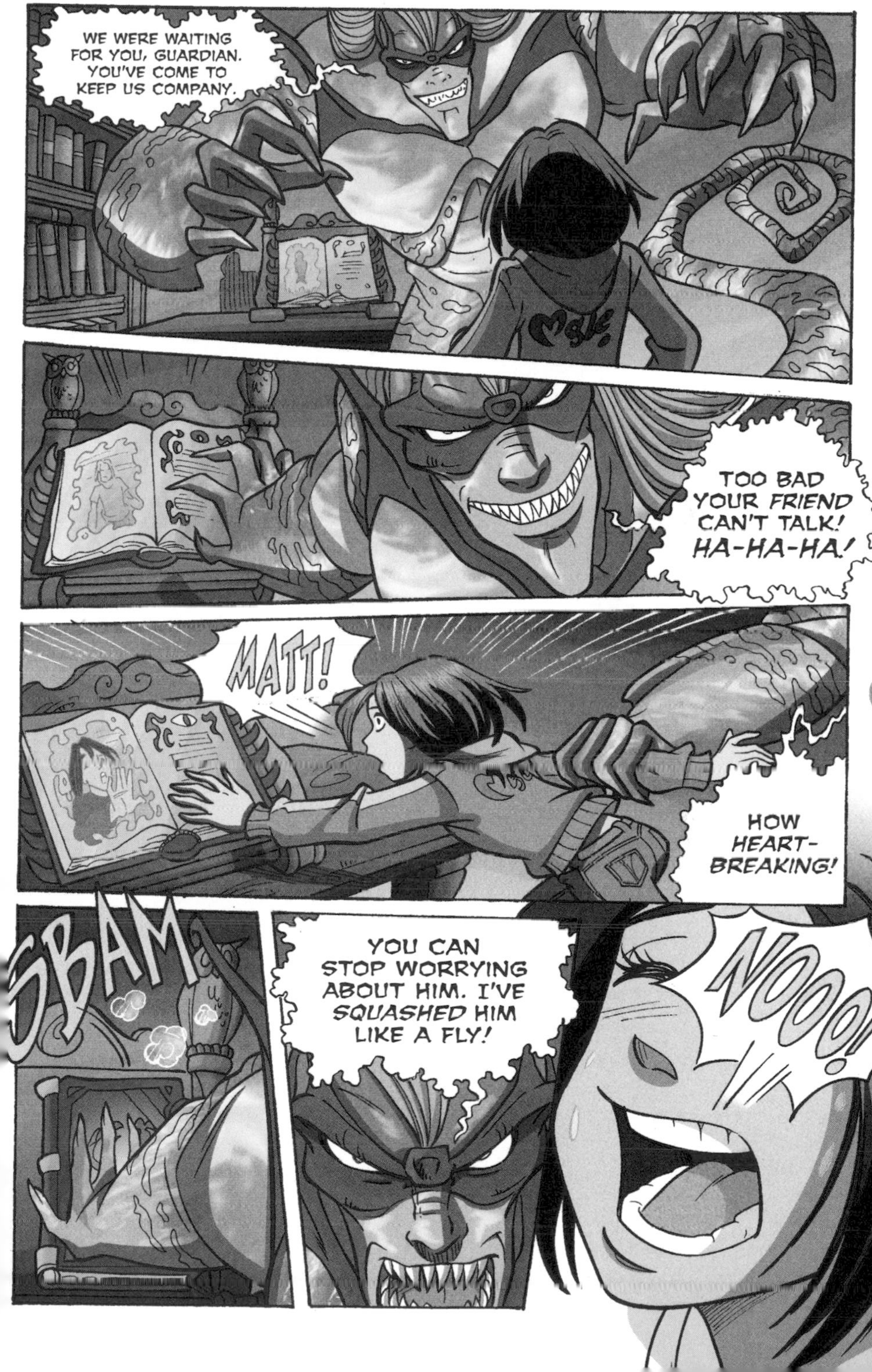

WE WERE WAITING FOR YOU, GUARDIAN. YOU'VE COME TO KEEP US COMPANY.
TOO BAD YOUR *FRIEND* CAN'T TALK! *HA-HA-HA!*
MATT!
HOW HEART-BREAKING!
SBAM
YOU CAN STOP WORRYING ABOUT HIM. I'VE *SQUASHED* HIM LIKE A FLY!
NOOO!

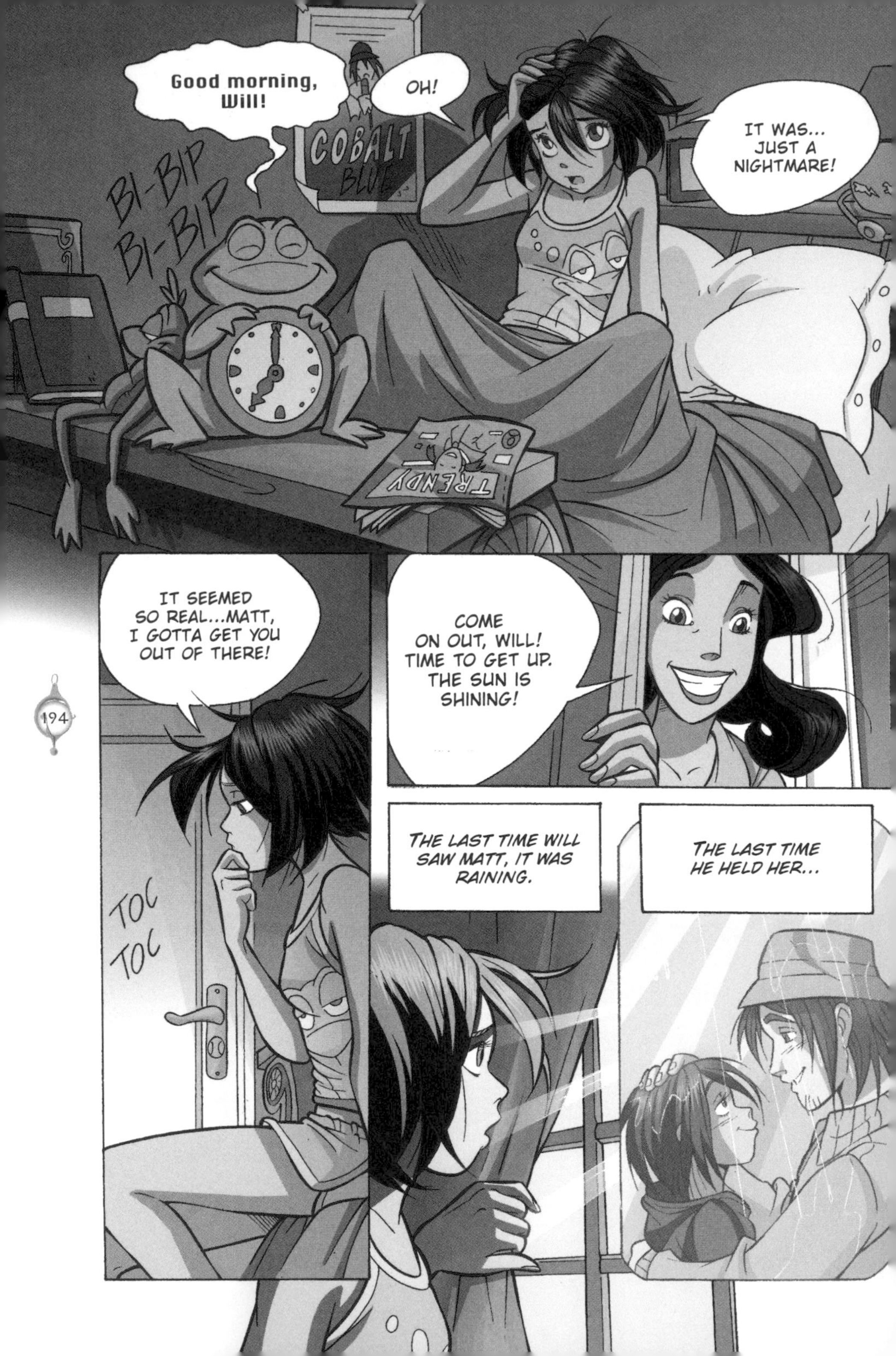
Good morning, Will!
OH!
BI-BIP BI-BIP
COBALT BLUE
IT WAS... JUST A NIGHTMARE!
TRENDY
IT SEEMED SO REAL...MATT, I GOTTA GET YOU OUT OF THERE!
COME ON OUT, WILL! TIME TO GET UP. THE SUN IS SHINING!
TOC TOC
THE LAST TIME WILL SAW MATT, IT WAS RAINING.
THE LAST TIME HE HELD HER...

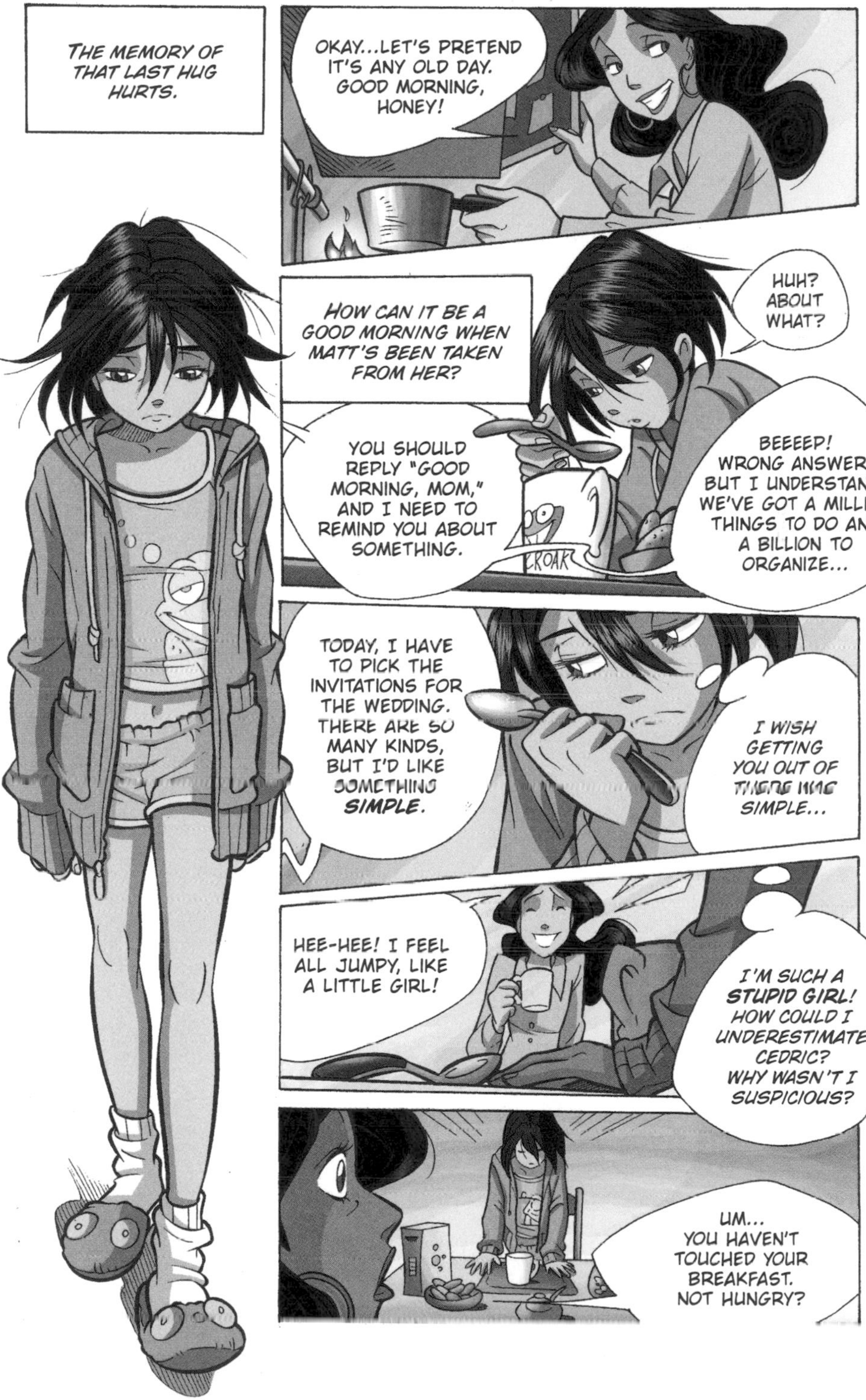
THE MEMORY OF THAT LAST HUG HURTS.
OKAY...LET'S PRETEND IT'S ANY OLD DAY. GOOD MORNING, HONEY!
HOW CAN IT BE A GOOD MORNING WHEN MATT'S BEEN TAKEN FROM HER?
HUH? ABOUT WHAT?
YOU SHOULD REPLY "GOOD MORNING, MOM," AND I NEED TO REMIND YOU ABOUT SOMETHING.
CROAK
BEEEEP! WRONG ANSWER! BUT I UNDERSTAND. WE'VE GOT A MILLION THINGS TO DO AND A BILLION TO ORGANIZE...
TODAY, I HAVE TO PICK THE INVITATIONS FOR THE WEDDING. THERE ARE SO MANY KINDS, BUT I'D LIKE SOMETHING SIMPLE.
I WISH GETTING YOU OUT OF THERE WAS SIMPLE...
HEE-HEE! I FEEL ALL JUMPY, LIKE A LITTLE GIRL!
I'M SUCH A STUPID GIRL! HOW COULD I UNDERESTIMATE CEDRIC? WHY WASN'T I SUSPICIOUS?
UM... YOU HAVEN'T TOUCHED YOUR BREAKFAST. NOT HUNGRY?

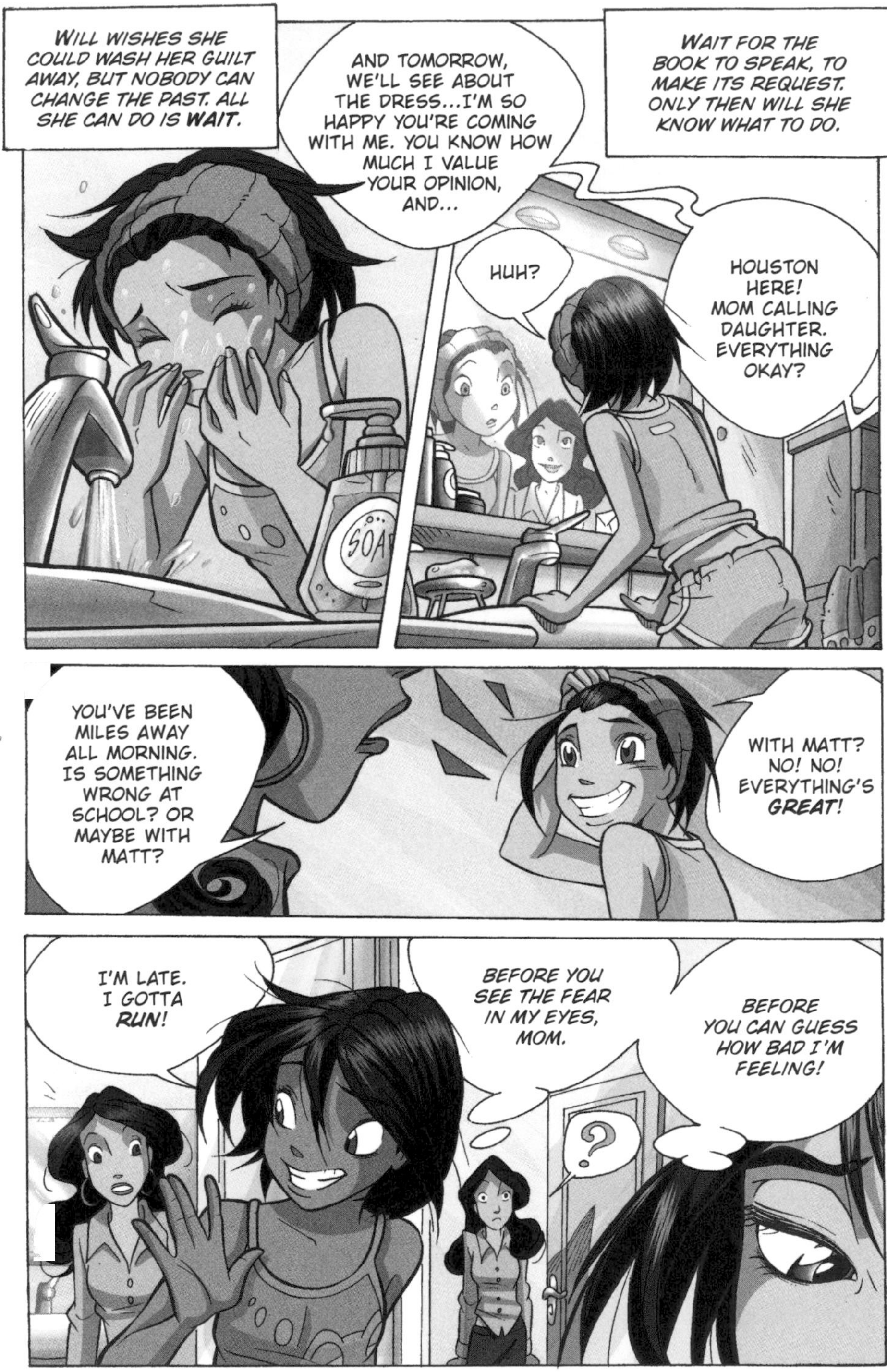
WILL WISHES SHE COULD WASH HER GUILT AWAY, BUT NOBODY CAN CHANGE THE PAST. ALL SHE CAN DO IS WAIT.
AND TOMORROW, WE'LL SEE ABOUT THE DRESS...I'M SO HAPPY YOU'RE COMING WITH ME. YOU KNOW HOW MUCH I VALUE YOUR OPINION, AND...
WAIT FOR THE BOOK TO SPEAK, TO MAKE ITS REQUEST. ONLY THEN WILL SHE KNOW WHAT TO DO.
HUH?
HOUSTON HERE! MOM CALLING DAUGHTER. EVERYTHING OKAY?
SOAP
YOU'VE BEEN MILES AWAY ALL MORNING. IS SOMETHING WRONG AT SCHOOL? OR MAYBE WITH MATT?
WITH MATT? NO! NO! EVERYTHING'S GREAT!
I'M LATE. I GOTTA RUN!
BEFORE YOU SEE THE FEAR IN MY EYES, MOM.
BEFORE YOU CAN GUESS HOW BAD I'M FEELING!
?

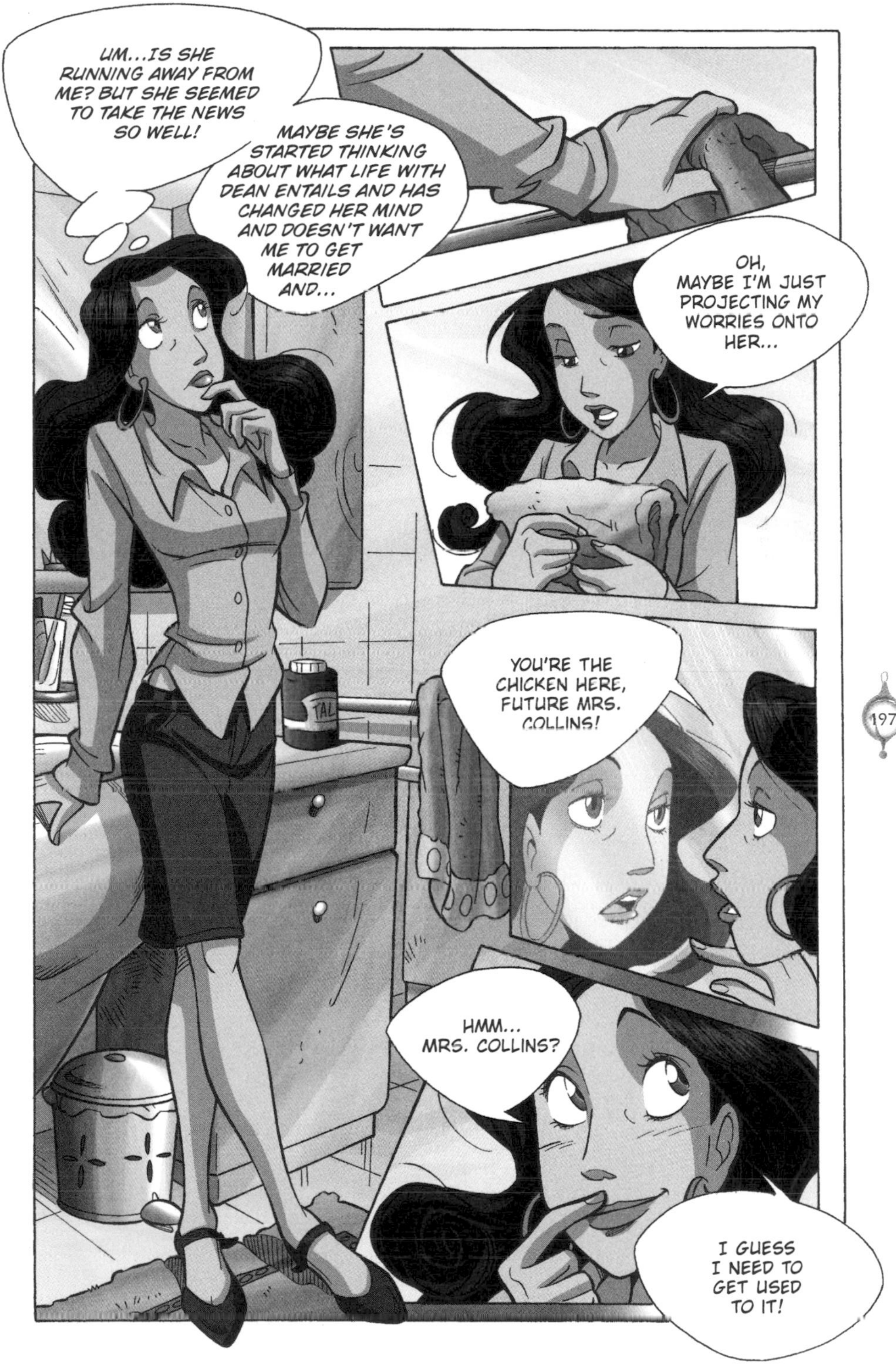
UM...IS SHE RUNNING AWAY FROM ME? BUT SHE SEEMED TO TAKE THE NEWS SO WELL!
MAYBE SHE'S STARTED THINKING ABOUT WHAT LIFE WITH DEAN ENTAILS AND HAS CHANGED HER MIND AND DOESN'T WANT ME TO GET MARRIED AND...
OH, MAYBE I'M JUST PROJECTING MY WORRIES ONTO HER...
YOU'RE THE CHICKEN HERE, FUTURE MRS. COLLINS!
HMM... MRS. COLLINS?
I GUESS I NEED TO GET USED TO IT!

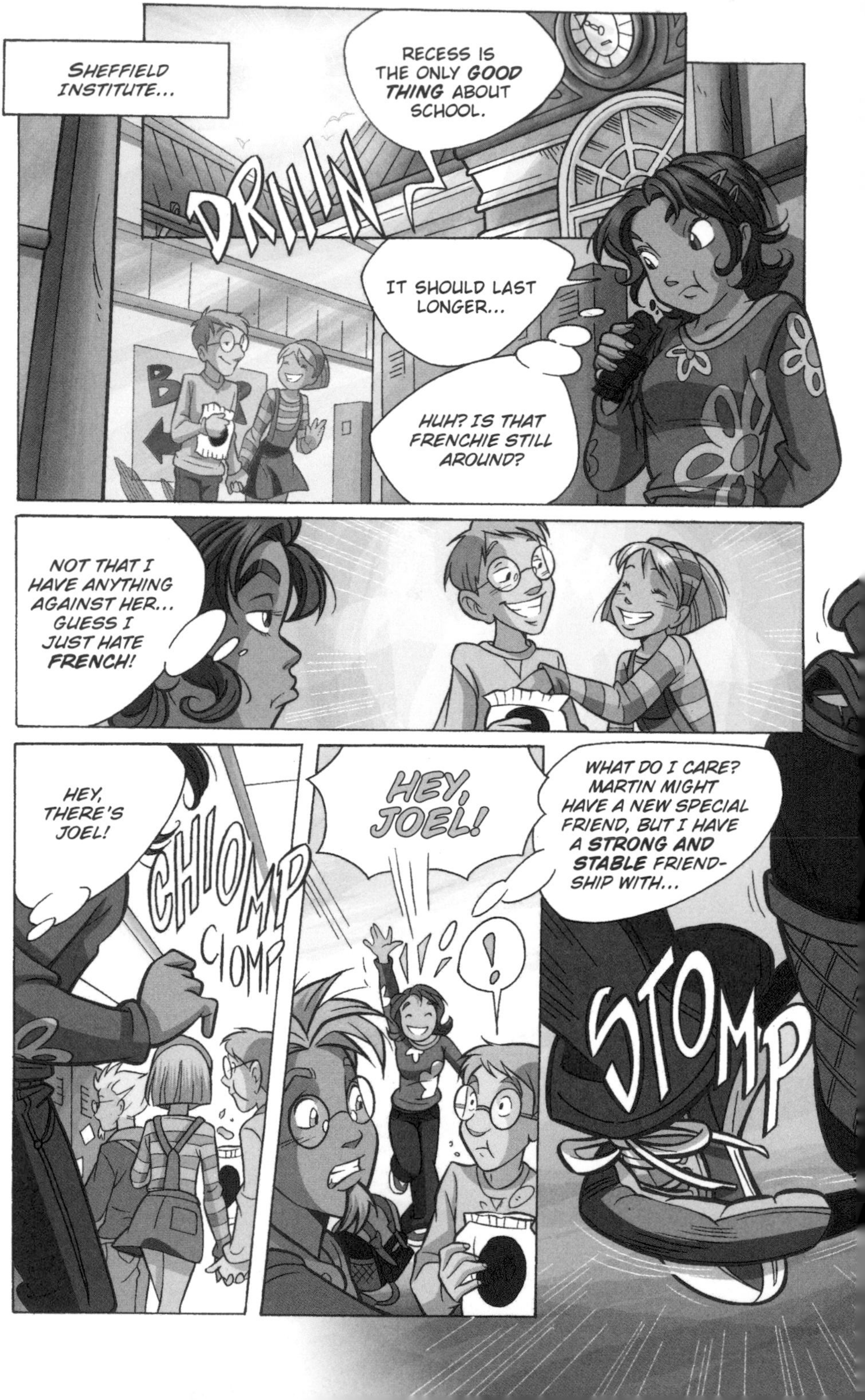
SHEFFIELD INSTITUTE...
RECESS IS THE ONLY GOOD THING ABOUT SCHOOL.
DRIIIN
IT SHOULD LAST LONGER...
HUH? IS THAT FRENCHIE STILL AROUND?
NOT THAT I HAVE ANYTHING AGAINST HER... GUESS I JUST HATE FRENCH!
HEY, THERE'S JOEL!
CHIOMP
CIOMP
HEY, JOEL!
!
WHAT DO I CARE? MARTIN MIGHT HAVE A NEW SPECIAL FRIEND, BUT I HAVE A STRONG AND STABLE FRIENDSHIP WITH...
STOMP

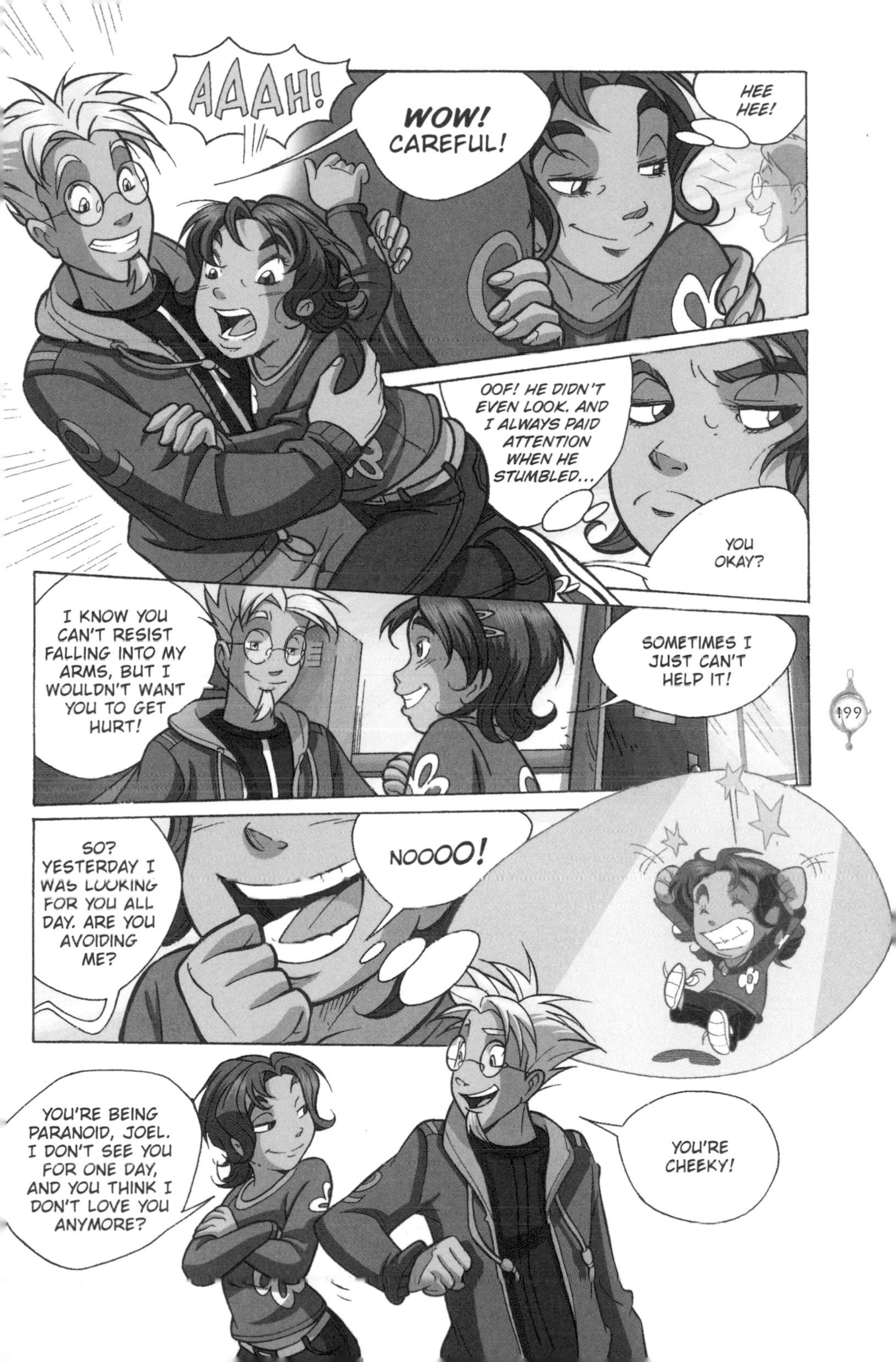
AAAH!
WOW! CAREFUL!
HEE HEE!
OOF! HE DIDN'T EVEN LOOK. AND I ALWAYS PAID ATTENTION WHEN HE STUMBLED...
YOU OKAY?
I KNOW YOU CAN'T RESIST FALLING INTO MY ARMS, BUT I WOULDN'T WANT YOU TO GET HURT!
SOMETIMES I JUST CAN'T HELP IT!
SO? YESTERDAY I WAS LOOKING FOR YOU ALL DAY. ARE YOU AVOIDING ME?
NOOOO!
YOU'RE BEING PARANOID, JOEL. I DON'T SEE YOU FOR ONE DAY, AND YOU THINK I DON'T LOVE YOU ANYMORE?
YOU'RE CHEEKY!

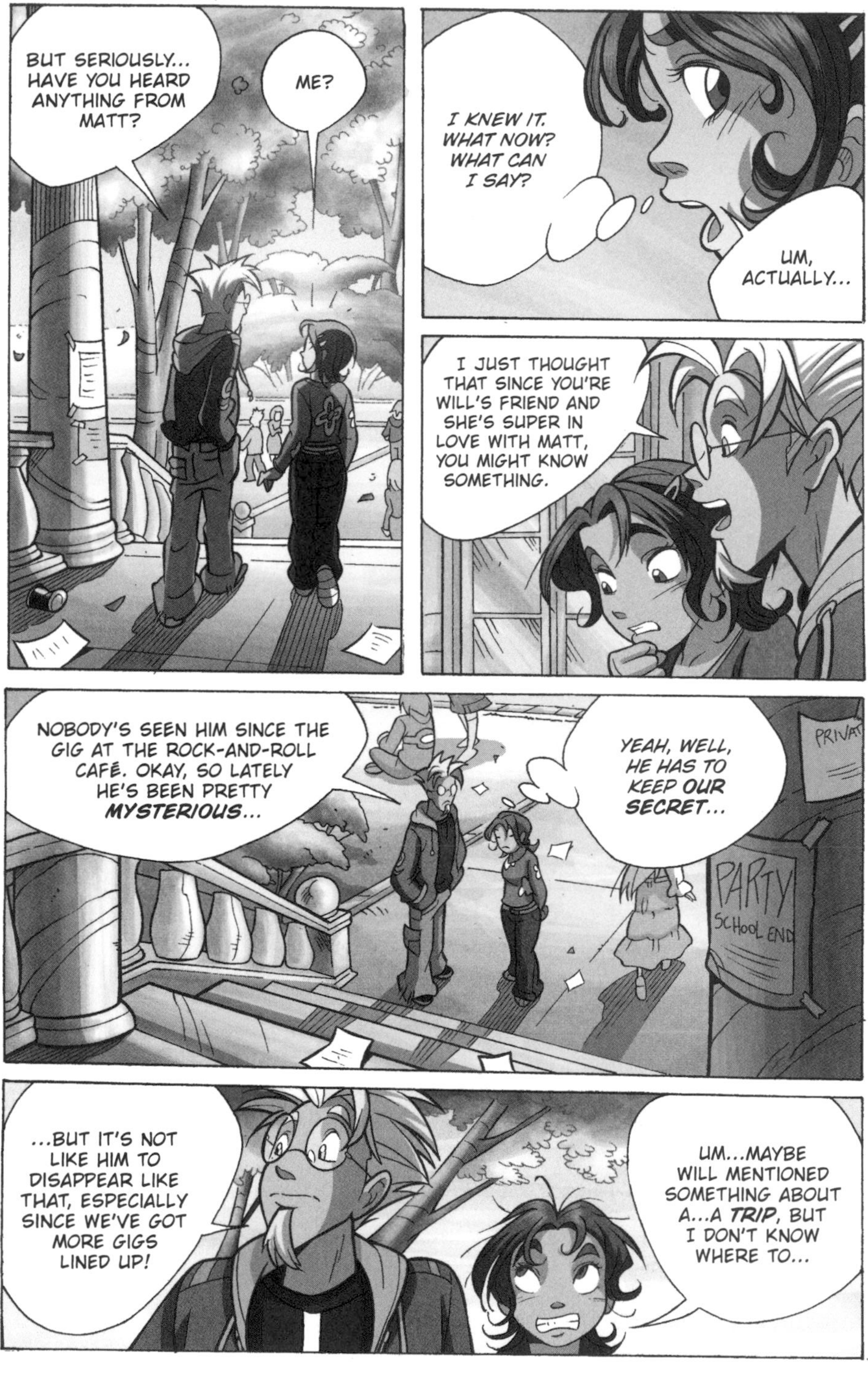

BUT SERIOUSLY... HAVE YOU HEARD ANYTHING FROM MATT?
ME?
I KNEW IT. WHAT NOW? WHAT CAN I SAY?
UM, ACTUALLY...
I JUST THOUGHT THAT SINCE YOU'RE WILL'S FRIEND AND SHE'S SUPER IN LOVE WITH MATT, YOU MIGHT KNOW SOMETHING.
NOBODY'S SEEN HIM SINCE THE GIG AT THE ROCK-AND-ROLL CAFÉ. OKAY, SO LATELY HE'S BEEN PRETTY ***MYSTERIOUS***...
YEAH, WELL, HE HAS TO KEEP ***OUR SECRET***...
PRIVAT
PARTY
SCHOOL END
...BUT IT'S NOT LIKE HIM TO DISAPPEAR LIKE THAT, ESPECIALLY SINCE WE'VE GOT MORE GIGS LINED UP!
UM...MAYBE WILL MENTIONED SOMETHING ABOUT A...A ***TRIP***, BUT I DON'T KNOW WHERE TO...

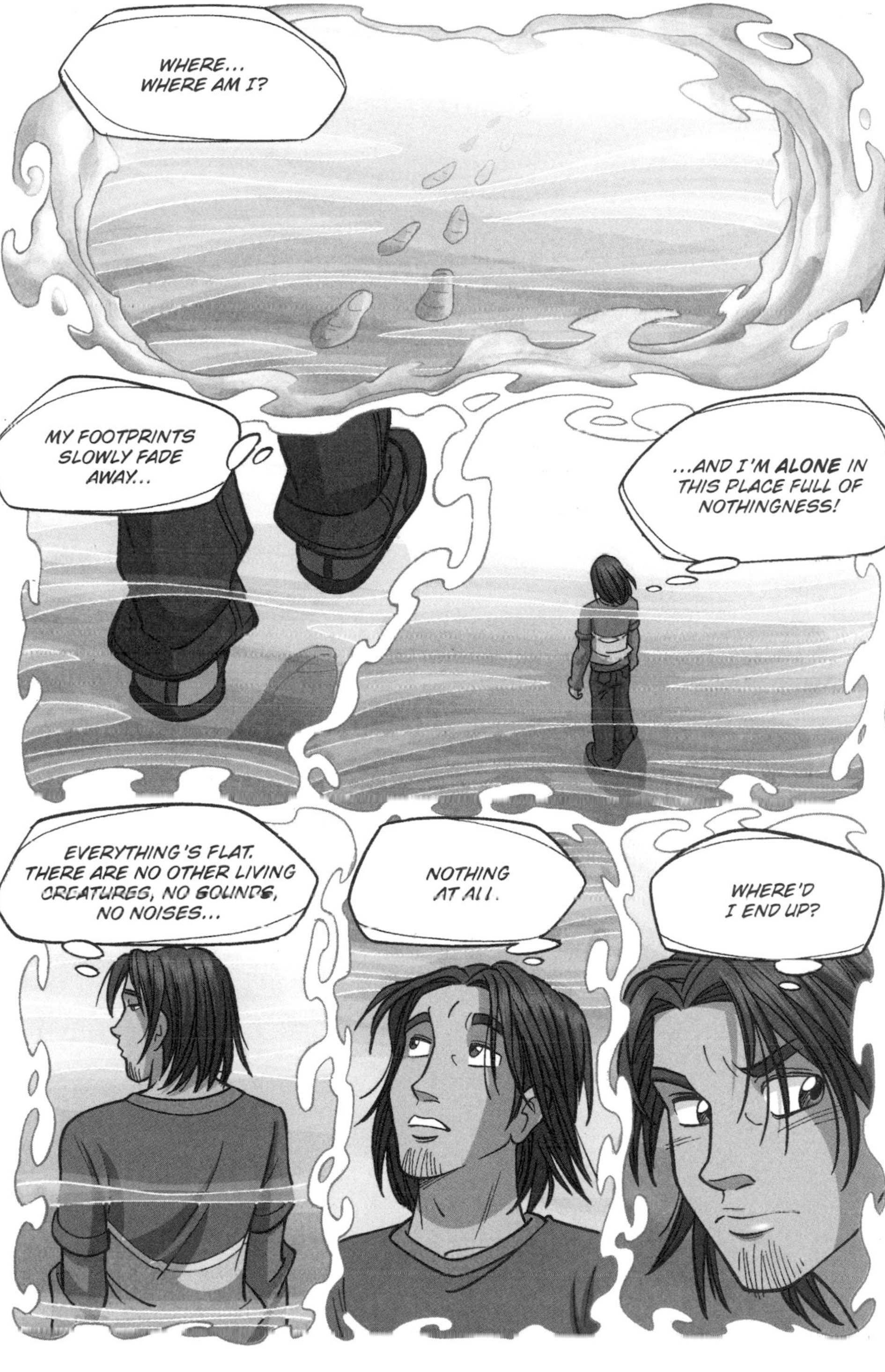
WHERE... WHERE AM I?
MY FOOTPRINTS SLOWLY FADE AWAY...
...AND I'M ALONE IN THIS PLACE FULL OF NOTHINGNESS!
EVERYTHING'S FLAT. THERE ARE NO OTHER LIVING CREATURES, NO SOUNDS, NO NOISES...
NOTHING AT ALL.
WHERE'D I END UP?

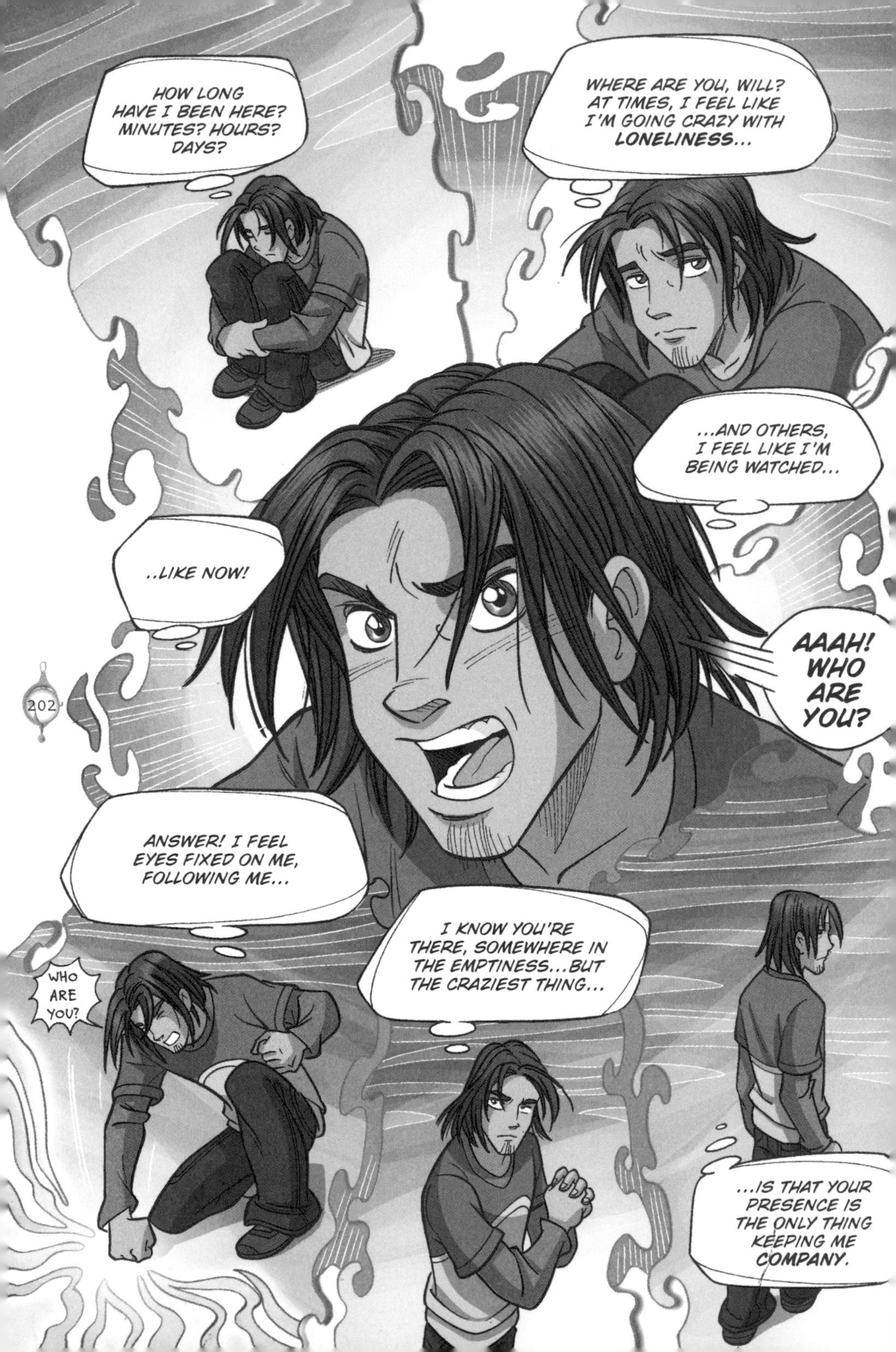
HOW LONG HAVE I BEEN HERE? MINUTES? HOURS? DAYS?
WHERE ARE YOU, WILL? AT TIMES, I FEEL LIKE I'M GOING CRAZY WITH **LONELINESS**...
...AND OTHERS, I FEEL LIKE I'M BEING WATCHED...
..LIKE NOW!
AAAH! WHO ARE YOU?
ANSWER! I FEEL EYES FIXED ON ME, FOLLOWING ME...
WHO ARE YOU?
I KNOW YOU'RE THERE, SOMEWHERE IN THE EMPTINESS...BUT THE CRAZIEST THING...
...IS THAT YOUR PRESENCE IS THE ONLY THING KEEPING ME **COMPANY.**

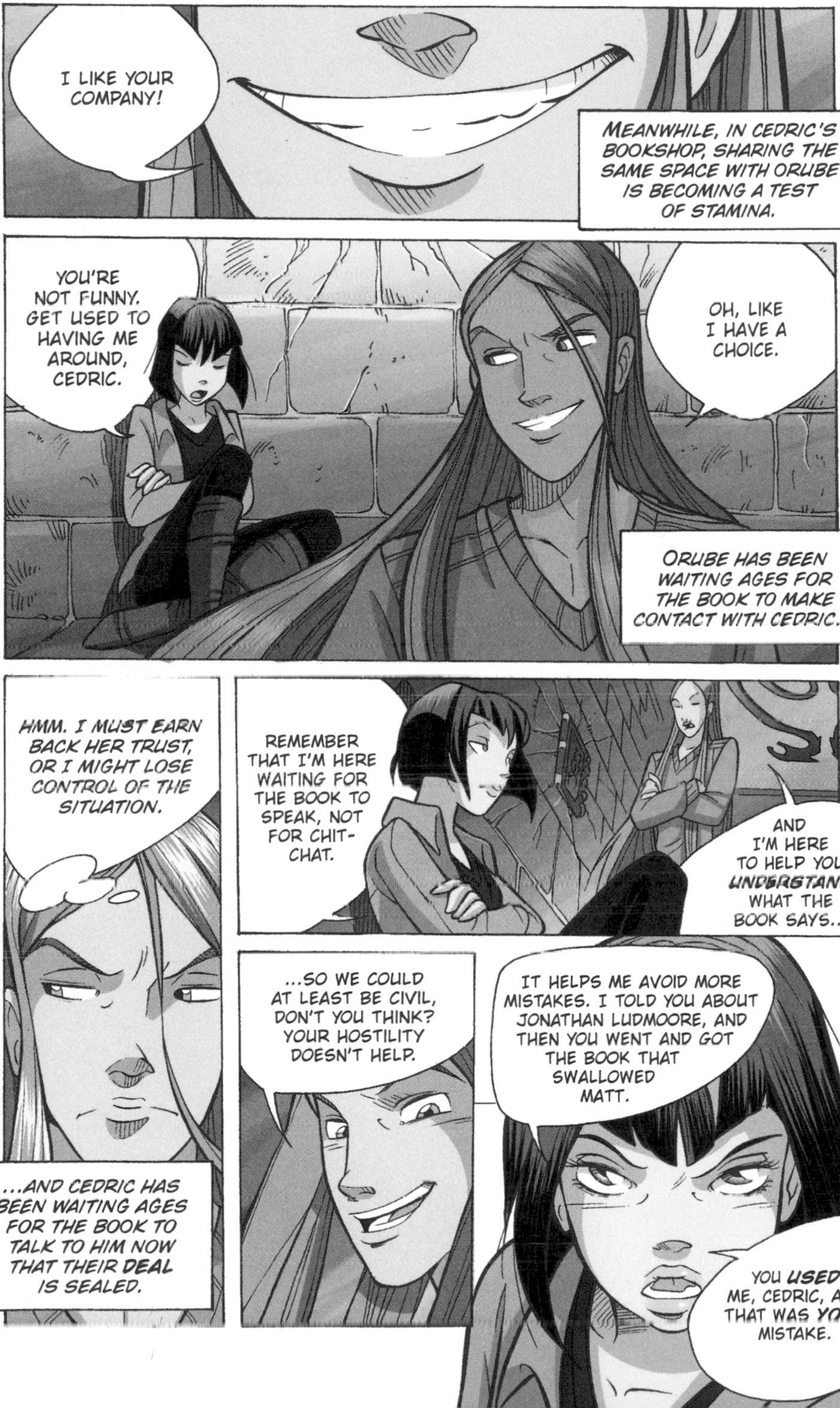
I LIKE YOUR COMPANY!
MEANWHILE, IN CEDRIC'S BOOKSHOP, SHARING THE SAME SPACE WITH ORUBE IS BECOMING A TEST OF STAMINA.
YOU'RE NOT FUNNY. GET USED TO HAVING ME AROUND, CEDRIC.
OH, LIKE I HAVE A CHOICE.
ORUBE HAS BEEN WAITING AGES FOR THE BOOK TO MAKE CONTACT WITH CEDRIC...
HMM. I MUST EARN BACK HER TRUST, OR I MIGHT LOSE CONTROL OF THE SITUATION.
...AND CEDRIC HAS BEEN WAITING AGES FOR THE BOOK TO TALK TO HIM NOW THAT THEIR DEAL IS SEALED.
REMEMBER THAT I'M HERE WAITING FOR THE BOOK TO SPEAK, NOT FOR CHIT-CHAT.
AND I'M HERE TO HELP YOU UNDERSTAND WHAT THE BOOK SAYS...
...SO WE COULD AT LEAST BE CIVIL, DON'T YOU THINK? YOUR HOSTILITY DOESN'T HELP.
IT HELPS ME AVOID MORE MISTAKES. I TOLD YOU ABOUT JONATHAN LUDMOORE, AND THEN YOU WENT AND GOT THE BOOK THAT SWALLOWED MATT.
YOU USED ME, CEDRIC, AND THAT WAS YOUR MISTAKE.

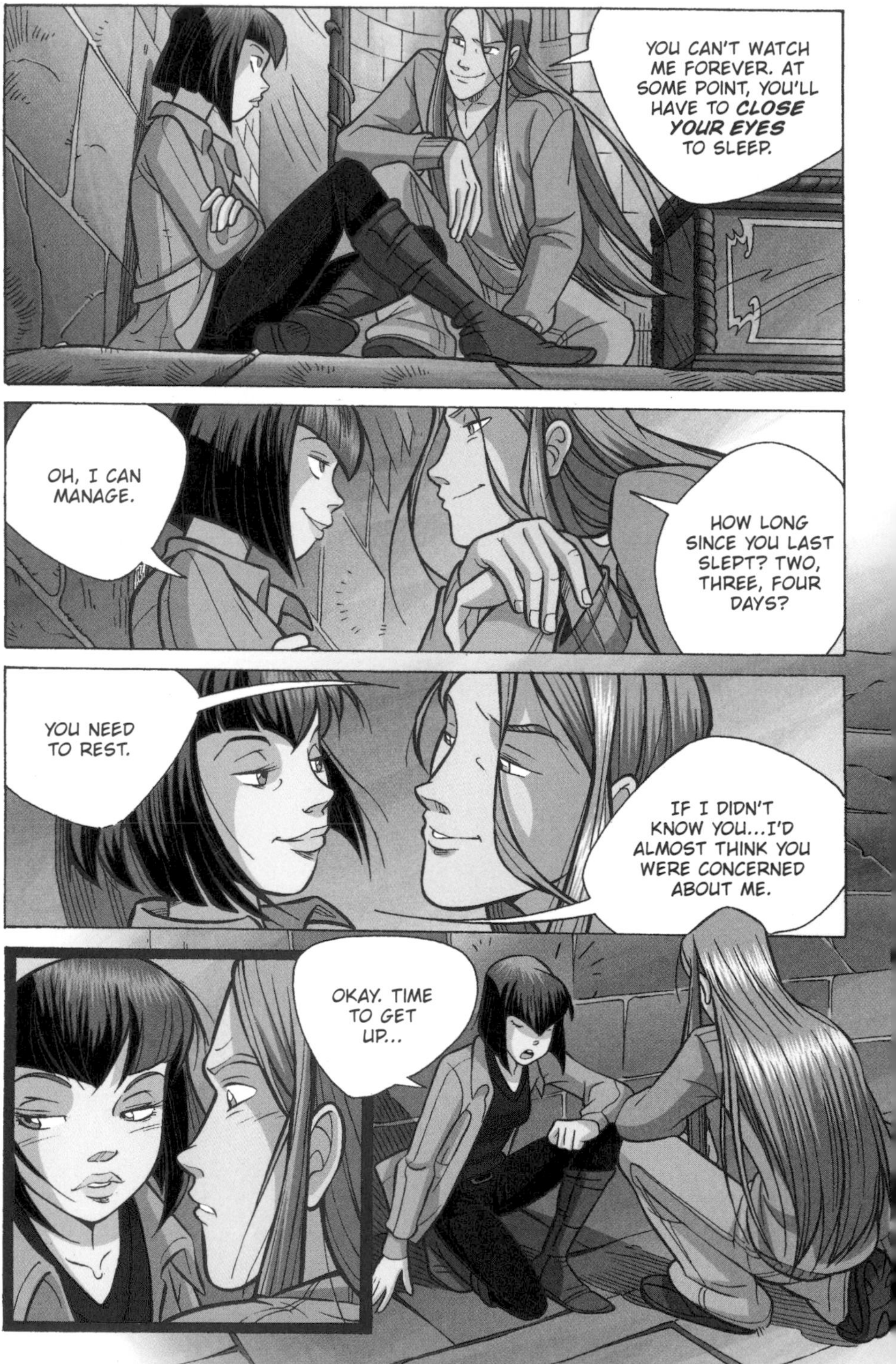
YOU CAN'T WATCH ME FOREVER. AT SOME POINT, YOU'LL HAVE TO **CLOSE YOUR EYES** TO SLEEP.
OH, I CAN MANAGE.
HOW LONG SINCE YOU LAST SLEPT? TWO, THREE, FOUR DAYS?
YOU NEED TO REST.
IF I DIDN'T KNOW YOU...I'D ALMOST THINK YOU WERE CONCERNED ABOUT ME.
OKAY. TIME TO GET UP...

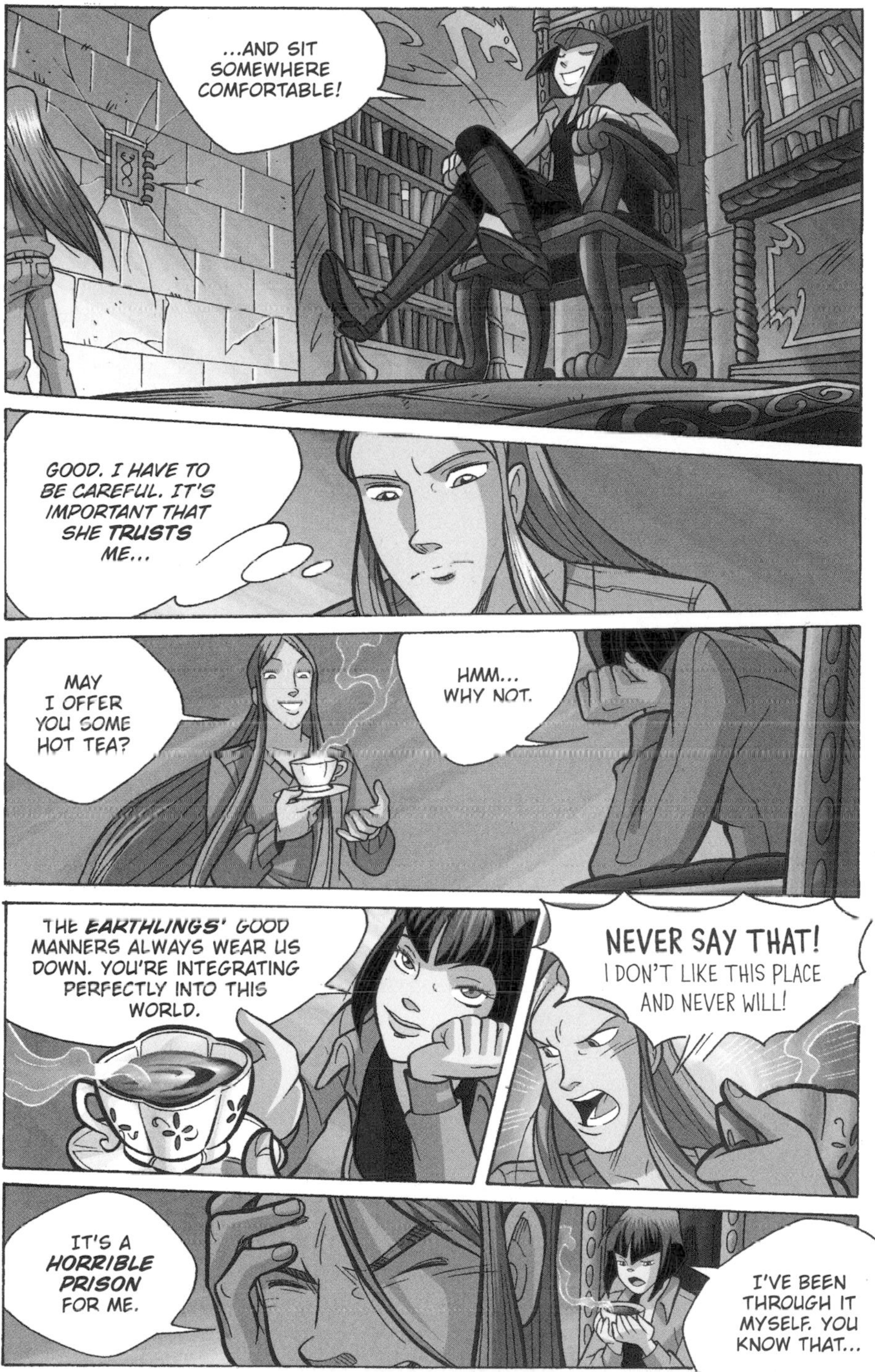
...AND SIT SOMEWHERE COMFORTABLE!
GOOD. I HAVE TO BE CAREFUL. IT'S IMPORTANT THAT SHE TRUSTS ME...
MAY I OFFER YOU SOME HOT TEA?
HMM... WHY NOT.
THE EARTHLINGS' GOOD MANNERS ALWAYS WEAR US DOWN. YOU'RE INTEGRATING PERFECTLY INTO THIS WORLD.
NEVER SAY THAT! I DON'T LIKE THIS PLACE AND NEVER WILL!
IT'S A HORRIBLE PRISON FOR ME.
I'VE BEEN THROUGH IT MYSELF. YOU KNOW THAT...

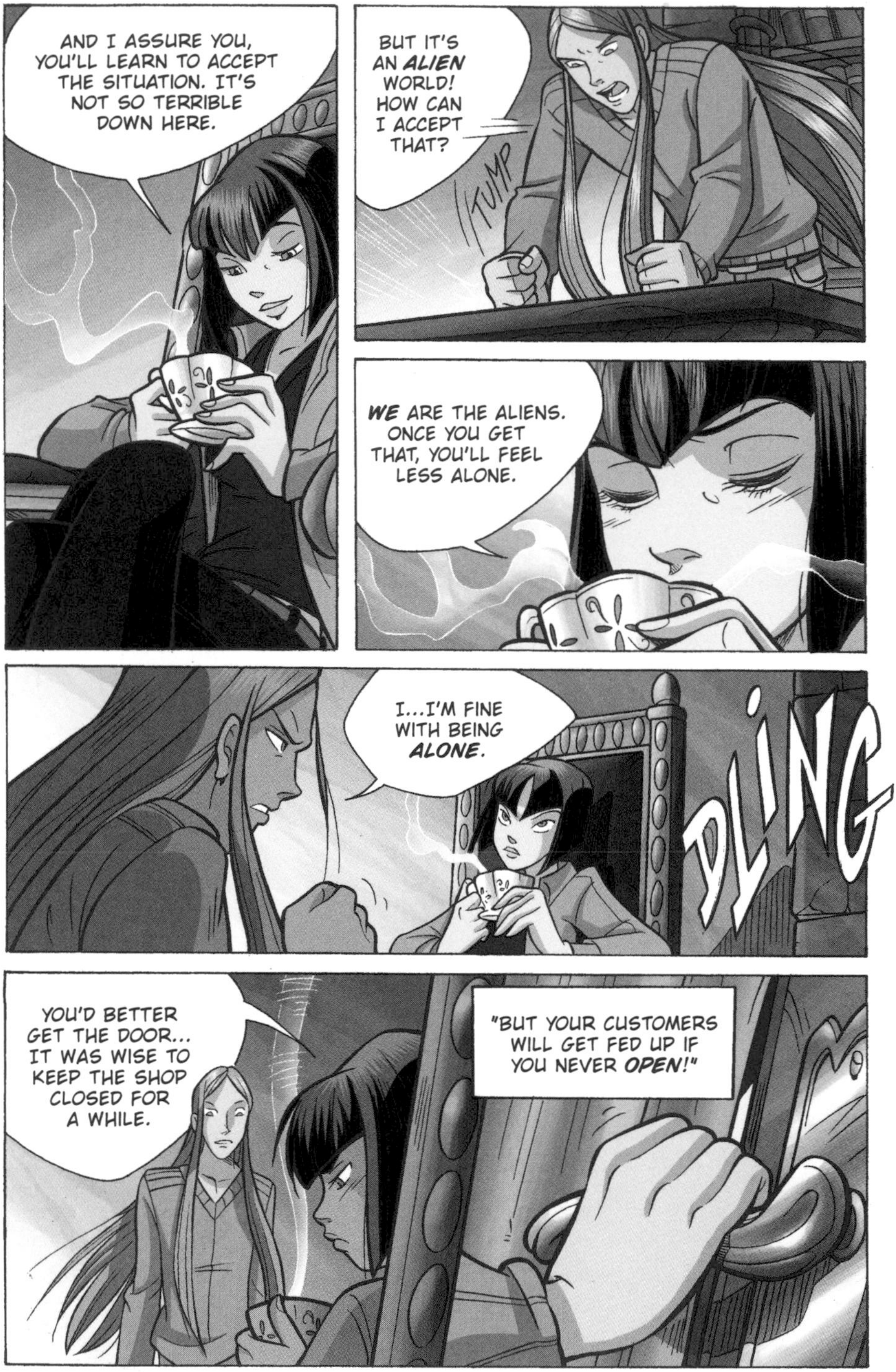
AND I ASSURE YOU, YOU'LL LEARN TO ACCEPT THE SITUATION. IT'S NOT SO TERRIBLE DOWN HERE.
BUT IT'S AN *ALIEN* WORLD! HOW CAN I ACCEPT THAT?
TUMP
WE ARE THE ALIENS. ONCE YOU GET THAT, YOU'LL FEEL LESS ALONE.
I...I'M FINE WITH BEING *ALONE*.
DLING
YOU'D BETTER GET THE DOOR... IT WAS WISE TO KEEP THE SHOP CLOSED FOR A WHILE.
"BUT YOUR CUSTOMERS WILL GET FED UP IF YOU NEVER *OPEN*!"

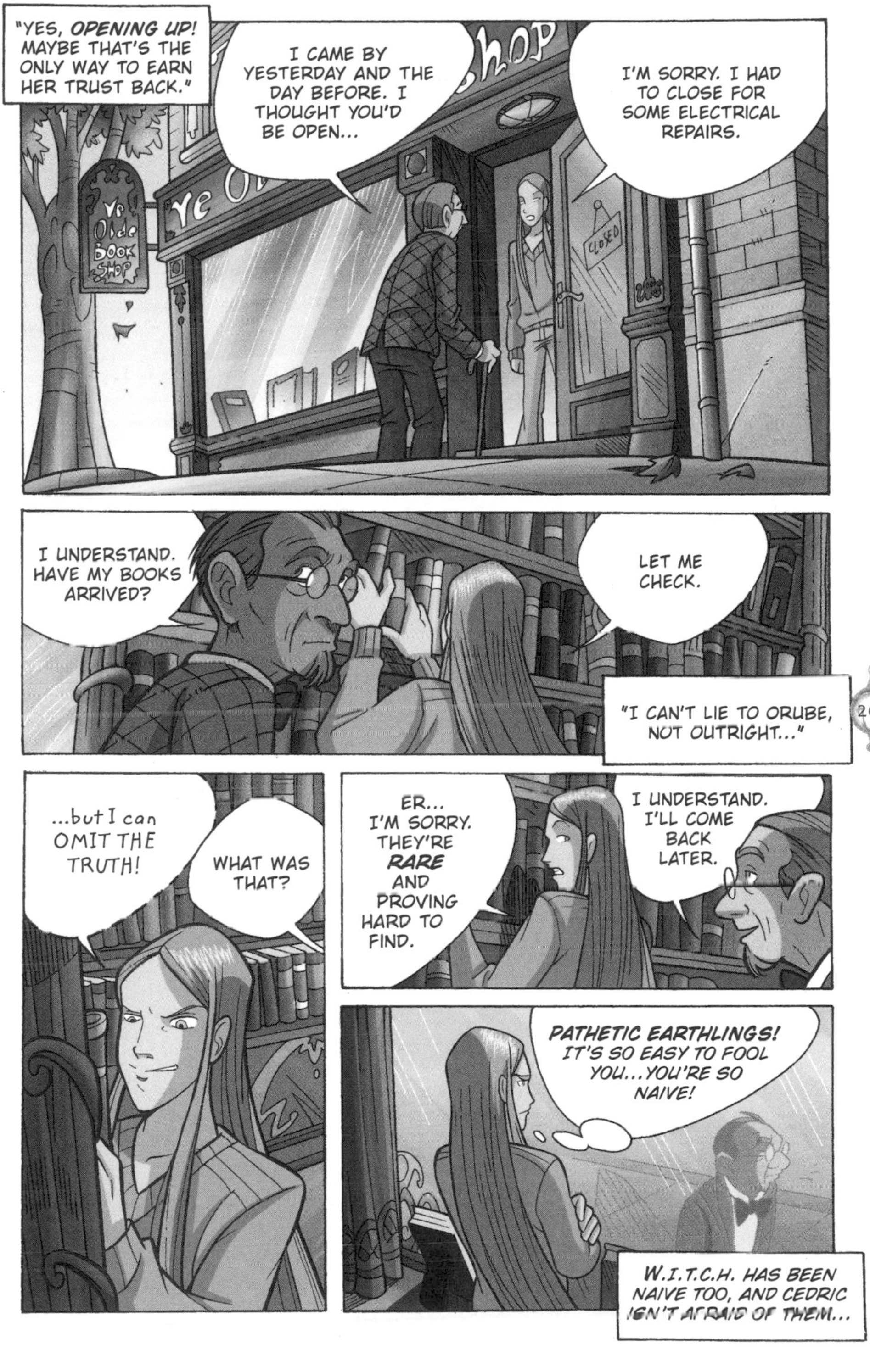
"YES, *OPENING UP!* MAYBE THAT'S THE ONLY WAY TO EARN HER TRUST BACK."
I CAME BY YESTERDAY AND THE DAY BEFORE. I THOUGHT YOU'D BE OPEN...
I'M SORRY. I HAD TO CLOSE FOR SOME ELECTRICAL REPAIRS.
Ye Olde Book Shop
CLOSED
I UNDERSTAND. HAVE MY BOOKS ARRIVED?
LET ME CHECK.
"I CAN'T LIE TO ORUBE, NOT OUTRIGHT..."
...but I can OMIT THE TRUTH!
WHAT WAS THAT?
ER... I'M SORRY. THEY'RE *RARE* AND PROVING HARD TO FIND.
I UNDERSTAND. I'LL COME BACK LATER.
PATHETIC EARTHLINGS! IT'S SO EASY TO FOOL YOU...YOU'RE SO NAIVE!
W.I.T.C.H. HAS BEEN NAIVE TOO, AND CEDRIC ISN'T AFRAID OF THEM...

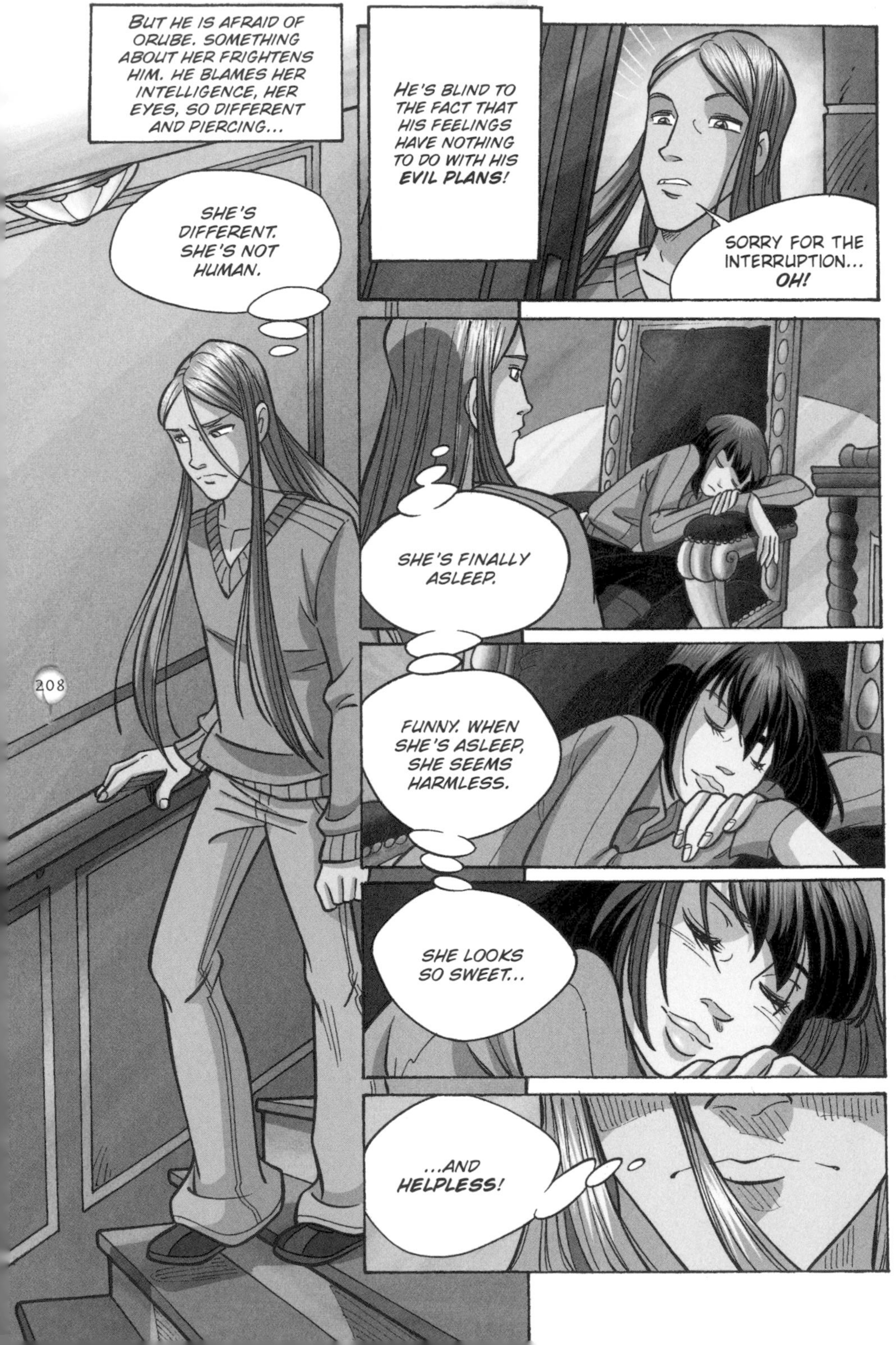
BUT HE IS AFRAID OF ORUBE. SOMETHING ABOUT HER FRIGHTENS HIM. HE BLAMES HER INTELLIGENCE, HER EYES, SO DIFFERENT AND PIERCING...
SHE'S DIFFERENT. SHE'S NOT HUMAN.
HE'S BLIND TO THE FACT THAT HIS FEELINGS HAVE NOTHING TO DO WITH HIS EVIL PLANS!
SORRY FOR THE INTERRUPTION... OH!
SHE'S FINALLY ASLEEP.
FUNNY. WHEN SHE'S ASLEEP, SHE SEEMS HARMLESS.
SHE LOOKS SO SWEET...
...AND HELPLESS!

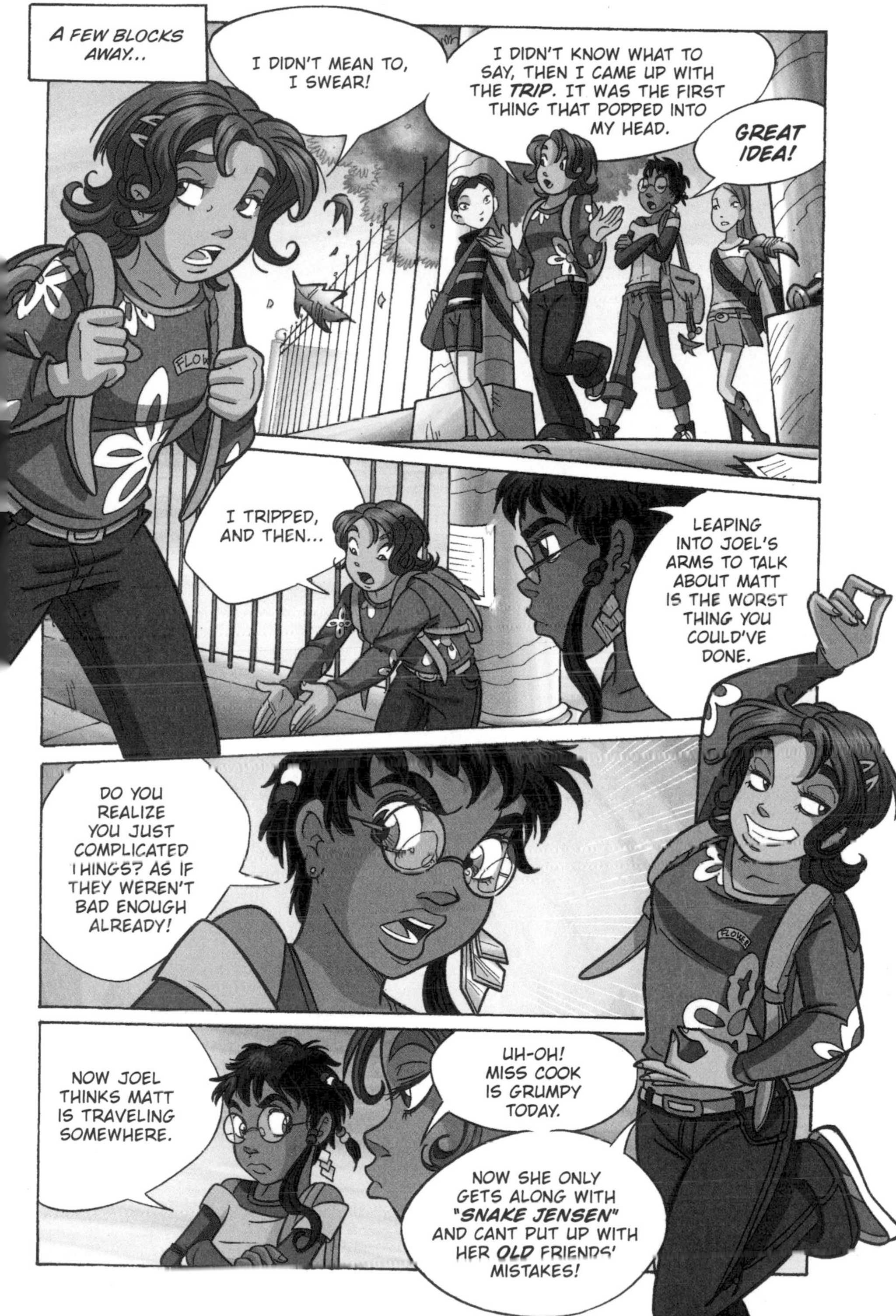
A FEW BLOCKS AWAY...
I DIDN'T MEAN TO, I SWEAR!
I DIDN'T KNOW WHAT TO SAY, THEN I CAME UP WITH THE ***TRIP***. IT WAS THE FIRST THING THAT POPPED INTO MY HEAD.
GREAT IDEA!
I TRIPPED, AND THEN...
LEAPING INTO JOEL'S ARMS TO TALK ABOUT MATT IS THE WORST THING YOU COULD'VE DONE.
DO YOU REALIZE YOU JUST COMPLICATED THINGS? AS IF THEY WEREN'T BAD ENOUGH ALREADY!
NOW JOEL THINKS MATT IS TRAVELING SOMEWHERE.
UH-OH! MISS COOK IS GRUMPY TODAY.
NOW SHE ONLY GETS ALONG WITH "***SNAKE JENSEN***" AND CANT PUT UP WITH HER ***OLD*** FRIENDS' MISTAKES!

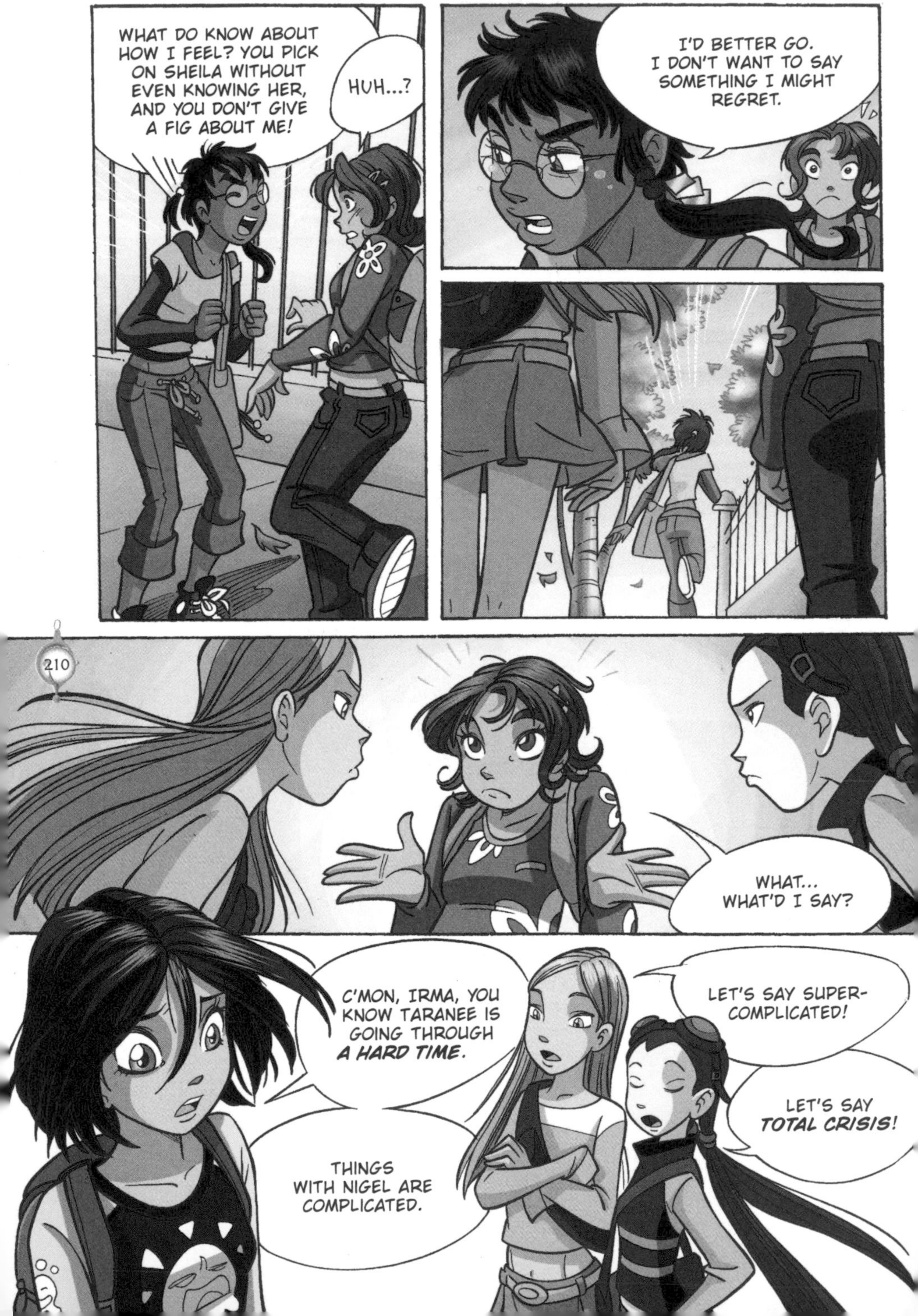
WHAT DO KNOW ABOUT HOW I FEEL? YOU PICK ON SHEILA WITHOUT EVEN KNOWING HER, AND YOU DON'T GIVE A FIG ABOUT ME!
HUH...?
I'D BETTER GO. I DON'T WANT TO SAY SOMETHING I MIGHT REGRET.
WHAT... WHAT'D I SAY?
C'MON, IRMA, YOU KNOW TARANEE IS GOING THROUGH ***A HARD TIME***.
THINGS WITH NIGEL ARE COMPLICATED.
LET'S SAY SUPER-COMPLICATED!
LET'S SAY ***TOTAL CRISIS***!

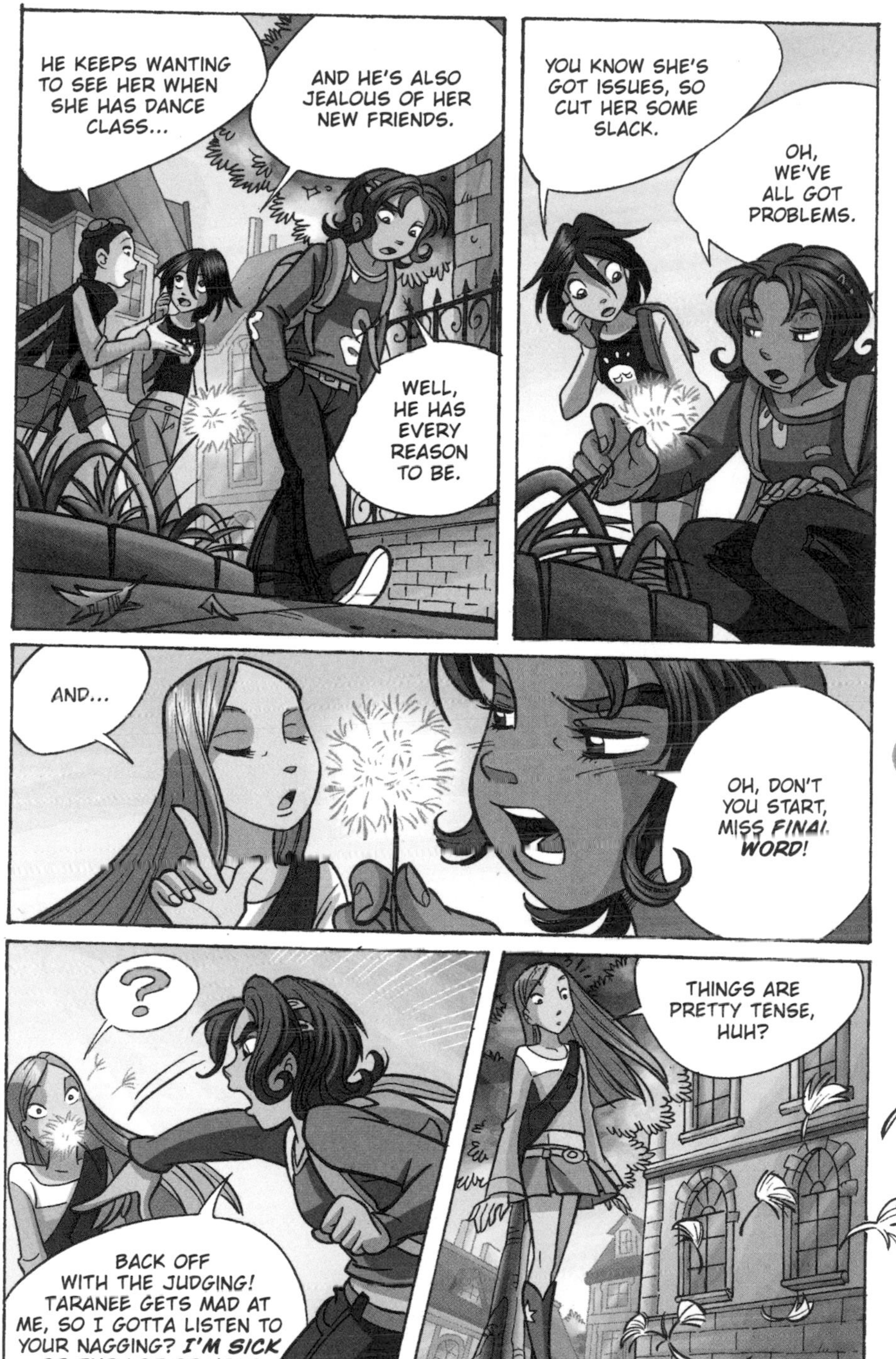
HE KEEPS WANTING TO SEE HER WHEN SHE HAS DANCE CLASS...
AND HE'S ALSO JEALOUS OF HER NEW FRIENDS.
WELL, HE HAS EVERY REASON TO BE.
YOU KNOW SHE'S GOT ISSUES, SO CUT HER SOME SLACK.
OH, WE'VE ALL GOT PROBLEMS.
AND...
OH, DON'T YOU START, MISS *FINAL WORD!*
?
BACK OFF WITH THE JUDGING! TARANEE GETS MAD AT ME, SO I GOTTA LISTEN TO YOUR NAGGING? *I'M SICK OF THE LOT OF YOU!*
THINGS ARE PRETTY TENSE, HUH?

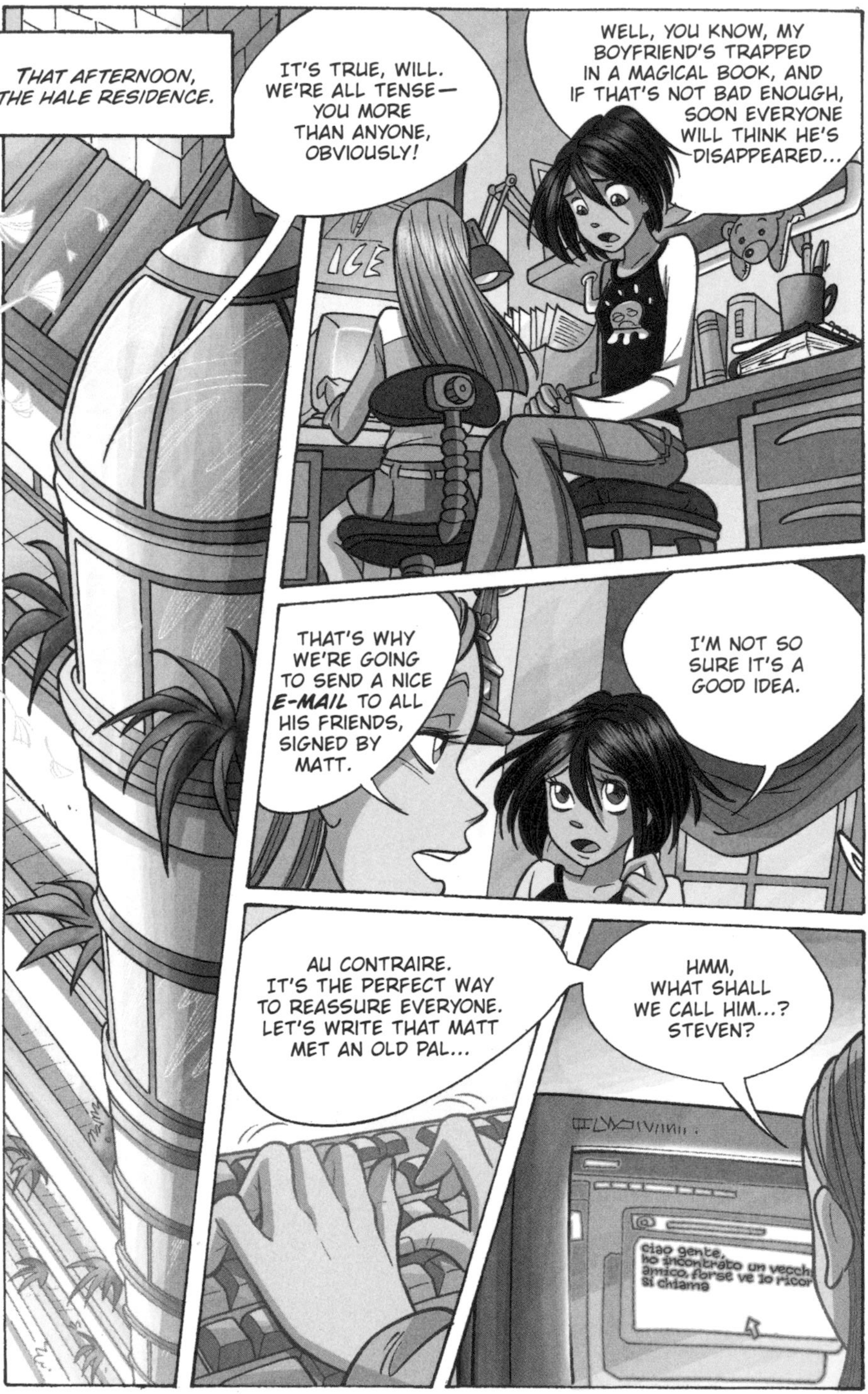
THAT AFTERNOON, THE HALE RESIDENCE.
IT'S TRUE, WILL. WE'RE ALL TENSE— YOU MORE THAN ANYONE, OBVIOUSLY!
WELL, YOU KNOW, MY BOYFRIEND'S TRAPPED IN A MAGICAL BOOK, AND IF THAT'S NOT BAD ENOUGH, SOON EVERYONE WILL THINK HE'S DISAPPEARED...
THAT'S WHY WE'RE GOING TO SEND A NICE **E-MAIL** TO ALL HIS FRIENDS, SIGNED BY MATT.
I'M NOT SO SURE IT'S A GOOD IDEA.
AU CONTRAIRE. IT'S THE PERFECT WAY TO REASSURE EVERYONE. LET'S WRITE THAT MATT MET AN OLD PAL...
HMM, WHAT SHALL WE CALL HIM...? STEVEN?
ciao gente, ho incontrato un vecch amico, forse ve lo ricor si chiama

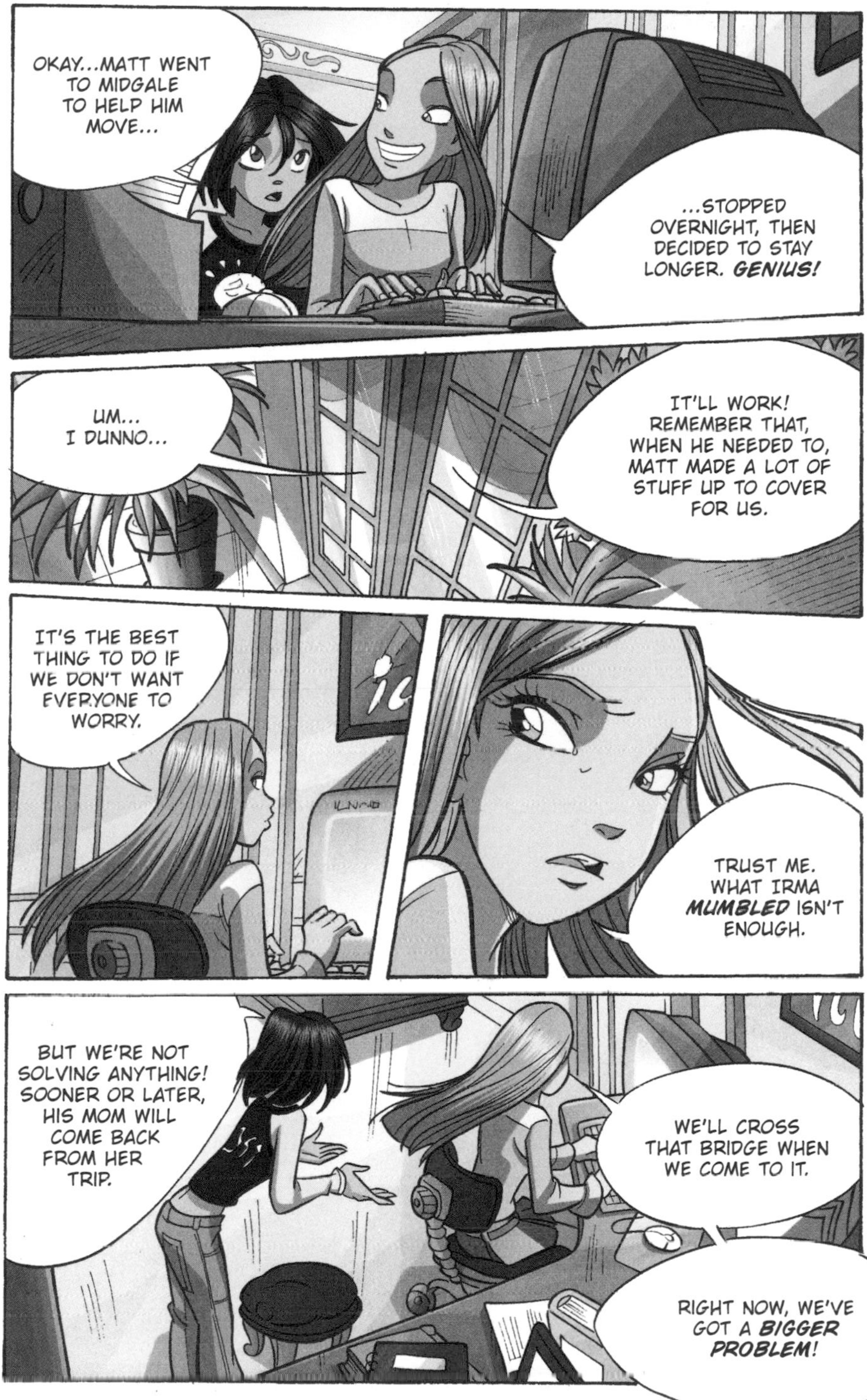

OKAY...MATT WENT TO MIDGALE TO HELP HIM MOVE...
...STOPPED OVERNIGHT, THEN DECIDED TO STAY LONGER. GENIUS!
UM... I DUNNO...
IT'LL WORK! REMEMBER THAT, WHEN HE NEEDED TO, MATT MADE A LOT OF STUFF UP TO COVER FOR US.
IT'S THE BEST THING TO DO IF WE DON'T WANT EVERYONE TO WORRY.
TRUST ME. WHAT IRMA MUMBLED ISN'T ENOUGH.
BUT WE'RE NOT SOLVING ANYTHING! SOONER OR LATER, HIS MOM WILL COME BACK FROM HER TRIP.
WE'LL CROSS THAT BRIDGE WHEN WE COME TO IT.
RIGHT NOW, WE'VE GOT A BIGGER PROBLEM!

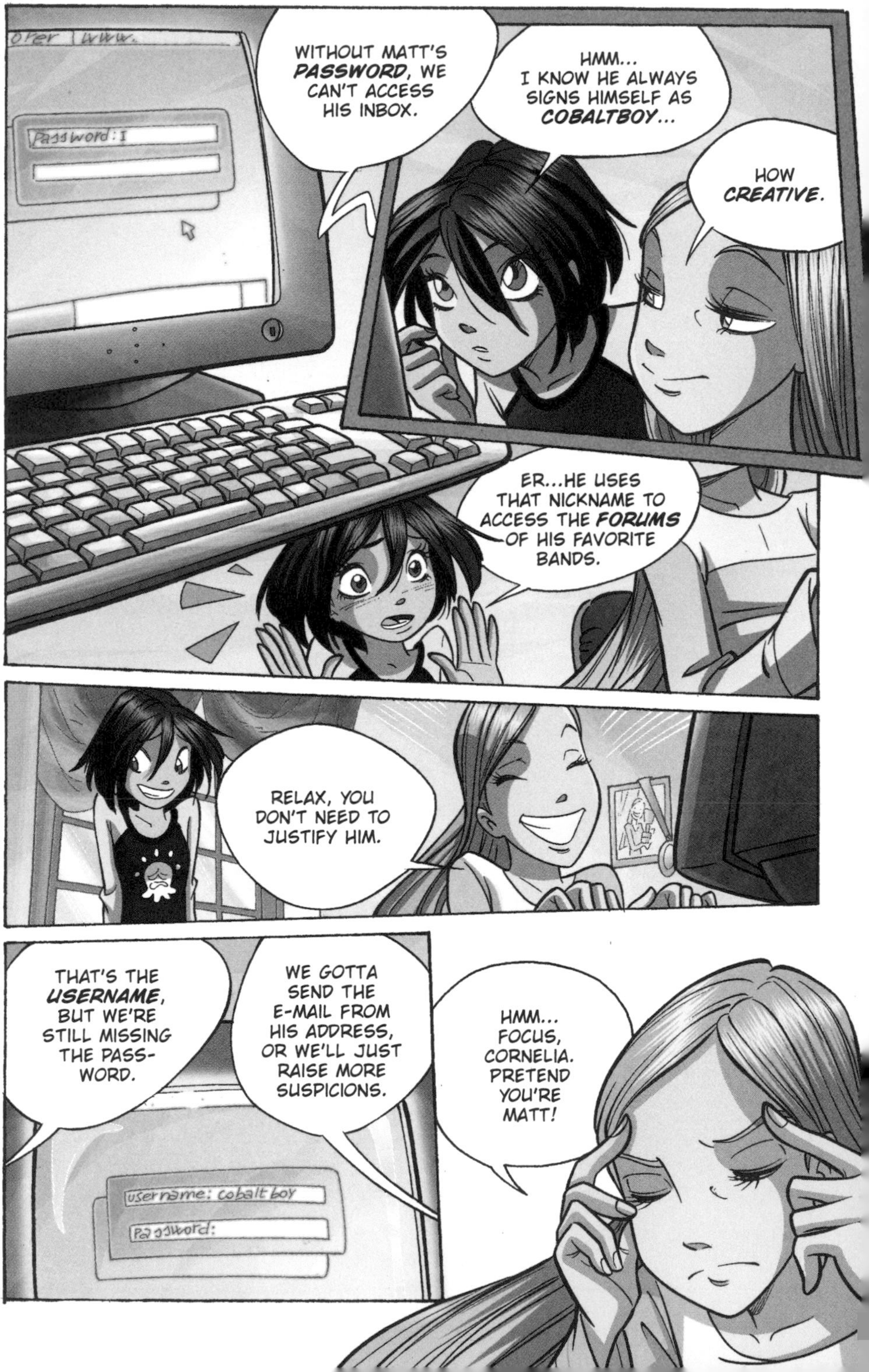

Password: I
WITHOUT MATT'S PASSWORD, WE CAN'T ACCESS HIS INBOX.
HMM... I KNOW HE ALWAYS SIGNS HIMSELF AS COBALTBOY...
HOW CREATIVE.
ER...HE USES THAT NICKNAME TO ACCESS THE FORUMS OF HIS FAVORITE BANDS.
RELAX, YOU DON'T NEED TO JUSTIFY HIM.
THAT'S THE USERNAME, BUT WE'RE STILL MISSING THE PASS-WORD.
WE GOTTA SEND THE E-MAIL FROM HIS ADDRESS, OR WE'LL JUST RAISE MORE SUSPICIONS.
HMM... FOCUS, CORNELIA. PRETEND YOU'RE MATT!
username: cobalt boy
Password:

214

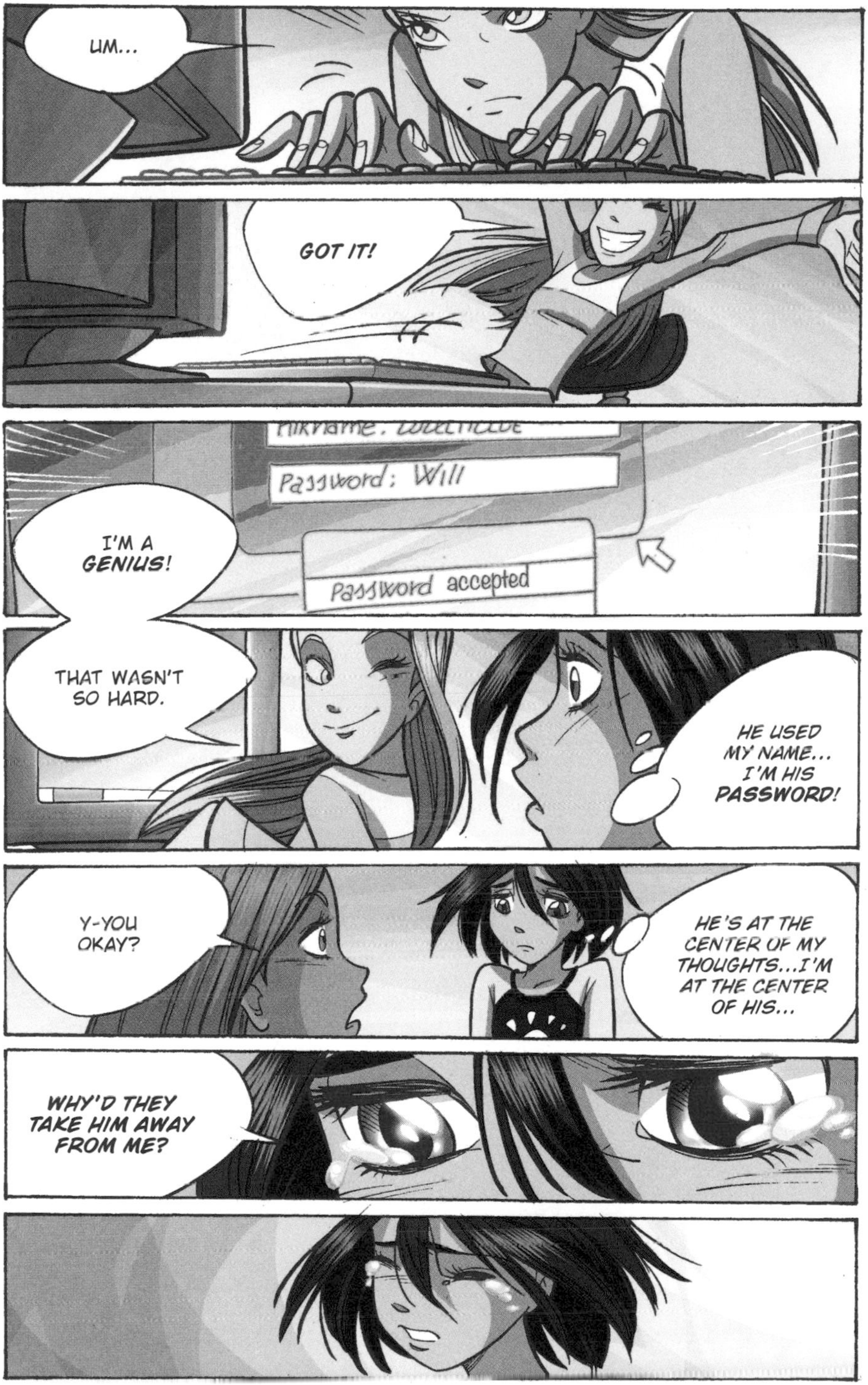
UM...
GOT IT!
Password: Will
Password accepted
I'M A GENIUS!
THAT WASN'T SO HARD.
HE USED MY NAME... I'M HIS PASSWORD!
Y-YOU OKAY?
HE'S AT THE CENTER OF MY THOUGHTS...I'M AT THE CENTER OF HIS...
WHY'D THEY TAKE HIM AWAY FROM ME?

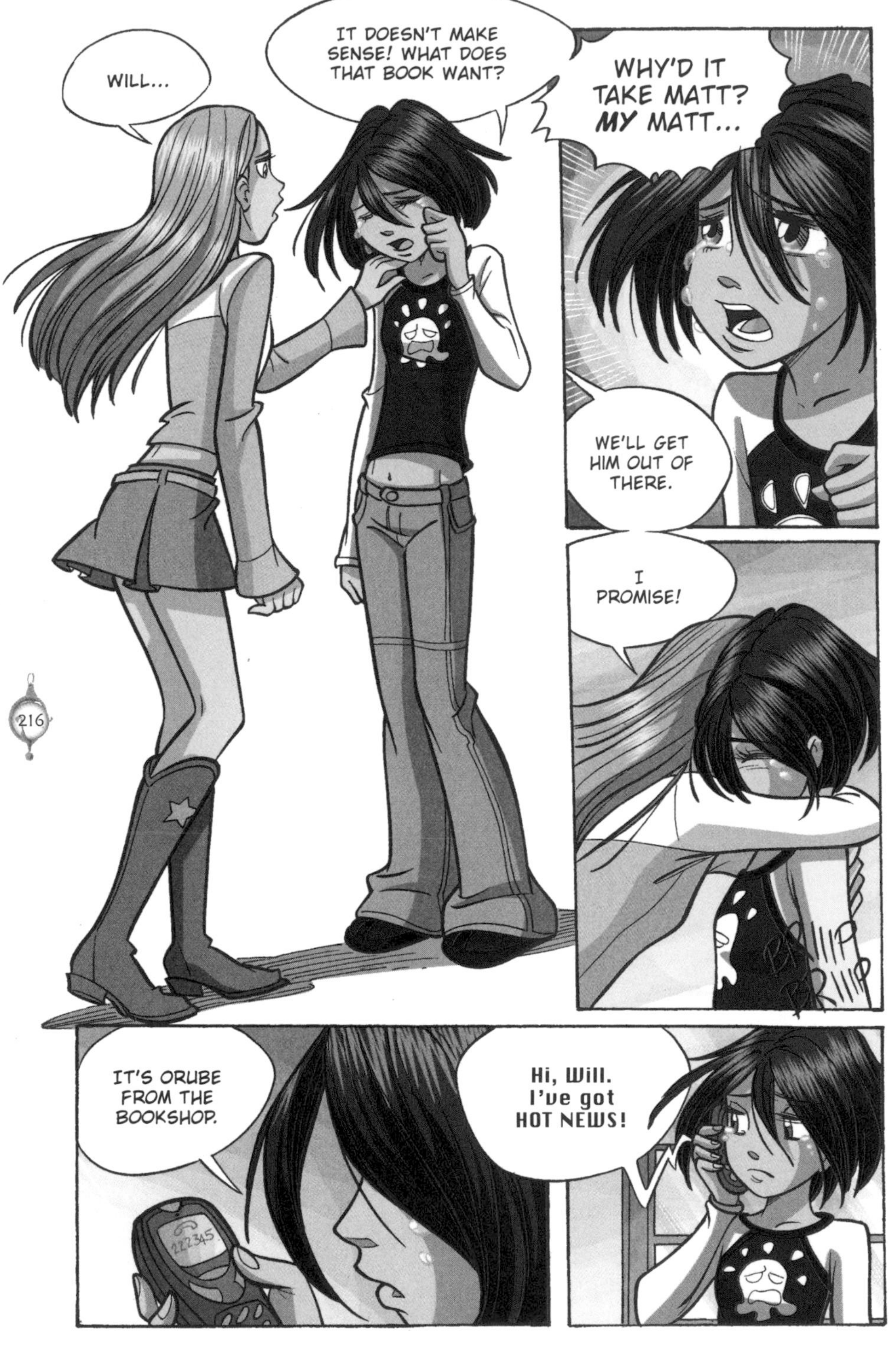
WILL...
IT DOESN'T MAKE SENSE! WHAT DOES THAT BOOK WANT?
WHY'D IT TAKE MATT? *MY* MATT...
WE'LL GET HIM OUT OF THERE.
I PROMISE!
BRIIIP BRIIIP
IT'S ORUBE FROM THE BOOKSHOP.
222345
Hi, Will. I've got HOT NEWS!

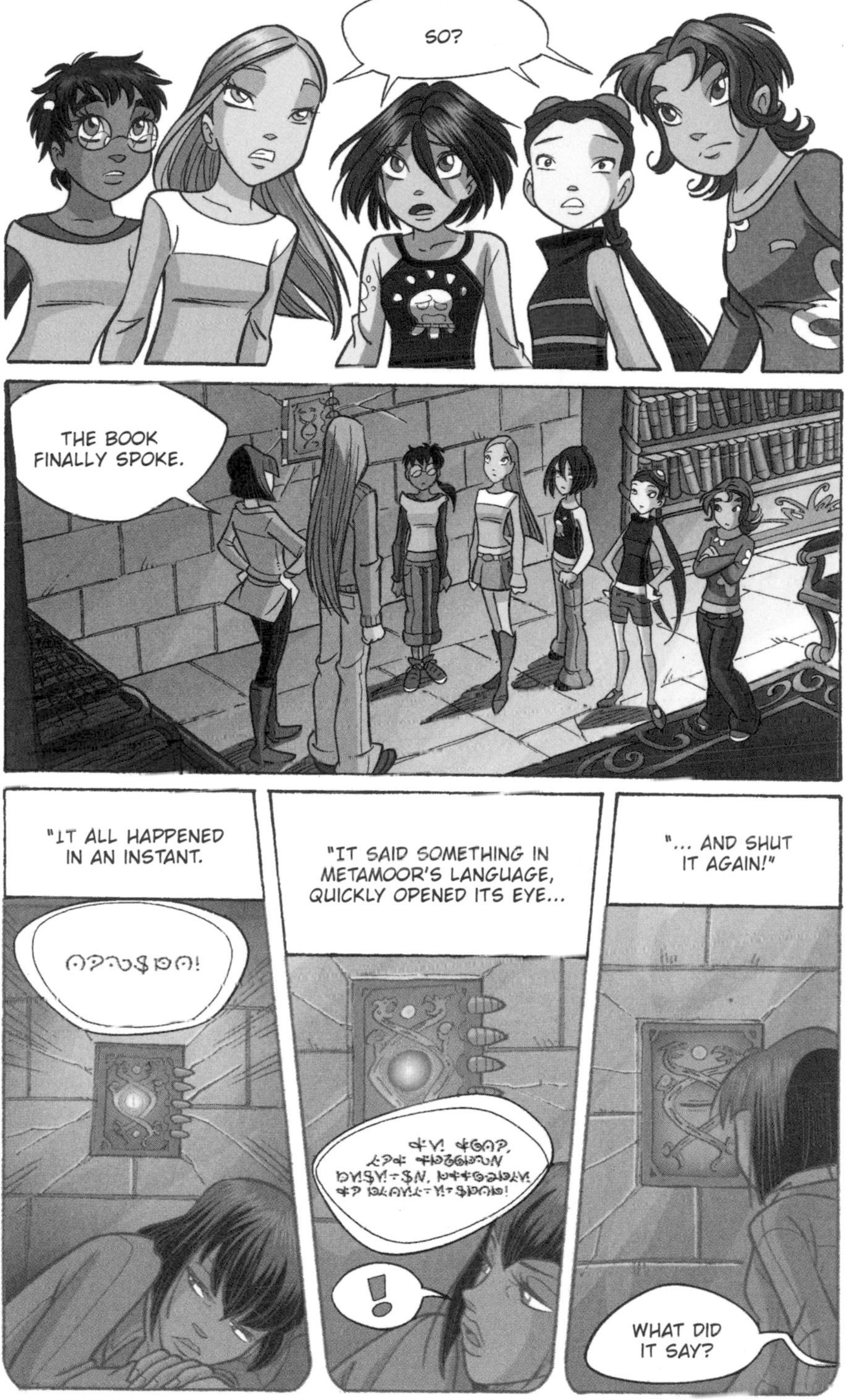
SO?
THE BOOK FINALLY SPOKE.
"IT ALL HAPPENED IN AN INSTANT.
"IT SAID SOMETHING IN METAMOOR'S LANGUAGE, QUICKLY OPENED ITS EYE...
"... AND SHUT IT AGAIN!"
!
WHAT DID IT SAY?

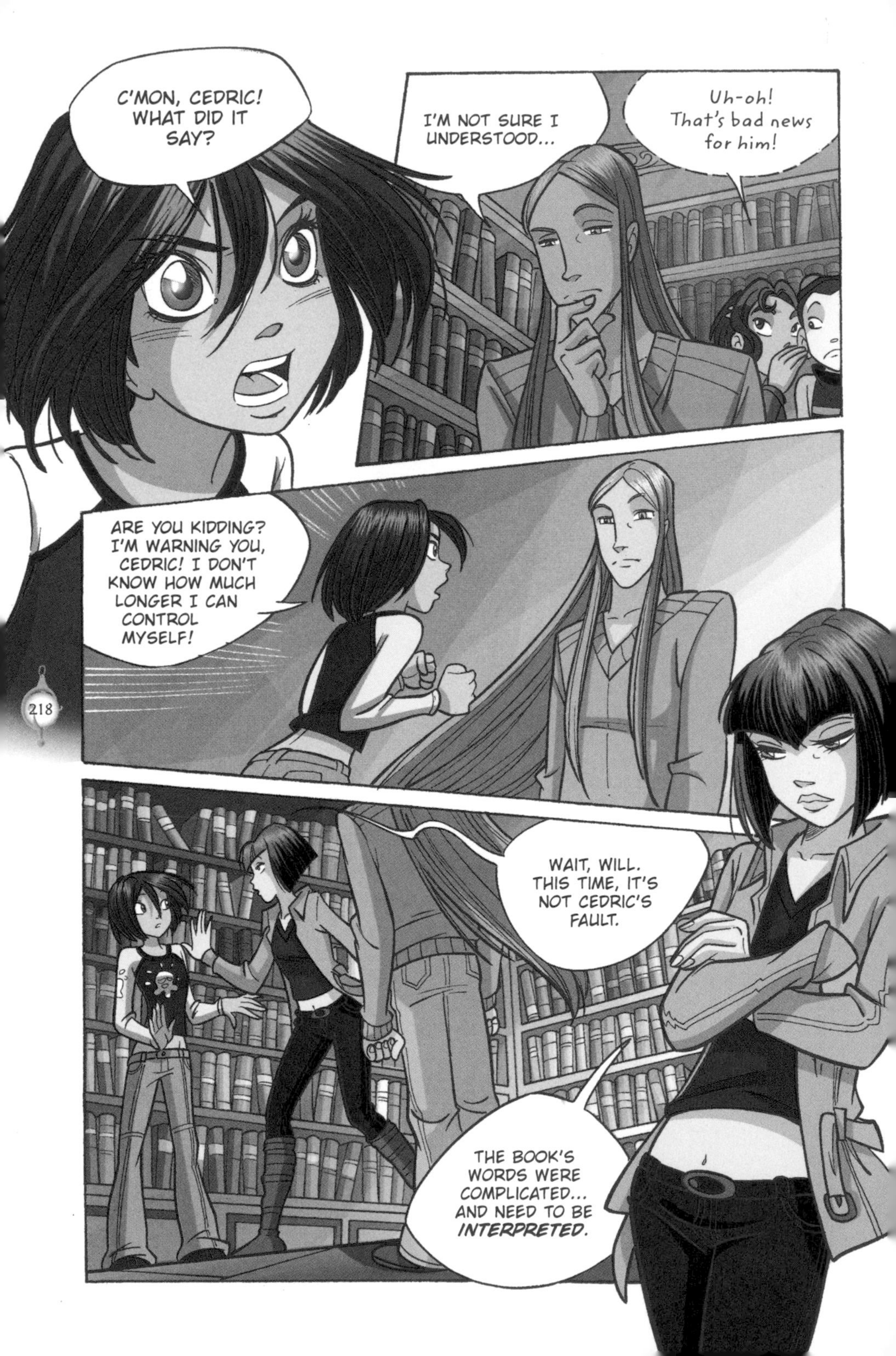
C'MON, CEDRIC! WHAT DID IT SAY?
I'M NOT SURE I UNDERSTOOD...
Uh-oh! That's bad news for him!
ARE YOU KIDDING? I'M WARNING YOU, CEDRIC! I DON'T KNOW HOW MUCH LONGER I CAN CONTROL MYSELF!
WAIT, WILL. THIS TIME, IT'S NOT CEDRIC'S FAULT.
THE BOOK'S WORDS WERE COMPLICATED... AND NEED TO BE *INTERPRETED*.

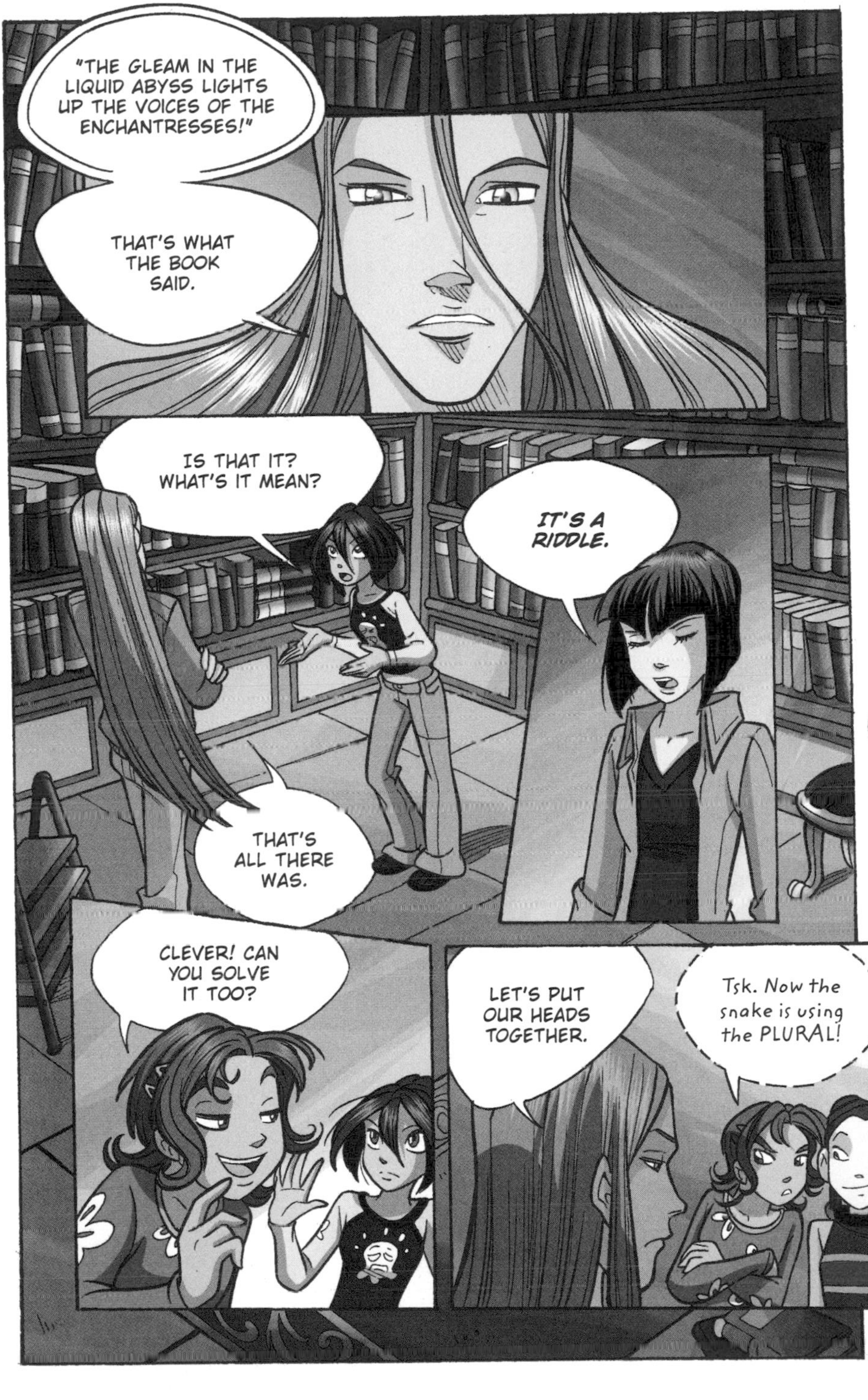
"THE GLEAM IN THE LIQUID ABYSS LIGHTS UP THE VOICES OF THE ENCHANTRESSES!"
THAT'S WHAT THE BOOK SAID.
IS THAT IT? WHAT'S IT MEAN?
THAT'S ALL THERE WAS.
IT'S A RIDDLE.
CLEVER! CAN YOU SOLVE IT TOO?
LET'S PUT OUR HEADS TOGETHER.
Tsk. Now the snake is using the PLURAL!

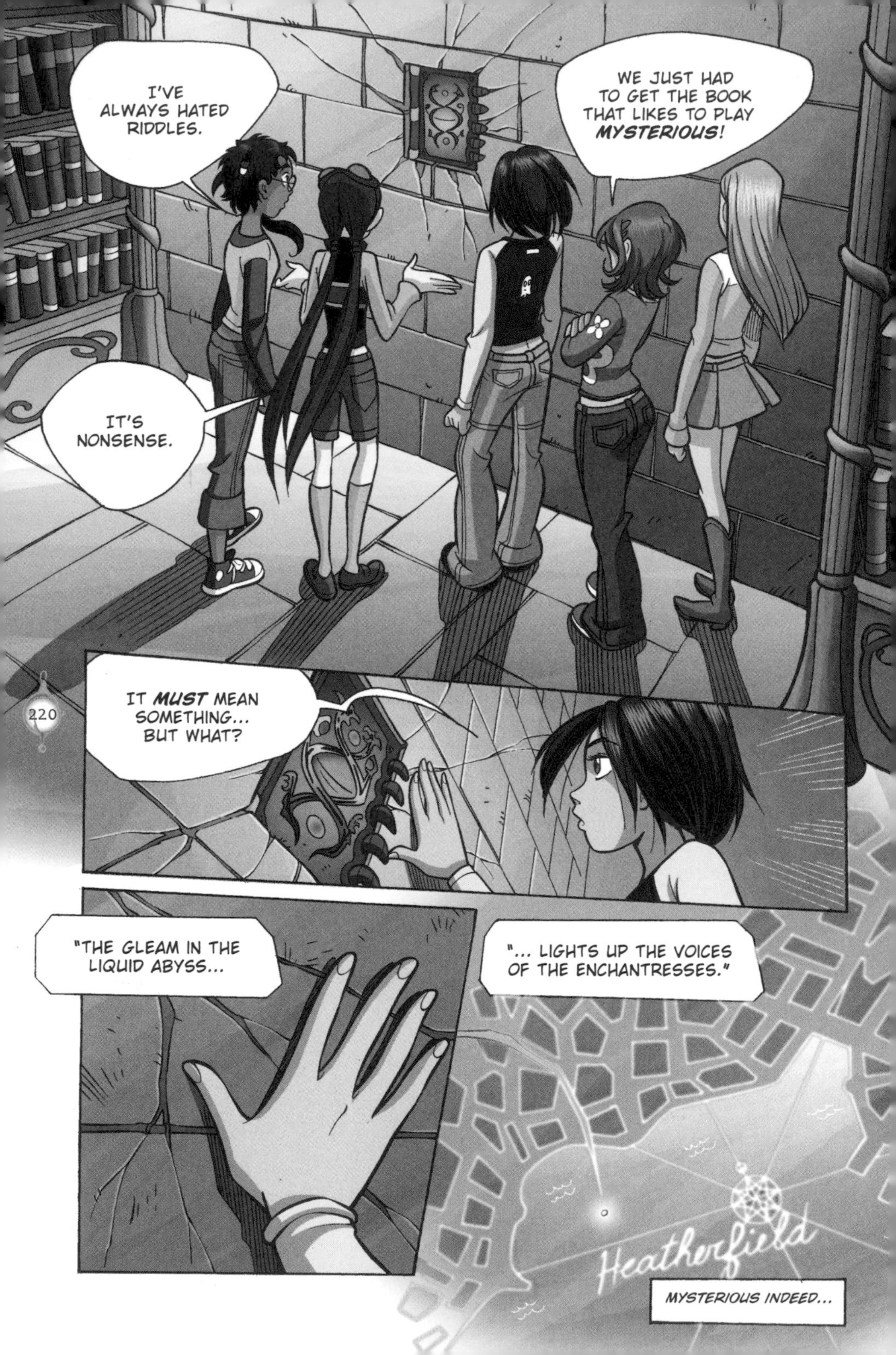
I'VE ALWAYS HATED RIDDLES.
WE JUST HAD TO GET THE BOOK THAT LIKES TO PLAY MYSTERIOUS!
IT'S NONSENSE.
IT MUST MEAN SOMETHING... BUT WHAT?
"THE GLEAM IN THE LIQUID ABYSS...
"... LIGHTS UP THE VOICES OF THE ENCHANTRESSES."
Heatherfield
MYSTERIOUS INDEED...

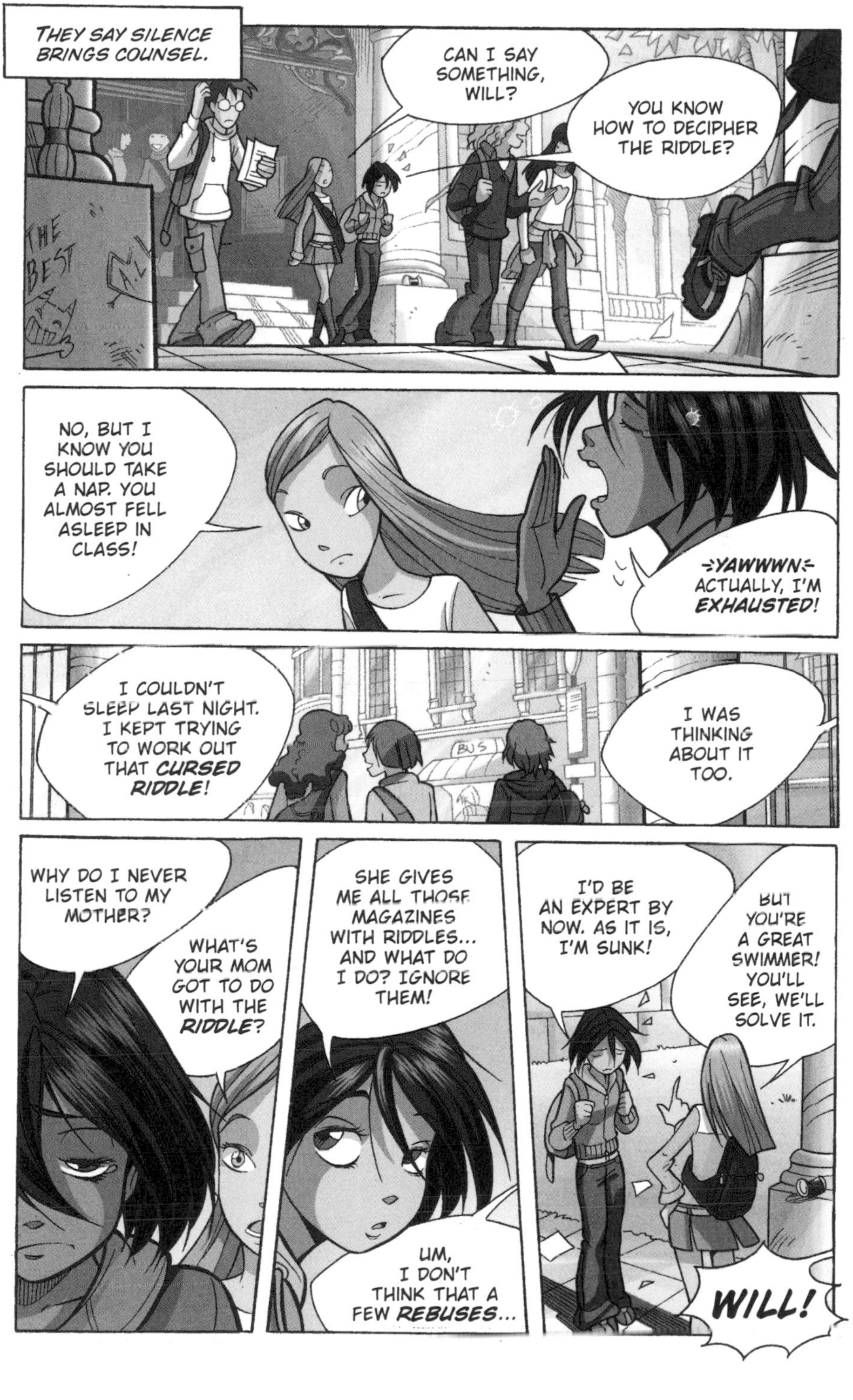
THEY SAY SILENCE BRINGS COUNSEL.
CAN I SAY SOMETHING, WILL?
YOU KNOW HOW TO DECIPHER THE RIDDLE?
THE BEST
NO, BUT I KNOW YOU SHOULD TAKE A NAP. YOU ALMOST FELL ASLEEP IN CLASS!
YAWWWN ACTUALLY, I'M EXHAUSTED!
I COULDN'T SLEEP LAST NIGHT. I KEPT TRYING TO WORK OUT THAT CURSED RIDDLE!
BUS
I WAS THINKING ABOUT IT TOO.
WHY DO I NEVER LISTEN TO MY MOTHER?
WHAT'S YOUR MOM GOT TO DO WITH THE RIDDLE?
SHE GIVES ME ALL THOSE MAGAZINES WITH RIDDLES... AND WHAT DO I DO? IGNORE THEM!
UM, I DON'T THINK THAT A FEW REBUSES...
I'D BE AN EXPERT BY NOW. AS IT IS, I'M SUNK!
BUT YOU'RE A GREAT SWIMMER! YOU'LL SEE, WE'LL SOLVE IT.
WILL!

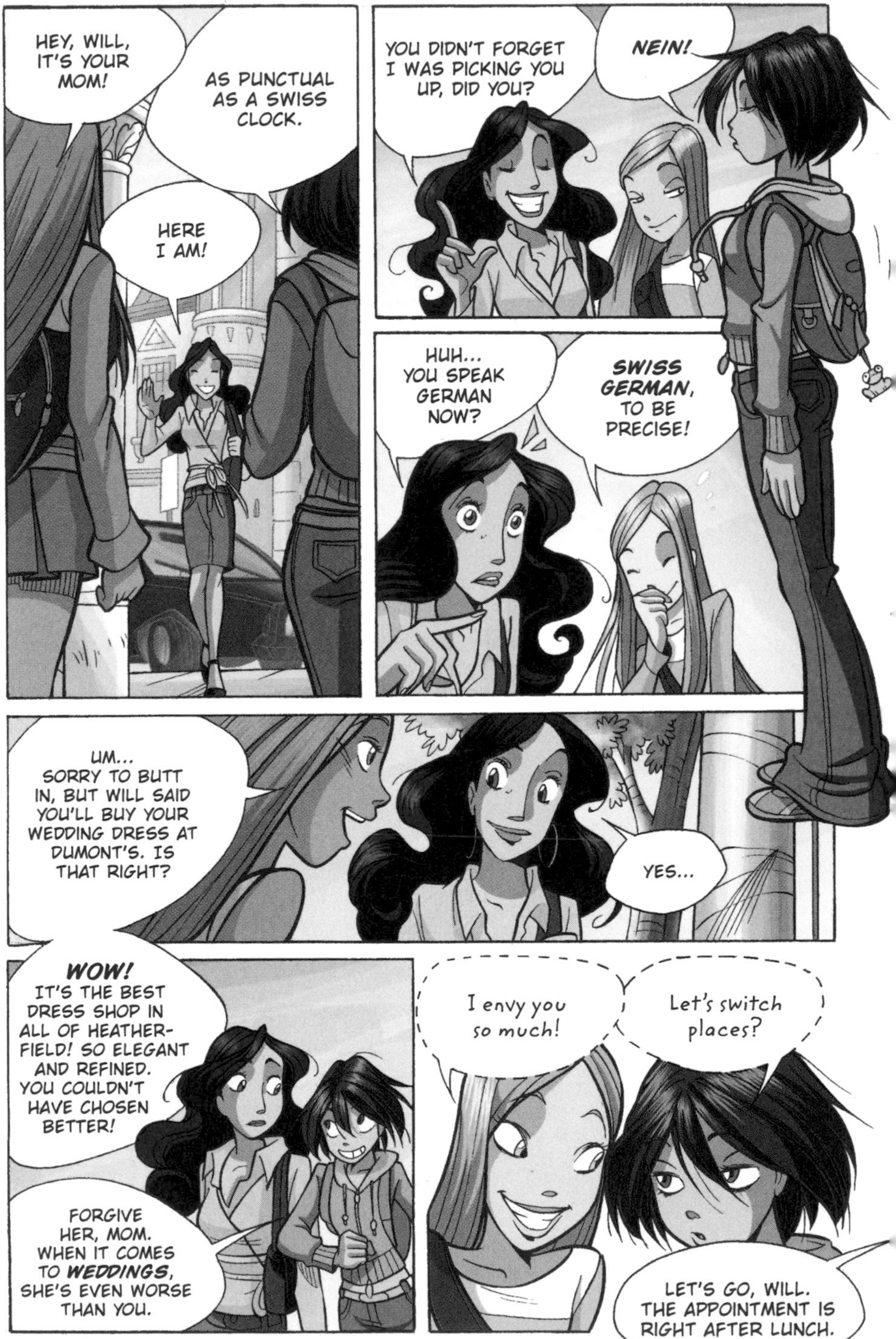
HEY, WILL, IT'S YOUR MOM!
AS PUNCTUAL AS A SWISS CLOCK.
HERE I AM!
YOU DIDN'T FORGET I WAS PICKING YOU UP, DID YOU?
NEIN!
HUH... YOU SPEAK GERMAN NOW?
SWISS GERMAN, TO BE PRECISE!
UM... SORRY TO BUTT IN, BUT WILL SAID YOU'LL BUY YOUR WEDDING DRESS AT DUMONT'S. IS THAT RIGHT?
YES...
WOW! IT'S THE BEST DRESS SHOP IN ALL OF HEATHER-FIELD! SO ELEGANT AND REFINED. YOU COULDN'T HAVE CHOSEN BETTER!
FORGIVE HER, MOM. WHEN IT COMES TO WEDDINGS, SHE'S EVEN WORSE THAN YOU.
I envy you so much!
Let's switch places?
LET'S GO, WILL. THE APPOINTMENT IS RIGHT AFTER LUNCH.

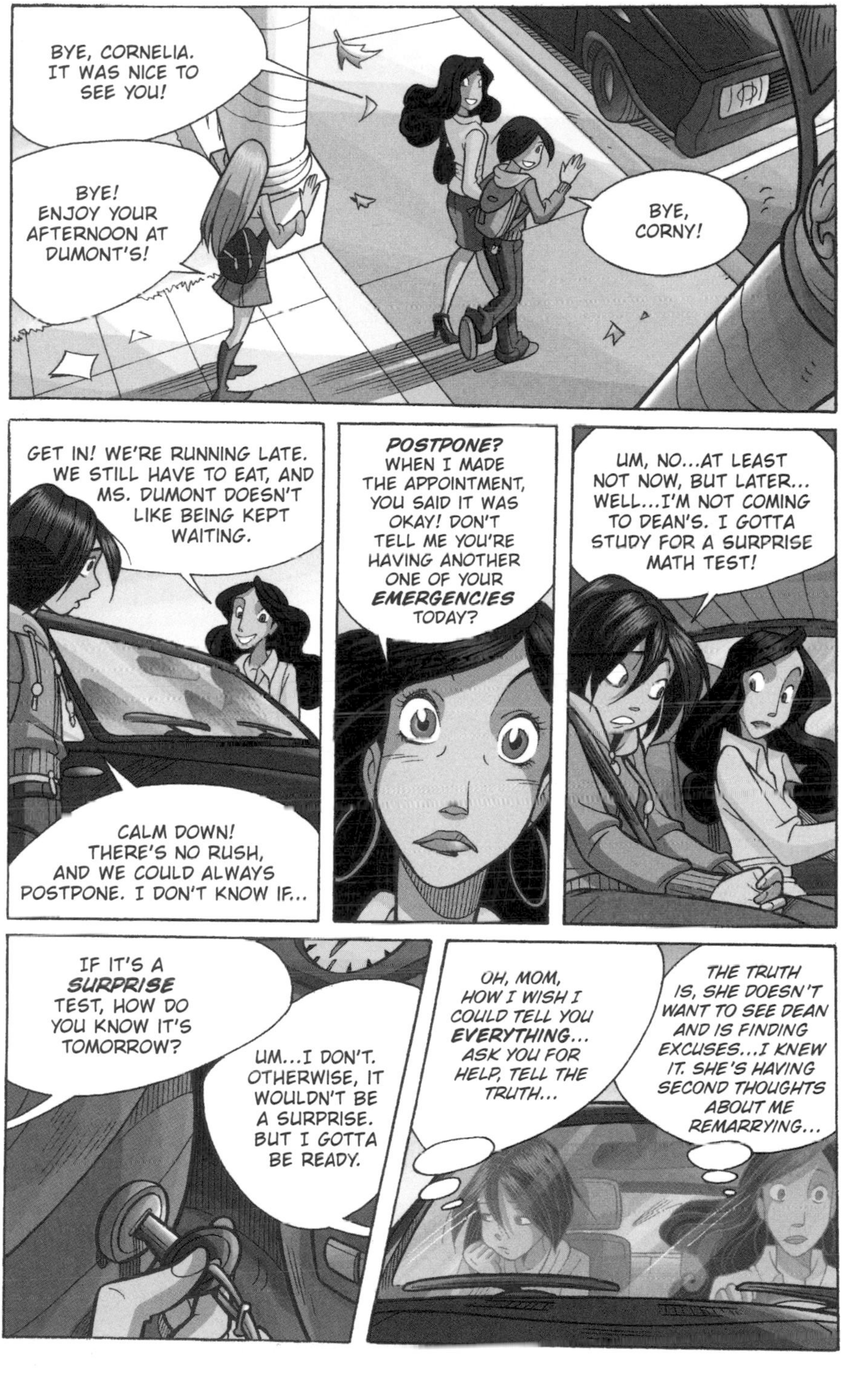
BYE, CORNELIA. IT WAS NICE TO SEE YOU!
BYE! ENJOY YOUR AFTERNOON AT DUMONT'S!
BYE, CORNY!
GET IN! WE'RE RUNNING LATE. WE STILL HAVE TO EAT, AND MS. DUMONT DOESN'T LIKE BEING KEPT WAITING.
CALM DOWN! THERE'S NO RUSH, AND WE COULD ALWAYS POSTPONE. I DON'T KNOW IF...
POSTPONE? WHEN I MADE THE APPOINTMENT, YOU SAID IT WAS OKAY! DON'T TELL ME YOU'RE HAVING ANOTHER ONE OF YOUR EMERGENCIES TODAY?
UM, NO...AT LEAST NOT NOW, BUT LATER... WELL...I'M NOT COMING TO DEAN'S. I GOTTA STUDY FOR A SURPRISE MATH TEST!
IF IT'S A SURPRISE TEST, HOW DO YOU KNOW IT'S TOMORROW?
UM...I DON'T. OTHERWISE, IT WOULDN'T BE A SURPRISE. BUT I GOTTA BE READY.
OH, MOM, HOW I WISH I COULD TELL YOU EVERYTHING... ASK YOU FOR HELP, TELL THE TRUTH...
THE TRUTH IS, SHE DOESN'T WANT TO SEE DEAN AND IS FINDING EXCUSES...I KNEW IT. SHE'S HAVING SECOND THOUGHTS ABOUT ME REMARRYING...

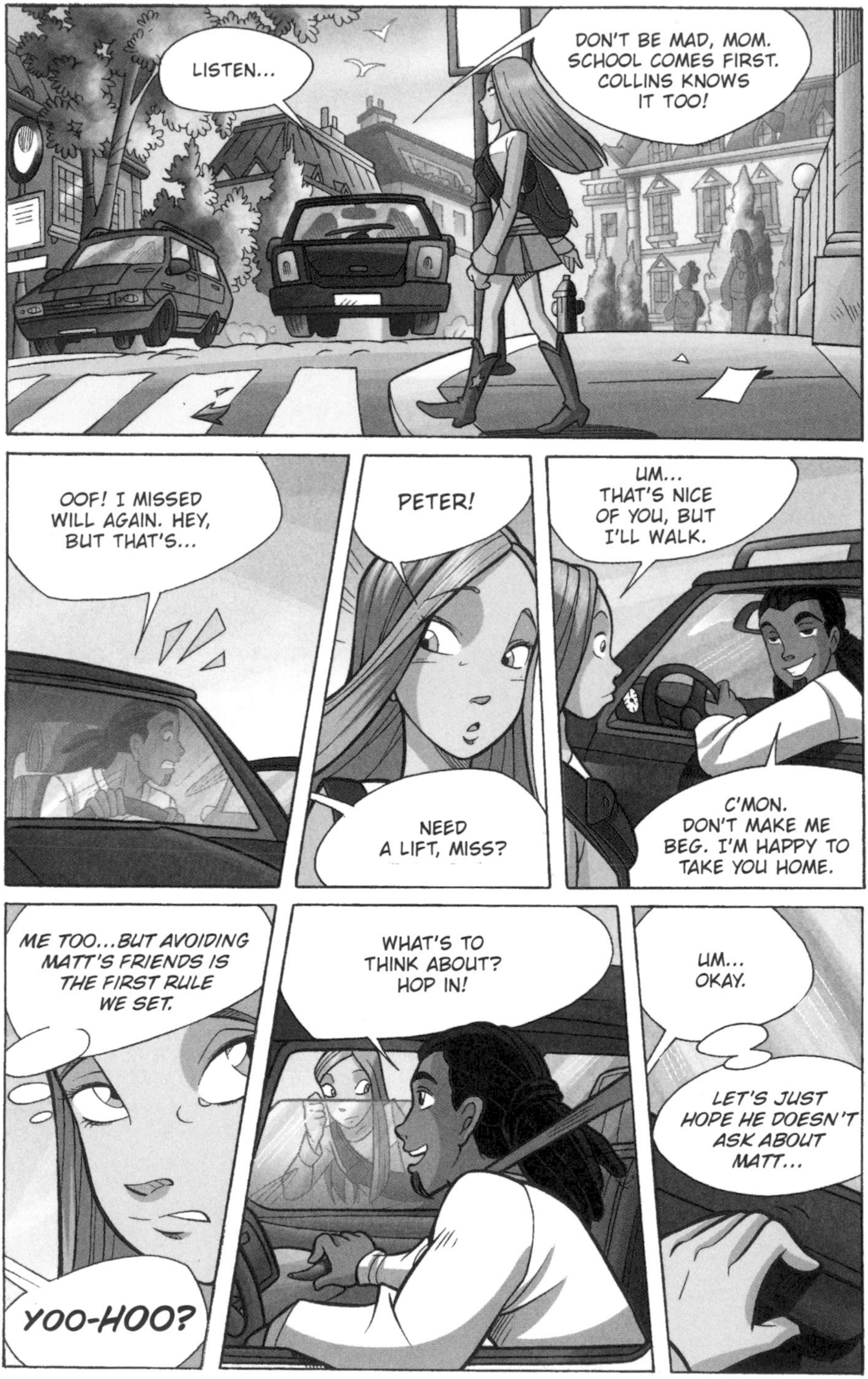
LISTEN...
DON'T BE MAD, MOM. SCHOOL COMES FIRST. COLLINS KNOWS IT TOO!
OOF! I MISSED WILL AGAIN. HEY, BUT THAT'S...
PETER!
NEED A LIFT, MISS?
UM... THAT'S NICE OF YOU, BUT I'LL WALK.
C'MON. DON'T MAKE ME BEG. I'M HAPPY TO TAKE YOU HOME.
ME TOO...BUT AVOIDING MATT'S FRIENDS IS THE FIRST RULE WE SET.
YOO-HOO?
WHAT'S TO THINK ABOUT? HOP IN!
UM... OKAY.
LET'S JUST HOPE HE DOESN'T ASK ABOUT MATT...

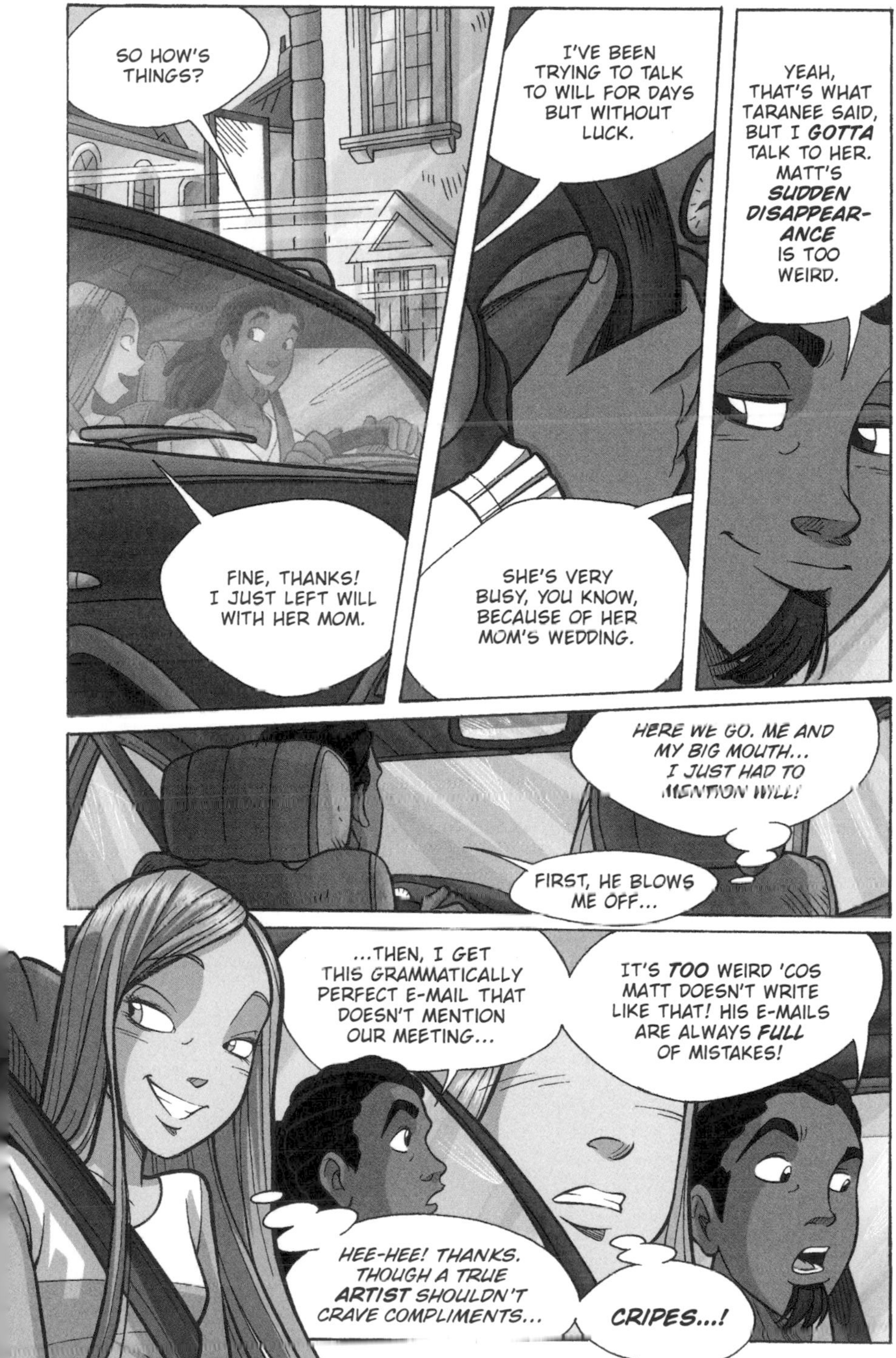
SO HOW'S THINGS?
FINE, THANKS! I JUST LEFT WILL WITH HER MOM.
I'VE BEEN TRYING TO TALK TO WILL FOR DAYS BUT WITHOUT LUCK.
SHE'S VERY BUSY, YOU KNOW, BECAUSE OF HER MOM'S WEDDING.
YEAH, THAT'S WHAT TARANEE SAID, BUT I GOTTA TALK TO HER. MATT'S SUDDEN DISAPPEAR-ANCE IS TOO WEIRD.
HERE WE GO. ME AND MY BIG MOUTH... I JUST HAD TO MENTION WILL!
FIRST, HE BLOWS ME OFF...
...THEN, I GET THIS GRAMMATICALLY PERFECT E-MAIL THAT DOESN'T MENTION OUR MEETING...
IT'S TOO WEIRD 'COS MATT DOESN'T WRITE LIKE THAT! HIS E-MAILS ARE ALWAYS FULL OF MISTAKES!
HEE-HEE! THANKS. THOUGH A TRUE ARTIST SHOULDN'T CRAVE COMPLIMENTS...
CRIPES...!

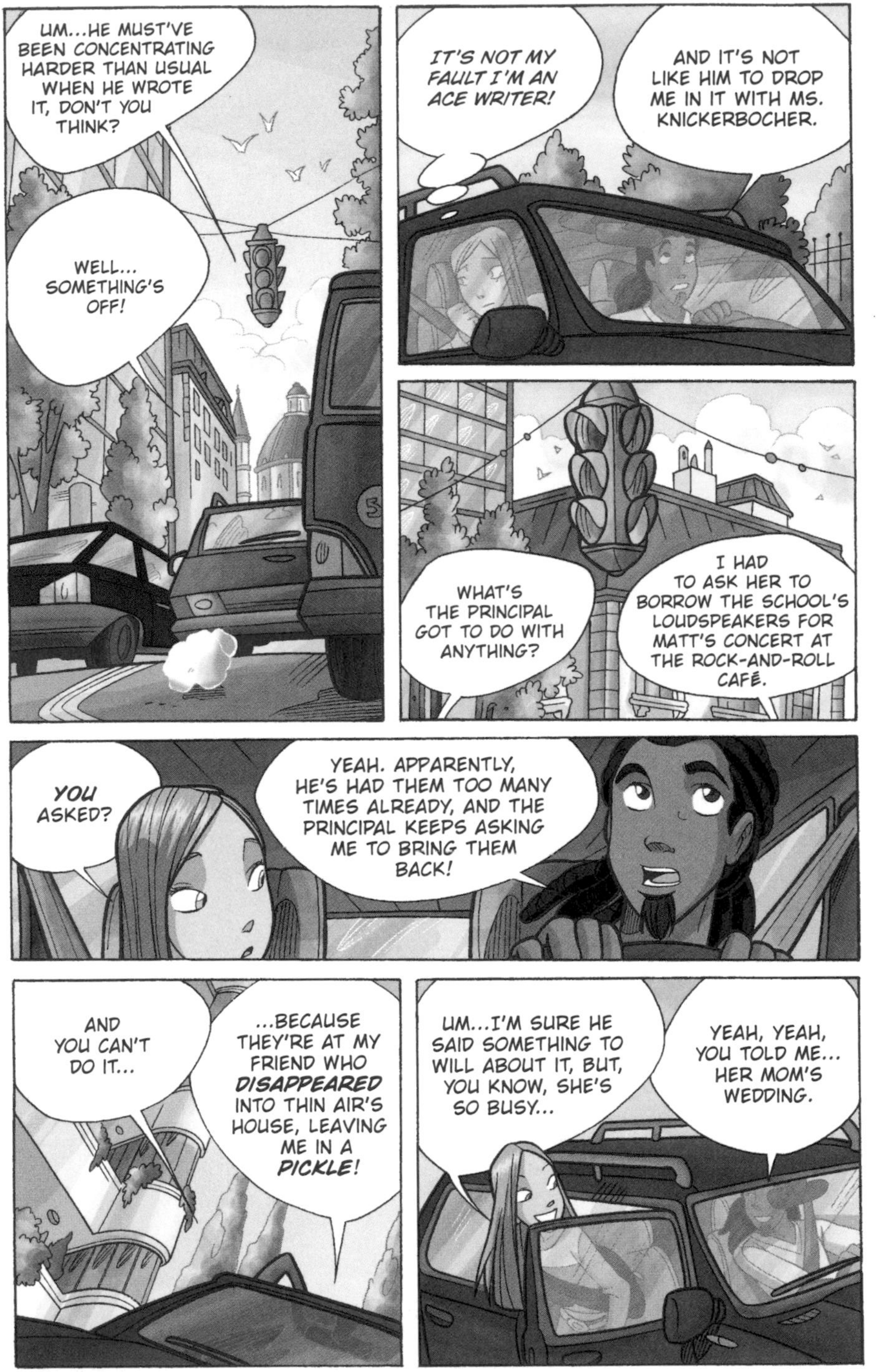
UM...HE MUST'VE BEEN CONCENTRATING HARDER THAN USUAL WHEN HE WROTE IT, DON'T YOU THINK?
WELL... SOMETHING'S OFF!
IT'S NOT MY FAULT I'M AN ACE WRITER!
AND IT'S NOT LIKE HIM TO DROP ME IN IT WITH MS. KNICKERBOCHER.
WHAT'S THE PRINCIPAL GOT TO DO WITH ANYTHING?
I HAD TO ASK HER TO BORROW THE SCHOOL'S LOUDSPEAKERS FOR MATT'S CONCERT AT THE ROCK-AND-ROLL CAFÉ.
YOU ASKED?
YEAH. APPARENTLY, HE'S HAD THEM TOO MANY TIMES ALREADY, AND THE PRINCIPAL KEEPS ASKING ME TO BRING THEM BACK!
AND YOU CAN'T DO IT...
...BECAUSE THEY'RE AT MY FRIEND WHO DISAPPEARED INTO THIN AIR'S HOUSE, LEAVING ME IN A PICKLE!
UM...I'M SURE HE SAID SOMETHING TO WILL ABOUT IT, BUT, YOU KNOW, SHE'S SO BUSY...
YEAH, YEAH, YOU TOLD ME... HER MOM'S WEDDING.

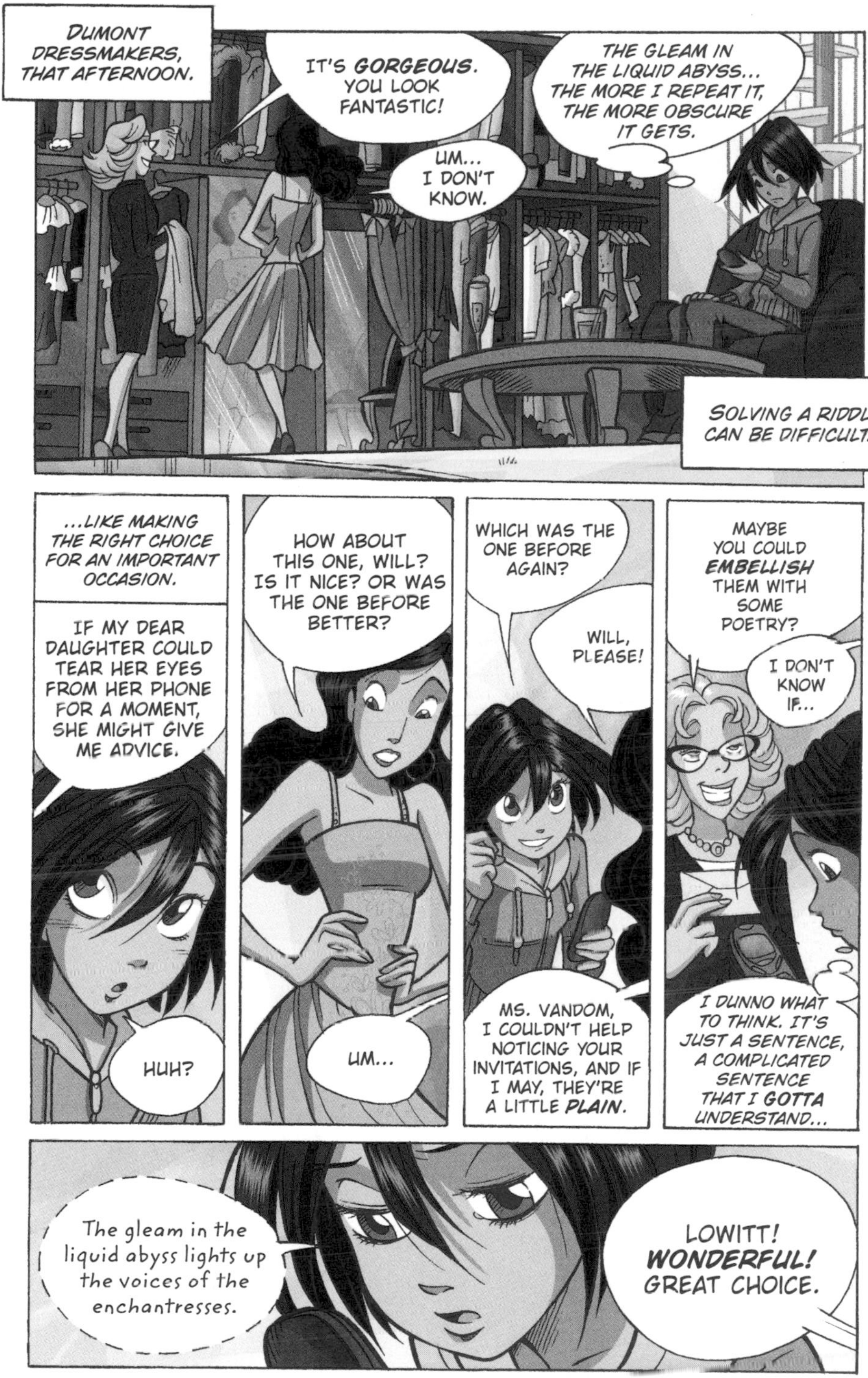
DUMONT DRESSMAKERS, THAT AFTERNOON.
IT'S GORGEOUS. YOU LOOK FANTASTIC!
UM... I DON'T KNOW.
THE GLEAM IN THE LIQUID ABYSS... THE MORE I REPEAT IT, THE MORE OBSCURE IT GETS.
SOLVING A RIDDLE CAN BE DIFFICULT...
...LIKE MAKING THE RIGHT CHOICE FOR AN IMPORTANT OCCASION.
IF MY DEAR DAUGHTER COULD TEAR HER EYES FROM HER PHONE FOR A MOMENT, SHE MIGHT GIVE ME ADVICE.
HUH?
HOW ABOUT THIS ONE, WILL? IS IT NICE? OR WAS THE ONE BEFORE BETTER?
UM...
WHICH WAS THE ONE BEFORE AGAIN?
WILL, PLEASE!
MS. VANDOM, I COULDN'T HELP NOTICING YOUR INVITATIONS, AND IF I MAY, THEY'RE A LITTLE PLAIN.
MAYBE YOU COULD EMBELLISH THEM WITH SOME POETRY?
I DON'T KNOW IF...
I DUNNO WHAT TO THINK. IT'S JUST A SENTENCE, A COMPLICATED SENTENCE THAT I GOTTA UNDERSTAND...
The gleam in the liquid abyss lights up the voices of the enchantresses.
LOWITT! WONDERFUL! GREAT CHOICE.

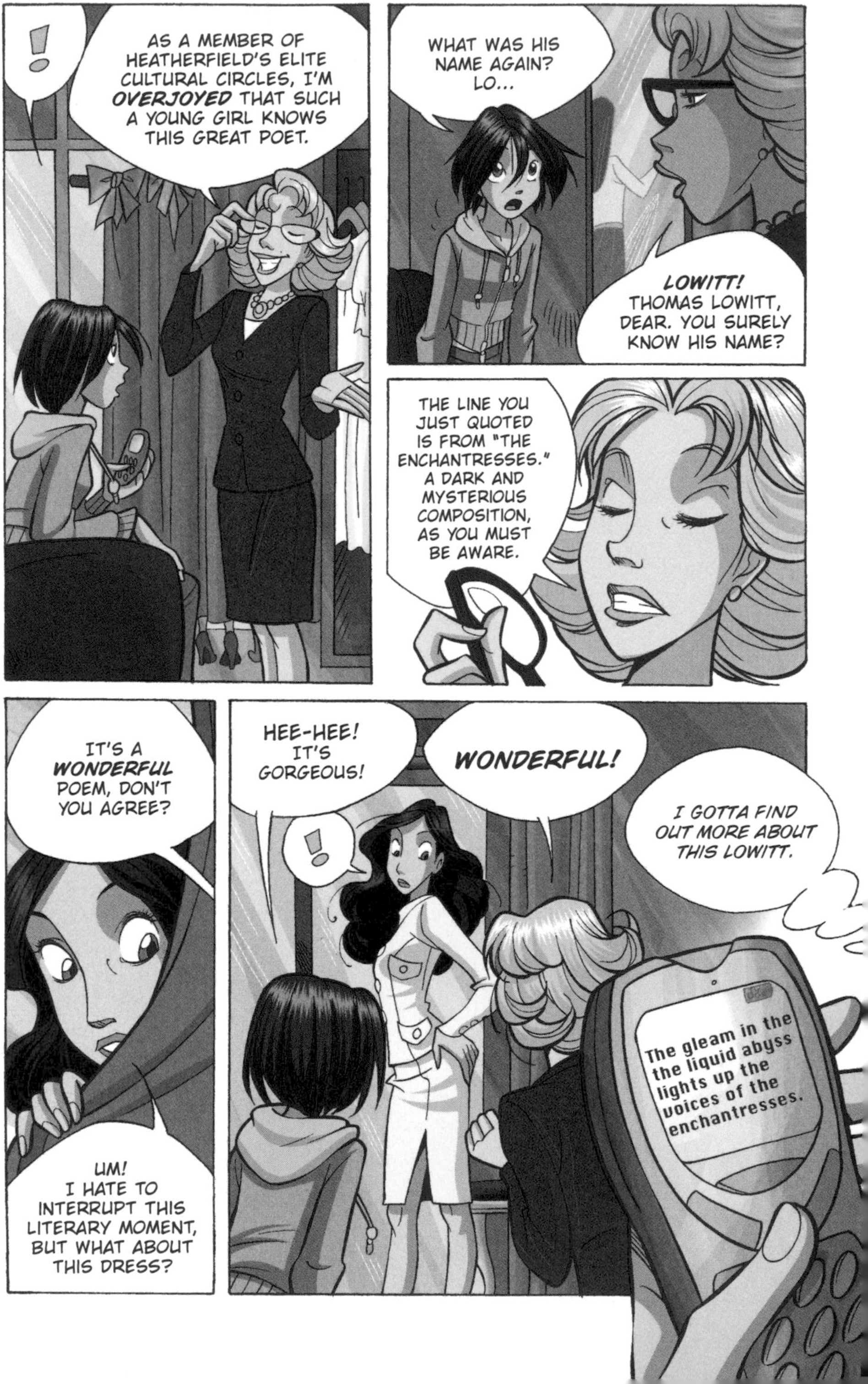
!
AS A MEMBER OF HEATHERFIELD'S ELITE CULTURAL CIRCLES, I'M OVERJOYED THAT SUCH A YOUNG GIRL KNOWS THIS GREAT POET.
WHAT WAS HIS NAME AGAIN? LO...
LOWITT! THOMAS LOWITT, DEAR. YOU SURELY KNOW HIS NAME?
THE LINE YOU JUST QUOTED IS FROM "THE ENCHANTRESSES." A DARK AND MYSTERIOUS COMPOSITION, AS YOU MUST BE AWARE.
IT'S A WONDERFUL POEM, DON'T YOU AGREE?
UM! I HATE TO INTERRUPT THIS LITERARY MOMENT, BUT WHAT ABOUT THIS DRESS?
HEE-HEE! IT'S GORGEOUS!
WONDERFUL!
!
I GOTTA FIND OUT MORE ABOUT THIS LOWITT.
The gleam in the liquid abyss the lights up the voices of the enchantresses.

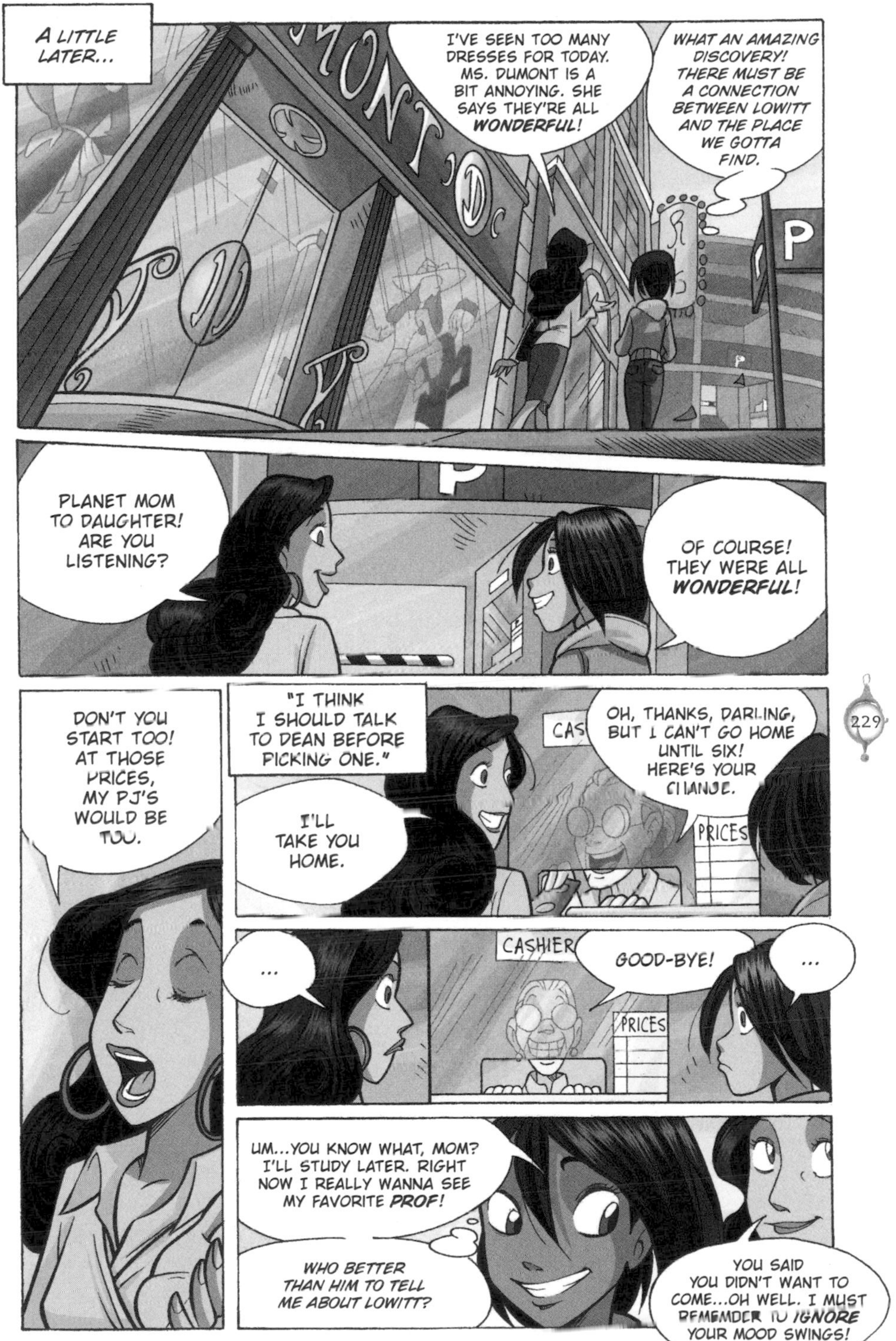
A LITTLE LATER...
I'VE SEEN TOO MANY DRESSES FOR TODAY. MS. DUMONT IS A BIT ANNOYING. SHE SAYS THEY'RE ALL **WONDERFUL**!
WHAT AN AMAZING DISCOVERY! THERE MUST BE A CONNECTION BETWEEN LOWITT AND THE PLACE WE GOTTA FIND.
P
PLANET MOM TO DAUGHTER! ARE YOU LISTENING?
OF COURSE! THEY WERE ALL **WONDERFUL**!
DON'T YOU START TOO! AT THOSE PRICES, MY PJ'S WOULD BE TOO.
"I THINK I SHOULD TALK TO DEAN BEFORE PICKING ONE."
I'LL TAKE YOU HOME.
OH, THANKS, DARLING, BUT I CAN'T GO HOME UNTIL SIX! HERE'S YOUR CHANGE.
PRICES
...
CASHIER
GOOD-BYE!
PRICES
...
UM...YOU KNOW WHAT, MOM? I'LL STUDY LATER. RIGHT NOW I REALLY WANNA SEE MY FAVORITE ***PROF***!
WHO BETTER THAN HIM TO TELL ME ABOUT LOWITT?
YOU SAID YOU DIDN'T WANT TO COME...OH WELL. I MUST REMEMBER TO ***IGNORE*** YOUR MOOD SWINGS!

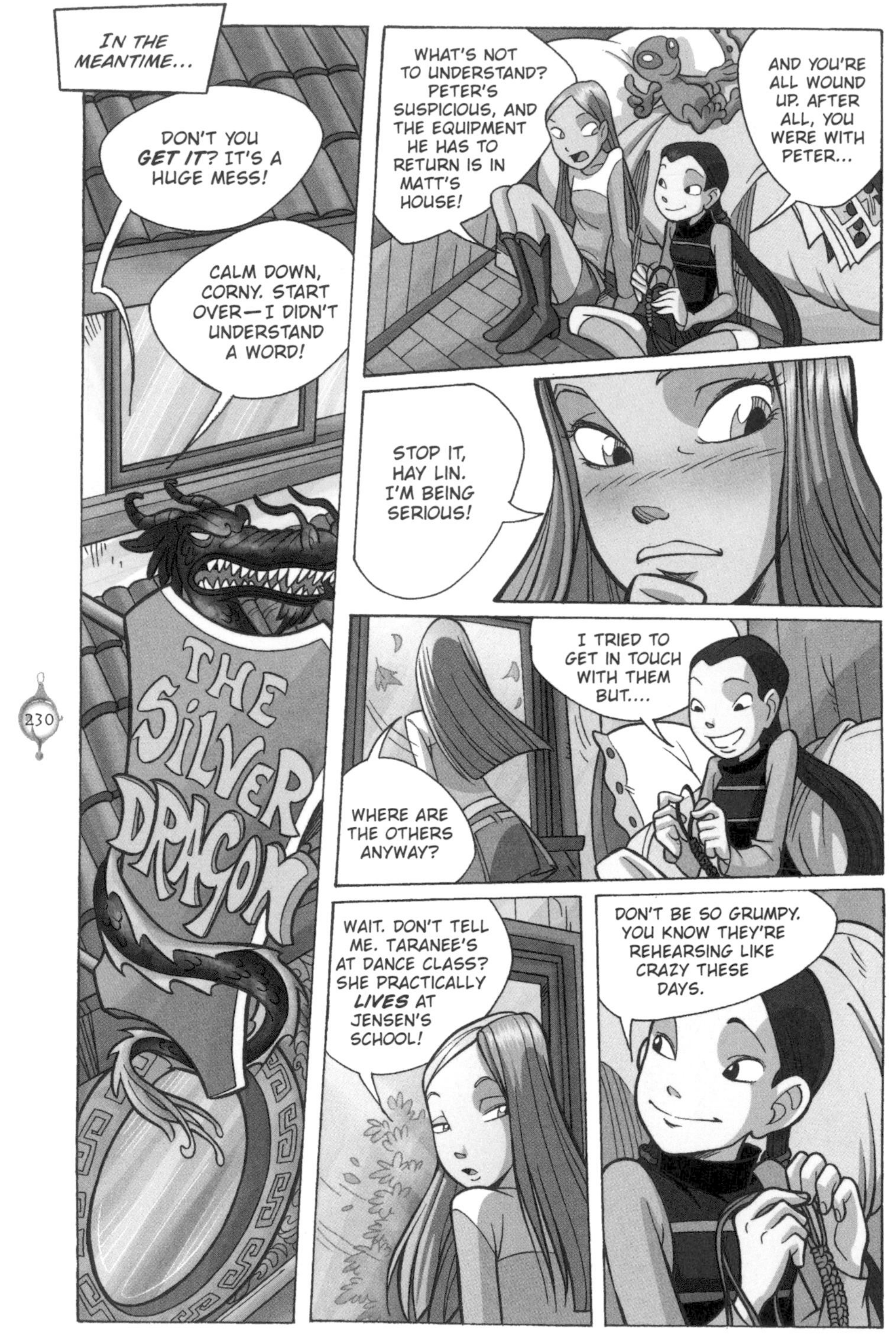
IN THE MEANTIME...
DON'T YOU GET IT? IT'S A HUGE MESS!
CALM DOWN, CORNY. START OVER—I DIDN'T UNDERSTAND A WORD!
THE SILVER DRAGON
WHAT'S NOT TO UNDERSTAND? PETER'S SUSPICIOUS, AND THE EQUIPMENT HE HAS TO RETURN IS IN MATT'S HOUSE!
AND YOU'RE ALL WOUND UP. AFTER ALL, YOU WERE WITH PETER...
STOP IT, HAY LIN. I'M BEING SERIOUS!
WHERE ARE THE OTHERS ANYWAY?
I TRIED TO GET IN TOUCH WITH THEM BUT....
WAIT. DON'T TELL ME. TARANEE'S AT DANCE CLASS? SHE PRACTICALLY LIVES AT JENSEN'S SCHOOL!
DON'T BE SO GRUMPY. YOU KNOW THEY'RE REHEARSING LIKE CRAZY THESE DAYS.

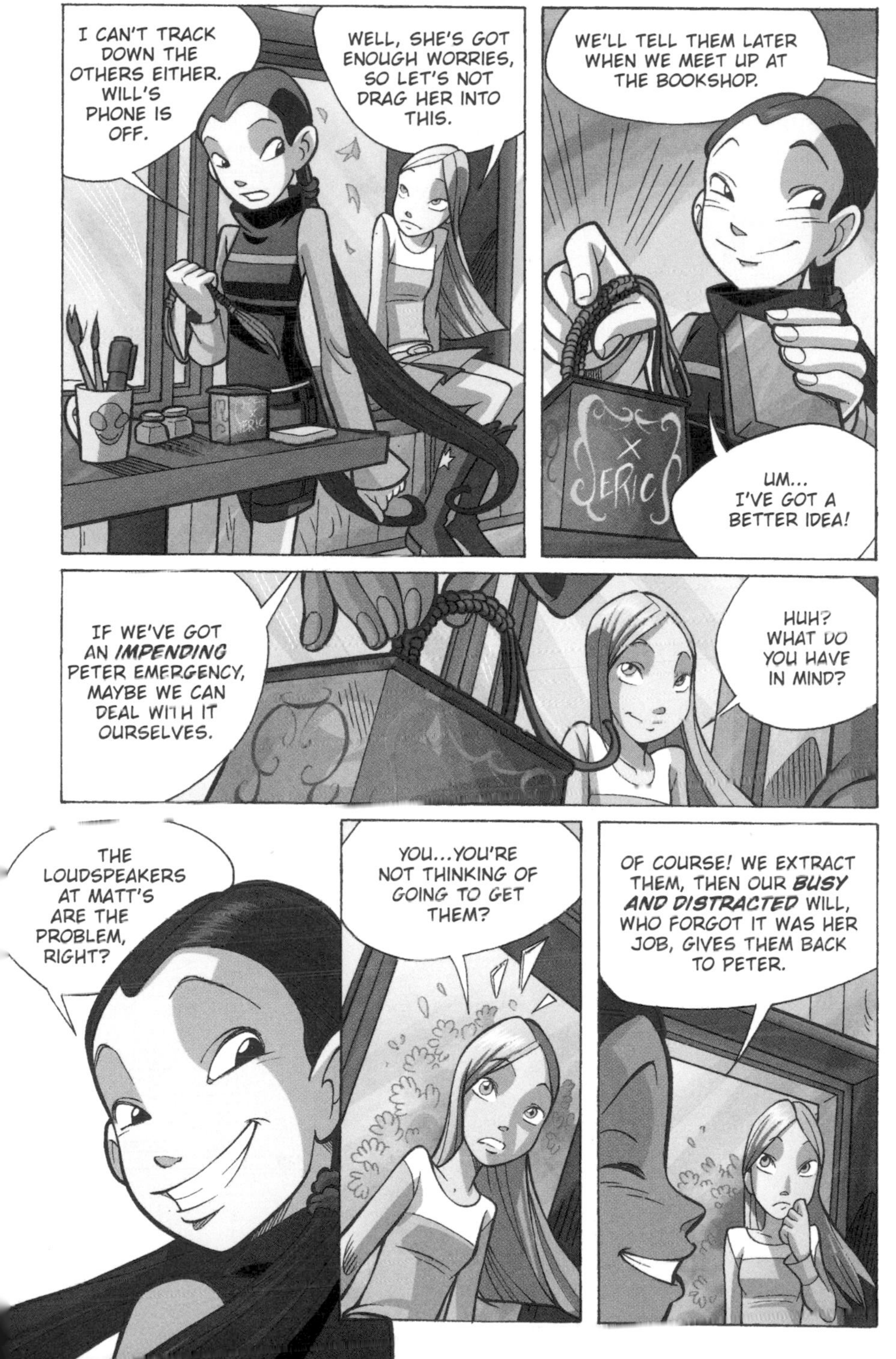

I CAN'T TRACK DOWN THE OTHERS EITHER. WILL'S PHONE IS OFF.
WELL, SHE'S GOT ENOUGH WORRIES, SO LET'S NOT DRAG HER INTO THIS.
WE'LL TELL THEM LATER WHEN WE MEET UP AT THE BOOKSHOP.
ERIC
UM... I'VE GOT A BETTER IDEA!
IF WE'VE GOT AN *IMPENDING* PETER EMERGENCY, MAYBE WE CAN DEAL WITH IT OURSELVES.
HUH? WHAT DO YOU HAVE IN MIND?
THE LOUDSPEAKERS AT MATT'S ARE THE PROBLEM, RIGHT?
YOU...YOU'RE NOT THINKING OF GOING TO GET THEM?
OF COURSE! WE EXTRACT THEM, THEN OUR *BUSY AND DISTRACTED* WILL, WHO FORGOT IT WAS HER JOB, GIVES THEM BACK TO PETER.

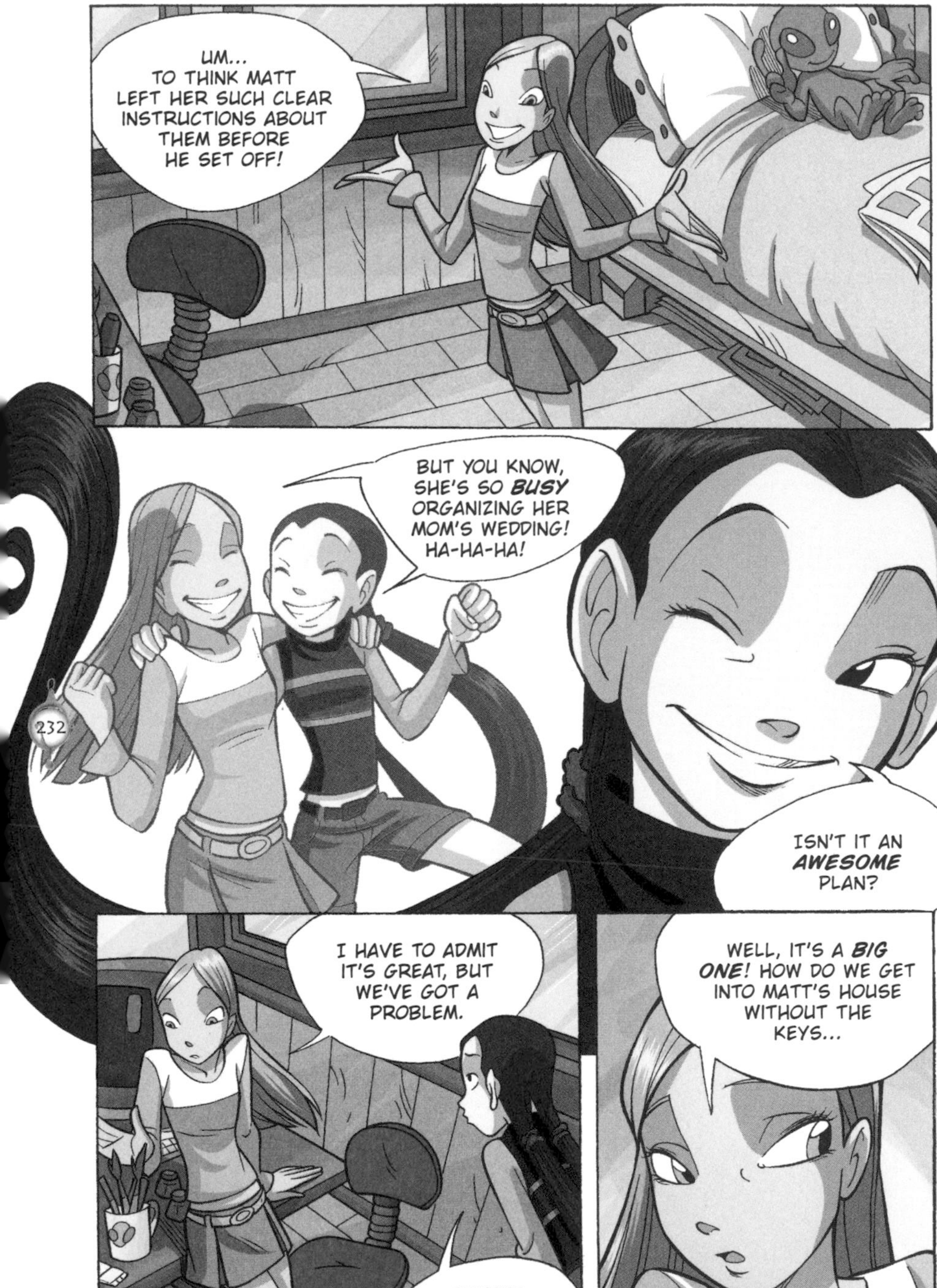
UM... TO THINK MATT LEFT HER SUCH CLEAR INSTRUCTIONS ABOUT THEM BEFORE HE SET OFF!
BUT YOU KNOW, SHE'S SO BUSY ORGANIZING HER MOM'S WEDDING! HA-HA-HA!
ISN'T IT AN AWESOME PLAN?
I HAVE TO ADMIT IT'S GREAT, BUT WE'VE GOT A PROBLEM.
ALWAYS SPLITTING HAIRS...
WELL, IT'S A BIG ONE! HOW DO WE GET INTO MATT'S HOUSE WITHOUT THE KEYS...

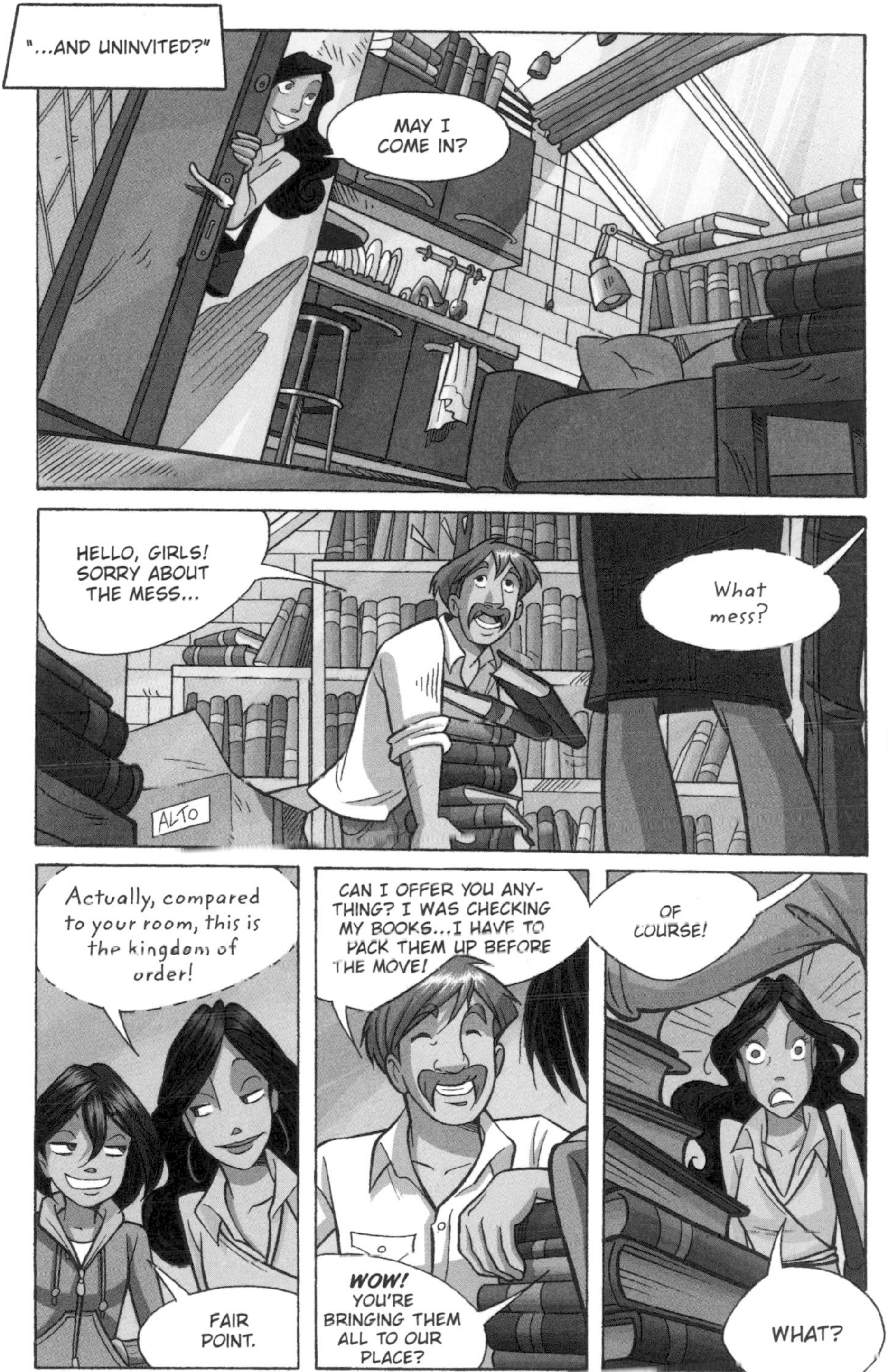
"...AND UNINVITED?"
MAY I COME IN?
HELLO, GIRLS! SORRY ABOUT THE MESS...
What mess?
ALTO
Actually, compared to your room, this is the kingdom of order!
FAIR POINT.
CAN I OFFER YOU ANY-THING? I WAS CHECKING MY BOOKS...I HAVE TO PACK THEM UP BEFORE THE MOVE!
WOW! YOU'RE BRINGING THEM ALL TO OUR PLACE?
OF COURSE!
WHAT?

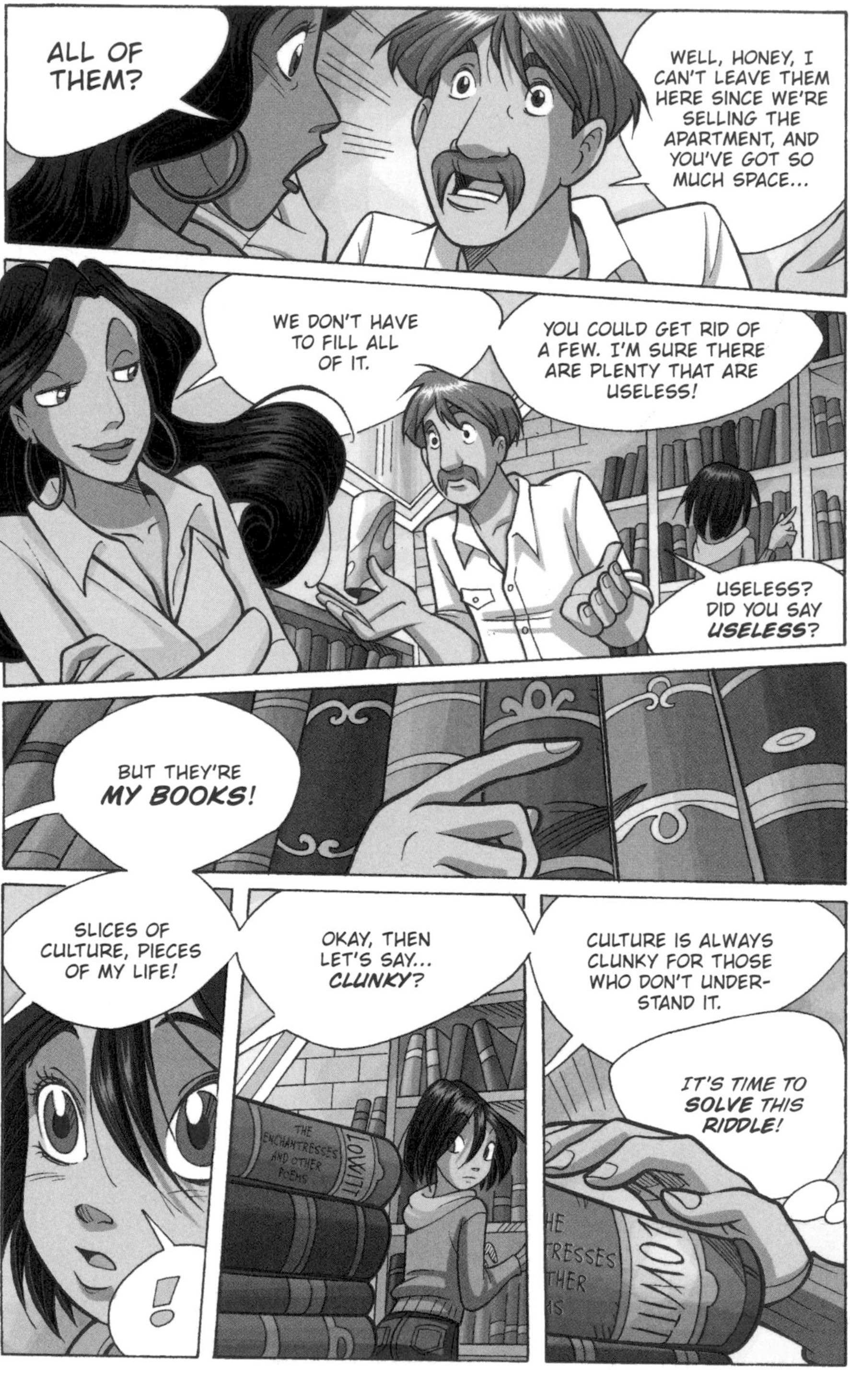
ALL OF THEM?
WELL, HONEY, I CAN'T LEAVE THEM HERE SINCE WE'RE SELLING THE APARTMENT, AND YOU'VE GOT SO MUCH SPACE...
WE DON'T HAVE TO FILL ALL OF IT.
YOU COULD GET RID OF A FEW. I'M SURE THERE ARE PLENTY THAT ARE USELESS!
USELESS? DID YOU SAY ***USELESS***?
BUT THEY'RE ***MY BOOKS***!
SLICES OF CULTURE, PIECES OF MY LIFE!
OKAY, THEN LET'S SAY... ***CLUNKY***?
CULTURE IS ALWAYS CLUNKY FOR THOSE WHO DON'T UNDER-STAND IT.
!
THE ENCHANTRESSES AND OTHER POEMS
*IT'S TIME TO **SOLVE** THIS **RIDDLE**!*

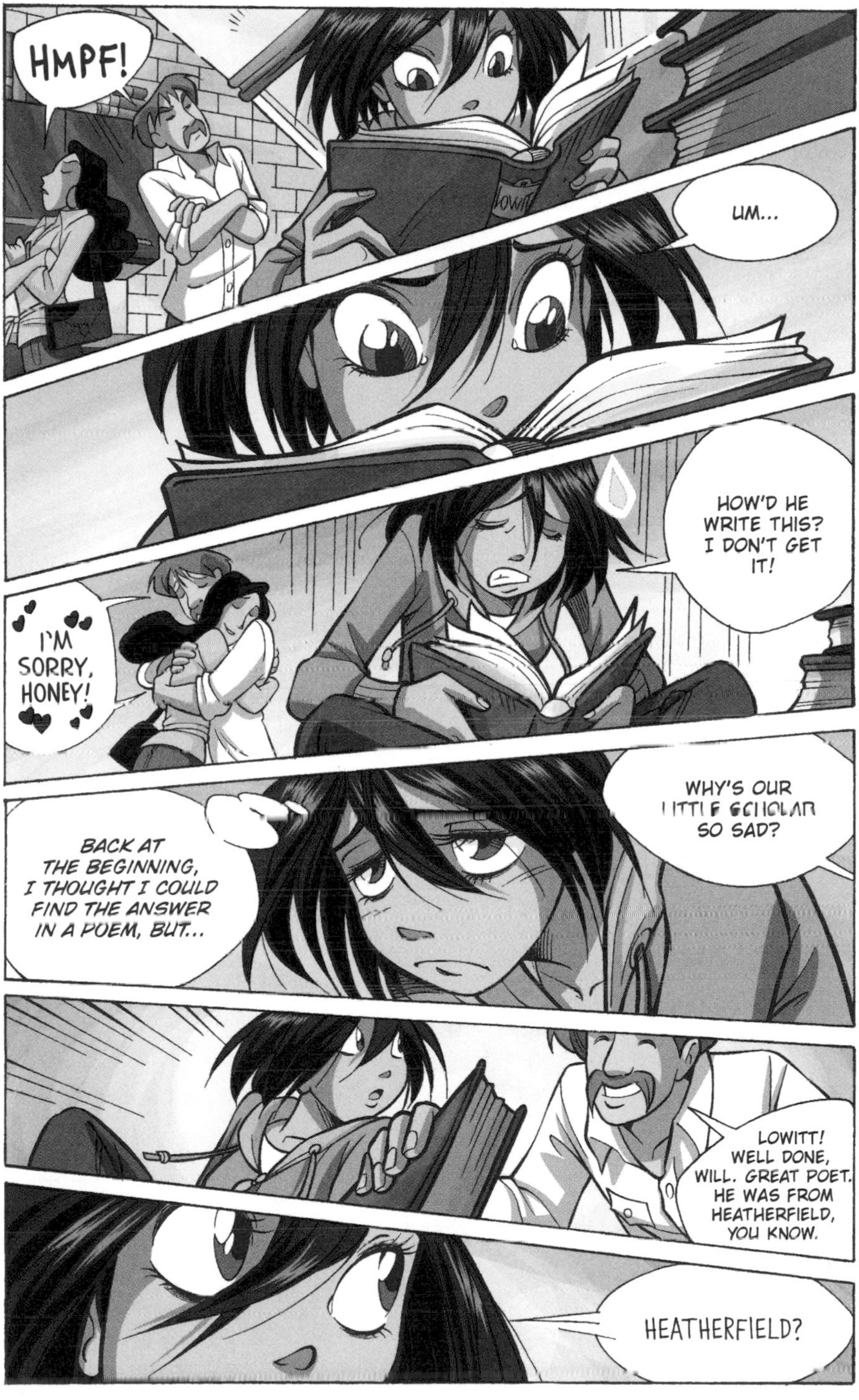
HMPF!
UM...
HOW'D HE WRITE THIS? I DON'T GET IT!
I'M SORRY, HONEY!
WHY'S OUR LITTLE SCHOLAR SO SAD?
BACK AT THE BEGINNING, I THOUGHT I COULD FIND THE ANSWER IN A POEM, BUT...
LOWITT! WELL DONE, WILL. GREAT POET. HE WAS FROM HEATHERFIELD, YOU KNOW.
HEATHERFIELD?

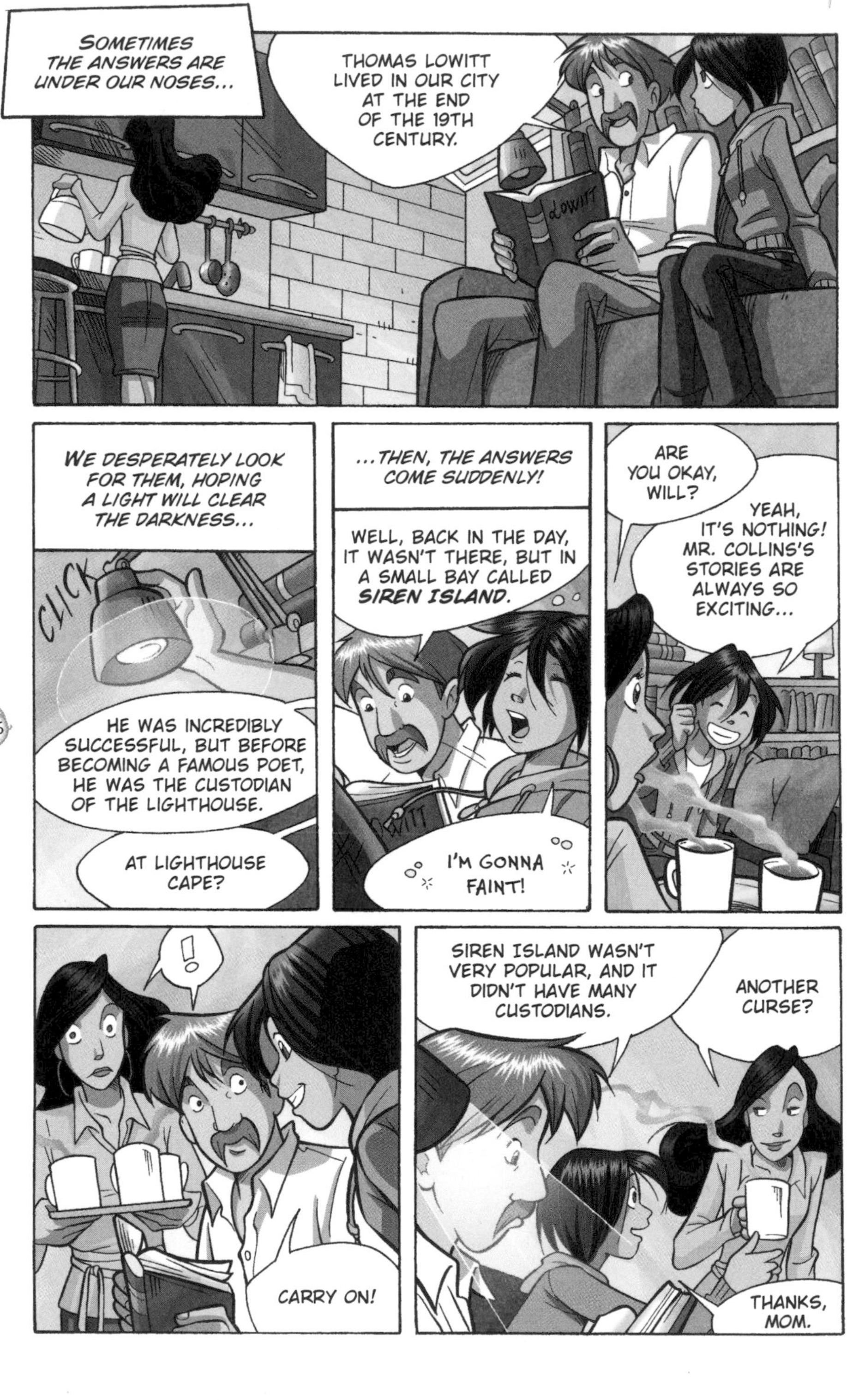
SOMETIMES THE ANSWERS ARE UNDER OUR NOSES...
THOMAS LOWITT LIVED IN OUR CITY AT THE END OF THE 19TH CENTURY.
LOWITT
WE DESPERATELY LOOK FOR THEM, HOPING A LIGHT WILL CLEAR THE DARKNESS...
CLICK
HE WAS INCREDIBLY SUCCESSFUL, BUT BEFORE BECOMING A FAMOUS POET, HE WAS THE CUSTODIAN OF THE LIGHTHOUSE.
AT LIGHTHOUSE CAPE?
...THEN, THE ANSWERS COME SUDDENLY!
WELL, BACK IN THE DAY, IT WASN'T THERE, BUT IN A SMALL BAY CALLED SIREN ISLAND.
I'M GONNA FAINT!
ARE YOU OKAY, WILL?
YEAH, IT'S NOTHING! MR. COLLINS'S STORIES ARE ALWAYS SO EXCITING...
!
CARRY ON!
SIREN ISLAND WASN'T VERY POPULAR, AND IT DIDN'T HAVE MANY CUSTODIANS.
ANOTHER CURSE?
THANKS, MOM.

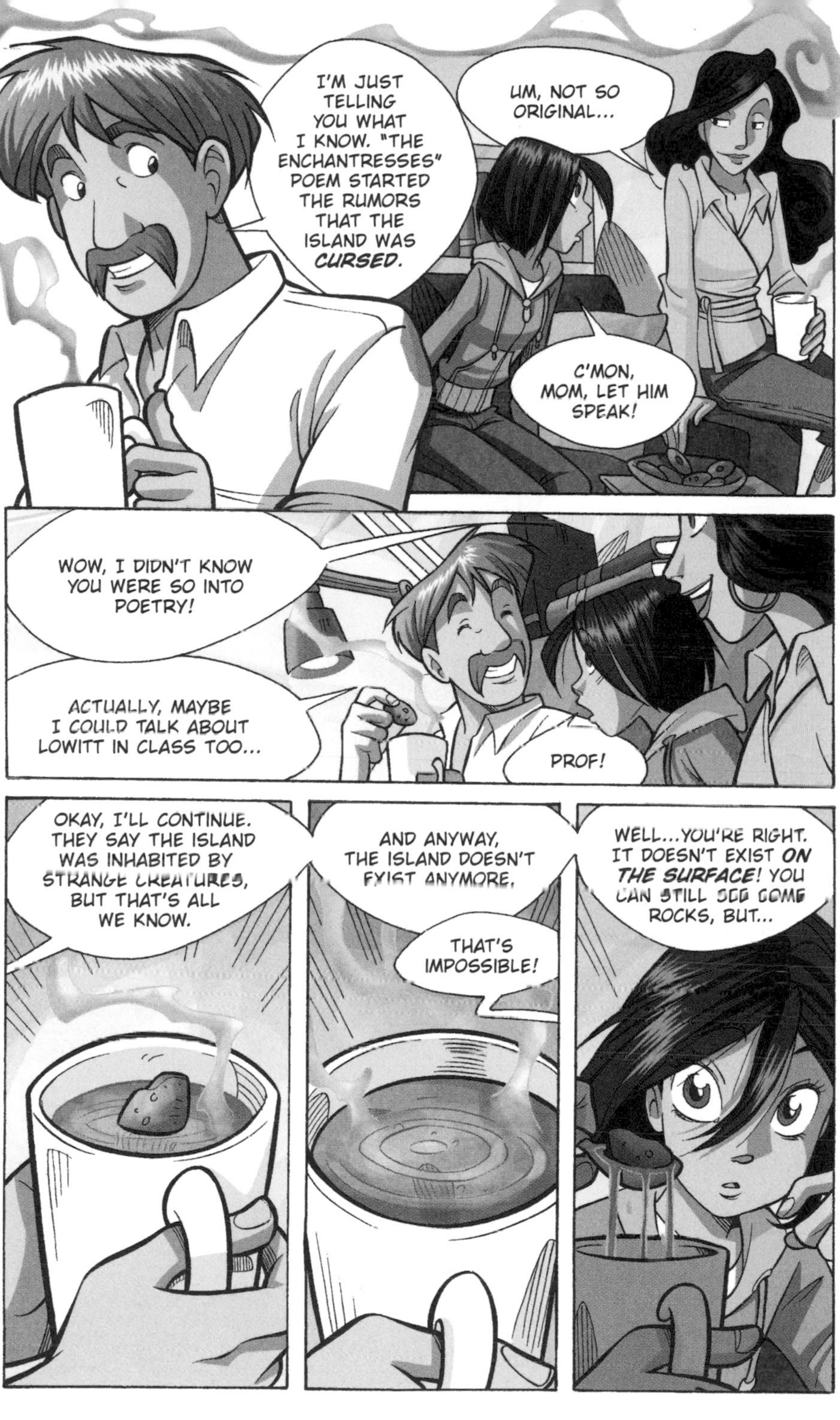

I'M JUST TELLING YOU WHAT I KNOW. "THE ENCHANTRESSES" POEM STARTED THE RUMORS THAT THE ISLAND WAS *CURSED*.
UM, NOT SO ORIGINAL...
C'MON, MOM, LET HIM SPEAK!
WOW, I DIDN'T KNOW YOU WERE SO INTO POETRY!
ACTUALLY, MAYBE I COULD TALK ABOUT LOWITT IN CLASS TOO...
PROF!
OKAY, I'LL CONTINUE. THEY SAY THE ISLAND WAS INHABITED BY STRANGE CREATURES, BUT THAT'S ALL WE KNOW.
AND ANYWAY, THE ISLAND DOESN'T EXIST ANYMORE.
THAT'S IMPOSSIBLE!
WELL...YOU'RE RIGHT. IT DOESN'T EXIST ***ON THE SURFACE!*** YOU CAN STILL SEE SOME ROCKS, BUT...

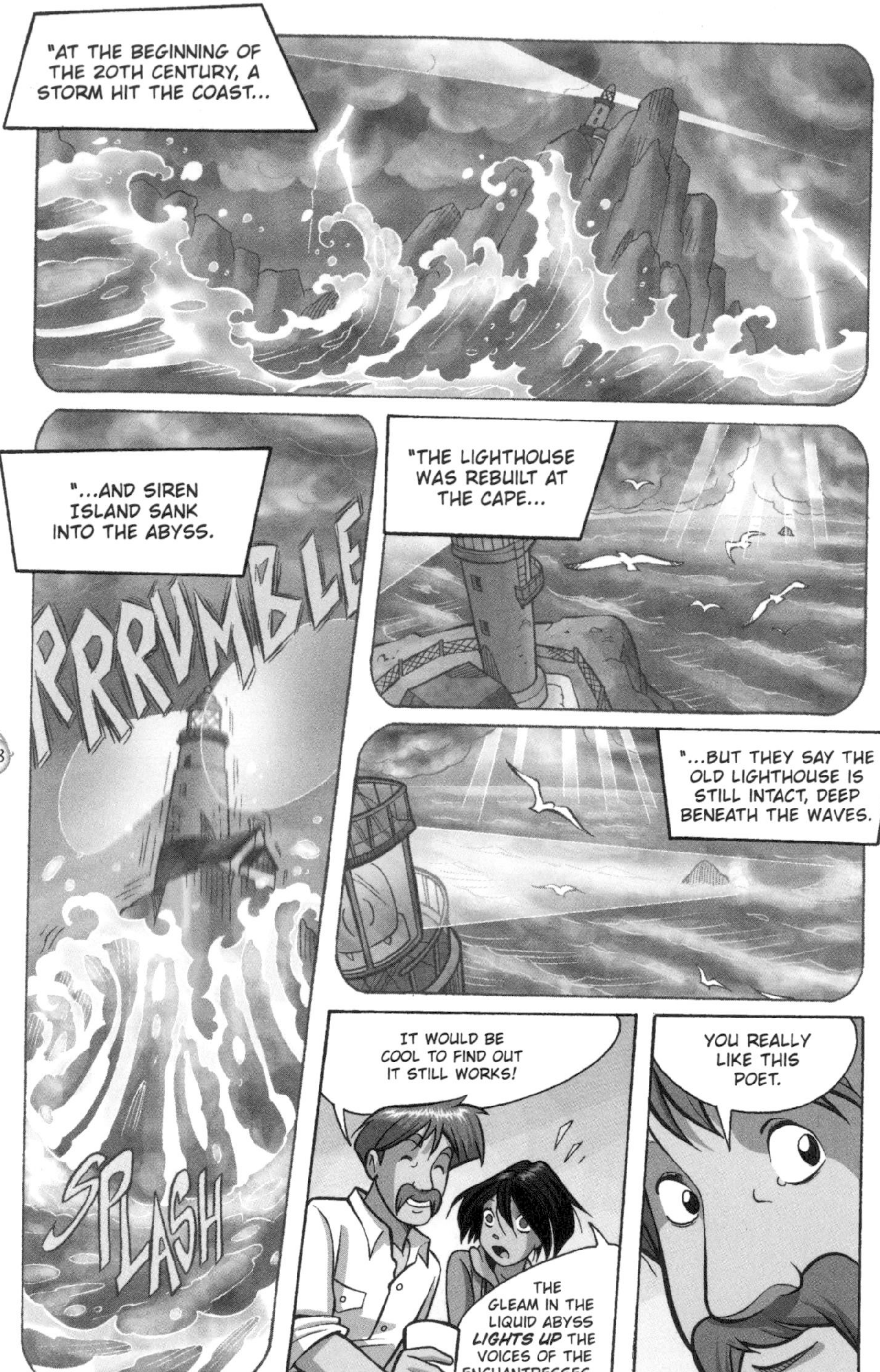
"AT THE BEGINNING OF THE 20TH CENTURY, A STORM HIT THE COAST...
"...AND SIREN ISLAND SANK INTO THE ABYSS.
PRRUMBLE
SPLASH
"THE LIGHTHOUSE WAS REBUILT AT THE CAPE...
"...BUT THEY SAY THE OLD LIGHTHOUSE IS STILL INTACT, DEEP BENEATH THE WAVES.
IT WOULD BE COOL TO FIND OUT IT STILL WORKS!
THE GLEAM IN THE LIQUID ABYSS ***LIGHTS UP*** THE VOICES OF THE ENCHANTRESSES...
YOU REALLY LIKE THIS POET.

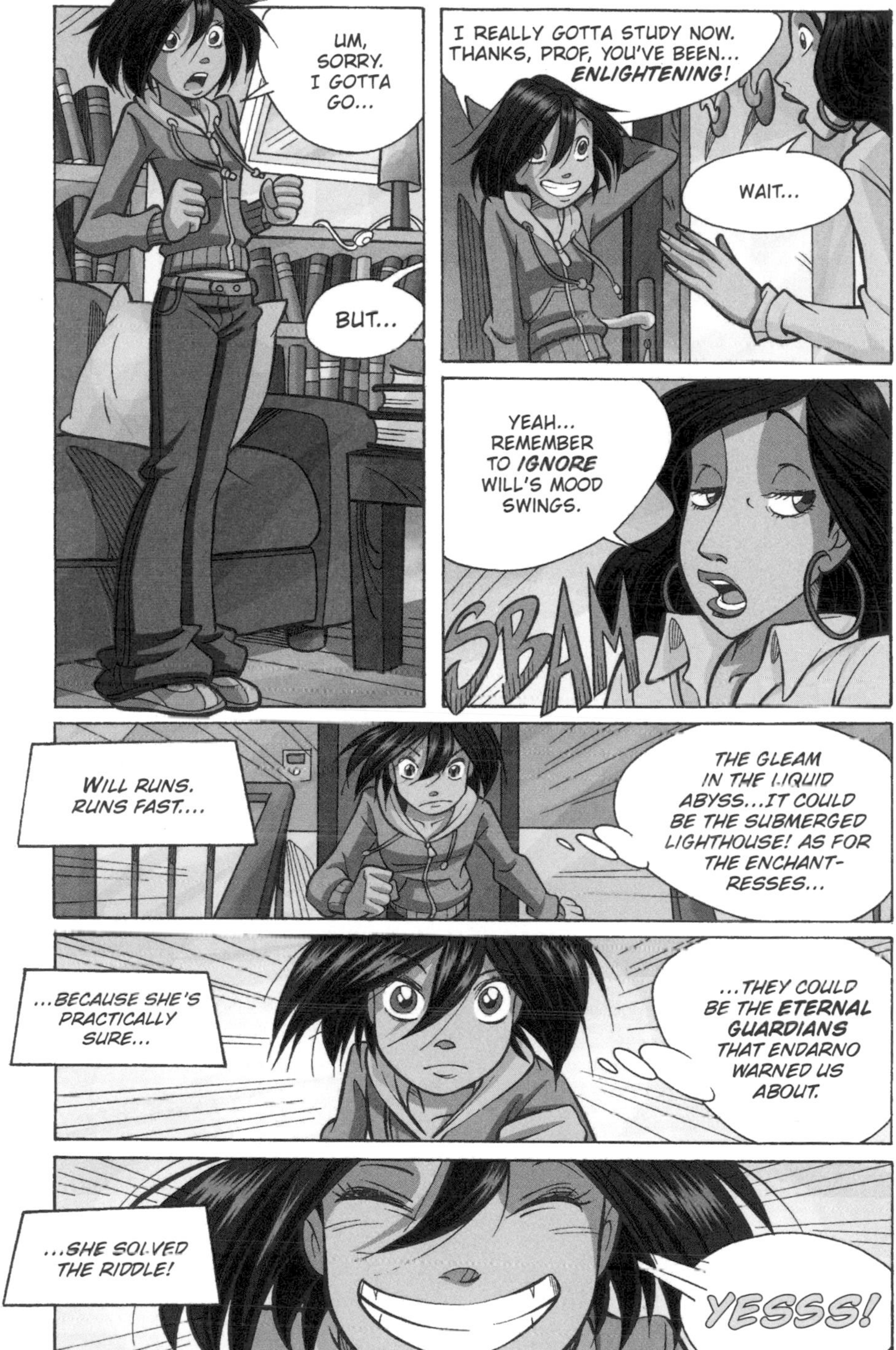
UM, SORRY. I GOTTA GO...
BUT...
I REALLY GOTTA STUDY NOW. THANKS, PROF, YOU'VE BEEN... ENLIGHTENING!
WAIT...
YEAH... REMEMBER TO IGNORE WILL'S MOOD SWINGS.
SBAM
WILL RUNS. RUNS FAST....
THE GLEAM IN THE LIQUID ABYSS...IT COULD BE THE SUBMERGED LIGHTHOUSE! AS FOR THE ENCHANT-RESSES...
...BECAUSE SHE'S PRACTICALLY SURE...
...THEY COULD BE THE ETERNAL GUARDIANS THAT ENDARNO WARNED US ABOUT.
...SHE SOLVED THE RIDDLE!
YESSS!

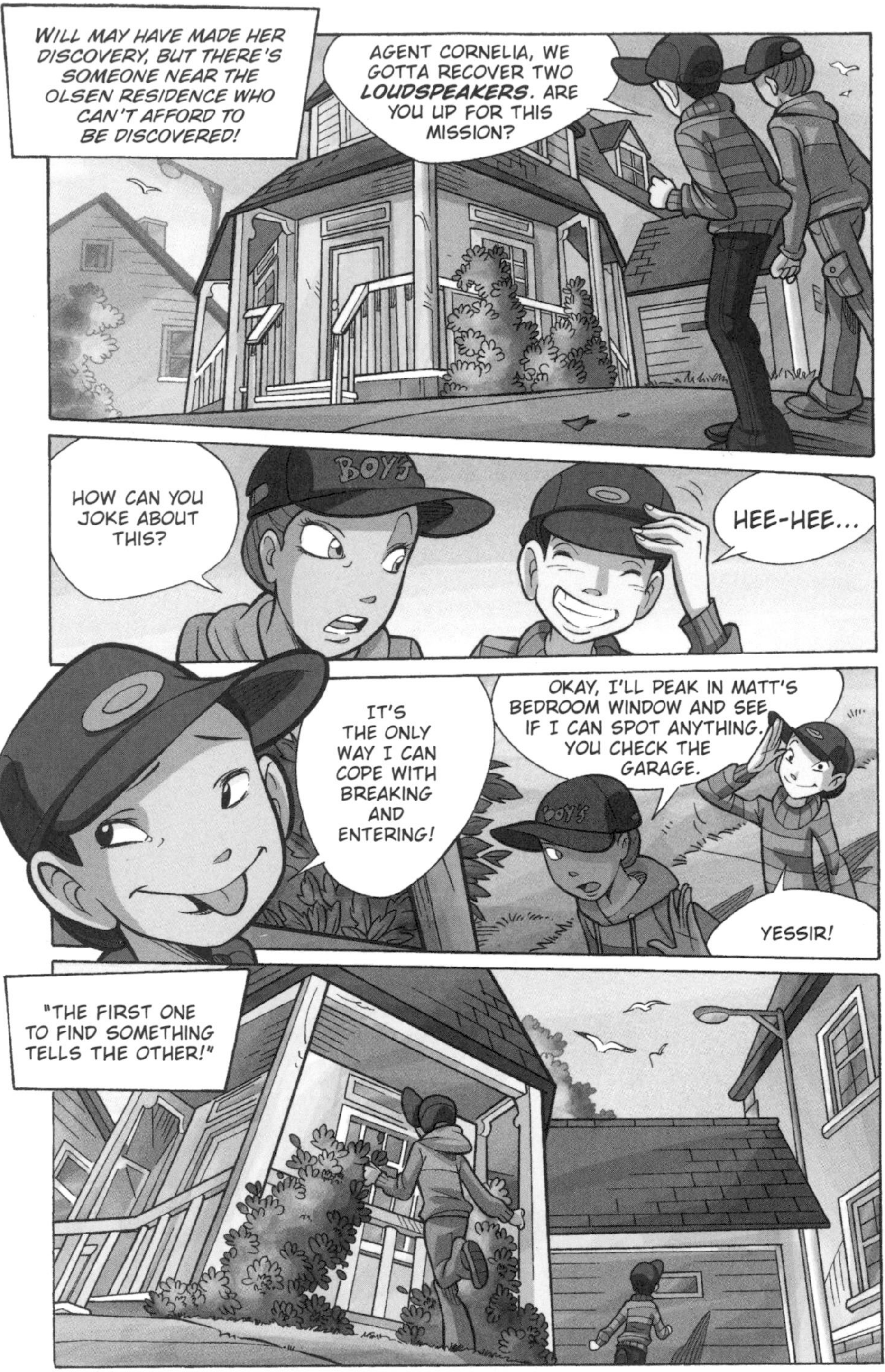
WILL MAY HAVE MADE HER DISCOVERY, BUT THERE'S SOMEONE NEAR THE OLSEN RESIDENCE WHO CAN'T AFFORD TO BE DISCOVERED!
AGENT CORNELIA, WE GOTTA RECOVER TWO LOUDSPEAKERS. ARE YOU UP FOR THIS MISSION?
BOY'S
HOW CAN YOU JOKE ABOUT THIS?
HEE-HEE...
IT'S THE ONLY WAY I CAN COPE WITH BREAKING AND ENTERING!
OKAY, I'LL PEAK IN MATT'S BEDROOM WINDOW AND SEE IF I CAN SPOT ANYTHING. YOU CHECK THE GARAGE.
YESSIR!
"THE FIRST ONE TO FIND SOMETHING TELLS THE OTHER!"

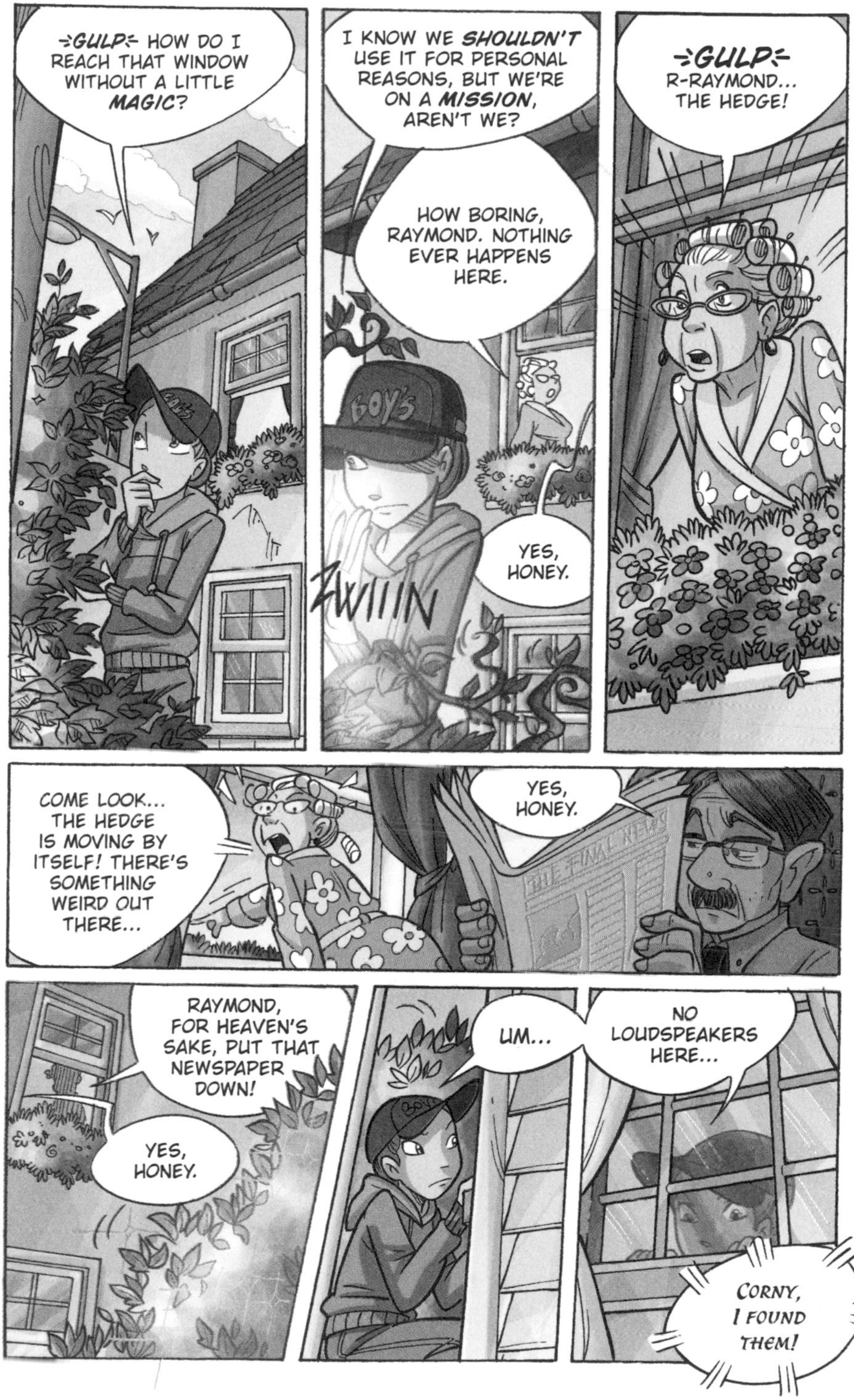
-GULP- HOW DO I REACH THAT WINDOW WITHOUT A LITTLE *MAGIC*?
I KNOW WE *SHOULDN'T* USE IT FOR PERSONAL REASONS, BUT WE'RE ON A *MISSION*, AREN'T WE?
HOW BORING, RAYMOND. NOTHING EVER HAPPENS HERE.
YES, HONEY.
ZWIIIN
-GULP- R-RAYMOND... THE HEDGE!
COME LOOK... THE HEDGE IS MOVING BY ITSELF! THERE'S SOMETHING WEIRD OUT THERE...
YES, HONEY.
THE FINAL NEWS
RAYMOND, FOR HEAVEN'S SAKE, PUT THAT NEWSPAPER DOWN!
YES, HONEY.
UM...
NO LOUDSPEAKERS HERE...
CORNY, I FOUND THEM!

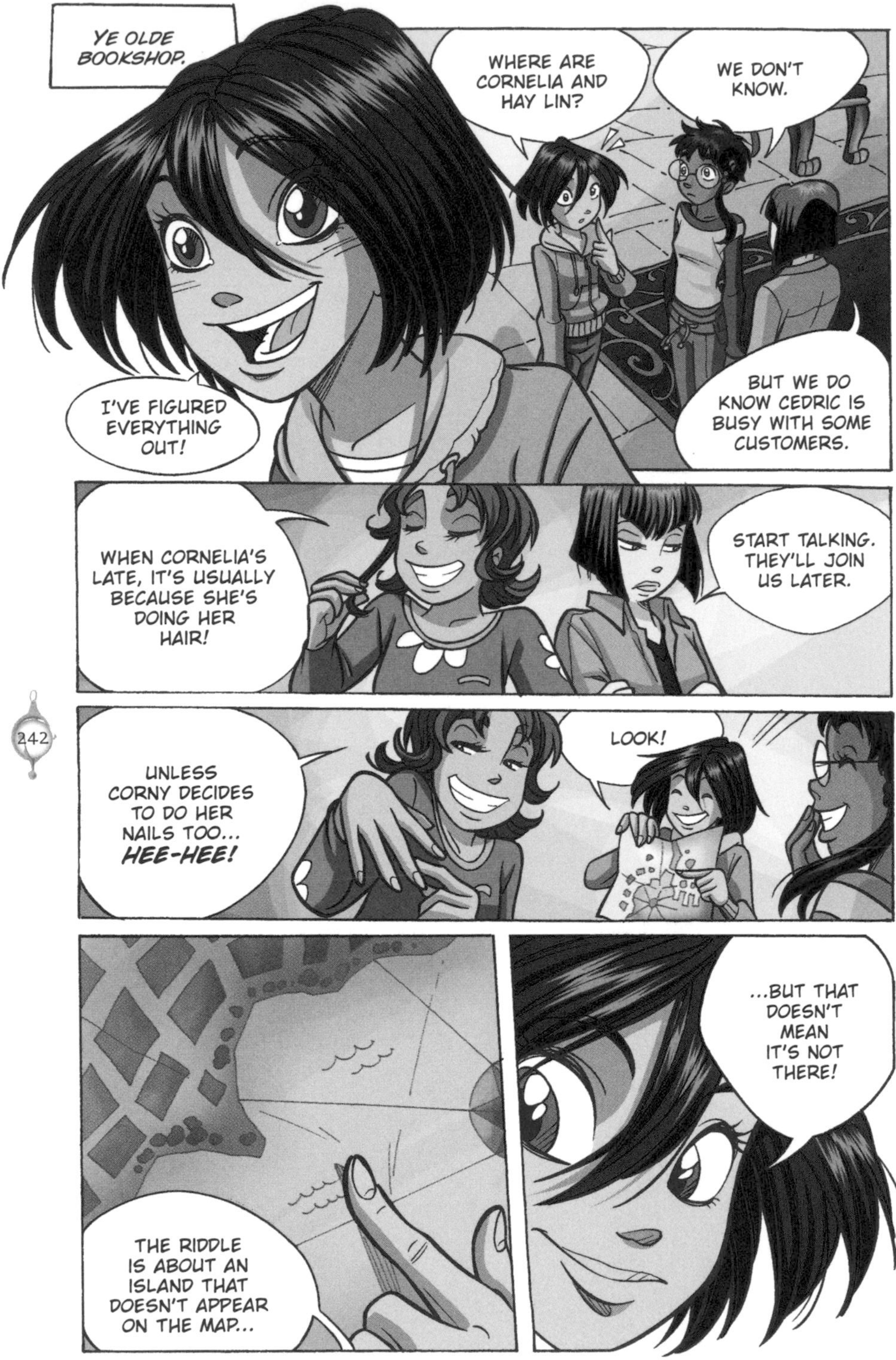
YE OLDE BOOKSHOP.
I'VE FIGURED EVERYTHING OUT!
WHERE ARE CORNELIA AND HAY LIN?
WE DON'T KNOW.
BUT WE DO KNOW CEDRIC IS BUSY WITH SOME CUSTOMERS.
WHEN CORNELIA'S LATE, IT'S USUALLY BECAUSE SHE'S DOING HER HAIR!
START TALKING. THEY'LL JOIN US LATER.
UNLESS CORNY DECIDES TO DO HER NAILS TOO... ***HEE-HEE!***
LOOK!
THE RIDDLE IS ABOUT AN ISLAND THAT DOESN'T APPEAR ON THE MAP...
...BUT THAT DOESN'T MEAN IT'S NOT THERE!

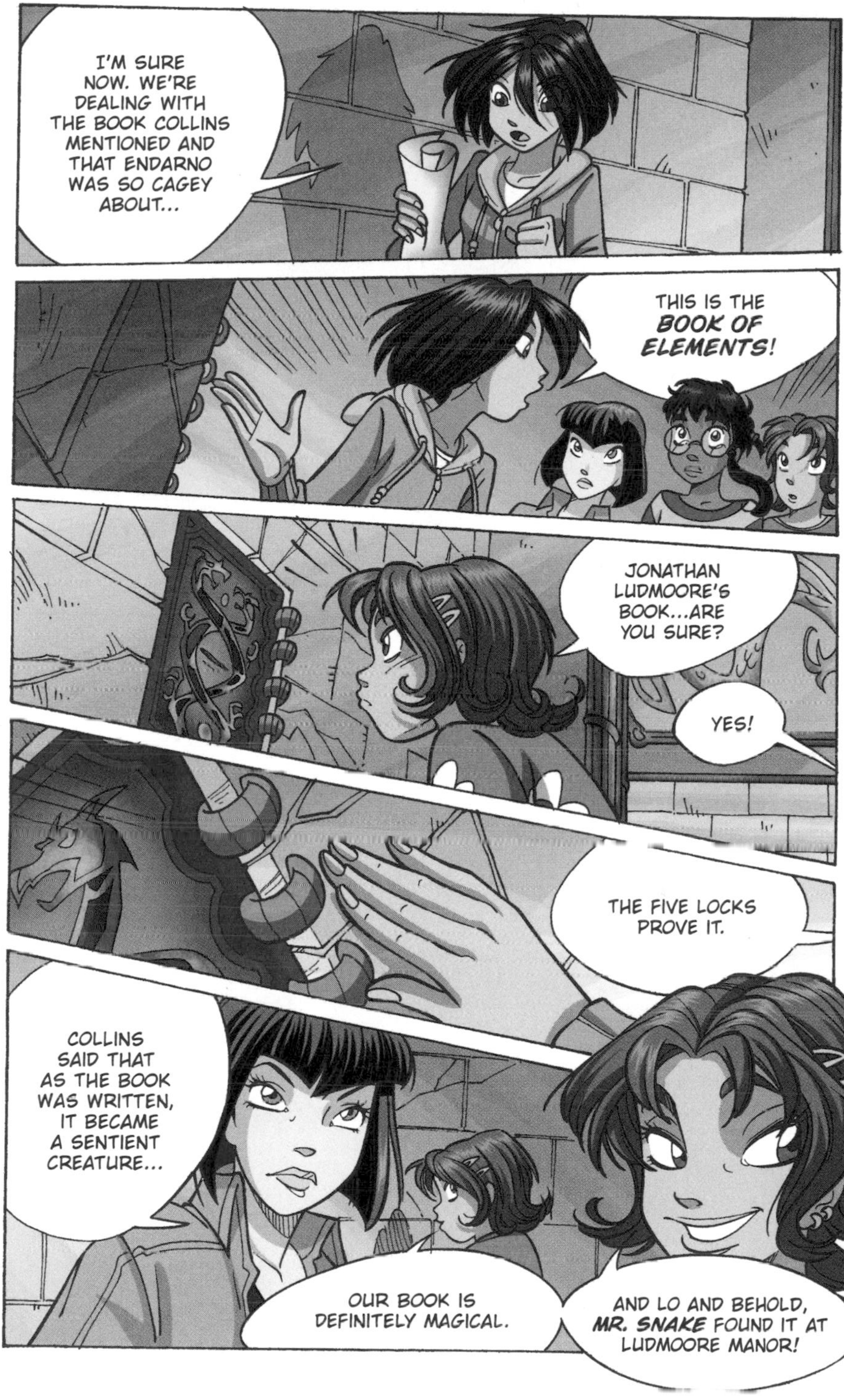
I'M SURE NOW. WE'RE DEALING WITH THE BOOK COLLINS MENTIONED AND THAT ENDARNO WAS SO CAGEY ABOUT...
THIS IS THE **BOOK OF ELEMENTS**!
JONATHAN LUDMOORE'S BOOK...ARE YOU SURE?
YES!
THE FIVE LOCKS PROVE IT.
COLLINS SAID THAT AS THE BOOK WAS WRITTEN, IT BECAME A SENTIENT CREATURE...
OUR BOOK IS DEFINITELY MAGICAL.
AND LO AND BEHOLD, **MR. SNAKE** FOUND IT AT LUDMOORE MANOR!

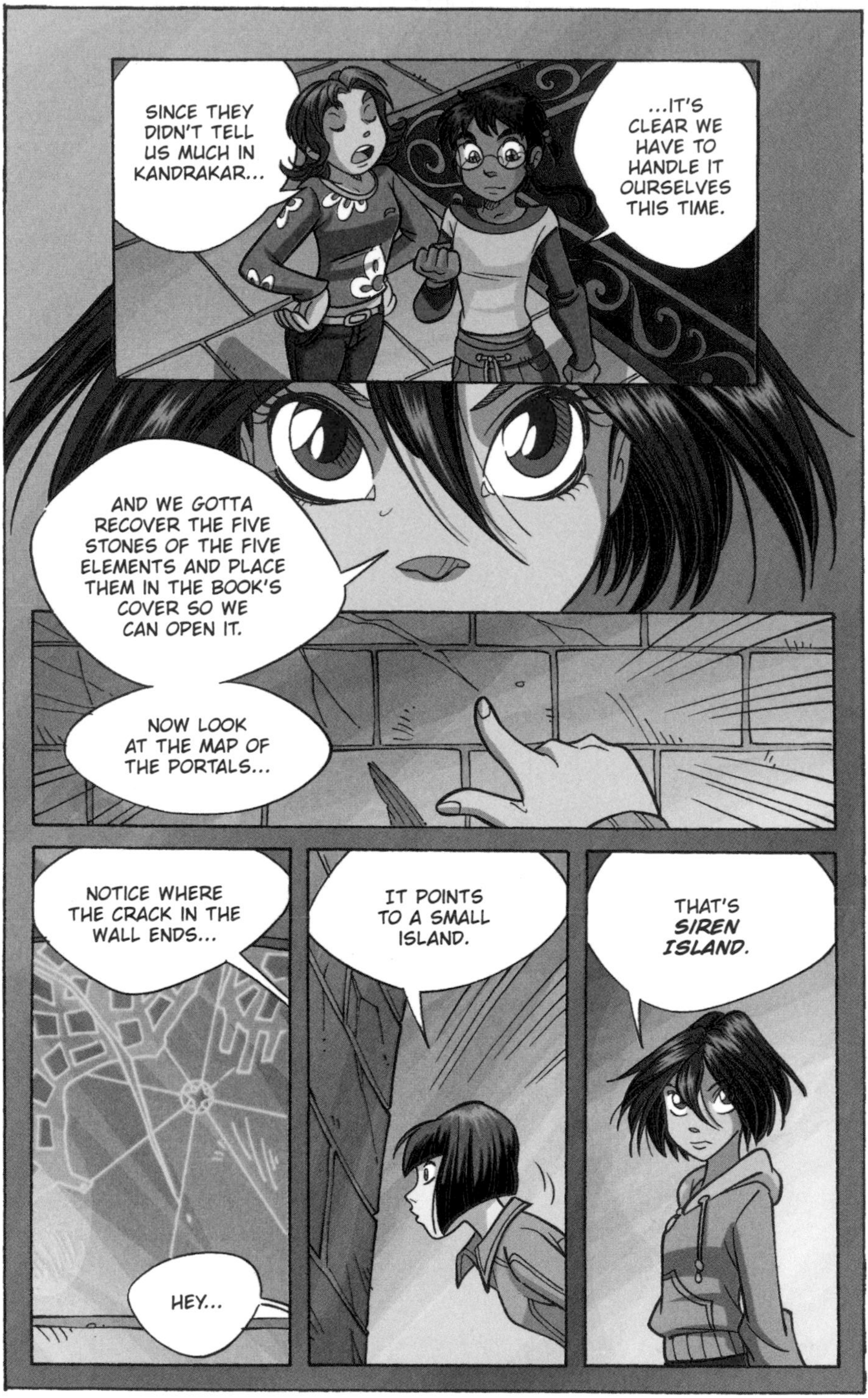

SINCE THEY DIDN'T TELL US MUCH IN KANDRAKAR...
...IT'S CLEAR WE HAVE TO HANDLE IT OURSELVES THIS TIME.
AND WE GOTTA RECOVER THE FIVE STONES OF THE FIVE ELEMENTS AND PLACE THEM IN THE BOOK'S COVER SO WE CAN OPEN IT.
NOW LOOK AT THE MAP OF THE PORTALS...
NOTICE WHERE THE CRACK IN THE WALL ENDS...
HEY...
IT POINTS TO A SMALL ISLAND.
THAT'S *SIREN ISLAND*.

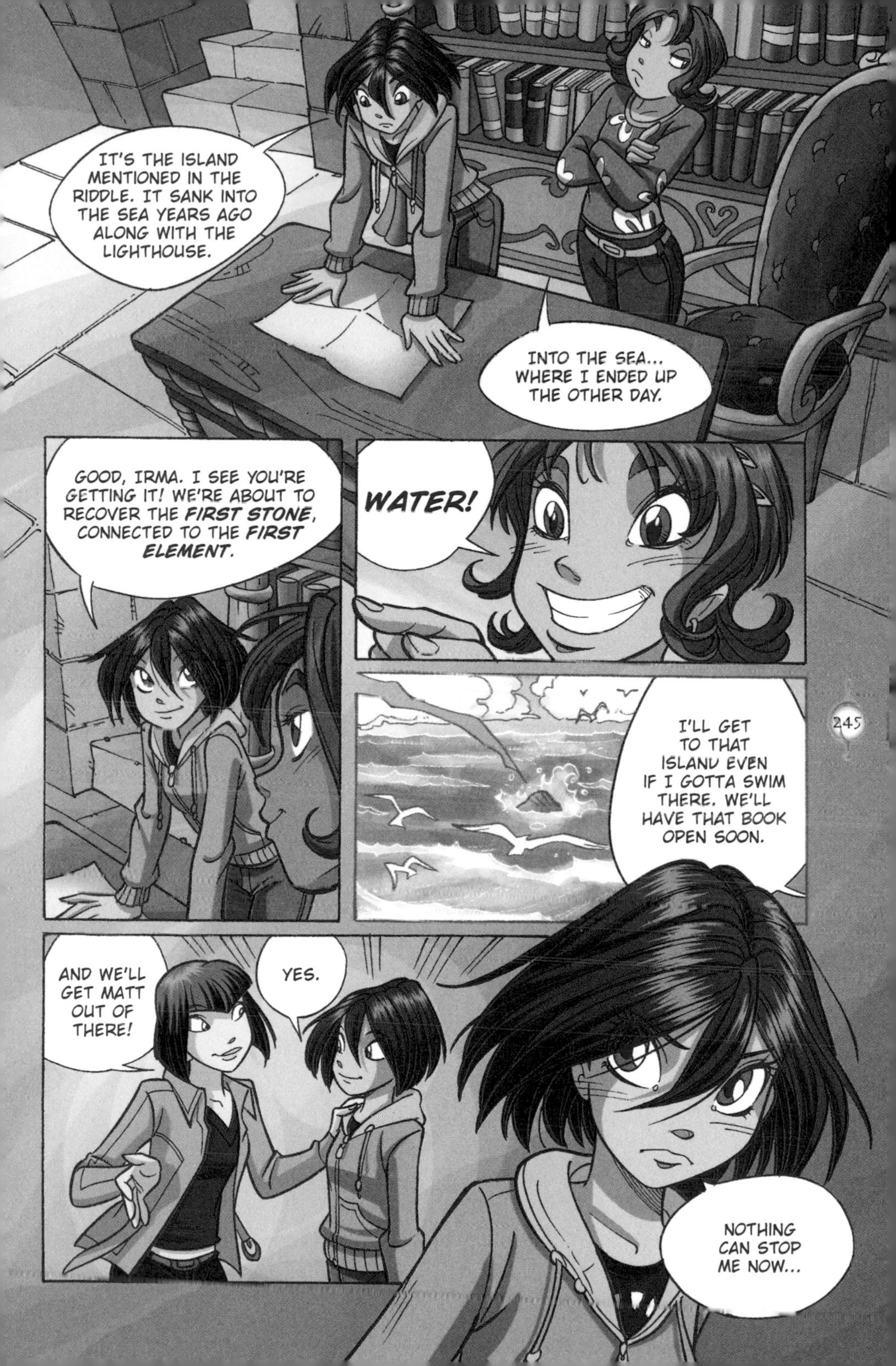
IT'S THE ISLAND MENTIONED IN THE RIDDLE. IT SANK INTO THE SEA YEARS AGO ALONG WITH THE LIGHTHOUSE.
INTO THE SEA... WHERE I ENDED UP THE OTHER DAY.
GOOD, IRMA. I SEE YOU'RE GETTING IT! WE'RE ABOUT TO RECOVER THE FIRST STONE, CONNECTED TO THE FIRST ELEMENT.
WATER!
I'LL GET TO THAT ISLAND EVEN IF I GOTTA SWIM THERE. WE'LL HAVE THAT BOOK OPEN SOON.
AND WE'LL GET MATT OUT OF THERE!
YES.
NOTHING CAN STOP ME NOW...

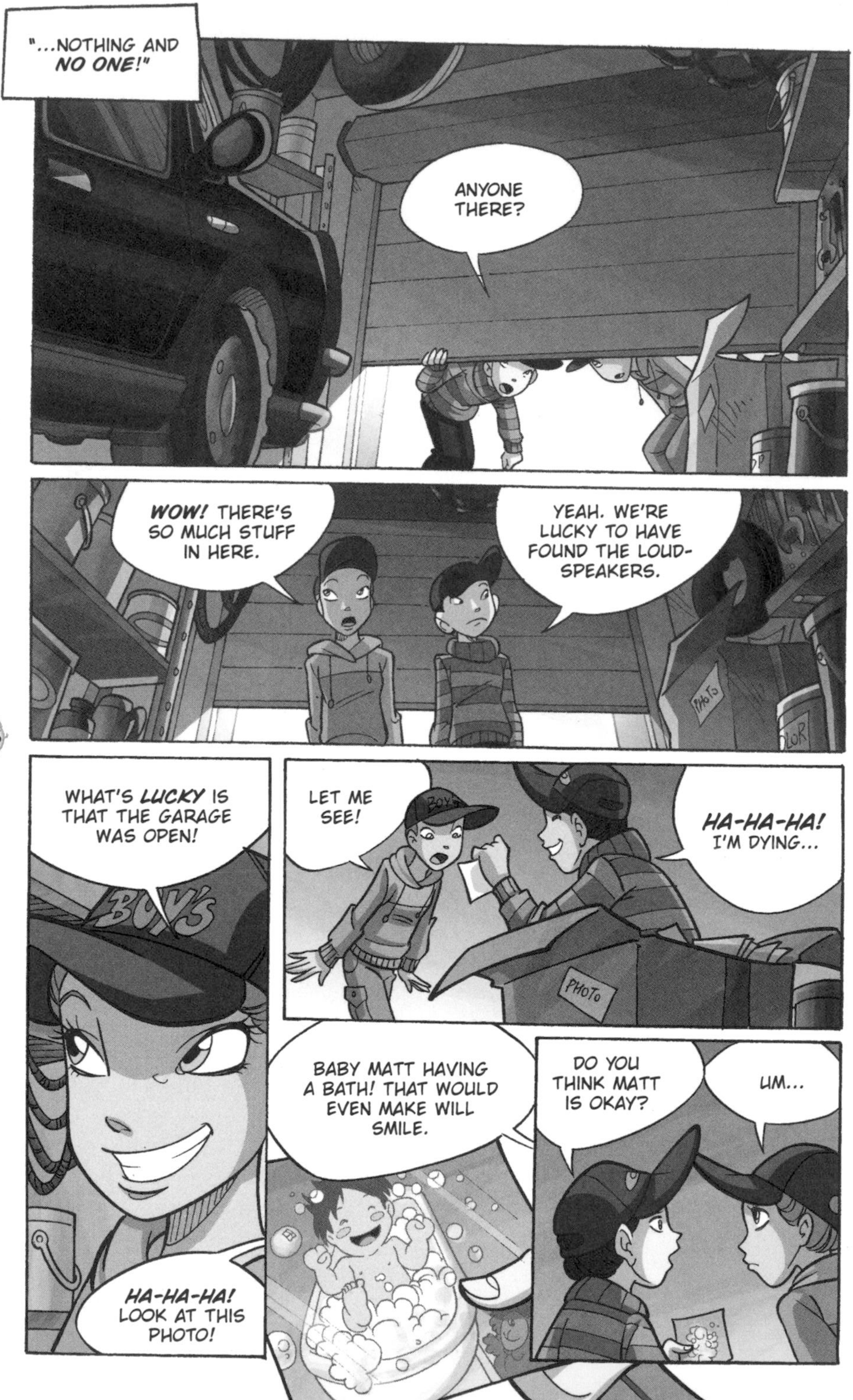
"...NOTHING AND **NO ONE!**"
ANYONE THERE?
WOW! THERE'S SO MUCH STUFF IN HERE.
YEAH. WE'RE LUCKY TO HAVE FOUND THE LOUD-SPEAKERS.
PHOTO
WHAT'S **LUCKY** IS THAT THE GARAGE WAS OPEN!
BOY'S
LET ME SEE!
HA-HA-HA! I'M DYING...
PHOTO
BABY MATT HAVING A BATH! THAT WOULD EVEN MAKE WILL SMILE.
HA-HA-HA! LOOK AT THIS PHOTO!
DO YOU THINK MATT IS OKAY?
UM...

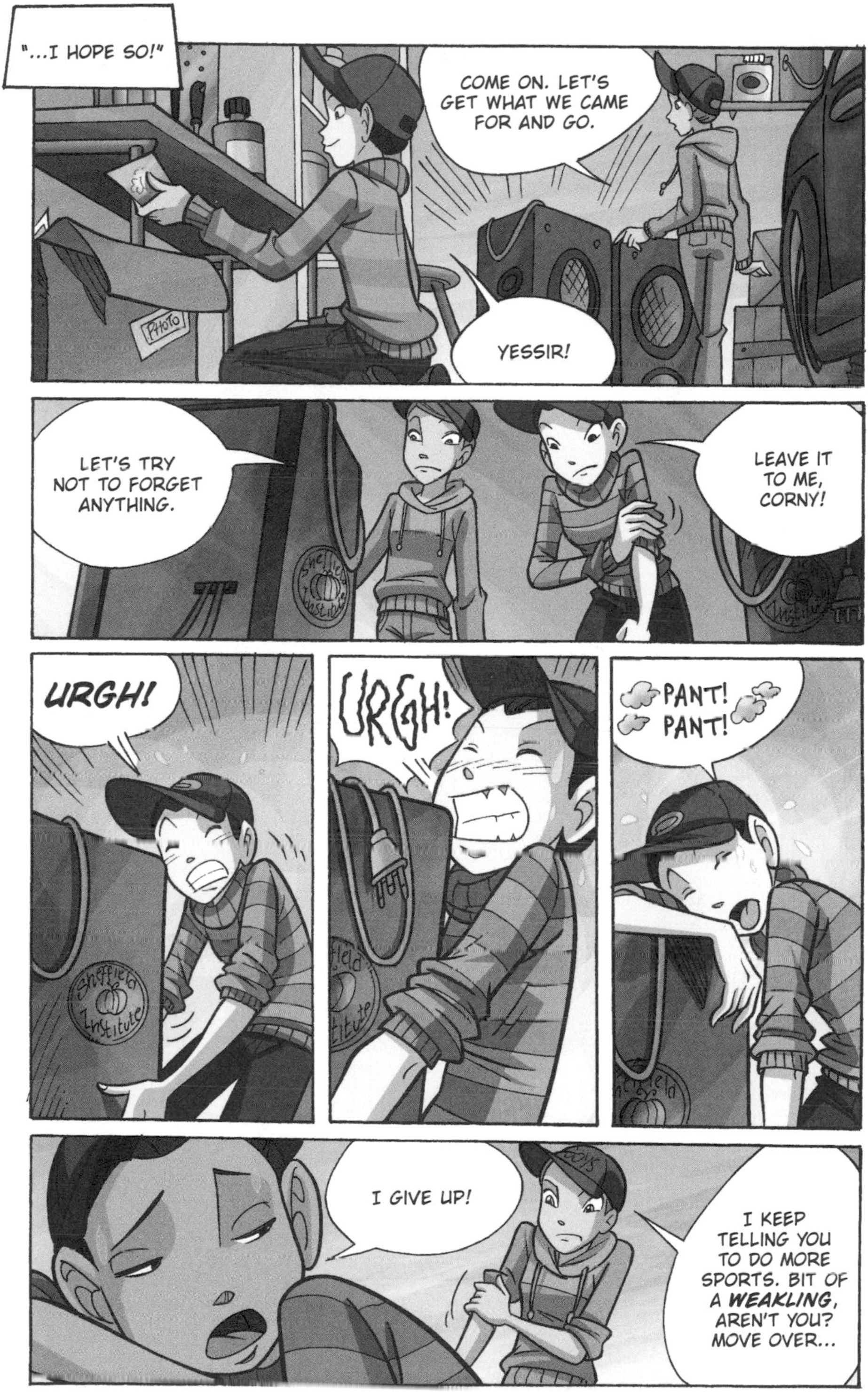
"...I HOPE SO!"
COME ON. LET'S GET WHAT WE CAME FOR AND GO.
YESSIR!
PHOTO
LET'S TRY NOT TO FORGET ANYTHING.
LEAVE IT TO ME, CORNY!
URGH!
URGH!
PANT! PANT!
I GIVE UP!
I KEEP TELLING YOU TO DO MORE SPORTS. BIT OF A WEAKLING, AREN'T YOU? MOVE OVER...

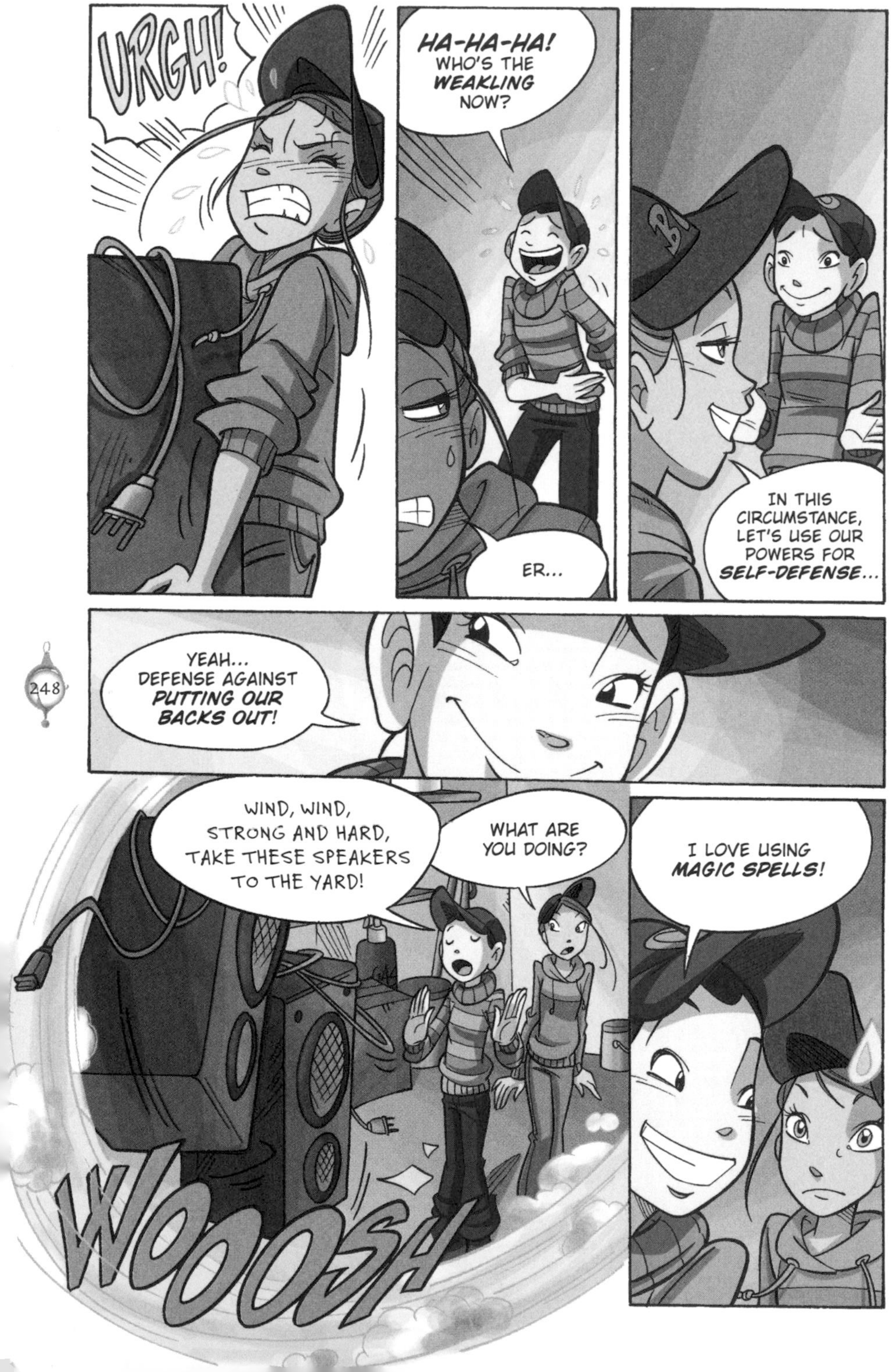
URGH!
HA-HA-HA! WHO'S THE WEAKLING NOW?
ER...
IN THIS CIRCUMSTANCE, LET'S USE OUR POWERS FOR SELF-DEFENSE...
YEAH... DEFENSE AGAINST PUTTING OUR BACKS OUT!
WIND, WIND, STRONG AND HARD, TAKE THESE SPEAKERS TO THE YARD!
WHAT ARE YOU DOING?
WOOOSH
I LOVE USING MAGIC SPELLS!

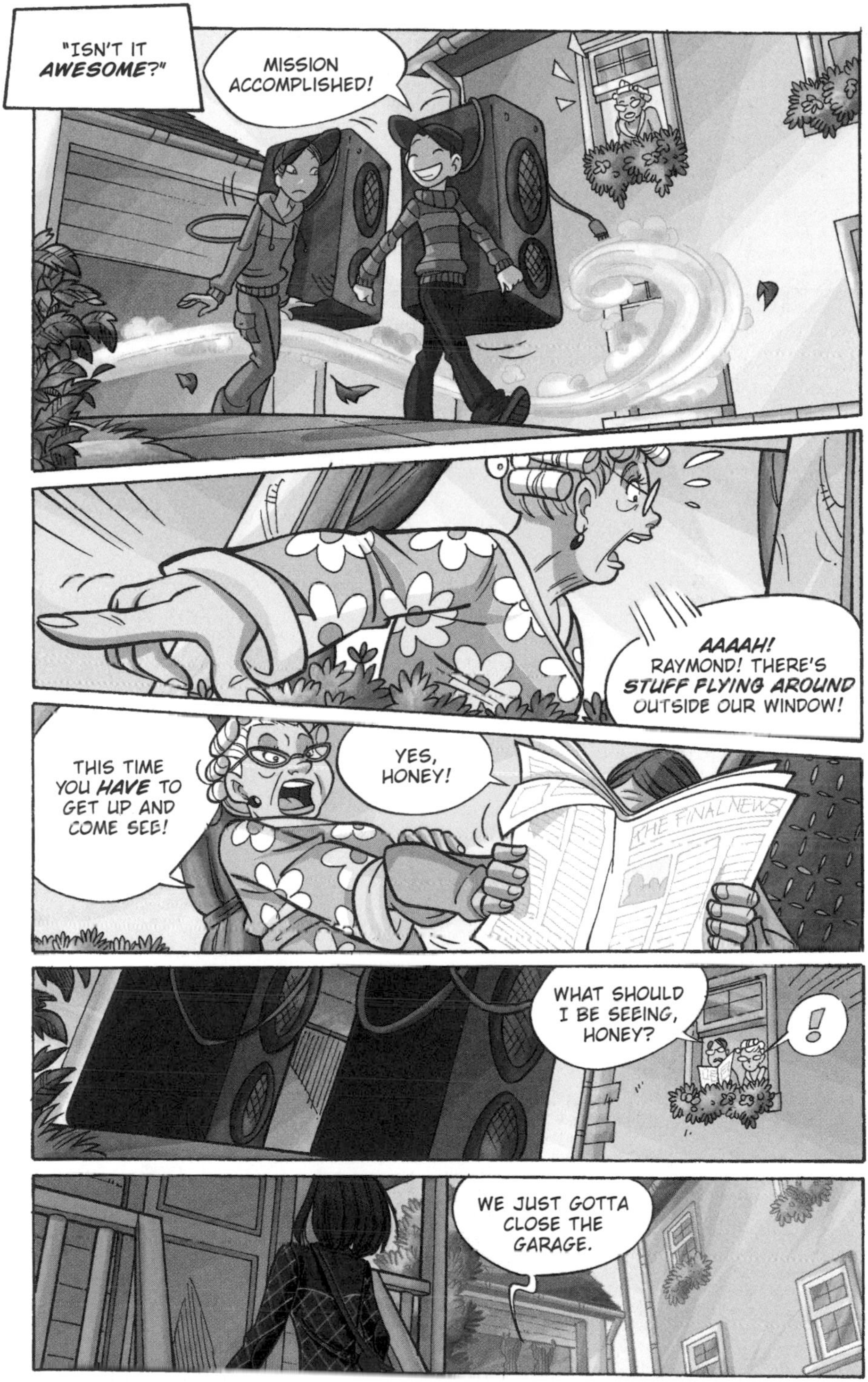
"ISN'T IT AWESOME?"
MISSION ACCOMPLISHED!
AAAAH! RAYMOND! THERE'S STUFF FLYING AROUND OUTSIDE OUR WINDOW!
THIS TIME YOU HAVE TO GET UP AND COME SEE!
YES, HONEY!
THE FINAL NEWS
WHAT SHOULD I BE SEEING, HONEY?
!
WE JUST GOTTA CLOSE THE GARAGE.

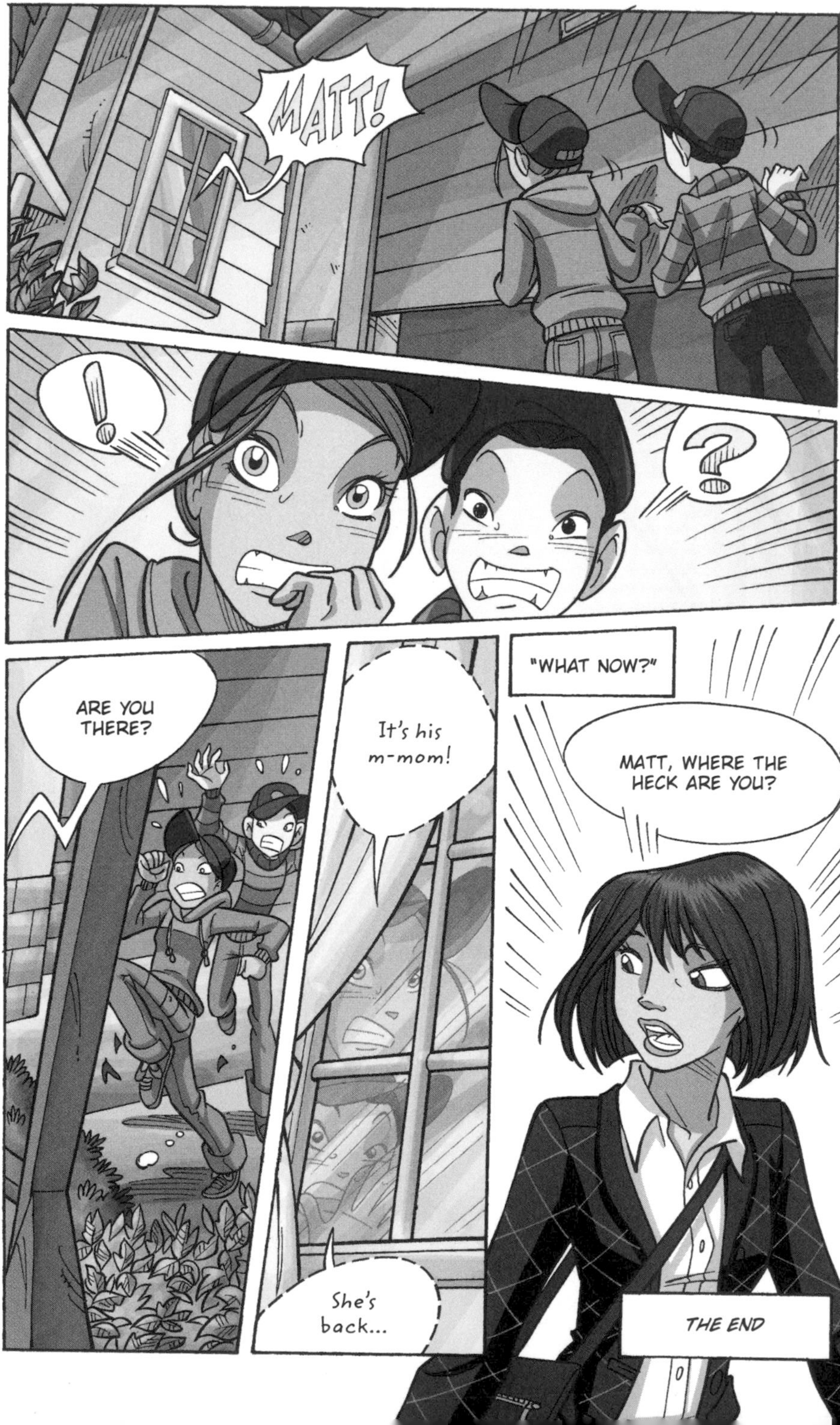

MATT!
!
?
ARE YOU THERE?
It's his m-mom!
She's back...
"WHAT NOW?"
MATT, WHERE THE HECK ARE YOU?
THE END

W.i.t.c.h.

Will Irma Taranee Cornelia Hay Lin

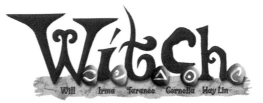

Read on in Volume 15!

W.i.t.c.h.

Will Irma Taranee Cornelia Hay Lin

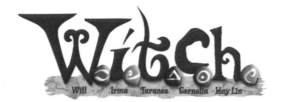

Discover the room of...

Explore Peter's Room

Taranee's big brother is friendly, funny, sporty, and absolutely irresistible! Let's explore his room.

- **Positive and cheerful** (and secretly vain), Peter Lancelot Cook is the big brother every girl would love to have!
- He's Taranee's **best friend**, a precious "ally", her rock, and... sometimes even her official driver!
- He doesn't know what "boredom" is: Peter is **always busy**! And always full of energy.
- He thinks he's great at almost **all sports**...and he's right! Forget about finding him home during summer: Between the **beach** and the **basketball** court, you can only see him at dinner.
- The only time when Peter feels **super lazy** is in the morning, when he has to wake up.
- Peter is a **bottomless well of ideas**: He always has new projects to suggest.
- He's very **creative**: Peter is great at drawing.
- He goes to Heatherfield Art Institute and isn't too fond of studying (but he's super smart). Sometimes, he gets away with it because he's so **cheeky**!

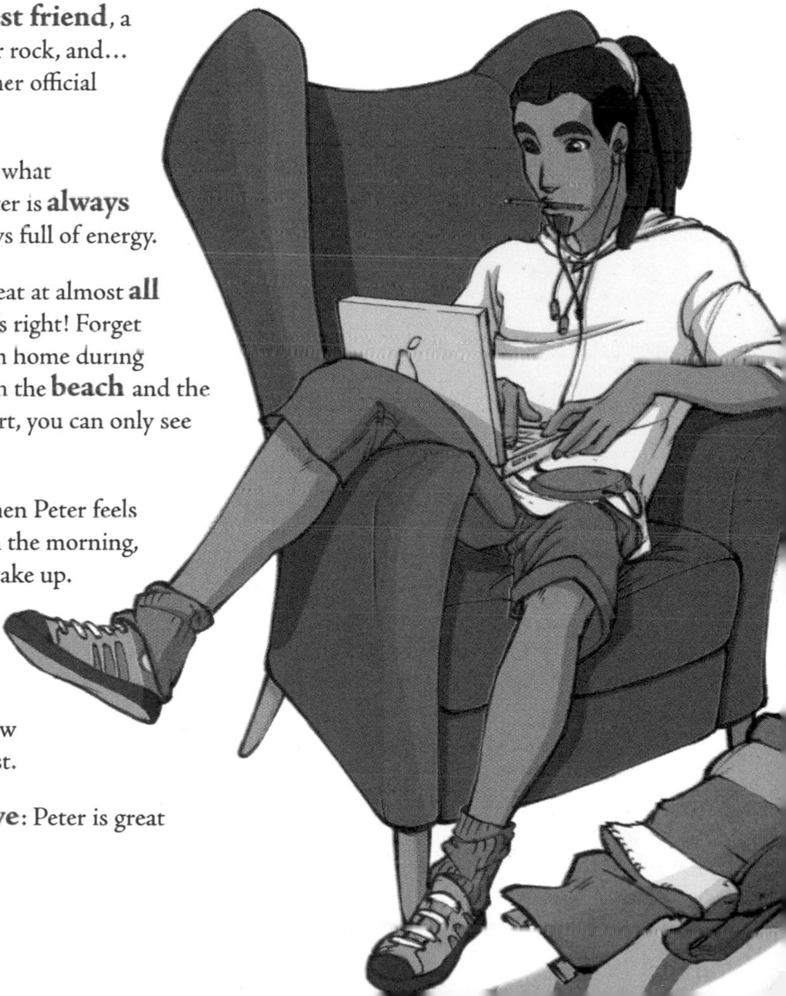

Exploring Peter's Room

Peter proudly displays the trophies he won at the high school basketball tournaments. He's an excellent player (and he loves to brag about it)!

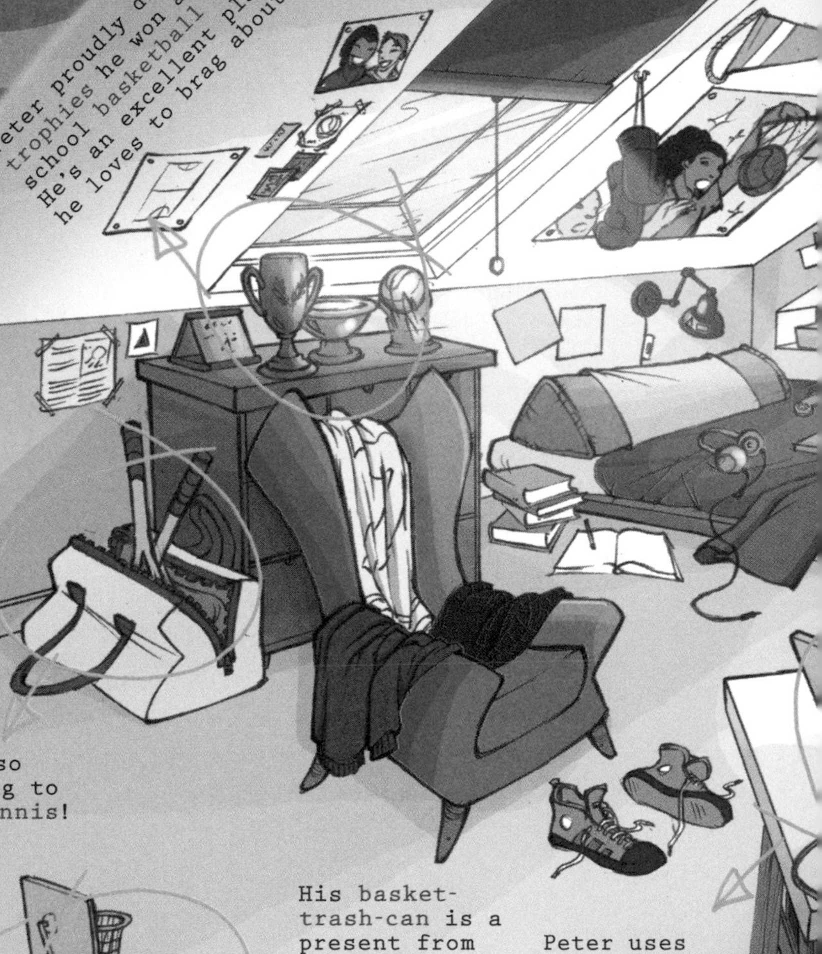

He's also learning to play tennis!

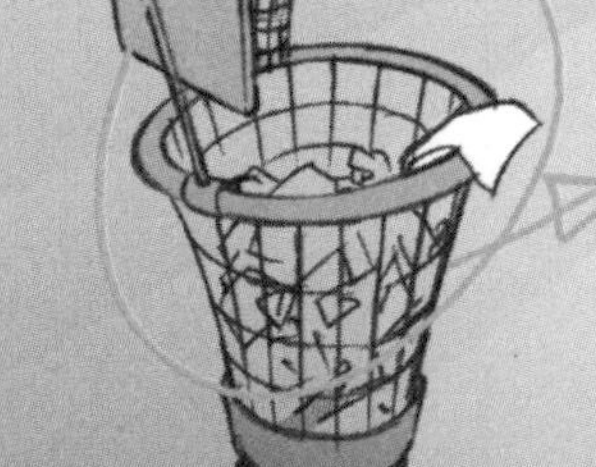

His basket-trash-can is a present from Taranee. When she saw it in the shop, she instantly thought of her big brother. After opening the present, Peter laughed for half an hour.

Peter uses the computer to keep in touch with his friends around the world and check the weather forecast before he goes surfing!

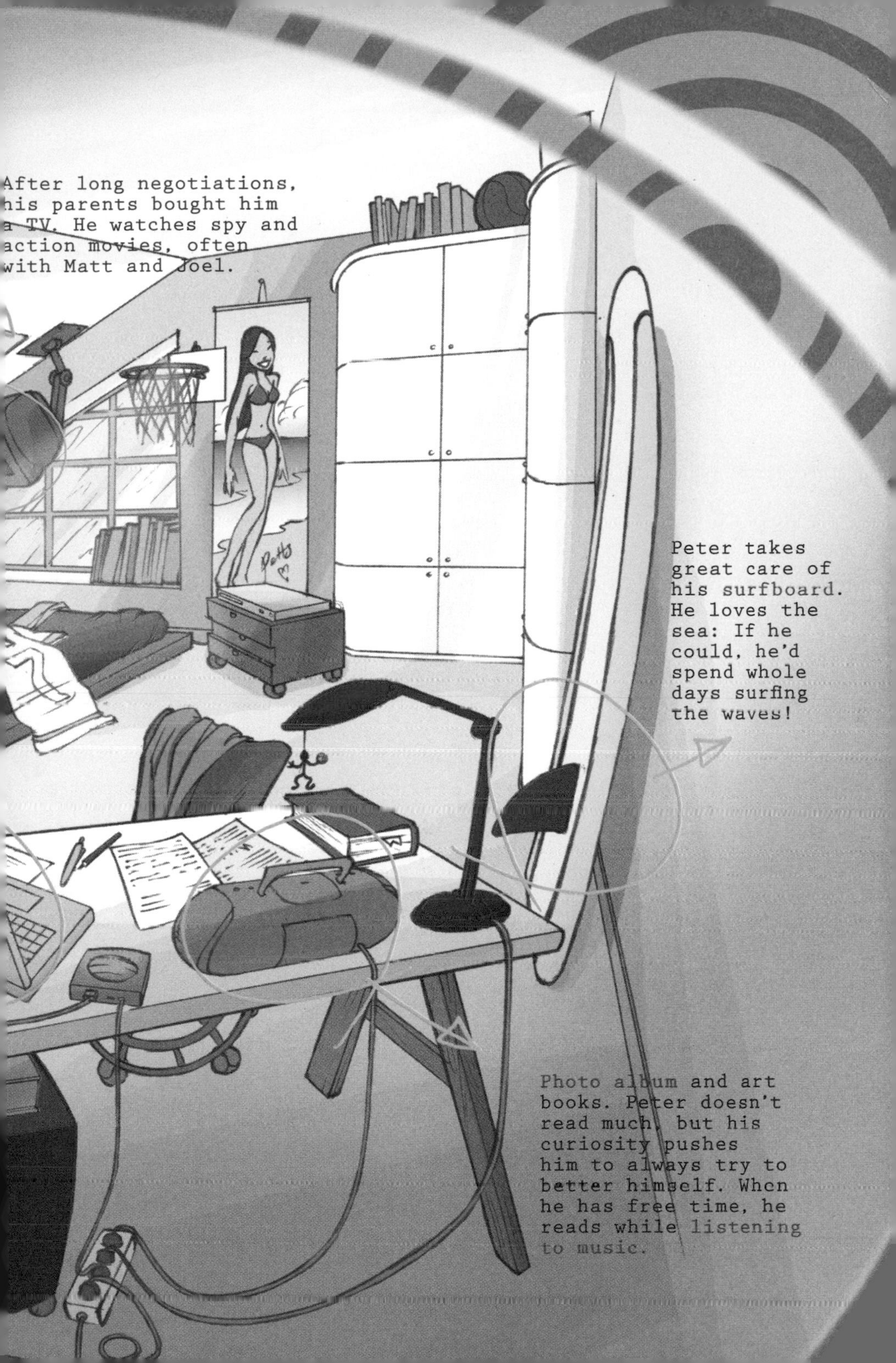

After long negotiations, his parents bought him a TV. He watches spy and action movies, often with Matt and Joel.

Peter takes great care of his surfboard. He loves the sea: If he could, he'd spend whole days surfing the waves!

Photo album and art books. Peter doesn't read much, but his curiosity pushes him to always try to better himself. When he has free time, he reads while listening to music.

Part V. The Book of Elements • Volume 2

Series Created by Elisabetta Gnone
Comic Art Direction: Alessandro Barbucci, Barbara Canepa

W.I.T.C.H.: The Graphic Novel, Part V: The Book of Elements © Disney Enterprises, Inc.

English translation © 2019 by Disney Enterprises, Inc.

JY
1290 Avenue of the Americas
New York, NY 10104

Visit us at jyforkids.com
facebook.com/jyforkids
twitter.com/jyforkids
jyforkids.tumblr.com
instagram.com/jyforkids

First JY Edition: January 2019

JY is an imprint of Yen Press, LLC.
The JY name and logo are trademarks of Yen Press, LLC.

The publisher is not responsible for websites (or their content) that are not owned by the publisher.

Library of Congress Control Number: 2017950917

ISBNs:
978-1-9753-8380-0 (paperback)
978-1-9753-8381-7 (ebook)

10 9 8 7 6 5 4 3 2 1

LSC-C

Printed in the United States of America

Cover Art by Manuela Razzi
Colors by Andrea Cagol

Translation by Linda Ghio and Stephanie Dagg at Editing Zone
Lettering by Katie Blakeslee

DANCING TO A DIFFERENT TUNE

Concept by Paola Mulazzi
Script by Teresa Radice
Layout by Emilio Urbano
Pencils by Manuela Razzi
Inks by Marina Baggio and Roberta Zanotta
Color and Light Direction by Francesco Legramandi
Title Page Art by Alessia Martusciello
with Colors by Andrea Cagol

ONE MORE HUG

Concept and Script by Teresa Radice
Layout by Gianluca
Pencils by Davide Baldoni
Inks by Marina Baggio and Roberta Zanotta
Color and Light Direction by Francesco Legramandi
Title Page Art by Davide Baldoni
with Colors by Francesco Legramandi

THE DAY AFTER

Concept and Script by Bruno Enna
Layout Federico Bertolucci
Pencils by Monica Catalano
Inks by Marina Baggio and Roberta Zanotta
Color and Light Direction by Francesco Legramandi
Title Page Art by Francesco Legramandi

THE RIDDLE

Concept by Bruno Enna
Script by Silvia Gianatti
Layout and Pencils by Alessia Martusciello
Inks by Santa Zangari and Roberta Zanotta
Color and Light Direction by Francesco Legramandi
Title Page Art by Alessia Martusciello with
Colors by Francesco Legramandi